The
Angel
Brings Fire

Book Four : *Children of The Fire*

(Second Edition)

by
Marcus B. Shields

For additional information about *The Angel Brings Fire*, surf to :

http://abfbook.telostic.com

For my daughter's children

Table of Contents

Prologue

Since *The Angel Brings Fire* is a multi-volume series, it is strongly suggested that the reader should enjoy Books One, Two and Three, *Angel of Mailànkh*, *Doubt Me Not* and *Angel and The Empire*, (respectively), before starting to read Book Four, *Children of The Fire.*

That said, it is recognized that for various reasons, some readers will have happened upon this volume of the series, without having convenient access to Books One, Two and Three.

We have therefore provided the following brief synopsis of the events of the previous three books, so that the reader can make sense of some of the characters and themes brought forward from the beginning of the novel.

Marcus Shields

Author

Angel of Mailànkh (Book One) revolves around the discovery of an extremely powerful female alien-being on Mars, self-described as "The Storied Watcher" a.k.a. "Karéin-Mayréij", who may or may not be an "angel" and who may or may not be Earth's only remaining hope of stopping a Doomsday comet named *Lucifer*.

The Storied Watcher manages to stow away on the Mars return vessel and while there, she learns of the planet's impending destruction. Fearing that there may soon be no-one left on Earth, the alien passes her secret gift – a supernatural power called *Amaiish* or *The Fire* – to the human astronauts who she encountered and befriended on Mars.

As a measure of desperation, Karéin-Mayréij resolves to destroy *Lucifer* in a 'death-run', powered indirectly by the enormous energies of Earth's Sun. And thus she does, although, at the close of Book One, it appears that she has sacrificed her life in the cause.

Doubt Me Not (Book Two) takes up the story of Karéin-Mayréij, after – much to her own surprise – she awakens after having crashed to Earth on a mountain-top in Idaho in the United States.

Badly wounded, hungry, cold, unable to speak intelligible English, having forgotten her true name and having lost almost all of her supernatural powers, she stumbles down to a truck stop, and has a few awkward initial encounters with citizens of America's near future. Calling herself 'Sari Tanak', she beguiles and befriends a down-and-out, forty-something floor-tile salesman named Bob

Billings, who, along with her and and an African-American woman named Whitney Claremont (plus children, Curtis and Melissa), are taken prisoner by a fundamentalist Christian cult called "The Klan of Jesus Christ".

However, the Storied Watcher's powers *are* returning, if painfully slowly, and she uses one of these – the same "cloak of invisibility" that enabled her to steal aboard the *Eagle* spacecraft, way back on Mars – to free Billings, the Claremont family and an orphaned Amerindian boy named Tommy George, from captivity. Together, the *ersatz* troupe locates and re-starts Billings' hidden, abandoned automobile. They begin a trip across-country, heading south to the salesman's home-base of Tucson, Arizona.

After a number of misadventures *en route*, 'Sari', Bob Billings, Whitney, Curtis and Melissa Claremont, along with Tommy George, arrive in Tucson and try to fit in to Billings' former "quiet, middle-class" lifestyle.

However, the United States of 2040 is a paranoid, declining society, obsessed with "subversion" of every type, and (though this fact is suspected by the Storied Watcher), she and the Billings party have been identified and tracked back to Tucson, not only by the omnipresent CIA but also by Christian fundamentalists (who believe the Storied Watcher to be "the spawn of Satan") and by a Russian SVR "sleeper" cell of spies, one of whom, "Misha", has been ahead of his American counterparts by a few days.

Feeling the imminent return of her greater abilities, 'Sari', who has by now become the salesman's mate, reveals her true nature to Bob Billings, and explains to him that since she now loves him and the others as her "family" (her second new "family", after the Mars mission astronauts in Book One), gradually, he, Claremont and the others (particularly Tommy George, who the Storied Watcher has adopted as a son) will begin to inherit the gift of *Amaiish*, in effect becoming among the first of a new race of super-beings.

Not really wanting to deal with all of this, Billings takes his alien lover to the floor-tile and home decorating business where he works, introducing her to his boss – Hugo Szabo – as a "secretary". Matters appear to be proceeding normally, when the Klan of Jesus Christ, arriving at the floor-tile-shop shortly after the CIA has staked it out, planning itself to capture or kill Karéin-Mayréij – "jumps the gun" on the American secret-police and attacks the building, causing heavy casualties on both sides.

As Book Two closes, knowing that she must flee and wait for her powers to fully return, the Storied Watcher pours out the gift of the *Fire* upon Bob Billings.

She departs with a dire threat to America's leaders : "Leave Bob, Whitney, Melissa, Curtis and most of all Tommy, free and unharmed... *or else*".

Angel and The Empire (Book Three) begins where *Doubt Me Not* left off, as Karéin-Mayréij, slightly wounded from the treacherous attack on the Tucson floor-tile-shop and beset by guilt at having allowed her second 'family' to have been so easily abducted by the authorities, has taken temporary refuge with "Misha", the Russian SVR spy. The Storied Watcher feels her greater abilities to be on the verge of returning, but she is still not powerful enough to directly challenge the U.S. government... so she must wait.

The alien-girl does not idly waste time, however, because – knowing that she may soon need to enforce her demands, that Billings, Whitney, Curtis, and Melissa Claremont and, especially, Tommy, be returned unharmed, she steals off to the Arizona desert, where she breathes life to a set of intelligent arms and armor, collectively named her 'war-children'.

Various other events – including the slow progress of a stolen, ex-Pakistani nuclear weapon, on its sinister journey to be used against an American target – occur. Eventually, Karéin-Mayréij hears of a 'special seminar', featuring the former NASA space scientists Hector Ramirez and Sylvia Abruzzio (with whom the alien-girl had conversed, during her travels through interplanetary space) being staged at the Hotel Tucson.

Suspecting a trap, but hoping against hope that she can communicate with someone who she trusts, the Storied Watcher attends the conference... only to be shot (though not seriously harmed) by one of the Klan of Jesus Christ's assassins, who she mistakenly assumes was sent by the President of the United States himself – a reasonable supposition, since, in the chaos that immediately ensues, Karéin-Mayréij is attacked in turn by CIA agents, acting on orders secretly given by the malevolent, power-hungry Director in charge of the Agency.

Unfortunately, neither the Agency, nor the Klan of Jesus Christ, nor the President, are in the least prepared for a battle against the ancient and mighty Storied Watcher, who – though still only able to access the least of her greater powers – is by now far beyond the abilities of mortal men, to contain or defeat. She makes quick work of the local CIA assassins, but then flies away from the Hotel Tucson, with two new followers – Misha, and a bounty-hunter named 'Wolf' – just before the U.S. Air Force is about to carpet-bomb the building.

Karéin-Mayréij steals off to a secluded cave in one of the walls of the Grand Canyon, in which she means to rest while bolstering Wolf's new-found, *Fire*-derived powers. Here, she is beset by the psychic backwash of a torture session inflicted by the CIA against Tommy; for, the U.S. government has realized that inflicting pain on her loved-ones, might hold the key to crippling or even killing the Storied Watcher herself. But the venture fails, instead both unlocking the Destroying Angel's greater powers and thoroughly enraging her with a resolve to destroy the United States from end to end.

This calamity is only narrowly-avoided, when Wolf and Misha manage to convince Karéin-Mayréij to instead attack symbolic targets, as a warning to the President as to what may come next. She leaves the two 'more-than-men' to carry this message back to the government, while she departs in a blaze of lethal glory, bound for the Mt. Rushmore National Monument.

To the amazement and alarm of many in the future United States, the Storied Watcher proceeds to methodically destroy the figures of the Rushmore Monument, a situation about which the President tries to mislead the American public, but to ensure that the message gets through, Karéin-Mayréij stops at a family restaurant, making a personal appearance on underground video in which she repeats her warnings as to what will happen if Billings and the rest of her adopted Earth family are not promptly released.

Meanwhile, important events have been occurring elsewhere, for – on the orders of the CIA director, undertaken without the consent of NASA or the Air Force – the former Mars mission crew consisting of Sam Jacobson, Cherie Tanaka, Devon White and Brent Boyd, has been involuntarily airlifted to the Agency's secret underground concentration camp, hidden in the wastes of the 1970s Amchitka nuclear test site in the Aleutian islands.

The unwilling, increasingly-suspicious four are hustled into a room in which the CIA intends to begin its "coercive interrogations"; but the Agency's brutal "doctors" and guards find the tables turned, as Jacobson, Tanaka, White and Boyd fight back with their new-found alien powers, quickly killing or incapacitating all around.

After pressing the survivors of this assault for information, the ex-Mars astronauts realize that Billings and the rest of the Storied Watcher's second family are also being detained in this same facility; and, fearing Karéin-Mayréij's likely reaction, were Tommy to die at the hands of the U.S. government, Jacobson and his team set out to explore the rest of this benighted place, hoping to rescue as many of the "new people" as possible.

Back at the restaurant, to protect the civilians in the vicinity against yet another indiscriminate attack that is about to be launched against her by the Air Force, the Storied Watcher streaks high into the Midwest sky, where she engages and utterly defeats a squadron of America's best fighter-planes.

Noting that these were directed by an airborne command-post, Karéin-Mayréij steals aboard this aircraft, where she easily brushes aside the feeble attempts to stop her, then orders the command-post's staff to open a communications channel with the President – who is preoccupied with an unrelated fiasco : one of his few remaining nuclear weapons has just been hijacked by parties unknown. He forces a frustrated Storied Watcher to wait for a chance to speak, then – secretly gambling that the CIA's plan to kill this bothersome, possibly-divine alien-being, by simultaneously "terminating" both the Billings and Jacobson parties, might in fact work – refuses to bargain in good faith with her, offering only half-truths and excuses.

At her wits' end, and at a loss to comprehend why the President "chooses to bluff with a hand of deuces", Karéin-Mayréij issues a final ultimatum to the crew of the airborne command-post, and as she leaves it, she relates what she will do next, to the intelligent weapons and armor that protect her...

"The President will understand that I mean *business*," she vows, "When I crush the capitol of his Empire – Washington, D.C. – and show that he is powerless to stop me."

As *Angel and The Empire* comes to an end, America's ruling elite would do well to set their sights to the western horizon... for, something ominous, their way approaches!

The Searching

About Those Eyes, Professor...

As the depth-indicator over the elevator-door showed their imminent arrival, Sam Jacobson – who had been more or less lost in reverie – stirred and warned the rest of the former Mars exploration team.

"Same tactical rules as in the corridor... right?" he requested.

"I *think* that it's clear – at least right outside the elevator door where we'll be getting off," countered Tanaka.

Her attractive, "wise-before-her-time" Eurasian eyes stared off into space, as if contemplating a thing unseen.

"And how would you – oh... *forget* it," ruefully grunted Boyd.

"Well, I *could* be wrong," allowed the Science Officer. "Just a feeling..."

"Guess we're 'bout to find out how psychic y'all is, Professor," observed Devon White.

"More and more, all the *time*," answered Tanaka; and the others couldn't tell if the remark was meant in jest.

"Top circle of the warm place, comin' up in about 3... 2... 1..." continued the African-American ex-astronaut.

The letters "SL-350" shone in baleful orange-red transitioning to white, above the doorway, as the downward motion of the elevator came to a slow stop.

Boyd, his demeanor more tense and expectant than nervous, fingered his gun and braced himself.

The elevator doors opened with a gentle 'swoosh', and a half-second later, the former Air Force and NASA pilot charged out into the dimly-lit corridor beyond, crouching reflexively to the left, then to the right, ready to shoot anything that might be foolish enough to move.

But there was nothing, at least not within range of the heightened senses of these four more-than-human-beings.

"Looks clear," whispered Boyd. "And half the overhead-lights are out... *strange*."

White, Jacobson and Tanaka filed cautiously out of the elevator.

"Yeah, strange, alright," offered the black man. "Wonder what it means... y'all think they might be goin' into lock-down?"

"Maybe – but if *that* were the case, I'd expect sirens, warnings over the loudspeakers, *et cetera*," noted Jacobson. "Usually this kind of thing indicates a power-out situation, like the facility has switched over to a backup-generator – but *we* couldn't have caused something like *that*... *could* we?"

"Don't think so," commented Tanaka. "Unless maybe a stray shot took out a power-conduit or something similar. It's *possible*... but I certainly didn't see anything like that. Anyway, the darker it gets – that works to our advantage –

and I can already feel my eyes adjusting. Do any of the rest of you see the warmth around the lights that are still 'on'?"

"Sombitch Pierre but I *can*," answered Boyd. "God – that's *weird*. Like you start to see it, when you need to."

He paused for a second, then added, "You know... it's very beautiful. Even in *this* setting."

"Don't think it's just the light thing," suggested White. "It *feels* a little warmer, background glow-wise, too. Maybe they started runnin' out of lead to shield the walls with, when they got down here?"

"Remind me to send a 'thank-you' card to the one who bestowed this little gift on us," mentioned Jacobson, "But while we're all marveling at our built-in night-vision goggles, I think we'd better figure out where we're going, and then start heading there ASAP. Devon – you got the map-card?"

"Right here," responded the African-American ex-astronaut. "I was lookin' it over – map for this level, that is – most of the way while we was comin' down on the elevator... but I'm afraid it ain't got a sign sayin' 'this way to the Billings family reunion'. 'Less you got a better idea, Commander, I guess we're gonna have to do this the old-fashioned way... like, knockin' on doors, one by one."

"I was *afraid* you'd say that," muttered Jacobson. "Well... if that's what we gotta do... that's what we gotta do. But how big *is* this level, exactly? At the very least, we need to consider how long it's likely to take, and where we'd be best off starting. Can I see that card-thing with the map?"

White handed the access-card to his former commander, and Jacobson studied it for several seconds.

"Not a *lot* of detail," he complained, shaking his head. "Now... if I'm reading this correctly, the floor-plan's more or less circular, with us at this point, here," – he pointed a big finger at a symbol near the middle of the card – "And this, and then *that* one over on the other side, those must be stairways... right?"

"Lemme see," requested White.

"Yeah... that's right, sir," he confirmed. "*Sort* of. The one, that's gotta be the stairs comin' from the level we just left... th' other one, I'm not sure... guess it might be an emergency 'scape-route or somethin' like that – but there's this 'lock' symbol on it, might be hard to get past... harder than normal, that is. But this elevator's more or less in the middle of the whole level, so it don't really matter too much what direction y'all want to head in."

By now, Boyd and Tanaka had come close enough to see the map-card's display, as well.

"Of course, we *could* all split up... that way we could each cover a quarter of the territory," proposed the Science Officer. "There would be *some* risk involved, but we could limit our actions to just finding out where the Billings party is located... then we could alert the others and go free them..."

"I don't think that's a good idea, Cherie," argued Jacobson. "If we ran into opposition, of anything like the sort we encountered above –"

"I feel pretty confident of my own abilities," answered Tanaka, with a disturbingly serene tone to her voice. "And all of you would be armed at *least* as well as any one or two guards who you might bump into – not that that's likely, considering our heightened senses –"

"I'd prefer to stick together, if it's all the same to you, Professor," opined the black ex-astronaut. "Besides... we're all assumin' that Billings 'n his folk even *are* on this level. Not much point in one of us gettin' captured – or worse – if we might have to just go on lookin' further down."

"Hear, hear!" agreed Boyd.

"Fine by me," retreated Tanaka, "I'm not going to press the point... but I thought I should at least *mention* it."

"Right," uneasily offered Boyd.

"So... where to, first?" asked White.

"It's all arbitrary anyway – so why not go clockwise, starting with 12:00, that is, north on the map?" said Jacobson. "Looks like they have a sort of hub-and-spoke layout, with a circular-corridor – the one we're in now, surrounding the elevators – and another one about halfway down the spike-corridors, toward what must be the far periphery of the level. We might as well do it in pie-slices – except there isn't any detail as to what exactly is in each section. They aren't even showing us where all the doors are... if this level is anything like the one above."

"Well, I doubt that they'd have somethin' on the legend like, 'here's where we do our sadistic torturing of detainees', Sam," commented Tanaka.

"What – y'all think they ain't *proud* of it, Professor?" remarked White, with equal sarcasm. "Don't know why – if they did it on TV, they'd prolly get another million votes for whoever's President this week. Just like they do with them hangin's."

"Yeah – and I bet you, the Agency gives out merit-badges for 'best use of the thumbscrews', or something," muttered Boyd. "It'd *suit* them. But we should get going – if they're sending anyone after us, they might try the elevator –"

"Already put it on 'hold'... or at least I *think* I did, Brent my man," cheerily pointed out the African-American.

"Something tells me that Sam's guess is right," noted Tanaka. "I just... *feel* like north's the right way. It's like I have an ache when I think of that direction. Intuition, I guess."

"Yeah... I guess," stated White.

"You want to take point?" asked Boyd.

"Let's do it the same way as we did up there," ordered Jacobson. "Worked for us... so far."

After the others nodded affirmatively, the two younger men, weapons at the ready, led the way through the semi-darkness, up the corridor to the north.

But after a few steps, Boyd reflexively checked his back, and had to suppress an urge to exclaim a warning.

"Professor – for *God's* sake... can't you do something about those *eyes*?" he whispered.

Who's On-Side... And Who's Not

"Harry – can you confirm her claim that Air Defense is about to attack her again?" requested the President. "Considering how well the *last* one seems to have gone... I may want to call the next one off, or use better weapons..."

"Checking, sir," answered Anderson.

"Listen, sir," slowly and carefully stated Bezomorton, "As you know, I'm the last one to suggest appeasement in a case like this, because it's entirely possible that this creature will just move on to even less reasonable demands at a later date... *but...*"

"Yeah, John?" countered the American leader, with an arched eyebrow.

"The point *is*, sir," pressed the Security Adviser, "She *does* have a point – about the Billings party, that is. I know that traditionally, our policy has been not to give in to blackmail – but why can't we at least let the alien meet this group of civilians somewhere?"

"Mr. President," interrupted DeWitt, "I presume he doesn't yet know about –"

"Gentlemen," wearily cautioned the President, "I had *hoped* that I'd have been able to keep the following information confidential; but, current situation taken into account, I believe that I now have no choice but to share it with you... are we *sure* this line is secure?"

"I'll switch the code over to an internal DoD cypher," proposed the Defense Secretary. "Please stand by... we may get a momentary interruption in the signal while the new encryption-layer's activated."

The screen went black for about two seconds. Then it re-appeared with the three familiar faces.

"So... here's how it is," began the President. "And there is new information that even *you* don't know, Harry, and Arthur. Before I say anything... will you two gentlemen pledge your *complete* loyalty to me, as your C-In-C?"

"Of *course*, Mr. President sir," reflexively replied the Air Force general, with an approving nod from DeWitt. "I'm already pledged to defend you – even at the cost of my own life."

"Same here," echoed Bezomorton.

"Well," said the President, "*That's* encouraging... because CIA seems to be headed in the exact opposite direction – a short time ago, I gave the CIA Director a direct order... which he simply refused to implement. I tried to fire him, but he replied that he's 'not subject to arbitrary dismissal in a time of national crisis', whatever *that* means, and then – here's the good part – he started to issue thinly-veiled threats about me 'having an accident', if I persisted –"

"You've *got* to be kidding," gasped the Security Advisor. "That's *treason!*"

"I wish I *was*," mordantly noted the U.S. leader. "And it gets *better*. Harry, Arthur... you guys remember that 'One-Two Knockout' plan?"

"I take it that Mr. Bezomorton is now entrusted with that information?" asked the Defense Secretary.

"Yes," confirmed the President.

"What are you *talking* about, sir?" asked Bezomorton.

"To make a long story short," explained the President, "Based on careful observations of the alien's behavior at the exact times when, according to them, members of the Billings party were, uhh, 'interrogated'... CIA drafted a plan to leverage the distress – that's the 'nice' way of putting it – inflicted on these captives, which is somehow indirectly transmitted to the alien – to make her, it, vulnerable to a more conventional attack. So –"

"Migod... no *wonder* she's furious with us!" muttered the Security Adviser. "But if this plan is such a great idea... then why isn't she dead, already?"

"The Agency thinks that it's just because we aren't, uhh, 'hurting' enough people who have a personal relationship with the alien," noted the President. "That's why they moved the Jacobson team to their holding-facility, but –"

"*What*?" uncharacteristically bellowed the usually-restrained Anderson. "You mean the Mars mission team? But *Mr. President* – they were being held under exclusive *Air Force* authority –"

"I know, I *know*, Harry," pleaded the U.S. leader. "Somehow – I don't know how, it may have been a faked communication, it may have been... who *knows* – the Agency-managed to get them transferred from the little 'hotel' that you, McPherson and I saw them in, to one of CIA's secret facilities. I can only assume that they are being – or are about to be – subjected to the same, uhh, 'techniques' as the Agency would be using on the Billings group. My problem now is that even if I *wanted* to give up the last, possibly-effective weapon that we've got to use against 'Karéin' – and I'm not sure that I do – the Agency is now acting like it's answerable only to itself. I'd welcome suggestions... if anyone *has* any."

"Why don't we just send in the Army and forcibly remove CIA's current leadership?" suggested Bezomorton.

"And completely cripple the functionality of my main intelligence-agency, while we have a stolen H-bomb in Louisiana and maybe three or four more Paki nuclear bombs being sent our way?" retorted the President. "To say nothing of the fact that they're also the only ones with a plausible weapon against the alien. All CIA would have to do would be just to whisper the location of this aircraft, to *her*... and I'd be dead in an hour. I'm afraid, gentlemen, that the director has me by the 'short and curlies'... I've already threatened him with forcible removal, but they know it's a bluff."

"We'd still have NSA, FBI and Secret Service," argued the Security Adviser. "They're all on *our* side... aren't they?"

"NSA is in like this with CIA, and the two of those together make FBI and the Service look like a junior high football-team playing in the NFL," countered the American leader. "We'd have to rely on the military... Arthur, not that I'm considering it, but... where do you think the loyalties lie within DoD?"

DeWitt hesitated for a few long seconds, then answered, "Mr. President... as I said before, *you* have my complete loyalty... and I believe that I could probably get the rest of the military to back you up – but note that in that scenario, we could end up with a *de facto* civil war between different departments of the Federal government. I don't think I need to detail the risks involved in *that* case."

"With at least one missing nuke and an enraged, ultra-powerful alien flying hither and yon, all the while," unhelpfully added the NSC Adviser.

"Sir," continued DeWitt, "There is another issue that you need to consider here : specifically, what GrayWar Corporation might do."

"What do you *mean*?" retorted the President.

"Well," explained the Defense Secretary, "That organization has almost as many men in uniform as does the entire Department of Defense – maybe more if we are only counting troops deployed domestically. They have roles *throughout* the government, including within DoD, CIA, FBI... even in the Executive Branch. If Mr. Duke – who I would remind you is ex-CIA, himself – threw his allegiance to the Agency, it could cause tremendous, almost insurmountable problems for us."

Gulping slightly, the President asked, "How likely do you think that is?"

"Impossible to say, sir," said the National Security Advisor. "Personally I think that it's not very likely... not because Duke is a 'nice guy', but just because GrayWar is so poorly-organized and so, uhh, 'unprofessional'. They have trouble even getting the laundry done properly at the INS facilities that they're supposed to be guarding – I'd be surprised if they could make much of a difference if someone tried to stage a *coup*. But that's just my opinion."

"We'll have to take that into account, I suppose," morosely observed the U.S. leader.

"Sir," interjected Anderson, "I'd like to propose that we immediately retrieve Jacobson and his crew from wherever CIA has spirited them away to. The Agency's in *flagrant* breach of your authority, my own authority and of the trust that both of us placed in them, on this matter – we need to get the Mars team back, ASAP. If CIA uses even their, ahem, 'normal' interrogation-protocol against Jacobson, Boyd, White and Tanaka, there's a good chance that one or more of them won't survive the process, or will suffer irreparable damage as a result of it. If that happens, we'll have lost an *irreplaceable* military asset –"

"Wait a minute," protested Bezomorton, "I realize that they're all celebrated astronauts, and that they have personal knowledge of the alien... but I'd hardly call all that 'irreplaceable', from a purely military perspective –"

"May I tell him, sir?" asked Anderson.

"Go ahead," said the President.

"To cut to the chase, Mr. Adviser," stated the general, "We have good reason to believe that the former Mars mission team has, somehow, inherited some of the alien's supernatural powers – for example, both White and Jacobson demonstrated a telekinetic ability, and did so right in front of the President. If they could teach these alien-powers to, say, the SEALS or Delta Force –"

"*Now* it makes sense!" sighed the Security Adviser. "And the Agency, knowing all that, was going to *torture* these guys... just on the off chance of dropping the alien? You've *got* to be kidding!"

"Air Force and I kept the new abilities of the Mars team secret – we only shared the information with Fred McPherson," explained President. "And I didn't authorize the interrogation of the Billings party, at least initially – I didn't even know that CIA *had* them, until much later. I only authorized the Agency to, uhh, 'stress' a few members of the alien's so-called family, and then, only after 'Karéin' had personally threatened *me*. It looks like CIA took my limited go-ahead as a *carte blanche* to do whatever the hell they want, to whoever they can snatch off the street or from the Air Force. My problem now is, even if I want to call off the whole program, I *can't*; possession's nine-tenths of the law, and they have control of all these captives. And the Director's *not* returning my calls."

"So where do we go from here?" inquired Bezomorton.

"As we all know, the options are limited," replied the President. "But here is what I'd like to do, if I can get full cooperation at least from DoD, preferably from the rest of the government – excluding CIA of course. First, Arthur, can you try to explain the situation, as tactfully as possible, to General Blanshard – don't come right out and ask if he'll support a military-based move against Langley... but just sound him out and see if he'll at least stay neutral, if we have to use some other arm of the government to deal with the Agency. Also, Harry – using only Air Force assets, can you see if there's any way to track down where CIA might be hiding the Jacobson and Billings groups?"

"I'll try, sir," agreed DeWitt, "But it goes without saying that doing so without arousing the suspicion of the Agency – they have a *very* sophisticated ability to intercept communications, after all that is their business – will be quite difficult, particularly because we have to cooperate with them on other issues such as retrieving the missing Louisiana weapon. If we *do* find out where these people are being held captive... what's the plan past that point?"

"I haven't thought that through," admitted the U.S. leader. "But knowing the location may give us – me – more leverage. Maybe even a rescue-operation. I don't know."

"For the record, Mr. President," requested Anderson, "I'd like to request the immediate return of the Jacobson team to Air Force custody. Failing that, a rescue-mission conducted by Air Force Special Forces may be necessary. With your permission, I'll start the necessary preparations."

"Permission granted," confirmed the President.

"Sir... I'm now getting confirmation of the situation in Midwest airspace," interrupted Anderson. "Unfortunately, it appears that my earlier assessment was correct – the alien encountered several squadrons of stealth-fighters and – there's no nice way to say this – knocked nearly all of them from the sky. I also have a report that she, uhh, jumped aboard one of these fighter-planes, tore off its cockpit with her bare hands and then used the opportunity to warn the squadron commander not to challenge her anymore."

"*Really*," offered the President.

"She – it – now seems to have left the AL-2C laser weapons-post, which is where she was during the just concluded conversation with the three of us," added the general. "Sir... I'd have to point out, in the current context, that from the alien's perspective, it may appear to her that she's exercising, uhh, 'restraint', in how she deals with us. From the available TacEval, there's little doubt that she could have destroyed both the laser-ship and the fighter-squadron, without regard to the body-count on our side – but although she inflicted grievous injuries on the aircraft's staff, she didn't actually *kill* anyone –"

"Are you suggesting that she's trying to be 'nice' to us, Harry?" shot back the President. "Threatening to slaughter millions of Americans or destroy the entire United States, doesn't sound like 'restraint'... from where *I* sit."

"I'd be the last one to recommend letting down our guard, sir," countered Anderson. "I'm just trying to point out that if the alien's military capabilities could have inflicted far more damage on us than has in fact happened... by definition, that counts as 'restraint'. My job is to assess actual enemy *capabilities*... not, *intent*."

"Fair enough – and I hope that everyone here can see why I didn't want to rule out CIA's idea for the 'Knockout Punch' thing, completely," commented the President. "Without something like *that* on our side... how are we supposed to negotiate with the damn alien, in the first place?"

"Is there anything that I can do to help, sir? On the Agency issue, I mean." asked Bezomorton.

"I want you to speak discreetly with Ochoa," answered the President, "And – without explaining our exact impasse with CIA – I need you to canvass their level of loyalty, should they be asked to replace some of the 'un-named Agency's' senior staff-members with people pulled from their own ranks... okay?"

"Will *do*, sir," agreed the Security Adviser. "Is anyone else to be in the know about this?"

"I want to keep any possible moves against the Agency completely confidential – if, of course, that's even *possible* against an outfit such as them – so I'm going to keep all of it confined to a few key personnel," instructed the President. "Specifically : yourselves, the Vice-President, my Chief of Staff, FBI and Secret Service. I will inform George, Jerry and the Secret Service chief myself, so you don't have to. Understood?"

"Understood, Mr. President," answered the other two, almost in unison.

"Let's get going, then," ordered the U.S. leader.

He cut the connection.

Payback Time For Assholes

I'm not getting any more feelings from the kid's direction, reflected Billings, as creeping fear – not just about his own situation, even though his nostrils were still redolent with the stink of burnt flesh and blood – gripped his mind.

He must've passed out.

Yeah... that's gotta be it.

Has to be!

Because the only other way that he'd drop off the radar-screen entirely –

He heard footsteps and – at the limit of his earshot – someone speaking into a phone or wall-communicator.

"Yeah?" muttered the voice. "Um-humm... guest is down here, getting the gears, as it were... kid's been sent back down to Level Three, though. Level Two, but I got *orders*, Level Four if we don't get anywhere by end of day... *what*? Doesn't matter to *me*... no, I haven't talked with anybody from up top today, but we were gonna get together after work hours, for canasta and zoo-porn... so? Well, send the GrayWar twerps after them... how hard can *that* be? I mean – where could they *go*? Um-humm? Well, that's *your* problem, not mine, but I wouldn't be worried... anyway, I got some fun work to do... right. See you in an hour or so. Out."

The footsteps headed back towards where Billings lay helplessly awaiting the next torment.

"Well... that's enough for our mutual little friend for today, Bob," interrupted the unctuous voice of the fake-doctor. "It seems that he can't go the distance... 'sensory-overload', that kind of thing – and we were just starting to have some *fun*... really *sucks*, you know? We gotta toughen him up a bit, I guess, so my friends have sent him off for a little well-deserved 'R-and-R', but not so much that he forgets why he's down here. Which leaves us just with... *you*."

You have no idea how happy I am to hear that, bitterly mused the salesman.

Means the little bugger's still breathing... hallelujah!

There's basically nothing left for you to do that you haven't done already... so go for it, asshole.

The 'doctor' leaned over his rigidly-restrained victim, leaning over Billings with hands planted on the side of the gurney.

"Now, Bob," he leered, "Since you haven't been getting the message very well up to now, I'm afraid that we're going to have to turn up the volume a bit."

He waved a stainless-steel instrument of some sort right in front of the salesman's face; the thing had a long handle, a tightening-screw and a circular end, with the inside face of this loop ridged by a razor-like cutting-edge.

"About that manhood that you're probably so proud of – I bet it's just as fat and out-of-shape as its owner is... right?" hissed the torturer. "So... I got an idea. We're gonna take an inch or so off the top, you know? Oh, sorry – I always get *that* one wrong, Bob ol' boy... I should have said, 'an inch or so, off the *sides*'. That, and, you don't need *both* of those balls of yours... do you? I mean, what would a chicken-shit little salesman do with a *real* man's balls – completely surplus-baggage, if you ask yours truly... and I think my fine colleagues will second that opinion. But we won't be doing all of this at *once*, of course. We got to do it *slow*, so... well, remember the whole 'no pain, no gain' thingie? Get my drift?"

Shit – I take that back! reverberated Billings' panicked mind.

So there is something you haven't done. Okay, I concede the point!

He tried to yell something, but his mouth was too securely wired shut, so all that came out was a pathetic-sounding yelp.

"Don't worry, though," sneered the pseudo-doctor. "For a pathetic, pug-ugly, way-over-his-little-head, two-bit sales-whore like you, it's not like you'll really need to *use* it that much, for the fun-stuff... right? I mean, after we're done here, you'll still be able to pee. *Just.*"

He paused for a second, then said, "Oh... but of course, I'll need to get my buddy to give you the old Nelson-lock while we get those pants down... we've got a strict 'no-go-it-alone' rule down here for this kind of entertainment – and rules *are* rules, don'tcha think?"

Billings noticed a few receding-footsteps, then heard, "Don't go anywhere – you got that? I'm sure you won't want to miss *this* one, Bob my man!"

Waves of panic and paranoia raced through Billings' beleaguered mind.

Gotta think fast – what to do – well, what the hell to do? he feverishly pondered.

Jaysus – despite the hours into days into God-knows-how-long of this non-stop pain, I feel strong, stronger than ever – feel like I should just tear out of these fucking straps and then snap his fucking pencil-neck...

I'm oh so close, but... what the hell is that... a voice, a mind... Tommy?

No, not him. Not the kid...

Whitney?

Can't be... haven't felt her presence in days... who the hell?

Sweet Mother of God, he thought.

If they're not from my group, the poor buggers who made the fatal mistake to get in my car up north – Tommy, Curtis, Melissa, Whitney – I'm so sorry, I didn't know it would come to this – then they got to be Gestapo types from this shithole – and they must have figured out some way to camp in on the CB-in-your-head trick.

Probably did that with some creative pulling out of fingernails, et cetera.

Which means, they can do to my mind, what they've so far only been able to do to my body.

Might as well give up now!

In a cold sweat, he stared at the pitiless florescent ceiling-lights, and realized,

But how do you 'give up', to pricks who do it to you, because they want to?

Damn you, Sari!

Damn you to hell!

It's your fault!

You fucked around with my head – made me fall for you... made me love you. Then you abandoned me and the rest of your so-called 'friends', to rot away down here...

We're just another bunch of unimportant 'mortals' – like the hundreds or thousands you must have chewed up and spat out, in all those fancy former lives of yours... right?

God, I wish I had never met you... I'd just be boring old Bob Billings of Tucson, Arizona, having a beer while watching the ball-game on TV.

Boring old life.

Safe, pleasant old life!

Damn *you!*

As tears of anger and frustration poured from his eyes, the salesman screamed, raged and strained furiously, against the brutally-tight restraining straps that seemed to envelop every inch of his frame.

He felt one or two of them loosen ever-so-slightly.

What the...?

Especially after all of this, I can't possibly *be strong enough to –*

He quickly put *that* idea down to wishful-thinking.

Oh God, he silently cried.

I'm sorry about all the bullshit I've done!

I swear, I'll give up the booze – I'll start paying child-support again – I'll start going to church – I'll do anything you fucking well want!

I'll even stop using cuss-words!

Same far-off mental-voices – feel like anger, concern –

What the H?

Sounds like firecrackers – a real sound, not this funky 'hear it in my mind' crap –

Oh, sorry, Big Guy... I know I promised not to – thought Billings, his state of mind changing rapidly from sheer terror to, well, sheer terror mixed with puzzlement.

A second later, he heard hasty, tripping-over-each-other footsteps, then a door slamming.

A latch clicked, followed by the sounds of something heavy being dragged across the floor.

"Get the fucking thing *secured!*" someone shouted. "Guards are *dead!*"

"Can't – I'm trying to call upstairs!" shrieked a second voice. "Who the hell took out the guards? What the – all I'm getting is this damn *music*, on the line –"

Ooo – ai-ooo – ooo-ai, repeatedly echoed an eerie, Celtic-sounding cadence, reverberating through the salesman's instantly-hopeful mind.

Migod! he frantically reflected.

Can it be?

No... not her... *sounds* so *close – so much the same, so* good – *but something's different...*

Thank you, Big Guy! he mentally added.

Got no idea what it is... but I'll take it.

Now the strength of a dozen – no, a hundred – men flowed down from... *somewhere*, into the brutalized, abused veins, bones, nerves, muscles and willpower of that ex-salesman, formerly Bob K. Billings Jr., of Tucson, Arizona. It danced through his body, regenerating life, confidence and courage, overpowering the intuitive human knowledge that a man simply *couldn't* rip off a straight-jacket.

Jesus, it feels almost like when I was with her... *almost...*

Oops – sorry 'bout that, he thought.

But *this* man, was no longer just, *a* man. And though the doing of it agonized his already-scarred flesh almost to the breaking-point, the same *something* let Billings over-rule his nerve-endings and keep straining.

With a savage howl – half-borne of pain, half of pent-up fury – he let loose a surge of rending, tearing strength that no torture-gurney had ever been built to withstand.

In their fives and tens, the accursed straps started to unbuckle and split.

Billings sat upright in the gurney, accosting the two shocked-looking pseudo-doctors, who had glanced over shoulders, upon hearing these sounds.

"*Hey motherfuckers!*" he cursed, with glowing eyes, through clenched teeth.

Wake Up, O My Brother

With a shudder reverberating through the surrounding walls, accompanied by a snapping-sound like somebody a mite too stout sitting on a plank, the locked door shattered into several large shards. These – not really stopped by whatever had been desperately placed just behind – collapsed backward into the room beyond.

The dozen or so bullet-holes in the door hadn't helped any, but it had actually been split apart by a blast of invisible force from Tanaka's scary-powerful mind.

Jacobson, White and Boyd didn't say anything, but the former Science Officer knew of their worry, anyway.

"I can only do this when things are *very* close," she had tried to explain.

The soothing words hadn't done a lot to reassure them.

Though there was a haze of suspended gyp-rock particles in the area of this forced-entry portal, the four victors of the shoot-out that had just happened in the corridor could easily tell that there were three people – well, okay, *two* biologically identifiable humans, and one other that the Mars mission-folk couldn't quite be sure of – inside the room.

The odd thing was... you would have thought that the two men who had been near the door, would be grabbing guns, firing at whatever was coming at them from outside. But instead – for some reason – they were both rushing *backward*, in the direction of whomever seemed to be about ten feet behind them.

"I think we cleared all the guards – Cherie, can you confirm that?" whispered Jacobson, from his crouching position down the hall.

"Except for whoever's in the room, past what's left of the door," agreed Tanaka. "I'm not seeing – not feeling – not *whatever* – anybody alive, except the three of them. *Oooh...*"

She paused, bent over with palms on thighs, as if to catch her breath. "Hooboy – did you guys feel *that*? A thought, communication like we do – but incoherent, raw hate –"

"Yeah," muttered White, still nervously fingering his gun, wisps of smoke issuing lazily from its muzzle. "Sorta like the vibes I got from y'all, Professor, just before we greased them two assholes at our first stop in this damn place... but even worse. Whoever he is – I *think* it's a 'he' – he's got *serious* issues."

Boyd was about to offer a comment, but he was cut off by more sounds of mayhem from within the room.

"Get a gun!" they heard, from the far-off reaches of the place. "What the *fuck* – grab him!"

There were more curses and screams, accompanied by crashing, shattering noises, gunshot-sounds and the 'thud' of something quite large being thrown against a wall.

A second later, through the diminishing remnants of the gypsum-dust and gun-smoke, the four Mars mission astronauts saw the crawling figure of a smock-clad *faux*-doctor, his legs evidently inoperative, trying desperately to clear the door for the corridor beyond.

"*Nooooo!*" he yelled, as something from behind the portal dragged him back inside the room. There were muffled shrieks, the sounds of punches and of something being smashed or cracked.

After no more than six or seven seconds, relative silence fell over the scene.

"There's still one guy in there," noted Tanaka. "Feelings of rage have ebbed somewhat. But he's getting faint."

"Well what do we *do*, just go in there and ask him for a business-card?" sardonically suggested Boyd.

"Whoever he is – I think he's on *our* side," offered Jacobson. "Judging from what he seems to have done to that 'doctor' that he dragged back in there."

"What if he's a gangster or terrorist?" cautioned Boyd. "If he's got a gun..."

"Chance I'll have to *take*," replied the former Mars mission commander.

Half-standing, now, Jacobson called out, "Hey – *you* in there! We're friends – not with the keepers of this place. We're here to free you. Lay down your weapons – we're coming in, on the count of five."

They waited for a few seconds, but there was no reply.

"Four... three... two..." Jacobson counted down.

Still, there was no answer coming from the battle-scene room.

"So... who wants to chance it?" he asked, turning to the others.

"I will," volunteered White. "But I'm keepin' my piece at the ready, don't you know."

Jacobson nodded appreciatively, and once more, raised his voice.

"Hey, you!" he shouted. "Major White is coming in to survey the situation. Make no hostile move – or we'll have to take you out. Do you understand?"

They waited a few seconds, but all was silent.

"Here I go," announced the black ex-astronaut.

Carefully, he stepped forward, avoiding the bodies of several GrayWar mercenaries – a few, shot dead by his own and Boyd's marksmanship, the rest sent to the next world by Tanaka's hellish lightening-bolts – while he approached the door.

White looked back at his comrades, got a 'go-ahead' nod from his former commander, and then quickly jumped into the room, spinning around as he exclaimed, "Hands *up!* Make a move and y'all *daid!*"

A second later, they heard, "Whoa! Y'all better come in here and check this out – looks like this dude tore them two apart with his bare hands... or somethin'..."

"Clear?" called Jacobson.

"Clear," affirmed White.

Rapidly, the rest of the team poured in to the room, whose accouterments looked unpleasantly like the first one to which they had been ushered, upon being introduced to this benighted place.

Much of the torture-room had been trashed – although not, apparently, by bullets or other mundane projectiles; instead, shattered, smashed things lay haphazardly strewn hither and yon, handles were torn from cabinet-doors, there were chairs with one or two supporting-legs missing, and so on.

Like the first chamber that had confronted the Jacobson team in the Amchitka facility, there were two gurneys in the middle of the place, but the larger one was rent and bent out of shape, with most of its restraining-straps seemingly torn by some superior force. The second looked like it had been normally-unbuckled.

The *faux*-doctors – including the one who had tried to escape, a minute or so before – who must have nominally been in charge here, were now quite dead, with arms, legs and necks twisted into impossible contortions. Their forlorn bodies bore ugly purplish, sub-skin, blood-swelling bruises – and also a few strangely green-tinted finger- and knuckle-prints, mutely attesting to a lethal assault by an unknown assailant.

"*Whoa*," whistled an impressed Boyd, looking at the third man. "You mean *he* did all *that?*"

They all turned their attention to the slumped, abused figure of pathos who now lay drooling and unconscious in a semi-fetal-position, against the far wall.

This man must have been in his middle to late 40s, and though, if standing up straight, he would have been of decent size – almost as tall as Jacobson, in fact – he looked like the prototype Mr. Average American; that is, rather too much around the gut, thinning hair and a flabby, out-of-shape physique.

The poor guy had evidently been here for a while, judging from his stubble-beard, bushy eyebrows, greasy, sweaty complexion and, most of all, the cruel, bloodstained and burned wounds, which scarred every uncovered part his body. His hands – the knuckles of which were bloody almost down to the bone – were still clenched into fists, though the man showed no signs of life, other than for fitful, faint breathing.

Tanaka dashed over to the unfortunate and tried to roust him.

"Hey, you – *hey* – do you *hear* me?" she stammered.

There was no response. Instead, the man's breathing became even fainter.

The color was draining from his face.

"We're losing him!" observed Jacobson. "Poor fellow... but at least he went out *fighting*."

"Yeah," agreed Boyd. "Guy robbed us of our chance to get back at those two bastards in the smocks – but I don't begrudge him the favor. I hope he knew he got his revenge, before..."

After staring sadly at the man with big, watering eyes, a shocked, pained look suddenly appeared on Tanaka's face.

"You don't *understand!*" she cried. "Brent, Devon – help me get him up – prop up his head and shoulders – *right now!*"

"Sure, Professor," said White, as he retrieved a head-pillow from one gurney and a blanket from somewhere else. "But what's th' big deal... this dude's almost done anyways, so why don't we let him go in peace... y'all want me to say a prayer, or somethin'?"

Jacobson crouched beside his former Science Officer and furtive lover.

"Listen, Cherie," he quietly suggested, "I don't blame you for caring, because this was a damn *brave* guy who fought to the last, rather than just be a victim, but... well, Devon's right. We don't have any first-aid gear on us, and anything that we find in here isn't likely to be good for someone in distress. We can try to make him comfortable, but we shouldn't take too much time about it... we'll have to get moving, soon. What with all the shooting –"

The woman turned her head and instantly, the other three were stopped in their tracks by the distant, other-worldly look upon her visage, accompanied with an equally weird eye-glow.

"*Professor –*" started Boyd, uneasily, but he was cut off.

"Robert – Bob – Mr. Billings – we're here – wake up, wake *up*, o my beloved *brother*," frantically chanted Tanaka.

She took hold of his shoulders and then embraced him closely, staring determinedly into his comatose, glassy eyes, and, not much to the surprise of the male ex-astronauts, little charges of white-purple energy began to issue from her forearms, transiting all over the man's upper-body, like the visible evidence of some kind of self-generated defibrillator-treatment.

Slowly, his breathing again became regular and his face, which had been pale as the proverbial sheet, began to regain its color. But the man was still out cold, numb to the rest of the world.

"What can I say but... 'wow'!" commented a duly-impressed Boyd. "I have a feeling that I already know the answer to the next question – but, Professor, how the hell did you learn to do *that*? And how'd you *know*?"

Now reclining side-saddle next to the apparently rescued torture-victim, with a far-off look, Tanaka replied, "Don't know, Brent... I was *desperate*... it just *came* to me, I guess – on both counts. Maybe like when you first learn how to skate, you think, 'why didn't I get it the first time', or something like that... I don't know. But enough about *me*. You heard... right?"

"Are you sure it's *him*?" inquired Jacobson. "Billings, I mean."

"Yeah, I am," she confirmed. "No doubt at all in my mind."

"Well... thank God for small favors," whistled Jacobson. "That's one down and four to go, I guess. Very lucky that you figured out *that* little trick, Cherie – you're encroaching on my specialty – but I'm not complaining. Good work."

He smiled warmly at his former Science Officer, a gesture that was immediately reciprocated.

"I don't want to dis' him, y'all understand," mentioned White, "But somehow this guy don't, I don' know, he just don't look too much like somebody who'd hang with a, uhh, a 'Storied Watcher'... he looks pretty damn ordinary... I mean, look at what's left of that beer-gut, I'd bet he can't do twenty push-ups even back wherever he got yanked off the street from. And besides... what was all that 'o my brother' stuff, Professor? If y'all don't mind my askin', that is."

"Because he *is* our brother, Devon," she replied, plainly and simply. "He's one of *us*. I can feel his thoughts – or at least I *could*, until he went out."

"*Wait* a minute," protested Boyd. "Didn't she specifically *say* that she wasn't going to do that? I mean – spreading this *Amaiish* thing all over Hell's Half Acre, down here? Because if he's been 'transformed', as we've been –"

"Brent's got a point," added Jacobson. "If she's been handing out *our* kind abilities indiscriminately –"

"Don't *sound* like her – that's for sure," White pointed out. "And if she did, maybe she made this poor ol' dude say that pledge that we had to do, up in the *Eagle*... that might 'splain it. Hey, listen, Commander... I'm gonna cover the door... okay?"

"Good idea," stated Jacobson, as the black ex-astronaut, gun again at the ready, fast-paced over to what was left of the portal and peered into the half-darkened corridor beyond.

"Anyone coming?" asked the commander.

"Negative, for now," answered White. "But I wouldn't count on it stayin' that way forever... we made a lot of noise back there, few minute ago."

"Yeah – you got it," echoed Jacobson.

Turning to address Tanaka, he started to say something about 'What do you think his condition is', but suddenly, the wounded man's eyelids fluttered and he began to mumble something.

"Mr. Billings – Bob – can you hear me?" quickly queried the Professor.

"Kid... forgive me... just don't have any more... out of gas," he slurred. "Don't let 'em get you... last ounce I got... from Uncle Bob... tell them I *tried*..."

He coughed, spitting up blood, and, with eyelids closed in a pained wince, moved his head slightly to one side.

"It's oh-kay," responded Tanaka, her tone patient, loving and reassuring, like a parent tending to a sick child. "Take some deep breaths... and take your time. I'm *here* for you now, Bob Billings."

"Bob here... Bob... whaaa... Sari? *Sari?*", he raved, semi-deliriously.

"Oh God, Sari!" incoherently stammered the wounded civilian, "I'm sorry, *so* sorry... ha, that's still funny, I think, don't you... didn't *mean* to say those things... about you... hurting, out of my head..."

Now the man came to, with a wide-eyed stare.

He regarded Tanaka with a mixture of joy, worry and panic and exclaimed, "Sari? *Sari!*"

A second later, the smile left the man's face, and, utterly confused, he muttered, "Hey... you don't *look* like... you *feel* like... *whaaa?* Who are *you*?"

"*Welcome back, Bob Billings, beloved brother of the New People,*" answered Cherie Teruko Tanaka, with a familiar, saturnine smile.

I'll Cross That River Jordan

Though the clean-cut, rather tall, twenty- or thirty-something Caucasian man had been here umpteen times, the size, grandeur and – despite the cheapishness of the strip-mall-bought rococo imitation-of-Notre-Dame statues, glowering down from upper places, everywhere – *severity*, of the place, never ceased to impress him.

Well, it's patterned after the Lord's own Heaven, after all, thought the man.

You'd expect it to get the message of respect, across to those favored enough to be allowed in here.

He approached the brass doors, smiling earnestly at the SWAT-geared gendarmes stationed on either side of the heavily-reinforced portal.

"Martin here, per schedule," he announced, to one of the guards.

"This is sanctified ground," grunted the gendarme. "You must say the proper words."

"I know," smiled the newcomer, reflexively adjusting his tie. "Stained with the blood of apostates... but purified with that of believers."

"The Holy Leader will see you, now, Brother Martin," acknowledged the man, from behind his mirror-visored combat-helmet.

He pressed a hidden button or switch of some kind on the wall immediately behind him, and, with a 'creak' sound, the huge doors slowly swung open.

Now, the clean-cut young man advanced to the threshold and peered inside.

This next room – really, more like the worship-hall of a cathedral, minus the pews, baptismal-font and podium – was mostly cloaked in shadow, except for subtle lights on the side-walls which accentuated the gargoyle-faces peering down from every angle.

At the far end, was a large hardwood desk, with the head-and-shoulders figure of a man – his features, as well, hidden by the oppressive gloom and majesty of the place – in an appropriately-large, leather-bound, reclining-chair.

"Come," demanded the man behind the desk.

After a quick bow, Martin advanced at an even pace, not looking back when the doors swung shut behind him. He stopped at a point perhaps ten feet from the desk, bowed again and looked up.

A half-second later, he suppressed an urge to shout in shock and surprise.

Slowly, the haggard, creased-leather face of his superior and mentor, was raised up from where it had resided on or near the surface of the desk.

The man's visage was streaked with the traces of tears, and the dark rings under his eyes – the pupils of which were subtly dilated – spoke of many hours without rest or sleep.

"*Blessed Brother –*" started Martin.

The Christian leader interrupted and motioned for silence with a shaken index-finger.

"Son," languidly stated Brother Harold, his characteristic Southern drawl now even longer than usual, with deep breaths taken on every phrase, "I didn't want you to see me like this... but... no, maybe it's better that you did... considerin' all that we have to go over."

"Sir... I don't mean to be impertinent, but... well... you don't seem like *yourself*, today..." stammered the clean-cut young man.

"I'm not," replied Harold. "If you'll bear with me... I will explain."

"Oh... of course," obediently agreed Martin.

"Take a chair," directed the elder man, pointing first to a plain, wooden seat to one side, then to a spot about five feet from the edge of the desk.

The younger man pulled the chair back to his place, which was now dead-center in front of the desk, at the designated distance.

Again, Harold's head sagged over his clasped hands, and for a moment, his young understudy was afraid that he'd collapse entirely. But after a few unpleasant seconds of complete silence, the Christian leader managed to again raise himself up and stare forward.

"You see... I have been prayin' for guidance continuously since we came into possession of the device – and, last night – the Lord took me to the mountain," explained Harold, speaking slowly and deliberately, as if half in a trance. "And God has revealed His plan to me. It's all clear to me now... *so* clear. It's just that I don't want it to happen... may it not offend the Lord in me sayin' this – but now, I think I know how our Savior felt, on the night before He was betrayed..."

"What... uhh... do you *mean*, sir?" nervously inquired Brother Martin.

"What I mean," answered Harold, "Is, the Lord told me – in a dream – what my fate is to be – and it's the same one as for the saints and martyrs, indeed, the same one that our Savior Himself had to endure. My days on this Good Earth are numbered, now; for it'll be *me* who must-do the deed – it'll be *I* who will have to send the Devil-Girl back to Hell, by lurin' it right next to my own side, and then... *I'll* hit that button on the device, son. *That's* how it must be done."

"Sir... *no!*" cried the younger man with genuine grief and indignation. "It can't *be!* There *must* be some other way!"

"I know that this must come as a blow to y'all," wearily noted the older man. "And God Himself knows... I've prayed and prayed and *prayed*, and I've *begged* the Lord for a reprieve, for this cup to be passed from my hands – but each time, the message has come back, clearer and firmer than before."

He paused for a second, and then continued, "No, my brother in Jesus... these are the orders that our Heavenly Father have given – not just to me, but to you as well – for just as Joshua had to take over from Moses at the verge of the Promised Land... it will be *you*, who will have to guide and grow this organization, and also keep it on the straight and true path of the One True Faith, after I've started my new life, with our Lord and Savior in Heaven. The cloak and staff will pass to *you*, Brother Martin... and I pray that you all will be ready for it – because the time is very near."

"Sir," whimpered Martin, with his own eyes now welling. "May we pray?"

"Let us pray," answered the Christian leader, offering his hand, which the other man grasped tightly across the desk-top.

"Holy Father God," invoked Brother Harold from behind squinty-closed eyes, "We humbly come to Thee today, as we fight the weakness of our pitiful, filthy, protestin' human flesh and try our best to follow Thy wise counsel of truth and justice. Lord... Thou hast given this Thy unworthy servant, who dares address Thee now, knowin' that he doesn't deserve even one *second* of Thy endless time – in Thy infinite wisdom, Thou hast given this here poor, useless sinner Thy blessed order to martyrdom, in the righteous battle against the accursed Spawn of Satan."

His senses reeling, the younger man tried to follow along, in his mind.

"We pray now, Lord," chanted Brother Harold, "That Thou might make us firm and true to this task, never thinkin' about self... make us crave death in Thy service, spendin' every wakin' moment readyin' ourselves for the final battle. Make us strong, Lord, give us courage to wield Thy Terrible Swift Sword with Thy Fortress of Lord Sabaoth, against the Muslim- and Devil-spawned Evil One, that She might be thrown by Thy mighty hand down to the depths of Hell, never again to plague this Thy chosen land."

"*Hallelujah*," whispered Brother Martin, as his mentor went on,

"Dear Lord, we know by Thy literal, inerrant word in the Holy Protestant Christian Bible, that our life on this here Earth is short and of no consequence whatsoever; but our *new* life, bought only by the sacrificial, Jew-spilled, agonized blood of our Lord and Savior Jesus Christ, is eternal – as is eternity in Hell, for those who dare to deny Thy supreme righteousness. Make us to always keep that fact foremost in our cowardly, inadequate, perverted minds, when we kneel, quakin' in fear before Thee after our deservin', sinners' deaths shortly to come... and then beg forgiveness for lifetimes of transgressions down here on Earth. Lord, we *know* we're worthy only of Hell; but we throw ourselves, terrified, at Thy feet, beggin' the mercy of Lord Jesus to ransom our dirty, pathetic, worthless souls. Let it be so, Dear Lord... this we pray with broken hearts, in Jesus' name... Amen."

"Amen!" breathed Brother Martin. But his hand was still tightly in the other man's grasp.

"Amen, amen, amen – let it be so, Dear Lord – amen!" added the acolyte.

"And also, mighty Father God," continued the severe man, "We now ask for Thy blessin' for Thy servant Brother Martin, who Thou hast selected to lead Thy flock here on Earth, after he who now addresses Thee does his duty and gives up his life in Thy faithful service. Thou hast spoke unto me and made me to pass the cloak of leadership to this man – an unworthy man of weak human flesh, just like me – but, Dear Lord... he's a man with a good, humble, Christian heart... and he'll do Thy biddin' and follow in mine own footsteps, if Thou will show him the way –"

"I *know* I'm not up to the task, Lord," interrupted Martin. "I can't *hope* to come *close* to the great accomplishments of a godly leader of men like Master Harold, who's been like my elder brother, wisely counseling and disciplining me since that wonderful day when first I was born again into the One True Church of Lord Jesus, and I don't deserve to take over for him. Thou already knowest that I'm inadequate in every way, but when that sad time comes – as Thou bid it do – that dear Brother Harold is delivered by the blood of Jesus into Thy merciful hands, between the tears pouring from my eyes... I'll get down on trembling knees and beg Thee for the Holy wisdom and strength of purpose that only Thou can bestow. I'm weak, corrupt and stupid, Lord... with Thy help, I can do *anything* – but without Thee, I'm nothing more than dirt, filth and garbage. Use me as Thou may will... and if that means I must shortly join my Brother Harold with Thee... I'm ready, Lord! I crave death, to do Thy bidding. May it be so... amen."

"Amen," echoed Harold.

With a fatherly tone, he instructed, "Son... the Lord knows you, as He knows me, as he has known each and *every* God-fearin' mortal since the first second that seed and egg came together in his mother's womb – and He has inerrantly made the right choice for both of us. Now, Feared Immortal Father God... we ask for Thy special blessin' for the quests of martyrdom and Christian leadership that Thou hast wisely laid upon us."

Martin nodded, gravely, as the Christian leader, preached, "Lord – we humbly pray that Thee find some way to pardon us sinnin' human bein's from the terrible, unforgivable transgressions of perversion, blasphemy, homo-sexuality, withholdin' of donations to Thy church, abortion, welfare, race-mixin', birth control, gun control, schools without Thy word to start the day, and – worst of all – lib-ral toleration of non-believers, that we foolishly allow, each and every day, hatefully ignorin' Thy life-givin' word of truth, law and life as given in Thy beautiful Protestant Bible."

"Amen," the younger man whispered.

"Set us on the straight path, O Lord," requested Brother Harold, "And especially make Thy unworthy servants Harold and Martin strong and without fear, for the great quests that Thou has laid before us. Father God, if even a *Jew* named 'Moses' could part the Red Sea with but a sneeze from Thy mighty nostrils... then, surely Thou canst gird us poor Christian sinners, to strike the Evil One down to Hell – let her burn and writhe in agony for all eternity – as she so richly deserves. In Jesus' lovin', gentle, merciful name, this we pray... amen."

"Amen," earnestly echoed Brother Martin.

He looked up at the other man. "How am I going to carry *on* for you, Master?" he plaintively asked. "I just can't find the *words*, like you do."

"Patience, Brother," counseled Brother Harold. "The words will come to you – as will everythin' else – if you just read your Bible and give your body, soul and mind up to the Lord. Release yourself from human cares and desires and just faithfully ask God to run you like His puppet... and you'll be okay. It has always worked that way for me... and I have no doubt that it will for you, too."

"God be praised!" intoned the younger man.

"Amen," added Harold.

"Okay, now, son... here's my plan," he started, the shadows of this place painting a gloomy fate on his face.

Failure To Communicate, Or Something

The anodyne, close-cropped, blue-eyed and dapper – despite the creased shirt, emblematic of a long day putting out organizational and political fires – figure of Jerry Kaysten reclined against the front edge of his White House Executive Branch desk, as he hastily wiped the mayo and mustard from his lips and strained to reach the mobile-communicator, its ring-tone playing his favorite, retro-70s punk "incoming-call" anthem.

No future, no future for youu..., it sounded, with an unmistakable, Rotten-Johnny snarl.

Didn't Bezomorton say something about that? mused Kaysten, as he fumbled for the "answer" button.

Well... as long as I drew the short straw and got stuck down here with the stunt-dummies, waiting for the Muslims, the alien and the Democrats to come collecting trophy heads, I should be able to end-run a rule or two, shouldn't I?

"Yo – Kaysten here," he rapidly fired off.

Something started being said from the device's too-small speaker.

"Umm-hmm," mumbled Kaysten, as he started to scribble pencil-notes on the back of a lunch-counter receipt. "Yeah, I'm the Chief of Staff – I seem to be in charge of all that, these days... sure, go ahead."

"Yeah... okay... I know, but things are a little, uhh, 'unusual' these days... you understand?" he went on. "It's all that Muslim-stuff – oh, no, couldn't agree more with you there – if I woke up one day and every last one of 'em had just vanished off the face of the Earth, I'd be –"

After a second or two, he apologized, "Sorry... didn't mean to ramble on there... I'm listening... you want *what*? No, that's just not *possible* – I'm sympathetic, please don't get me wrong – but since Horn took off to parts unknown, I'm still catching up on a lot of loose ends on the political-front, I guess this is one of them, I'm doing the best I *can* – we're interviewing for a replacement... what's *that*?"

The Chief of Staff rolled his eyes and listened patiently, then asked, "Well... why can't we send somebody from the Cabinet – I don't know – maybe the Secretary of State? Yeah – I *know* he's a Jew, but for Chrissakes – no offense meant – they're on *our* side. Okay then... how about the *Vice*-President, or somebody from Defense... you folks are big on the military, right? I can probably get you a General, an Admiral... what about an amputee war-hero or two? We got lots of those who we can pull from Walter Reed – even got some missing everything but their heads, you should *see* 'em, fuckin' *amazing*, or – "

More incoherent babble confronted Kaysten's ear, then he again spoke up.

"Look... what we have here is a 'failure to communicate'," he complained. "However much money you give to the Party – not that we don't *appreciate* it, you understand – but the President's schedule is usually made up months to a year in advance, you can't just – what? Well – I can pass on the message, but I really doubt that the answer is going to be any different... yeah? Yes, of *course* he and the First Family are here – as a matter of fact, he's in the Oval Office right now... oh, come *on*, that's just some kind of stupid conspiracy-theory – do you think we could pull off *that* kind of a stunt for months on end? I'm sorry, but I can't discuss... you know, the old 'national-security' thing... right? Anyway, I'll see what I can do, but don't get your hopes up... maybe in the summertime... what?

"Not a chance!" complained the Chief of Staff. "We couldn't even – look, I'll tell you what – since we *do* appreciate all the support that your organization has been giving to the Party year after year, I'll ask him personally on your behalf, but I pretty much know what he'll have to say... once we know what the score is, then we can talk again and get something firmed up... umm-humm? Sure! How about in a week or so – by then I should know. Right. Oh – no problem, we're always happy to go show the flag, gotta keep that old base happy, you know? Okay, great – have a nice day. You too. 'Bye."

As he hit the "hang up" button, Kaysten shook his head.

Fucking Bible-bangers, he self-harangued.

Since we got the voting-machines all rigged up... who even needs *them, anymore?*

And fuck Billy Horn too – wherever the hell he is.

Wasn't it his *job to schmoozle with these hillbillies?*

It ain't mine... and it sure ain't the President's, thought the Chief of Staff.

But, he realized, *I guess I'll have to call the Old Man and ask him anyway, just so it's* him *who's saying 'no'.*

¡Agarra Sus Armas, Muchachos!

"*Mira!*" shouted someone from the back of the van.

"*Oyeme, cholo* – we *got* to stop somewhere! And I ain't jokin'!"

"*Que tal?*" demanded the driver, as if he didn't already know the answer.

"Gustavo is lookin' *real* bad, *hombre... real* bad," argued the voice. "Come *on,* man, pull the fuckin' truck over so we can at least get that shit he puke all over the place, washed out... *comprende?*"

The driver turned and looked anxiously at the navigator.

"What you think, *cholo?*" he inquired. "*Usted sabe, el jéfé* say that we wasn't s'posed to stop 'till we get past the 'burbs... meet up with the *muchachos* from the *barrio* there."

He raised his voice, addressing the *Maras* in the back.

"What's *wrong* with him, *hermano?*" the driver asked. "Fucker got the flu or somethin'?"

"*Yo no sabe,*" came back the reply. "He just get sick all of a sudden – that's all. Bunch of us not feelin' too great, either – me *duele en la cabeza... comprende?* Come *on,* man, just for *cinquo minutos,* then we get goin' again, *de acuerdo?*"

"I don' know either, *hombre,*" argued the navigator. "It's gettin' dark again, an' since them last two detours I'm not even sure where we is, an' with all these road-lights out it's fuckin' *impossible* to tell – ain't even no McDonald's signs lit up, worse than Houston, *cholo* – I don' know *how* you keepin' this *camion* on the road – an' we *got* to find the right side-street so we's can get into the City past the Man – *el jéfé* say he had it all figured out, *pero no se olvide,* he also say 'if you *putos* off by even one block, them Crips gonna have you balls for snack-time'... *me entiende?* I guess we *could* just pull over for the night in that big park we passed back there – you know, the one on the right – an' try it in the mornin'... but we be late then. You want to chance it, *cholo?*"

The driver seemed lost in thought for a moment or two, but then he stated, "No, I don' think so... you see that sign few miles back there?"

"Only got a glimpse of it, *amigo*," replied the navigator. "But I think we still on 60."

"Thought it said 'Yorba' somethin'," pointed out the driver. "That's in L.A... *verdad*? An' the last route-sign I see was *noventa*-somethin'... but it's so fuckin' dark, *hombre*, if you'd just let me turn on the lights, for once –"

"Hey, come *on*, you fuckers," yelled a voice from the back of the van. "*¡Que el aire huele aqui!*"

"*Tenga paciencia – ya casi llegamos*," the driver tried to order, shouting over his shoulder.

"*Si hombre*... but didn't *el jéfé* say the turn-off was in Chino?" nervously inquired the navigator. "*Espera un momento, permítanme referirme a mi mapa.*"

"*Por supesto, hombre*," replied the driver, turning his head slightly to address the other man. "But I don' think we can keep them *muchachos* stuck back there much – *¡LA MIERDA!*"

Desperately, he jammed on the brakes, to avoid the barrier of half-nailed-together two-by-fours, sandbags and oil-drums, that had suddenly loomed alarmingly-close in the headlights; but this sent the maps and various other items in the van's cabin, flying in various directions, while the navigator's head slammed brutally into the dashboard.

With the squeal of burning rubber, the vehicle – its wheel-base only barely able to deal with the momentum of the sudden deceleration – lurched and tilted from right to left and then back again, but eventually came to a fitful stop.

Dazed – with blood pouring from his nose and lips – the navigator mumbled a curse in Texas-street Spanish, as he tried to get his wits about him.

Something guttural and menacing sounded from outside, on the other side of the barrier.

It sounded like a warning, in English.

"FUCK! Roadblock!" shouted the driver, as howls of protest started coming from the *Maras* in the cargo compartment. "*Espera, yo voy que –*"

With reflexes honed from dozens of similar, earlier encounters with law-enforcement, he quickly threw the van into reverse and tried to speed backwards into the welcoming safety of the darkness. But this maneuver was rewarded with a loud "pop", as both rear tires went flat in no more than a second or two.

"Ohh, *fuck*, my head hurts..." complained the navigator, as he wiped the blood from his beard.

From outside, they now heard an ominous demand, delivered by megaphone.

"Exit of the van – *now!*" it ordered. "You're prisoners of the White Aryan People's Christian Army, on cause of resisting lawful arrest! You have ten seconds... or you'll be shot like *dogs!*"

They could just hear another voice from somewhere outside, saying something like "I think they're fuckin' wetbacks in there, Aryan Lictor Captain... probably more of them cock-suckin' taco-asses tryin' to sneak in from Mexico."

"*¡Agarra sus armas, muchachos!*" cried the driver, about three seconds before the shooting started.

Just A Lil' Ol' Walk In The Park

"Take a few deep breaths... take your time," counseled Cherie Tanaka, with an uncanny bedside-manner that would have made Florence Nightingale green with envy.

Every word that she issued during those first few minutes seemed to give the man some implausible succor; although, judging from the punishment that he had recently endured, it was miraculous that he was the least *bit* coherent.

"Better... better now," he mumbled, with the color slowly returning to his cheeks. "But – uhh, no offense, lady – I just thought that you might be someone... uhh... *else*, that's all. I mean, you sure sounded – *felt* – like – "

"Like... who?" disingenuously inquired Boyd.

"This isn't, uhh, going to make a lot of sense," muttered the ex-prisoner, "But... well, you see, her name is 'Sari'... she's kind of my girlfriend, and I had this crazy idea that she was on her way to spring my sorry ass out of here... but hey, I'll take you guys... any port in a storm... you know?"

"Quite a storm – you got *that* right," commented Jacobson, as he scouted the entrance-way for signs of movement.

White sat down, cross-legged, beside Billings, and said, extending a hand, "I'm Devon White, formerly U.S. Air Force, just like my homie Brent over there, Captain Jacobson as well – he's the big guy, by the way. Nice to get to know y'all, Mr. Billings... mind if we call you 'Bob'?"

Limply shaking the black astronaut's hand, the salesman replied, "Oh, for sure, Devon... nice to meet you, too, and that goes for all of you. No, let me take that back – I'm damn *lucky* to meet you all. I guess I owe you my life... did the best I could, but I'm no hero..."

Boyd crouched down, looking intently at the man.

"Yes, you *are*," he countered. "You have *no* idea, Mr. Billings."

Billings winced in pain and slumped back.

"Where are my shoes?" he grumbled. "They take 'em off you when they start... oh, *there* they are," he added, with a wheeze.

"Hey... take it *easy*," admonished Tanaka. "We *know* what you've been through, Bob – I'm trying to help, but there's only so much I can do, without getting you to a hospital... and I'm afraid there isn't likely to be anything like that, around here."

"You don't *say*," muttered the ex-victim. "Actually, you know – funny thing is... it *is* an awful lot like a hospital down here, with the one exception that the 'doctors' are here to make things *worse*... not better. Kind of like what we got back in Tucson... but at least they don't cancel your health-insurance when they 'operate' on you."

He paused for a second or two, then gratefully remarked, "And, just for the record... I sure *could* feel you 'helping'... that's *so* weird... thanks so much..."

Tanaka smiled serenely as White chuckled, "Man's got a sense of humor – damn useful down here, and that's no lie. But listen, Bob... about this, uhh, 'Sari' chick... that what y'all called her?"

"Nothing visible down the corridor," interrupted Jacobson. "But we had better figure out what to do with Mr. Billings... I don't think we want to hang around here too much longer."

"For what it's worth, I don't remember seeing too many guards in this rat-hole," offered the salesman. "By the time people get here, they're mostly not in any shape to fight back. Oh – but as to my, uhh, girlfriend – well, her name's 'Sari' – 'Sari Tanak'... at least that's what she told me. I realize this might not make a lot of sense to you guys, but – you see – she's... uhh... a little weird... okay, a *lot* weird – not the kind of person that you'd want to get on the bad side of... you know? So I had this idea that she'd... no, I guess you *wouldn't* know... would you? Look, I can explain this, but it might take some time –"

Now Cherie Tanaka, the first-blessed by a latter-day 'angel', lowered her head with closed eyelids; and from somewhere, a stirring, ethereal song began to invade the consciousness of all the super-mortal beings, in this small oasis of subterranean enlightenment.

A second later, she slowly raised up her head and opened her bright-glowing, *Amaiish*-powered eyes, staring intently at Bob K. Billings, Jr..

"*No*, Bob," she cooed, with regal demeanor, "I don't think it will take any time at all... because we both know *who* we're talking about... *don't* we?"

"*Holy sh* – wait a minute!" stammered the salesman. "I *thought* I recognized you – you're – you're one of those *astronauts*... right? The ones who were on the Mars mission, the ones who they told us dug up – while the comet was –"

"Bingo!" quipped Boyd, pointing an insouciant finger at Billings.

"Y'all one fast learner there, Bob my man," joked White.

"Listen, I don't want to make any more enemies – I got enough of those for six lifetimes, down here already – but are all of you, uhh... like... like... *her*, now? Not that it would make any difference to yours truly, of course," he prevaricated. "Why, some of my best friends are space-aliens!"

"Well... that's probably a *good* thing," commented Boyd. "How's it go, again? Oh yeah – you gotta learn to love yourself, first. To appreciate your own best qualities, in somebody else."

"Huh?" replied the confused salesman.

Now, after a gesture requesting White to take up the sentry station, it was Jacobson's turn to sit down beside the convalescing torture-victim.

"Listen, Mr. Billings," he related, "You've been through a lot – and ordinarily we'd try to introduce some of the following information to you more gradually... but given what we had to do to get to this room in the first place, I'm concerned that we might have set off some alarms – thus we might be attacked by a larger force of guards at any moment, so this is going to come at you rather fast... bear with me, okay?"

"Believe me, Captain," countered Billings, "If you knew what I've already seen – been through – you'd know that nothing you're likely to say to me, is going to surprise me very much... so go for it."

"Fair enough," agreed the former Mars mission leader. "And by the way, please call me 'Sam' – as I believe Devon mentioned, all of us who had previously been in the Air Force – well, we've kind of resigned our commissions, you know?"

"The fact that you had to *shoot* your way in here, made me suspect something like that," wryly offered the salesman.

"We're no more down here of our own free will, than you are," explained Jacobson. "Except that – thank God – the 'gifts' that your, uhh, 'girlfriend' bestowed upon us, have progressed a little further in us, than they have in you; so, we had more of a chance to get ourselves free, then come looking for yourself, as well as –"

"*Wait* a minute," demanded Billings, with an air of worry. "What do you mean, 'gifts', and what do you mean, 'in me'?"

"How's it feel to be in the space-alien club, Mr. Bob?" interjected White.

"Like – *her*?" asked the salesman, pointing at Tanaka, whose song and eye-glow started to tactfully wane.

A second later, he hastily added, "Listen... please, sorry – I take that back, I just meant –"

"Bob," she spoke, in an eerily familiar, kindly voice, "What Sam means is, while we were up in space with your 'girlfriend', she *changed* us – made us better, more powerful in every way – the noble and loving Storied Watcher gave us the gift of using the previously-unknown energy called *Amaiish*, or, 'the *Fire*', is how you'd call it, in English – and it appears that she's done the same for you. You're one of *us*, Bob; her power lies upon you, it grows in you, just as it does in the rest of us."

"That's... uhh... great... really... *great*," warily muttered Billings.

She approached closer still and took hold of his hand.

"Bob," said Tanaka, "We'll talk more about this later... but there are a few things that I think you need to understand, right up front. One, the gift of *Amaiish* is the greatest thing that has ever happened to the human species, since our ancestors learned how to use fire – it's *that* important. Two, as far as we know, once it takes hold in a person, there's no way to turn back the process – which is probably the only thing that kept you alive, while the bastards in charge of this dungeon were doing their worst to you."

Billings looked away, reflectively.

Then he replied, slowly and ruefully, "Yeah... yeah, you gotta be right about that. They were killing me... *killing* me! But somehow... I got through it. I even thought I heard her voice, now and then... but..."

With a knowing-nod, the former Mars mission Science Officer continued, "Thirdly, Bob... the Storied Watcher must have a very special place for you in her heart, because she told us that she would only give her gift to the very few people who she completely trusted... and four, don't be scared by me, how I look, or what I can do. When you see my eyes, the power flowing through my veins – can you *feel* it, Bob, yes, I *know* you can – you're seeing your future, as well as that of our entire race. *Welcome* it. You're *greatly* blessed, man."

"It's just a bit... *much*, you know," he observed. "And God, you sound so much like... *her*."

"I was the first one that she entrusted with this amazing gift," explained Tanaka. "And I came to know Karéin-Mayréij on a very close basis... she's like a *sister* to me... like the most wise teacher who I've ever –"

"I hate to interrupt, Cherie," Jacobson mentioned, "But we've *got* to get going again in the next few minutes... if Bob can move at all. How you doing?"

Slowly, with each fiber of his being talking back and not saying anything that you'd want your Great-Aunt Harriet to hear, Billings rolled over, propped himself up on all-fours and came to a sitting-position.

"*Damn*," he gasped. "Feels exactly like when they were going at me, just before you guys showed up... I mean, I'm *hurting*, I know that... shouldn't be breathing – shouldn't be crawling – let alone trying to escape from some top-of-the-line shit-hole like this... but *something's* keeping me going. I'd say this is one of those 'out-of-body-experience' thingamajigs... but I'm still very much stuck in this old hide... sorry. Yeah – I guess I *can* get to my feet... but don't expect any nine-yard dashes, you know?"

"Well understood," noted Jacobson. "And – by the way – welcome to the joys of *Amaiish*. If it's of any interest, I've already taken at least one rifle-round in the leg, on this little expedition – and so far, the Storied Watcher's 'gift' has been able to fix it up better than new... not something that I'd advise you try testing if you can avoid it... but comforting to know is there, when and if you need it."

"I'll take... your word... for it..." forced Billings, as his sweat-bedecked brow furrowed in discomfort, while, wheezing and straining, White and Boyd helped him gradually to his feet.

"Well, now, *that* wasn't so hard... was it?" maliciously commented Boyd.

With palms on thighs to support his thorax, Billings complained, "Compared to *what*, my friend? Having your fingernails slowly pulled out, and your guts filled with industrial-strength toilet-bowl cleaner? Yeah – I'd have to say that after all they threw at me, why... this is just a lil' ol' walk in the *park*."

He coughed, weakly.

"Bob, my man, y'all and me, we got somethin' in common," noted White.

"Like?" grunted the salesman. "Oh, wait... *I* know... we're both former members of the human race, now members of... God *knows*, what. And we're both stuck down in some damn Men-In-Black prison, where if they're feeling sympathetic they kill you *fast*, as opposed to slow. Am I close?"

"Havin' a sense of humor – that's how y'all 'n me's alike," confirmed the black ex-astronaut. "Keeps yours truly from goin' nuts, don't you know."

"I'll take your *word* for it," echoed Billings. "And... thanks for the uplift, in both senses of the world. Listen... if you all don't mind, before we get going... I got two questions..."

"Go ahead," said Jacobson. "Quickly, though."

"I guess what I'm asking is," requested the salesman, "Where the hell *are* we, exactly? On the map, I mean. Uhh... if you know. And, you're saying that we've got to get out of here – okay, I *get* that, those guys who we both, uhh, wasted, they're bound to have a few friends come looking for them – but where exactly are we going? What's the plan, Stan?"

"Well, since we first managed to overcome these so-called 'doctors' and the guards who tried to subject us to the same treatment that they gave yourself – that was up on the first level above this one, by the way – we've been improvising," explained Jacobson, "And there are still a lot of details that we don't completely know... but, briefly, this entire prison seems to have been built in a former nuclear weapons test-hole on the island of Amchitka – that's in the Aleutians... Alaska, if you're not up on your geography. We've got a partial map of the facility, and we're using it to track down yourself, as well as –"

"Alaska... *Alaska? Wait* a minute," protested Billings, as the others noted the color returning to his face, with unnatural rapidity. "You mean you could've just buggered on out of here – but you went down – further in, I mean – just to find *me*? Not that I'm complaining... but why the hell am *I* so important to you guys? I mean, you're all Uncle Sam's chosen few, and I'm just a –"

"*Bob*," interjected Tanaka, "Apart from the fact that you're one of us – and that's something that makes your safety a priority, right by itself – there's another, even more important reason."

"Which would be?" inquired the salesman. "By the way... I think I'm mobile, so if you want to get going..."

"Right this way," ushered Boyd, in the direction of the wrecked door. "I think I got all the ammo that was left around here, Captain," he directed, to Jacobson. "Unfortunately, only three clips, both from those dead guards out there, are salvageable; those two guys that Bob tore apart – wish I'd been there to lend a helping-hand, let me say for the record – they were using small-caliber hand-guns, rounds won't fit in the auto-rifles. But I took the pistols anyway... figured it can't hurt to have a sidearm."

"Good work," agreed the Mars mission commander. "Let's go."

Tanaka took Boyd's place supporting Billings' much larger frame.

"You see, Bob," she related, as they stumbled forward, "We know about you and your friends – when you were being abused, images of what was happening, the *pain* of what was happening, too – these came to my mind, Brent's as well. God *damn* them, when I get a *chance* – but anyway. It's some kind of empathetic communication that Teacher gave to us, along with *Amaiish*... it's unpredictable, sporadic – we don't know how to control it, really –

but when it shows up... hooboy, do we *ever* know that we're, uhh, 'in contact', especially if the other person's experiences are unpleasant. I had bad dreams – visions, call them what you will – of people being tormented... you following me, here?"

"Perfectly," confirmed Billings. "And reluctantly. I thought all this stuff showing up in my head was just a dream – just wishful-thinking – or a nightmare... I guess not. Owww..."

"You okay?" asked White.

"Only hurts when I laugh," muttered the salesman. "Oh, and when I move, breathe and who *knows* what else. Don't even *ask* about goin' the john... okay?"

"Should do, Mr. Bob," joked the ex-astronaut, "But only after about a quart or so of Sergei's Stolchi – oh, you don't know him, do you – he was a Russian, up on the space-ship..."

"He must have been with Sari, so he's one of you... one of *us*... right?" asked Billings, staring idly forward.

"Yep," remarked White, as, a good two man-lengths behind Boyd, they traversed the doorway. "Lucky bugger, he don't work for Uncle Sam... didn't get tied up in all this shit. Far as I know he's still up there – but maybe he's back in Russia by now. Can't be worse off than us... right?"

"I'm sure there *is* worse," argued Billings. "There's *always* worse."

"Yeah... reckon y'all right 'bout that," ruefully agreed White, looking down.

"So just after we, uhh, overpowered the two men who had been assigned to torment us – this is on the first floor, like Sam explained earlier – we interrogated one of them and managed to get some information about yourself, and the people with you," Tanaka stated. "There was an African-American woman, and a child, a boy –"

Billings dug in his heels, bringing his two supporting-assistants to an unexpected, dead stop.

"He's *alive*, you know," nervously insisted the salesman. "Tommy – Tommy George – that's his name. Listen, Cherie – you don't mind if I call you 'Cherie', do you? We've *got* to find him, Whitney, Curtis and Melissa, too – before it's too late! Because if we *don't* –"

"We already know why, man... we already *know*," offered White, with unusual seriousness. "But just so we's all on the same page, why don't y'all explain that out a bit."

"Sari considers Tommy to be her son, adopted of course... he's an Indian boy from up north – might be an orphan – but definitely a runaway," explained Billings. "Look... I don't know exactly how to say this, but... well – she's *very* protective of him, of all of us, yours truly included – and, remember how I told you, 'I wouldn't want to get on the wrong side of her'? So... I was right in there with the poor kid when they started doing the old nine-yards on him, and not just once... I lost count... Jesus, *I* could hardly put up with it, Sari's weirdo-crap helping me out, or not. It just broke my *heart* to see those pricks abusing his little body. I *tried* to help him – I really *did*, I *swear* I did... I couldn't *move*..."

Tears welled to the man's eyes and he hung his head.

"Something's wrong back there," whispered Boyd to Jacobson.

"It's okay, Brent," whispered back the commander. "Bob's just telling what's been going on. Not a pretty story, as you can imagine. Let's stop for a minute... keep your eyes peeled."

"Roger that," answered Boyd, fingering his gun as he concentrated both his new and old senses to survey the far reaches of the corridor.

"Bob," counseled Tanaka, "If you don't want to talk about this – we'll understand."

"No... it's okay," he countered, wiping his eye-sockets with a bloodstained shirt-sleeve. "It's... it's important that you know. The gist of it is – what they've been doing to me, they've been doing to Tommy, that I know for sure – and, no doubt, they've been doing it to Claremont and her two kids, as well – the bastards *told* me as much..."

"Are they all still alive?" anxiously demanded the Science Officer. "Whitney Claremont... that's her name? Is she the African-American woman?"

"Yeah, that's her name... her kids are Melissa, about 14 or so, Curtis, he's Tommy's age," stated Billings. "But as to whether they're alive, or where they are, or where Tommy is, now – God, I wish I *knew*. I think I remember them saying something about 'Level Three' for where they were taking Tommy... the others, I got no idea. But lookit – what I was going to say is, about Sari –"

"You mean, 'Karéin-Mayréij' – *that's* her name, you know," corrected Tanaka.

"*Whatever* the hell she's calling herself, these days," shot back the salesman. "That's not important, and I can't remember how to pronounce that damn... uhh... whatever name it was, that you said, anyway. What *is* important, is – if she gets here and finds Tommy's gone... she told me what she'd do, and not just to the lucky ones in the immediate vicinity... to the whole fucking *country*, in fact –"

Sam, come here – you'd better hear this, sent a determined-looking Tanaka to her former commander.

"Shit!" exclaimed an astonished Billings. "I *heard* that. No – *didn't* hear – just like Sari would talk into my head... you mean *you* can do, it too?"

Without saying a spoken word, Tanaka replied,

Yep. We're still learning... so now's a good time for you to do some pick-up lessons.

But we're trying to talk normally when it's safe to do so... this is a little secret that we'd like to keep 'just among ourselves'.

"Roger, wilco... whatever," attempted the salesman.

"I've got Brent on recce," announced Jacobson, who had stepped back to be closer to the three of them. "What's so important?"

"Bob?" prodded the Asian-American woman.

"I was just saying, Captain," explained Billings, "That Sari – you know, Little Miss Martian Goddess – she told me specifically that if the government, or anyone, so much as parted our hair the wrong way, she'd flatten the whole U.S. of A.. with what's gone down so far in here, especially with Tommy... let's just say that I wouldn't want to be in the vicinity, when she gets the bad news..."

"We had feared much the same thing, from the first time that we suspected that you, Tommy and the others might have been the Storied Watcher's, uhh, 'second family', down on this planet," commented Tanaka. "But why would she have let you all be abducted, in the first place? She's powerful enough to shatter a *comet*, after all –"

"Oh... *that's* easy," countered the salesman. "When she told me all this, she also said some bafflegab about, 'after my fall to Earth, my powers had all but vanished – but they're coming back, and it won't be long until I can reduce this 'America' to a smoking ruin, if your fool President mistreats my family"... when I first ran into her, which was in some nut-case religious prison-camp up Idaho way – she was already plenty strange, but not 'blowing up whole *nations*' strange... know what I mean?"

"Which," interrupted Tanaka, addressing Jacobson with a nod, "Undoubtedly explains why she couldn't find, or free, *us*, either. Maybe we really *are* on our own, Sam..."

"Let's hear the rest of the story, before we assume that," suggested the former Mars mission commander.

"So... by the time we all got down to my place in Tucson – that was via ol' Bob's trusty car, incidentally," continued Billings, "Well – let's just say that in a shoot-out between say your average police department and Sari, I'd have picked her 10 times out of 10. But the spooks who came after both of us, when we were at my workplace – they were on a whole new *level*, compared to your garden-variety cops... 'Men-In-Black' stuff, you know. She told me that she didn't feel up to fighting them, at that point, and had to leave me there... the rest is history."

"Pity they couldn't have waited just a few weeks longer," commented Jacobson. "Then this whole fiasco might never have happened."

"Somehow I doubt that, sir," countered White. "You know them CIA-boys, whole government in fact – either they control somethin', or they waste it... been that way down here in the good ol' U.S. of A. for some time, don't you know – they'd probably just have thrown more firepower against her. I just wish that I had given Miss Storied Watcher more of a heads-up on what she was goin' to find, if and when she showed up on Earth. But – as y'all will recall – she didn't seem very confident about comin' back, when she set out from the *Eagle*, for the last time. Her and us... we just had too much to deal with, too fast, I guess."

"And," added Tanaka, "What the government was trying to do with Karéin, Bob and his group as well, is pretty much the same thing that they wanted to do with *us*... remember, Sam? I don't blame her a *bit* for being furious with them!"

"Sari got a good look at how things really work for average Joes like yours truly, starting when I ran into her, Claremont and the kids, up at the Jesus-Jail in Idaho," noted Billings. "For someone with her, uhh, background, she sure caught on, fast. Did I mention she's pretty hard to bullshit?"

"She's had a few hundred thousand years in which to learn how to tell lies from the truth, you know," remarked Tanaka, with the hint of a smile.

"Look, everyone – I can't reasonably argue any of this, given what we've already been through," observed Jacobson. "But with all of it in mind, we've got to figure out where we go from here. So far, I think our best bet is just to try to find the rest of Bob's family – that is, Claremont, her two kids and – most important of all – this 'Tommy', heal them up as best we can and then try to get all of us out of this accursed place, as quickly as possible."

"Great idea," agreed Billings, "Because the faster I get out of here, the better – but, uhh, once we get out... where do we *go*? I don't suppose there's somewhere that we can catch a plane or a boat – not that I have my credit-card on me, anymore... and even if there *was* some transportation available, they'd just come looking for us again... wouldn't they?"

"We sort of hadn't thought through much of that... we're several hundred meters down below the surface of an isolated Aleutian island," replied Jacobson. "And if – *big* 'if', by the way – we find some way to make it topside... I'm afraid that there doesn't seem to be any civilization anywhere nearby. Furthermore, your observations about the likely behavior of our government are, unfortunately, probably correct, so..."

"*So?*" asked Billings, arching an eyebrow.

"The bottom line, Bob," admitted Tanaka, "Is that other than for trying to rescue you, Whitney and the kids... we don't have a *clue*, as to what we do next. We're making this all up as we go – that's about the long and short of it."

"Can't you guys just – I don't know – flap your wings and carry us off into the sunset, or something like that?" complained the salesman. "Sari went on and on about 'how in another week I'll be able to outrun a rocket', or some-such nonsense. How about Hawaii – no, I guess they'd look *there*, too... okay, I *got* it – one of those South-Sea places, or New Zealand – would that be too far? To fly to, I mean."

"We... uhh... *levitate*, Bob," sheepishly mentioned Tanaka. "We haven't quite figured out how to fly... *yet*. By the way, all of us can attest that Karéin wasn't exaggerating, about the 'flying'-thing, that is – within a few days of her being on-board our spacecraft, she was zipping to and fro, at hundreds of thousands of kilometers per hour, in a total vacuum. If I were you... I'd believe *everything* that she says, about what she'll eventually be able to do."

"Since you've, uhh, 'known' her longer than I have, you'll get no arguments about that, in the long-run," allowed Billings, "But for right now – I don't suppose you could maybe 'levitate' us all the way to Hawaii, just for a quick stop-over... could you?"

"I can't speak for Sam and the others," nonchalantly replied the professor, "But I'd probably be able to get you – say – five miles off-shore of Amchitka; after that, you'd sort of be swimming your way to Waikiki. In 50-degree water, that is. I think you'd be doing well to last a half-hour... maybe 40 minutes, on a good day. That's with no waves, you understand."

"Swell," muttered Billings.

"Yo, Bob – good joke there, my man!" grinned White. "But y'all forgot to say, 'an' here I didn't bring my trunks'."

"What?" stammered the salesman. "Oh, wait, *I* get it... heh. Totally unintentional, actually. But I suppose that means, 'Hawaii's out'... right?"

"'Fraid *so*," deadpanned Tanaka, with an arched eyebrow reminiscent of her lost *sensei*.

"Look – this is a subject that we're going to have to deal with later," requested Jacobson. "But Bob... do I remember hearing you saying something about Tommy being on, a, uhh, 'Level Three'? That sounds like one below where we're at, right now. You don't know where Claremont and her children are being held?"

"Yes, and no," answered the salesman. "But the truth is... I know next to nothing about the layout of this place, if that's what you're asking. They had me blindfolded most of the time, except when they took it off to show me what they were planning to do to me."

"More or less what I'd have suspected," grunted the Mars mission commander. "Hey, Brent – can you hear?"

Boyd nodded, one eye still on the corridor beyond.

"I think we're going down one more level in pursuit of the rest of the Billings party," proposed Jacobson. "Does the way look clear to the elevators?"

"Near as *I* can tell, yes," answered Boyd. "But I'd advise against it. Unless they're totally stupid around here, they're bound to have disabled it, or worse – what if they have it remotely rigged to just stop in between floors? We could be trapped... we'd be at their mercy."

"'Mercy' is in short supply around here... or hadn't you noticed," commented the salesman.

"No *shit*," agreed White. "Well, Commander... like I said before we fished out Mr. Billings here – we do got two sets of stairs, or at least I think that's what they are – on this little map-card thang. Gonna take us a few minutes to get to either one of 'em... I'd suggest the one on the west, 'cause it don't seem to have that 'lock'-symbol on it."

"Agreed," replied Jacobson. "Devon, you want to lead the way?"

"No," said the black ex-astronaut, "But what I 'want', that ain't been relevant for some time, I guess. Brent... y'all want to take my place holdin' up ol' Bob?"

"It's okay," protested Billings. "I think I can walk on my own, now. Just be gentle... it's my first *time* being with space-aliens, you know?"

He got a malicious, obscene look from the two former pilots of the *Eagle* spacecraft.

"Well, on second thought... maybe not my *first* time with a space-alien," he said, with a thinly-disguised grin-and-wink.

"Ah... I *see*," observed Tanaka. "*That*, would sort of explain the 'no pledge' thing."

"The *what*, thing?" asked a perplexed Billings.

"Bob my man... I can see we gonna have a *lot* to talk about, when this shit all taken care of," offered a smirking White.

"Gentlemen – I'm using that term loosely, it seems – and ladies, if you're *quite* ready," ordered Jacobson. "Let's get on our way."

Gerald... I Saw A UFO

Notwithstanding the myriad troubles of these times – like endless terrorist scares, frequent episodes of mass-murder by some loser 'going postal', intermittent race-riots, shrieking 'synth-slam' music on the radio (the oldie stuff that you could bear listening to, was now only on the satellite-channels... and we all know how *that* turned out), sky-high prices for admission to anything, steadily-increasing restrictions on how much gas, booze, coffee and toilet-paper that you were allowed to buy, not to mention how much cash you could take out of your bank-account – as Mr. Average American, you decided to take your family for a nice, uplifting trip to that legendary capital city, its polished-marble monuments shining in the bright spring sunlight, like a for-once-it's-authentic talisman to The Universally-Envied American Way-Of-Life.

Okay, so had you frog-marched the kids, the dog and the Significant Other, into the car and headed off to D.C..

That would be another way to put it.

But – being a good, upstanding, white-bread American family – you had kept the A/C going all the way in, ostensibly to deal with the heat that seemed to last nearly all year, but also to keep out that yellowish muck that passed for air these days; you had navigated past the pervasive police and military roadblocks and had managed to look the other way when the gangstas on every other street-corner challenged your stare.

God only knows how you found a place to park – it had taken almost an hour and a near-fight to claim the spot as some old, craggy-nosed geezer pulled out his late-model Patriotic, and fifty bucks – but, you were finally... there!

The Mall!

Washington, D.C.!

And to *think*, your feet were now planted on the very same soil that had supported luminaries such as Nixon, Reagan, Palin, all three "President Bushes", Bachmann, Beck, Cruz and Limbaugh!

It would make a red-blooded American guy feel, well... red-blooded.

Okay... a bunch of others like that black preacher-guy (hard to remember his name, after it had been excised from most of the history-books and the network), and all those hippies, had also been here; but one didn't bring up the subject, if one were wise.

There were stories of people who 'talked too much' about such things, just... *disappearing*.

"Better safe than sorry", as the old saying goes.

After all, even the District – along with the rest of the states – they were *all* "Red States", these days... right?

Ever since that little 'accident' that had so unfortunately befallen that half-Black guy, whatwashisnameagain, so many years ago, the new 'normal' – actually, a lot like the old 'normal', right after the second big war in the last century, what with women being pushed back into the home where they belonged, and the minorities' votes starting to just... *vanish*, when counting-time came around, courtesy of new laws and a few 'tweaks' to those computer voting-booths – had come back into fashion.

Things had settled down and folks pretty much got to knowing what the rules were – even if they weren't that happy about having to rent out half the house to some damn seven-person Latino famil, just to pay the bills, even if they weren't thrilled with having to work to seven p.m. each night and on Saturdays at Wal-Target, for the same reason.

But the H with all of that – you were now in the *Capital*, with Mssrs. Lincoln and Jefferson staring down over you!

Where to *start*? Where better, than the Washington Monument – its huge, marble-granite-and-sandstone obelisk thrusting its patriotic, masculine potency aggressively into the hydrocarbon-yellow sky!

Now, the line-up was pretty long, even though there were mostly only white-folk in it; "ghetto-dudes can't make it past the roadblocks", somebody had explained. None the less, and despite another ten-dollar charge just to get two kids in to and out of the Port-A-Potty, half-way along, you were now almost at the bottom entrance.

God – that thing is *big*, you had thought, as you stared upward at the marble-clad sides of the obelisk.

There was more interminable waiting.

A guy came by selling "genuine-imitation-substitute chocolate-bars, it's for charity to support our boys fighting in Cuba" – the real ones cost twice as much, due to a shortage of something-or-other – and the kids wouldn't be denied.

Whammo! Another ten bucks, down the drain, while you tried to get that funny-electro-rock song out of your head.

Damn thing was getting louder and louder – stirring, uplifting, must be one of those new ones that the Army uses to get the grunts psyched up for a battle, would have been quite a nice listen-to – if you could just have turned it *off*.

That's when you injudiciously stepped a bit out of line and called forward and backward, "Could whoever's got that boom-box, *please* use your headphones?"

Some teenage girl shrugged and commented, "Dunno, mister... it's comin' from *everywhere* – I tried every channel on my MicroApple player and it's all I can hear. Freaky... eh?"

"Must be a promotion," offered a pretty young twenty-something. "They're doing that all the time these days. Buyin' all the airtime, that is."

Then, someone pointed at a different part of the sky.

There was something approaching, *fast*; and it *was* glowing like the mother-of-all-shooting stars, as it circled overhead, with the unwanted, weirdo-music started to roar from both the heavens and the earth.

"What the hell's *that*?" the other man shouted.

"Gotta be them Muslims – maybe them Chinks," argued a good ol' boy with a rotund belly and a baseball cap. "Somebody call the police, or the Army, or the Park Service!"

"*Told* you that one day we'd see a UFO... didn't I, Gerald?" proudly exclaimed a housewife.

"Uh-oh," you finally managed, as you saw the *thing*, changing course and heading straight for the upper-reaches of Mr. Washington's personal monument.

Turn Your TV On, John

From his way-too-small office aboard this poorly thought-out substitute for the "real" Air Force One – try as one might, there was just no way to get a purpose-built set of communications-gear, plus military crew and Executive Office staffers, into a commandeered 747-900 airplane – John Bezomorton hit the "Connect" button.

After a few seconds of encryption-imposed back-and-forth, the National Security Adviser established a connection – faint but still easily audible – back down to the "real" White House.

"Yo, Kaysten here," sounded a familiar voice.

"It's John here – I'm up in the alternate location," spoke Bezomorton. "Returning your call."

"Hey, John," answered the Chief of Staff. "How're things up there?"

"Miserable," complained Bezomorton. "Effin' galley-stove died yesterday, we're down to only microwaved sandwiches. And there are ten-minute waits to use the one remaining washroom – the other's been on the fritz since the first day we set out, and we can't stop long enough to get it fixed. So –"

"That's the shits, guy," interrupted Kaysten.

"Yeah... whatever. Well – about your call, anyway –" asked the Security Adviser.

Bezomorton had never particularly liked Kaysten, nor the now-defunct Billy Horn – nor any of their huge coterie of political fixers, parasitic gold-diggers and hangers-on. These guys took up an endless amount of the President's time for no apparent good reason; but – depressingly – the Old Man seemed to revel in this stuff. He would leave NSC memoranda sitting unsigned on his desk for weeks on end, instead spending the time on nonsense like writing personal letters-of-condolence about a luckless foot-soldier for Uncle Sam, or like campaigning on behalf of some "nobody" local candidate.

If he didn't like the affairs of state, then why'd he run for the damn office in the first place? silently thought Bezomorton.

Truth is – as little as I want to admit it – the Boss likes doing Kaysten's crap much more than he likes doing mine... or Anderson's, he mused.

Difference is – considering the headlines these days – Jerry's got no choice... he's got to play second fiddle to the real world...

Not that it makes me any happier, about having to work with him... the self-aggrandizing, smooth-talking little twit.

"Uh-huh," temporized the Chief of Staff.

"I suppose you already know what the answer is... right?" parried the Security Adviser.

"Did you ask him directly?" inquired Kaysten.

"*Look,* Jerry," Bezomorton shot back, "You *know,* it's *completely* out of the question."

"Yeah... but for Christ's *sake,*" retorted the Chief of Staff, "We're not asking for the real thing, here – we're simply talking about having the stunt-doubles show up on a podium, far-away from the audience – all picture- and video-gear confiscated at the door, of course – for an hour or so, at some isolated banquet-hall down in Dixie. Completely unannounced ahead of time – and we'll get the whole lot of 'em back to D.C. before the press even finds out that they're gone. I don't see what the risk *is* here... frankly."

"DeWitt and I already *discussed* this – we even brought in Ochoa – on top of it, and all three of us are of the opinion that the risks are both very real and *still* way too high," argued Bezomorton. "What if somebody in the press – or anybody, say, a renegade member of these Bible-Bangers out there in the audience, somewhere – *does* manage to get a clean picture of the decoys? That could blow our entire cover-story... as well as throwing the country and the economy instantly into a panic over the 'where is the President' issue – not to mention instantly telling both the alien and the Muslims that he's not, in fact, in the White House. We simply can't afford to give it – uhh, *her* – the slightest additional targeting data to use against us –"

"John – you don't seem to appreciate my *position* down here," protested Kaysten. "I wanted to get the VP off the plane and in front of the Jesus Brigade in person; you nixed that – okay, fine... then, I tried to get them to go for somebody high-up in the military, all leave has been canceled – I grant you, I should've foreseen that one... *now,* what am I supposed to do?"

"Well –" Bezomorton tried to say, but Kaysten went on.

"I'm getting calls twice a day from the Majority Leader, asking crap like 'when's the next time that I can get Mrs. Mildred Shithead from Poughkeepsie, in the Oval Office for an autographed Gold Star Campaign-Contributor Commemorative Photo'," he complained. "Point is... with each passing day, maintaining this little scam is getting harder and harder to pull off. If we could stage the Dixie event, we'd have something concrete that we could throw back at those jackasses down at Disney News –"

"Hate to have to say it this way, Jerry," commented Bezomorton, "But that's *your* problem, not mine – fixing things like *this*, well, that's why you get paid the big bucks. Listen – I gotta go – I'm late for a NSC conf-call, starts in two minutes –"

Kaysten sounded like he was going to launch into one of his trademark whining protests; but abruptly, his voice appeared to be addressing someone else, evidently someone within earshot down in the White House.

"Hold on, John," he demanded.

Barely, Bezomorton could make out, "No – I'm *busy*, I'm on the line to – what the *fuck*? Where?"

There was a gasp, then the Security Advisor heard, "Jesus H. *Christ!* Yeah – get them *out!* What? Well wherever you take them... how the hell would *I* know? No, not the safe-bunker, that's reserved for the real – Yeah! *Go!*"

"Jerry – what's going *on* down there?" exclaimed a worried Bezomorton.

Though this telecom-link was protected by the second-to-best computer-encryption and compression that the military could come up with, still, it began to resound with a now-familiar New Age electro-Celtic-rock anthem.

Ooo-ooo-ooo-ooo, came the haunting chords of the song, as Kaysten tried to advise,

"Turn your television on, John."

What's 'Er Name Again?

Thump-thump-thump went the receding noise of the helicopter-blades – their sound echoing more and more faintly from the red-and-gray walls of this scenic location – as the craft that had borne the party flew away.

"Got to tell you Minnie... but I got a *bad* feelin' 'bout this," grumbled Boatman, his eyes tracking the helicopter until it disappeared over the deepening shadows at the top of the canyon. "Just too easy for the bad-guys – whoever they may be – to try for a shot at *her*, but then smoke us all down here... and nobody'd be the wiser."

"There are chances to everything," philosophically replied Minnie Chu, as she shook the dust from her FBI-issue female agent's garb. "Including, 'doing nothing'."

She turned to address the bounty-hunter. "You say that this was where she did it – that is, where she, uhh, 'tested' you – right?"

"Just about where you're standin'," confirmed Wolf. "Don't know if that fancy gear that you guys got back at your home-base can prove it... but if you'd been right there, a few days ago, well... let's just say that you'd have quite a hot-foot."

"I'll take your word for it," answered the FBI team-leader. "But, Will – you mind scraping up and bagging a few samples? Can't hurt to have some physical evidence, in case she doesn't show."

"She *will*," promised Misha.

"I just wish we had brought some folding-chairs, maybe a tent and sleeping-bags," complained Ramirez. "You guys know, it gets plenty *cold* out here in the desert, at night?"

"Well... *duh*," replied Hendricks, as he dutifully knelt down and used a pocket-knife to dislodge some of the scorched sandstone on the canyon-floor. "I wanted 'em to drop us a trailer and Neo-connection so we could pass the time watching football... but the Director said 'no dice'. What a party-pooper, eh?"

"'Nothing that might make the alien think that we're setting a trap – not even the communicators – unless it's us calling S-O-S for evac'... remember?" explained Chu, as she reclined against a large rock. "This is likely to be the only chance we *get* to call her. We certainly wouldn't want to scare her off."

"I got *news* for you, lady," grunted the bounty-hunter. "If she thinks she's bein' set-up... 'scarin' her off' is gonna be the *least* of your problems. It'd be more like, 'she'll vaporize this here part of the Canyon, and everythin' for the next twenty miles'."

"*Told* you I had a bad feelin' about this, Minnie," muttered Boatman, shaking his head. "We all's so deep-down here that we probably can't even get a cell-signal out, if we *do* get into trouble."

"You wouldn't get a chance to hit the 'call' button, pardner," commented Wolf.

"Are you sure about that... about *her*?" inquired Abruzzio, in the direction of the bounty-hunter. "Somehow that just doesn't sound like the Karéin-Mayréij that Hector and I spoke with, before..."

"She's had some bad experiences, since landin' down here, darlin'," answered the bounty-hunter. "You might say it's put her a bit off on the whole U.S. of A. thing... as we discussed while we were up in that copter. If I were you –"

"I think my friend is being somewhat – how do you say in English – 'over dramatic' about this," interrupted Misha. "The Storied Watcher is not the type to hurt or kill people who she does not know – at least if they have not done anything stupid to provoke her. Furthermore... when she sees us here, that should be a positive factor in and of itself – since, after all, Wolf and I are *supposed* to be helping her, ahh, 'interface' with the American government. Just keep your guns out of sight and I do not think that we will any problems."

"Of course,...if we *do* have problems, we're probably all dead," unhelpfully observed Hendricks.

"We'll do that," agreed Chu. "About the guns, I mean. So... should we start?"

"Might as well," replied Wolf.

"Wait a minute," interjected Boatman. "If you all's the choir... who's the director? The lead-singer, I mean."

"Do we got to have one?" asked Ramirez.

"Beats *me*," remarked Abruzzio. "I've never done this before, and there's no scientific method behind it – however, it stands to reason that if four voices calling out Karéin's name are 'good', then seven would be 'better'... why don't we have *everyone* join in?"

"I have a terrible singing-voice," argued the third agent. "Count me out."

"Listen, Ms. Abruzzio – I *would* join in," warily noted Chu, "But I'm concerned that if the alien heard it, and then realized that the voice was coming from someone with whom she wasn't, uhh, 'familiar', she might be offended... which would be a *bad* thing."

"I think that is highly unlikely," countered the Russian.

"But it *is* possible... isn't it?" pressed the FBI team-leader.

"*Anything* is possible," he allowed.

"Yeah... but if she hears only the voices of her personal glee-club – no offense to you guys, by the way – calling, then shows up and sees all three of us standing around, she might get pissed just by that," warned Hendricks. "Might look like an ambush. Maybe at least one of us FBI-folk ought to join in, that way she'd know that there's extra company coming to the party."

"Otis?" said Chu, looking at the black agent.

"Minnie, you can't be *serious* –" he protested.

"Didn't you tell us that you used to sing in the church choir, back in St. Louis?" needled Hendricks.

"I'm not going to order you," cajoled the FBI team-leader, "But Will may have a point. There's a risk in us joining the chorus – but there might be a bigger risk in the alien showing up and being surprised. Who's to say? If you don't want to do it, I suppose the duty falls to me."

After a pause of two or three seconds, with an immensely-uncomfortable look on his face, Boatman turned to address the bounty-hunter.

"So... how the hell you say her name, again?" he asked.

Just A Little Off The Top

At first, on the top observation-deck-level of the Washington Monument, they heard the Destroying Angel's beautiful – but foreboding – war-song. Its tune was mostly delivered to the subconscious; times being what they were, most of the electronic-junk – including mobile-media-players – had been confiscated at the entrance-gate.

But as she approached, the chords and orchestration of this arcane melody began to issue from the air itself – not to mention from the very *stones* of the place.

The Storied Watcher circled the obelisk once – twice – thrice – trying to send a mental-warning to its fascinated – but understandably-fearful – inhabitants. It mostly went for naught – their conscious minds were too closed, too hostile to new ideas, too... *ordinary*, for the message to fully get through.

Maybe it was the robustness of the stone-construction of the thing, or possibly it had to do with the thickness of skulls; but on this day, she was not disposed to wait.

Sterner measures are needful, sent Karéin-Mayréij, to her war-children.

There – perceive ye thus?

The viewing-window, on the north-side.

Vœran Fàiagàryuu, – to mine hand!

Weaklings, are they... for all that confronts us, is unenchanted stone!

The two or three humans who had been staring, slack-jawed, at the spectacle from behind this particular portal, were very lucky to have guessed that remaining there would be a *bad* idea. They only just were able to leap out of the way, before the shining, singing whatever-it-was, was seen to be barreling right at them.

Reflexively – though, if truth be told, she needed not so to do – the Storied Watcher tensed and flinched slightly as the obelisk's outer wall disintegrated under the lethal kiss of *Vœran Fàiagàryuu.*

She crashed through the side of the Washington Monument, a few-score meters from its pointed top, sending an outward-rocketing explosion of marble-and-sandstone rubble showering down on points below, along with a cloud of dust and debris billowing onto the observation-deck.

Please forgive, sent the alien, to her kindred.

My cringe is not something that ye should emulate.

It is just that it is a long time since I have swum through stone by the power of my Fire.

One loses confidence... but it will return... so I swear.

Most of the crowd of Average Americans on the top-level had, by now, had the good sense to head for the exit-stairs, causing an ugly Hobbesian scene as one clawed past another for presumed safety further below. But three or four, perhaps realizing the futility of trying to get past this madding crowd, had tarried behind.

Remember, children... just strength, force of arms, and fire, counseled the young-looking woman.

They cannot bear the death-shine, and they perceive it not.

I want them to fear and cower... not to... die.

Now, the fire-enveloped, glowing-eyed visage of mighty Karéin-Mayréij confronted the humans, and she let loose a cruel, brutal wave of heat – almost, but not quite, enough, to burn exposed flesh – in all directions.

"You have thirty seconds to flee," she spat. "Elsewise... I suggest that you learn how to fly, because where I now stand – and all above – this, will soon be going on a nice trip to nowhere."

"But we can't get *down*," pleaded a man. "They're all bunched-up, at the stairs –"

With the floor hissing and smoking in protest of her every move, the Storied Watcher calmly walked over to the stairway-entrance, which was still choked with shrieking, arguing tourists.

A few looked behind to see the frightening figure from whom they had no escape, and these ones yelped in alarm.

With a thinly-disguised look of contempt, the Karéin-Mayréij promised, "Here – I will fix your problem."

She opened her palms as if giving a benediction; but instead of a blessing, what descended on the floor on either side of the metal spiral staircase was more akin to a pile-driver, as the stone tiles shattered, leaving the top of the staircase essentially unsupported.

A second later, the alien's telekinetic-attack fell upon the sides of the staircase itself, stretching and rending these like taffy, until the top-parts of the passage downwards were almost twice their original width.

"See? *Lots* of space now," she taunted. "Maybe no longer – ahh – 'up to building-making codes'; but do not worry about that... the stairs will support you long enough to get your sorry peasant-hides, down from here. Now, *go*... or start growing feathers."

"*What?*" whimpered a teenager, as even more panic seized the crowd, with people madly trampling over each other.

"Fifteen seconds," nonchalantly replied Karéin-Mayréij, with a menacingly saturnine smile.

A moment later, after another suffocating, pain-threshold wave of heat, she flew out of the Washington Monument, through the same blasted-apart portal from whence she had come.

Ooo-ooo-ooo-ooo, wailed the song of the Storied Watcher, as she counted away the seconds.

Ten... nine... eight..., she silently sent to the war-children.

Such is how the humans learn to count.

The music played so loudly, that a low vibration started to affect the entire obelisk.

What is that, Vîrya I'ëà'b'? reflected Karéin-Mayréij.

What shall I now do?

Three... two... one, she counted.

And behold the waxing greatness of thy mother.

Do ye not feel it, little ones?

A fraction of a second later, the eye-lenses of *Virya Ahn'jë* almost met an untimely end, as they only just danced out of the way of the Storied Watcher's raging, *Amaiish*-fueled death-gaze, in time.

An entire level of the Washington Monument, just above the observation-deck, began to disintegrate, as the Destroying Angel floated around the obelisk, with the *Gaze of the Watchers* steadily bisecting it like some kind of other-worldly buzz-saw.

Art mighty thou indeed, Mother blessed! soundlessly remarked a host of half-awed minds.

Bob's New Signature-Phrase

For all of his skills in interplanetary-navigation, White had to apologize to the others, as he had mis-read both the key-card's scale, and its orientation : the group had to backtrack twice to stay on course. And – because the place was much larger than they had anticipated – it seemed that this level was bigger than the one above.

Progress down the facility's endless, eerily-silent corridors, past its intermittently-spaced doors and entrance-ways, had been painstakingly-slow.

Can't blame my astronaut-friends for stopping and carefully scouting out each corner and junction, reflected Billings.

They may be space-alien gods and goddesses by now...

But they don't want to get shot, any more than yours truly.

Two cheers for them...

"Clear?" whispered Jacobson.

"Yeah... much as I can tell," answered the African-American ex-astronaut, *sotto voce.*

"But it's one H of a long way down there to the next level," he added. "And my Mars eyes is givin' out a bit more than half-way – same thing down in the shaft as up here... near all the lights seem to be out. Brent... y'all want to try?"

"Yeah," agreed Boyd.

He crept out on to the fire escape-like thatched-metal-landing on all fours, trying at all costs to avoid making noise.

Carefully, the ex-U.S. Air Force Major surveyed the gloomy depths of the square-walled stairwell; but no movement confronted his eyes, ears or other senses.

"Devon's right – damn hard to tell, but I sure can't see anything," remarked the ex-astronaut. "It's got to be at least thirty meters down there... I'd feel better if the Professor verified my opinion, though."

"Let me have a look," requested Tanaka.

There was that now-familiar, dim glow in her eyes, as she scanned back and forth, up and down.

She turned to Jacobson.

"I can't see anything, either, Sam," she noted, "But... I have a queasy feeling about this."

"What do you *mean*, 'queasy'?" nervously inquired Billings, who was just behind the woman. "Is that 'queasy' like, 'the strychnine that they fed me for breakfast, gave me heartburn', or like, 'we're going to get our heads blown off, ten seconds from now'?"

"It's 'queasy' like, 'I don't have a clue why... but something tells me that we're asking for trouble, by going down the stairs'," stated Tanaka. "It just doesn't *feel* right."

"Well... *that* just gives me the ol' warm and fuzzies, doesn't it?" muttered the salesman. "Is this 'more than a feeling'? Sari used to say that she had a sixth-sense that would warn her, when she was about to walk into a trap."

"I honestly don't *know*, Bob," replied the professor. "It doesn't feel any different than it did before I met the Storied Watcher – and I've been wrong both before and after."

"As little as I like the idea of chancing it, especially if Cherie isn't one hundred per cent in agreement," interjected Jacobson, "What, realistically, are our options, here? We ruled out the idea of using the elevator, except as a last resort, and... Devon, didn't you say that the other stairs had some kind of 'security' symbol on them?"

"Yeah... it's a lock, like on them Neo-sites... see?" explained White, showing Jacobson, Billings and Tanaka the key-card. "I dunno what it means, exactly – but this set of stairs in front of us here don't have it... as y'all can see. Could be anything from a bunch of Claymore-mines to a bicycle-lock, for all I know."

"Point is," continued Jacobson, "If we're going to try to find the rest of Bob's party, we *have* to get down there... and there's no guarantee that the other stairs – or the elevator, or any part of this place – is going to be any safer than what confronts us here. Unless we want to call the whole thing off –"

"*You* can," interrupted Billings. "I won't – I'll keep going after them as long as there's an ounce of breath left in me! I pretty much figured my sorry ass was grass, from the time I first woke up in here... I may as well go out, trying to do something noble. Won't make up for all the other crap in my life – but when I finally end up in front of Saint Pete, I figure maybe they give Brownie-points for extra effort... you know?"

Jacobson's face showed a wry smile, and Billings noticed that somehow it was easy to discern, even in the half-light.

"Just pulling your chain, Bob," chuckled the former Mars mission commander. "You've neatly summed up how all of us feel. But do any of you want to double back and try either the elevator, or the other stairs?"

"As little as I like the idea of going against the Professor's intuition," commented Boyd, "I like the idea of doing *that*, even less. We've probably woken up every guard in this whole damn facility by now, and they'll be sure to follow our trail... militarily, our best option is to keep them guessing as to where we go next. It's not a *great* option – but it's one of the few available to us. Remember... they probably don't know that we've got the key-card. They may not realize that we have some ability to intelligently choose what route we take... especially considering the size of this place."

"Leave me out of the 'intelligently' stuff," quipped Billings. "I only just passed high-school."

"Y'all could have said the same thing, 'bout bein' dumb enough to sign up for the Air Force," grunted White. "Nice interestin' trip to Mars... fuckin' *bad* time back on Earth, don't you know. Anyway, Captain... I vote to try the stairs. I'll even go first, if y'all want me to."

"You and me together, bro'," volunteered Boyd. "I'll cover your back. Rest of 'em can stay up here and keep an eye on us."

"Any objections?" asked Jacobson.

"I want to stay up at the landing, with a clear line-of-sight to them," requested Tanaka.

"Huh?" said Billings.

"Just a *precaution*," replied the professor.

Jacobson nodded to White, and, with Boyd a step or so behind the black ex-astronaut, the two cautiously stepped out on to the spiral staircase.

Speak to me... or think to me, as best you see fit, sent Tanaka to White.

It'll mostly be talkin' the old-fashioned way, came back the reply.

Takes some concentratin' to do this mental walkie-talkie stuff... and I'd prefer to keep my mind on my gun, if y'all don't mind.

"Yep," quietly confirmed Tanaka, as Boyd and White continued down.

"Bob – take hold of my hand," she added.

"Sure... but I already *got* a girlfriend, and we're, uhh, kind of *serious*... you know?" mentioned Billings.

He grasped on to Tanaka and inquired, "Any reason for this?"

"Maybe none," murmured the Eurasian-American woman. "Maybe a whole *hell* of a lot. Sam – remember back in the *Eagle?* When she..."

Jacobson nodded and sent a knowing look to Tanaka, whose half-serene gaze was totally focused on her two compatriots who were going down the stairs.

"What the H – I'm hearing a tune in my head, like a song you can't stop thinking about –" complained the salesman.

"Good... and I hope you know what you're doing, Cherie," quietly noted Jacobson, as he, too, kept his stare on the scene below.

"Half-way down," whispered Boyd, as loudly as he dared push the volume. "Hold on – Devon, over there – d'you see –"

Suddenly, there was a beam of light from somewhere up on the wall, just past the point where the two men had passed.

A klaxon screeched out a menacing howl.

As the searchlight washed over them, White and Boyd crouched instinctively, guns at the ready; but they could see no obvious target, except perhaps for a box-like contraption that was slowly extending from the wall-side opposite to the one from whence the light was issuing.

A voice bellowed out, "Freeze, prisoners! Hands over your heads, or you'll be shot *dead!* There will be no more warnings!"

Ooo – ai-ooo – ooo-ai, sounded a weirding riposte, its stirring chords oh-so-close to those of her mentor, as charges of other-worldly energy started to infuse Tanaka's body, extending like chain-lightening from her trunk to her extremities.

A shocked Billings tried to yank his hand away from the professor's grasp, but for perhaps a half-second, until she herself broke the connection, he was unsuccessful, and the *Amaiish*-stuff shot into his body, as well.

Half-stunned, with steam or smoke issuing from his palm, the salesman collapsed backwards, falling midway between the first part of the upstairs platform and the corridor from whence the group had originally come.

"*Trap!*" yelled White.

With unnatural haste, he raised his gun and fired at the light source.

Rifle-rounds ricocheted hither and yon, to little apparent effect : the ex-astronaut was firing right into the glare, and even *his* elevated senses couldn't easily acquire a target.

A second later, a crackling, staccato-sound, accompanied by rapid-fire flashes, began to issue from the box on the opposite side of the wall.

Mercifully, the thing must not have been perfectly auto-targeting, because its aim – probably under the remote control of some guard, somewhere else in the complex – was not immediately lethal; its rounds impacted on the stairs just below Boyd and White, apparently in a maneuver intended to stop the forward progress of the two men.

But then, one shot evidently hit Boyd square in the chest, throwing him backward, head against the railings, as if sucker-punched.

As the moaning, agonized man put his hand over his breast to cover a smoking, sizzling wound, White tried desperately to drag him out of the line-of-fire.

"*Brent!*" wailed Tanaka.

They were pinned. Though some of the incoming bullets were deflected by the metal-ribbing of the stairs, and while White alternately dodged and fired as best he could, it could be no more than a few seconds before the remote operator's aim would improve enough to end the days of the two ex-astronauts.

Now, with her personal war-song wailing, Tanaka took leave of Billings and Jacobson.

Like some impossibly-lithe gymnast, she careened at break-neck speed in and out of the spiral staircase, using its upright-parts as hand-holds and, where necessary, as a fulcrum.

Cat-like, she somehow dodged a hail of gunshots, and came to a three-point landing between White and Boyd.

Immediately, a shimmering, wall-like field of... *something*, appeared above the three. A fusillade was unleashed against this from the gun-box, to utterly no effect, as each bullet simply vanished or was sent careening off into the darkness, upon coming into contact with Tanaka's force-shield.

"Crouch – and shoot the damn thing when I tell you!" she demanded, her eyes lit up like Sirius.

But before any of those halfway down the staircase could implement these orders, to the dismay of the entire party of refugees, a *second* searchlight now illuminated Billings and Jacobson, on the platform above.

As it did, the firing-box started to swivel to point in the direction of the two men.

Jacobson raised his gun to fire, but his aim wasn't any better than had been White's, a few seconds earlier.

If I scramble back down the corridor, it'll target on him, thought Billings' racing mind.

I don't have to out-run the bear... I only have to out-run you... right?

The firing-box was almost in alignment, now.

A second more, and it would have a clear shot.

No, not going to do that – he's a good man – you owe him your life, Bob old boy, realized Billings.

And shit – is this what they mean about, "your life passes in front of you"...

No – not like that.

Like everything's... slowing down?

I can see the damn thing moving, but in slo-mo... what the F...

Hey – I've been here before, haven't I?

Yeah... up at the Jesus-Jail...

She made it dark, darker than a coal-mine – didn't she?

I wonder if...

Oh, come on, Bob!

That was Little Miss Martian Goddess – not a floor-tile salesman from Tucson, Arizona, don't forget Winona...

But didn't she say, 'just imagine it – believe in your greatness – and –'

Well, slo-mo or not, only one tick of the clock left...

Jacobson, you and me – we go bye-bye together, one way or another...

Here goes...

Now, a *different* kind of shimmer appeared on the top-platform.

For a split-second, Tanaka, and White, also Boyd, though the latter man was doubled up, grimacing, could still sort of see Billings and Jacobson, like the momentary glance of something that you see on a TV-screen, before it loses the signal entirely.

Then, every trace of the two men on the upper-platform just... *vanished.*

There was still the occasional flicker of disturbed light from the place; but to the unaided human – even, more-than-human, eye – there was simply... nobody there.

"What *the* –" gasped an amazed Tanaka.

But White was more purposeful, and this time, he aimed straight at the firing-box, which was clearly visible due to the leaking side-glare of the two searchlights.

"Eat *this*, mother*fuckers!*" he shrieked, crouching in sniper-posture, a half-second before the professor moved her force-field out of the way.

The firing-box was reasonably well-armored, and it might even have survived the six or seven precision-aimed shots unleashed against it by the black ex-astronaut; but in the following seconds, both it – and a goodly amount of concrete and connecting wire, as well – was savagely torn from the wall, by a crushing blow from Tanaka's energized mind.

Then, White drew a bead on the second searchlight, shattering it with a well-placed rifle-bullet, as Tanaka turned her fury at the glare of the first one, which disintegrated with a loud "pop".

The half-darkness returned.

"Yo man – sorry, I tried to draw their fire, man," stammered the African-American ex-astronaut, his voice choking.

"Rain – check – on – the – 'goodbye speech'," Boyd forced out, from bended knees. "*Shit*, that hurts... must have been a small-caliber round... flak-jacket stopped it... but I feel like I was just on the wrong end of a charging rhinoceros..."

"Oh... thank *God!*" sobbed Tanaka.

White's shoulders slumped in relief.

"Y'all need some time there, bro?" he asked.

"No," answered Boyd, as he uneasily stumbled to his feet, still wincing with every twist of his torso. "Kind of *figures*, I guess... damn thing wouldn't need high-velocity rounds just to stop unarmed prisoners... they don't want to chip the concrete on the walls after all, ha ha... must have been a SMG or something like that, in the turret. I can still function fine – but let's stop at the first dispensary for some Aspirin, you know?"

"I wouldn't trust anything in the medicine-cabinets here," observed the woman.

She looked upward.

"Guys?" called the professor, as loudly as she dared.

Then, with Boyd painfully bringing up the rear, White and Tanaka hurried back up the stairs.

"Bob, Captain, y'all still there – *shit!*" cursed White, as he stumbled over the still-invisible bulk of the crouching Jacobson and Billings, on the top platform.

They might still be able to see or hear us, even if the lights are out, broadcasted Tanaka.

So no more talking –

Let's all get back down the stairs, sent Boyd.

We can regroup at the next landing, or wherever is just beyond.

Slowly, Jacobson emerged from the shroud of darkness that had mysteriously enveloped him, and he followed White and Tanaka downward.

Where's Bob? sent White.

I don't see the man.

"I'm up *here*," whispered Billings, just within earshot of Tanaka and Jacobson. "I can't figure out how to turn the damn thing off... and I can't see more than an inch in front of my face."

Here... I'll come get you, messaged Tanaka, as her music ebbed.

She stole past her three male comrades and extended her hand to Billings, noting with bemusement that it seemed to vanish up to about the elbow.

Let's hope they aren't recording this, communicated Jacobson.

And... by the way, Bob... well done – damn *well done!*

I owe you!

"Don't clap... just throw money," muttered the salesman, *sotto voce*, as, effectively blind, he awkwardly and invisibly felt his way down the twisting staircase.

After twenty-or-so seconds of this cautious fumbling, they were at a bottom-landing, very similar to the one that they had left behind.

"Brent – you okay?" asked Jacobson, upon noticing that Boyd was moving more slowly than usual.

"Took a pistol-caliber round from that remote-control gun-turret up there on the wall, but the flak-jacket stopped it... still hurts like hell, though," explained the ex-Air Force major, matter-of-factually. "I'm lucky they must have run out of budget to put a real assault-rifle in the damn thing... otherwise I'd probably be pushing up daisies by now."

"I felt the impacts on my screen," added Tanaka. "They *did* feel lighter than what I encountered out in the corridor... so I think Brent's right about the gun in the thing."

"Thank God for small blessings," commented Jacobson. "But I'm worried that we're running out of cat-lives. Anyway... we've got to get out of here – there's obviously no doubt that they now know where we are."

There was a locked, reinforced steel-and-something door – certainly crowbar-proof at the very least – with a small glass-window at eye-height in its middle, blocking their way.

"Devon?" whispered Jacobson.

"Tried it, Captain," answered White. "It don' wanna open."

"Fine," growled the former Mars mission commander. "Cherie, you've had your fun... now it's *our* turn. Brent, Devon, when I give it the boot – give it a little head-rush, you know what I mean?"

"Perfectly," acknowledged Boyd.

"Would it interest you to know," he added, "I'm not getting headaches, any more?"

"Fuckin' *ay!*" inveighed the African-American ex-astronaut.

"Okay – one – two – *three!*" inveighed Jacobson.

The big man – his attack suffused by a smaller, less brilliant, but still very evident, example of the body-lightening that had earlier displayed on Tanaka – took a run at the door. As his boot made contact with it, there was a loud crashing-sound, along with a dimly-sparkling, blue-green flash.

The door flew apart from its anchorings, as if it had been made of wet cardboard. It went a short distance into the brightly-illuminated corridor ahead of the group, then slowed and stopped after about ten feet.

"Let's get out of here," suggested Jacobson.

The rest of them quickly complied, and – with Boyd and White in the vanguard – they all moved into the corridor.

"*Whew!*" gasped the still-invisible Billings. "Remind me not to get into an ass-kickin'-contest with *you!*"

Jacobson turned to Billings – or, at least, to where he fancied the salesman to be located – and replied, "Believe me, Bob... I've been building a mental list of arses that I intend to kick into next week, when and if we get our own ones out of this place. We've all got our own favorite little skills, I suppose; and – for the record – I had the help of Majors Boyd and White... but listen, personally, I don't have a problem with you going around, uhh, 'cloaked' like that... but did you say something about not being able to see, up there? Can you see me, now?"

"I can't see jack *squat!*" complained the salesman. "It's just like how it was with Sari – err, Kar-whats-er-name. She mentioned something about 'it keeps out all the light-waves, bends them into pretzels'... or whatever. When *she* used it, you might as well have been down in a coal-mine without a flashlight... very much like I seem to be, now."

"Y'all don' *really* want me sayin', 'y'all look *so* much better like that', Bob?" joked White.

"Ha, ha, ha," muttered Billings. "Don't any of *you* know how to turn it off?"

"None of us can do it – so we can't teach you from experience," remarked Tanaka. "But... I have an idea."

"Which would be?" asked Billings.

"Well, how did you turn it *on*, to begin with?" inquired the professor.

The salesman stopped and pondered for a few seconds, then explained, "Not sure, exactly... but it was like I wanted to hide... when that light fell on me and your Captain, there, I figured we'd be sitting-ducks... I kind of wished that I could hide, that I'd go dark... I knew what it was like to be inside this weirdo-shroud when Sari did it – so I dreamed of the same thing happening, and... presto."

"So do the reverse," suggested Tanaka. "Imagine that you really *want* to be noticed. That you *want* to stand out."

"And I'd do that... *how?*" demanded Billings.

"Just do whatever you last did, when you wanted to catch someone's attention," counseled the woman. "And here's something else – in one of my own first lessons, after the Storied Watcher gave me the gift of the *Fire*, she also mentioned that it'd be easier to do, if I associated the use of a particular ability with a 'key-word'... that is, a word or phrase that would remind me that it's time to energize, or de-energize. You get the idea?"

"No... but here goes, anyway," muttered Billings.

For a few seconds, concern began to build within the former Mars mission crew, as the salesman had fallen dead-silent.

Then, in the blink of an eye, there was a flicker in the air.

"*Taxi!*" exclaimed Bob K. Billings, Jr., formerly of Tucson, Arizona, as he appeared in full view.

Fix The Facility, Please

"You already have my own confirm-codes," announced the pleasantly anonymous figure at the other end of this uber-secured video-link, his IBM-button-down-style, navy-blue suit and red tie contrasting dramatically with the sparse, concrete-walled underground meeting-room from which the transmission was originating.

"And I can see you, sir," he stated, "But I need your challenge-response."

"My values are Top Dog, ID-value is Anthill 456, Geranium 89, Torus 3A," answered the CIA director. "I won't have a lot of time for this conversation. We have a few chain-of-command issues to deal with back here, and I'm in the middle of dealing with those. Let's have the report, most important topic first."

"In fact, there's only *one* thing, sir," mentioned the other man, "But it's a Level Three event. We need operational instructions."

"What is it?" inquired the director.

"Lapse in communications with the Amchitka facility," noted the understudy. "You may remember that you wanted to be informed, if anything unusual occurred there."

"That's correct," confirmed the CIA chief. "Is this some kind of technical-glitch?"

"Doesn't look like it, sir," explained the other man. "Primary and backup circuits are both still up and they seem nominal... but we're not getting all the check-ins that are called for by protocol. We set off the beeper at the other end, but part of the facility isn't reporting."

"Which part?" asked the director.

"Level One," said the man in the navy-blue suit. "They've missed two checking-intervals, so far. There's been nothing for over ten hours."

"What about the other areas?" said the director.

"Reporting as usual – except, the GrayWar-boys are investigating what appears to be an electrical-problem," elaborated the other man. "Issue there is, as you know, they aren't supposed to go down into the facility – even to the guard-posts – without being first escorted there, by our people. About four hours ago, the Legion-contingent sent a message that the Agency-staff on Level One weren't answering a page. So they're stuck at the surface-elevator, until they can find someone to take them down to the service-room."

"I *knew* this was going to be a problem... I mean, using the mercenaries in place of our own people – it just complicates *everything*, even if Mr. Duke used to be an Agency-man... but what with all these budget-restrictions..." complained the director. "Anyway – this *could* be something innocuous, but what worries me is, the Amchitka facility is the one where we sent the Mars astronauts to join the Billings party for our special program. Do we have a track on the whereabouts of these two groups?"

"Our people from the lower-levels report the Billings group all accounted-for and are held securely," reassured the blue-suited man. "Last check we had for the Jacobson team was that they were going through the reception-process... all checks were nominal. That was quite some time ago."

"I see," acknowledged the director. "Well... for the time being, keep trying to raise the Level One facility-people – and when you do, tell them that I want to *personally* speak with them – I won't *tolerate* this kind of sloppy work! You can tell them – on my behalf – 'one more screw-up and you'll be joining the patients of our fine facility, to find out what things look like from *their* perspective'... you hear?"

"Loud and clear, sir," confirmed the other man. "I'll do that."

"Top Dog out," concluded the director.

Rose-Garden Strategy

Despite repeated attempts by the Park and District Police to clear the entire Mall, a ten-person-deep crowd had gathered to ring the Washington Monument, in its hour of travail.

"Dadd... is that pretty music coming from the shiny thing that's flying around the big tower?" asked a cherubic six-year-old.

"I don't know, cupcake," answered a Middle American father. "But it sure *is* nice, isn't it? I just wish it wasn't so loud... I can hardly hear the radio over it. Mildred... are there *any* stations that don't have that music playing?"

"Uh-uhh," replied a frumpy housewife, shaking her head. "They all got it, but it's fainter on the digital ones. I think – *whoa*, Kelvin – lookit *that*!"

A gasp came from the crowd, as a scintillating, yellow-and-white-and-gold beam of *something*, suddenly blazed from the UFO; the ray struck the Washington Monument about five-sixths of the way to its top, sending yet more chunks of shattered stone and other debris – over and above what had been shot out, after the *thing* had blasted its way in to the observation-deck, then back out again – hurtling down to the base of the obelisk.

"Not them Muslims, *again!*" angrily shouted a man.

Ooo-ooo-ooo-ooo, echoed the song, as the UFO began to float sideways, its death-ray slicing a deep and almost perfectly horizontal gash in the side of the Monument.

It continued thus – then relented for a few seconds, then fired again – leaving gaps where the structure of the obelisk was left undisturbed, repeating the pattern as the *thing* kept circling, hundreds of feet in the air.

"Ladies and gentlemen – this area is *dangerous* – you're ordered to disperse and leave the Monument site, *immediately!*" bellowed a policeman, from behind a bullhorn. "Park Police are authorized to –"

OOO-ooo-OOO-ooo, echoed the war-song, yet louder and more haunting, its Celtic-electro-rock theme mixed impossibly with something like the biggest, most melodic classical orchestra that you had ever heard.

A few of the more impressionable started to sway and step from side to side, as if involuntarily learning a new dance.

"*Omigod!*" yelled someone, as the stupefied crowd saw what was now happening.

"Will you look at *that!*" exclaimed several more.

With the side-cut inflicted on the Washington Monument now complete – it looked very much like the "scissors-go-here" markings on a retail sewing-pattern – the UFO darted to position itself directly above the point of the obelisk, in so doing neatly placing itself out of range of the few police and soldiers who had the temerity to take pistol- or rifle-shots.

A shudder issued from the tower, all the way through the nearby ground, reverberating through the feet of the onlookers.

With a cracking, groaning sound, another shower of debris shot out of all sides of the beleaguered building, at the cut-line.

OOO-ooo-OOO-ooo, continued the song.

Then – after perhaps a half-second – the top-part of the Washington Monument just... *lifted off*, tagging about ten meters behind the UFO like some kind of bizarrely-shaped carnival-balloon, leaving the rest of the obelisk truncated, flat-topped and forlorn.

What was now floating through the District of Columbia sky, without any apparent means of propulsion or support, must have weighed *hundreds* – if not *thousands* – of tons.

Lazily – at a speed of no more than a few tens of miles per hour – it drifted northward from Seaton Park, crossing Constitution Avenue and causing many traffic-accidents, as dumbfounded drivers stared in amazement and consternation about what was going on, three hundred feet over their heads.

From far-off, the roar of military jet engines sounded ominously; and – when the UFO had almost reached the center of the Ellipse – five or six little puffs of smoke appeared at random locations on the ground, as concealed Secret Service agents launched man-portable surface-to-air missiles against the *thing*.

At first, these lethal high-tech arrows tracked faithfully against the target, which must have had an easily distinguishable heat-signature. However – as the projectiles reached a point perhaps half-way toward the UFO – there were more weird sounds overlaid upon its now half-familiar song, and those watching the event with binoculars could just make out two small projectiles of some sort being launched against the missiles.

There was a blue-colored flash on one side, followed rapidly by a yellow-orange flash on the other; then, every one of the SAMs either detonated prematurely, or fell, stone-dead, to the ground.

"It's heading toward the White House!" shouted more than one of the onlookers.

This warning was bang-on : while sirens and claxons wailed all over the place, the UFO and its gigantic cargo floated over E Street, drawing small-arms fire from multiple directions, although these puny bullets had the same effect as would the proverbial snowflake on the bosom of the Potomac.

As the mysterious, glowing, singing, *thing* reached the South Lawn, the top remnant of the Washington Monument began to rotate in the vertical plane, performing a 180 degree turn, until its pointed aluminum tip was facing almost precisely straight downward.

All of a sudden, whatever ethereal force had been holding this trophy aloft, released its grip, and gravity did the rest : the obelisk's top careened downward as if rocket-propelled, and a second later, with an earthquake-like "boom", it buried itself deep into the lawn just below the South Portico.

Shrugging off a fusillade of automatic-weapons-fire without the slightest apparent concern, the UFO streaked around the South Lawn's new ornament, blasting an inscription into its southward-facing side, before abruptly changing course and landing in the Rose-Garden, no more than twenty meters from the eastern door of the Oval Office.

"Check *this* out, Mario!" shouted an amazed tourist-onlooker, sharing his binoculars with a friend, from a blocks'-distant perspective. "That space-ship-thing – it ain't no flyin' saucer – it's a *person*, long hair in a pony-tail... looks like a woman, some kind of shiny black duds she's wearing – *whoa!* Cops is rushin' her – what the hell, po-lice flyin' every *which* way, like they was shot out of a cannon – look there, one of 'em's goin' right through that window – oh my *Gawd!* Door to the White House just *shattered* into a million pieces..."

The onlooker froze, feeling the point of a gun-barrel in the small of his back.

"Put that down and get your hands in the air!" exclaimed a gruff, National Guard voice. "You're ordered to leave the D.C. ADIZ, *immediately!*"

"Hey – take it easy there, soldier... I don't want no trouble, you know?" answered the man.

"Then *move!*" growled the gendarme.

Turning to face the other, the civilian said, "Fine, fine – we're goin'... but you mind if I ask you somethin'?"

"What?" shot back the SWAT-geared gendarme, the words "GrayWar Legion" faintly evident on the shoulder of his uniform. "Make it *quick* – we have to search every building within six blocks in the next twenty minutes."

"It's 'bout that humongous big thing that she dropped just this side of the White House," stated the tourist. "I got a good look at it with the spyglasses, just before you showed up. What you s'pose it *means?*"

"I don't follow you," countered the soldier.

"Well... we're all figurin' that this is some kind of 'terrorist'-thing, so I expected somethin' in that-there Muslim writing," explained the tourist.

"But all it says", he added, "Is... 'Free My Family Now, You Coward President... Or Else'."

Ah – You Are Someone "Important"

I admire the bravery of these body-guard-men, silently counseled the Destroying Angel, as her fearsome being and living war-accouterments calmly walked past the smashed Rose-Garden door, in so doing intruding on the highest inner-sanctum of U.S. political power : the Oval Office.

They jumped against us from diverse points, and would have seen their flesh char and disintegrate on the scales of young Vìrya Ahn'jë, *or have it be ripped apart by the edge of her elder-sister.*

It was thus merciful that we propelled them backwards.

A few broken bones, a few glass-cuts... a small price to pay compared to being crippled for life... think ye not?

Are blessed Mother wise thee, replied many small mind-voices.

One other thing, Daughter Burning-Mountain, requested Karéin-Mayréij.

I pray that thou should hold in thy fire with every mote of thy will, especially that which comes from thy feet.

We trod upon a fine carpet here, inscribed with the kingship-symbol of this "America" empire; and it would be disrespectful to deface it with boot-prints.

Why? asked the war-children.

Because, dear ones, replied the alien-girl, *When we insult, we do so by design, not by happenstance.*

Such is playing the game of politics – fear not to assert one's dominance... but do so only when the time and place is right.

Now the Storied Watcher's expert eyes, their perceptive-abilities enhanced yet further by the new-found and growing powers of Vìrya Ahn'jë's spectacles, scanned the entire scene.

Very useful, dear Daughter, to have the exact locations of the little electro-com-pu-ter things, displayed easily for thy Mother to see.

Daughters – I beg ye – help me to befuddle the dull minds of the spying-techno-boxes that are artfully hidden, around here.

There are so many... I might miss one or two.

Yea, Mother, replied the armor and the shield.

The Oval Office was deserted – no surprise there – but, apart from the shattered exterior-door, there was no more than superficial damage to the rest of the room.

Unfortunate that my first venture here is as an enemy... not what I would have wished for, mused the Storied Watcher.

Much history has been made, in this place... and it is of dignified structure and decoration – a tee-vee screen in one wall, a few techno-recording-cameras here and there... must have been used for those lies that were broadcast recently – but other than that, the room looks like a Temple of the Law.

If only these Americans obeyed their own laws...

Now... what did the Neo-Net picture-things say? she recalled.

This, I recall, is a goodly-sized palace – certainly not as large as some that I have frequented in earlier times – but it was built as a residence, not as a fortress.

The com-pu-ter network said that in an 'emergency' – and what we do here, that would no doubt qualify, ha ha – the plan was to 'evacuate' the President by air, in one of those airplanes with the big propeller on top.

Well, we perceive nothing like that yet... but children, if ye note its advent before thy Mother does – hesitate not to advise me.

Vìrya Ahn'jë – I see no war-guards in here, but there are the life-forces of several humans retreating rapidly down the hall past yonder inside-door.

Shall we see where they are going?

Yea, came back the enthusiastic response.

Too sounds right stronger left than, closer Mother be must they.

The old-fashioned lock on the door leading to the interior hall of the West Wing lasted a quarter-second against the Storied Watcher's telekinetic-attack, and she stepped out into what appeared to be a 2-way nexus, with halls going to the north and west.

From a corner at the far north-end, two dark-suited Secret Service agents crouched and fired repeatedly, their hollow-point bullets alternately bouncing off and vaporizing on the young-looking woman's instantly-raised protective-bubble.

Væran Ss'éth'ch'... if ye please, sent Karéin-Mayréij.

To make fear and deter – not to kill.

Return when they go away.

With an eerie, chiming sound, the blue-dagger rocketed up the hallway, its aura of brutal, Stygian cold leaving a thick coating of frost on walls, ceilings and the floor, while the bullets passing by in the other direction, fell frozen and useless.

About three meters in front of the Presidential bodyguards, *Væran Ss'éth'ch'* came to an abrupt stop, floating in mid-corridor and projecting his elemental-attack slowly forward, with the frost-coating creeping toward the dumbfounded Secret Service agents.

The men got the message and retreated around the corner.

Ever scrupulous of the carpeting, Karéin-Mayréij now slightly levitated as she entered the west-leading hallway, streaking down it much faster than a human Olympic sprinter could have managed.

Just ahead and to one side, there were chaotic noises, with human voices shouting incoherently.

Hmm, she procrastinated.

Noises coming from in there, room in the far south-west corner... what is this title, "Chief of Staff"?

Ah, well – probably, most these courtiers have already been evacuated, so I must start somewhere... if I am lucky, I will find someone to throttle.

A second later, the doorknob leading into this place crumpled like a discarded piece of notepad, as a fine hardwood-door crashed open, revealing a tastefully-decorated, oak-and-mahogany executive office-room, scarcely smaller than that of the President himself, except more cluttered with books and paperwork.

The alien-girl floated in to the room, coming to rest on her feet, about a foot or so past the broken doorway, as *Væran Ss'éth'ch'* rejoined her leg.

Bang – bang – bang, reverberated gun-shots from two more Secret Service agents, who had positioned themselves on either side of the door to the hallway.

This attack was rewarded first by a look of bored contempt by the Storied Watcher; then, with a quick gesture of her mail-clad index-fingers, both men were lifted off their feet and, as if thrown by some giant's-hand, propelled through the large picture-window leading westward to the south White House lawn.

"Do not worry," she mentioned, in a *faux*-friendly voice, from under her 'static-on-TV', eye-obscuring weird-sunglasses, to the two other humans who were cowering under the large, 1840s-style wooden desk, near what was left of the window. "There *is* a little blood – but I weakened the glass before I threw these two body-guards out of here. They will live... if they are wise enough not to bother me any more."

There was no answer, although the pained breathing of the fugitives was as obvious to the alien-girl, as would have been an open cry of distress.

"Oh-kay... fine," she muttered, using her mind-force to upend the desk backwards, in so doing blocking access to the window and revealing two Caucasian men – one, a lanky, clean-cut, long-faced guy with thinning blond hair expertly arranged to cover up impending baldness, and another who looked very much like... the President.

"You might as well stand up," requested Karéin-Mayréij, with an insouciant smile. "I can slay you with ease, either way – but presumably you would prefer to die on your feet? Such is a more noble way, in which to meet one's fate."

"You – you're the *alien*... aren't you?" stammered the blond man, as he unsteadily got up. "*Please* don't kill us!"

He flinched against the waves of barely-tolerable heat, issuing from every point on the alien's form.

"Ah... *that* is why you are in this 'Chief of Staff' office, then?" inquired the Storied Watcher. "*You*, there – arise, too, or I will have my war-children give you a fine incentive. Let me see... yes... it *comes* to me! Perhaps by burning off your toes, one by one? Would that, ahh, 'work for you'?"

The other man, dressed in a conservative business-suit, reluctantly complied, holding his arms straight up as he arose.

"Oh, no need to do *that* – please put down your arms," instructed the alien-girl. "Make the wrong move, and you will be dead before you can blink an eyelid, anyway. Now – to answer your question, sir... yes, I *am* the 'Destroying Angel of the Many Worlds', Karéin-Mayréij, by name; who is called the 'Storied Watcher', and who calls your President and empire to account, for wrongs done to me and my family. And *you* would be...?"

Sullenly, the two men just stood mute.

"I *see*," she cooed. "Someone i*mportant*... right?"

"We're just ordinary staffers –" started the first man.

Pointing to the second man, young-looking woman taunted, "*Really?* You look very much like the portraits that I have seen of the President, also, he with whom I spoke back at the ho-tel back in the desert city. *Strange*, though... I perceive deception... and I would have expected many more body-guards, to protect such a, ahh, *distinguished* ruler, who fancies himself the 'leader of the Free World'. And *you*, the tall, graceful-looking one, with the hair akin to mine own – I *know* you from somewhere; your thoughts smell familiar... you, too, were at that little confrontation in Tucson-town... were you not?"

"Sorry – you must have me confused with someone else," evaded the first man. "But thanks for the compliment... I think."

He tried to force a weak smile.

"I have many thousands of your years of learning how to tell when someone is lying to me, you know," she shot back, while crossing her mail-clad arms. "And there is an easy way to deal with this, with, shall we say, the least, ahh, discomfort to yourself. My dear lover – Bob Billings – was in the habit of carrying a number of little cardboard cards with him, so that others could remember how to contact him after being introduced. You would not happen to have a 'biz-ness card'... would you, sir?"

Fuck! thought the man.

What do I do now... *they're right in –*

"In the little metal-case, within your biz-ness-suit... are they not?" remarked the Storied Watcher, with a malevolent smile of her own. "You really *should* remember that you deal not with some ordinary 'terrorist', here, my friend; you are risking your life against a creature whose powers you cannot *comprehend*... let alone defeat. Let us have a look... shall we?"

The front pocket of the man's suit-jacket almost ripped off, as his business-card-holder was seized and propelled by the alien's telekinetic force.

"I would not want it to burn or melt," explained Karéin-Mayréij, "So I will just have a look at it, from a distance."

The case flew open, revealing the top card within it.

"Ahh," she cooed. "'Mister Jerry Kaysten, White House Chief of Staff'. Well, now... *there* is a fine prize – would you not agree? But nothing, compared to having your master, also within my grasp..."

"Why don't you grab *his* business-card and find out," stammered the first man, desperately thinking of any way to keep talking and thereby stay alive.

"Because I already know that he is just an impostor," mockingly riposted the Storied Watcher. "Your minds are an open book to me... at least, when you lie so crudely – I can hardly *help* but notice. Tell me, Mister Fake-President... how much are they paying you, to be the blood-sacrifice for the transgressions of the, uhh, 'real thing'? A nice 'college-endowment' for your children, and flowers on your grave every week-end, perhaps?"

"I... uhh... don't know..." muttered the *faux*-President. "They said it would be... uhh... an *honor*, that I'd be doing it for my country – and besides, before I went in for the plastic-surgery, they told me the only serious threat was the Muslims, oh and of course the occasional nut-case with a plastic gun... that was before *you* showed up... no offense meant, Madam. If you mean to take my life, I'm ready... it was part of the bargain, I gambled... guess I lost..."

"Ha – well, if you really *had* offended me, you would be a small pile of ashes by now," replied the Storied Watcher, with perhaps a hint of genuine sympathy. "But for the record... it demeans me to snuff out the lives of helpless opponents; I am not a *cruel* Destroying Angel... *most* of the time, that is. In the future, I suggest that you should find a better master to be a food-taster."

"Can I go, then?" requested the second man, hope against hope.

"Not until I get a satisfactory answer to my next question," she demanded. "Which is to our fine 'Chief of Staff', here."

"Yeah?" said Kaysten.

"If I were to kill the President... who would succeed him?" inquired Karéin-Mayréij.

"The Vice-President," he replied.

"And *that* man is... where?" asked the alien.

"You *know* I can't tell you that," said the Chief of Staff, trying to constrain the sweat forming on his brow. "But he's not here."

"And *you* know that if I wanted to, I could invade your mind and pull out this information by force... it is something that – if I were you – I would try, at all costs, to avoid having happen. Very, very painful – and sometimes, the, ahh, 'side-effects' cannot be repaired. Does the phrase, 'happy idiot' mean anything to you, Mr. Kaysten?"

"*Please...*" he whimpered, upon wobbly-knees.

A saturnine smile came to her lips.

"But I believe that I have a better idea," commented the Storied Watcher. "You see... it occurs to me, that this 'Vice-President' of yours is not likely to be much more honorable than he who now postures as the king of this state; and – in any event – there will be plenty of time for me to effect such a change, should doing so be necessary. Now I have another question... is it true that our impostor-President here, is shown to the American peasantry, in place of the 'real' President, wherever he may now be hiding?"

"That's the whole *idea*," confirmed Kaysten. "So the country sees its President at work in the White House, on a daily basis. 'Stability', 'business as usual'... that kind of thing, you know."

"And, therefore... should Mister Substitute-President issue an order, it would have to be followed... would it not?" she suggested.

"I... uhh... well... I don't think..." muttered the Chief of Staff.

"You, well, do not think... *what*?" she pressed.

"Only the actual *President* can issue a policy-directive, and have it carried out," offered Kaysten.

Uh-oh, he thought.

I see where she's going, here... fuck, fuck, FUCK!

"Maybe later – if you are still alive by then," she deadpanned. "Three reasons : I do not know you very well yet; 'sleeping with the enemy', as I believe you humans say in Eng-lish is not advisable, unless it is by way of alliance; and why you use the act of physical love and pleasure as a curse-word, I cannot fathom. Oh – and you would be burned to ashes, upon the touch of my skin. Oh-kay... *four* reasons, then!"

Her goofy-looking – girlish, but fang-adorned – smile, would have been hilarious, were it not so foreboding; the effect was completely bizarre, as the Chief of Staff and the *faux*-President were confronted by a creature considerably shorter than either of them – but one with a godly, majestic aura, a fire-bedecked suit of shimmering black armor, lethal-looking archaic weapons, and sunglasses whose lenses looked like an un-tuned TV-set.

"*What?*" spoke Kaysten, his mind feverishly alternating between suppressing an urge to laugh, restraining a desire to get down on his knees to worship, while trying to deal with the realization that she really *was* reading his thoughts.

"You see," she explained, "This trick that your regime has crafted to fool the peasantry – it *is* most convincing... is it not? Were it not for my ancient skills – and these cannot be exercised except in close presence – it would have been very difficult for me to have detected that Mister Fake-President, is other than the actual ruler of your empire. Indeed... when earlier, I spoke with your 'President', who knows... perhaps I spoke with this man to your side, or another such duplicate. But it matters not; because if, now, he speaks on *my* behalf, and issues the appropriate commands..."

"It won't work," protested Kaysten. "The real President will simply countermand the orders."

"If I was the average, gullible American peasant, or army-soldier," countered the Storied Watcher, "How would I know the difference?"

"But the Government has ways to..." the Chief of Staff tried to argue.

"Start walking," curtly interrupted the alien, pointing to the doorway. "Both of you. I presume that you know where the President's office is?"

"I don't suppose I have a choice?" asked Kaysten.

"No," commanded Karéin-Mayréij. "Oh, and... that techno-thing in your other pocket – that is your personal 'cell-phone'... is it not?"

"Yeah," confirmed the man. "Go ahead, pick my brains for the access-code, not that you need to... right?"

"I will refrain – so long as you will enter it when I so request," she pleasantly replied. "Is it one of those that can make a mov-ee-recording?"

"Yeah, it is... so what?" asked the Chief of Staff.

"Good," inscrutably remarked the alien-girl. "Now, *move...* or you will find out a new meaning for the word, 'pain'."

A split-second later, Kaysten's bewildered, overwhelmed mind was invaded by a thought clearly not his own.

No – you will not, it reassured.

I will not hurt you, Jerr-ee – you are not a bad person... let us be friends.

Please – ahh – 'play along with me', it continued.

If the Gods so will it... let my love fall over you and show you the way toward nobility.

"What the...?" gasped Kaysten.

Uncomfortably, the two men headed for the door, with the Storied Watcher floating after them, her burning feet levitating a few centimeters or so above the floor.

More body-guards approach from the west and around the corner behind us, noted the alien, to her war-children.

Væran Ss'éth'ch', again I call on thee... what is that?

Yes – thy Mother understands, Little Fire-Tooth – but thy brother is better suited for this task... as his touch – unlike thine own – cannot set off a conflagration which then consumes this building.

Remember the big airplane, with the hot-gaze, coming from its nose?

All chances in war even out in the end... as thy Great-Aunt will attest.

The blue-dagger again shot from her right leg, heading for the west-most corridor of the White House ground floor, turning all it passed into a choking-cold imitation of the depths of the Antarctic.

With a perfunctory glance to the corridor extending north from the Oval Office – the hallway was still mostly frozen solid, and it showed no signs of hostile activity – Karéin-Mayréij compelled the 'stunt-double' President and the Chief of Staff, to enter the West Wing's most important room.

"Presumably you are used to sitting in this fine, leather-bound chair," she mentioned to the second man, pointing to the President's seat, behind the Oval Office desk. "And look – writing-paper, right here... how convenient!"

"We tried to get him to do everything on the digital-flexi-surfaces and on the computers," interjected Kaysten, trying to lessen the tension, "But he's kind of old-fashioned, you know... hence the pen and paper."

"Well... I need not a quill, or a stylus, or any other such," noted the Storied Watcher.

She floated over to the desk, and, with a wave of her hand, a page-worth of easily-readable inscriptions began to burn into the surface of the writing-pad.

After about ten seconds, she was finished.

"Behold what I direct you to read, when we turn on the cameras," she demanded, addressing the *faux*-President.

"And... if I don't?" he nervously inquired, reflexively straightening his tie, as he positioned himself in the seat.

"Oh... in that case, regrettably... I shall have to kill you, in front of the cameras," explained Karéin-Mayréij, her voice cool and mockingly precise. "Do not forget to give us a nice big smile, just before I splatter you all over the office."

"I... uhh... *see*," he stated, pale-faced with fear.

"It is nothing *personal*, you understand... so please give me no reason to harm you," offered the alien-girl, as she kissed the little blue dagger that had now returned to her person, leaving a trail of ice behind it. "I will give you a few seconds to review the material. But your 'Secret Service', and the local police, some war-soldiers as well, are re-grouping some distance away; they are planning an assault – and though this be no threat to myself, both of you might be hurt if they attack before we are finished. Jerr-ee Kaysten – do you know how to operate the cameras?"

"Since there's apparently no point in trying to deceive you," commented the Chief of Staff, "The answer is, 'yes'. But nobody will believe it, you know."

"We will *see*," said the Storied Watcher. "You and I will stay out of the camera's field-of-vision, while our friend here, ahh, 'gives us the performance of his life' – which will either be a short or a long one, depending on how faithfully he acts out the part. Tell me... will this transmission be sent to the tee-vee networks?"

Shit! thought Kaysten.

After we did that last set... did they turn off the network-feeds?

I'd go to the Media Control Office... but what if they don't realize what's going on?

"Not... not right away," he stalled.

"But it *will* go on to the little storage-thing that is in the camera... will it not?" pressed the young-looking woman.

"Yeah – but when those guys out there get back in here, they'll *never* –" he tried to argue.

"Leave that to *me*," retorted the alien. "And – by the way – may I have your cell-movie-phone, please?"

Without a reply, the Chief of Staff retrieved the small device from his pocket. To no-one's surprise, it flew by itself to the grasp of the Storied Watcher, with little wisps of smoke or steam issuing from the points where her infernal grasp came into contact with it.

"Please position the camera and turn on the shining tee-vee lights to either side," requested the Storied Watcher, "And no tricks – each one will cost you a finger or toe... your choice of which."

I jest, of course, Jerr-ee, implanted a thought, into his consciousness.

I do not hate you – and I would like to be your friend and your teacher – but you must trust me... even if what I do, affrights your soul.

Shortly... you will know why.

"What happens if I screw up more than ten times?" he tried to joke.

"Then two things happen : I operate the camera myself, and you will not have a leg to stand on," amicably replied the alien-girl.

"*Right,*" mumbled Kaysten, and – by now completely out of bright ideas – he unenthusiastically fumbled with the video-apparatus' controls, as he moved the camera to where it had been only a few days earlier, its view-field confined to the head and shoulders of the false-President, behind the Oval Office desk.

"Ready as I'll ever be," muttered the Chief of Staff.

"You can use my first-name, if you want," proposed the alien. "Are you ready to, ahh, 'shoot'? I give you the count of five – then begin the broadcast."

"Uhh... okay..." replied a befuddled Kaysten.

"Five... four... three... two... one... you are, ahh, 'on'," announced the young-looking woman.

As the *faux*-President began to speak, his steadfast tone and polished delivery made it immediately apparent that he was no rank amateur at this type of subterfuge.

"Good afternoon, my fellow Americans," he began, his surgically-enhanced voice sounding virtually identical, except to the alien ears of his captor, to that of the real President. "This is the President, speaking to you from the Oval Office, with an important special announcement. Recently, there has been a dispute between the Government and the powerful alien-being named 'Karéin-Mayréij', alternatively referred to as the 'Storied Watcher'; but, I'm happy to report that today, we have concluded an agreement with Karéin-Mayréij that will resolve this issue."

Over 'puter out wire nets 'lecro pulses to other, beloved Mother, revealed *Vìrya Ahn'jë,* to the Storied Watcher.

Trace but far so only.

"While some of the details remain to be worked out," continued the stand-in, "Here is what I have committed to do, on behalf of the United States."

"First," he rattled off, "The Armed Forces, on pain of court-martial, are directed to cease all hostile actions against the Storied Watcher, and to stop tracking her movements. Second, I am ordering the immediate release of five individuals, namely, Mr. Robert K. Billings, Jr., of Tucson, Arizona; Ms. Whitney Claremont, of Detroit, Michigan, plus Ms. Claremont's two children, Melissa and Curtis Claremont, and, most importantly, the boy known as Tommy George, of Nebraska, to be re-united under the custody of the Storied Watcher, at a time and place of her choosing, to be communicated to myself within the next several days. I am also ordering the release of all members of the former Mars expedition team and all other illegally-detained political prisoners currently held by the United States, including but not limited to a list of specific individuals that will be provided by Ms. Mayréij, at a later date."

"Third," concluded the actor, "The United States will issue a written apology to the Storied Watcher, expressing our sincere regret for the mistreatment of the individuals mentioned above. Conversely, Ms. Mayréij has provided me with her own statement of contrition for the property-destruction that she has lately inflicted upon various national monuments. She has told me of her deep regret for any suffering that she may have caused to American citizens, and has promised to personally heal the wounds so inflicted, also making restitution, where a complete recovery cannot be provided."

The *faux*-President concluded, "In summary, my fellow Americans – with today's agreement, which was freely and voluntarily entered into by my Administration, we have avoided what would have been a disastrous and futile battle against a powerful and determined opponent. We hope and pray that in the future, the United States can work productively with the Storied Watcher, to advance the causes of peace and justice, in an atmosphere of mutual respect. God bless each one of you... and God Bless America."

Kaysten turned off the 'Record' button.

"I'm probably risking my hide," he observed, "But where the hell did you figure out how to write a speech like *that*?"

"I read books," matter-of-factually stated Karéin-Mayréij. "Perhaps you should also develop the habit of doing so."

"Reading sort of, uhh, went out, with virtual-reality video-games," explained the Chief of Staff. "And since Disney bought out half of NeoNet and replaced most of the news-shows with game-shows, people don't really pay a lot of attention to anything *but* that. They might not even *watch* what we just filmed."

"Sam Jacobson... I need to have a talk with you, regarding your description of your fellow Americans," ruefully muttered the Storied Watcher, shaking her head. "I think that Bob used the term, 'bill-of-goods'... well, it *would* be – if any of you could *read* it."

"Am I done, now?" asked the *faux*-President. "May I go?"

"Not just yet," answered the alien-girl. "One more thing. Here – take Mr. Kaysten's cell-phone-box, if you please."

The communicator floated over the desk, depositing itself in the *faux*-President's hand.

"What do you want me to do?" he inquired.

Turning to the Chief of Staff, she said, "First, give me the recording-chip from the vid-ee-o camera – the one that we just used to preserve the speech."

Daughter Burning-Mountain, preserve it, let it not affect by thy aura... keep this thing safe, for a few minutes, she silently sent to Vîrya Ahn'jë.

And while ye all have this thing – absorb its essence, if ye have time.

Call on thy Great-Aunt and sisters for help, that they also gain by the lesson.

Me teach dear learn and cold like Mother keep little Ice-Tooth I, came back the private voice.

Kaysten popped a small, 100-petabyte memory module from the device and held it out for her.

The thing was instantly snatched from his fingers, and it disappeared somewhere within the folds of the Storied Watcher's body-suit.

"Next... come beside me," she ordered. "We shall both look straight at our friend the actor : a nice portrait of man and *Makailkh*. Tell both of us – how does one activate the mov-ee recording feature of this cell-phone?"

Mother issues tooth-venom dear, silently exclaimed an alarmed *Virya I'ëà'b'*.

Why?

Trust m – and fear not! sent the Storied Watcher simultaneously to both Kaysten, and her war-children.

Not in any way accustomed to the alien's telepathy, the partly-dazed Chief of Staff was only able to slowly say, "Oh... that's easy... you just hit the red 'Rec' button on the bottom of the display... see it?"

He stumbled forward and stood next to her, although he could barely tolerate the heat afflicting that side. "You don't have to enter my code," added Kaysten, "Unless you're sending the video somewhere."

"Yeah... I think I got it," replied the *faux*-President. "Let me know when to start."

"Go ahead," said the Storied Watcher. "Are we 'on', now?"

The man behind the desk nodded affirmatively.

"Greetings," spoke the alien-girl, looking directly at the mini-recorder in the Chief of Staff's mobile-communicator. "This warning-message is for the President of the United States of America. You now see Karéin-Mayréij – the Storied Watcher – side-by-side with Mr. Jerr-ee Kaysten... who, I am told, is one of your most close and valued courtiers. Is that not correct, Jerr-ee?"

This will sting a little bit and you will sleep, she silently counseled.

But in the long-run... you will realize how lucky you are about to become.

You are greatly-blessed, man... prepare yourself!

Kaysten saw the *faux*-President's face blanch, with the latter man's eyes staring in fear; but the Chief of Staff was somehow frozen and could neither move, nor turn his head to see what had set off the worry in the other man.

"So far, Mr. President," continued the Storied Watcher, her four sharp teeth starting to slowly extend, "Despite the cruelties that you have repeatedly inflicted on my family, and indirectly upon myself, I have tried to be... *restrained*, in how I deal with you. I have attacked some of the monuments of your 'empire' – taking pains to avoid killing American peasants or foot-soldiers – but you have ignored these warnings. Regrettably, you have not yet received the message – and, unfortunately, to demonstrate that I, ahh, 'mean business'... I now have only two choices left : I can either kill *indiscriminately*... or I can –"

Suddenly, with some kind of faintly gold-tinged liquid dripping from her incisors, the Storied Watcher shot upward, pivoted in mid-air, and sunk her fangs deep into the Chief of Staff's unprotected neck.

The poor man's eyes rolled and glazed, and he let out a pathetic groan as he slumped to the floor, landing with a 'thud' at the alien's feet.

Alternately wiping and burning blood from her savage teeth, Karéin-Mayréij stared at the cell-camera, and snarled, "Mr. President, I hope that this shows you... I will not be trifled with, any longer! This man," – she pointed at Kaysten's crumpled body – "Met his fate, *quickly* and easily. I can make it take much, *much* longer, when I come to visit *you*. To make things easier, I have arranged for, ahh, 'yourself', to make a con-cess-ion speech, which will shortly be delivered to your tee-vee stations; I would advise you to comply with these commitments and take credit for them; and I will expect to see Bob and my family released forthwith. Or... *else!* Have a nice day, Mr. President."

She mentioned to the *faux*-President, "You may stop recording, now, sir."

With a trembling finger, he hit the "Off" button and whimpered, "What... uhh... what now?"

"Simple," instructed the alien-girl. "One, put the cell-phone in your pocket, and ensure that the first person from your government who you meet, he or she should see the recording that we just made, immediately. You may tell them, 'all is not as it seems'. Can you do that for me?"

"Y-yes," he stammered, as he stuffed the device away.

"And two," continued the Storied Watcher, pointing to the ruined portal leading out to the Rose-Garden. "See that door?"

The man nodded.

"*Use it*," she commanded. "I would suggest that you keep your hands above your head, when you leave here... regrettably – as I have discovered – these American soldiers have a bad habit of, ahh, 'shooting first and asking questions later'."

Though nearly paralyzed with dread, somehow, the *faux*-President managed to coax his leaden legs to carry him outward.

Just before leaving the Oval Office, he took one last glance at the frightening creature that, to all appearances, had casually murdered the hapless Jerry Kaysten.

She was crouched over the Chief of Staff's body, with a strange, translucent barrier, looking like a huge, barely perceptible soap-bubble, enclosing both Karéin-Mayréij and her apparently-lifeless prey.

"I am not so bad as you believe," she murmured, with an inscrutable smile.

A song, beautiful but ominous, began to rise, from all directions.

Ooo-ooo-ooo-ooo...

The *faux*-President raised his arms and – no fool he – ran for his life.

Hell, Level Three

So far, since they had descended to "Hell Level Three" – as White had dubbed the current floor – there had been two more brief fire-fights. Both of these had resulted in near-instant death for small numbers of GrayWar Legion mercenaries; but after hours more of searching, neither the former Mars mission crew, nor their ex-salesman tag-along, had seen hide nor hair of Billings' friends from the northern car-trip.

There had been endless numbers of securely-locked doors, with little evidence of anything at all behind them. The place gave an eerie impression of a "hotel still waitin' for most of its guests", as White had sardonically put it.

The encounters had, at least, provided them with the most important tools, for a place like this : guns and ammo. Even Billings was now toting an auto-rifle; Boyd, White and Jacobson had been duly impressed by his ability to use the thing – a fact that two camo-suited gendarmes in the last fire-fight, had found out about, in the proverbial "hard-way".

Of course, the salesman *had* suddenly appeared as if from "nowhere", with his itchy finger on the trigger... and *that* certainly hadn't hurt his action-hero style, either.

"I dunno," complained the black ex-astronaut, as the group paused, just to one side of a corner in the corridor. "We done just about this whole *level*, Captain; there's only this section, here," – he pointed at about a quarter of the map-card – "That we ain't been to."

"Any mental-messages yet, Cherie?" inquired Jacobson, of the professor.

"A lot of general bad karma," evenly replied Tanaka, "But most of it's coming from... *below*, as far as I can tell."

"Just what I wanted to hear," muttered Billings. "I suppose this means, 'further down into the belly of the beast'... right?"

"Maybe," evaded the former Mars mission commander. "Devon – can I see the card?"

"Here," offered White. "Layout's more or less like the last level – 'cept neither of them stairways got the 'lock' symbol on it. But, uhh... as y'all know already – usin' them stairs probably ain't too good an idea..."

"Yeah," murmured Jacobson, as he studied the map-card intensely. "Having almost been killed on the last set of them, I'd tend to agree with you on that."

"Thing *I'm* worried about," opined Boyd, "Is simply how long we've been down here. We've been amazingly lucky in only encountering scattered opposition... I can't explain why the response to our break-out has been so slow, but we *got* to figure that sooner or later, even these twerps from GrayWar will get their asses in gear and come after us in a serious way. I don't know how many of them that there are in this facility; but given the size of the, uhh, 'inmate' population, you'd have to assume maybe fifty to a hundred, possibly more. I'm not sure we could handle –"

"We can't stop looking... if that's what you mean, Brent," interrupted Tanaka.

"I wasn't suggesting that, Professor," retorted the ex-astronaut. "But – for the record – I *do* think that we should making plans for when, God willing, we eventually find the rest of Bob's friends. For example... if we have to go another level further down – or two, or three, or ten – do we fight our way back out? Do we take the same route that we took to go down? And – assuming we make it as far as Level One – what happens if they blow that big elevator-shaft – the one leading to the surface? They could trap us down here..."

"Maybe they already *have*," unhelpfully remarked Billings.

"Or they might just drop some big bomb on our nice lil' ol' heads, to seal us in here real good," added White.

"A nuke – a H-bomb, that's what you mean... right?" asked the salesman, in a 'more-worried-than-usual' tone.

"Y'all want the 'good' news or the 'bad' news, Bob my man?" replied White.

"Both together," requested Billings. "Like a martini – the gin offsets the vermouth, you know?"

White's grin beamed, lifting the spirits of the rest of the group. "Like the way y'all put that, Bob," he said. "But as to the facts of the matter... talk on the street before we ended up in our first jail down here, was that the Armed Forces was just about out of nukes, 'cause they shot 'em all off against Mr. 'Lucifer'... unless they believe we's a much more important target than I *think* we is... maybe they won't waste any of the precious few on us. That's the 'good' news."

"And...?" asked the salesman.

"'Bad' news is," elaborated White, "Air Force has got all sorts of conventional bombs – some of 'em's tens of thousands of kilos heavy, that could *easily* take out a hole this deep... I think. So..."

"So when we hear a big 'bang', then we hide under the good Professor's little, uhh, 'bubble'... that's the plan?" proposed Billings.

"I'm becoming stronger every minute, Bob," counseled Tanaka, "But I doubt that I could stop something *that* powerful. Pistol-shots, easy-peasy; rifle-bullets, they hurt a bit, but still not hard to manage... I might even be able to stop a hand-grenade, on a good day – but a *bomb*? Sorry to disappoint you... but that's a 'no way, José'. The shock-wave from something like that would probably crush me, the minute that my back hit an unmovable object. Assuming, of course, that I wouldn't already be dead from the feedback –"

"What do you mean... 'feedback'?" asked Jacobson.

"It's hard to find English words for, Sam," explained the woman. "I *feel* each impact against the shield – the energy that gets released when that happens, it comes back to me – but it's raw, crude, painful, not compatible with me... 'uncooked' *Amaiish* is the best way I can describe it. If I got a bomb's-worth of it all at once... God, I don't want to even *think* about it. Remember what Karéin told you might have happened, if you hadn't been ready to use her power, when she, uhh, 'channeled' it through your body, back on the *Eagle?*"

"Yeah... I sure *do*," ruefully confirmed Jacobson. "'Ouch' and double 'ouch'. Okay, point taken."

"So if they *do* drop a bomb on us," pressed Billings, "What do we do... run? Pray? Maybe get out our Wile E. Coyote umbrella and wave 'bye-bye' to the camera?"

"Ain't nowhere to run *to* – or hadn't y'all noticed," laconically remarked White.

"Look, everyone," interrupted Jacobson, "This is one of those many issues that, as of yet, we don't have a good solution for... and we could debate it forever, but –"

His commentary was interrupted by a high-pitched cry – faint but still disturbingly evident to the more-than-human ears of the group – issuing from somewhere ahead.

Five sets of eyes cross-interrogated each other.

"Could that be Claremont?" suggested Boyd.

"Can't tell, but doesn't *sound* like her... I don't *think*," offered Billings.

"Her daughter, then?" argued Tanaka.

"Don't know... never heard her scream," answered the salesman. "Thank God for *that*."

Again, they heard a faint, heartbreakingly agonized wail, from the same direction.

"*Jesus*," breathed Billings.

As if in physical pain, he bent over, almost hyperventilating.

"Bob – you okay?" demanded a worried Tanaka.

"Yeah," he replied, in an unconvincing tone.

Billings paused slightly, then, wincing and shaking his head, added, "No. No, I'm *not*... you see, I know what it *feels* like... but I had Sari's weirdo-stuff to keep me going... I can just imagine what she's... but... anyway..."

He quickly wiped his eyes, hoping that the rest wouldn't notice.

The gesture was futile, but was regarded compassionately by all the former Mars crew.

A pall of disgust – mixed with fear and a nice, thick overlay of anger – descended on every member of the group.

"Could be any one of potentially *hundreds* of women – or girls – who they're doing their, uhh, 'thing' with," reminded Boyd. "If we get sidetracked, where do we stop –"

"Fuck *you!*" spat Tanaka. "I'm *going!*"

She straightened up, as if to stride forward.

"That's *enough*, Cherie!" remonstrated Jacobson, his voice sharp. "Brent had a *duty* to remind us of that. If he hadn't... I *would* have. We may not be able to help everyone who's been trapped in this monstrous place... and that's a fact that we have little choice but to face."

"Y'all both right, I reckon," interrupted White, his eyes sad but determined. "We can't forget the objective, that's for *damn* sure... but sometimes, we got to take a detour, y'understand? Least... that's how I see it. And every second that we sit around bullshittin' this thing – them mothers gettin' another twist of the screws in on whoever they got in there. I say, we get goin'."

With her own composure nearly at its breaking-point, Tanaka said to Boyd, "Yeah... okay... I know what you're saying... but it's getting so that I'm *feeling* these things, as much as hearing them... sorry, Brent. Didn't really *mean* it... you know?"

"I know," softly assured Boyd.

"But I'm *still* going," declared the woman.

She was relieved to see a businesslike nod of acknowledgement from her former Mars colleague.

"Yeah," muttered Jacobson. "You're... you're right, I suppose – we have a moral-duty to give whatever help we can. But let's do this *properly* – if for no reason other than to stay alive for the next one."

He paused, looked up, and commanded, "Ladies and gentlemen... battle-stations, if you please."

Silently, they put their guns to the ready and advanced down the corridor.

Elissha

They were now in the corridor outside a locked, reinforced door; and from the other side of that, they heard the same pitiful, high-pitched wailing that had so disturbed them, from five or six doors' down.

"No! *No!* Please, Mister – *please!* Please – *no!*" screamed a small, desperate voice.

In the silence outside, a wave of primal emotions – ranging from raw hate to disgust – enveloped the more-than-human team.

I give them the 'pizza's ready' knock – Cherie gets the door – Bob drops out of sight and sneaks around the back... Brent and Devon waste whomever needs it... ready? sent Sam Jacobson.

The former Mars team all sent back mental-confirmations, but Billings – 'still strictly a one-way-CB', as he had self-described – merely nodded affirmatively.

Three... two... counted off the former Mars mission commander.

A shrill, pained, cry beset their ears.

One...

Jacobson did his best impression of a Hallowe'en prank.

Knock, knock... knockity knock knock.

"Who's *that?*" called a male voice, from somewhere inside.

Jacobson did not reply, though the low sobbing coming from further inside the room, sorely tempted him to.

There was a pause.

"You hear a knock?" spoke the man on the other side of the door, far-off but still very audible to the ears of the team.

"No," replied another, female-sounding voice.

"Here – I'll go see," declared the first one.

"But we're on *lock-down!*" complained the inside-woman. "Escaped 'guests' – didn't you hear? Until GrayWar get their boys down here, we're not supposed to –"

"Ah, don't worry – just keep the little bitch *busy* for a sec... probably the GrayWar-boys doing the rounds," flippantly requested the first voice. "Get the car-lighter out – will you? We still gotta do the cheeks and the squishy-parts, you know," he added.

Jacobson and the rest of his team heard footsteps approaching, over a backdrop of a child's hysterical crying.

"Whoever's out there, we need your call-code," demanded the male voice on the other side of the door.

The fury coming from deep within Cherie Tanaka washed over the four others like a *tsunami*. They saw her trunk start to light up from inside – like some kind of bizarre super-human lava-lamp – as her song began to reverberate from here, there and everywhere.

Ooo – ai-ooo – ooo-ai, called the music; and, just before he vanished from sight, the salesman came to realize that it sounded deeper – richer, with more ethereal accompaniment – than when he had first been rescued.

Something like adrenalin, but *far* more potent, poured into his bloodstream.

Again, the child wailed.

They heard a slap, and a curse.

"If there's somebody *out* there, you need to –" peevishly complained the male voice.

That was, in fact, the last thing that this man would ever say; in mid-sentence, the door was struck by the pile-driver force of Tanaka's enraged mind, combined with one of her trademark lightening-discharges. Its remains flew inward as if shot out of a cannon, striking the inside-man and splattering his battered body against the opposite wall.

Billings clumsily shuffled in, blind, though still strangely aware of his surroundings.

Cradling his gun, he went leftward on the wall that separated this room from the outside hall, the sounds of mayhem all around him.

"You sumbitches get the *fuck* away from that *kid!*" he heard someone – probably White – yell.

"Who the hell are *you* –" shouted the female voice.

"Oh my *God!*" gasped Tanaka, a wave of mental-grief emanating outward from wherever she must have been.

There were sounds of a brief struggle – a muffled curse – and a "thud", as if someone was being tackled.

"Got her, Brent?" spoke Jacobson.

"Yeah," confirmed Boyd's voice. "Guy that was behind the door – he's *had* it, though. No effing loss..."

Shit, thought the salesman.

Please God, don't tell me it's –

"*Taxi*," he muttered, and the darkness fell, revealing another torture-room, very much like the ones where so much pain had lately been inflicted on him.

Except... in this case, although there were two gurneys, they were both occupied by pre-pubescent children – a fair-skinned boy, perhaps 8 to 10 years old, and a similar-looking girl, probably slightly younger.

Both were clad only in filthy-looking, blood-and-urine-stained underwear briefs and panties.

Not Curtis, not Tommy, not Melissa, Billings reflected, with guilty relief.

But... kids!

Jesus H. God – not more kids.

Please. No more. Please!

With White and Jacobson standing close by, Tanaka's telekinesis ripped away the straps holding down the girl; and – when the latter was brought to a sitting-position – Billings could see that her body had been cruelly-abused, with burn-marks, bruises and half-open wounds, all over it.

The child had a dazed, vapid countenance, and she stared hollowly-forward as if in a trance, despite Tanaka's desperate embrace.

"It's *okay*, baby," softly consoled the professor. "It's *okay*, okay, all okay – you're *safe* now, honey," she sobbed.

Billings asked, "What about the other one? Why aren't you undoing *his* straps?"

A sad shake of the head from White told the salesman all he had to know, on *that* front.

"Yeah... I *see*... all right," Billings managed.

Now Jacobson's gaze, infused with a sullen anger that none of the Mars team had previously seen, turned ominously toward the pasty-faced, corpulent Caucasian woman, dressed in a parody of a nurse's smock, who was being held tight in Boyd's grasp.

"*You're* responsible for this... *aren't* you?" he accused.

The woman half-pursed her lips and she initially remained silent, letting out only a small yelp of pain as Boyd twisted her arm and frog-marched her over to where the boy's terribly-afflicted body lay restrained.

"Have a good *look*, bitch!" hissed Boyd into the woman's ear.

Not really wanting to – but knowing it was a duty – Billings followed, and when he saw the evidence of what had been done to the dead boy – especially, a ghastly grimace of fear and pain on the murdered child's little face, a mute testament to interminable last Earthly moments of horror – the salesman almost fainted, steadying himself against one of the gurneys only with considerable difficulty.

He managed to go over to Tanaka, helping her comfort the girl, and looking down with tear-filled eyes upon this luckless, helpless, pathetic creature.

White walked up in front of the nurse-woman.

Abruptly, he slapped her hard, on the right side of the face.

"Answer the fuckin' *question*, 'ho!" he snarled.

The woman remained tight-lipped.

"Okay," spoke White, with a seemingly indifferent shrug of his shoulders.

Then, with no more warning than before, he punched the left side of the woman's jaw, striking her with such force that when her eyes fluttered back to consciousness, she began to spit out fragments of teeth, along with blood.

"*Devon –*" started Jacobson.

He took another look at the *faux*-nurse.

"Oh, the hell with it... *forget* it," retreated the ex-commander.

"It was... it was *him*," evaded the captive. "I didn't do it."

"Oh, *right*... I *see*," taunted Billings, looking up across the gurney that had held the girl. "Well – you assholes *always* work in twos... don't you? As I can *personally* attest."

Jesus, he thought.

What happened to the boy – if Sari hadn't built me up with the Mars-stuff – could have been me...

The salesman's cold-sweating face, was ashen.

"It's all *lies*," she haughtily prevaricated. "What do *you* know?"

"Only that your sorry ass has at most about five minutes more to live," he savagely retorted. "Four fifty-nine... fifty-eight..."

"*Wait!*" protested the woman. "I need medical-attention – I think you beasts broke a tooth –"

"Shut the *fuck* up!" growled Boyd, as his muscular grip twisted one of the woman's arms into an even less comfortable position.

"Honey," Tanaka half-whispered to the girl, who was now being cradled and rocked while the Eurasian ex-astronaut sat in a nearby chair, "Me and my friends here – Bob, Sam, Brent and Devon... we're *your* friends, too, and we'll never let *anyone* hurt you, ever again – we *swear* it... don't we, guys?"

In their own ways, three of the four vigorously confirmed this assertion.

Now Billings crouched down beside Tanaka and her diminutive companion. He added, "Listen, kid... sorry, don't know your name yet, but... I'm Bob, Bob Billings – you can call me 'Uncle Bob', or just 'Bob', or whatever you want... but the thing *is*, see, what they did to you – they did that to *me*, too... so if you need somebody to talk to about it... you can talk to me... you know?"

Still obviously in shock, the child managed to nod affirmatively.

"I'm Cherie," continued Tanaka, "And we can get used to each other little by little, but... there's one thing that I need to know. Do you think you can tell me the honest truth, hope to die?"

"Bad choice of words –" cautioned Jacobson, but the girl's faint, timid voice cut him off.

"Yes... Cherie," she whispered.

"Okay," said Tanaka, looking intensely at the child. "Now... tell me... about that lady over there... did she do any *bad* things to you?"

The girl nodded.

"Any *very* bad things?" inquired the professor.

Again, the girl nodded, this time with more force.

Tears poured down her little face, undoubtedly in the remembering of a nightmare all-too-real.

"I know this must be very hard for you... I'm *sorry*," apologized Tanaka. "Just one more. Did she do anything to the little boy over there?"

Now the girl seemed to come out of her stupor, and she shouted, with a child's simple anger, "He's my *brother* – and she *killed* him!"

"You lying little –" shrieked the *faux*-nurse, until Boyd's wrist-lock put her into agony.

"I... *see*," coldly observed the former science-officer.

She turned to Billings.

"Bob," requested Tanaka, "Can you look after our new little friend, here, for a minute or two?"

"Uhh... *sure*," replied the salesman.

Tanaka arose, and Billings sat where she had, holding the girl on his lap.

"Uncle Bob will look after you, sweetheart," he informed her. "So will all of us. That's a *promise*."

The atmosphere became yet more thick and ominous with every footstep that Tanaka took, until she had come in front of both Boyd and his pinned captive.

With unsuppressed fury, Cherie Tanaka stared at the woman.

"I'm second-in-command of this entire *level*," negotiated the *faux*-nurse, blood-and-spit-slobber staining her chin. "I don't know *who* you people are – or how you got free – but I'm *warning* you... you're in a lot of trouble, as it is, and there's no way out of here! Now... if you let me go, when the guards get here, I'll be lenient... I'll put in a good word for –"

"Y'all *hear* that, Professor?" sneered White. "Bitch gonna put in a 'good word' for us niggaz. Well, ho'... if I was *y'all*... only 'good words' that I'd be worryin' 'bout, would be in the Lord's Prayer... don't you know."

There was a cruel, savage smile on Tanaka's face, and her eyes were – much to the amazement and consternation of the captive – starting to shine with a blue-and-white glow.

"You're a woman, too," whined the *faux*-nurse. "You wouldn't hurt me, would you? I'm appealing to... to *sisterhood*. It would be *inhuman* to do anything to me!"

"Brent – take her outside," ordered Tanaka.

"*Cherie*," plaintively argued Jacobson, his eyes desperately interrogating the rest of them.

"Don't want to *hear* it, Sam!" she shot back. "Don't even *try!*"

"Team, we can't just –" the former commander started; but again, he was interrupted.

"Not when it's *kids*, Captain!" forced Boyd through clenched teeth, as he gave the *faux*-nurse's arms a brutal, cracking twist. "Not when it's *kids*. If you convince the Professor... you won't convince *me*."

"We's all fed up, sir," added White. "Ain't gonna put up with it no more. Bottom *line... sir*."

"Yeah, I suppose we aren't... *are* we?" helplessly commented Jacobson. "Well – for the record – as much as I don't like saying so... we can't leave her *here* – possibly to get let loose on the world again when those GrayWar-pricks show up, paying no penalty – and we obviously can't take her *with* us. So..."

"Nooo!" shrieked the woman. "You wouldn't *dare*! Guards! *Guards!!*"

"We shouldn't watch this, kid," quietly advised Billings. "Uncle Bob is going to make it real dark for a little while, and I want you to cover your ears... okay?"

The child nodded, and instantly, both she and the salesman – along with the seat that they occupied – vanished from sight.

"*Wow*," came a small voice from the apparent nothingness.

From the perspective of those who stayed in the room – Billings and the girl, a sad-faced plus a defeated-looking Jacobson – they saw, or heard, a grimly-determined Boyd, accompanied by a fatigued-looking White and a furious Tanaka, drag the self-styled 'nurse', kicking and screaming, through the door and into the hallway outside.

"I have *nothing* in common with you, nor does any real human being... though I'm not one of *those*, any more," they heard Tanaka inveigh. "But I *do* have a regret – that I can't make this take longer... like, a *week*, or so."

"Y'all give my regards to them Nazis, down in the warm place, bitch," they heard White curse.

There was a sickening, pathetic-sounding groan, and the noise of something falling or being thrown to the floor.

Then, they heard a muffled 'bang' – and another – as made by a small-caliber gun fired at close-range. There was one more shot; and, finally, all was silent... save for pained breathing, for many long seconds.

When he was certain that the dirty-business was finished, Billings dropped his cloak with a weak invocation of 'Taxi'.

He asked the child, "Well... *that's* over with – thank God. Listen, kid... you got a name?"

The little girl looked up at him with sad, half-trusting eyes.

"I'm Elissha," she replied.

A Slight Change Of Plans, Mr. President

The unmarked, nondescript facsimile of the "real" Air Force One aircraft had stopped for refueling, at an equally mundane second-tier USAF base, just outside of Fairbanks.

The President – having just awoken from a fitful sleep – was sick and tired of being cooped up in the aircraft, as he had been since God-knows-when.

So – despite the advice of his bodyguards – he had descended the mobile step-thing to the tarmac; here, reclining on the fold-up chair that a lieutenant had thoughtfully brought down, he took deep breaths of cool, clean Alaskan air and admired the towering forests, not too far-off in the distance.

Suddenly, the spare, no-nonsense, leather-skinned face of Arthur DeWitt appeared in the entrance portal leading back to the airborne command-post. A second later, he was joined by Bezomorton.

Both of the men looked thoroughly alarmed; or – perhaps – "panicked" would have been a more accurate adjective.

"Mr. President," called the Defense Secretary, "There's an update on what's been going on down in D.C. – you had better come see this."

The Chief Executive shook his head.

"I already *know* what the score is, with the damn alien," he grumbled. "What'd she do *this* time... write swear-words all over the Bill of Rights at the Archives? I've had *enough*, for now. When do we get airborne, again?"

"This is *different*, sir," protested Bezomorton. "We *really* think you should –"

"If it's so important, then come down here and give me the good news yourselves," complained the President.

"As you wish," replied the National Security Adviser.

He huffed and puffed as he hurried his paunchy frame down the stairs; then, flanked by the much more in-shape DeWitt, stood in front of the still-sitting President.

Bezomorton was carrying something, perhaps a mobile-communicator, in his hand.

"So... what *is* it," wearily inquired the President.

"Sir, I'm afraid I have some *very* bad news," stated Bezomorton, "And I know it's probably going to be even more of a shock to yourself than it was to me, so –"

"Just give it to me straight, John," retorted the President.

He saw a pained expression on the man's face, and in so doing, knew that this was something more than the usual 'bad news'.

"Alright," replied the Security Adviser. "As you know, sir... we have reason to believe that the alien, after having vandalized the Washington Monument, went on to attack the White House itself; but we had, of course, planned for that eventuality, by having the decoy, false 'President' there as a confidence-building measure –"

"Is he okay?" demanded a worried Chief Executive. "She go after him?"

"Yes, and yes," answered Bezomorton. "You aren't going to *believe* what she forced him to do... I'll get to that later, but he survived the incident – for reasons that we still don't clearly understand, the alien let him go."

"So what's the *problem*?" asked the President.

"The National Security Council had earlier made the determination that to maintain the cover-story involving the fake 'President' and the alternate 'First Family', we would rotate certain high-level members of the Executive Branch – excepting yourself, of course – in and out of the White House, so that in case the media suspected something, we could show them 'the real thing', as it were. This week, Jerry Kaysten had been assigned to be in that role..."

"What *is* it?" pressed the President, seeing the look of loss on Bezomorton's face.

"I'll let you see for yourself," answered the Security Adviser.

He held up a mobile-communicator, with a flip-out digital video-screen several inches wide.

A video began to play. It started with, "Greetings, this warning message is for the President of the United States of America..."

With serious demeanor, the President listened to the Storied Watcher's litany of complaints.

Then, Bezomorton and Symington saw his face turn ashen-gray. The man's eyes started to well up.

"Oh my God... *Jerry!*" his grief-filled voice softly murmured.

He turned to address Bezomorton.

"Are you *sure* that she – I mean –"

"Unfortunately," answered the National Security Adviser, "After we re-took the White House, which happened less than an hour ago, the Secret Service did a complete search to flush out the alien, in case she was still hiding there... but it appears that she had left some time previously. However... they *did* find what may be the pattern of a human body, burned into the floor of the Oval Office, and some of the personal effects found at the scene indicate that the victim was almost *certainly* Kaysten. For the record – he was an excellent Chief of Staff, and I never doubted his loyalty to either yourself or the United States... I'm *sorry*, sir."

"I'll second that opinion," echoed DeWitt. "Mr. Kaysten died while doing his duty, in the service of his country. No finer epitaph can be written for any of us, sir."

"Have we made arrangements for a, uhh, memorial-service?" requested the dazed and crestfallen Chief Executive.

"Before we get to *that*, sir," replied Bezomorton, "I think you should see the *next* video."

"What are you *talking* about?" sputtered the President. "You mean, from the alien?"

The National Security Adviser nodded.

"*Fine,*" muttered the President, his voice infused with anger and frustration. "When I find out where she taped all these things, I'm going to send whoever owns the studio to –"

"It was actually made in the Oval Office, sir," remarked Bezomorton. "By the 'stand-in' President, apparently under duress by the alien; it was found on a video-recording memory-unit from an Oval Office movie-camera – the same one, incidentally, as we did the pre-recorded speeches that you, yourself, made, some time ago. Here it is."

Again, the communicator showed some moving pictures, starting with the words, "This is the President, speaking to you from the Oval Office..."

"Oh... come *on!*" complained the President, when the movie was over with. "*Nobody's* going to believe that – but just to be on the safe side... make sure the damn thing gets put away somewhere real safe. Like in a bonfire or at the bottom of the ocean, for example."

"I'm afraid it's too late for that, sir," retorted Bezomorton. "It looks like a copy has already leaked on to both the TV-networks and NeoNet – we're still trying to determine who was responsible, and needless to say they're going to end up 'disappearing' – but in the meantime, we have a serious command-crisis to deal with."

"What do you *mean?*" inquired the American leader.

"Sir," interrupted DeWitt, "The issue is – if you recall – in this video, the alien appears to have compelled the 'fake' President to issue a series of misleading commands... which of course conflict with your *own* standing orders, to the Armed Forces. When I first heard of this, I got in contact with General Anderson, General Blanshard and Admiral Halford about the matter, to ascertain how each branch of the Service was reacting... and basically, we've got a *mess* on our hands."

"*Surely*, Mr. Secretary," shot back the President, "They can't believe that I'd give up and appease the alien, like I – I mean, my 'stand-in' – does on this video... *can* they? Look, John – we need to get a retraction sent out to the networks, *immediately!* We've got the ability to do our own recordings on board this aircraft... right? There's not a *minute* to waste. Let's get going."

The two other men stood mute, for a few uncomfortable seconds.

"What are you waiting for?" demanded the President.

"Sir," stated the National Security Adviser, slowly and carefully, "I've also been in contact with General Anderson, as well as with the Vice-President... both of them are standing by for the discussion that we need to have next. I think I should let them participate directly... may I activate the connection?"

"I don't know what this is all *about*," complained the President, "But go ahead... I assume that this link *is* secure... isn't it?"

"Of course, confirmed Bezomorton.

He entered a key-combination on the communicator, and – by the miracle of high-tech wizardry – the device's screen now showed the picture of Harry Anderson on one side, with that of the Vice-President, on the other.

"Hello, Mr. President," spoke the general.

"Likewise," added the Vice-President.

"Well, Harry... George," started the President, "I suppose you're both aware of what's been going on down at the White House? With the alien's callous murder of Jerry, as well as this fake speech that she somehow sent out to the networks, I mean. I can *tell* you... after finding out what she did to my Chief of Staff, it's 'gloves off' against this creature – I want her *dead* – and I don't *care* how that happens! But while we're at it... how do you know that I'm, uhh, 'me', and how do I know that you're, 'you'?"

Both Anderson and the Veep politely chuckled.

"I guess we'll just have to trust each other on *that* one, sir," mentioned Anderson.

"I guess," echoed the President. "Anyway... John's telling me that based on today's crisis, we have something more than usual to discuss. Which is fine by me... I was planning on calling a Cabinet-meeting for later today, anyway. John, you may proceed with whatever you had to say."

"Can both of you hear me?" inquired the Security Adviser.

"Very well," affirmed the Vice-President. Anderson nodded.

"Okay... so, I'll get right to the point, Mr. President, sir," stated Bezomorton, slowly and hesitatingly. "As everyone here's aware, apart from the alien's brutal and pointless murder of the Chief of Staff, we're now confronted with a serious challenge... namely, 'Karéin's creation of a faked speech, containing the false assertion of a 'deal' between herself and yourself, as well as a set of misleading orders to the Armed Forces, instructing them to cease military operations against the alien."

"Skip it, John," interrupted the President. "We're all aware of the background."

"Err... right, sir," mumbled Bezomorton. "I'd feel more comfortable if General Anderson were to explain the next part... General?"

"Gee – thanks for *nothing*, John," quipped Anderson, trying to sound upbeat. "But I suppose it *does* fall to me. Mr. President, the bottom line here is, the alien has evidently staged an effective attack on our command-and-control infrastructure, cleverly targeted at its weakest link... namely, the credibility of orders issued by the Commander-In-Chief, that is, yourself. She sure *is* a resourceful opponent... isn't she?"

"I don't like where you're going with this, Harry," muttered the U.S. leader, "But I'll hear you out. Go on."

"Well, sir," continued Anderson, taking a deep breath, "I've spoken to the other members of the Joint Chiefs, and we have all reluctantly come to the same conclusion : as long as we maintain the current – uhh – leadership-structure, the alien could basically repeat the same stunt, any time that she wanted to do so, for purposes of slowing down or disrupting our military activities. Therefore –"

"Wait just a minute – just an effing *minute!*" retorted a flustered, nonplussed President, jumping to his feet as he spoke. "Just get the fake

President *out* of there, for God's sake! Put him somewhere where the damn alien can't find him or shoot him! You can't seriously be *suggesting –*"

"Sir," interjected Bezomorton, "Don't forget – we have three other 'stand-in doubles' for yourself, located in various semi-secure facilities... she could go for any of those ones."

"So get rid of *them*, too!" argued the President, sweat showing on his brow. "Put them in one of your wonderful 'deep holes in the ground' and throw away the key. Then we – I mean, I – issue some *authentic* orders and tell the military to ignore anything else. How hard can *that* be?"

"Mr. *President*," argued Anderson, trying to be as diplomatic as possible, "While in the long-run, some of the measures that you have described might, indeed, mitigate the alien's ability to confuse the Armed Forces, we have a near-term command-crisis to deal with... and also, we have to consider seriously what this creature's *next* moves might be, given how she has pulled off her most recent attack. All of us here – I believe – are of the same opinion as are the Joint Chiefs, about our only *practical* way of depriving her of this category of options."

"And *that* would be?" listlessly queried the American leader.

"The bottom line, sir," proposed Anderson, "Is that both the National Security Council, and the Chiefs of Staff, believe that for the good of the country, we would all be best off if you would agree to a, uhh, 'temporary retirement', until this business with 'Karéin' can be dealt with."

Weakly, the President – or, 'soon-to-be, ex-President' – managed to laugh.

"Sounds much more like a 'permanent' retirement to me," he protested. "CIA's in on this... right? Don't *tell* me, let me guess what comes *next* – you offer me, plus all the stand-ins, up on a silver plate for the alien to do her worst with; she gets her 'revenge' for 'slights real or imagined', flies off into the sunset somewhere, and everyone – except for yours truly, of course – lives happily ever after. Sorry, gentlemen; you'll have to come up with a less obvious way for me to commit suicide. Can we get back to work, now?"

With a hurt look that might have been genuine, Bezomorton explained, "No... with all due respect, sir, that's not at *all* what the NSC had in mind. The point here is, first, to deprive the alien of even the *theoretical* ability to mimic your person, therefore your command-authority, until we can track 'Karéin' down and put an end to her; and second, since she seems to have developed a personal, uh, 'hate' for yourself, having you out of the, uh, 'picture' – sorry, sir, there was probably a better way of putting that – might help defuse the situation and buy us some time."

"Yeah... and delivering my corpse to her would also do quite nicely," snapped the President.

"Mr. *President*," shot back Bezomorton, sounding hurt at the implication, "We're simply proposing that you announce that you're temporarily 'retiring' for health-related reasons; nominal control of the military, as well as the title of 'Commander-In-Chief', would then follow the Constitutional line of succession to the Vice-President, who'd act as a proxy for your own decision-making, as regards the authority of the Executive Branch."

The President looked long and hard into the communicator.

"George," he plaintively asked, "Please don't tell me that this was *your* idea."

The Vice-President, showing his default cynical grin, shook his head.

"I'm coming in late on this whole thing," he claimed. "But *look*, Clark... I think you're missing the point. This plan that NSC and the military have cooked up – it's not about painting you out of the picture... not permanently, as I understand it. The idea is simply to be able to say to the stupid voters – as well as the Armed Forces – 'don't believe anything that you hear from the former President, because anything that you *do* hear, is just a pack of BS from our little alien-friend'. Remember... they don't have any 'stunt-doubles' for *me* – so she can't kidnap one of *them*, and get him to do the same crap that we all just saw on TV. So I think –"

"This is all *bullshit!*" countered the American leader. "What are you going to do, George... just head down to the Oval Office and wait for her to turn *you* into a smear on the floor... like she did to poor old Jerry?"

"I ain't *that* stupid," parried the Vice-President. "My position is – and I think that John, Arthur and Harry are also of one mind on it – that the 'everything's just fine, dandy and normal' thing went out with having the top of the Monument, made into a South Lawn ornament. If you know what I mean."

Silently, the President's eyes shifted from the images of Anderson and the Vice-President, to the faces of Bezomorton and DeWitt, and back again.

After a few more painfully long seconds, again, he spoke.

"As far as I'm aware, there's no precedent for *any* of this... and under the Constitution – we *are* still casually referring to that, aren't we, or am I wrong *there*, too – there's certainly no *legitimate* way to do this, if I choose not to resign," he remarked. "So above all else... I need to know one thing."

"Yes, sir?" asked the National Security Adviser.

"Do I, in fact, have a *choice* in this matter?" demanded the President, summoning up whatever dignity that still remained.

"Sir – we have serious concerns about being able to guarantee your safety on a continuous basis, should you elect to turn down this plan and remain the nominal – as opposed to the actual – Commander-In-Chief," carefully stated Anderson. "At least until the 'alien' issue is dealt with, of course. After that, the plan is for you to renounce your 'retirement', and for the Vice-President to relinquish the Oval Office, back to its original owner."

"We all know that once I'm 'out' – I'm *never* going to be back 'in'," defiantly answered the President. "So... no deal! I'm still the duly-elected leader of this country – and I intend to remain so. Now –"

"Everyone on this call has been contacted by the Agency," interrupted Bezomorton, with as much of a poker-face as he could muster. "They're *strongly* in favor of this move. They emphasized that your safety – and that of your family – might... uhh... be in *jeopardy*, if you were to remain in your current role... *sir*."

"Oh... for *sure*," sarcastically retorted the President. "How *nice* of them."

"If this means anything, sir," commented Anderson, "CIA also stated that the only thing protecting our own families, from threats of this nature... was the Agency's domestic wet-operations staff. The director warned us that these could just as easily be used against us... as for us. So you can see what's motivating us, in this situation. I'm sorry, sir – not what I would have wanted... *that's* for sure."

The President – a stunned, disbelieving look on his face – fell silent for a couple of long seconds, and then said,

"I have one condition."

"What would *that* be, sir?" asked Bezomorton, trying all the while to sound as 'professional' about the matter, as he could manage.

"I need the personal word of honor, of everyone present here – as well as of anyone else who is involved in this little *coup*," pleaded the President, "That whatever you, CIA, or the alien, do to me – you'll leave my wife and family *out* of this."

"Of *course*," quickly agreed the National Security Adviser. "I don't think that any of us would have a problem with that... correct?"

The others on the conference-bridge all nodded positively.

"I think the Agency will go along with that," mentioned DeWitt. "Since a similar promise was given to all of us."

"The only consideration is," noted Bezomorton, "We'll also have to keep your family-members secluded... since they might be considered as a target by the alien – not to mention the Muslims."

Crestfallen, the ex-American leader turned his back to the Defense Secretary, the adviser and his communicator.

"Well, gentlemen," he quietly commented, looking at the dark, tall boreal forests, "I'll make my peace with God... then, you can put a speech in front of me. My guess is that the Agency will get all of you, before they come for *me*. Three weeks, if you're lucky; three hours, if you aren't."

Bezomorton and the general uneasily regarded each other, both unsure of what to say.

A cold, light Alaskan breeze blew across the tarmac, as the President stood silent, and, at length, the two others walked back up the stairs.

Tucumcari In Her Sights

She had been streaking invisible and low over the cornfields of Middle America, going as fast as she dared, in a steadily-losing race trying to keep up with the setting sun.

It had been *hours*, now, with her ridiculously-fragile, unconscious captive-cum-passenger, who rode uncomfortably upon the concave inner-surface of

Vîrya I'ëà'b, her force-shield more or less offsetting the infernal heat and radiation coming from her younger sister – in so doing keeping Jerry Kaysten, alive.

The mental stress of constantly having to avoid terrain-obstacles, while adding the occasional 'zig-and-zag' to throw off any of the Americans' tracking-systems, was beginning to wear upon the Storied Watcher.

Soon, we shall have to stop and rest, little ones, counseled Karéin-Mayréij.

Thy mother's fatigue builds – all this bobbing-and-weaving, much more tiresome it is even than flying a thousand-fold faster, unto the firmament – and though we would survive an unfortunate collision with one of these 'high-tension wires'... our new brother Jerr-ee, might not.

Yet I am not inclined to waste so much as a second, ere we arrive at our destination... ah – I hate a compromise...

Man this Mother carry why all at? asked the blue-dagger.

So is important why he?

What said voices that and are calling late family thy if save we?

As far as thy mother knows, there are only six humans who know how to call for me, Little Ice-Tooth, explained the alien-girl.

One is dear Bob – and, though it pains my heart to say – the words that come to my mind do not smell much like his own; so, those who call, must be either of the two space-scientists, or my friends 'Wolf' or 'Misha', who I left back near the 'Tu-son' city, in the desert-realms.

If it were Bob, be ye all assured, Mr. Jerr-ee would at once be down on the ground, and we would be flying to my tormented lover faster than anything has ever done, in the skies of this world.

For now, we must be content with a speed that does not cause our human friend's bones to shatter, his flesh to melt or his thinking-nerves to shut down, she continued.

Such are the joys of accommodating humans... but we have great plans for this man... so accommodate, we must.

Silently, the weirding-troupe flew on for at least a half-hour more, and the Storied Watcher was now so tired that she thought she *must* land. But presently, she heard her name being called, and this again fortified her determination.

Vîrya I'ëà'b', use all thy arts to protect him... but still let him taste our life-force... a repast of nobility and might, implored Karéin-Mayréij.

A voice calls from the south-west; and now, I think I know where it bids us to go.

Like Mother Jerry beloved I, murmured the little shield.

Dreams his hear I. Good fearless inside hard acts his he – but heart is.

Would if pet him my thou I as.

Please?

The Storied Watcher did not hide a wry smile, as, ever faster, she hurtled past the Texas Panhandle, with Tucumcari in her sights.

The Recruits

___

Say It One More Time

"This is a *total* effin' waste of time," muttered the third agent. "We've been here for *hours*, now... how much is enough?"

He looked up at the long shadows falling over the canyon-walls.

"It'll be night-time soon," he peevishly added.

Chu did not reply.

"What's the matter... 'scared of the dark, there, son?" taunted the bounty-hunter.

"Nope," answered Hendricks, evenly. "But I don't feel like campin' out without a tent, *with* a few rattlers and scorpions to come cozy up wherever I decide to flake out... it's a 'city-boy'-thing... you know?"

Smart-ass, thought the FBI team-leader.

But God bless Will... he's giving as good as he gets.

"Look, Minnie – if I have to say that, uh, 'woman's' name one more time, I think I'm gonna develop an allergy to the letters 'K' and 'M'," grunted the massive, rotund black man. "You gotta admit... young man's got a *point*. This-here thing was a fine idea – an' I don't blame you for having given it a good try – but... I think it's time that we just called back to H.Q. and cut our losses."

"You really *think* so?" idly replied the Asian-American FBI-agent. "Why now, and not an hour ago... or an hour from now? Or two... or four?"

"Well, for one thing... I'm gettin' *hungry*," complained Boatman. "And yes, folks, I *know* what y'all thinkin', yours truly's got a bit more on him for livin' off the land, than the rest of you does... but you know, Agent Chu, I get cranky if I don't eat... remember?"

"Oh... we wouldn't want to have *that* happen," quipped Chu, with a wry smile. "And I don't think I'm giving away any secrets here, by admitting I'm disappointed – I've got no idea what to say to the Director, about wasting boatloads of operational-time and umpteen thousands of his dollars, when we come back with nothing but some clothes covered with canyon-dust, to show for the whole thing. Listen, though... how do the *rest* of you feel about packing it in?"

"I dunno," sighed Ramirez, with a weary shrug. "We *have* been down here a long time, and I'm getting hungry, too... ah, I will hang around, if any of the rest of you also want to do that."

"I *hear* you, Hector," commented Abruzzio, "And I certainly *could* use a shower and a nice, clean bed – but this is likely the only chance that I'll ever get to meet a real... *alien*. Ms. Chu, I'm sure you can appreciate why, if the choice were up to me alone – okay, me and Hector – we'd want to tough it out as long as we can."

"Believe me," remarked Wolf, "When Little Miss Flyin' H-Bomb *does* make her appearance... it'll be well worth the wait – *that's* fer sure."

"I would like to stay a bit longer, if it is not too much trouble, Agent Chu," requested Misha, with precise politeness. "We *do* have a water-source down here – the pool at the foot of the waterfall, that is – and from my own point-of-view, I do not relish heading back to the kind embrace of the U.S. government... frankly, considering my, uhh, 'vocation'... I am rather amazed that your Director allowed me to come along on this trip, at all."

"These are unusual times," offered Chu, "And perhaps they call for unusual exceptions to the rules."

"I hope so," agreed Abruzzio.

"Okay – *okay*," muttered Boatman, throwing up his big hands in a mock surrender gesture. "I guess I'm out-voted here... but can I at least ask, 'how much longer do we keep this stuff up, before we call it 'a day'?'"

"I vote for ten minutes," deadpanned the third agent.

"As long as it takes, maybe?" countered Abruzzio.

"That's, uhh, quite a variance, between the two," observed Chu. "How about we split the difference and say, 'another two hours'? By then it'll be pitch-dark... we can call for the chopper and be back home before midnight, or thereabouts."

"Sounds good to *me*," said the black agent, with quick relief. "That way we'd at least save Mr. Hendricks over there, from all them rattlesnakes."

"And the sand-flies... don't forget the sand-flies, man," cracked the third agent. "They're real *bad* down here... or so I'm told."

"Well, I don't think I want to –" started Wolf, but he was cut off by Boatman.

"Okay... well, just in the interests of us not hangin' around here one second longer than necessary... whose turn *is* it?" he asked.

"I think it's Ramirez's", suggested Hendricks.

"No *señor*," protested the Mexican-American scientist. "I went just before Sylvia – and she was the last one before we took our last break."

"Wiiilll," remonstrated Chu. "I haven't heard *you* doing the chant lately... *have* I?"

"Aw, Ma, do I *gotta*? I don't *wanna!*" whined the third agent, doing his best Dennis-The-Menace impression.

A friendly-but-firm look from his superior told him all he needed to know; so Hendricks reluctantly got up, shrugged and walked some distance away.

Facing the waterfall, he began to lazily chant, "Karéin, Mayréij... Karéin, Mayréij... Karrie Ann... Kandy Darling... Kool Kool Kitty..."

"For God's *sake*, Will," complained Chu, "It's only fifteen minutes, anyway, then somebody else steps in... try to stick to the *script*, will you?"

"Yeah... sure... whatever," mumbled Hendricks, with another indifferent shrug.

He re-started the chant.

"Karéin-Mayréij... Karéin-Mayréij... *Karéin-Mayréij...*"

Six pairs of astonished eyes and ears turned to regard the third agent, upon hearing his last invocation.

Hendricks' words seemed to take on a melodic, Stentorian tone; they ricocheted like fireflies off the canyon-walls.

From somewhere, a song echoed in the distance, as the faint chords of some fast-paced song began to issue up from the ground.

Ooo-ooo-ooo-ooo...

Stunned – and way more than a little apprehensive – the third agent just stood in place, wondering what to do next.

"Uh-oh," gasped Boatman.

"Goes to show, 'careful what you wish for', pardner," stated Wolf, with a triumphant smirk, "'Cause it looks like you just got it."

"It is truly *amazing* music... isn't it?" observed Abruzzio, with a look of wonder on her face.

"*Claro que sì,*" agreed Ramirez. "I can't believe this is really *happening,* Sylvia!"

Ooo-ooo-ooo-ooo...

Two or three of them felt a slight breeze.

"FBI-people – you know the drill," ordered Chu, moving hastily into action. "Behind the rocks, far-away from our guests – Wolf, Misha – back to back with Sylvia and Hector, in the middle. And, let me remind you... no guns, *anywhere* – holster 'em, boys, if they aren't already."

"She can detect them, anyway," reminded the Russian. "But it would be a – how do you say – 'good-will gesture', none the less."

"Alright... now let's go over the agenda," quickly continued the FBI team-leader. "First, we explain to her that –"

"I am listening... but should I take notes?" interrupted a light, melodious voice, issuing from an unknown direction.

"Who *said* that?" demanded a perplexed Boatman, looking nervously from right to left, upwards and downwards.

Even in the diminishing light, several of the rest of them could see a broad smile appearing on the faces of both the bounty-hunter and the Russian.

"Welcome back, Storied Watcher," called Misha, to nowhere in particular. "You can de-activate your hiding-cloak, if you like. Nobody here will try to harm you."

"You will feel a wave of hot-stuff," warned the disembodied voice. "Do not be afraid... it will not hurt you."

Then, in much less than the blink of an eye, the legendary Storied Watcher stood in front of the group, between the four clustered close together and the pool leading to the waterfall.

Behind her, the dimly-lit figure of... *someone* – his butt inside the concave inner-surface of something that looked like a Chinese cooking-wok – slowly floated down to rest on the Vishnu schist bedrock.

She was true to her word; a flash of heat, like an unwisely opened ceramic-curing-kiln, washed over the group.

"*Oh my... God,*" gasped Abruzzio. "It's really... *you*... isn't it?"

"The same, dear friend, Sylvia," announced Karéin-Mayréij, in a gentle, friendly tone of voice. "And... greetings and love to you, too, Hector, who helped guide me to my last quest."

At this, *Vîrya Ahn'jë*'s TV-interference pattern glasses disappeared somewhere, revealing the Storied Watcher's shining eyes.

"Hello," was all that the nonplussed Ramirez, who was, despite trying to prepare, far from ready for the godly countenance of the alien, could think of to say.

The Storied Watcher went down on one knee and added, "I apologize most sincerely for that unfortunate business at the hotel... but my heart rejoices in the knowing that the both of you have survived."

Rising up, she continued, "Now... I recognize you, Sylvia and Hector, and my friends, 'Wolf' and Misha, as well... but who are these people behind the stones... ah, *you*, over there," – she pointed to a large rock – "You are... 'Minn-ee-Choo'... are you not? And the big man behind the other, he is 'Boat-Man', with the third one being 'Hen-driks' – the one whose voice I heard last... correct? I ask you to keep those guns of yours put away, if you please – I have had more than enough shooting, for the time being. What are these three doing here? Misha, did you invite them?"

"How the *fuck* she know our names?" whispered the third agent, in Chu's direction.

"Be cool," counseled the bounty-hunter, motioning for calm as he spoke. "They're from the government, but –"

"The *'government'*?" exclaimed the alien, her voice rising rapidly, with after-echoes of her war-song issuing subtly from hither and yon. "The *American* government? But this kingdom *hunts* me, Wolf! Especially after what has, err, 'gone down', earlier this day –"

"We can *explain*, Karéin!" interjected Misha, with equal alacrity. "These three – you may as well get up and show yourselves, I can assure you that hiding between a rock will not be any real protection against the Storied Watcher, anyway – are from the American 'FBI'... which, as you probably know, is one of their intelligence-agencies; but do not worry about this being a trap – it is the opposite, in fact. They have some important information, if you will stand down your guard and speak with them."

The young-looking woman looked slightly behind, for a half-second and instructed, "Protect Jerr-ee, *Vîrya I'ëà'b'*. And keep watch on the skies – lest anything, ahh, feel that it is time to fall upon our head."

She turned her head back to regard the rest of the group, crossed her arms in front and called out, "Then I will listen to what you have to say, eff-bee-ai people. But no tricks, please! The first of you who calls our location to the President's air-warriors, will be smitten unto dust, in the next quarter-second. It also will not work, as many American fighter-pilots have lately discovered... they now have, ahh, a new appreciation for their para-choots. Do you understand?"

"There's fire all *over* her," nervously whispered Ramirez to Abruzzio.

It's like waves of... I don't know *what, coming from her,* reflected the female scientist.

Ooh... what a strange feeling... warm, nice... come *on, Sylvia, keep it together,* concentrate...

"Uhh... perfectly," hesitatingly replied Chu.

Okay, here goes nothing, she thought.

I might as well get killed right in front *of her, as cowering behind this damn rock.*

The FBI team-leader came up from her crouch and walked slowly in the direction of the fearsome being.

"This is gonna be *good,*" whispered Wolf to Misha.

"You had better hope so," replied the Russian.

A smoking, mail-clad finger pointed at the FBI-agent, who came to a stop just at the limit of where the Storied Watcher's infernal aura became painful.

"You are Agent Minn-ee-Choo... correct?" she inquired.

"How do you *know?*" idly asked Chu. "We haven't been introduced."

"Maybe when we get to know each other... *better,* I will tell you," replied the alien-girl, with an oddly-sympathetic-looking expression. "So what is this 'information' that the fine U.S. government has for me, today? After my last few encounters with your President, I would have thought that – ahh, as my dear companion Bob Billings used to say – 'there is not much more to talk about'."

"Maybe there isn't," allowed Chu, "But for what it's worth... here goes."

"Um-hmm?" nonchalantly replied Karéin-Mayréij.

"It's... well... it's like... *this,*" stammered the FBI-agent, sweat on her brow, and not from the heat.

What am I doing, *in front of this being?* silently shouted Chu's half-panicked mind.

She can read my thoughts – *she can kill me on a whim – this was a* crazy *idea – I should run –*

Suddenly, another idea appeared to her psyche, as if from nowhere.

Do not fear me, Minn-ee, reassured an ethereal voice.

I can smell evil and duplicity from a long way away.

You are pretty and attractive – you smell nice.

I will not hurt you – the opposite, in fact.

Let us be the best of friends... or even... more *than just 'friends'.*

A wary and most confused FBI team-leader, stood dumbfounded.

"If you are interested – my war-children confirm my assessment," noted the Storied Watcher, with a wan, albeit sharp-toothed, smile.

"Your... *what?*" responded a befuddled Chu.

"Never mind... I will explain *that*, later," remarked the Storied Watcher. "So what does your government want to say to me, at this late hour?"

"Well," started Chu, regaining some of her composure but knowing not how, "The Director – he's my ultimate superior, other than for the President, of course – he has asked me to relate two messages to you : one, that he requests that you not attack us any more –"

"My dear, lately-lost lover, Bob Billings, had a saying for such idle talk, after all that has gone on before your President and myself," retorted the young-looking woman. "I believe that it went, 'yadda yadda yadda'... or something alike."

Only barely-suppressing an urge to laugh out loud, Wolf chimed in, "Yeah, that'd be about it... wouldn't it, Karéin?"

Karéin-Mayréij did a sarcastic half-curtsy, to acknowledge this jest on the part of a follower.

"Wait – there's *more!*" protested Chu. "The second and more important thing is, the Director – our whole organization, in fact – we believe that the actions that seem to have offended you – and here I'm referring to the kidnap and mistreatment of Mr. Billings, Mrs. Claremont and the rest of the people who you have called your 'family' – may have been carried out without the President's knowledge and probably without his consent. So –"

"You know," commented the Storied Watcher, quizzically arching one eyebrow, "I have had conversations with this 'President', in which it certainly seemed to *me*, that he was taking credit – or responsibility, or call it what you will – for these transgressions; which, by the way, are ongoing, as we speak. You are also pleading on the part of a leader who has *repeatedly* lied and who has repeatedly tried to *murder* me... as my friends Wolf and Misha can personally attest. A difficult case to make... would you not say, Agent Minn-ee-Choo?"

By now, Boatman and Hendricks, reluctantly acting out of loyalty to their team-leader, had cautiously come out of hiding, approaching from behind Chu.

The black man stated, "Listen there, lady... we all knows that there's been some bad blood between you all and the President – but what Minnie's tryin' to say is, 'we think that whoever's behind all this stuff with your family, they're tryin' to jack the President, too... you gotta *understand*, yes, he's the head honcho and all that – but he don't run everybody in the government like a puppet... some of 'em got their own agendas... you know?"

"I have had several thousand of your lifetimes in which to have learned the ways of court-intrigue," reminded the Storied Watcher. "But if – against all common sense, I agree to consider this line of discussion – what real evidence can you provide me with, to support your argument?"

"I'll tell you what we know," said Chu. "First, Storied Watcher – uhh, is that the right thing to call you?"

"Either that, or 'Karéin-Mayréij'," confirmed the alien-girl.

"Okay," continued Chu, "From the first point at which you landed on Earth – up north in Idaho, that is – on orders issued directly from the President, FBI has been trying to locate you, communicate with you... the entire *idea* was precisely to avoid the kind of dispute that has now occurred. You have to understand, Ms. Mayréij –"

"It is just 'Karéin-Mayréij' – or 'Karéin' for short," imperiously corrected the alien-girl. "As much as so admitting reveals my loneliness... I do not *have* a clan-name."

"*Right*," hastily replied the team-leader. "Anyway... my team – that is myself as well as Agents Hendricks and Boatman – we've encountered repeated, hard-to-explain problems... roadblocks, missing-witnesses, disappearing-evidence, false leads... and so on. For example, we were apparently very close to being able to contact you just after you arrived down in Tucson with Mr. Billings, and were planning to do so, but then – and here you *have* to believe me, Karéin – *someone* – someone *else* – staged the attacks on the Billings residence as well as his workplace –"

"Just a *minute*," interrupted the Storied Watcher. "Misha... did you not tell me that from what you had observed – while you were, ahh, 'working for your previous employer' – that the big black cars which captured Bob, Whitney, Tommy and the others, were 'the kind that the American spies always use'?"

"That is true, Karéin," agreed the Russian, "But do not forget – the United States has *many* different secret-police agencies... those vehicles could have been from any of these. Or from someone masquerading as one of them. Remember that in the incident at the 'Tile Store', the black cars *themselves*, were attacked by a bunch of ordinary-looking American citizens. There is something 'involved' happening here, I believe."

"Yes... possibly... go on," stated Karéin-Mayréij, addressing Chu. "And you can then try to talk your way out of how your government tried to murder me, while at the hotel. But before you do – Sylvia, Hector, again I must humble myself and ask for your forgiveness, over what transpired there. As I flew away – with my new-found friends Wolf and Misha close to my breast – I was sick with fear and regret that the Americans' bombs might have struck either or both of you dead... but I did not dare turn around and try to rescue you... not with the amount of firepower that the President had arrayed against me. I am *sorry*, friends."

"It's okay," sympathetically answered Abruzzio. "And if it's of any interest, the government – some political-hack named 'Kaysten', specifically – they wanted us to tell you a lot of pompous-sounding nonsense about 'you have to do what we say, or else'... that kind of thing... we warned them that it would backfire – which it obviously did."

"But we remembered your message," added Ramirez, earnestly. "We *called* for you."

"Yes... you *did*, beloved friend!" answered the Storied Watcher, hoping that they could not see a tear evaporate from her cheek. "You *did!*"

"May I... uhh... continue?" requested Chu.

"Please *do*," said the alien-girl.

The others noticed that she had briefly retrieved a small amulet from inside her burning body-mail, and had whispered something to it, in a totally-incomprehensible tongue.

"So," explained the FBI team-leader, "The bottom line here is, Ms. Karéin-Mayréij – within FBI, we believe that while there definitely *is* a branch of the U.S. government – possibly more than one branch – who indeed *could* be considered as your 'enemy'... looking at the matter strictly from your point-of-view, of course, we think that whoever this is, they may have maneuvered the President into the current confrontation with yourself."

"And why would that be any matter to me, Minn-ee Chu?" countered Karéin-Mayréij. "My powers – already far beyond your conceited little empire's ability to defeat – grow minute by minute; and as sure as the sun rise in the morning, I *will* track down this 'President' of yours, and I *will* either make him sue for peace on my own terms... or I will off with his untruthful head. Why should I *care*, who within your government, intrigues against who else? I can slay all, regardless! And I have sworn a vow of revenge against your President – it would be shameful for me to renege on that. You ask me to put aside the sword – to abandon my lover, my friends and my beloved, orphan *son* – just on a *theory*, uttered by a faithful spy-woman who is likely tutored to make me forebear... until the President thinks he has another weapon that can work against me. Do you then think me so gullible?"

"But... but..." stammered a frightened, desperate Chu, "If we can work together... perhaps we can defuse the situation without any further, uhh, 'damage', to any of the parties involved. This is a good-faith request on the part of the Director of the Federal Bureau of Investigation; and – by the way – the President does *not* know that it is being made. The Director is risking a *lot* – his career, for sure, possibly his *life*, as well – by extending this offer to you."

Chu stopped talking.

The humans all held their breath, while another thought appeared in the team-leader's befuddled mind.

Tamp down your anxiety, dear Minn-ee – I know *that your pleas are sincerely-given.*

Stay true to your heart... wherever it may lead you.

At length, the Storied Watcher offered, "You know, Agent Minn-ee-Choo... every last atom of my heart *wants* to believe what you say – but we must face facts, here. Even if it *is* true, my loved-ones... my *son* – woe be the dark day – are *still* being cruelly-abused on account of me; and the only reason why I stand alive in front of you now, is because I have defeated every one of the many attempts on my life, that have been directed against me by your President's spies and warriors. Not *enough*, Minn-ee-Choo... not enough!"

"But there is *another* reason why you should consider her offer, Storied Watcher," argued Misha.

"Yes, my friend?" she asked. "And why would *that* be?"

"Because it is the right thing to do," he replied, simply.

Karéin-Mayréij fell silent for a few seconds.

Then she turned to address Abruzzio and Ramirez.

"Hector. – Sylvia – I know your dispositions – your minds – and they are innocent," slowly remarked the Storied Watcher. "Free yourselves from any fear of retaliation by these people, or by *anyone*... after I crush his armies and scatter the President's body to the Four Winds, I can provide you with safety, knowledge and power, for the rest of your lives, as you see to live them out. You have both experienced the duplicity and treachery of which this government of yours is capable... if the matter were up to *you*, what would you have me do?"

Ramirez and Abruzzio shared a nonplussed look.

"You go first," demanded the Mexican-American scientist.

"No – *you*," countered Abruzzio. "I'm still thinking."

"Well... okay..." nervously stated Ramirez. "I don' know, Karéin... I think that maybe she's leaving somethin' out... but it kind of makes sense what Ms. Chu is sayin'... I can tell you, from what I used to see down in the *barrio*, all *Los Federales* used to do is get in each other's way, whether it was the immigration-police, or the border-police, or the FBI, or... whoever. Most of the time, they didn't know what they were doin', and – no offense meant, Ms. Chu – and their way of compensating for it was just to beat *la mierda* out of folks, until they'd get a confession. "Not smart... but big" – that's how we would say it in Spanish... you know?"

Karéin-Mayréij regarded him with a knowing smile. "I have heard the same thing from some others of your clan, Hector," she noted. "Sylvia?"

"Karéin," forced Abruzzio, "You must realize that neither Hector nor I are comfortable in advising you on something that might make the difference between life and death for so many people... I can only appeal to the values of fairness and mercy, that someone like you must have adopted, over the ages –"

"You are assuming that I *am* a merciful and moral being," interrupted the alien-girl. "That is a dangerous assumption, when dealing with a far more powerful creature – it is one that has almost cost me my own life, several times in the past. However... fortunately, you are right. I *am* someone who believes in justice and kindness... or, at least – though this be a conceit – I *fancy* myself as such. Time will tell... will it not?"

She smiled, insouciantly.

"*Look*, Storied Watcher," cajoled the female scientist, "What it *really* amounts to is, 'what do you have to *lose*, by suspending hostilities for a short while, until you can evaluate the truth or falsity of the FBI's theory'?"

"*Easy*," retorted the Storied Watcher. "Every *second* that I waste, is another second that they have to torture my son! Do you have any, ahh, 'kids... Sylvia?"

"No... I kind of gave up a personal life for my job," answered Abruzzio. "But I guess I'd feel much the same way that *you* do, if I were faced with someone doing the same thing to my own son or daughter. Let me ask you another question – and I'll understand if you don't want to answer it – but... how close are you, to being able to track down where your family is being kept?"

Suspiciously, the alien-girl's gaze swept from face to face.

"Before I reply," she demanded, "I need a pledge from all of you, that you will not reveal what I say, to *anyone* outside this group. Do you so swear?"

"Yes," echoed from all.

"The truth is," admitted Karéin-Mayréij, in a small voice, "I do not, uhh, have a *clue* where they are."

A tear in plain sight, evaporated from her cheek.

"I cannot – I cannot *abide* by it!" she wept. "Were someone to tell me, I would be there in scant minutes, the dungeon-keepers would be burnt to ashes, my loved-ones would be free... and all this would be over with. It makes no *sense!* I have tracked lost friends into the deepest tombs of the Nameless One and thence rescued them, or at least given them the peace of death... I have gone to other worlds, other dimensions... but I cannot find a salesman, a peasant-woman and three children... not to mention beloved Sam Jacobson and *his* brave crew. There is no smell-trail, no... *nothing!* Thus, why my only recourse has been to apply pressure to the leader who, it appears, controls their captivity. But he lies to me – evades me – at every step."

"Please believe us, Ms. Karéin-Mayréij," interjected Chu, "If FBI knew, we *would* tell you, and damn the consequences... as it is now, we *don't* know – but we may be able to help. I can't *guarantee* anything – that needs to be said up front – but the Bureau's pretty damn good at getting to the truth on these kinds of things... it just takes *time*, that's all."

The Storied Watcher went over and sat down on a large rock, its surface hissing and steaming as she reclined upon it.

She motioned 'come hence', first to Wolf and Misha, then to Abruzzio and Ramirez.

"Have a seat," she commanded; but neither of the scientists could approach closer than perhaps a yard, while the bounty-hunter and the Russian – to the amazement of the FBI-agents and scientists, and though wincing at the brutal heat issuing from her – came right next alongside Karéin-Mayréij.

"Have you seen the most recent events that have transpired between myself and the American government?" she asked.

"What do you mean?" replied Misha.

"The, ahh, 'Washington Monument', the 'White House'... or what is left of each of those," stated the alien-girl.

"*Uh-oh*," muttered Boatman.

"*Told* you they should have let us bring a TV-receiver down here, dude," complained the third agent.

"You all would'a just been watchin' sports on it anyway," retorted the black FBI-agent.

"Listen, Karéin," inquired a bemused Wolf, "You didn't *whack* that fucker – the President – did you? Not that I'd *mind*, if you did."

"Ha!" she ruefully noted, "You have a *lot* to learn about warring against a guileful opponent, my friend. Did I encounter someone advertising himself as, 'the President', in this 'White House'? Yes. Was he, in fact, the, uhh, 'real thing'? No, of course – so I set him free, after, ahh, convincing him to make a nice movie for distribution on the tee-vee networks, on my behalf. However, I *did* bring along a little sou-ven-eer from that palace; namely, the man who sleeps yonder guarded by my war-child shield, *Vîrya I'ëà'b'* – his name is 'Jerr-ee Kay-stan', and he is apparently one of the President's most trusted advisers. I thought that –"

"*The* 'Jerry Kaysten'?" interrupted an incredulous Abruzzio. "The one from the hotel?"

"Just a *minute!*" protested Chu. "You mean that you kidnapped the President's *Chief of Staff?*"

"I would not call it 'kidnapping', Ms. Minn-ee Choo," diffidently remarked the alien-girl. "More like, 'an exciting, all-expenses paid adventure vay-cay-shun, which will change you, for the rest of your life'."

"I'd bet you she'll even throw in free drinks, somewhere, pardner," quipped Wolf. "One lil' taste and you wake up a day later, feelin' mighty *strange*... as I can personally attest."

"Can you not be serious, just for *once?*" grumbled Misha, in the direction of the bounty-hunter.

"Guess you never enjoyed the 'Fixin'-To-Die-Rag'... did you?" Wolf answered back.

The Storied Watcher giggled maliciously.

"What we do *now*, Minnie?" whispered Boatman. "Can you *imagine* what the Director's gonna say, if we let her just fly off with that guy bein' held hostage?"

"Not that you, or he, could do anything *about* it," cautioned Karéin-Mayréij, with an obligatory raised, flame-touched index-finger. "But anyway, Jerr-ee – when he wakes up – and by the way, Wolf, my kiss lies upon him as I had proposed to do for yourself, back in the cave –"

"*Thought* I saw a smile on the bugger's face," muttered the bounty-hunter. "Now I know *why*. I guess he got the full treatment... right?"

"Even with the protection of my stalwart child *I'ëà'b'*, he would have died, being so close to me when I flew away from the President's palace in Dee-Cee," explained the Storied Watcher. "It was *necessary*. Besides, he is greatly-blessed, and a mighty chance I took, in giving him my gift. I hope that he be worthy."

"What the hell they talkin' about?" whispered Hendricks.

"I don't know – but we have to assume that the Chief of Staff may now be *compromised*," warned Chu, *sotto voce*.

"Have you people not yet learned that 'whispering' works not against me?" taunted the alien-girl. "But I will save you the trouble of speculating. I *bit* Jerree, and injected a special type of venom into his bloodstream – one that brings immediate, prolonged, sleep – but which makes the person, uhh, *compatible*, with the essence of my power. If you would like, I can do the same for Sylvia and Hector."

"Gee, thanks... I think," hastily replied Ramirez, while Abruzzio's face went white.

"I suppose you all might think this is a stupid question," demanded Boatman, "But why just *them?* If you're fixin' to turn people into zombies, then why not get yourself some FBI-zombies along with them two scientists?"

"Not *smart* enough, I bet," unhelpfully cracked Hendricks. "She probably only wants zombies with a PH.D."

"I didn't even finish high-school, pardner," joked Wolf, while Misha stewed.

"You're *kidding*, man!" deadpanned the third agent. "I'd never have guessed!"

"It is not *that*," remarked Karéin-Mayréij, before Wolf could talk back. "First of all... my gift does not turn you into a 'zombie'... take my word on this, human, I have seen plenty of *real* 'zombies' – the walking-dead, I mean – and you would not be so flippant about it, if you were more familiar with the evil and anguish that those creatures both are, and endure."

"*Riight*," uneasily spoke the third agent.

"And besides," argued the alien-girl, "Do Wolf and Misha sound like mindless robots? Either of them can tell me to, ahh, 'eff-off', whenever doing so occurs to them – hopefully, that will not happen too frequently, but it is something that I will not control. Secondl... if you knew what this kiss of venom *really* does – and also understood the fullness of it – you would be down on your *knees*, begging me for but a taste."

"Like being able to use your hand to snuff out candles... or a blowtorch or two?" asked Chu.

"That is just the *start*, Minn-ee-Choo," answered the Storied Watcher. "But we are getting 'off track', as dear Bob would say. I now address my trusted friends, Wolf and Misha – and I tell you, right up front, that I am *not* willing to stop my war against the President : to do that, when I have sworn an oath of revenge, would be craven and shameful. His warriors would then correctly judge me a coward, who cannot make good on her threats. But... I was thinking..."

"What?" inquired the Russian.

"Need it be said – the same offer I gave to Hector and Sylvia is also upon you – I *can* and likely *will* kill anyone who threatens you, on account of me, so you have no reason to appease these 'eff-bee-ai' people, or any other followers of the President, for that matter," explained Karéin-Mayréij. "And though I cannot simply surrender in this conflict... *if* Ms. Minn-ee-Choo and her fellow-spies can provide something concrete in terms of information that might lead me to brave

Bob and poor Tommy, the others as well... perhaps, I *could* agree to a temporary truce – a 'cease-fire' – as I believe the people of this world call it."

Thank God! simultaneously thought both Abruzzio and Chu.

"I might even accept something that would identify *who*, precisely, is behind the abuse of my family," continued the Storied Watcher, "Assuming, for the moment that it was not the President, after all. Then I would track down the responsible evil-doer, and wring the knowledge of where my family are being kept, from his or her foul mind... one second before that person meets the cruelest death that I can devise. Perhaps I *could* see fit to do that, as a token of good faith."

"Good thing she's willing to 'compromise'," incautiously whispered Hendricks. "I'd hate to see what would happen if she isn't."

"You can turn on your tee-vee to get a foretaste, Will Hendricks," answered the Storied Watcher. "Wolf? Misha? What say you?"

"I kinda still want to see you kick Mr. Fancy-Pants President's ass all the way into next week, Karéin," commented the bounty-hunter. "He *deserves* it – not just for the shit he's done to you and this 'Billings' dude and your kid, but also for what him and his bum-buddies been doin' to this sorry ol' country for the past umpteen years... but... hey! If it works for *you*, I'd say – 'you go, girl'. I got one question, though."

"Umm-humm?" she pleasantly replied.

"Just what exactly *did* you do to the Washington Monument?" pressed Wolf.

"Oh, I – ahh – decided that its top quarter-part would look better if it were planted in that nice big lawn and garden, on the south-side of the White House palace," nonchalantly explained the alien-girl. "I also wrote a warning on one side of the top of the obelisk, after I deposited it... pointy-side down, of course."

"*Please* tell me you wrote 'Fuck *You*, Mr. President'", cajoled the bounty-hunter, scarcely able to contain his glee.

Hendricks was also about to burst out laughing, until he was 'shushhed' by Chu.

"I *was* sorely tempted," admitted Karéin-Mayréij, with an insouciant smile, "But on the advice of wise *Vìrya Quü'j*, instead, I just warned the President to surrender my family. Noble *Quü'j* felt that this would count as a measure of, ahh, 'restraint'."

"Forgive me interrupting – but, who did you say was advising you, on that?" asked Abruzzio.

"*Vìrya Quü'j*", repeated the Storied Watcher, retrieving the little amulet and showing it to the group.

"You mean... the *locket* was talking to you?" inquired the scientist.

"Oh... she is much more than just a 'locket', Sylvia," remarked the alien-girl. "*Vìrya Quü'j* is just as much alive as anyone here, and she is older and more wise than any of us... even, myself. She has been my companion and defender in times much darker and less hopeful than what we contend with now... and her powers against evil magic are surpassed by none."

"Uhh, 'magic'," mumbled the third agent. "*Riight.*"

"If only you *knew*, Will Hen-dricks," countered the Storied Watcher. "My other war-children – for example stalwart *Vîrya Ahn'jë*, the Burning Adamant Mountain, in whose mail I am now clad – are much younger; they do not have their, ahh, 'grandmother's wisdom and insight... yet they, too have the force of life. Their own powers are formidable, and they can use them with or without the adjunct of my own. And... if *Vîrya Quü'j* agrees, when we have better times, Sylvia, Hector... I will let you speak with her. As a woman of science, I think that you will find her counsel very interesting."

"And them CIA-boys down in the hotel was gonna smoke her with a few guns," commented Boatman. "Shee-*it!*"

Karéin-Mayréij shot the black FBI-agent a prideful, fang-toothed smirk of acknowledgement, then did a slight bow.

Abruzzio turned to Chu.

"You *must-do* what she's asking!" passionately demanded the scientist. "Do you *understand* what kind of scientific knowledge is at stake, here? I can't *believe* that the government's been trying to kill her... I'm ashamed to be an American, right now, I have to tell you."

"Join the club, pardner," muttered Wolf.

Imperceptibly, the humans – Wolf and the Russian, as well – saw the godly alter ego of the Storied Watcher leak through her semi-human guise, as her haunting music played subtly in the surroundings.

"You know, Sylvia... you sound very much like my dear friend Cherie Tanaka, when you speak in the desire of truth – the knowing of things – and the vanquishing of ignorance," kindly commented the alien-girl. "When it is over, Hector and you – Cherie as well – you shall all work with me, so we can share our wisdom, and rejoice in so doing. This I *swear.*"

"This is very touching... but what *I* understand, Professor," measuredly stated the FBI team-leader, "Is that the survival of our entire country, may depend on us coming to some kind of an agreement, here. Not much point in worrying about science, if we're all dead beforehand, I'd say."

"Something tells me, Karéin," interjected the Russian, "That all is not as it seems. Furthermore – earlier on – I could not honestly have recommended agreeing to Ms. Chu's plan, because the chances of a double-cross would have been very high – they *still* are, but the difference now is, you are – ahem – more than capable of defending yourself, in that case. So I think that it is worth the risk. May I, however, request one thing?"

"Of *course*," she said, lowering her flame-flickering gauntlet over his hand and squeezing the latter affectionately.

Misha winced for a second, but then seemed none the worse for wear.

"Sylvia... look at *that*," whispered an awed Ramirez.

"*Incredible*," was all that Abruzzio could think to say.

"You know that I trust you, beloved friend," mentioned the Storied Watcher. "We are all, ahh, 'playing for high stakes', here. Do you really think this course of action is likely to be more productive than me just tracking down the President – wherever he may now be hiding – and then wringing his foul neck, until he reveals the truth?"

"I know that it is not my place to ask this, especially after Wolf and I ended up sitting in an American jail, as opposed to faithfully executing the plans that you had given us," requested Misha, "But... wherever you decide to go, after this issue is resolved, I would like you to take me there, with you. Right now, my choice is probably between an American lethal-injection – for 'being a spy', and a Russian firing-squad – for 'being a traitor'. I do not know what the alternative with yourself would be... but it can scarcely be worse."

"I *have* seen worse," responded Karéin-Mayréij, "Like several human lifetimes in the bondage of living death, for example... but fear not, friend! I will *not* abandon you – and woe betide anyone who tries to hurt you, on account of me."

She turned to address Chu.

"Minn-ee," she firmly, but, politely demanded, "Please communicate to your Director, that Misha is not to be imprisoned or punished, in any way. Or *else.*"

"Look, Ms. Karéin-Mayréij," Chu tried to argue, "I can *ask* the Director, of course, but not even *he* can over-rule the laws –"

Again, they saw the flaming, cautionary, index-finger.

"Or *else!*" warned the alien-girl. "I am not interested in these so-called 'laws' of yours, which seem to apply only to peasants who have no skill-at-arms. Oh – and by the way – this also applies to Wolf, as well. Touch not a hair on his nice, bushy head... *understood?*"

"*Told* you, lady," taunted the bounty-hunter.

"Right..." uneasily stated the FBI team-leader. "Well... I will communicate your request to the Director, but does that mean that you... uhh... *accept* his proposal?"

The Storied Watcher stared intently at Chu, and for a few seconds, Misha and Wolf were afraid that the alien might have been using her mental-domination powers; but, eventually, she replied,

"For the time being... yes. I give three days, or until I find my loved-ones of my own device, Ms. Minn-ee-Choo of the eff-bee-ai. You may use your cell-phone box-thing to speak to your superior – but I caution, 'no tricks' – and in specific, please do not enable the vid-ee-o-tee-vee-recorder-thing on your little box... I do not want our surroundings being used to target us on a map. You saw what happened down in the Tucson hotel, when your government tried to do that – how many of your city-blocks were blown up... do you remember?"

Misha uttered a Russian oath of relief, *sotto voce.*

"All too well," answered Chu.

Fumbling and cursing her nerves for unsteady fingers, she hastily attempted to enter call numbers and codes, into her mobile-communicator.

Korey's Clean White Blanket

"Any luck?" inquired Jacobson.

"A lot of nasty-looking chemicals – acids, bases, other corrosives, as far as I can tell – and there are a bunch of them that I can't even *guess* at... not much else, although I *did* get some clothes that we can put on our new little friend," replied Boyd, as he deposited what he had been able to scrounge from the cabinets of this benighted place.

"By the way," he added, "There were a few pistol-rounds, but they're the wrong caliber for the side-arms that we've got. We can use them in the hand-gun that the dead guy over there had, which gives us one more pistol with twelve shots in it. That's about it."

"Devon?" asked the former mission commander, addressing the black astronaut.

"'Bout the same as my bro' Brent, I'm afraid," stated White, "But I found us some food – not sure I'd want to eat anythin' that was meant for their lips, if y'all understand what I'm sayin', Captain. Yo! Just a minute – what's *this* – hey, maybe we hit the jackpot – check *this* out!"

He held out a handful of key-map-cards.

"Yeah... but we've already *got* one, right?" observed Tanaka, as she gently rocked the child, taking note of every half-millimeter that the small eyes got closer to being completely closed.

"Hmm... let me see," requested Jacobson, holding a finger in the air to signal a pause.

"Hold on – yeah, you may be right there Devon... you may be *right*," said Jacobson, with waxing interest. These ones look different, somehow; they're more detailed... definitely worth taking along. I'm just guessing – but didn't that woman who we... *you* know... didn't she say something about being 'second-in-command', or something? If that's the case, she might have had more elevated credentials to go from one level to another... right?"

"Well then... she actually *did* leave something positive, as her, uhh, 'estate'," commented Billings, from his slumped, back-to-the-wall position, on the floor. "Who'd a thunk it."

Tanaka ruefully nodded.

"Wouldn't have changed *my* mind," she muttered, staring off into space.

None of them wanted to re-start *that* topic, so Jacobson changed the subject.

"Well, listen, folks," he started, "We've taken a few minutes now so that the young one there can catch her breath – and I hate to be the task-master here – but we had better start thinking about getting on the move, again. I suppose we try to figure out these new cards, finish this level... then dive even deeper-down?"

"I *guess*," answered White, with a half-hearted shrug. "But – uhh – we now got a bit of an unexpected tactical handicap... you know? Not that I mind, y'all understand – but what if we get into another gunfight, with the kid taggin' along? I mean... that's gonna *seriously* crimp our ability to maneuver."

"We obviously can't leave her here," argued Tanaka. "And the only other choice would be to have one or more of us stay back here, or in some other hiding-place, to guard her. I thought we decided earlier that it's 'one for all and all for one'... remember?"

"Yeah," agreed Boyd, reflexively scratching the back of his head, as he pondered. "I don't think that it would be advisable to split up now, anyway – not with our limited egress-options. Devon has a very valid point – I'd feel *terrible* if the girl got hit by a stray bullet, on account of us. Professor – unless anyone has a better idea, I'd suggest that we keep Elissha as close as possible to yourself... that way at least she'd have your force-field to protect her."

"Worse things could happen than to have her right next to me," said Tanaka with a smile, as she gave the almost-sleeping child a motherly kiss on the head.

"Or I could keep her and then just go bye-bye, the minute that we see any of those jackasses in the SWAT-suits," offered Billings. "Oh, excuse me, kid. Sorry, Uncle Bob said a bad word there. Cover those little ears... okay?"

"Invisibility doesn't stop bullets," countered Tanaka.

"Except if you're my girlfriend, and you get the best of both worlds", grunted the salesman. "Well – I'm not going to press the point... I never *was* that good with kids."

"Could have fooled *me*," gently chided Jacobson. "I think having Elissha stay with Cherie for the time being is the best of a bad set of options, so –"

"You know... there *is* one other consideration that we haven't thought through," interrupted Boyd.

"What?" asked Jacobson.

"I don't know exactly how to put this, Professor," explained the former Air Force astronaut, "So I'll just speak my mind. When you use your version of the 'gift' that Karéin gave us – especially when you, uhh, 'crank up the volume', for example when you power up your shield or fire that whatever-the-hell-it-is at the bad-guys – I can certainly sense the *Amallsh* coming from your direction. Don't get me wrong... it's a pleasant feeling, for sure... but like all the rest of us, I'm getting so that I can tell what kind of power you're putting out – and it's now so high that I wonder what it might do to Elissha, if she were right next to you."

"Man's got a point," added White. "The kid's just one of them ol'-fashioned, obsolete human-type things... she ain't got any affinity to this weirdo-stuff that little Miss Angel stuffed into our hides. Don't forget... yours truly first zeroed in on the Storied Watcher, back on Mars, just by measurin' the raw energy-output that was bein' given off around her. That's probably *way* over what you got goin' there, Professor – no offense meant, of course – but what if it acts on the girl, as if she was standin' next to a nuclear-reactor... I mean, ionizin' radiation and all? That'd be a *hell* of a thing..."

"You're speculating wildly, both of you," complained Tanaka. "There's *zero* reliable evidence supporting this theory."

"Only because we ain't seen anybody die from *Amaiish*-poisoning, yet," retorted Boyd. "Look, Professor – you may be right, and I'm not going to bet good money on the supposition that it's going to happen – but... shouldn't we err on the side of caution?"

"Bob was an ordinary human, too – *he* came into close proximity of the Storied Watcher for an extended period of time, *he* didn't undergo our little initiation ceremony – and *he* turned out all right," Jacobson interjected.

"Yeah, but, I... uhh... well, I got to know her a bit better than I think the kid's going to get to know any of us, if you know what I mean," sputtered Billings. "Maybe that counts as my free pass into alien-land."

"Y'all *think*?" mocked White. "I dunno, Captain, but – again, no offense to y'all – but my vote's gotta be for the kid to go with him... kinda the best of a bad set of alternatives, if y'all understand what I'm sayin'."

Tanaka shot back, "Haven't any of you considered that *he's* giving off *Amaiish*, as well? Or is he doing that 'bye-bye' trick of his, with something he learned out of a Houdini-book?"

"I don't read a lot of books... only newspapers, and then only the sports-section... and the comics," mentioned Billings, with a shrug.

"You know – there are *so* many things that I could say to that," quipped Jacobson, "But just to avoid this degenerating any further, I'll spare you. If this *Amaiish*-stuff is, in fact, dangerous to the girl – a proposition that I by no means accept, by the way – then it'd make sense to keep her as far-away as possible from the most powerful source of the energy. If she starts to show the symptoms of radiation-poisoning, we'll have to consider our options, at that point. If not, then of course, we'll put her back by your side. Does that sound reasonable?"

Tanaka sat, stony-faced, for a few seconds, looking with sad eyes at her precious young friend.

Eventually, she protested, "Even if I accept your explanation – which I don't, because I refuse to believe that the Storied Watcher's gift would make any one of us dangerous for ordinary humans to associate with – a kind of cosmic 'booby prize', wouldn't you say – to steal a page from Brent's playbook, implementing this is likely to be very impractical. By your own reasoning, I shouldn't power up my shield *at all*, nor should I use my burst of force in combat... either of those make me reach deep-down and use a *huge* amount of the *Fire*. Are you guys willing to give up those weapons – possibly at the cost of our lives – just on the *chance* that this theory is correct?"

Jacobson pondered and then said, "I wish I could give you a straight answer to that, but we're pioneers, here... it's all guesswork."

"And what do we do if – more likely, when – we meet the next 'plain old human' that we want, or need, to rescue?" argued Tanaka. "Such as Bob's friends, for example. Sure hope we don't run out of rifle-bullets, boys."

"For what it's worth," commented Billings, "Whitney told me that being with Sari had made her 'better', in more or less the same way as it did for me... okay... *almost* the same way. For example, she – Claremont, I mean – you should have *heard* her singing, after a few days on the road with Little Miss Martian. Afterwards, Whitney told me that ability was completely new... she had been in the choir back in Detroit, but only because they didn't have too many other volunteers."

"What 'bout her kids?" inquired White. "Y'all think they one of 'us'... or one of 'them'?"

"Don't know," admitted the salesman. "Something tells me that Tommy – if, please God, he's still alive – wouldn't have any trouble taking in anything that we can dish out. As for Curtis and Melissa... your guess is as good as mine."

"This is a bridge we'll have to cross when we come to it," noted Jacobson. "I can only hope we don't free some of these poor captives down here, only to find that the presence of their 'liberators' ends up being lethal to them."

"Yeah... not to mention, to all our families back home, when and if we get out of this place," glumly mentioned Boyd.

"It's all BS, anyway," grumbled Tanaka. "She wouldn't *do* that to us!"

"Hope you're right, Cherie," answered Jacobson. "Let's limber up, folks."

Along with a couple of the others, he slung an auto-rifle and began preparing to leave, but, unexpectedly, the child awoke upon hearing the activity.

Wide-eyed, she grabbed on to Tanaka in a vice-like embrace.

"*Nooo!*" protested the little girl.

"Shhhh," gently counseled the professor. "Hey, *hey* there, sweetie... you'll wake the neighbors."

"What are you *doing!*" whined the strangely-agitated child.

"We're going to leave, now," explained Tanaka, "But don't worry, Elissha dear... you can come with us. We'll take you home, when we get out of here."

"*Noooo!*" wailed the girl.

Billings had gone over to Tanaka's side, by now.

"Hey there, trooper," he cajoled, "What's so bad about getting out of here? I got to tell you, your Uncle Bob was pretty glad to get out of the room that *he* got put in... why aren't you?"

"I don't want to leave Korey!" sobbed Elissha. "They *killed* my mommy and my daddy. Korey's the only one I have left in the whole wide *world.*"

"I... I... *see,*" half-whispered Billings, hanging his head. "Listen... kid... I..."

He couldn't force any more words out, no matter how he tried, so he stood up and looked away.

Sari – where are *you?* his mind cried out.

"It's okay, darling... it's *okay*," stammered Tanaka, tears streaming down her cheeks, as she forced the child's head down over her shoulder and patted the woebegone little one's back.

"Curse them – curse them to *hell!*" fumed the professor, trying to avoid the child seeing the rage clouding her eyes. "What *are* these people – these *scum* – what are they capable of... where's the *end* of it..."

For some reason, White had closed his eyes.

He seemed to be saying something under his breath.

Tanaka bit her lip to stop her quivering chin.

"I can't leave him – *can't* leave him, Miss Cherie!" whimpered the child. "They'll come back... they'll come *back* and do bad things to him, again. I *know* he's gone, Miss Cherie – but I won't let them do that. I *won't!*"

"So *now* what do we do, team?" plaintively demanded Tanaka.

At this, the black ex-astronaut, his feet moving slowly, as if resisting every inch of the way, managed to squat down beside the mother-and-distraught-child scene made up by Tanaka and her young charge.

"Listen, Elissha," he offered, with the quiet, dignified *gravitas* that the others saw only rarely, "All of us here – includin' yours truly – we all got kids, and we all know what y'all goin' through... in our hearts, we're all prayin' for your brother, and we all know that he's on his way to a better place, where he won't be hurtin' any more. I really *believe* that, honey... I really *dŏ.*"

Something new – an electric-hymn, notably different from what they had heard when Tanaka unleashed her own power – was playing in the distance.

The child had turned her head to look at White, who gave her a second to absorb what had been said.

Then he continued, speaking softly but authoritatively, "Now... there's a lot of really mean-folk in here, and some of 'em – y'all right 'bout that – might be comin' back to do bad things to your brother. We can't stay here to prevent that entirely, and we can't take Korey with us... but, Uncle Devon, he's got a special trick, which can probably make it *awful* hard for them bad people to try anything."

"What... what *kind* of 'trick'?" suspiciously demanded Elissha.

"I'll cover Korey in a big heap of ice and snow," explained White. "Really *cold* snow – so they'll freeze their dirty hands off, if they even *touch* it – and it'll be clean and white and silver and a good place for your brother to sleep in an' get ready to meet the Lord. But I can't do that... unless y'all give me the go-ahead."

"He's my *only* brother," quavered Elissha, her little eyes filled with tears, matching Tanaka's own. "My *only* one!"

After another second, she added, "Give him a nice big blanket, Mr. Devon... give him one to keep him safe, *forever!*"

"I *will*, darlin'... as the Lord My God is my witness – I *swear* it," spoke the black astronaut.

"Devon – are you *sure* you can...?" asked Jacobson.

Now White, his countenance purposeful and inspired, stared forward, away from meeting the glance of any of the others.

"Captain," he forcefully commanded, "Get everyone out of here."

"Well, we were going, anyway, but... alright," concurred the former Mars mission commander. "Come on, everybody."

One by one, Billings, Jacobson, Boyd, then Tanaka, with the child held tightly around her midriff in monkey-hug style, filed out of the room and into the corridor.

Elissha gave the woman a kick.

"I want to *see* him do it! Or I'm not going!" demanded the girl.

"I... uhh... okay," allowed the professor.

She tarried by the outer side of the portal, and the others saw a look of astonishment come quickly to her face.

White, his demeanor eerily calm and confident, at first knelt by the dead boy's gurney; then, the ex-astronaut slowly rose to his feet, placing his hands about a foot over Korey's lifeless body.

A rock-spiritual played in the psyches of everyone at the scene.

At once – it hit Tanaka and the girl first – there was a wave of numbing, choking cold, and – to the amazement of all the onlookers – the very *air* around the gurney began to congeal.

In two or three seconds, the entire gurney assembly was covered in a solid block of snow-dusted ice, with little rivulets of the same stuff extending in a radial-pattern from the edges of its central mass. Most of the rest of the room started to resemble the interior of an Antarctic cabin with a broken-in window.

Tanaka tried to enter the room to congratulate her male compatriot; but the cold within made her feel like the very *life* was being drained away, and out of concern for the child's welfare, she rapidly retreated.

White – with a fine coating of frost over nearly his entire body and fatigue-ringed eyes – followed and met them in the hallway, as his music started to ebb.

"*Impressive*," congratulated Jacobson. "Cherie – I'd say that as of about one minute ago, you just got some new competition in the 'alien Olympics'. At least that's what it looks like from here."

"I don't mind sharing the prize," admitted the woman. "It's *lonely* up here."

"I'd shake your hand," commented Boyd, with an envious stare, "But I'm afraid it'd be like licking a flagpole in February."

"Yeah," said the black ex-astronaut, "But there's a warm heart in this-here chest, don't you know."

He came next to Tanaka and addressed the girl.

"See?" he remarked. "I don't think those bad people will get in there, anytime soon. And I asked God to send a whole bunch of angels to watch over Korey, and to help him fly up there with 'em, when he's ready. I hope that works for y'all, darlin'."

Elissha nodded, the tears again flowing uncontrollably.

"Goodbye... Korey... *my brother!*" she choked, with a child's simple wave.

"Let's... let's get *out* of here," managed Jacobson.

Silently, the group of six moved out, past a mangled, blanket-covered *something*, lying in mute testament to the wages of sin.

Daughter Tornado-Diamond-Curtain

"It'll be pitch-dark in another few minutes," advised Chu, in the direction of the Storied Watcher. "How much longer are you going to need?"

"Hopefully... not too much longer," replied the alien-girl, her gaze never leaving Kaysten's somnolent face as she crouched next to the incapacitated man, his backside still resting in the inner-surface of the little shield.

"He is coming slowly out of the dream-world," she noted. "*Vìrya I'ëà'b'* confirms that. It is interesting, you know – she has become quite close to Jerr-ee, in the time in which she has been protecting him."

"Karéin," inquired Abruzzio, who, along with Ramirez, had also come to rest next to the Chief of Staff, "Do you mind me asking you about that?"

"Not at all, Sylvia," said Karéin-Mayréij. "Just as long as you understand that there may be things that would be, ahh, 'unwise' for me to reveal, in the presence of these eff-bee-ai people – who, though they be friends right now – could revert to being my enemies."

"Yeah... can't blame you there," agreed the scientist. "Well – what I wanted to know is... you've been referring to some of these items that we've seen on you, as if they were, uhh, 'people'... like the shield there, for example. What exactly do you *mean* by that?"

"Just what it sounds like, Professor," matter-of-factually stated the Storied Watcher. "That is what they *are*."

"Sorry, but I'm not getting you," said Abruzzio.

"There we go again, with this Eng-lish thing about 'getting' this and 'getting' that," grumbled the alien-girl. "I will speak plainly : my war-children – including *Vìrya I'ëà'b'*, for example, as well as *Vìrya Quü'j* – though in her case, she is venerable and could not be considered as a 'child'... are *alive*. They think, dream, quarrel, hope, fear and speak... they are aware of their state-of-being – not exactly like as do you or I – but in a manner very similar. Perhaps most importantly... they desire love and give love back; they wish to grow in knowledge and wisdom. In this, my war-children are no different from any other sentient being."

"That's... *amazing!*" commented the female scientist.

"It certainly *is*," added Ramirez, "But... where did they come from? I don't remember seeing anything about a bunch of armor, from the recordings on-board the *Eagle* and *Infinity*. Did you hide them away on board, when you left Mars?"

"Ha... no, Hector," answered the Storied Watcher. "Though there *are* others, who sleep secure now, in the deep reaches of *Mailànkh...*"

Her eyes took on a far-away stare, for a few seconds, then she continued, "To answer your question, though... I gave birth to all of them, except for *Vìrya Quü'j*, that is. You could consider me their 'mother' – they are my children."

"If you don't mind me sayin', Karéin," joked Wolf, "Considerin' the size and shape of some of them things, that must have been kinda... *painful*, you know?"

"Boy, he shore likes to *push* it... don't he?" muttered Boatman.

"Ah – that is just my big friend's sense of humor," nonchalantly replied the alien-girl. "But if you are asking if they came out of my woman-hole, as would a human-child... the answer is, 'no'. Just as there are many, many types of intelligent beings in this universe who look, think and act nothing like you or I, there are also many ways of giving life... and some of these are not, uhh, 'biological'. As for my war-children, I used knowledge and powers from places long ago and far-away, to breathe the spark of life into *Vìrya I'ëà'b* and her sisters and brothers. Behold, therefore, where, before, they were only inanimate-items – a sword, a shield, *et cetera* – now, they live as separate entities, as a human-child lives apart from his or her mother. And their mother loves them very much, by the way."

"*Wait* a minute," interjected Hendricks. "Did you just say that you took stuff that was just lying around, and made it – uhh – 'alive'?"

"I would not say that they were just 'lying around'," stated Karéin-Mayréij, "There is a story behind *that*, too. However – if I understand what you mean, Will Hen-dricks – I would have to say that the answer is, 'yes'."

"So's that mean you could, like, take my cell-phone or my key-chain, and make it come to life?" incredulously pressed the third agent.

The Storied Watcher allowed herself a low chuckle of amusement. "Breathing the life of the *Makailkh* into a mobile com-mun-ee-kator – now *there* is a fine idea!" she quipped. "What weirding-powers would you have me infuse in it, Will – perhaps 'immunity to tell-ee-phone network money-costs', or some-such, mighty ability? I am afraid that it does not work that way, though. An item to which one wishes to gift life... it must be a treasured companion, one who will accompany you through all of life's trials and battles... it must have some *spirit* in it, from the start. I hate to disappoint you – but that is how things have been, ere the dawn of time."

"Aww, damn," complained Hendricks. "And there's all those 1-900 things I could have –"

"Just as good," chimed in Boatman. "You make that-there thing magic, all it's gonna do is get you into ball-games without buyin' a ticket."

Now, the alien-girl, her eyes dimly aglow, her body outlined with a godly aura in the half-light, sent the third agent a very strange look.

"But in *your* case..." she started.

"Come over here," ordered Karéin-Mayréij.

"Yeah... okay... I guess," complied Hendricks, very unsure of himself.

Haltingly, he came over to where she was seated, next to the still-sleeping Chief of Staff.

"Bend over so that I can see your face and upper-body more clearly," she demanded.

Reluctantly, the third agent stooped as low as he could.

His face was very close to her own, and the man could instantly tell how far out of his depth he was, in dealing with this being; her fresh-faced, teenager-like attractiveness – evident at any range – was simply *overpowering*, like every schoolboy's secret, unrealized dream of 'having' the perfect supermodel.

The Storied Watcher reached up and ran her fingers over the gold chain that Hendricks usually kept semi-hidden, behind his tie.

Though she did not come in direct contact with his flesh, each finger-stroke sent electric thrills up and down his spine.

God – I can hardly keep it in my pants, warned his alarmed mind.

"You know, Will," she counseled, "If you would give life to something, I would start with *this*. It is something dear to you... is it not?"

"Yeah... I guess it is," he stammered. "It's... uhh... it's like a religious-thingie, from my Dad... he was in the Army in Pakistan about twenty years ago, when they first went in... gave it to me just before he passed away... Dad told me it kept him safe while he was over there, told me to wear it all the time... kind of a souvenir, you know?"

"No... it is *not*," she contradicted, with a light shake of the head.

The alien-girl's voice was gentle, warm and considerate, but her stare was deadly-serious.

"Just a sou-vee-neer, that is, Will Hen-dricks," she stated.

The crickets stopped chirping, all of a sudden, and the air became heavy. The humans' attention was drawn inexorably to the alien's portentous words. Dignified, electric-hymnal-music sounded dimly in the distance.

"This little chain binds you to your father, and to your ancestors, as well," patiently explained the Storied Watcher, as if delivering a high-school science-lesson. "You want the secret of breathing the living-power, young agent of the eff-bee-ai? I will tell you. Take hold of your neck-chain every night as you can, sing to it, play good music by your own hands as well; tell it that you cherish and respect it, think back to the memory of your father, remember the good times with him... his strength, what was noble about him... why you *loved* him."

As she intoned these words, a frightened, awed, but simultaneously thrilled Hendricks thought, *J.H.C., no* wonder *those two warned me about the "whole different level" thing... what a rush... if I live through all of this, that is...*

With the choral-music raging through human bloodstreams, Karéin-Mayréij continued, "Honor all those in your line who came before you, and dream of those who will come after you; tell each link of this thing that it is *special* – that it will bind your successors to your clan as surely as it holds fast with the next of its kind. Above all else, give thanks that your parents gave *you* life – and pray to your God that your chain should be blessed with the spark of awareness, also such abilities as were meant for it, as judged by the spirit-world."

What could he do, but nod?

"Thus," she instructed, "If you be worthy and your God favor you, perhaps your prayer should be answered; but this may take much time – many years, possibly – and you must persevere with *faith*, as you pour your own spirit and life into what you would in turn give the blessing of being... for nothing with a consequence such as this, comes without the greatest of effort. You are a mortal and you do not have my arts to help you along – but hear my words, man, the doing of this *is* within your grasp, if you will but *believe!*"

Is this how an angel sounds when she's talking? reflected a shocked Abruzzio, absentmindedly wiping a tear.

Listening to her is like hearing all those beautiful church-hymns – but this is real, right here, right now...

Five minutes ago I was talking with her like one scientist to another... now I want to get down on my knees and worship her...

"And the knowing of it will come to you in a vision," concluded the Storied Watcher. "You will hear a voice that is not a voice, speaking when you slumber; it will be different from the sounds in any other dream. When you wake and concentrate on your chain, you will hear that voice again – at first, like a whisper in the back of your mind – but later, as loud and clear as you hear me, right now. Afterward, you must teach your new companion in the ways of the world, just as you would teach a newborn babe – but *this* child will live on, long after you are gone, and it will sing the story of your life to your own human children, and theirs, and the ones after those, even unto the end of the marking of space and time. *That*, is how it works, Will Hen-dricks."

"And the government wants to *kill* her," muttered Ramirez. "If what she's sayin' is *true – Dios Mio*, the *implications –*"

Abruzzio's wide-eyed, awed astonishment required no word from her lips.

"Can't be *true*," stammered Chu. "*Can't* be. Every rule of science says that this kind of thing is just superstition –"

"It *is* true, my friend," argued Misha. "All one need do, is see these 'war-children' of hers, in action... that will dispel all doubt. Knowledge available nowhere else, my friend. *Nowhere* else!"

He stopped for a second, as if pondering something, then added, "And *I* have such a locket, as well – a memento from the Patriarch. These are said to protect one, when danger is all around."

"Indeed," affirmed the alien-girl, with a knowing look. "And you should do as I counseled this young man, forthwith. The *Fire* is within you... a, ahh, 'head-start', as it were."

The third agent, utterly at a loss about what to say, remained stooped over the Storied Watcher for a few seconds. Then, without a word, he stumbled backward, staring at the chain.

The Storied Watcher turned to Ramirez.

"Here," she said. "Help me lay Jerr-ee down on the ground, for I have something to show you about what manner of being comes to life, by these blessed arts."

The air slowly went back to normal, as the music tailed off.

Abruzzio and Ramirez complied, and they were only slightly surprised when they saw the buckler float unaided upward, to take a place on her left arm.

Then she mumbled something in her incomprehensible language in the direction of the shield. It left the alien's arm and hovered within easy reach of the two scientists.

"*Touch* her," commanded Karéin-Mayréij. "She will not harm you... nor is this a brain-control trick. If your bodies had been, ahh, 'made more compatible' with my war-children and I – by the gift of my kiss, that is – Vìrya I'ëà'b' could speak directly to your minds; but as matters are now, you must be in contact with her."

Abruzzio looked at her compatriot. "I don't know, Hector... do you think we should...?"

"Ain't that the shield that sliced the arms off them CIA-boys back at the hotel?" demanded a suspicious Boatman.

"Yes, she is," admitted the Storied Watcher, speaking to the black FBI-agent. "And her powers are *much* greater now, than they were on that unhappy day. With so much as a thought on my part, her edge could slice yonder big stone," – she pointed to a rock at least two meters thick – "Clean in half, and keep going after that. Or she could simply fly fast at it, and knock it back by a handsome distance. Vìrya I'ëà'b' has many other powers that I care not to discuss; after all, she *is* a living child-being, and I should safeguard her privacy. Now, with all that said... Hector, Sylvia, why not run your fingers across her side-edge... you know, the one that can dismember you, in a tenth-of-a-second?"

"That doesn't sound like, uhh, too good an idea, Karéin," evaded Ramirez. "I mean, that's gotta be *sharp*... right?"

"See for yourself," replied the alien-girl.

She pointed to the shield with an open palm.

"What's the *matter?*" cracked Wolf. "Ain't none of you boys ever patted somebody's pet Rottweiler? If it don't like you, there goes your hand... same thing, more or less."

"Yes, but guard-dogs can't fly, or cut you in half... at least with one bite," argued Boatman. "I bet with yours truly, they'd take two or three."

"That's why we love you, Otis," wryly noted Chu.

"Well, look, Sylvia," proposed the Mexican-American scientist, "I guess *one* of us *should* try it... and the other one takes notes – just in case the, uhh, 'guinea pig' ends up not survivin' the experiment, you know?"

"I'm not going to stop you, if that's what you mean," answered Abruzzio.

"I'll take that as a 'yes'," said Ramirez.

Warily, he extended a hand and gingerly touched his index-finger to the bottom-part of the shield, immediately withdrawing it, as one does when touching a potentially hot surface.

"I guess I still can point at things," he joked. "So here goes nothing."

Now, with all the humans – except Wolf, who feigned disinterest – staring intently, Ramirez touched his index-finger to *Vîrya I'ëà'b'*, this time maintaining continuous contact with the shield.

He looked stunned, staring blankly ahead.

"Hector? *Hector!*" exclaimed a worried Abruzzio.

"It's... it's okay, Sylvia," slowly spoke Ramirez, while the others wondered if he realized that he was now grasping the buckler on either side of its lethal edge.

"This is... it's *incredible*, man," he gasped. "I can *hear* it – hear *her*, sorry there, *chica* – talkin' in my head... I'm communicating with her... can't tell if the words are in Spanish or English, but somehow, I'm sendin' them back and forth."

He paused for a second, then said, "Hey there, Little Miss Shield – I gotta go for a bit, but I'll be back."

He let go of the thing.

"Sylvia – you *gotta* try this," he demanded, with a look of utter amazement. "It's like – I don't know – like havin' your brain plugged right into Neo... no, I take that back, it's *better* than that. You can hear the thing *thinking* – it sounds like a kid... a girl, but I don't know how I know that... there's really no words to describe it."

"*Vîrya I'ëà'b'* actually *does* know a few words of Spanish, and a few other Earth-languages as well," explained the Storied Watcher. "Remember – she, and all her brothers and sisters, also *Vîrya Quü'j* – are connected to my own intellect, when we journey together. I teach them what I know... and already, they are starting to teach *me*."

"What could they possibly teach *you* about?" inquired Abruzzio. "From our conversations while you were in space, my understanding is that you're, ahem, a little older than anyone here... including these living creations of yours."

"Well... let us just say that some of my war-children are better-attuned to the techno-stuff of this world, than am I," mentioned Karéin-Mayréij, with a saturnine smile. "Oh – and by the way, while we were talking – before I, ahh, 'put most of them to bed' – my war-children have been, ahh, 'learning' about how your little talking-box, works. They told me that it is very intricate and sophisticated... they are most impressed with the craftsmanship that has made it. But they will figure it out, very soon, now."

"*She-it!*" chuckled Boatman, who had taken a seat on the nearest large rock. "You know, Minnie... that explains a lot of things, I guess. Like why the bugs didn't hear nothin'."

"We're not supposed to talk about that, you know," cautioned Chu. "But this is, uhh... very interesting, to say the least. These weapons that we saw on you... they look like *medieval*-stuff – swords and shields – we never considered the possibility that..."

"Did you think that I would just sit around and fall as a helpless victim of your techno-weapons?" remarked the alien-girl, with an air of smug satisfaction. "For the record, Ms. Minn-ee-Choo – your friend is not telling me anything that

I did not already know. On *my* side, I reveal this information, weighing off the risk of allowing you to know too much, against hoping that your government will be deterred by what you learn while you are with me. I may not get this balance right... but it is a chance that I believe that I must take."

"How, exactly, are these 'war-children' of yours, learning about technology, Karéin?" pressed Abruzzio. "I mean... Hector and I tracked your progress since the Jacobson team first encountered you, in that cave on Mars. We all thought it was remarkable, how quickly you adapted to what must have been very unfamiliar circumstances, what with the appearance of the astronauts... however, it's *one* thing to teach a living, breathing, intelligent being how to use a telephone or a dishwasher – but how would you teach that to a shield? What would be its sphere of reference?

"Why not just ask *Vìrya I'ëà'b'* for herself, Sylvia?" teasingly replied Karéin-Mayréij.

"I... I don't think I should..." stammered the scientist. "I mean..."

"There's nothing to worry about, Sylvia," assured Ramirez. "But if you don't wanna do it, that's okay... I can just ask her – the shield – on your behalf."

Abruzzio bit her lip, torn by the conflicting desires of insatiable curiosity and fear of the unknown.

"Oh, the *hell* with it!" she muttered. "Go ahead – read my mind, take it over, if you will – you've probably got better ones to play with, anyway."

Quickly, she extended her hand to grasp the shield from above and below near its edge, and instantly, her visage took on the same astonished look that the group had seen from Ramirez, a few minutes previously.

Except that there was an incredulous, overjoyed smile, this time.

"Oh... *wow*," breathed the scientist. "Hector... this is just *amazing*, I can hear her talking... yes... hello to you, too... I'm sorry, little one, I don't know how to pronounce your name... I'm Sylvia, I know your mother... why thank you, I'd love to be your 'auntie'! I did my best to help your mom – and that was before you were born... So what was I going to ask? Oh, yeah... I wanted to know, about the computers, how do you... *what*?"

Abruzzio started laughing, then regained her composure.

"Well... I don't think you can do *that*, even if it worked with the 'dumb-ass techno-critters' – did your mother say that was what they are?" she spoke, as if to nobody. "A human being is *different*, you see... don't be sad, I'm sure that he will come to love you too, but it takes *time*, you see, you have to get to know him better... there, *there*... oh, we have *so* much to talk about... I want to be your friend, and so does Hector... what? Yes, he's the 'hoo-man' who just spoke with you, that's right... okay. I'll tell him... I *promise!* Got to go, but I will be back... bye-bye..."

Abruzzio slumped backwards, her head hanging from the fatigue of utter bewilderment.

"This is all... too... *much*," she managed. "I could... I could feel her mind running all over my own, trying to learn as much about me as quickly as she could – it didn't hurt and I could tell that it was innocent, but it's a *scary* experience... I felt naked, helpless –"

"So it *is* some kind of mental-domination thing... isn't it?" suspiciously demanded Chu.

"Minn-ee," explained the Storied Watcher, "If I wanted to control your mind, you would be *groveling* at my feet right now. What Sylvia refers to is that Vîrya I'ëà'b' is still young – and, like a human child – sometimes her curiosity overcomes her, uhh, 'judgment'. Have you never had a little one who pries into places of your house, where he or she should not go? You humans must all remember that the only way my war-children can truly perceive the world – although this is slowly changing, and their senses are good enough to let them function on their own – is through my own eyes. They hunger to know... to grow and to progress. And I would ask Hector and Sylvia, as the friends that I know they are, to help them in this journey. Will you?"

"What scientist could turn down such an opportunity?" quickly concurred Abruzzio. "Is there any chance that we could get one or more of them, into an... uhh... laboratory?"

"Sylvia..." cautioned Ramirez.

"I can ask them, when this is all over," replied the alien-girl, "But do not forget – Vîrya I'ëà'b', her brothers and sisters too – they are all independent beings, with minds of their own. Just like it is with Jerr-ee... the decision will be up to them. You may want to ask 'Daughter Tornado Diamond-Curtain' yourself, next time you parley with her."

"That's the shield... right?" asked Chu.

"It is one translation of the words that you hear in her name," answered Karéin-Mayréij. "There are others."

Abruzzio was about to continue with her line of questioning, but she was interrupted by a low moan coming from Kaysten's direction.

They heard a cough.

"Looks like he's coming to," remarked the FBI team-leader. "Is there anything we can do to – uhh – help bring him around?"

"If 'bring him around' is what I think it is," replied the alien-girl, "The answer is, 'no'... he will be light-headed and disoriented for a few minutes, but he will be, oh-kay."

"*Ohhhhh...*" moaned the man.

All of a sudden, to the obvious consternation of the Storied Watcher, the little shield flew over to Kaysten and landed on his chest.

"Vîrya I'ëà'b'," cautioned Karéin-Mayréij, in a parental tone.

But the shield just rocked back and forth, as if resisting being pulled off.

With his eyes still closed, he muttered, "So... now... what... happens..."

"Take your *time*, Jerr-ee," counseled the Storied Watcher. "You are with me – that is, with Karéin-Mayréij. "I have stolen you away from the 'White House' palace... you are safe, but we are far-away, in the big southern canyon, along with some friends of mine... and some, ahh, 'acquaintances', who I have made."

Unexpectedly, he winced and laughed a bit.

"Oh, *stop* it – that *tickles!*" protested Kaysten.

His hands reached out to grab the shield, and the minute that he touched it, he stopped fidgeting.

"Yes, I like you too..." he muttered.

Then his eyes opened.

With a startled look, the Chief of Staff exclaimed, "What the – where –"

"Ain't you never been to the Grand Canyon, there, pardner?" sarcastically questioned Wolf. "Oh, wait a minute, I know – you all couldn't get your limo, down here... right?"

By now, the Chief of Staff had more or less come to.

He propped up his upper-body with arms behind and surveyed the scene.

"Who the *hell*?" he complained.

A second later, his gaze fell upon the Storied Watcher, and he added, "Oh... it's *you*, there... funny, you don't look nearly so... *impressive*, without that suit of armor..."

"Well, what did you *expect*, Jerry – my only, ahh, 'change of clothes', is from that 'Salvationary Army' place, and it is challenging just keeping it intact, when it is hidden within the folds of *Vîrya Ahn'jë* – go and see what *your* clothes look like, after storing them inside an oven for a few hours," she answered. "And for the record – after our little trip, your own suit needs a good pressing, too."

Now Chu crouched down close to Kaysten.

"Mr. Chief of Staff," she said, "I'm Minnie Chu of the FBI – I don't know if you remember me, but I was with the Bureau liaison-team down at the Hotel Tucson, just before the incident that occurred there... I'm here with Agents Otis Boatman and Will Hendricks –"

"Yo," called the big black man, while the third agent smiled and waved.

"Oh... so you're here to get me out? *Fantastic!*" remarked Kaysten. "When do we leave?"

A second later, he winced.

"*Owww,*" he protested, looking at *Vîrya I'ëà'b'*, who had nestled herself into his chest around the belt. "What's *that* – oh, no, never mind, I guess I... know... but look, *you*," – he pointed at the shield – "No more tickles and bites – you *hear* me?"

"Looks like you picked yourself up an alien stray-puppy there, Mister Kaysten," joked Boatman. "But I'd advise you all to give it lots of positive-reinforcement, if you know what's good for you. In the 'keepin'-my-body-in-one-piece' category, that is."

"Nonsense!" contradicted the alien-girl. "*Vîrya I'ëà'b'* would *never* hurt Jerr-ee... *would* you, dear child?"

The shield gave off a weird, barely-perceptible squeaking-noise, and wiggled a bit more.

The Storied Watcher sighed and shook her head.

"Why don't you tell it that you'll put it to bed without supper?" maliciously suggested Wolf. "That always worked for my gf's kids."

"First off – *Vîrya I'ëà'b'* and her brothers and sisters do not 'eat'... at least not in the way that you may think," countered Karéin-Mayréij. "And second – if *your* child flies off in a pout, *you* will not have to pursue it through the skies or the very earth-rock, at several thousand kil-o-meters per hour."

Another odd sound, halfway between a chirp and a giggle, issued from the shield.

"Too fuckin' *much!*" commented a laughing Hendricks.

"I was going to say, 'I could write *books* about this'," interjected Abruzzio. "In fact... I could write *encyclopedias.*"

"Look, Mr. Chief of Staff," continued Chu, "We realize that you've had sort of a rough ride in getting all the way out here – and you may still be suffering some of the after-effects of it, so please stop me if I'm going too fast... but I need to bring you up to speed on what has happened in between the incident at the White House and now. May I begin?"

"I'm not sure I want to know," muttered the man, "But go ahead."

"Well, briefly, sir," said the FBI team-leader, "After she invaded the White House and took yourself and the 'stand-in' for the President hostage, the Storied Watcher rendered you unconscious with what she described to us as her 'kiss', which is in fact a bite, that injected some kind of alien-substance into your bloodstream, the effects of which we're still not sure about –"

"Yes – you *are*," admonished the alien-girl. "I *told* you! All that it did was let Jerry fly safely at close-quarters with me. And it gave him good health and long life, as well."

"That's what *she* says," neutrally commented Chu. "She also told us that this, uhh, 'kiss' of hers, shouldn't affect your judgment or ability to reason, particularly about the Storied Watcher herself. Is that true, sir?"

"Is *what* true?" he asked.

"Do you feel yourself to be under her mental-control, sir?" demanded the team-leader.

"What?" he replied. "Oh... no, not at all."

Kaysten pointed a finger at the Storied Watcher.

"Listen, *you!*" he complained, "You've got a *lot* to answer for, young lady!"

The alien did a mock curtsy, and diffidently replied, "I am not so 'young', actually. Ah – maybe my best years are behind me... do you think?"

"You're not so cute, without that weirdo-gear all over you, either," he quipped.

While its mother shrugged nonchalantly, the little shield fidgeted and rocked back and forth, causing another pained expression on the face of the Chief of Staff.

"Not, *you*," he apologized, in the direction of *Vîrya I'ëà'b'*. "*Her*."

The shield let out another strange, edge-of-hearing sound and quieted down.

"*Riiight*," spoke Chu. "So anyway, she – Karéin-Mayréij, that is – spirited you away to here... she claims so that she can 'educate' you – we're not so sure about that... but there's little that we can do about it. Furthermore – as of a few minutes ago – the Storied Watcher concluded a tentative working-agreement with the Director for her to temporarily call off her – uhh, 'campaign' – against the United States, in exchange for the Bureau's cooperation in tracking down whomever within the Government is responsible for the abduction and torture of the Billings party –"

"Wait a minute," interrupted Kaysten. "Did you say, 'within the *Government?*'"

"Yes," confirmed the FBI team-leader. "Sir... I'll relate the full story behind this to you when we have more time, but basically – the Director, as well as many other agents of the Bureau – including, incidentally, myself, Agent Boatman and Agent Hendricks – have had our internal investigations under Project Red Rover systematically blocked and subverted, by someone on the 'inside', for reasons as yet unknown. Up to now, the Director has kept this point-of-view under tight wraps, for reasons that I shouldn't need to explain; but given the urgency of the situation with *her*, the Bureau had to undertake a private initiative to make contact with the Storied Watcher and see if we could work something out. Which – I'm happy to say – we seem to have been able to do."

"Your government is – how would Bob say – 'on probation'," mentioned Karéin-Mayréij. "It would be *most* unwise of your President to spoil his reprieve."

"*Surely*, Agent Chu," warily stated the Chief of Staff, "The Director must be aware of the implications of doing something like *this*... behind the President's back? And that I'd have to tell him, the instant that I can?"

"He is... and we are," professionally confirmed Chu. "But the Director's of the opinion that to have alerted the President to the plan, would almost certainly warn whomever is behind the abduction of the Storied Watcher's 'family', as she calls them. The Bureau's unanimous that our approach is in the best interests of the country. We're hoping, frankly, that you'll come around to seeing things our way."

"I... uhh... won't answer that, right now," evaded Kaysten.

He looked up at the Storied Watcher.

"Is it okay for me to get up with... uhh... *her*, on top of me?" he asked.

"I would assume so," remarked the alien-girl. "*Vîrya I'ëà'b* has told me that she likes you. Therefore she will refrain from – ahh – slicing you in half."

"Of course, women are known to be fickle... *human* women, I mean," unhelpfully added the Russian.

"Sexist," grumbled Chu, while Misha just smiled.

Shaking his head, the Chief of Staff slowly stumbled to his feet, with the shield still tightly adhered to his chest.

"This is bloody *awkward!*" complained Kaysten. "But every time I try to shake it off, I get this really annoying, itching feeling."

"You sure it isn't 'the heartbreak of psoriasis', dude?" joked Hendricks.

"The *what?*" asked a perplexed Storied Watcher.

"Nah... probably diaper-rash," chimed in Wolf.

"What?" said a confused Karéin-Mayréij. "He is a grown man – but Jerr-ee, if you need to clean yourself, you can use yonder pool, by the water-fall –"

Kaysten glowered.

"I'm fine!" he protested. "Your friend there in the cowboy-boots, has a big mouth."

"You *noticed?*" sarcastically muttered Misha.

"*Behave* yourselves!" remonstrated the Storied Watcher, to her two understudies. "You have free-will – use it responsibly, and chastise not each other – neither still our friends, brothers. I do far too much boasting and threatening talk myself... and I expect to be told when I am, ahh, 'crossing the line'. Let us antagonize and war on the big issues... not on trivial insults."

"You *too*, Will," ordered Chu, wagging a finger at the third agent.

Hendricks, the Russian and the bounty-hunter wisely fell temporarily silent.

"Sorr-ee," continued Karéin-Mayréij, addressing Kaysten. "I misunderstood, with this Eng-lish... one never knows if words really mean what they seem to say. But... anyway... *Vìrya I'ëà'b'* has told me that she has considerable affection for you, Jerr-ee. And in fact – were it not for her skills – you would still have died while flying with me, across the country. If I were you, I would try to be nice to her."

"Look at the *bright* side of it," added Wolf. "If it was that suit of *armor* that she wears, and it took a-likin' to you – you'd be roast toasties by now."

Speak told up thee not to, came the little voice of *Vìrya I'ëà'b'.*

Thee why defy I can cannot?

Because I am thy mother, little one... and they are not my sons, silently replied the Storied Watcher.

All freedom shall come to thee in time, beloved daughter Tornado-Diamond-Curtain; but thou must learn much about this world, before that day.

A barely-audible whining sound issued from the shield.

"Or the two daggers," commented Misha. "Wolf and I have both had them rather close by us... the experience was not pleasant – but for *you*, it would have been much worse than that."

"Yeah... kinda like what's left after a frozen steak gets thrown into a curin'-kiln," confirmed the bounty-hunter.

"Neither *Væran Ksé'l'ch'* nor *Væran Ss'éth'ch'* would want to harm any of my friends... nor even anyone with whom I do not have a known quarrel," indifferently offered the alien-girl. "Then again, they *are* but children – they *do*, ahh, 'rough-house' every so often, unfortunately."

"Most kids don't 'rough-house' at 500 below... or 5000 above," observed Wolf, with a wicked smile.

"Absolute zero is approximately minus 273 degrees Celsius," corrected Misha. "There is no such *thing* as 'five hundred below'."

"There is, if you never took all that 'science' stuff in high-school, pardner," retorted the bounty-hunter.

Abruzzio sighed and rolled her eyes, while Hendricks whispered to Boatman, "Yeah... and my guitar-amp goes up to '11', too."

"It shore is good seein' you in one piece, Mr. Chief of Staff," stated the black agent, trying to get back on topic. "Because after what we saw goin' down at the White House – on TV I mean – we all thought you was a 'goner'."

"They put *that* on TV – the thing where the other guy was filming us?" asked Kaysten. "What about the one that she had us do – with the 'stand-in' for the President – where he's telling everybody to 'lay down your guns' and all that?"

"That one went first, followed up by the one where she, uhh, laid the bite on you," recounted Chu. "There seems to be a bit of a PR-war going on, over the airwaves, right now. As of when my team and I headed off here, the Government was in the midst of a frantic campaign to regain control of the debate and assure the public that the real President, *is*, in fact, in charge of the country. There was talk within the Government of martial law being declared... but the problem was, 'who are the Armed Forces supposed to believe'."

Kaysten turned to address the Storied Watcher.

"Was all of this really necessary?" he demanded. "Not to mention the crap at Rushmore, and dropping the top-half of the Washington Monument into the South Lawn. Oh – and let's add to that, flying me off to here... wherever 'here', happens to be."

"Grand Canyon... remember?" snorted Wolf. "I'd have voted for puttin' you on top of Old Faithful in Yellowstone... but that's just 'me', I guess."

"In answer to your question," explained the Storied Watcher, with a half-shrug, "I arrived at that hotel, fully ready to, ahh, 'talk things over'... and I was rewarded by being first shot in the back, then by being attacked from all directions by people dressed very much like my eff-bee-ai friends over there, and then by having a number of huge bombs, dropped on my head – all presumably the 'gifts' of your nice little American government. I have already made penance to Sylvia and Hector, for having endangered them, by showing up there, in the first place. If you knew what I was – and am – capable of doing to this empire of yours, you would say that my actions so far, have been quite... *restrained.*"

"She was going to wreck your entire *country*, you know," warned Misha, in Kaysten's direction. "We – that is Wolf and I – dissuaded her... I *hope.*"

Karéin-Mayréij sent the Russian an affectionate glance.

"You owe my friends Misha and Wolf a great deal," she remarked. "Let us hope their counsel is not in vain."

The alien-girl slowly walked over to be closer to Kaysten, then continued, "And that is an interesting subject... do you not think? You see... it was not just out of friendship, or wanting to have a hostage, that I brought you to this place."

"What do you mean?" he asked.

"*Well*," she coolly mentioned, "I hoped that if I could remove you – a senior courtier of your President-Emperor, that is – away from the entrapments of the American state, you might be able to, ahh, 'fill me in on' what has *really* been going on, within the deliberations of your government. I am sure that Minn-ee Choo and her team, also her 'Director', would want to know, too."

Kaysten tried to remain silent.

"Let us be frank, here, Jerr-ee," cajoled the Storied Watcher, "We both know that what your President has said to me – equally to the peasants of your country, about the whereabouts and captivity of Bob, Tommy, Whitney, Curtis and Melissa, not to mention Sam Jacobson and his valiant space-adventurers – is a parcel of lies. Now that you have no spies or army-men looking over your shoulder, do you have any additional information to reveal?"

"What happens if I don't tell the truth... or if you think I'm not telling the truth?" nervously asked the Chief of Staff.

"Nothing," answered the alien-girl. "Except that I will be very disappointed in you; and, I will think less of you."

"The Storied Watcher has given the Director her personal assurance that you won't be harmed," interjected Chu. "My team will hold her to that."

"As if you *could!*" retorted Wolf.

"There is no need to goad them, good companion," cautioned Karéin-Mayréij, in the bounty-hunter's direction. "What you say is true – I *could* kill everyone here, with only a thought – but Minn-ee and her team are pledged to defend their leaders – Jerry among them – even at the cost of their own lives. There is honor in such bravery, and shame when one much greater, crushes the weak, without risk to self. So you have nothing to fear from me, Jerr-ee – but you *do* have something that would be terrible to lose."

"Uhh... *what?*" he demanded. "I don't follow you."

"I would hope that someday you would... and *that* is what you have to lose," she replied, with a hint of the godliness leaking out, again. "But for the time being, all that I request, is a little *information.*"

"As our friends from FBI can probably attest, it'd be *treason* – that's a death-penalty offense, by the way – for me to divulge the internal discussions of the White House," offered Kaysten. "But what I *can* tell you is... the President's just about at his wits' end about you, Ms. Mayréij. Originally, he just wanted the Government to be the first to get in touch with you, sit down and make some arrangements... you know? So we set up the thing in Tucson – as Ms. Abruzzio and Mr. Ramirez are no doubt aware, I was in charge of that event – and we were hoping that by staging it, we'd get another chance to set the record straight. But something – uhh – went wrong... you gotta *believe* me, it was the *opposite* of what the President intended."

"You withhold the whole truth, Jerr-ee," pressed the alien-girl. "I have *ways* of knowing when a mortal is doing that."

"How would *you* know?" evaded the Chief of Staff.

Because you are starting to know, too, she sent to his surprised mind.

Close your eyes and reflect, man.

Think deep-down – my power – the Fire *– lies upon you – it grows within you... ask my beloved daughter, who cleaves now to your chest, for guidance.*

Soon... you, too, will know instinctively, when someone tells a lie.

A second later, came another message.

You will also know when someone like you, *is living a lie... and is thereby denying who he really* is, *Jerr-ee.*

I do not judge humans because of stupid prejudice.

I will not judge you, if you will accept my love... even if you desire me not, as man desires woman.

An air of concern circulated between the others, as, for a few seconds, Kaysten did not say anything, instead staring vacantly into space with an astonished, half-panicked look.

Eventually, he managed, "Okay... I hear you... I *get* it."

"You get *what*?" asked Boatman. "She ain't said *nothin'* to you."

"She does not *have* to," commented Misha. "There are ways of communicating that do not involve speaking with one's lips."

"Ms. Abruzzio," asked Chu, "Is this what you were referring to, when you told us about the 'message' that she –"

Yes, it is, came the mental response, from she knew not where.

And the fact that you now so clearly perceive my thought... means that you *are changing, too.*

Chu gulped.

"I... *see*," she nervously offered. "What if I don't *want* to?"

"Easy," remarked the Storied Watcher, out loud. "Then move yourself away from me. But you had better do so quickly, and make it nice and far... say, ahh, the top of yonder canyon-wall, would do."

"You *know* I can't do that... neither can Will or Otis," protested the FBI team-leader. "We're under *orders!*"

The alien-girl shrugged, nonchalantly. "Oh well, then," she purred.

"Can't you turn it *off*?" demanded Chu, with desperation. "*Please!*"

"Not as far as I know," explained Karéin-Mayréij. "And I *would* not – even if I could. The blessing that my presence bestows is as much part of *me*, as your ancestry or the sound of your voice is part of *you*. I will not deny who I am, nor who I will become... nor should you."

The music was playing again, and out of the corners of eyes, the mortals again could see the awesome countenance of the Storied Watcher.

"But you're trying to *change* who I am!" argued Chu.

"I am not 'trying' to do anything, Minn-ee Choo... my new *sister*," countered Karéin-Mayréij. "It happens naturally – without any effort on my part – for those who I favor. With each passing second, you – and everyone here – are becoming more – so *much* more – than 'just a mortal'. Why not accept my trust, my gift and my love, in gratitude, woman? Do perfect health and another hundred years added to your lifespan, mean *nothing* to you? It is your *destiny!* Do you think that you were brought here by happenstance? There is a *purpose*, to all things."

"Uh-oh," muttered Hendricks. "Any chance we can call that helicopter, after all, Minnie?"

"Wait a minute," interrupted Boatman, addressing the Storied Watcher. "I thought you said that you had to *bite* us, or some such nonsense, before –"

"That makes it better, and makes it happen faster," stated the alien-girl. "But if you are in my presence, and my arts tell me that you are a follower of the Holy Light... it will happen, anyway."

She arose and walked over to the big black man, and, to his obvious discomfort, embraced him, laying her head on his massive chest.

"Be my friend," she quietly inveighed. "And thus, be... *strengthened*."

"Look – it ain't that I don't *like* you," stuttered Boatman. "But you goin' too *fast* here, you know?"

"Who knows how much time remains to us, before the hour is urgent," replied the Storied Watcher, regarding the black man from a perspective way under his much taller face.

"Hey – congratulations on joinin' the club," cracked Wolf, a cynical smirk on his face. "But hey, Karéin – don't the Russkie and I get brownie-points fer campin' on, first? After all... I had to *shoot* a man, to get to run with you."

"A friendship forged in the fires of war, is like a well-tempered sword – stronger than one that has never been so hardened," replied Karéin-Mayréij, with a friendly nod toward the bounty-hunter as she slowly let go of Boatman. "But my love and blessing fall upon *all* who now hear my voice. I only ask that they accept it. *Be* with me... be *part* of me – with all my heart, this I pray!"

Somehow, the desert stars shone brighter, and previously-hidden colors started to show themselves to the eyes of the humans in this place.

"Otis – Will – get as far-away from here as you can, as long as you can keep us all within eyesight," commanded the FBI team-leader.

"But Minnie... it's just about dark out there," argued Boatman. "Director told us all that we had to –"

Damn, silently reflected the big FBI-agent, his mind racing with excitement and real fear, for the first time in decades.

I knows I should get my ass the hell out of here – but I can't – feet don't wanna go...

Should pray to the Lord... but...

What if she's on His... side... somethin' keeps tellin' me...

"It would not be far enough, anyway," commented the Storied Watcher. "Your fellow eff-bee-ai agents would have to be *much* further away. And some roads, are not for turning back upon."

"Funny," mentioned Hendricks, "Is it just my imagination... or is the last bit of the sun reflecting off something up there? No moon, but I can see all sorts of stuff now –"

"Karéin," protested Abruzzio, "As a scientist, I find this fascinating... I feel... *funny*, in a nice way, but... Ms. Chu has a valid point. It's unfair of you to impose this, uhh, 'gift' – as you call it – upon the rest of us, without our informed consent. I'm asking you to stop the process. *Please*."

"Yeah, I mean – leaving aside all the other issues – we're supposed to be doing an, uhh, 'objective' analysis of yourself," added Ramirez. "How can we do that, if you're, uhh... changing us into something other than a 'real' human being?"

"I *cannot* stop it – not without denying who I am, or without making myself defenseless – which I will in no way do, and besides... you have a choice," countered the alien-girl. "You can walk about a mile, or more, in any direction. But, Hector... does it *feel* 'bad'? Do you feel any the less able to think – to reason – to make your own decisions? If you must walk... walk with *me*, man! And bring your friends on our journey, that I might teach them... thereby showing my special love, to all who hear these words."

She bowed her head, her hands reverently folded.

Uh-oh, realized more than one of the soon-to-be-ex-humans.

Here it comes...

But they could do nothing; and – subconsciously – each one knew it.

Dumbfounded, Ramirez hesitated, involuntarily biting his lip.

"I would have to say that it feels... *wonderful*," he admitted. "The opposite of 'bad', in fact."

As the ethereal music played gently in the nether-regions of human psyches, the Mexican-American scientist looked up to the heavens.

"*Dios mìo*... it sure *is* pretty... isn't it?" he quietly observed. "Look at the little ones... I've spent my whole life looking at the sky, you know... but I never saw them before... not like *this*..."

Ramirez' voice tailed off.

"What's *happening* to us?" whimpered Chu, as she struggled to maintain her famously-professional presence. "Not what I wanted... not what I wanted... not... what I wanted... what I want... I *want*..."

"I never did drugs," absent-mindedly remarked Abruzzio. "But I see things... *new* things... how can it be *real*, how can it have all been just round the corner, just past our finger-tips... this is *terra incognita*... Karéin, I'm asking you, please..."

"Your beautiful world – how it *really* is, Sylvia," quietly answered Karéin-Mayréij, like a tutoring parent. "How the Immortal Light meant her children to see it – thus to love it, treasure it... and *preserve* it. Let thy favored eyes be opened, woman... friend... *sister*."

Hymnal-music played faintly, from everywhere and nowhere.

A shooting star passed by. Its tail was iridescent, sparkling, so much *better* than in even the best childhood memories.

Was it a dream?

Mutely and reluctantly, six now more-than-human glances passed uneasily from one to the other, then back again, all around.

Shine!

"How's she doing?" inquired Jacobson, his attention divided equally between the query to the salesman and the corridor leading to the stairs, dead-ahead.

"Okay... near as I can tell," offered Billings, "But she's been very quiet – sleeping a lot – that's why I'm carrying the kid over my shoulder like a sack of potatoes... feels like a *ton*... I forgot how heavy they get, I guess. Or maybe it's 'how out of shape Bob still is, in spite of the alien health-club membership'."

"Y'all need me to spell you?" asked White, with a quick glance back from his point-position.

"Nah – I'll get by," demurred the salesman. "I'm, uhh, kinda getting *used* to her... you know?"

White grinned, knowingly.

"Y'all ain't so bad," he said.

"Don't tell anybody – you'll spoil my *image*," grunted Billings. "*Especially* don't tell my boss... wherever the hell, he is. Did I mention that the buggers got *him*, in the same raid where they grabbed yours truly?"

"No – really?" asked an interested Tanaka. "What was his name?"

"Hugo... Hugo Szabo," mentioned Billings. "You know... you're not supposed to be friends with your boss – it's a 'business-thing', I suppose – but I sort of broke the rule with Hugo... he's not a bad guy, I gotta say. Damn good sales-manager. We go *way* back, been through a lot of adventures... *sales*-type adventures, I mean – we thought *those* were exciting, ha ha. I sure hope he didn't get stuck in here, especially on account of me. I'd never forgive myself."

"Yeah," acknowledged the woman. "Being around you – or being around *us*, myself included – that hasn't been too great a thing, for anyone."

"Yeah," reluctantly confirmed Billings, momentarily hanging his head.

"Anyway," interrupted Jacobson, "We've cleared the rest of the level, and nothing but corpses – thank God, nobody that Bob knew – so I think we've got to head downwards again, unless anyone else has a really bright alternative idea. At least we were able to get something to eat and drink back in that last room, but I'm a little worried about Elissha... not like a kid to refuse food, after how they must have been starving her. Bob – are you *sure* she's alright?"

"Seems okay to me – a little pale, maybe, but considering what she's been through... I *did* get her to have some water, she could just be fussy," commented the salesman. "Curtis and Tommy were both that way, when we were all together... used to drive both Whitney and Sari nuts. I remember Sari saying things like 'I can shatter *worlds* and crush Demon-Princes... but I can't make a small boy eat his breakfast or politely wipe his nose'... God, I *miss* those days..."

His voice tailed off.

"You know, Sam," reflected Tanaka, "It was nice to find some food and water that wasn't poisoned... I've never been enthusiastic about snack-bars and energy-drinks, mind you, but... I think I'm starting to understand what Karéin told us about 'I can go for centuries without sustenance, as long as I have *Amaiish*'. It's a strange feeling – I mean, before we found that rations-locker, I *knew* I was quite hungry and thirsty... but somehow, it didn't matter. I didn't have the fatigue and weakness that a normal human would suffer when deprived of nourishment. Have any of you had the same experience?"

"Same here, Professor," observed White. "I liked havin' a meal – taste in my mouth, that is – but somethin' was tellin' me that it's a 'nice to have'... not a 'must-do'. And I gotta admit, it also felt – uhh, *disrespectful* – answerin' the call of nature back there, what with all that's been goin' on in those rooms... but even if this *Amaiish-stuff* could keep Miss Angel alive while she's zoomin' from star to star... I can't imagine how she could do that for years, without takin' a dump."

"When you gotta *go*... you gotta *go*," quipped Boyd. "There's a *lot* of outer-space in which to hide a turd or two, after all."

"If and when we ever see her again," noted Jacobson with a sad smile, "I'll make sure to ask her about that. But in the meantime... about the map, with the stairs – Devon, is this the one?"

"Appears to be," confirmed the black ex-astronaut. "But if y'all look on the card – see here – they got this little symbol by these stairs... looks like a 'skull and crossbones', near as I can tell. So..."

"Let me see," requested the former Mars mission commander.

"Brent – you'd better have a look, as well," he requested.

Boyd stepped back and arched to see the map-key-card.

"Little as I like to admit it, I think Devon's right," he confirmed. "And after how I just about got a nice big hole drilled through my gut at the last place – need it be said, I'm anything *but* enthusiastic about trying our luck on this set of stairs... but what are our options? Elevator's probably *crawling* with guards – or booby-trapped, or both – and the other set doesn't go down past this level. If anybody has a better idea, for God's sake let me know."

"Well... if we know that we're likely to be going up against a prepared position, we had better have a good tactical-plan," suggested Jacobson. "Assuming that the defenses are similar to what we encountered before – not always a safe assumption, I know, but we have nothing else to go on – I have an idea. Want to hear it?"

"As long as it doesn't involve yours truly," interjected Billings.

"As a matter of fact, you're the star performer," replied Jacobson.

"Look – I'm a *civilian*," complained the salesman. "I barely know how to fire a gun."

"Y'all smoked them guards pretty good, a ways back, there Bob," cheerily stated White.

"Haven't you heard of a lucky shot?" argued Billings.

"Weren't too 'lucky' for them GrayWar muthas," remarked the black ex-astronaut, with an appreciative shrug.

"Anyway," interrupted Jacobson, "Whatever your relative level of military-training, Bob, you have the ability to make yourself, uhh, 'scarce', real fast. We can turn that to our advantage, in a situation like this. Judging from the map, the layout of this set of stairs looks very similar to the other one – so what I'd propose is that you do the old Houdini-thing before we embark downwards, taking either Brent or Devon with you... I'll let them decide who gets to be the 'volunteer'."

The salesmen tried rolling his eyes, but none of them took the bait.

"So," continued the Mars mission commander, "When you get to the bottom of the stairs, shout the 'go' signal to us up here. Cherie will walk out onto the top landing, and as the gun-turret trains on her, your partner below, pops his head and gun out of the hidey-shroud, and the good Professor and he, blast the thing from both directions... if one misses, the other should be able to get a clear shot and take it out. With me, so far?"

"Gee – thanks for making me, the one who wears the bulls-eye," sarcastically commented Tanaka. "But I suppose I'm the only one with a force-field – so I get to play 'Ms. Lucky' today... so be it. What about Elissha, though?"

"I'll stay behind with her, until the coast is clear," replied Jacobson.

"*Way* behind," requested the woman. "I'm not 'safe' to be *around*... remember?"

"Ain't *nowhere* here that's safe to be around, Professor," observed White.

"I don't want to seem like I'm not hot to trot here," continued Billings, "But I can't see more than a foot or so in front of my nose when I have that, uhh, *thing*, going... and I had enough trouble just making it down the last set of stairs. I don't relish the idea of doing that, while somebody is nice and cozy behind me and bullets are flying in every which direction. Can't we just have the Professor let fly at the damn thing, the minute when it turns on the light? From up top, I mean."

"'Who dares, wins'... you ever hear that one, before, Bob?" half-joked Boyd.

"Yeah, and 'you can always tell who the pioneers are, because they've got the arrows in their backs'... sounds about the same to *me*," argued the salesman.

He thought for a second or two more, then said, "Wait a minute – how about this – if you're so convinced that me trying to sneak in there is such a good idea... why don't I get on the Professor's back, then we both float up there, like, she 'levitates' me, yeah, *that's* it – we could get so close that we couldn't *miss*."

"Hmm," mused Tanaka. "Sounds crazy, but... okay, Bob. Let's try it, just as a test."

She bent slightly over and rested her palms on the upper-parts of her thighs.

"You mind?" requested Billings, pointing to the somnolent child while addressing Boyd.

"Dumbest question in recorded history, man," replied the astronaut, with a smile as gentle as his touch as he retrieved the girl from the salesman and nestled her into a shoulder.

"I got kids at home... thought I'd be in the back-yard playing catch with them..." mumbled Boyd, with a sad, far-away look, as softly patted Elissha's back.

"Yeah... well, *I* got some too... and they're all down here," remarked the salesman, in the same melancholy tone.

Then he got behind Tanaka, placing his arms around her shapely, much slimmer midriff; but the moment that he did, he realized what male-on-female biological-function that the scene was reminiscent of.

Billings coughed and blushed a bit.

"Are you... umm... 'ready'?" he asked. "Look – if we could do this the other way around – with *you* behind *me*, I mean..."

"Ahh... the things we do for *science* – right, Bob?" said the woman, with a wry smile. "But don't worry about it – believe me, I'm sure we've both been in – ahem – more *compromising* positions, before... haven't we? Here goes."

She closed her eyes, and as she slowly opened them, the glow of *Amaiish* was more evident than it had ever been.

From far-off, Cherie Tanaka's now-familiar *ooo – ai-ooo – ooo-ai* song started to play, its chords subtle but unmistakable.

Slowly, the duo began to levitate. But after a few inches, ridge-marks of strain began to show on the woman.

She winced; then, breathing deeply – almost hyperventilating – Tanaka collapsed to the floor, with Billings deposited unceremoniously on top of her back.

The music waned and vanished.

"*Cherie!*" exclaimed an alarmed Jacobson. "You okay?"

"Never... uhh... better," muttered Tanaka. "Bob... do you mind?"

"Oh – of course," replied the abashed salesman, gingerly lifting himself up and off.

The woman rolled over and sat up.

"Well, there's another beautiful theory killed by an ugly set of facts," she ruefully commented.

"Listen... I *know* I could stand to lose a few pounds in the ol' gut, but –" protested Billings.

Tanaka shot him a strange glance.

"No – it wasn't *that*, Bob," she explained. "I think I could have easily lifted you right *out* of this accursed place, if there didn't happen to be umpteen levels of floors between us and the surface. It was something else completely – a weird feeling, like my power was flowing out of *me* and into *you*... and the more that I tried to use in lifting the both of us up, the more energy I lost. I was starting to feel pretty light-headed... I knew that I had to give up, or I could have passed out."

"Now, *that's* something new," observed Boyd. "Professor – do you have any idea what was going on, there? Scientifically, I mean."

"Beats *me!*" she replied, shaking her head. "Maybe it's some kind of other skill that Bob has... a vampiric-effect – drains your *Amaiish* or something like that? Your guess is as good as mine."

"Any chance you can turn it off, Bob?" asked Jacobson.

"That would assume that I know what 'it' is... or how to turn 'it' on," retorted the salesman.

"I'll take that as a 'no'," professionally noted the Mars mission commander. "So I think we're back to 'Plan A', team... unless there are any other bright ideas."

The rest of them stood silent for a second or two, so Jacobson requested, "That being the case... Devon, Brent, which one of you is going with our human Stealth-weapon, there?"

"I 'spose Brent ain't much on gettin' shot halfway down the stairs again," stated White, "And for the record, neither is yours truly... but I guess it's only fair that I take the next bullet... kinda even things out."

"You aren't taking *any* rounds, on my behalf... you *hear*?" answered Boyd, while shaking his finger at his fellow ex-astronaut. "I'm good to go, Captain – so if you need a 'volunteer' –"

"I think Devon beat you to it, Brent," offered Jacobson, with a smile. "But there'll be a 'next time', be of no doubt about that... so if taking pistol-rounds is your cup of tea, you'll get plenty of chances."

"Just what I wanted to hear," muttered White. "Might as well get it over with sooner rather than later, I guess... what's gonna be the 'open-fire' signal?"

"Anything but 'Tax-*you* know', if you don't mind," demanded Billings.

"Since we're so damn far underground," suggested Tanaka, "How about 'subway'?"

"Works for *me*," agreed White. "'Specially as what I had in mind, y'all might not want to be sayin' that kind of thing in front of Sleepin' Beauty there."

"It's the *thought* that counts, anyway," said Jacobson. "So go on thinking in that direction... you'd probably just be catching up on how I feel, about this whole mess. Devon – position yourself behind Bob, and both of you, keep your heads well down – if you get into trouble, freeze in place, we'll do more or less the same as we did last time... right, Cherie?"

"That was 'exciting' – way *too* 'exciting'," complained Tanaka. "Like... it was exhilarating, because I could tell that my powers were growing as I used them – pushed them to the limit I mean, but it was terrifying at the same time – one little slip-up and, 'bye-bye baby'... you know? So let's keep this one boring and on plan... okay?"

"Damn straight," confirmed White, as he grabbed Billings from the rear-flank.

"Hey, Bob – how's it feel bein' my main man?" he joked.

"We're just good friends," muttered the salesman, in the direction of the other three, who were looking on with scarcely-hidden, bemused smirks. "I think they passed a law in Tucson about that kind of stuff, anyway. You get caught, you'll do a year or more in a high-security jail like... uhh... like the one that we're stuck in right now, as a matter of fact. No – I take that back – probably a much *nicer* jail than we're in."

Ruefully, he shook his head.

"Well... there y'all go, bro'," said the black ex-astronaut. "Nothin' to lose, whatever y'all aimin' to do."

"The only thing I want you to aim, is that rifle you're toting there, my friend," retorted Billings. "Can we get going?"

"Just a second," requested Jacobson. "Brent... if you're helping Cherie cover from up here, you'll have to pass the little one off on me."

Boyd nodded and re-transfered the child, who made a few whimpering-sounds, but whose eyelids mercifully stayed closed.

"Anytime, Bob," commanded Jacobson, hoping that none of the others could notice the tears coming to his eyes, as he cuddled the girl next to his neck.

Whatever becomes of us, great Karéin-Mayréij, he silently thought, *get this beautiful small one, safely out of here.*

"Here goes *nothing*," started the salesman, *sotto voce*.

He closed his eyes and, after a second or two of what was evidently considerable concentration, he and White vanished from sight.

"*Damn*, Bob," they heard White curse, "Y'all ain't kiddin' about this thing bein' dark as a Delta night... I can't see *shit* in here!"

"You *think*?" replied the salesman's voice. "Roach trap for sunbeams and moonbeams, guy – 'they check in... they don't check out', you know? And if it's any consolation – *I* can't see jack squat, either... we'll have to feel our way down. Sari had some way of letting in just enough so she could still navigate... wish she had taught *me* that trick..."

"Straight forward – about ten paces – then you're at the top of the stairs, gentlemen," explained Jacobson, taking a quick look outward from the door. "Might just be my imagination... but this stairwell looks quite a bit deeper than the other one – I'd keep it down to a whisper if I were you, until you get to the bottom and call out, since some of the defensive-devices might be voice-activated. Ready?"

"Already stepping out," called Billings. "Like molasses in January – but we're moving."

"Brent, Cherie... your turn," said the former Mars mission commander, as he stepped backward, taking care not to give the child any good reason to wake up.

The Asian-American woman and the ex-astronaut now advanced to either side of the door, its substantial bulk propped open by a well-placed carrying-bag.

Since you shouldn't make too much noise, Bob, sent Tanaka to the void ahead and past the portal,

If anything goes wrong – let your mind call out to me.

"Yeah," she quietly confirmed, in Jacobson's direction. "I see structure there – maybe 25 meters or so below this set of stairs. Hold on, I'm getting something –"

Sound... just... like... her, came a confused jumble of thoughts.

Hate... this... mental... crap... never... could... get... used... to... it...

That's Bob, alright, interjected Boyd's mind, as he shared a wry smile with the professor.

Awkwardly, the Billings-and-White pair – their footsteps anything *but* well-coordinated – shuffled down the stairway, with the salesman barely able to refrain from cursing after repeated collisions, both with the astronaut's boot-tips and obstacles on the route.

Meanwhile, the rest of the troupe – further above – sat and waited, holding their collective breath.

Made it... I think... sent White.

Ready?

Ready, confirmed Tanaka's thoughts.

With her song playing dimly in the background, the more-than-human woman, a faint, translucent field-shield in front, slowly walked out on to the platform.

Less than a full second later, Tanaka was brightly illuminated by a floodlight.

"On your knees – hands behind your head, bitch!" ranted a loudspeaker voice. "We start shooting in three seconds!"

"Subway," called the woman, loudly and clearly.

"*Fuckin' subway!*" yelled White, his head and shoulders appearing suddenly from nowhere, way below.

With grim, experience-guided determination, he loosed a fusillade of rifle-shots at the light-source, and this time, White didn't miss; the searchlight was blown apart with the black astronaut's first barrage, with the accompanying gun-turret being reduced to junk a second or so later.

"Wow!" exclaimed Tanaka, with a serene smile. "*That* went smoothly – bastards didn't even get a shot at me. Good work, Devon –"

"Uh-oh," warned Jacobson, from behind her. "Cherie, I'm hearing voices – boot-steps, too, *lots* of 'em – from back down the corridor. Brent, I've got the child... can you cover the rear?"

"Do my best," assented Boyd, as he quickly moved to place himself to the aft of Jacobson and the girl, with the former Mars mission commander between Tanaka and himself.

The ex-astronaut crouched in firing-position and concentrated, for a second.

"You're right, Commander," he grimly muttered. "At least ten of them – maybe more, further back. We got twenty to thirty seconds, at most."

"*Shit!*" sounded a voice, probably that of White, from below.

"*What!*" shouted Tanaka.

"Heard a ricochet off the far side of the door, man," replied White. "Think they're shootin' at it. Didn't get *that* one through, but – *damn*, there's two more –"

"Let's get our asses *out* of here," demanded Billings' voice.

"Can't," yelled the alarmed woman. "They're *behind* us, too!"

"They're just 'round the corner," announced Boyd, as Jacobson, holding his precious, still-sleeping cargo, hurried out on to the platform.

The big man grabbed the pack-sack.

"Don't try to shoot it out, Brent," he commanded. "Get your butt out here with us – we'll bar the door!"

Gotta think fast, come on, Cherie Teruko Tanaka, she desperately mused.

O power from above, a plan, give me a plan *– wait – yes!*

"Listen – all of you," she called out. "We're *trapped* – there's a small army behind us up here, and God knows how many behind the other door, down there. But there's another stairway below us – I'll levitate us down."

"I thought we're too heavy for that," shouted Billings.

"I didn't say I could get you back *up*," retorted Tanaka. "But *down*... that, I can probably handle. Get to the middle of the stairs – *now!*"

She motioned to Jacobson and Boyd, and hurried downward.

Ratta-tattta-tatta, echoed the sounds of bullets reverberating against the far side of the bottom-door. A round – then another – smashed through the small glass-window in its top-half, and dents started to show up all over the side facing into the stairwell.

"Gotta be a shitload of 'em on th' other side," cautioned White. "Door can't take it – gonna bust – wait a minute, *I* know what –"

"How do we know what the hell's down there –" protested the salesman.

Billings stopped in mid-sentence, shocked by the waves of elemental cold now coming from the man beside him.

Condensing air – like steam – was coming from White's nostrils and mouth.

The area felt like-stepping out of a sauna, into the cold of a Finnish winter night, as a shroud of ice started to envelop the bottom-side door.

"Brent – get in here!" demanded Jacobson toward his former understudy, who was on one knee, poised in classic ambush-position.

Suddenly, at least three SWAT-garbed gendarmes rounded the far corner down the upper hallway. They instantly opened fire; but their aim was ragged, and they missed Boyd by a country mile.

However, two bullets hit the corridor-facing side of the door. Their kinetic-force slammed the thing tightly-shut, leaving the ex-astronaut temporarily alone, facing three – no, it was four, five, or more, now – hostile, and well-armed, enemies.

Inside the stairwell, Jacobson reflexively dashed down to hand the child to a nonplussed but enthusiastic Tanaka, while on the other side of the closed door, Boyd's mind raced in end-of-life experience fashion.

No time to get back and open it – I'm a sitting-duck – they'd get me in the back for sure, he mentally cursed.

If it wasn't so damn bright in here – if there was a light switch, turn it to shadow, I'd have a chance –

Then, in a tiny fraction-of-a-second, to the mutual astonishment of both the trapped ex-astronaut and his opponents... that was exactly what happened.

A veil of Stygian blackness enveloped the entire corridor, for as far as Boyd could see – and, inexplicably, he still *could* see; very well, in fact.

My God, Karéin... is this what it looks like to you? he silently thought, with time weirdly slowing in his favor.

It's pitch-black – my human eyes can't see a thing – but the bastards are still right there in front of me – the hot-color – the life-color – the energy-color... plain as day.

Yes, it is... isn't it? something told him.

Like what my mind saw through your memories, those dreams of mad, forbidden places, from long ago and far-away...

Oh, how blind *I was as a human – how totally without the picture...*

"What the –" sounded a panicked shout from the milling mass of confused gendarmes.

The urgency of the here-and-now snapped Boyd out of the daydream, and his military-training took over from there : methodically, he drew a bead on his first target, firing two lethally-effective shots, one aimed at the midriff, the second at the head.

A scream echoed from the other end of the corridor, as the ex-astronaut selected his second victim, aimed and fired, to the same fatal effect.

His heat-seeking eyes could easily see a splash of warm blood splattering all the GrayWar mercenaries, beside where Boyd had put a bullet squarely through a visor.

"Legion, *advance!*" screamed a harsh voice, from behind the darkness. "Rush the position!"

Brent, came a thought, *hang on – Elissha's with Cherie – I'm opening the door –*

More gendarmes clumsily scrambled into the corridor-to-corridor crossroads at the far end of the hall, and though they were firing wildly, Boyd – holding his ground and exacting a terrible toll, while so doing – knew that he was heavily out-gunned; if nothing else, he'd soon run out of bullets.

High-velocity rifle-rounds whizzed perilously close to his low knee and then his ear. One plowed into the wall just in front and to the right of him, sending painful shrapnel into his thigh, while more shards impacted in the chest.

God, if it weren't for the breastplate – no, fuck that, it won't stop a direct hit from a rifle-round –

Despite Boyd's frantic mental signals, the darkness-thing was fading.

In frustration, he shuffled to the left, hoping to throw off his enemies' aim.

The clock still ticked away at normal-speed – he *knew* that, could perceive time just fine, thank you – but somehow, the movements of the gendarmes began to look torpid, like a movie played at three frames per second.

To his dismay, the ex-astronaut's mind again started to wander.

The thing *that exploded in the sky when I shared your deep memories...*

The terrible light and more-than-light – *the smoke poured from your clothes, from your skin...*

You writhed in pain... then adapted, drank it in, thrived *on it...*

The burning eye of God – or was it the Devil –

Now, a new war-song – fast, powerful, thrilling – began to reverberate from everywhere and anywhere, as – though he was paying no attention and did not take note – Boyd's body flashed with charges of the *Fire*, playing up and down, side to side.

Destroying Angel – you know my thoughts – hear me now – send it forth!

And as suddenly as had come the dark – starting at a point about a foot in front of the surprised ex-astronaut's gun-grasping hands – the corridor in front of Brent Boyd was flooded with roiling, arcing energy-charges of an infernal, sizzling brilliance, as if every molecule of the air had transformed to a miniature magnesium-flare.

Beams of light and more-than-light shot backward through the door view-port just behind the ex-astronaut, to the alarm of all those inside the stairwell; to them, it looked exactly like a previously-undetected million-candle spotlight.

Screams and moans – along with confused shouting, curses and the sounds of men falling and colliding with each other – issued from the faraway posse of gendarmes, and there was a nauseating smell of melting, burning building-material.

With overwhelmed visual-nerves, Boyd fell backward, only narrowly missing the edge of the door as Jacobson swung it open.

"Brent! You *hit?*" shouted the concerned former commander, seeing a prone Boyd grimacing and massaging his eyes with finger-tips.

A half-second later, even Jacobson was doing the same.

"God *damn*, I can hardly *see* you – there's some kind of shining-thing ahead of us... hold on... *got* you – kick, if you can't stand up –"

"Whoa... too close to the flash-bulb," muttered the ex-astronaut, as he awkwardly crab-crawled out on to the stairway-platform.

Jacobson shut the door, fastened its handle in the 'lock' position and braced it with a piece of railing that he had apparently torn out with bare hands.

"Can you see?" he asked. "What the hell did you *do* out there, Brent?"

"Not sure," gasped Boyd, as he struggled to get up. "But I set them back a bit, I'll wager."

"There's *smoke* coming from your hands, you know," remarked an amazed Jacobson.

"Guess that's my little specialty – black as Lady Midnight and white as Old Man Sun – but I'm not sure if it's more of a danger to us or the bad-guys," ruefully noted Boyd. "Captain... I'm still seeing stars – but my vision's slowly coming back. I'm sort of mobile... what are we –"

"Rounds comin' fast 'n furious down here," echoed White's worried voice. "I froze it up real good... but they fillin' it with lead, don't think that ice is gonna stop rifle-rounds forever –"

"Brent – we're going to float down to the next-level stairs, below us," advised Tanaka. "Get over here!"

She turned her head and said something softly to the little girl, who was rubbing her own eyes and whimpering, now.

Guided by his former Mars mission commander, Boyd stepped down the stairs as quickly as he could. As he reached a point just above where Tanaka and her young charge were positioned, White and Billings approached from the other direction.

The black man's face took on a duly-impressed demeanor.

"Whoa, Brent my man, y'all look... *different*," White offered. "A *nice* kind of 'different', that is. Them hands of yours is *hot*, bro, my Mars eyes is tellin' me."

"Yeah, well... a bridge was crossed up there," confirmed Boyd, "Or *burned* up there – don't ask me which. I greased a lot of them – but there are more to come... not a good idea to go back that way."

He peered over the railing.

"Professor – you *can't* be serious!" protested the ex-astronaut. "It's *got* to be fifty feet down to that level... my eyesight is anything but 20-20 right now but even *I* can tell. Did I hear you say we're supposed to just *jump*?"

"Not as in 'free-fall'," countered Tanaka, "I'm going to float us all down there... but don't count on a return-trip – that's beyond me. I don't see any signs of activity down there, but we can't be sure that they don't have any more of those damn gun-things on the walls... so if we run into the same defenses below, that we encountered up here, we'll have to act *fast* to take them out – same way we did a minute ago. Got that?"

"Damn straight," agreed White. "I been countin' – I still got plenty of rounds in my clip. I'm probably good for another two fire-fights, long as they're short ones. And I know more or less where to shoot at... had two chances to get the tactical down, by now."

"I think I just evolved a new weapon, up there in the corridor," offered Boyd, with an air of thinly-repressed satisfaction, "So even if I run out of bullets... I should still be able to fight. But make sure you close your eyes when I, uhh, 'let fly'."

"I can sure attest to *that*," ruefully stated Jacobson. "Took me a minute or two to be able to see *anything*, after Brent lit up my life, up there. It looked like staring right at a halogen-headlight, from one foot away."

"Yo, bro'," congratulated White. "I freeze 'em... y'all fry em! Bag 'em up for TV-dinner, don't you know."

Boyd grinned. He exchanged a proud high-five with the black man.

"Sam – can you get the railings?" requested Tanaka. "Otherwise we'd all have to climb on top of them... no problem for *me*, but I don't think any of the rest of you took gymnastics."

"I'll try," replied the commander.

He took hold of the right-side guard-rail, closed his eyes and flexed his not inconsiderable shoulder-muscles, grunting and breathing deeply to offset immense effort.

Blue-green flashes ran up and down the big man's back, and the metal in the rails began to bend backward, toward the inside of the staircase.

"*Whoa*," breathed White, *sotto voce*. "Look at *that* – ain't no *way* one man could do such a thing, without a junkyard-press –"

"Olympic weightlifting is only for genuine human types," reminded Billings. "They'd make you pee into a bottle and give you a one-way ticket home."

"There goes my gold medal, I guess," muttered Jacobson, his face grimacing as he pulled. "Pity – I actually made it to the state-finals in high-school..."

A fusillade of rifle-rounds reverberated against the frozen lower-door, and one or two also sounded against the upper one.

With the guard-rail bent to about knee-height, Jacobson brought a savage boot down on top of it, and it collapsed so as to leave a wide gap.

"Listen, Cherie – the kid – I mean, we've been exposing her to our energy," he advised. "All of us together, plus gear, must weigh several hundred kilograms... you'll have to power up *substantially* to avoid a crash-landing. You'd better give Elissha to Bob, is what I mean."

"Yeah – okay, fine – complete waste of time... but whatever," muttered the woman.

"Hey, sweetie," she gently counseled. "You can keep those eyes closed; Uncle Bob is going to take you for a few minutes... okay?"

The child nodded, falling effortlessly into Billings' outstretched arms.

"I guess I'm – we're – supposed to be as far-away from you as possible, right?" he inquired.

She nodded in the affirmative, then, with arms outstretched in preparing-to-dive fashion, turned to face the void.

"Best thing, I think, is for us to balance out the weight – so Bob, you and Elissha go on my far left, Devon between you and me, Sam on the far right, Brent in between on that side," suggested Tanaka. "All of you guys grab on to my arms – *tightly*."

"What if this doesn't work?" complained the salesman.

"Depends," matter-of-factually answered the professor.

"Depends on *what*?" he pressed.

"Simple – assuming we hit the stairs below, if you're below whoever falls on top of you, then you break more bones... your rib-cage, probably, too," she noted, with a half-shrug. "If you're the 'impactor' as opposed to the 'impactee', then you break fewer bones. Oh... and if we *miss* the target and my skills fail us, then we reach fatal velocity about three seconds later, give or take a second or two."

"Wonderful... remind me to give you a few lessons in 'how to sell your customers on a concept'," mumbled Billings.

A rifle-shot smashed through the lower-door's view-port and careened off the opposite wall. Another reverberated against the upstairs portal.

They could hear voices on both levels, still relatively far back, but approaching.

"Of course... you *can* stick around here and take your chances," remarked Tanaka.

"I sell a lot of stuff by being the 'least worst choice'," retorted Billings. You've sold *me*, professor."

He turned to address the child.

"Now keep those little eyes closed, honey," he cooed. "Uncle Bob's not going to let *anything* bad happen to you."

I hope... his mind involuntarily broadcast, as the others shuffled into place.

"Ready for a jump into the unknown?" announced Tanaka, shifting her gaze first to the right, then to the left.

"Call it a 'leap of faith', Professor," said White, in his serious voice. "I'll go for that."

Silently, the shining-eyed woman nodded in acknowledgement.

Ooo – ai-ooo – ooo-ai, came her song, strong and determined its melody, as she led them off the stairway, down into the dark below.

Welcome To The City Of Angels

"Oh-kay," cheerily announced Karéin-Mayréij, as her weird dark-shroud started to ebb, mercifully revealing random points of light and the patterns of something more than an amorphous black nothingness, for the first time in an hour or more. "We have arrived. You can move off the rock, now. Oh... but watch your step – it is night-time, and I made our traveling-platform as thin as I dared, but even so... human bones are so fragile... are they not?"

"Yeah, I know – we's all just little lost lambs," muttered Boatman.

The Storied Watcher showed a smile that could be seen, even in the dim glow of the two or three street-lights that were still operative.

In a split-second, her war-garb – except for the little shield, which for unclear reasons remained floating in front of the Chief of Staff – vanished, and again the alien-girl was dressed in disheveled street-clothes.

They were in what appeared to be a large, trash-polluted open-air plaza, with vandalized pieces of backyard furniture strewn haphazardly to and fro.

The walking-surfaces of the area were mostly pitted, cracked concrete tiles, but here and there were sizable patches of open dirt that might, at one time, have looked like green-space; upkeep on these must have lapsed long before the recent disturbances, and there was now little left except the sun-withered and forlorn remnants of lawn-grass.

Large buildings and half-wilted palm-trees loomed in the darkness of the periphery of this place, and there was an eerie, untoward quietness, here.

She gave a slight curtsy and made a stewardess-like gesture.

"Damn well about *time* that we landed," complained Kaysten. "Hasn't anybody told you how disorienting it is, flying around in that thing, without knowing where you're going?"

"That is only if your eyes are blind to the greater types of radiation," replied the Storied Watcher. "I will allow that your world is much more beautiful if viewed in the full spectrum, even at night... but as I said, back in the big canyon, I dare not make my bubble transparent, except to a very few, ahh, 'seeing-rays', lest your fine Air Force track me... excuse me – track *us*. I presume that not being able to see the scenery, is preferable to dealing with a few death-missiles, coming your way?"

"You could say that, I suppose," ruefully allowed the Chief of Staff. "But I just wish I could have seen out the window so I knew what's going on."

"Give it time, Jerr-ee," tutored Karéin-Mayréij. "Soon enough... you will."

"*Riight,*" mumbled Hendricks.

"Listen, Karéin," apologized Abruzzio, "I'd like to say 'sorry', for having gotten air-sick while we were up there... I don't travel very well, I guess. Sometimes I even have trouble on a *normal* flight, and..."

"Well – thank God for that shield," interrupted Kaysten. "You sure weren't kidding when you said that nothing could get by it. I guess I owe your 'Vera Ee-yah-be' one... this is a top-of-the-line Italian suit, I paid ten grand –"

"She has had to defend me against worse attacks than human-bile," noted the Storied Watcher. "I made her proof against dragon-breath, for example. Oh – and please work on how you pronounce her name – you will hurt my war-daughter's *feelings*. Children are very sensitive to such things, after all."

"This is all interestin', no doubt," interjected Boatman, "But... you mind tellin' us exactly where, 'here', is? I see a few lights – office-towers 'n such, all 'round – but even if you dropped that hidey-thing of yours, it's still pretty damn dark out there. We in a city?"

"If I remember the maps correctly," answered the alien-girl, "Welcome to downtown Los Angeles, Otis Boat-man. I picked a park – or, at least, a place with grass, bordered by four streets on each side. Therefore, there is a line-of-sight, whereby intruders can be detected. Until we figure out where we shall make our camp."

There was a momentary, stunned, silence. Then Chu spoke up.

"You can't be *serious!*" she protested. "Didn't you know that this whole *city* is a 'no-go zone'?"

"From what I have been told by your President, Minn-ee Choo," indifferently observed the Storied Watcher, "Your entire *country* is a 'no-go zone', for myself. How, then, can this place be any worse?"

"*I'll* tell you," Chu shot back. "Ever since the, ahem, 'comet-incident', and since the confusion that followed close behind it, most of Los Angeles has been taken over by the gangs – criminals who'd kill anyone for a half-hit of synth-drugs. There's no law or authority here, anymore : the Director told the President that it would probably take an entire army division to clear out the *Maras*, Bloods, Crips and other gangs and restore order. The last I heard, the project was on indefinite hold, partly because of the Muslim-bomb situation and partly because the Armed Forces were preoccupied with hunting down you. Karein, do you understand what I'm saying?"

"Umm-hmm," confirmed the alien-girl, a wan smile barely visible on her face. "*Perfect*, then!"

"You talkin' *shit* there, girl," argued Boatman. "Droppin' us all down here in the middle of a gang-war, and no cops, no Army, no National Guard, anywhere in sight... how can *that* be 'perfect'?"

From somewhere far-off, there was the 'tinkle' of breaking glass, and the *crack-crack-crack* sound of gunfire.

"Well... if this is somewhere that your police and Army dare not go," remarked the Storied Watcher, "Then it is kind of a *good* place for me."

Wolf guffawed, but then commented, "Look, Karéin, I hear you... I guess it might make sense from your point-of-view, but Chrissakes – even if them gangstas can't get *you*... what about the rest of us? I mean... little miss Chinese FBI over there ain't makin' any of that up – these gangs down here, they're some mighty mean *hombres*... only thing she got wrong is, they won't just dust you for a hit of synth, they'll do it just for fun – I can *personally* attest to that, seen it happen more than once. Besides... unlike them FBI-people, me and the Russkie don't even have a piece on us – we'd be sittin' *ducks* out there, minute we turn the wrong street-corner. My vote's for gettin' out of here, pronto."

"Perhaps our American spy-friends could be talked into lending either you or I, one of their weapons?" mischievously suggested Misha.

"Give my gun to some *Russkie*, in the middle of downtown Gang-War U.S.A.?" retorted Hendricks. "You already know what the answer is."

"The simplest thing is just to get us out of here," pressed Abruzzio. "Karéln, this is a *very* bad-place to spend our time in. The government tried to keep the situation off the news-networks – but pretty much everybody knows what has been going on in the L.A. area, ever since... well, *you* know. You're *needlessly* endangering all of us, by placing us here! Can't you see fit to put us all back on the flying-plate and take off for somewhere, anywhere, else?"

"And where would *that* be?" countered Karéin-Mayréij. "So far, almost everywhere I have gone, what has inexorably followed my presence, has been a massive and indiscriminate attack, supposedly aimed at myself – but, in fact, ultimately directed against those unfortunate enough to have been in my vicinity. Now – if what you say is true, and most of those who remain in this city are brigands and savages – well, then, at least when your Air Force drops some bombs where it *suspects* that I reside, those who will so be killed, may actually *deserve* it. Does this not seem fair to you?"

"I hate to admit it," mentioned Ramirez, "But she *does* have a point, Sylvia. I don't like being stuck down here any more than you do... but where would you have her hide out? At the top of the Sears Tower, or the Astrodome? You *saw* what happened at the Hotel Tucson. We barely got out of there with our lives."

"How about another country?" said Chu. "Why does it have to be in America, anyway?"

"Yeah... New Zealand's nice this time of the year," proposed Kaysten.

"Hear, hear," echoed Hendricks. "I'd even settle for Australia... nice beaches, man."

"I have seriously considered doing that," replied the Storied Watcher. "But there are several big reasons against it. One, your American empire respects no borders or jurisdictions, when it comes to dropping bombs against those to whom it takes a dislike. I desire not to trigger a war – possibly waged with these atom-smashing bombs – between the United States and some other country, simply by becoming a target and having peasant-citizens of the latter kingdom slaughtered in the crossfire; then, yet *more* blood would splatter on to these hands – and when *I* kill, it is for my own purposes... not by mishap or proxy. Two, my quarrel is with the government of your empire – not any other – and it would be shameful to hide elsewhere and pretend to conduct my campaign from a 'safe haven'. There is no honor in combat without risk, but double be the *dis*honor to a so-called warrior who cravenly hides her body behind helpless hostages –"

"Like me?" interrupted the Chief of Staff.

"You are no 'hostage', Jerr-ee," she replied. "You may walk away, any time you want to."

"Hey, and all you gotta do is talk your way past the Bloods, the Crips and the *Maras*," quipped Wolf. "You got insurance, pardner?"

"No... but I got an army, navy and air force that's looking for me," riposted Kaysten. "Who you got looking for *you*, smart-ass?"

The bounty-hunter was about to raise his voice, but his erstwhile mistress cut him off.

"Three," she continued, with a far-off sound to her voice, "A feeling tells me that I am closer to discovering where my beloved family is being kept captive and is being abused. This knowledge is just out of reach, thus most frustrating... but with each hour, my powers of perception wax stronger. If I stay here, perhaps..."

"Storied Watcher, do you mean to say that Billings and the others are *here*, in the Los Angeles area?" inquired the Russian.

"I do not know, Misha," she answered. "I do not believe so... but I am not sure. All I *do* know, is that it *will* come to me, eventually. It always *does*. And... there is a fourth reason."

A gentle but determined tune played ethereally in the minds of the sort-of-humans who were arrayed around the alien-girl.

"What's reason number four?" requested Chu.

"You are not yet... *ready*," stated Karéin-Mayréij.

"What the H you *mean*, 'we're not ready'?" demanded a confused Boatman. "Not 'ready', for *what*?"

"For the *Fire* to flower within you all, as she must – ere a great test, come to pass," obliquely remarked the Storied Watcher.

"Uhh... yeah... whatever *that* means," sighed the third agent, while Ramirez and Abruzzio exchanged knowing glances.

"So you're *not* going to fly us out of here?" asked a crestfallen Kaysten.

The alien-girl, deep in thought, shook her head.

"Not until it is time to go," she eventually said.

"Well, that's just fuckin' *great!*" complained Hendricks. "So we're stuck in downtown fuckin' L.A., in between a fuckin' million gangstas, who out-gun us by a fuckin' *thousand*-to-one. Who's for a *cheeseburger*?"

"Gave 'em up when they made the cheese in 'em one hundred per cent 'edible-oil' shit, as opposed to ten per cent real cheese," related Wolf. "And we *ain't* out-gunned... at least not with *her* around. But you got a point there, pardner – Karéin, what *are* we s'posed to do... just hang around here, until you figure out the whole damn puzzle?"

"When I am in a strange city," offered the Storied Watcher, "It is usually a good idea to find a place in which to stay. Minn-ee – I assume that there are hotels, inns, *et cetera*, in this area... are there not?"

"Of course there are – or, there *were*, before law and order fell apart," explained the FBI team-leader. "They're probably all abandoned by now, or maybe they're gang-occupied... who knows. Karéin, this is *crazy* – staying here, I mean. It's like we're locked inside a maximum-security prison, with all the guards either dead or having fled for their lives, while it's the *inmates* that have the guns. Can't you reconsider?"

"Those who are 'locked in' with *me*," malevolently pledged the young-looking woman, "Will learn, *who* should fear *who!* As, I believe, your own government has come to understand."

"I like how that sounds," commented Kaysten. "The first part of it, I mean."

An alien curtsy came his way.

"For the record," spoke Chu, "I think this is a *very* unwise decision – but as you are obviously aware, there's little that any of us can do to influence it... so I suppose we have no choice but to go along with you, if only because we'll have a better chance of survival by staying all together. This city's *crawling* with criminals, many of whom we know from experience, will 'shoot first and ask questions later'... so can I at least request that Agents Boatman, Hendricks and I, be allowed to keep our sidearms at the ready?"

"No problem, for the time being," answered Karéin-Mayréij. "But later, these 'guns'... they will not seem so formidable, to you."

"Huh?" inquired the third agent.

"You will find out, Will Hendricks," she replied.

"Where does that leave Wolf and I, Storied Watcher?" asked Misha.

"Not to mention Hector and myself," added Abruzzio.

"All of you stay close-by me, when and if danger besets us," ordered the alien-girl. "Wolf, Misha – give the innermost positions to Sylvia and Hector, for you – my disciples, I mean – you will be much less subject to gun-bullets... do not let them get a good shot at your head or heart, but almost all else you should be able to withstand, though perhaps not in comfort. For my two scientist-friends, I will bid my war-children guard you, as necessary; but be warned, their presence may prove... *uncomfortable,* until you become, uhh, accustomed to it."

"What does 'accustomed to', mean?" uneasily asked Abruzzio.

"It means, 'becoming used to enduring extremes of heat and cold, that would quickly kill a normal human being'," stated Misha. "Like Ms. Chu and her friends saw us do, with the cigarette-lighter, back in the FBI station."

"Wait a minute," requested Boatman. "You sayin' we can do *that,* now?"

"If I am inferring correctly about what happened there," explained the Storied Watcher, "The answer is, eventually... yes. But my blessing was received gratefully by Wolf and Misha – whereas for the rest of you, it has been, ahh, a 'nice surprise'... the benefits come as they will, in any case, and do not always appear at the same pace. So I advise you not to *assume* anything, until we can be sure. When your power develops, I will know... and so will you."

"This is all very interesting," interrupted Chu, "But let's not forget that we're standing out in the open, in the middle of a gang-controlled downtown. Some of those guys might be able to *see* us, right now, dark as it is. Shouldn't we get moving? To get some cover, I mean."

"Certainly... would you like me to lead?" suggested the alien-girl.

"Please do," agreed the FBI team-leader. "Karéin, I'd suggest that I follow you, flanked by Wolf and his Russian friend, the three of Mr. Kaysten, Mr. Ramirez, and Ms. Abruzzio in a group next, Will and Otis to cover the rear – that way we'll at least have some firepower in each direction. Okay?"

"Oh-kay," confirmed Karéin-Mayréij. "But it matters not. You are all completely safe in my custody, anyway, as indeed you would be even in the deepest Catacombs of Meph'èl –"

"Huh?" asked Hendricks. "What's *that*?"

The Storied Watcher fell silent for a couple of seconds, and the minds of the ex-humans all felt a wave of unease.

"A huge, dark labyrinth deep underground, under high mountains, very far-away and very long ago," she recounted. "One that was inhabited by evil, monstrous enemies, whose cruel arts would make your 'gangstas' look like little children. Several times, I was called upon to rescue friends who had become trapped there, usually after foolish quests for treasure or fame; and so I did, but let us say, it was a... *challenge*. The shadow-shrouded stone halls of that place hold the bones of many... it offers no second-chances to the unwary."

"Not on Earth, I'd presume –" inquired a fascinated Abruzzio.

"No," reflectively replied the alien-girl. "My birth-world... I believe."

"Can we continue this conversation indoors?" demanded an impatient Chu.

"Of course," allowed the female scientist. "Lead on."

The troupe assembled into more or less the marching-order that the FBI team-leader had suggested, and then began to slowly march across the plaza toward what the alien pronounced to be the north-east end of the place.

They passed collections of heaped and randomly-discarded garbage, various graffiti-covered walls and modern art-items, as well as a large, raised concrete-structure that might, at one time, have been a reflecting- or wading-pool, except that there was no remaining trace of water, except for spots of dried-up brine.

About halfway, Ramirez stopped momentarily and pointed to a figure grotesquely slumped against a large ceramic pot.

"Look at *that!*" he half-gasped.

"Yeah... sure stinks... don't he?" noted Wolf.

"Have a little *respect*, for God's sake," remonstrated Abruzzio. "That was once a living person."

"Nothin' new, darlin'," countered the bounty-hunter, with a shrug. "In *my* line of work, sometimes I used to deal with two or three a week like that."

"Good that it's so dark," commented Kaysten. "I can't really see the gory details... and I don't want to."

"I can," said Ramirez, simply.

Behold... I open your eyes, came an unrequited thought.

But with the revealed beauty, comes the also-revealed ugliness.

He knew from whom it had issued.

"Well... hate to agree with Mr. Bounty-Hunter there, but it ain't nothin' that we ain't used to seein' while doin' field-duty for homicide, either," observed Boatman. "But judgin' from the smell, and it shore *is* bad – damn, even worse than I remember it bein' in the old-days – he must have been there for a week or so... maybe more. Goes to show y'all how things is, 'round here."

"The victim may have been armed," professionally remarked Chu. "And we're short of weapons. Will, Otis – which one of you wants to check?"

"Come *on*, Minnie!" complained the third agent. "I already *got* a gun, and I don't want to get near... *that*. Probably crawling with bugs 'n shit, too. Hey – but my bro' here has more experience doing forensics, so –"

"Oh *no*," protested Boatman. "I ain't fallin' for *that*. When I do the CSI-stuff, they always give me them rubber gloves –"

"Here," muttered an exasperated Storied Watcher, falling out of line.

She advanced quickly to a place just in front of the corpse, then went down on one knee, holding her hands together in a prayer-like gesture, softly intoning some kind of invocation.

"What you *doin'* there, lady?" asked the big black agent.

"I beg the spirit-world – and this unfortunate stranger's soul – to forgive disturbing these remains," she quietly explained. "For I know not if he followed the Light, or the Twilight, or the Dark; and his personal God might take offense, if I show not proper respect... I must ask that the loyalty of his personal weapon should thus be released, again to war in the defense of another mortal. One should do this, if there is time, though sometimes it is not possible – the Gods understand that in the fury of battle, it may be necessary to, ahh, 'cut corners' and grab a fallen comrade's sword, without much ceremony."

She bowed her head, said another alien prayer *sotto voce*, and concluded, "And if any of you are interested... my greater self has come to know that this warrior did not suffer over-long; there is no shroud of spirit-pain here... he has gone on in decent and rightful manner to the Planes Beyond. All is as it should be, for the final breaths of a mortal man. There... it is *done!*"

Abruzzio crossed herself.

There was a rustling-sound, though the Storied Watcher did not actually touch the corpse; then, a pair of metal objects, the light reflecting dimly off their polished-surfaces, floated up to be in front of her face.

This was followed by successive, invisible bursts of heat and cold, and a wisp of smoke or steam issuing from both items.

"A hand-pistol, and an extra clip of bullets for it," noted Karéin-Mayréij. "I am not expert in such matters, but I suspect that it is fully operational. Who among you will take this weapon? It has been released from the spirit of its former owner... and as well, cleansed of the stain of blood and crawling-things."

There was an uneasy silence for a few seconds, then Wolf said, in an unfamiliar, subdued tone, "Well... I suppose I should claim the prize, Karéin, if nobody else wants it. Funny, though... like I said – I've seen a lot of stiffs, but it's just the way you say that, about riflin' through what he's got on him, you know... kind of makes you *think...*"

"There is nobility in you, though you try to bluff past it, dear Wolf," answered the alien-girl, as she handed the gun to the bounty-hunter. "I have killed many times, mostly for good reason... yet after each, I have done my plea for the spirits of my enemies – that they be released, that they find their way to destiny in the Further Realms. *You* should learn to do so, as well. It will be a step on the path to greatness."

"What was that movie that had, 'killin' a man – that's a hell of a thing', in it?", observed Boatman. "Same as you there, Mr. Bounty-Hunter... I seen a lot of dead folk in my time, but I never got used to it... don't 'spect that I ever will."

"'Amen' and 'Hail Mary', to *that*," added Abruzzio.

"No objections?" asked the Storied Watcher, in Misha's direction. "I could make Wolf and you, ahh, 'flip a coin', for the honor of inheriting this weapon."

"I *do* know how to use a gun," mentioned the Russian. "But I would suspect that my American friend, has lately had more experience in using one against 'gangstas', and such. If another one becomes available... may I ask to have it?"

"Soon, you will not *need* a 'gun'," stated Karéin-Mayréij. "But the answer is 'yes' – and thank you for being considerate."

I miss the mo-tel room... and the bed that was there, she sent to him, and Misha smiled enigmatically, upon receiving the thought.

Wolf checked the weapon over with an expert's-eye, carefully enabled the safety and stuck it through his belt, barrel-down.

"Don't want to change the subject," interrupted Ramirez, "But there's a sign here – *see?*"

He pointed to a dark, flat object just ahead.

"Hmm," murmured the Storied Watcher. "Yes... I can see it easily – 'Purr-shing Square', reads the inscription. Does that mean anything to you? For, I am familiar with the landmarks of this empire, only at – ahh – a 'high level'."

"Shore *does*," affirmed Boatman. "Been down this way a number of times doin' gang- 'n narcotics-traffickin' investigations; last I remember, there was a bunch of upscale ho-tels in the direction we's headin' in, also some clothin'-stores, some restaurants... Regional Director took me to a good steak-dinner in one of 'em, while back. Well... at least we's in a *nice* part of L.A. downtown, I guess. City Hall's a few blocks up from here, by the way."

"How do you figure we're in a 'nice' part of town?" complained Kaysten. "You been looking-around, lately?"

"Lots of tourist-attractions, man," joked the third agent. "You just gotta *look* for them."

"Could have been worse, Mr. Chief of Staff," answered the black agent, with a philosophical shrug. "She *could* have dropped us in Compton, after all. Or the South Side."

"Those are bad-places – worse places?" inquired the alien-girl.

"You could say," deadpanned Hendricks. "Difference is, with the way things are downtown nowadays – after you did that little number on the comet, I mean – it's not safe for us pale-faced guys, but over in places like Compton or East L.A., it hasn't been safe for the better part of a hundred years or so."

"East L.A. isn't safe for the people who *live* there, either," Ramirez pointed out. "One of my uncles was shot in a gang-war there, ten years ago."

"Ahh... I *see*," echoed the Storied Watcher. "Like Whitney used to tell Bob and I, about her homeland, in De-troit... where those who look like her and your stalwart friend Otis there, live apart from the fair-skinned Americans... right?"

"Pretty much," agreed the third agent.

"Well, I got me a decent place back in St. Louis," remarked Boatman. "Mixed neighborhood. It's only the poor-folk who get stuck down in places like Compton or Detroit way, most of the time. But it's been gettin' harder to move up the ladder, so to speak, for some time now... I *do* have to admit that."

"Funny," she reflectively replied. "You know... I wonder how things might have been different, had my dear, faithful friend Devon, been the first to unearth me, back on *Mailànkh*... instead of Sam and Cherie."

"Huh? Oh... *I* get it," said Abruzzio, with a wry smile. "Like you told Sam Jacobson, on the *Eagle?*"

"Yeah," replied Karéin-Mayréij, in an equally far-off tone. "That is my destiny, I suppose, Sylvia – some things remain the same – but never the same person twice... you know?"

"Maybe in time I *will* come to know a small part of it, Karéin," answered the scientist. "So much about you is, uhh, 'alien', to the likes of me."

"Re-discovering who I am 'this time', is always a strange experience for me, too," offered the alien-girl. "I never will become used to it... of *that*, I can assure you. Meanwhile – whatever manner of being we may be – the goodness in our hearts and the enlightenment of our minds unite us; but unreason and superficial, outward-things... those, divide us. Sadly... it is nothing unique to Planet Earth."

"Shall we continue?" requested Chu.

"Yes – let us go on," concurred the Storied Watcher. "There is a sign saying 'Bella-Vista Inn', a few hundred paces yonder. We can make camp, in there."

"You know," mentioned Misha, bending forward, "I can almost discern the letters – but in this poor light, I should not be able to. *Amazing!*"

"Many more, 'amazing' things lie in your future, friend," softly replied the alien-girl. "Scarcely now, can you imagine them."

Upon hearing this, exchanging uneasy glances as they walked forward, the FBI-agents allowed themselves a brief respite from surveillance.

From a couple of blocks away, came the sound of squealing tires and multiple gunshots.

"Keep your guard up, guys," warned Chu. "Otis – I've surveyed the entire area... nobody in sight, despite the noise over there – you or Will see anything?"

"Negative," answered Boatman. "I ain't *never* seen downtown L.A. as deserted as *this*."

"I guess all the clubs aren't doing too well these days," commented the third agent. "But same here. *Thought* I saw somebody dash behind one of those buildings off to the right as we were walking... but it could have just been my imagination."

They had come to a wide expanse of polished, *faux*-marble, museum-style steps. Ahead, there was the facade of what must have, at one time, been a five-star hotel, with a colonnaded, out-jutting entrance, a taxi drop-off way between the stairs and the remnants of a pair of thick, tempered-glass front-doors.

"Bullet-marks all around the entrance," remarked Hendricks. "See 'em?"

"Yeah," confirmed Boatman. "Minnie... want me to scout the place out?"

"As you have not yet learned how to bend light-beams, so as to hide from mundane vision," interrupted the alien-girl. "Though I sense no-one inside, just to be, ahh, 'on the safe side'... I will do it. Minn-ee Chu, protect our party while everyone waits here, if you please."

Continuing gunfire echoed in the distance, inducing the FBI-agents to look hastily over their shoulders.

"Okay," unenthusiastically agreed Chu, as – to no-one's surprise – the Storied Watcher vanished from sight. The buckler, however, did not go with its mistress, instead continuing to hover just in front of the Chief of Staff.

"Let's at least get up to the taxi-way... we're not as much in the open, there," ordered the FBI team-leader.

The rest of them quickly complied, and after a lapse of no more than eight to ten seconds, the familiar, teenager-slim figure of the Storied Watcher again popped into view. She was just inside the building, on the other side of the shattered glass-doors.

"Holy *shit*, Karéin – you don't waste any time, do you?" exclaimed the bounty-hunter. "You *sure* nobody's in there? You can't have gone too far –"

"Actually... I have been through most of the first level of this place," answered the alien-girl. "And it *is* deserted – although I am not certain about the upper-floors. When I go on a spying-mission, if the terrain is suitable, I usually go in hidden-guise, and my feet touch not the ground – much faster than walking, and thereby I leave no foot-prints. On *this* world, I have the extra advantage that I need not fear magical traps and snares. When *those* are around, one must be considerably more... *careful*. One false move, and... how would dear Bob have said it... you are, ahh, 'well-done toast'."

"I can't interest you all in a promisin' career in the Bureau... can I?" grunted Boatman. "I bet you'd be a lot better at the undercover-stuff, than I was. I was a little too, uhh, *conspicuous*, 'specially when I'd sit down for dinner."

"Speaking of that... you see a salad-bar in there?" joked Hendricks. "I'm *hungry*... but I don't want to end up like *him*."

The Storied Watcher was about to reply to this wisecrack with an admonition about politeness, but Misha cut her off.

"She already told me that she is not interested in working for Mother Russia's SVR," he noted. "I doubt that her attitude would have changed."

"As I have told Sam Jacobson – and I assume that he passed on the message to Sylvia and Hector," stated Karéin-Mayréij, "I seek not to rule humans, nor do I want to be enmeshed in your endless political- and religious-disputes; and still less, do I desire to be a foot-soldier – or a spy – in some army or police-force. But thanks for the compliment, Otis Boat-man – I know that it is sincere. Now... you should all come inside, for there are sounds of warfare out in the streets. Of course I would protect against any such issue... but best that we avoid the matter entirely."

"You got *that* right, young lady," muttered Kaysten, as he broke ranks and, followed by the shield – which was tagging along like a stray-puppy – went rapidly past the Storied Watcher, into the hotel.

A few seconds later, the entire troupe had assembled in the lobby. To their mutual amazement, they saw that there were still a few LED-lights, lending feeble illumination to what otherwise would have been a tomb-dark area.

At one time, this had evidently been an upscale-place, judging from the remnants of its former plush, chrome-and-glass décor, although the window-curtains, and indeed everything else of convenient size and appreciable value, had already been carted away by looters.

The lobby had been heavily-vandalized, and upon closer inspection, it was evident that the word "BLOODS" – spray-painted in bright red in at least five different locations – had first been over-written each time, by a blue-tinted "CRIPS", then by the moniker "W.A.R." done in white, finally by the elaborate, serifed "MARAS" name in green, white and red.

The graffiti was accompanied with the usual swear-words, death-threats against unknown gangland-figures and obscure, urban turf-marking symbols.

The area still contained its original, leather-bound waiting-divans, just to one side of the entranceway, even if these were pock-marked by knife-slashes, bullet-holes and large stains of what was undoubtedly dried blood. There were also burn-marks and bloodstains on the lush, red carpeting; but, judging from the thin film of dust on most horizontal surfaces, it has been some time since the last battle had gone down, in here.

"This place sure *has* seen better days," remarked Ramirez.

"Kind of reminds me of what the Tucson hotel looked like... *before*," added Abruzzio. "Bullet-holes, they can fix, but..."

"Anybody mind if we take a breather for a few minutes?" asked Kaysten. "Man, I wish there was something to drink – AC's out, no surprise there – and I bet the water-mains are dry, because of all the gang-stuff."

They heard the voice of Wolf, who, along with Misha, had been exploring everywhere within eyesight of the group.

"We're in luck!" he announced, proudly displaying four plastic soft-drink-bottles, two in each hand. "Bar-fridge back there behind the reservation-desk – ain't cold, door was left open, I guess – but they're sealed... should still be good to drink. By the way, I checked the till – been cleaned out, not a *dime* left. There's a lot of drawers 'n cabinets 'n such back there, but they're all locked tight... couldn't pry 'em with my knife. Maybe Miss Goddess can give it a try?"

"Sure, in a few minutes – after we head upstairs to find our camping-room," answered the alien-girl. "I do not believe that it is a good idea to stay here permanently – this room is too exposed to the street – but a few minutes may be oh-kay, as long as we do not make too much noise, or start any fights –"

"I was meaning on *asking* you about that," interjected Kaysten, in the direction of the Storied Watcher, as he grabbed one of the bounty-hunter's pop-bottles and sat down in a high-backed, stuffed chair.

"You know," he complained, "This whole fiasco could have easily been avoided, if you had just been a little more, uhh, *reasonable*, when we were all down there. I organized the event – as your scientist-friends will attest – and all we – the Government, I mean – all *we* wanted to do, was make contact with you, have a talk, take you out for dinner... that kind of thing. After all... it was an American space-team that dug you up on Mars, gave you a nice warm space capsule to ride in, back to sorry old Earth – I'd have thought that you'd be a little *grateful*... why'd you go ballistic on us? What did you have to *gain? Owww!"*

He winced and half-cringed, as the shield made a peculiar whirring-sound and impacted in an un-gentle way, with the back of his head.

The Storied Watcher wagged a remonstrative finger at *Vìrya I'ëà'b'* and lectured, "Thy mother can fight her own battles, little-one – please refrain from doing that to Jerr-ee... he is still mostly a human, after all... and thy weakest attack might do him much harm."

The buckler let out another strange noise and retreated slightly to a hovering-position, behind and above the Chief of Staff.

"That's quite some groupie you've picked up on the way there, pardner," quipped Wolf. "If I was you, I'd be nice to it, as well as its mother – were you listenin' when she mentioned how it can cut through a few feet of concrete with that edge it's got on it?"

"*Vìrya I'ëà'b'* would *never* do anything like *that... would* you, dear?" huffed Karéin-Mayréij.

The shield shuddered, sending out an oscillation that all around could feel.

"You are quite safe, Jerr-ee," continued the alien-girl, through clenched teeth. "But to give an obvious answer your presumptuous question... with no provocation at all on my part – except for words – your spies *shot* me! When that happened... what was I *supposed* to do? Perhaps, stand still so that your President's assassins could cleanly kill me, without, ahh, staining the meeting-room carpets?"

"Wait – *wait* a minute," protested Kaysten. "The President didn't *mean* for all that to happen! It was all a *mistake –*"

"Could have fooled *me*, pardner!" shot back the bounty-hunter. "If Little Miss Martian Firecracker here hadn't air-lifted the Russkie and me out of there, we'd probably have been greased by the Air Force, when it bombed the place... like a lot of other bystanders no doubt were... 'collateral-damage', you know."

"Like, just about, both Sylvia and me," commented Ramirez.

"Bottom line is, Mr. 'Chief of Staff'," growled Wolf, "I don't know what things look like from up there in your candy-ass little White House office... but down here on the street, everybody *knows* how them Feds really work – all them 'disappeared' folk, wars goin' on all over the place with no end in sight... I got Army-friends who done seven tours overseas and they *still* get tapped for another one – it's all *bullshit*, man! And now it's caught up with you and your big daddy President. Fuckin' about *time*... if you ask me."

"While my bounty-hunter friend is perhaps not being as diplomatic as he could be," added Misha, "If this all was a *mistake* – then how do you explain the repeated assassination-attempts? All your President had to do, was to order the release of the captives and refrain from further hostile actions. Instead, he – or someone in your government – chose to *wildly* escalate the conflict, in the false belief that they could eliminate the Storied Watcher, before she became powerful enough to effectively resist. The burden of proof now rests on your Government, sir. If I were our alien-friend, I would be wary of believing *anything* that requires the slightest trust, on her part."

"The reason that we're all standing here together, right now," interrupted Chu, "Is that the Bureau's Director is aware that something *has* gone seriously wrong, in how this entire matter has been handled – and he's doing his best to get to the bottom of it and not let the situation escalate further. However... we're not getting a lot of forensics done from downtown, gang-controlled Los Angeles... are we? Karéin, it was *you* who set the deadline on how long you'd wait for a believable answer. It's hardly fair for you to plunk all of us down here, completely cut off from our investigative support-systems, and then expect us to dig for the truth."

"I will concede that point," allowed the Storied Watcher, "But what did you *expect* me to do – just turn up at your eff-bee-ai headquarters building, check in with the, uhh, 'reception-desk', and then hope for the best? I must assume that those who have repeatedly tried to murder me, are still out there... and still am I their target. How you resolve the pledge made by your Director, is not *my* concern – but in our last conversation, I believe he said that all you had to do was to, ahh, 'keep me out of trouble'... so, here we are. Do you see 'trouble' – for example, a nice laser-eye bomb, falling from above – in any direction?"

At that precise moment, gunshots sounded in the distance.

"Oh-kay... not, ahh, *much* trouble," muttered an embarrassed alien-girl.

"Karéin," offered Abruzzio, "I know that what you're saying is true, from your perspective – Hector and I have both known that, ever since you spoke to our minds, on that awful day down in Tucson. But if you never trust *anyone* in the Government – for example, Ms. Chu and her agents of the FBI, if all you rely on, is force of arms – then you're giving those among them, who believe only in authority, an easy excuse to keep hunting you. I'm afraid Wolf is partly right : there *are* some very ruthless, determined killers who work for the Government... they may miss once or twice, but eventually... they *won't* miss. Do you *really* think that you can win a war against a superpower like the United States?"

Ominous waves of pride and cold contempt flowed over the group like an unexpected Arctic breeze.

"My sister Sylvia, my love is to you – but you could not be more wrong," warned Karéin-Mayréij. "You – and all here – have so far seen but a *fraction* of the *Fire*, within this body. 'Can I win a war against your President's army', you ask? I will leave it to Jerr-ee to tell you what happened, when last I ran up against the 'mighty U.S. Air Force'. Speak the *truth*, man!"

"That's – uhh – 'classified information'," evaded Kaysten.

"I'm sure we can keep a secret," replied Boatman.

"What about *him*?" argued the Chief of Staff, pointing at Misha.

"If the nature of this information is as I think it is," sniffed the Russian, with an indifferent shrug, "I am sure that Russian military intelligence is already well-aware of it. But if you want my pledge not to reveal what you say... fine. I am technically no longer a SVR agent, anyway."

"I don't think I can – *oww!*" yelped Kaysten, as the shield gave him another, if less forceful, head-butt.

"*Vìrya I'ëà'b'*, I bid thee to *refrain!*" scolded the Storied Watcher.

"Okay, okay – I get the *message*," he retreated. "Just so you know what she's referring to... before she carried me off from the White House, there was an – uhh, encounter – between her and and four squadrons of fighter-jets over the Midwest. The military wasn't very forthcoming about the result... but we heard that things didn't, uhh, go very well for us."

"I will enlighten you, Jerr-ee," remarked the alien-girl, in a forceful, haughty tone. "After I had – ahem – visited one of your Air Force's airborne battle-ships, I soared high; and there, your military sent several-score of their fighter-planes against me and my war-children. They fired many volleys of the seeking-arrows – 'guided-missiles', I believe is how they are called – meaning to kill us. When next you speak with your President and his advisors, tell him that in *that* battle, my war-children and I *did*, indeed, face a challenge : namely, 'how to tear these aircraft into little pieces, without, in so doing, slaughtering the human pilots within each one'. Fortunately – though at some slight additional risk – we found a way, since your fighter-planes do not fly very well without wings or tail-feathers, after the shattering kiss of my half-son, *Væran Fàiagàryuu*, relieved them of those."

She paused for a second, then continued, "I relate this only to point out that I could *easily* have destroyed thousands of your President's foot-soldiers... but it is dishonorable to kill helpless opponents, if I run no personal risk. However... with the endless variety and ingenuity of the weapons that the American war-machine might employ, it *is* – unfortunately – possible that I might only be able to defend myself, by unleashing really *powerful* counter-attacks. These abilities are necessarily indiscriminate... and many people might be killed by their use. It would be shameful for me to have to do that – but if trapped, if 'forced into a corner', as Bob would say – doubt me not... I *would* do it!"

There were moments of silence, interspersed by more far-off cracks of gunfire.

Eventually, Abruzzio spoke up, turning to address Kaysten.

"You know, Mr. Chief of Staff... Hector and I had already given the Government a considerable amount of data on Karéin's ability to travel and maneuver in outer-space at very high speeds – something that she clearly demonstrated on several occasions. What on Earth – pun intended – made the Air Force think that they could shoot her down like a target-balloon?"

"She was flying faster than Jacobson's spacecraft, you know," added Ramirez, "And *that* was the fastest manned object ever launched by NASA. What were they *thinkin'*, over at the Pentagon? They *had* to know that it wasn't gonna work. And that it was just gonna piss her off."

"They did a fuckin' good job, on the second point... right, darlin?" asked Wolf, of the alien-girl.

Silhouetted by the half-light, the Storied Watcher slowly nodded assent.

"I struggle to contain my anger, dear friends," she admitted. "I know that it corrodes my morality, my nobility... I am ashamed of who I have become. With each scowl, wish of ill-will or – even worse – mortal-blood-shed – I lessen and demean myself. Still... if one remains sanguine in the face of the basest of evils, done to one's kin... is *that*, not just as bad as righteous fury?"

None dared respond.

"You'll have to ask *them* about how they handled the situation," eventually offered the Chief of Staff. "Here again... the military doesn't tell us political-folk a lot about tactics or strategy... best I can do, is mention that they may have thought that she was, uhh, kind of 'off her game'... that was the rumor."

"They had that *half*-right, Jerry," explained the Storied Watcher. "I had a *terrible* fall, after unleashing my greatest, justly-forbidden power against the comet that menaced your world – I was fully prepared to die... and it is ironic, in a way; I have seen uncounted legions of mortals come to the end of their lives and thus, I hope and pray, transition to the spirit-world... all my countless years, I have wondered what it must be like, to die... to be really *dead*, I mean. But – for better or worse – I woke up, *nearly* dead, in the snows of yonder mountain north and east of here... and for several long days, I was very weak. If you had wanted to destroy me, then would have been the time... but you missed your chance! All your President can now hope to accomplish, is to kill those unfortunate enough to be *around* me, when next he strikes."

"Gee... *that* just gives me the warm-and-fuzzies," muttered the third agent.

"*Stay* with me, Will Hendricks – this I plead," she answered, in a tutoring voice. "For I have wonders yet to show you; and soon, you will be able to shrug off most mundane attacks, in any event. As for the bombs and missiles – well, we will just have to hope that we do not attract the President's attention... hence, why we are here, in this rather derelict place."

Ramirez could not suppress a yawn.

Sheepishly, he addressed both the Storied Watcher and the others.

"Sorry, folks," he said, "But it's been, uhh, a long day... you know?"

"Know what you mean," agreed Kaysten. "Even after you – young lady – you knocked me out stone cold back in D.C., and I ended up sleeping on your little cross-country flight, I'm still pretty tired, myself. Anybody want to check for somewhere to sleep, upstairs?

"I'm *terribly* stressed and fatigued – a bit hungry, too," added Abruzzio. "I want to find a nice cozy bed somewhere... but somehow I know that I could go on for another three days, if I had to... there's something *unfamiliar* lighting me up from inside... I guess it's what those drugs are supposed to feel like..."

Karéin-Mayréij silently beamed at the scientist, with a knowing, appreciative smile.

"Let me go first," proposed the alien-girl. "I determined this floor to be free of potential enemies – but I know not what lies in wait above. There is no electric-power flowing through the el-ee-vator – that was apparent as I stole past it, so we will have to use the stairs. Until, that is, you all figure out a way to travel upward, without using your feet."

"Huh?" demanded Hendricks.

He was met by another saturnine, self-satisfied, alien smile.

The first floor was laid out with the reception-area in its middle, with parallel corridors to the right and left and the now-moribund elevator-assembly also in the center, well behind the front-desk-complex.

The Storied Watcher now led the group to the left, stopping at what was evidently a stairwell, just on from the elevators.

The door leading to the stairs swung open without a touch, though Wolf and Misha could instantly feel the use of the alien-girl's telekinetic-abilities. The stairwell looked ominously dark, as it was illuminated only by intermittent emergency-lights.

"Oh *man*... what a *stench*," complained Kaysten.

"More dead people, no doubt," remarked Chu.

The Storied Watcher floated into the stairwell.

"Aye," she confirmed. "Below us, on the way to the car-parking-basement. Several of them... and it appears that they have, uhh, been deceased for a few days, at least. But I perceive no weapons that can be salvaged. I will say a silent prayer for their souls – but my vote would be for us just to continue upward. What say you?"

"Sure... long as we take the stairs on the *other* side to get back down," muttered Boatman.

"Fuckin' *ay!*" agreed the third agent.

"Let us go, then," commanded Karéin-Mayréij.

She began to float up the stairs and quickly vanished from sight.

"Where the hell she *go*?" inquired Kaysten.

"Up there, somewhere," stated Ramirez.

The shield, which had deposited itself on the back of the Chief of Staff, gave off a *sotto voce* chirping-sound.

"Oh, right... *I* get it," he muttered, apparently to no-one. "Mommy will be back in a minute. Swell. I mean... thanks."

In the darkness, he rolled his eyes.

"So we follow her... up the stairs, I guess?" asked Kaysten.

"Well, I'm gonna –" spoke Wolf; but then he stopped, with his hands motioning for silence.

"You hear *that*?" he warned, with an alarmed tone.

Pop – pop – crack, came a sound that seemed considerably closer, than had been the previous cascades of gunshots.

"Yes," confirmed Misha. "Very near. And some shouting, I think in Spanish, English also –"

"*Fuck!*" cursed Hendricks. "Effin' gangstas are shooting it up out there, and I hear it now too... comin' our way –"

"Dark or not – we better get our asses *up* there," demanded Boatman. "Fast as we can, without makin' the homies know we's on their turf. Let's *go!*"

Somehow, their eyes had no trouble making out each stair-step, though intuition told each member of the group that it should not have been so : the place was dark enough that a good flashlight should have been necessary.

Huffing and puffing while trying to keep newly-sensitive ears perked for more sounds of mayhem, they stumbled ever upward, passing the second floor, then the third, then all the way to the sixth, before Boatman called for a temporary halt.

"*Whoa,*" he gasped, sweating and forcing the words under his breath. "I *know* I's out of shape, but..."

Scarcely-winded, Chu came to his defense.

"If it's any consolation, Otis," she consoled, "You were sounding like that, after only *one* set of stairs, back at the office... so give yourself a pat on the back. You're doing a lot better than you were, just a few days ago –"

She stopped and pondered for a second.

"Well it ain't the clean livin', Minnie – and you're right, I ain't got the same *kind* of bein' wiped, after runnin' up here... so *that* means..."

"I don't know if this Mars-shit makes you lose weight, too, pardner," joked Wolf. "But over here, feels like my hairline ain't recedin', any more."

A faint voice called from slightly above.

"Just one more set of stairs to go, friends," implored the Storied Watcher. "All the floors below seem to be deserted, but I decided to choose a place for our camp, on the level where I now reside."

With a few groans and curses, the group again clambered upward, coming out into a faintly dank-smelling, carpeted corridor, dimly-illuminated in the same manner as had been the stairwell.

"Seventh floor," wheezed Kaysten. "Why not the sixth... or the sixteenth? Not that I'm asking to have to climb any more damn stairs."

"My dear lover Bob Billings used to say that to humans, 'seven' is an auspicious number," replied Karéin-Mayréij. "May it be so."

She glided to Kaysten's back and rubbed the shield, as a parent would ruffle a child's hair.

"Thy war-brothers and war-sister envy the trust I place in thee, Daughter Tornado-Diamond-Curtain," she cooed. "Thou wouldst have protected Jerry well. It is *lonely*, being away from all of us... is it not?"

The little shield named *Vîrya I'ëà'b'* issued another one of its barely-perceptible, chiming, gurgling-sounds.

"But remember – thy place remains with all of us, when we gird for war," added the alien-girl, addressing the buckler.

It apparently did not answer.

"I am just glad this isn't a really *big* building," opined Ramirez. "Some of them have a seventy-seventh floor, you know."

The Storied Watcher cruised over to the Mexican-American scientist and gave the nonplussed, but appreciative man, a hug.

"I will have to remember that, Hector," she stated, warmly. "For the next time when I fly through one of your cities, and need a place to perch."

"All well and good, Karéin," interrupted Abruzzio, "But we hurried up here because there were the sounds of a gun-battle below – possibly inside this very building. Were you aware of that?"

"Yes," replied the alien-girl. "It was fortunate that we removed from the ground floor, when we did. I think that is where some of this took place – but it was on the other side of the building from where we entered, and it does not appear that you were noticed or followed. I will remain vigilant and will tell you immediately, if I detect this conflict should come closer to where we are now."

"So where you picked out for us to be stayin'?" asked Wolf. "Hope it's somewhere with a beer-fridge."

"I did not check for that," she answered. "Just a big room with a large window facing outward, whereby we can easily survey what goes on outside, and a cooking-area – I am, however not sure if any unspoiled-foodstuffs yet remain there – and two, uhh, 'suites', one to either side. I wanted a place with a lot of beds... as you humans are usually not disposed to taking repose next to casual acquaintances... correct?"

"Well I ain't sleepin' with the Russkie... if *that's* what you mean," grunted the bounty-hunter.

Misha blew him a sarcastic fake kiss.

"Follow me," requested the Storied Watcher, and so they did, navigating through the tenth-light to a door at the north-east corner of the floor.

An observant Kaysten looked at the closed, locked portal and commented, "Key-card entry system... as up-to-date as you get in a five-star. Everything else here is locked shut, except for the few that we saw that were forced open... how'd you get in there?"

Insouciantly, Karéin-Mayréij took hold of the door's opening-handle; there was an almost imperceptible glow of *something* issuing from her fingers, and the locking-mechanism instantly gave way.

"I *told* you, Jerr-ee," she said, "Both I and my war-children – though we be in no way born to the knowledge of such – have come to be accustomed to speaking the electro-cant of the techno that you have, everywhere. It is difficult – there are so many dialects – they speak so *very* fast, and they all seem to want the little 'up' and 'down' pulses arranged in a particular way – but fortunately, we need not maintain long conversations. And the tech-minds are generally forgiving, if we make a mistake – we can try again and again, until we communicate correctly."

She now addressed the buckler.

"Is that not correct, dear child?" queried the alien-girl.

The shield cooed and hummed, apparently in the affirmative.

"So you can, uhh, talk to my cell-phone... in binary?" inquired Hendricks.

"Not yet," answered Karéin-Mayréij, with a saturnine, hint-of-sharp-tooth smile and an arched eyebrow. "But... give us *time*."

She opened the door.

"I bid you all enter," requested the alien-girl, and without much further ado, the crowd in the hall marched in.

"We shall bivouac here," she stated. "And take care not to flip any light-switches or light any torch-fires – we do not want to draw undue attention to ourselves, and the skylight from yonder big window at the far end of this room should give us enough illumination to go about our necessary duties."

The Storied Watcher had not been exaggerating about the nature of the place that she had selected for their stay; in better days, this must have been a first-class business-suite, or a honeymoon-suite, because its large, outward-facing picture-window had a sumptuous view of central- to northeast- Los Angeles, with the Harbor Freeway – pockmarked by abandoned vehicles of every type – just visible to the north and west, while due north-east, they could see the flame-scarred walls of the building that had, earlier, served as City Hall.

The city looked eerily dark and quiet; and from this perspective, it was obvious that if any of the inhabitants of other similar high-rise suites were still in there, they were also keeping a low profile : nary a room-light could be seen in any of the other hotels and condo-buildings in the downtown area. Perhaps one out of every five street-lights on the avenues far below, was operational.

As for the room itself, there was a sunken, pillow-strewn central-area in the main room, with a private kitchen on the right, a large, jacuzzi-tub-equipped washroom on the right – of course, there wasn't any power to run the thing, although it still did contain quite a bit of tepid water. Interior-doors on both the right and left led to secondary bedrooms on either side.

"Wow... *nice*," offered Abruzzio, "But God – is it ever *stuffy*, worse even than out there in the rest of the hotel – air-conditioning must have been out since all the bad-stuff started to happen... oh, look, there – this is one of the ones where you can open a window. Hector... can you lend a hand, please?"

The two of them struggled a bit but then – much to the relief of the rest of the group – they managed to pop open two small windows, one in the washroom and another near the kitchen-area.

In flowed the cool night air – refreshingly clean for once – since the vast majority of the automobiles of the Los Angeles Basin were now at a stand-still.

The suite was decorated in the minimalist, *faux*-1960s, Space-Age style that had – along with other retro-habits such as workplace-smoking and "discouragement" of female workforce-participation – come back into fashion three Presidential terms before that of the current occupant of the White House. But – much to the third agent's disappointment – the flat-panel television-display turned out to be as non-functional as all the other electrically-driven appliances, and – to no-one's surprise – the phone- and computer-lines were "out", as well.

The room looked as if it had been quickly vacated; some paper-money had been left out in the open, and the closets, upon closer inspection, turned out to have an extensive collection of upscale men's and womens clothes. The dessicated remnants of some last meal, sitting forlornly on a counter-top, were quickly disposed of.

Wolf and Misha explored the kitchen, while the others alternatively explored elsewhere or just relaxed by removing shoes from aching feet.

"Lots of stuff in the fridge," said the bounty-hunter, "But no power for weeks... cold-stuff's all spoiled, judgin' from the smell... I ain't takin' any chances with it. There's some fruit-juice and some bottled-water, though – *that* might still be good, I guess. And there's beer in here... but shit! Warm beer – *that's* a waste for sure... anythin' in the cupboards there, pardner?"

"I think the situation is better for dry-goods," remarked the Russian. "Several sealed packages of potato-chips, tortilla-chips, other snack-foods, crackers and something that looks like Melba-Toast – also sugar, flour, salt and various condiments... hmm, what is *this*? Ah, yes, dried meat-snacks... uhh, 'beef-jerky'... that is how you Americans call it... right?"

"Damn – and if we could just get a ball-game up on the TV, we'd have the start of a party there, guy," peevishly commented Hendricks.

"Probably not much of a party," answered Misha. "But there is enough in here for a partial meal for everyone here, if we allocate portions evenly."

He took out a bowl from under one of the serving-counters, put it in a sink and turned the tap. For three or four seconds, water poured out; but then, there was a coughing-sound and the flow dried up.

"Residual water in the tubes," he noted, professionally. "Make sure that you do the same, for the bathroom – we are lucky that there was enough pressure to get this little bit out... considering how high-up we are. I would ask everyone not to flush the toilet, as the water in its holding-tank might be very useful."

"*Ewww*," mocked the third agent.

"I will fly somewhere and fetch some, if needs be," proffered the alien-girl. "Is anyone thirsty enough to merit doing that –"

She stopped in mid-sentence, then changed the subject.

"More gunfire, from far below," warned Karéin-Mayréij. "But it is more or less directly underneath us. This is not very good news – I should go to investigate. *Vìrya I'ëà'b'* – stand thee guard over the rest in here, and use all thy arts of alerting, if thee please. I shall be back very shortly."

Hide thy brothers and sisters, who sleep in the nave of the ceiling, with the light-beam-bending thing, silently sent the Storied Watcher, to the shield.

Use thy push-arts to maintain them there and reveal them not, excepting if war come to this place – then bring thy young-sister, Vìrya Ahn'jë, *and the others to life, leaving them in the command of venerable* Vìrya Quü'j, *foremost to protect the humans from harm.*

Thus be thy next test of trust, little one.

Dark my dear cast Mother I cloak them over, replied Vìrya I'ëà'b'.

Own now thou remove thy can. Best very do I.
Come promise Jerr-ee I nice harm no to.

The alien-girl let out a sigh, which, in futility, she hoped than none of the humans would be able to hear.

"Karéin," remonstrated Chu, "Are you *sure* this is necessary? I mean, we could just lie low, in here, they might not even –"

"You forget that I can travel while invisible to human eyes," mentioned the Storied Watcher. "And I *considered* just trying to hide... but the problem is, all the rooms in this ho-tel have only one way in or out – if one must walk, of course. I would feel more comfortable if I at least knew whether we are on the edge of a skirmish, or of a full-scale war. In the latter, armies are usually more thorough, in ensuring that all traces of the enemy have been rooted-out and eliminated. Do not worry, Minn-ee-Choo; but, I would advise you to post someone near the door, to listen for anyone who comes this way. If you can hear them, then you will know that it is not me."

"Yeah... okay," said the FBI team-leader, as the alien-girl disappeared from view, transiting the door with a gentle, quick open-and-close.

"Well, we're on our own, I guess," announced Chu, to the rest of the group.
Then her glance fell upon *Vîrya I'ëà'b'*.

"Okay... maybe not *quite* alone," she added.

Swiftly and invisibly flew the uncomfortably-alone Storied Watcher, downward, from floor to floor.

Yea, Karéin-Mayréij, you miss them... do you not? came a wry thought.

Yet... you have gone for eons by yourself.

Let not your mind wander into such topics... for you would then grieve the others – whose life-force also sprung from thy breast – who you had to leave on the other worlds...

Where are they, now?

"*Mé'aj'h,*" she involuntarily cursed, *sotto voce,* wiping a tear.

Trying to gather her thoughts and forget sad memories, she allowed her feet to come to rest upon the carpet.

Suddenly, her ears were confronted by barely-comprehensible shouts and gun-shots coming from below, yet the sounds were uncomfortably-close – they should have been detected two floors above, had she been paying proper attention – and the alien-girl silently scolded herself for this lapse.

They cannot see me, in any event, she thought.

The sounds approach – no need to go further...

And... sound not the psycho-music, I pray ye Powers Above – for here, I desire stealth – not announcement...

The Storied Watcher withdrew her legs, secured by her outstretched arms, into a ball-position, then floated up to the ceiling.

She waited.

Mayhem was not long in coming; for – after not more than ten to twenty seconds – the north stairwell door burst open. Through it, crashed a pistol-armed man, who outwardly looked and was dressed much like the bounty-hunter, except slightly shorter, dark-maned and with a more tanned, heavily-tattooed complexion.

He was bleeding profusely from multiple wounds, at least two on the left leg and another in the trunk.

"MMierr...da..." she heard the man gasp, as he collapsed in the hallway, his blood slowly leaking to stain the formerly-immaculate carpeting.

"*Santa Maria, me...*" he gasped; then, his lips stopped moving.

Just another brigand whose life fast goes the way of all who live only by the sword... no concern of mine, she reflected.

No, wait... something different about this one... what?

Not possible – humans cannot live, with the mark of that, upon them, especially, not when the glow is so strong...

Did not notice it at first – was not expecting to see it... but definitely there...

It makes no sense!

Where could he have encountered it?

But why should I care?

Too quietly for even alert human ears to hear, the same *Makailkh*–tongue curse as before, came to her lips.

Why demand so, ye voices? she silently complained.

Why bid ye save this unworthy gutter-soldier?

Have I not enough, yet with to contend?

But as she looked at the bleeding, crumpled figure on the floor twenty paces in front of her, a strange, unrequited feeling of pity and empathy fell over Karéin-Mayréij, and she wiped another uncalled-for tear.

I know not why, mortal, she mused,

But your days are not yet ended.

I hope you are worthy of what I now do – for reasons that I know not why, and still I know that I must ever be faithful.

Free will, you humans!

For good or ill... stupid or enlightened!

Free to choose the unstraightened path!

Would that I could experience it, as do you all!

Her telekinetic grasp closed over the half-conscious man. After deftly removing the gun from his hand, the Storied Watcher draped his long, muscular arms over her shoulders, enclosed him in her cloak-of-darkness and flew a retrograde course, toward a temporary sanctuary of her own making, far above.

Everything Is Fine, Fellow-Citizens, Just... Fine

By now, there had been so many of these "urgent announcements from your Government", that the Average American had almost stopped paying attention; however, what with the chaotic events that had recently occurred in the National Capitol, even Mr. and Mrs. John and Jane Doe, could scarcely help but turn on the TV, for *this* one.

Jaws dropped all over the country, after what was seen, just after the obligatory announcement, "... and now, the President of the United States".

For the elderly face with the 'used-car-salesman' eyes that appeared behind the desk within the hastily-repaired Oval Office, was *not* the familiar one, for whom a select few of America's citizens, had occasionally been allowed to vote.

"Good evening, my fellow Americans," began the former Vice-President. "I'm speaking to you, after having been sworn in as President of the United States, less than a half-hour ago, at a time in which our great country is in a state of emergency. The purpose of my speech to the nation, is to inform everyone of what the situation is now, and of how the Government will resolve it."

He paused for a second or two, then stated, trying his best for a fatherly, reassuring tone, "Now... the first thing that you are all probably wondering about is, 'what has happened to the former President'. Let me set everyone's mind at ease : he's alive, and along with the former First Family, is being kept in a safe but secluded location."

Taking a second to pause, the *nouveau*-President gravely intoned, "However – I have to tell you tonight, that our former President *was* seriously injured by the alien-being alternatively calling itself 'Karéin-Mayréij' (or the 'Storied Watcher'), in this dangerous, anti-American creature's recent attack on the White House. Therefore, he has requested that I take over as President, until he's fully recovered from his injuries... which, regrettably, are extensive. I have reluctantly accepted this un-sought duty, out of my deep love for the best interests of the country."

"What all Americans need to know," elaborated the ex-Vice-President, "Is, despite the faked video produced by the alien, which was, intended to give the false impression that she – or it – has reached an 'agreement' with the United States – any such assertion is absolutely untrue. Your Government is still fully in charge of the Armed Forces and other state resources and we will *remain* firmly in charge. The Army, Navy and Air Force are now on a state of high alert against further terrorist attacks by this malicious, murderous and unpredictable creature, and we have an equally high level of confidence that her next move against us, will be her last."

Again, he paused, cleared his throat, and continued, "In the meantime, I'm asking all Americans to ignore any further messages that claim to come from the 'Storied Watcher', equally so the many, unfounded rumors that are now circulating regarding her, since these can only serve to divide and confuse us. If you encounter this being, she, or it, is to be considered armed and *extremely* dangerous : do *not* approach or follow her! Instead, you must immediately report her location to your nearest local police or military facility, and then remain indoors while waiting for further instructions from your Government."

Looking intently at the camera, the *nouveau*-President added, "We don't know what has caused this being to turn on America; the Government has consistently extended our hand of friendship – but, sadly – our entreaties have been rebuffed, and for reasons known only to itself, the alien seems to have started a war against us. This has, unfortunately, already resulted in hundreds of casualties among the brave men of our Armed Forces. But this 'Karéin-Mayréij' would have done well to have read a few history-books, before she picked a fight with us – because she would then have discovered that America isn't in the habit of losing wars, once they're imposed upon us."

Waving a cautionary finger, he warned, "Americans should know that your Government prepared to use whatever amount of force is necessary to rid the world of this vicious creature – and, in that light, you should also understand that while we will do our level best to avoid civilian casualties, the alien's cowardly habit of hiding in well-populated areas, may make some collateral-damage, inevitable. We don't take such a possibility lightly... but it's obviously better than having to submit to slavery, under a tyrannical, unstable monster such as this so-called 'Storied Watcher'. We have no other choice, and we're sure that all patriotic Americans will support us, as we defend our republic."

Did the new American leader suppress a smirk? Only the freeze-frame analysis later would tell, because in a split-second, he was back to his methodical, well-planned mode of delivery.

"So," he explained, "As you'll no doubt appreciate, given the unique nature of this threat, the Government has had to take some unusual, extra measures to combat it. First of all, I am today announcing a heightened state of national emergency, over and above what had previously been implemented to deal with the still-ongoing risk of Muslim nuclear terrorism. Most of you won't notice anything different going on, but there will be certain new restrictions on media news-reporting and how you use NeoNet, and there also will be strict penalties for anyone suspected of spreading false rumors, since doing so appears to be one of the alien's favorite tactics for sewing confusion and dissent."

"Specifically," proclaimed the former Vice-President, with obvious relish, "The transmission of false information with the purpose of subverting the Armed Forces is now subject to the death-penalty, with all trials pertaining to this rule to be held in special, closed-session processes. Other, already-existing regulations – for example, the dissemination of anti-draft or pro-Islamic propaganda, will be strengthened – and, beginning today, the right of *habeas corpus* is rescinded for cases involving national-security, although not for ordinary criminal cases, which will continue to be dealt with by the state court system."

"Finally," stated the *nouveau*-President, "Because our country is now confronted by a threat to its very existence, we are," – he let out a quickly-suppressed cough – "Calling on Almighty God for His divine aid, in the same plain, honest way that countless American soldiers have done in foxholes, all the way back to the founding of our republic. Effective today, a special, oath of Christian loyalty will be required of all public-sector staff, including – but not limited to – members of the Armed Forces; and, we have scheduled a number of public rallies, to be jointly conducted between the Government and our chosen partner, the Southern Baptist Hallelujah Klan of Jesus Christ, to let the Lord know that we plead for His help, in defeating the menace of the 'Storied Watcher'. I would hasten to add that all Christian denominations, including Roman Catholics and even Mormons, but excluding non-mainstream groups such as Unitarians, will be welcome at these events, for we need all the," – again, he reflexively coughed – "All the spiritual-help that we can get."

"In summary," he concluded, "My fellow Americans... these are trying times. We face many enemies – both internal and external – but we have prevailed over everything that has threatened us in the past, and – with God's help – we *will* do so this time, as well. Your Government is counting on your patriotic support, as we go about the difficult business of ridding the world of 'Karéin-Mayréij'; and we will expect nothing less, from each one of you. God bless us all... and God bless America!"

At the Aspen Down-Home All You Can Eat And Keep Standing Chicken And Ribs Restaurant, Ms. Danielle DuBois swore an oath and changed the channel on the overhead TV-display back to the basketball-game.

"Well – *that's* something, isn't it," offered one of the white, middle-aged, beer-gut males, who sat at the bar.

"Wasn't that guy the Vice-President, before?" asked another.

"Not sure... I think he was the, uhh... the *money* guy... wasn't he?" suggested a third man. "Or was he that Secretary of State... like, the one who used to go to Europe, before they closed down most of the flights?"

"*Couldn't* be," argued the first man. "He's a *Jew*. They can't be President."

"Don't ask *me*... don't pay no attention to politics," grunted a trucker. "But it's good that they're makin' everybody a Christian. 'Bout *time* that we got back to basics... if you ask me."

"What about them, uhh, them Budists and them atheists... or whatever they call themselves?" inquired the first bar-goer.

"They can convert, or go fuck 'emselves," chuckled the trucker. "That's what *I* think."

"*I'll* drink to that!" cheerily echoed someone, hoisting a Miller Full-Bodied.

"Gosh, darn it," DuBois quietly muttered to herself.

And to think that if I only had known... *I could have turned her in.*

I Hate That Smell

"Professor – *Professor!* I think we *overshot* – still going down – for God's sake, is anyone listening to – *OWW!*" shouted Billings, a half-second before he collided with a very firm and solid, horizontal metal-surface.

Somehow, he managed to hold on to the little girl, so she felt hardly any impact at all, despite the salesman coming to rest on the walkway in very unceremonious fashion; that is, butt-first and butt-down.

However, more out of imitation than genuine alarm, Elissha still began to cry, until Billings lowered his voice and said to her,

"Hey... wasn't *that* a fun ride?"

There was still fear on the child's face, but she managed to giggle, even so.

Tanaka and White had been agile enough to avoid pratfalls upon impacting with the metal walk-way, but Boyd and Jacobson hadn't been so lucky, and both of them had to scramble back to their feet.

A rifle-bullet pinged off one of the walls, far above.

"Anybody hurt?" asked Tanaka. "I tried to slow us down as much as I could, but I had to move us laterally as well... that used some go-juice, I guess."

"Tactical!" quickly called Jacobson. "Threat-assessment – scan the area."

"Don't see any gun-turrets, sir," replied Boyd. "But there's something up there, ball-shaped, just below the –"

His voice was cut off by the glare of a spotlight, which focused on himself and Tanaka. But this time, the expected guttural warning did not come – indeed, there was no sound at all, save the gun-shots from the previous level, which were coming at a worrisome pace, now.

"What you make of it?" commented the black astronaut. "I was 'spectin' to be shot at, by now... *wait* a minute..."

He stood at attention, sniffing the air.

"You smell *that*, Professor?" he demanded.

"*Gas!*" exclaimed Tanaka. "Making me dizzy – we've *got* to get out of here – Bob, cover up Elissha!"

"Which way?" shouted Billings, as he forced the child's face into his upper-body. "Doors on either side – "

Jacobson didn't hesitate : with clenched teeth, flinching as if trying to throw off a swarm of angry bees, he charged to the left, his trademark blue-green power-up glow in full force; and the others fancied that they heard a new song – deep, dark, determined, it was.

Juggernaut-like – moving at amazing speed considering the short space in which he had to run – the former Mars mission-commander crashed headlong into a strongly-reinforced door with another blue-green flash, on impact.

The thing was knocked flat, torn from its hinges as if nothing at all had been holding it in place.

"*Come on!*" he yelled, from atop the door.

The others needed no extra encouragement, and they rapidly followed Jacobson to the opposite side of the portal.

In hurried glances forward, it was immediately apparent that this was the darkest prison-corridor that they had yet entered : the overheads were almost all out, with maybe one emergency-light every ten meters still functional, and there were a few bullet-holes and scorch-marks on the walls, here and there.

"Brent, Devon... you functional enough to help me get this thing back up?" asked the big man. "We got to block the gas!"

"Yeah," affirmed White, wheezing and gasping as he spoke, for he had been the last one to get out of the walkway-area.

He grabbed one side of the downed door along with Boyd, while Jacobson took hold of the other. The three men rapidly threw it back into position, but, without its normal fastenings, the door wobbled precariously.

"Here... stand back," ordered the black ex-astronaut.

Jacobson and Boyd complied, and they felt a wave of frigid air fly backward into the corridor, as White's alien-power welded the door firmly into place, covering the entire portal with enough ice to make it certainly air-tight.

"*That* oughtta hold it," claimed White. "Damn... I still feel like I just woke up from the mother of all hangovers. Few more seconds out there, in *that* shit..."

Ruefully, he shook his head.

Boyd coughed.

"You got *that* right, man," he muttered. "I took two – maybe thre – whiffs of it... and I was already getting rubber-legs."

"Yeah... I sure know what you mean," added Tanaka. "Must have been some kind of knockout-aerosol; and judging how it affected us – remember, our physiology is probably far more robust than before – a normal human might very well be *killed*, by exposure to – oh my *God*, Bob, what about Elissha!"

Billings looked down at the child.

"Sweetie?" he prodded. "Honey? Uncle Bob, here – wake up – wake *up* – uh oh, Professor, we need *help*, here, *pronto* –"

All of them rushed over to surround Billings and the girl. Tanaka put one hand on the child's forehead and another on her neck, just below the jaw.

"Cold sweat – she's unconscious!" worried the professor. "I can barely feel a pulse. Bob, may I take her, please?"

"Yeah... sure," he answered, handing off the girl.

"Elissha... Elissha... come back to us, sweetheart," pleaded Tanaka, her eyes full of maternal instinct, as she cradled the child in her arms, rocking back and forth. "We love you, we need you... come back... come *back*..."

There was a warm, gentle feeling, all around, and it came from Cherie Teruko Tanaka.

The little girl's eyelids fluttered. To the immense relief of the rest of them, she yawned, puckered her nose, opened her eyes and mumbled,

"Ewww... that was *stinky* air, Ms. Cherie. I couldn't *breathe!* It's real dark in here. Can you see me?"

Beaming, the science-officer gently laughed and replied, "You got *that* right, sweetheart. And we all can see you just fine. How are you doing?"

"Better," said Elissha. "But I still feel kind of yucky. When are we going to stop for lunch, Ms. Cherie?"

"Soon, baby-girl... *soon*," prevaricated Tanaka. "Until we do, you should try to get a little more sleep... is it okay if I give you back to Uncle Bob?"

The professor sounded anything *but* enthusiastic.

"I guess it's okay," answered the child, "I like him a lot, too... but he doesn't smell as nice as you do."

"Your Uncle Bob hasn't had a bath in, ahem, a long while," interjected Billings. "*That's* why. But I'll keep you away from my armpits... okay?"

"*Promise*?" demanded Elissha.

"Pinky-swear," committed the salesman, making a gesture.

Reluctantly, Tanaka handed the girl back to a grateful Billings.

"You know, you kind of grow on a guy," he offered, to Elissha. "But do me a favor... don't puke on my shirt... okay? It's already smelly enough."

"You're *silly!*" she giggled, while laying her head on his shoulder.

Now Jacobson spoke up, saying, "Listen, Brent, Devon, Cherie – I've been looking down the corridor... I don't see anything for a couple of hundred feet – mind you, it's pretty dark in here, worse than anywhere else that we've been, so far... you see those bullet-marks?"

"Yeah," confirmed White. "Seems like somethin' *heavy* been goin' down, 'round here – I *could* be wrong, but I think there's marks of both rifle and pistol-rounds in there... a *lot* of shootin' – that's for sure."

"I'm also not hearing anything from back behind the door that we just secured," added Jacobson. "What about the rest of you?"

"Negative," stated Boyd. "I doubt those guys up there know where we went – unless there was someone manually releasing the gas, who might have clued them in. They might find out when they see the bent guard-rail... but if I was them, I'd think that we jumped and didn't make it."

"But there's no bodies on the walkway," argued Billings.

"They'd probably think we missed it," countered Boyd.

"You got a point, Major... so what level does this make us being on?" inquired the salesman.

"At least one lower than we were before," unhelpfully quipped Tanaka.

"Well... what I *mean*," pressed Billings, "Is that with what went on up there, we missed much of the level that we jumped down from. What if –"

"We'll just have to hope that isn't the case," replied the Asian-American scientist. "Because if the rest of your friends are on *that* level, then they're probably pretty well-guarded, judging from all the firepower that was coming from the door that Devon froze up... up there."

"Well, we *do* have at least one advantage," observed Boyd. "Another totally-weird thing... I can *see* how dark it is... but I can, like, see right *through* it – which might give us the first shot... is it the same for the rest of you?"

"Um-hmm," serenely affirmed Tanaka.

"Same here," mentioned Billings. "'Weird' ain't the right word, Major... it's like parts of it, the bullet-holes, those splotches of I-don't-wanna-know what, are in Day-Glo, but *not* Day-Glo... I just wish I could see through that damn hidey-shroud that I cooked up – excuse me, that *Sari* cooked up – oh, sorry, kid, cover those little ears, Uncle Bob keeps forgetting..."

To his satisfaction, he discovered that Elissha had again nodded off.

"I'll try to give you plenty of warning, if I have to let fly with my, uhh, new ability," elaborated Boyd. "It's probably pretty bad if used suddenly against normal human vision, and I'd strongly suggest that you not look right at it, with the Mars eyes we all seem to have inherited. Tell you what – I'll call out, 'Shine'... okay?"

"'*Shine*'," remarked White. "I *like* that, man – but I guess I need one, too... lemme think... hey, I got it. How 'bout, 'Sno-Kone'?"

"Sounds good to me," opined Jacobson. "But why *that*, in particular? Why not just, 'ice'? That'd be only one syllable."

"When I was a kid," explained the black ex-astronaut, "We were pretty poor. I could only get one of them 'Sno-Kone' things, when we went to the State Fair. Kinda nice memories... y'all understand?"

Boyd chuckled.

"Better than we got down here, otherwise, bro'," he said.

And inwardly, he thought,

I've had some good buddies, Devon – but you're in a class all your own... and I don't care if you hear that.

Call me 'homie', man, came back the silent answer.

Only white-man I'd call a 'brother', or who I'd die for, these days... 'cept maybe for Captain, soon as he learns to like soul-food.

They both cracked up.

"I missed most of *that* one, because I was thinking something through," said Tanaka, "But I got the good vibes, as it were. And just to inform you all, I guess I'll keep mine to one syllable – faster to call out. 'Shield' for the force-field, 'Sword' for the, uhh, lightening-bolt. Understood?"

Several of them nodded, but Boyd spoke up.

"As long as *you* understand, Professor," he warned, "That if you raise that 'Shield' of yours, make sure that you're *behind* me; or – if you're in front – for God's sake, make sure that you drop it before I fire off my own little alien-power... I have a feeling that if my attack bounces backwards off the inside of your force field, the results could be very, uhh, *bad*, for us."

"How 'bad' would 'bad' be?" idly asked Billings.

"'Bad', as in, 'staring right at a billion-Watt flashbulb... or maybe, standing in front of a small H-Bomb'", answered Boyd, with undisguised pride.

"I'll take your word for that," quickly conceded the salesman. "You got what he said... right, Professor?"

"You *bet*," confirmed Tanaka. "If Brent's attack is anything like my own... well, there is the possibility that we'd just absorb the *Amaiish* that powered it... but I recall Karéin saying something about, 'it can be converted to normal types of energy, when used as an attack'... certainly not something that I'd like to test, with my own life. But if we have to react quickly, Brent, or if it's difficult for us to communicate, I think you shouldn't fire until it's either completely safe to do, or until we have a chance to co-ordinate our actions... that way, I'll know that I can protect us, without causing a disaster. Do you have a problem with that?"

"Not at all," concurred the former Mars mission pilot. "We have a saying in the military – 'friendly fire – *isn't*'. If I'm gonna get wasted down here... I'd prefer not to be the cause of my own demise."

"Damn straight," agreed White.

"For the record," offered Jacobson, "Having seen both of these powers in action – Brent's one looks different than yours, Cherie; it's much brighter... more photons, less electricity, maybe... oh, and as for me, I just punch things... I'll communicate 'kinetically', as it were. And, Devon – mind if I ask you something that's been on my mind, since back in the room with, uhh, Elissha's brother?"

"Sure, Cap'n – no problem," said the black ex-astronaut. "What is it?"

"Well – my own alien-ability can only be used, uhh, 'within fist-swinging range', and both Brent's and the Professor's seem to line-of-sight, at least at the distances that we're likely to encounter down here, but... from how far-away can you freeze things? If you even *know*, of course."

White's brow furrowed, as he pondered this question for a few seconds.

Then he replied, "Not sure if I can really answer that and be sure of it, sir... but I hate to say, I don't think I can make somethin' at the other end of the building into a Popsicle, 'much as I'd like to. All I *can* say is... when we were back there – up on the last level, that is – I tried freezin' up the door that y'all and Brent crawled back through, just after he let loose with his own little Mars-thang – but it didn't work... felt kinda like when y'all reachin' out for something with your hands, and it's just too far-away – like I can't quite touch it... you know? But within – say, twenty feet or so – I'd advise y'all to bring your thermal-underwear... bet I could make it pretty chilly, anywhere within there."

Jacobson smiled.

"I'll remember that," he stated. "As soon as I can find somewhere with a change of winter-clothes that'll fit me."

Then Tanaka addressed Billings.

"What about you, Bob?" she asked. "About the 'keyword' thing."

"Oh, I'll stick with 'Taxi' –" started the salesman, only to find himself instantly enveloped in his trademark cloak-of-shadows.

He couldn't see anything, but could easily hear the muffled guffaws.

"Okay, *okay* – 'Taxi'... round-trip!" muttered Billings, as he popped into view.

Immediately, he could see White's face, contorted painfully and tearfully as he desperately tried to avoid descending into gales of laughter.

"Meter runnin', there, Bob?" managed the black ex-astronaut.

"Save the tips, folks," Billings grunted. "I got nowhere down here to spend 'em."

"Now that *that's* dealt with," professionally continued Jacobson, "I think we should be on our way, again... even if Brent was right about the confusion that's probably happening upstairs, it won't take those goons from GrayWar and whoever's in charge of them to get back on the trail –"

He stopped.

"You hear *that*?" he asked.

"What?" replied Billings.

"*I* heard it," mentioned Tanaka. "Shouts, far-off... maybe, gun-shots –"

"What direction?" demanded Boyd.

A second later, he added, "Wait – *I* got it too... way off to the right, I think."

"Yeah," confirmed White. "Copy that. Somebody yellin'... shootin', too... should be too far-away for human ears... can't make out the words, though."

"Wait a minute," protested the salesman. "This makes no *sense* – *we're* the only ones on the lam down here... right?"

"Maybe not," suggested Jacobson. "There's obviously somebody else who's not happy with someone else again, on this level... I suppose it could just be a screw-up – that is, two or more groups of guards firing at one another, each thinking that the other's us – after all, the lighting's marginal here... if it's like this all over, it would be easy to make a mistake. But... somehow, I doubt that. Let's face it, folks, we're, uhh, pretty *distinctive*, once the shooting starts –"

"Captain," interrupted Boyd, "This may be the first real break we've gotten, since we managed to escape from what they were planning to do to us, up on the first level. We can use the situation to our tactical-advantage... what I *mean* is, if we get attacked by the guards, we try to lead them in the direction of the other side – whoever that is. The rest comes naturally."

"Or we get caught in a crossfire between two groups of heavily-armed psychos," Billings pointed out. "Whatever side they're both on, it's unlikely to be ours... right?"

"I'm not suggesting that we deliberately head in their direction, or that we try tracking them down," replied the former Air Force astronaut. "Just... let's keep this idea in the back of our pockets, in case we get sandwiched, through no fault of our own. We could all hunker down in that hidey-thing of yours, Bob, crawl out of the line-of-fire, and wait until the coast is clear to get away. It's a contingency-plan... something that you learn to do when you're in the military... that is, if you want to survive a battle or two."

"We'll keep that in mind," agreed Jacobson. "However... you're certainly right about not heading in the direction of trouble – especially, with Elissha to worry about. There's another T-junction just at the edge of my field-of-vision, ahead – and since the noise is coming from the right, I vote we go left, when we get there. Any objections?"

"Yeah," muttered Billings. "We *know* that the damn corridors are all crawling with gun-totin' crazies... so why do we have to go walking down them, in the first place? I mean, Commander, you've got quite a knack about smashing through doors and walls – if I had *my* way, we'd surprise 'em real good... by making a few 'unexpected appearances' through the gyp-rock, you know?"

"My shoulders – my hands – they *hurt*, after doing the door, Bob," patiently explained Jacobson. "I'm pretty sure that if I had tried that, a few months ago, I wouldn't have had much of skeleton left... as it is now, I'd prefer to only use my power on things that I *know* can't take more punishment than I can. If it's all the same with you, that is."

"Just make sure to tell the next bunch of those jackass guards 'sorry I ran into you', after you wipe them off your boots," joked the salesman.

Billings looked over his shoulder.

"Good... she's still asleep," he added.

"Yeah – but Sam," interjected Tanaka, "Did you *know* that you could safely whack the door back there... without injuring yourself, I mean?"

Jacobson fell silent for a second or two, with a pensive, far-off look.

"No... I guess I didn't," he quietly admitted. "But it *had* to be done... and the hell with the consequences."

"Truth or consequences – and we's *already* way down in Hell," remarked White. "Least I can make it properly cold... when and if."

Jacobson smiled appreciatively and shrugged in faked nonchalance.

"Let's go," he commanded.

Kiss Of Life

"Open the door... let me *in*, if you please," requested the Storied Watcher's pleasantly feminine, yet authoritative voice.

"Think we should?" asked Boatman, with mock indifference. "Didn't she say somethin' 'bout, 'if you can hear me... then it ain't me'?"

"Well – it's pretty simple," answered Abruzzio, who was standing in the vicinity of the black FBI-agent. "If you can *see* her... then you'll know that it's 'her'. And if you can *hear* her – but you can't *see* her – you'll *also* know it's 'her'. Right?"

"You are learning quickly, Madame Professor," offered Misha.

"I bid that you open the door... and quickly!" demanded the alien-girl, from out in the hallway. "I do not believe that I was followed – but let us not *assume* so!"

"I think you can let her in, Otis," assented Chu.

None of them saw what stole through the portal as Boatman provided entry to the room; but they were all unpleasantly amazed when they saw what appeared a second or so later, in the shallow pit in the main living-area.

Yes, there *was* Karéin-Mayréij, as expected; but her clothes were stained with the slowly-leaking blood of a badly-wounded, unconscious Hispanic man, who the alien-girl had evidently been carrying over her shoulder, from wherever she had come. This unfortunate was dressed very much like Wolf, although he was slightly shorter, with a more lean, not-an-ounce-of-body-fat frame, and his goatee-beard was oddly reminiscent of that of the bounty-hunter.

As gently as she could, the Storied Watcher deposited him prone on the floor of the central depression, hovering over him like a concerned parent. The man's pock-marked, otherwise olive-colored cheeks, had a dull and sallow complexion, with only the faintest traces of respiration showing in his chest.

"Here... take his gun," she requested of Misha.

The Russian quickly complied.

"Karéin – what is the *meaning* of this?" he protested. "This man looks very much like a gangster – one who has apparently been on the losing-end of a gunfight. Why did you bring him back up here?"

"I do not know," evaded Karéin-Mayréij.

"Whaddya *mean*, 'you don't *know*'?" pressed Kaysten, who, along with all the others, had hurried over to the scene after Boatman had closed the door. "Didn't you tell us back there at the Canyon, that you've got all this stuff figured out ten moves in advance... or something like that?"

"Yeah, that is correct, Jerr-ee... it is *exactly* what I said," muttered the kneeling alien-girl, while her hands raced over the wounded man's body, lightly touching him in some sort of exploratory-gesture.

"*Well?*" he demanded.

"Sometimes... I am *guided* to do things," she offered, avoiding his glance.

"By who?" inquired Hendricks.

"By 'Boodda', God, Allah, the Santie-Claws... or that big rabbit who brings sweets in the spring-time," she peevishly retorted.

"What about the Tooth-Fairy, man?" snickered the third agent. "Doesn't *he* have a say in any of this?"

"Him too... on alternate Temple-days," she quipped.

Several of the onlookers smirked at the joke, while silently pondering the implications of what was being said.

The gangster's body shuddered, then stopped moving altogether.

"He's stopped breathing, Karéin," advised Chu.

"This boy's *daid!*" remarked Boatman.

"Ach! You are all too right – his life-force ebbs... this man will go to the Planes Beyond, unless I act forthwith," warned the Storied Watcher. "Here... help me prop him up, as I prepare – I must roll up this sleeve."

Misha and the bounty-hunter quickly complied, but Wolf kept up the barrage of questions.

"Listen, Karéin," he asked, "Far be it for any of us mere humans to be callin' you back on anythin', but... maybe you're not familiar with them tattoos on the arm that's in front of you?"

"Yeah... what *about* them?" she murmured, with eyes closed, as if deeply concentrating on something-or-other.

"That's the call-sign of the *Maras* – Latino street-gang, that is – 'case you didn't know," explained the bounty-hunter. "Pretty fuckin' mean *hombres*... slit your throat for a peso or two, then use your head for a basketball, just for fun. If he got shot up like he is – that's kind of rough justice... you know? What I *mean*, to be blunt about it, is... 'not worth savin'. An' he's a 'goner' anyways... why try?"

Now, Karéin-Mayréij was swaying in place, humming a strange mantra, and its subtly-powerful chords reverberated through all the onlookers.

Time slowed down; but with each torpid click of the second-hand, the ex-humans felt themselves being somehow empowered, strengthened and fortified.

Half-stunned, they could do naught but observe.

"'Not worth saving', you say..." she breathed, with the music having taken over by itself, in the background. "*Yea* – I come in the name of the Almighty... not only to rescue the just – but even to light the path, for those who have lost their way... to give a *second-chance...*"

"May thee be worthy of this kiss... never to use thy gifts for wrongful-things," prayed the Storied Watcher.

Her eyes opened, shining star-bright, and to the collective shock and fright of the eight ex-humans, they saw four cruel, vampire-like, venom-dripping fangs suddenly bared.

In an instant, Karéin-Mayréij bent over and sank these deep into the crippled gangster's arm, leaving her teeth in his flesh for at least a full second, before withdrawing and wiping the blood from them, then again coming to an upright, knees-down position.

The man's body stiffened, then convulsed for a second or two; he coughed, let out a pathetic groan and then collapsed as if having taken his last gasp.

The music and supernatural atmosphere quickly subsided, while the alien-girl again shut her eyelids and took several deep breaths.

"I'm gonna be *sick*," whimpered a nauseated Kaysten. "Is *that* what you did – to *me* –"

Still closed-eyed, with a trace of blood faintly evident on her lower lip, she replied, "What is, ahh, the matter, Jerr-ee... do you want another bite?"

Kaysten raced for the bathroom.

Two seconds later, unpleasant sounds issued from that direction.

"So much for the spare water in the toilet-tank," grumbled the always-practical Russian.

Finally, the Storied Watcher, visibly drained from the experience, re-opened her eyes and wobbled to her feet.

"Hey, Karéin, you look a little pale... maybe you should sit down," suggested Ramirez.

"Yes... I should..." she agreed, depositing herself on the top part of the center depression, looking down on the somnolent man whose arm bore the four puncture-marks made by the young-looking woman's fangs.

Ramirez and Abruzzio each took a seat on either side of her.

"You see," explained Karéin-Mayréij, with a dizzy, pained tone, "Seh-bast-yann was all but gone... he had already begun to step into the spirit-world. To bring someone in such a state back... requires *immense* power... drains me..."

The Storied Watcher's hands clasped together at her waist, and her head bent over her knees. She was gently rocking back and forth.

Abruzzio put an arm around her mentor's shoulder, which, the others silently noted, seemed to be gratefully accepted.

"Take your time," stated the scientist. "Tell me if you're not good to talk."

"No... fine... oh-kay..." replied the alien-girl, her voice barely audible.

"Karéin," inquired a simultaneously fascinated-and-dreading Abruzzio, "Are you saying that he was... *dead*?"

"Yes... no," equivocated Karéin-Mayréij, as she forced out the words. "Sort of. You humans over-simplify everything – the end of life in this plane... this dimension... it is not one stage, one event, you see... it is a *series* of steps, physical, mental and psychic changes – some subtle, some obvious – these may all come at once, if a mortal body is instantly destroyed, like if I were to... to vaporize one of you, with powerful fire-energy... but given time and the proper rituals, the final voyage can be made easier, less stressful... and no, I do *not* know where you go, after you have... departed. Not... exactly. *If*, in fact, you always go... *anywhere*. I have wondered about this, over countless of your lifetimes... there are theories... legends... once or twice, I have seen a glimpse... of..."

"So... he *wasn't* dead?" demanded Boatman.

"As you would understand it," slowly replied the Storied Watcher, "He was no longer, alive. Neither, was he fully... dead. My kiss – my venom – also the gift of my life-force – poured out into him and incidentally into yourselves as well, those brought him back... but reaching so far, *mightily* strains my soul, in ways that you cannot know. I will have to rest for a while, as will he... it may be several hours before enough of his body- and mind-power are replenished, for him come back from the land of dreams."

"Karéin," quietly remarked Chu, now also crouching beside the alien, "What *are* you?"

"My sister... do you not already know?" she replied, staring right past all the others.

Keep it together, thought the female FBI team-lead.

Only one person could do that – *ever – just a story in the Holy Book... right?*

After a few seconds, mercifully, Misha stepped in to change the subject.

"Karéin," he asked, "You said that this man's name was, 'Sebastiàn'. Do you know anything else about him – gang-affiliations, his reason for being here – last memories, and so on?"

Again, the alien-girl closed her eyes, as she tried to concentrate.

"His mind thinks in the Spanish-language – with is relatively new to me – and it was already shedding its mortal cares and tribulations, when I salvaged his soul back to this plane," she stated. "It is disrespectful and offensive to the Gods, to probe overmuch – indeed, it can be very dangerous. To touch minds with the dead, that can bring death in turn – it is a step that must *never* be undertaken, until one's own time has rightly come to an end! But, to, uhh, answer your question... he is a warrior for a bandit-army, I think... and there is something else..."

Now it was Abruzzio's turn to incredulously shake her head.

She looked up and regarded each of the near-humans in the group, in turn.

"We *have* to protect this being – at the cost of our own lives!" passionately exclaimed the scientist. "Do you realize what she has just revealed, here? Tens of thousands of human generations have wondered – and now, here it is – do you *understand*?"

"Thanks, noble sister of Cherie Tanaka," offered the alien-girl, with a weak, wry smile. "I know so pitifully little truth, of this most fundamental subject. But behold, how what I *have* learned, is freely-given, to you, brothers and sisters."

"Yeah," added an awed Boatman. "Laws-a-mercy, we shore do... *understand*."

"Amazing!" admitted the Russian. "But... you said that there was something else, about this man?" he asked, addressing the Storied Watcher.

"He has the power-energy-particle-shine-aura," noted Karéin-Mayréij, as if the others could easily understand what she meant. "*Most* odd – it would certainly have killed him eventually, had not the bullet-holes thus afflicted poor Sebastiàn. But I cannot figure how one such as a, uhh, 'street-gangsta', would come into prolonged contact with a large substance of such as this."

She yawned. "Ah... another mystery, on top of the several-score that already beset me," she mumbled.

"I'm afraid I don't *get* you," offered Chu. "What 'aura' is this?"

"Hmm... I guess that your eyes have not yet been opened to see it," explained the alien-girl. "That ability will come in time, no doubt. But what I meant is... it is the glow given off by the radiation-giving elements, the unstable ones from whence the energy-particles are prone to leak. You know – 'you-rain-eeum' and 'ploo-tone-eeum'... those are how you humans call the most well-remembered of these materials... though verily, there are many more. As I said... it would take a *lot* of this stuff, to have it rub off on him, and –"

"*Whoa!*" warily exclaimed Hendricks.

He jumped back by a meter or more and added, "You mean this guy's... *radioactive? Shit!* Listen... can't you carry him somewhere nice and far-away from all us pasty-fleshed little human guys? How about somewhere like – I dunno – five miles offshore?"

"Relax, Will Hen-dricks," counseled the Storied Watcher. "While I appreciate your concern – yes, it *would* be dangerous for a human to be too close to this man – for *you*, the opposite is the case. Why not lie by his side, and thereby take drink of the power-specks which emanate from his body... while you can. The glow slowly ebbs, after all... why not use it?"

"You know, Karéin," commented Abruzzio, "You're more or less openly implying that we're not... *human*, any more."

"Yeah," quietly acknowledged the alien-girl. "You are not. Or, rather, 'no, you *are* not'. I have trouble with confirming a negative, in Eng-lish. Sorr-ee."

"I was meanin' to ask you all 'bout that," mentioned Boatman. "Like, 'thank you for askin' us if we wanted to'. With all due respects, of course."

"Did you stop to think," searchingly countered Karéin-Mayréij, "That you and I might have been... 'guided'... to do *that*, as well?"

Double-keep it together, self-advised Chu, as the group fell silent for another few seconds.

But in their minds, they all heard far-off, graceful, hymnal-music.

"*Riight*," uncertainly offered the third agent.

Kaysten's rather-more-pale-than-before face, now appeared in the bathroom-doorway.

"Damn – *that* was unpleasant," he complained. "Did I miss something?"

"Uhh... yeah," responded Chu. "We just found out that our gangster-friend here, is, well, he's... *radioactive*. Although Karéin is saying that since she, uhh, *changed* us, it shouldn't hurt us. Or maybe the opposite."

"You... don't *say*," stammered the Chief of Staff.

He looked at the alien-girl.

"You expect us just to *trust* you on that?" he demanded.

"Compared to what you have had to trust me with, already, Jerr-ee," she answered, "A little atom-glow cannot be *so* much worse... can it?"

"All right, all right – I *get* it," he irritably observed. "But can you please do me a favor... no more with the *teeth*... okay?"

The Storied Watcher put up one hand, with all fingers except the thumb crossed together. She stared insouciantly at Kaysten, then quickly flashed a malicious, fang-bedecked smirk; then, in the next eye-blink, retracted her teeth so as to present an apparently normal Colgate smile.

"My, Grandma..." started Hendricks.

"No, it's just the index-finger and the second one," corrected the bemused bounty-hunter. "What *planet* you comin' from, dearie?" he joked.

"I would tell you, if I remembered," she said, not missing a beat. "But I suspect that you might find pronouncing its name, to be difficult."

The Storied Watcher yawned.

"I should rest," she proposed, as she reclined, head supported by folded hands, across the demi-steps leading up from the bottom of the room's central 'pit' to its main floor-level.

"*Vìrya I'ëà'b'*, bring down thy great-aunt and siblings, please," she added.

In a split-second, the neck of Karéin-Mayréij was first adorned by the tiny amulet; then her figure was covered by the dark-shimmering scale-mail, skull-cap, belt, gauntlets, foot-pieces and cape of *Vìrya Ahn'jë*, the flame-flicker of the latter, uncomfortably close to the floor. After this came the two lethal daggers, *Væran Ksé'l'ch'* and *Væran Ss'éth'ch'*, depositing themselves on her left and right legs, respectively, with their auras of heat and cold apparently not affecting their mistress' lower extremities.

Væran Fàiagàryuu, his cruel blade dimly alternating green-red-blue, came to rest upon the young-looking woman's upper-body, above *Vîrya Ahn'jë*; but he was then covered by the little shield, which sat atop the sword and body-armor like a weird, round sentinel.

"So... you just gonna catch forty winks like that... right there?" inquired a nonplussed Boatman.

With eyelids now closed, the alien-girl replied, "Indeed... I hope that my doing so, does not offend you. May I ask you eff-bee-ai people to guard the door, and... can you please move our new friend, to one of the beds in yonder sleeping-quarters, beside the bath-room. It will be more comfortable for him there – and perhaps he will heal faster, if he is not so close to my war-children."

"More and more amazing... even though it, like, *hurts* to be so close to her," observed Abruzzio, after shuffling backward in a near-panic, when the armor and weaponry made its appearance. "Hector... can you hear their voices?"

"Sì," confirmed the Mexican-American scientist. "Very faint... like little *señorita* Eee-Ab, there... but different. You know, Sylvia, I'd try to touch them – to talk, I mean, like we did with her, but... well, man, with that armor – it'd be like holdin' hands with a blowtorch! Hey, Karéin – don't want to interrupt your little nap there... but, you ain't gonna set fire to the place... right?"

"I have asked *Vîrya Ahn'jë* to, ahh, 'turn down the bar-bee-cue flame as low as it goes', so also have I done for *Væran Ksé'l'ch'*; oh, and his war-brother promises to extinguish any conflagration," lazily replied Karéin-Mayréij. "Besides... *Vîrya Ahn'jë* assures me that you have at least ten degrees more – as humans reckon – before her essence will ignite the elements within what I now lie upon... but keep some water handy, ahh, 'just in case'... oh-kay?"

"You can be *shore* of that," pledged Boatman. "You all don't mind if we use what's left in the toilet-tank, do you?"

"No problem," she answered, barely suppressing another yawn. "Funny, though... I do not remember needing sleep, like humans... *ach*, perhaps, friends, the changes are not all in one direction... dream with me, dear children..."

She fell silent, as eight more-than-humans exchanged "what-to-do-now" glances.

Finally, Wolf walked as close as he dared, looked down at the strange scene at his feet, and proposed,

"Tell you what... I'll get the fella's shoulders."

Hang In There, Ladies

"I'm hearing sounds from all directions – closer on the right and ahead, further away on the left," whispered Boyd, as he stepped back from the four-direction junction between the corridors. "Can't see anything, though."

Should we switch to the mind-talking-thing? sent Tanaka.

"Only if you don't want any feedback from yours truly," muttered Billings. "Funny, you know – I think I *had* the hang of it, when I was with Sari... but now, I'm 'receiving' you fine... it's just the 'sending'-part, that I'm having trouble with."

"Your feedback is *always* appreciated," under-stated Jacobson. "But as moving silently is one of our main advantages, you'll understand if we think rather than talk... right, Bob?"

"Did I mention I'm not much up on thinking, either?" retorted the salesman.

"Shut up, Bob, y'all gonna make me laugh out loud... which is a *bad* thing, I guess," quipped White, briefly turning his head to address the three adults, plus one somnolent child, behind him and Boyd.

He looked at Elissha. "How she doin'?" inquired the black ex-astronaut.

Billings shrugged.

"Sleeping like a baby – thought I felt a bit of a sweat on her forehead a minute ago... but it's probably just my imagination," he replied.

A worried look was on Tanaka's face, even though it was too dark for human eyes to have seen it.

"Okay – to the left," ordered Jacobson.

Rapidly, the group stole past the corner, heading off at a right-angle to the corridor from which they had entered this level of the underground prison.

"Damn – sounds of heavy shit *everywhere* down here," complained White, *sotto voce*, after they had gone no more than fifty feet or so. "Y'all hearin' that?"

"Yeah... but not like with Elissha," noted Tanaka. "Shouts, but not from torture – like somebody's arguing, or fighting – from more than one direction –"

"Shots?" asked Jacobson. "Like back to the right past the intersection?"

"Nope... don't think so, Captain, just voices –" started White.

"Flashlights – far-off – but dead-ahead!" warned Boyd.

A second later, he spoke up again, saying, "Funny – they were going everywhere, aways off... but then they just disappeared. Nothing there, now."

"Do we go back?" suggested Billings.

"Towards the shooting, you mean?" inquired the former Mars mission commander. "I don't think that'd be wise."

"So?" pressed the salesman.

Over a few seconds there was silence, save for a few more far-off gun-shots and distant human voices.

But presently, White proposed, "S'pose I'd best go on recce, then."

He got up from his crouch, but was countermanded by Boyd.

"Listen, man... I think I'm better off doing that," argued the ex-astronaut. "I don't have Bob's stealth ability, but you haven't seen my own little dark-trick, yet... if I get into trouble up there, I'm pretty sure I can turn off the lights long enough to confuse the Bejeezus out of 'em and get back here. That is – unless Bob wants to volunteer for the mission."

"What do *you* think?" defiantly countered Billings. "I already *got* a job!"

He rubbed the little girl's back with genuine affection.

"Hey, Bob – y'all learned the first lesson of bein' in the Army," joked White.

"And what'd *that* be?" idly inquired the salesman.

"Easy," replied the African-American ex-astronaut. "Don't 'volunteer' for nothin'."

Billings sighed, wearily.

"Here I go," announced Boyd.

With his gun in classic military 'ready-to-fire' stance, the former Mars mission pilot advanced cautiously, but rapidly, down the corridor. His enhanced senses were pressed to the limit, as he tried to keep the power-activating thoughts available, in the back of his mind.

He passed a door on the right.

Screams – pain – back in there – but they've got to be through a bunch of walls, judging from the faintness of the sounds.

Better not tell the Professor... she'll go off on the 'do-gooder' thing...

Shit, Brent, what's wrong *with you – how can you just turn your back – no, gotta concentrate on the objective...*

Okay – the door twenty feet ahead, on the left – that has to be the one that I saw the flashlights around... right?

Whoa... voices, lots of 'em, damn clear now – what the?

Sounds like Spanish... well, so what – there must be Latinos in here, gangsters, some poor bugger nationalist that the CIA snatched out of Cuba, after we invaded the second time...

Moans, man, bad *vibes, hurt, sorrow... omigod –*

What's that*... behind the door and the wall, but no doubt about it...*

One of us? No, wait... more than... one of us?

There was more shouting from behind the door, and, weirdly, something that sounded like singing. Boyd heard footsteps.

Better get the H out of here, he realized.

Stepping backward almost as fast as he had approached, Brent Boyd, ex-U.S. Air Force Best and Brightest, disappeared into the tenebrous quarter-light from which he had come.

Perhaps five seconds later, the door opened, but *this* time – mercifully there were no flashlights; for had those inside been so equipped and had they aimed in his direction, the astronaut would have been plainly-visible, at least for the split-second before he could have triggered his first, new-found ability.

Boyd didn't know much Spanish, but he could make out something that sounded like a curse, along with words like, *"No hay nadie"*.

The door slammed shut, as the ex-astronaut retreated back down to the place where the others had encamped. He noticed that White had gone to the back of the group, and was now covering the rear, toward the intersection.

"Well?" softly demanded Tanaka.

"You're not going to *believe* this, Professor," responded Boyd, "But there are some of *us*, down there. I think they're in the room with the flashlights."

"Some of 'us'?" remarked Billings. "We, are all here... that is if you count the kid, as being 'us'."

"No, Bob," counseled Tanaka, her voice raising with excitement. "What he means is, 'some of... *us*'."

"As in, 'us', as distinct from *Homo Sapiens*," added Jacobson.

"In other words – 'jackpot'!" commented White, never taking his eyes off the corridor in the direction from which they had come. "Fuckin' 'bout *time*, if y'all ask me. Now all we gotta do is figure a way *out* of this-here shithole."

The salesman stood and puzzled for a second or two, then, a look of shock, mixed with apprehension, appeared on his face.

"Holy *Sh –!*" he exclaimed, rather too loudly. "Brent – Major, I mean –" he stammered, *"Who?* They *okay?* Listen – we gotta go *get* 'em –"

"Wait... *wait* just a second," cautioned Jacobson. "If we want to get these people – not to mention ourselves – out of here, alive, we have to think this through. Brent – full report, please. Are you sure you're right about the, uhh, 'others'?"

"As sure as I am of *anything* down in this hell-hole, sir," replied the ex-astronaut. "As I came back down the corridor, I checked for it carefully... I concentrated on it, and I could *feel* your presence – all of you except Elissha, that is, perhaps what I'm sensing your 'auras', or the, uhh, *Fire* that you're giving off, or whatever – and it was *definitely* the same sensation when I got down near that door. Incidentally – it felt like there were two distinct individuals, in there... that's the good news. The *bad* news is, the place is crawling with Spanish-speaking male voices –"

"How many?" interrupted the former Mars mission commander.

Boyd thought for a second or two, then offered, "Hard to say... but probably five to eight of them, at the very least – there were several voices, multiple tones. Some of them were arguing, and – I know how this is going to sound – but there was singing. Like they were having a party, or something."

"Armed?" asked White.

"Couldn't tell," answered the ex-pilot. "But I wouldn't bet *against* it."

"Based on Brent's account of what's going on, further up the corridor," opined Jacobson, "Unlike the last few situations where we've run into other parties down here, there seems to be a chance that whoever these guys are, they aren't guards – and they may not be as well-armed as us. That may imply a change in our tactics, in this case... especially because if we just burst in there shooting, we could be endangering the lives of the, uhh 'non-humans' who Brent claims he sensed, behind the door."

"All fine and dandy, Commander... but what are you suggesting, that we just knock and say, 'excuse me, but have you got any space-aliens in there'?" argued Billings. "But whatever we do, we've got to make sure that none of, err, us 'space-people', wind up dead. Remember... if Sari shows up and finds out that we could have saved Tommy, but screwed things up so badly that he got shot –"

"Umm-humm," confirmed Tanaka. "But you've answered your own question there, Bob – we've got nothing to lose by knocking on the door and politely asking to be let in – maybe the people in there are escapees, just like us. They might even welcome us... I think it's worth a try. How about you, Sam?"

"I forgot to mention," noted Boyd, "That I was receiving some, uhh, pretty *bad* thoughts, from inside that room – vague – unfocused, not mental-communication like *we* can do... but it sure felt like someone in there was not enjoying himself –"

"Like they were being tortured?" immediately interrupted Billings.

"No... not exactly... if I'm interpreting it right," answered the ex-astronaut.

"You *sure*?" pressed the salesman.

Boyd held up his hands in protest.

"What do you want me to *say*, Bob?" he complained. "I was trained to fly fighter-planes and spacecraft with a little light auto-rifle duty on the side – not to play remote-access psychologist, for God's sake."

"Yeah... okay," relented Billings, albeit unenthusiastically.

"Look," continued Jacobson, "Maybe the best way of dealing with this is, we send one person down there to knock on the door, if possible go in there and find out what the hell's actually going *on* – volunteers would be appreciated, of course – then that person can evaluate the situation. Remember that if we use anyone other than Bob, our 'scout' can call silently for help, if –"

"I'm not into 'volunteering'," interjected Billings, "And even if I *was* – or if I *could* do the mental walkie-talkie thing – over my dead body am I gonna get captured by those Gestapo types and put up on a gurney, again... right, sweetie?"

He looked down at Elissha.

"Geez, Jacobson... I dunno about the kid," he added, worriedly. "She's sleeping like a log, and she's breathing fine, but..."

Tanaka put her hand on the child's forehead.

"Damn," she cursed. "Bob's right – there's *definitely* something wrong with her, but I can't tell exactly what it is... her skin feels clammy. We have to get Elissha some real medical help... sooner rather than later..."

The Eurasian scientist's voice trailed off, in obvious frustration.

"Is she in immediate danger, Cheri?" demanded Jacobson.

"Don't know, Sam," muttered the woman. "Just don't know."

"All the more reason why we need to get this next thing over with as quickly as possible, so we can at least get out of the corridor... I *hope*," sighed the Mars mission commander. "The question is, 'who goes up and knocks'?"

"I'll do it," quickly volunteered Tanaka.

"I was gonna suggest –" started White.

"It's okay, Devon," reassured the scientist. "Remember – to whoever's in there, I'll probably look like a single, unarmed woman... nothing *threatening*, kind of thing?"

"*Riight*," said White, with a wan smile. "Well, Professor – don't take this the wrong way... but I wouldn't want to meet y'all in a dark alley... you know?"

"Let's hope I don't have to show anyone why," answered Tanaka.

"Now that *that's* settled," stated Jacobson, "I think the best thing to do, from a tactical point-of-view, is for someone – Brent, I guess – to go down the corridor past the door, just far enough to be out of the range of human night-sight... that way we can cover the forward-approaches, while the rest of us wait the same distance away, on the other, nearer side of the door. Devon, keep covering our rear-flank... okay?"

"Got it," affirmed White.

"Let's get going," requested Boyd, and without much further ado, he and Tanaka set out down the corridor, followed by the others, about ten meters further behind.

Soon, the ex-astronaut had disappeared into the shadows on the far side of the door, while Tanaka stood in front of it.

Brent, she sent.

You were right...

Same feeling, as when we found Bob – weaker, but more than one –

Stand firm, O my brothers and sisters, the ordeal will end – we're coming, coming for you –

Slowly, as if pondering the consequences of so doing, she extended her arm, hesitated for a second or two more, and then lightly rapped on the portal.

"Hello?" she called, still keeping the volume as low as possible.

The chaotic noises from the other side of the door ceased immediately.

"*¿Que va?*" sounded a gruff voice.

"It's me – Cherie Tanaka – I'm outside, I'm alone... I'm unarmed," announced the woman, trying to sound convincing. "Please let me in. I'm, uhh, afraid of being all by myself."

Yeah, Professor... y'all tell 'em, unhelpfully sent White.

There were muffled, Spanish-sounding voices, as if a debate of some kind had broken out. This was followed by a brief period of silence.

Then the door opened.

The scientist squinted and raised a hand over her eyes, as she was bathed in the illumination of two or three flashlights.

Then, abruptly, someone from inside the room seized her other arm, roughly pulling her inside.

The door slammed shut.

Cherie! sent an alarmed Jacobson.

For two or three agonizing seconds, there was no response; but, eventually, a thought washed over all the more-than-humans in the outside corridor.

I'm okay, she broadcasted.

Latinos – banditos – rough-looking – five of them – three big white guys with beards, muscles and tattoos – and...

Two black females in the corner, cowering – they're *the ones, Sam, our dear kin –*

Billings tugged on Jacobson's sleeve.

He whispered, "Ask her what they look like... the girls, I mean."

There was confused, rapid talk – in both Spanish and English – coming from inside the room.

Are you safe? sent the big man.

Are they armed? And Bob wants to know about the females.

"Hey there, take it *slow...* okay?" came Tanaka's voice, from inside. "Lots of time to have some... fun..."

A second later, her mind again spoke silently to her compatriots.

Three guesses about what kind *of fun,* she sent.

Hard to move, act, talk and mind-think at the same time...

Don't see any guns, but they all got knives... woman's thin, thirties, girl's a teenager...

Now a mind that rarely spoke, sounded a clarion-call.

Whitney! Melissa! sent Billings.

It's me – the asshole with the gut and the car – hang in there, ladies!

And it was followed by a psychic-signature that the more-than-humans – except perhaps for one of them – had never before heard.

Lord... that y'all? she called out.

Take us now, Lord – we's sufferin', Lord –

He has heard your prayers, sisters, came the powerful, utterly-faithful thoughts of Devon White, directed toward the room.

Be strong, y'all... deliverance is on its way!

"You can take 'em off yourself – or I'll do it *for* you, bitch," growled a gruff, Anglo-Saxon voice, on the other side of the door. "*Pretty* little bitch... ain't you? I *like* 'em slim, you know."

Uh-oh, sent Boyd, trying to maintain his conscious concentration on surveillance of the darkening corridor in front, while he tried to simultaneously keep track of events from behind and to his left.

If that's the Professor *he's trying to molest –*

Just call it 'ball-lightenin', yo! mentally-replied White.

Even a blind man, could have seen the evil smile that showed on the black astronaut's face.

"Fuck *you, puto!*" came a Hispanic voice. "Who said she was yours?"

There was a 'thud' from inside.

Down on my duff, beside the girl and woman, came Tanaka's mind-message.

God, that guy can't have had a bath in –

"Well... I thought you had your fill with them nigger-bitches over there in the corner, *hombre,*" argued the first voice. "Besides... she looks almost half-white, 'cept for them dink-eyes on her – only fair that she gets a nice *pink* pork-sword... not some damn brown one –"

"Listen – there's something you need to know –" spoke Tanaka.

"Shut the fuck *up!*" demanded the first, Anglo-Saxon voice. "Don't you know the score here, bitch? Better be *nice* – or I just might let Mister Taco-Gangsta here do what he wants... and he ain't nearly so *gentle,* as me. Don't take *my* word for it – just ask them two ghetto-spooks 'side you... they'll tell you how it goes."

Dear sisters, sent Tanaka.

Come close.

Drink from me.

Sam – on the count of three, I raise the shield.

We're in the far right corner.

Do whatever you want.

Understood, came back the reply.

"Come *here, chiquita,*" sounded a Latino voice. "¡Gonna have *una fiesta, tu conmigo!*"

One...

Two...

The salesman, along with all save the humans, felt the *Fire* surging, from within the room.

Party's over, motherfuckers! he thought, neither knowing nor caring if the message was received.

Three.

And... 'Shield'!

"¡Carajo!" shouted a second, different, Hispanic voice. "¿Que pasa? –"

Ooo – ai-ooo – ooo-ai, came Tanaka's now-familiar, wailing song.

Jacobson's blue-green-flashing boot smashed the door flat off its hinges, and – in the next second after he barged into the room beyond – a lesser man would have been immediately unnerved by the large group of big, tough-looking gangsters and street-thugs, into whose domain he had intruded; but the Mars mission commander, no mundane human he, just stood and glowered.

Three or four of the ruffians reached for concealed knives.

A half-second later, in dashed Boyd and White, with automatic-rifles very clearly at the ready.

"Make one wrong move," yelled Jacobson, "And we shoot!"

"What the *fuck* –" exclaimed one of the white thugs.

"Okay, Bob – you can come in, now," called Jacobson.

This place was different from most of the others, being much larger, and more rectangular in layout, compared to the square dimensions of the other ones. It might – at one time – have been a conference- or meeting- area, because there was a long, oval table in its center, surrounded by ten or more comfortable-looking reclining-chairs, with a coffee-and-condiments serving-area on one side.

On the far, smaller-length wall, along with the familiar, ominous signs of mayhem in the form of dull, red-brown blood-stains, there was an audio-visual screen of some type, as well as various dials and controls embedded in the table.

To the interest of several of the more-than-human party, the table also contained a large number of randomly-distributed binders and loose paperwork, as if whomever had been using these documents had to leave in a hurry.

Billings, with the child glued to his shoulder, shuffled in. His gaze fell upon Tanaka and two African-American females, all three still encased in a shimmering force-field.

"Oh God – *Whitney – Melissa!*" he cried. "Professor – let me *in*, let me talk to them –"

Tanaka arose, and in the same instant, her bubble disappeared, while Billings, still with child in arms, dashed over to the dazed, disoriented-looking black women.

The salesman got down on his knees and, between poorly-concealed sobs, began to softly whimper something to the two.

As she walked by the gangsters to rejoin Boyd, Jacobson and White, Tanaka approached the big, heavily-tattooed and bearded white biker-type with a huge beer-belly, who had, only a few moments before, been man-handling her.

"You've been *awfully* lucky today," offered the Asian-American scientist.

"Yeah? How you figure that?" he replied, uncertainly.

"Because," indifferently mentioned Tanaka, "If you had actually tried to *rape* me... you'd be a pile of ashes, by now."

"That's *bullshit*, bitch!" he bluffed.

"Sam," she remarked, "We need to seal the portal... don't we?"

As a bemused Jacobson nodded assent, the scientist's eyes started to glow, causing the biker to reflexively take a step backward. Her telekinetic-power caused the broken-in door to self-levitate back to a closed position, and a second later, she extended her index-finger in the precise direction of where the latch and lock of the door had been.

"*Sword!*" she inveighed.

A sizzling, multi-colored lightening-bolt jumped from Tanaka's finger-tip, striking the mechanism straight-on. It smoked and melted, leaving flicks of flame hither and yon.

"Devon?" she solicited. "Oops! Looks like I started a *fire*, there... *my* bad. Mind cooling it off?"

"Why... my *pleasure*, Professor," he insouciantly replied.

White walked over to a point about two meters in front of the door. He stared intently, his outstretched hands arranged, claw-like.

"Sno-Kone," was *his* invocation; and in a half-second, a suffocating, freezing blast washed over the portal, icing everything within close proximity into an solid mass.

Even as far-away as Tanaka and the others were standing, the super-Antarctic cold of the black ex-astronaut's attack made them wince and involuntarily step back.

"Of course... if y'all don't like that whole 'ashes' thing," challenged White to the biker, with a dismissive shrug, "I can set y'all up with my *own*, special English. 'We be chillin'... don't you know?"

"What's *he* do?" asked one of the other white bandits, pointing at Boyd.

"Wanna *see?*" threatened the ex-pilot, stepping aggressively forward, slinging his gun over the shoulder and preparing to roll up his sleeves.

"Uhh... *no*," muttered the gangster.

"*Smart* decision," hissed Tanaka, through tightly-clenched teeth. "I'll bet there would've been even *less*, left of you."

"But look at the plus side... you'd have a real *nice* shine," maliciously commented Boyd.

"What the fuck *is* you, man?" demanded one of the Latino gangsters, perhaps the leader. "You some kind of fuckin' crazy-ass guards, or somethin'?"

"Oh no – we're not guards... far *from* it," explained Jacobson. "As a matter of fact... we've been fighting a sort of war with the assholes who run this place, ever since we were unlucky enough to end up here."

"Yeah... but you got them guns," argued one of the bikers, gesturing at the rifles that Boyd, White and Jacobson were carrying. "Same as them gay-boys from GrayWar is slingin'."

Jacobson walked slowly and calmly over to his interrogator.

The former Mars mission commander was only slightly shorter than the ruffian, but – even with the slight gut that had been acquired, courtesy of too much good food and too little exercise, after arriving back on Earth – the other man probably outweighed Jacobson by a good fifty pounds, or more.

Despite this, there wasn't the slightest hint of fear or intimidation in the commander's eyes.

"Look – maybe we're not 'communicating', here," indifferently stated Jacobson. "Frankly... neither I nor any of my team gives a *shit* about who you think we are... and we've already killed enough people on the way down here so that a few more, won't trouble us in the *slightest*. So if I were you, my friend, I'd shut that big damn mouth of yours –"

Sam... cautioned Tanaka's mind.

Let me handle this my *way*, retorted Jacobson's own.

These guys only understand one kind of language.

The biker yelled "*fuck you!*" and lunged at the former Mars commander's throat with a crude, home-made dagger, and, despite a quick dodge, actually landed a strike, tearing Jacobson's right tunic-sleeve and drawing some blood.

This triumph was short-lived, however; for in the next second, there was an unpleasant cracking-sound, as a blue-tinted, more-than-human boot hit the biker's left knee, sending the thug crashing to the ground, alternately cursing and moaning in pain.

Then, Jacobson's kick again made contact, propelling the crippled biker – who must have weighed two-fifty or more, if he weighed an ounce – at least three mans'-lengths toward the rest of the criminals.

White and Boyd stepped forward, brandishing their rifles.

"Back *off*, muthafuckers!" commanded the black ex-astronaut. "Get yo' asses in the far corner there... 'fore we forget that 'thou shalt not kill'-thing."

The Mars mission commander pointed at his groaning, sweating victim.

"Presumably, you buggers aren't so stupid as to not get what your chances are, if you end up like *him*... and there's a lot more where *that* came from," he growled. "Who *wants* some?"

Mutely, the other gangsters started to slowly retreat.

"Brent – Devon – cover 'em," ordered Jacobson. "I've got to see what's going on with Bob and Cherie, over there."

With grim determination, White and Boyd nodded, never taking their eyes off the muttering, scowling group of thugs, who had moved back to the far quarter of the place.

Now Jacobson hurried over to where Billings – the child still draped over his shoulder – had knelt in front of the two black women.

"*Melissa... Whitney...* come on – *say* something..." pleaded the salesman.

"Traumatic shock," diagnosed Tanaka. "Their *eyes* – just staring."

And it was true. Both of the African-American women just looked vacantly at their rescuers, as if on some kind of perverse drug-trip.

"Cherie, I'm no expert," opined Jacobson, "But don't people come out of a state like this, eventually?"

"*Sure* they do, Sam," replied the scientist. "But it can take hours... sometimes, days. You want to hang around here that long, with that crew of white and brown trash cooling their heels in the corner, all the while?"

She looked down, compassionately.

"They're so... *beautiful*, you know," she quietly remarked, running her hand through the elder female's hair. "I see it, I *feel* it, deep within them... our beautiful, noble sisters..."

A tear showed in Tanaka's eye.

"So what do we do?" asked the salesman, grasping for straws. "Professor, *do* something!"

The Mars mission science-officer closed her eyes and pondered for a few seconds, then spoke up. "Break through – yeah, that's it – *has* to be it. Bob, Sam – would you back off a bit, please... not sure how this might affect Elissha."

She got down on one knee, in front of the two dazed females.

"Yeah... okay," complied Billings.

Both men stepped backward, until they were halfway between Tanaka and the Boyd-White team, who still stood on guard against the crowd of gangsters.

"*Shield*," spoke Tanaka, and instantly, her shimmering bubble appeared in place.

Now the minds of all the more-than-humans echoed with the Eurasian-American scientist's escalating entreaties.

Sisters... wake up... hear me...

No – you can't *go back,* can't *hide...*

We know *it hurts, but the worst is over...*

My mind reaches to you, sisters...

Come out!

A wave of pain, fear and resentment washed over the group, to the point where White and Boyd almost blacked out.

The gangsters sensed this, and were about to advance upon seeing the two ex-astronauts become dizzy and flinch momentarily; but then Boyd and White shook off the effect, and again the guns were raised into firing-position.

The bubble vanished.

There was a moan from the direction of the three females.

"Ohh... sweet baby *Jaysus!*" came a teenage voice. "We still here – still *here* – in the bad-place, Momma," it whimpered. "*Hold* me, Momma!"

"Take her," ordered Billings, as he quickly handed the girl to a well-understanding Jacobson.

"Hey... *hey!*" consoled the salesman, as he dashed over to the two black women and knelt beside Tanaka, in front of them. "Whitney – Melissa – it's *me,* Bob – Bob Billings –"

The teenager's eyes looked up, and instant amazement was on her face.

"*Bob!*" she exclaimed. "That really *y'all*? Oh yeah – praise *Gawd!* But... what y'all *doin'* down here, Mista Billins?"

Billings, his eyes watering, tightly embraced each of the women, in turn.

"Pretty much the same thing as you and your mother, sweetheart – pretty much the same thing," he gasped. "But thank to *these* damn fine people," – he gestured at a beaming Tanaka, Jacobson, White and Boyd – "I – we – we've got a chance... hope..."

He looked at the African-American woman, who was now sitting up straight, clearly fully awake, but also, strangely silent.

"Well, Whitney," mentioned the salesman, "I know you and your daughter have been through a lot, but... don't I get at least a 'hello', for showing up with the Sam Jacobson and Company Cavalry, here?"

The woman opened her mouth, but all that came out were gurgling, incomprehensible, baby-talk sounds.

Melissa looked down at the floor.

"Momma ain't got no *tongue* left," she quietly explained.

Unable to deal with this, Billings involuntarily looked away.

He began to sob.

Tanaka's shoulders slumped; then, with furiously pursed lips, she hissed, "Just when I *thought* I had seen every *possible* kind of cruelty..."

She held out a hand to Claremont.

"Dear sister," spoke the scientist, with chords of power playing through half-human minds, "We'll make good on this – we *will* give you your voice back. This I promise with all my heart... but now, I must speak to your mind –"

Whitney Claremont – blessed friend of Bob Billings and the wise and great Storied Watcher, savior of Earth, Angel of Fire... do you hear me? sent Tanaka.

With an astonished, but informed, expression, the black woman nodded.

She was about to try to stand, but was dissuaded by Billings.

"Hey – take it *easy* there, Whitney," he cautioned. "They gave me the whole treatment... and if what you and Melissa got was anything like *that*, you'll need a few minutes to regain your strength."

He paused for a second, then looked at the woman, and cried, "You'll sing again, Whitney – I *know* you will!"

"They did *awful* things to Momma 'n me, Mista Billins," whimpered the teenager. "They beat me up, used them metal-thangs... burned me, cut me open... it hurt *bad* – so bad! Ah prayed to the Lord and begged Him to take me home, but all ah got was a nice feelin', as if He was sendin' me His peace... but then they tied me down, and they... they..."

Her chin quivered, and again, the salesman rushed in, to hold her tight.

"Melissa... Whitney..." he managed, in a choking voice, forcing out every word. "If I hadn't gotten you in with Sari and me... up north, I mean... I didn't know that any of this was going to happen – no – that's not right – she *told* me, warned me... sort of... but I didn't *listen*, didn't think it'd *happen* this way! God – I'm *so* sorry... please, *please*... if you can find it in your hearts to forgive me..."

"It ain't yo' fault, Mister Bob... we both knows that," answered the girl, compassionately. "Right, Momma?"

Claremont nodded, then planted a kiss on Billing's beard-stubble cheek.

"Thank you – *thank you* so much – you don't know how much that means to me, ladies," he quietly replied. "And I'll get you both out of this... I *swear* it!"

"Listen," interrupted Tanaka, "I know you all should have some time to grieve together, and we'll make sure that you get it... but right now, I need to know – these guys that Majors Boyd and White – they're the two with the guns, by the way, and they're on our side – but the gangsters that had you in here, before we arrived, did they *do* anything to you? Anything... *bad*, I mean."

"Just th' *usual*," muttered Melissa. "Y'all knows what ah mean."

"*Really*," coldly replied Tanaka. "Which ones?"

"Don't honestly 'member," stated the teenager. "Momma 'n ah, we's pretty much used to it, by now – 'least that's what ah thought, but guess ah just passed out, after th' second or third one went at me... weren't the *first* time, since they put us in them black cars, back in Tucson, y'know..."

Tanaka stood up. She addressed the girl.

"Melissa... you said that you couldn't tell which of these bastards raped you, is that right?" she requested, neutrally.

"Yep, that 'bout the size of it," confirmed the teenager.

"*Well* then," remarked Tanaka, through clenched teeth, "*That* being the case, the only fair thing to do would be to vaporize all of –"

Her eyes were glowing and there was a furious look on her face.

To the astonishment and worry of the two African-American women, this was accompanied by bolts of energy crawling up and down the scientist's trunk.

Her hand was raised, pointing at the gangsters, who alternately cursed and tried to crouch.

"Okay – *okay* – Cherie!" quickly interrupted Jacobson. "*Enough!* I *know* what you mean... but there's a difference between 'justifiable homicide' and 'premeditated murder' – right? Leave them alone, unless they're stupid enough to provoke us, on their own. They're not worth wasting a Watt of *Amaiish* on."

"Well... I'd be willin' to waste a few bullets," muttered White. "I'm sure I wouldn't miss a clip or two, don't you know."

"*Am* – what?" asked Melissa, as she wobbled up to a standing position.

"*Amaiish*," explained Tanaka, with her glowing eyes still focused malevolently on the gaggle of gangsters in the far corner. "It's the limitless power of the mighty Storied Watcher – Karéin-Mayréij by name – who you and Bob knew as 'Sari Tanak'... and it's what almost certainly kept you alive, in captivity down here. You're one of *us*, Melissa, and so is your mother; you're part of the new, better-than-human race. Now tell me... what, should I do with the bastards over there, on the other side of the room? Fast or slow? I can make the hurt that they inflicted on *you*, look like a fucking walk in the *park*..."

The teenager walked over to position herself next to the scientist, studying with fascination the weird energy that roiled throughout the latter's body.

"Miz Cherie," murmured Melissa, "Ah knows what y'all's fixin' to do – an' ah gots to admit, wid what they done to Momma 'n me, they'd deserve it... but..."

"Umm-hmm," grimly confirmed Tanaka, her finger still threatening doom.

"We's *Christians*, in our fam'ly," noted the teenager. "And in the Bible, it say that we 'sposed to forgive people – even if they sin real bad, 'gainst us – like, twenny time a day... or was it fifty... oh... ah forgets. So ah guess ah'm aksin' y'all to let 'em be. If that's alright."

Billings noticed that Claremont's hands were folded in prayer-fashion.

"Yeah... alright..." reluctantly relented Tanaka.

Slowly, she lowered her arm and extinguished the surge of her alien-energy.

"God *bless* you, Melissa," breathed the salesman, wiping a tear. "You and your mother... you'll get even dirty ol' *Bob*, past those pearly-gates."

Claremont rolled her eyes, but she none the less sent Billings a smile of acknowledgement.

And... 'Amen', came the mental voice of Devon White.

I think that's what the Angel would say, soul sisters.

"You have these beautiful, merciful, noble more-than-women who you abused, to thank for your lives," called the Eurasian-American scientist, in the direction of the gangsters. "But next time... I *won't* ask for a second opinion! *Got* that, scumbags?"

Sullenly, the thugs and brigands in the corner stood and waited.

"Listen, y'all," half-shouted White. "I'm gonna take down my gun and deal with my homies, but Brent still got a bead on you – make one move, y'all *daid* before y'all make it to the door. Y'all understand what I'm sayin'?"

The gangsters glowered, but a couple of them nodded.

"Okay," spoke White, as he lowered the rifle and went over to Claremont and her daughter.

By now, the black woman had managed to stand up.

The African-American ex-astronaut extended a vigorous handshake to the two newfound escape-party members.

"I'm Devon White, used to be U.S. Air Force," he announced. "Damn nice to meet y'all, sisters... and if it means anythin', I'm a Christian too, so we already got that in common... this-here guy with the other gun, he's Brent Boyd, Major, that is. Cap'n Jacobson – he's carryin' Elissha, she's a kid that we rescued one level up – he's in charge of the whole show, and I guess y'all already know Professor Tanaka and good ol' Bob, we sprang him further back. Should I give 'em the lowdown, Captain?"

"Please do," agreed Jacobson. "But keep it brief... I bet Brent's arm is getting tired, holding that gun up, I mean. Bob – you mind taking Elissha, again? I need to be in on this."

"Oh... sure," answered the salesman.

He received the child and walked off by a few paces, gently bouncing the little girl in mock-father fashion.

"Not half as 'tired' as my trigger finger is 'itchy'," warned Boyd. "It's not so heavy when you use a little mind-push to levitate it... you know?"

"Well, there you *go*," said White, with his cheery smile. "So here it is. See, we – the Commander, Brent, the Professor and yours truly, also a Russian guy who y'all ain't met yet – we was all on that trip to Mars that y'all might have read about awhile ago. We dug up Little Miss Storied Watcher, took her to Earth... then she did her thing and saved this sorry old planet... but after that, we kinda lost track of her, I guess. We're still not sure what happened next, but she must have showed up in the U.S. of A. and had some kind of, uhh, *misunderstandin'* with the President... because all of a sudden they's at war or somethin', and anybody – y'all, Bob, your kids, or us – who had met her, the Government, they come to think of us as, uhh, 'weapons', to be used to take her down with –"

"What y'all mean, Major Devon?" interrupted Melissa. "Sari, she *wicked* powerful – ain't no *way* they could do *nothin'* to her –"

"I hear y'all, sister," replied White, "But y'all stay with me a minute here... okay? See... looks like the muthas who are runnin' this place – that's the CIA, by the way – they cooked up some idea that if they could hurt *us*, that would hurt Karéin, too, long-distance wise –"

"Who *that*?" interrupted the teenager. "Y'all mean Sari?"

"Yeah – that's her real name," explained the black ex-astronaut.

"Although, while we were all together back on the *Eagle* spacecraft," added Tanaka, "She *did* mention that she apparently has had twenty to fifty different, 'real', names, over the ages."

"Well... *whatever* she's callin' herself these days," continued White, "Them guys in the Government threw everythin' that they *had* against her, torturin' us-wise, I mean – and though we can't be one hundred per cent sure, it don't look like it worked... so their next step might have been to just kill us –"

"That don' make no *sense*, Major Devon!" protested Melissa. "As the Lord's mah witness... we ain't done *nothin'* 'gainst the Gov'ment!"

"Neither did *we*, honey – me and my space-team, I mean," commented Jacobson. "None of us can think of a good reason for the Government's actions, in this case... but what we *can* be certain of, is... 'we're on our own', now. At least we have each other, and, Melissa, Bob wasn't bluffing, when he promised you that he – and we – we'd get you and your mother, the rest of your loved-ones, too, out of here –"

Claremont, her eyes squinting in frustration, tried desperately to talk.

"Ah thinks ah knows what Momma want to say," offered Melissa. "Like, 'where *is* we, 'zactly'... an', 'where is Curtis'? Oh, an' Tommy, too, ah 'spose."

"Where *is* we, sister?" answered White. "Well, I'd say, 'Hell'... but if y'all want somethin' more precise, we're several hundred feet down below the surface of an island, up Alaska-way... nice little prison that the CIA set up to be 'out of sight, out of mind'. And as for your bro'... I'm sorry, we don't quite know – but we *ain't* gonna stop lookin' 'till we find him... Tommy, too. Just like we all promised, hope to die, that we'd keep lookin' until we found y'all and Mrs. Claremont, there. Y'understand?"

"Yessir," acknowledged the teenager, with a serious, grateful look.

She hesitated for a second or two, then, uneasily, inquired, "But... ah means... if we's all that ways far down, an' we got them spies 'gainst us, maybe th' whole *Army*, too... how we gonna make it back out?"

"I'll be honest with you, Melissa," replied Jacobson, "We haven't figured all of that out... yet. However, it's not as if we're totally helpless, either. We've got guns, some other military weapons, but even if we didn't... you *saw* what Devon and the Professor were capable of doing... right?"

"At first ah thinkin it was, like, in a dream – with th' door, ah means, Mister Captain Sam," answered Melissa. "But then ah wake up, an' ah sees Miz Cherie, pointin' at them guys, and... well... it's like in them comic-movies that they got on Curtis' little player-thang."

Tanaka moved to be in front of the teenager, then embraced her arms just below the shoulders, in motherly fashion.

A young African-American jaw dropped, upon seeing the glow in the Professor's eyes, accompanied by a surreal, soft, background *ooo-ai* melody.

"Melissa... dear daughter... beloved sister," counseled the scientist, "I'll say to you, what was said to Bob, only a few short hours ago : the blessing of the Storied Watcher lies upon you and your mother, as well. You're already *so* much more than an ordinary human being,... and you will become more powerful still, in time. I don't know how you'll evolve – each of us, has his or her own special alien-ability – for example Devon's is cold, Sam's is, uhh, 'ass-kicking' – but *trust* me, child – it grows within you now. I can *feel* it. You're going to be a *super-heroine*, Melissa. All you have to do, is stay alive, long enough for your powers to show up. How does that make you feel?"

"Ah'm not sure, Miss Cherie," fidgeted the teenager. "But if ah know mah brother, ah bet Curtis, he be *wicked* happy 'bout it."

Claremont rolled her eyes and tried to say something.

"The Professor speaks the truth, Melissa," stated Jacobson. "Your exposure to Karéin-Mayréij – especially as she considered you to be a friend – has set you on the same path as the rest of us... that is, 'to go where no human has before'. We don't know where it's all going to end... but for now, we all have to make the best of a bad situation and hope that the powers the Storied Watcher has given us, will be enough to get us out of here. And – speaking of that – Cherie, however much we'd like to give those bastards in the corner their due reward, we've got to be *practical;* they're of little use to us, and we can't turn our backs on them for so much as a second... my vote would be just to kick 'em out.. With how things are down here, they probably won't get very far, anyway. What you say?"

Tanaka's visage clouded.

She hesitated, then replied, "It goes against everything that I believe in, justice-wise; and I don't think it should be *us*, that makes the decision, particularly since it wasn't *us* who these sons of bitches abused. I think it should be Whitney and Melissa who decide."

The former Mars mission commander turned to address Claremont.

"Whitney," he quietly requested, "It's up to you and your daughter – we could tie 'em up, or we could give 'em a taste of what they did to both of you, or... we could simply kick them out the door and let nature take its course. There's three options, for you. Why don't you hold up the corresponding finger of your right hand – that way we'll know what you want us to do."

Claremont, though tongueless, still managed to let out a grunt that sounded like a hoarse, guttural laugh.

She held up her middle digit in the classic "third-finger salute" style.

"Momma say, 'let 'em go... and let the Lawd deal with 'em," related Melissa.

A knowingly smiling Jacobson nodded.

"I like your way of putting that, Whitney," he chuckled. "And your daughter makes a good translator – I've been told that half of *that* profession, is communicating what someone *should* be saying... as opposed to what they actually *did* say."

He turned to Boyd and White.

"Listen, guys," said Jacobson, "Cherie and I have been consulting with our two new party-members, here, and we've reached a tentative decision to kick those guys in the corner out of here, but to take no more steps against them. Do any of you – you too, Bob – have an objection?"

"I was kind of hoping that one or more of 'em would try something funny," muttered Billings, "Just so you could give them another taste of that boot of yours, Jacobson. But I guess it's up to Whitney and Meliss... so, yeah... go ahead. Less I have to look at those assholes, the better."

"'Long as y'all know, next time I run into 'em down here, I might be shootin' first and askin' questions later, Captain," unenthusiastically offered White.

Boyd just nodded, with a cold look on his face.

Jacobson walked over to the edge of the table and accosted the gangsters.

"Hey, all of you – yeah, you *heard* me!" he called. "Here's your *second* lucky break, today : Melissa and Whitney – they're the two women who you raped, in case you didn't bother to ask their names – they've decided to live up to their beliefs and let you just walk out of here. So –"

One of the Latino gangsters interrupted.

"An what if we don' wanna go, *chico*?" he defiantly shouted back.

"Oh... that's *easy*," answered the space-commander, his eyes steely-serious. "If you aren't out that door within five seconds of when I say, 'go'... we'll simply *kill* you."

"Seven of us and only four *hombres* among youze," challenged the gangster. "I cut you up *good... puto!*"

"I *heard* that!" hissed Tanaka, stepping forward, with the *Amaiish*-bolts dancing through her body.

A second later, she was joined by Boyd, who had slung his gun over a shoulder. The ex-astronaut's hands were enveloped by a dull, whitish-yellow glow. Thin wisps of smoke issued from his palms and finger-tips.

He held his hands up toward the gangsters, and bellowed, "*Midnight*".

Instantly, the far corner disappeared into a black shroud of nothingness. It looked similar to – but was somehow slightly different from – the power that had earlier been demonstrated by Billings; with the latter, you could see past the hidden more-than-human, but with the Boyd dark-trick, it looked like everything had been covered in a faintly-shimmering, roiling, velvet curtain.

Curses and shouts of near-panic came from the darkened area.

"That's the one that you'll *live* through, jackasses!" spat Boyd. "The *next* one, you won't... unless you've figured out how to live in a microwave-oven. Captain – you'd better tell them to get the fuck *out* of here... the power's calling me, *begging* to be let loose... I'm honestly not sure how long I can resist it..."

And the near-humans heard a new song; strong, deep and determined, were its 'from-somewhere', up-and-down chords.

"They can still hear me... right?" asked Jacobson.

"Far as I know," answered Boyd.

"Hey... assholes!" exclaimed the former Mars mission commander. "Time to go! You got ten seconds! Nine... eight..."

He looked behind, at the door.

"Oh... uhh... Devon... would you mind?" he asked.

"I'll help him," volunteered Tanaka.

Together, the telekinetic-powers of the woman and the black ex-astronaut ripped the door again off its hinges, sending shards of shattered ice into a mess, through which a confused crowd of cursing, angry, humiliated thugs awkwardly slipped and slid as quickly as possible, into the near-dark corridor outside.

Finally, all of them – save the crippled man who had foolishly challenged Jacobson earlier – had left, apparently running off to the right.

"*Damn!*" gasped an amazed Melissa Claremont.

For this, she received a grunt and a light slap from her mother.

"Sorry for cussin', Momma... but that was *wicked* impressive!" gushed the teenager.

Claremont nodded in agreement.

Gradually, the darkness in the corner of the room abated, as did Boyd's song and hand-glow.

"Coming soon – to a young lady near *you*," stated Tanaka, with a wry smile.

Melissa beamed, excitedly.

Now, White turned to Boyd.

"She ain't kiddin', bro... *damn* impressive!" he remarked. "But I got a question... if y'all don't mind my askin'."

"Sure... what?" replied the ex-pilot.

"Well... what's this 'Midnight' thing?" inquired White. "I thought it was, uhh, 'Shine'... wasn't it?"

"That's for the *other* one," explained Boyd. "Like, the ten billion-Watt light-bulb trick. I had to think of something to use to warn you all... and besides, 'Taxi' was already taken... right?"

"Well, I wouldn't have minded if you had wanted to use 'Taxi' –" mentioned the salesman.

Immediately, he disappeared.

"Hey, Bob... where y'all go?" asked a surprised Melissa, while Claremont stared in amazement.

"Taxi," came a disembodied, sighing voice.

A sheepish-looking Billings re-appeared.

"Oh... wow!" exclaimed the teenager. "That just like Sari do, Mista Billins!"

"You *got* it, kid," muttered the salesman. "I must have picked it up from her, on the way... but – for the record – I would've preferred her to have taught me how to fly, so I could airlift all of us out of this accursed place. Oh well... can't have *everything*, I guess."

"Maybe that will be Melissa's calling, Bob," offered Tanaka. "Or Whitney's. Who can tell the future?"

"I'm just hoping that there *is* one," he replied. "For us, I mean."

What's that, Whitney? interrogated the energized mind of the professor.

Yes, you're right – I see glimpses of it, too; and though you may believe it is just a dream –
There is *a future... and it burns bright –*
In the corner of your eye... just past the horizon, sent Cherie Teruko Tanaka.

Not So Bad A Job After All

The new President turned to address the Air Force General's age-lined, grandfatherly face, only slightly more elderly-looking than his own.

But at least he managed to keep all of his *hair,* silently noted the former Vice-President.

"Ready, sir?" asked Anderson.

"Yeah... okay," answered the *nouveau*-President.

He motioned to an orderly, who was standing just outside the Air Force One conference-room.

A clean-cut, young male Air Force lieutenant nodded, spoke something into a mobile-communicator and hit a control-button, then removed himself from the area after closing the meeting-room door.

The bland poker-face of the CIA director appeared on a view-screen.

"Hello, Mr. President... and may I offer my congratulations on your new position," offered the man, his lips barely moving.

"*Still* not used to being called that," demurred the *nouveau*-President. "But thanks. Can we get down to business, please – why'd you request this call?"

"Oh... has General Anderson not told you, sir?" answered the CIA director, with probably-feigned surprise.

"The good General and I only just had a chance to sit down and go over a lot of things," said the replacement President. "So why don't you fill me in?"

"Very well," replied the director. "I assume that you're aware of 'Operation One-Two Punch'... are you not, sir?"

"Yes I am," replied the American leader. "It didn't *work*... right?"

"Not... *exactly*," stated the CIA director. "The Agency has had – and continues to have – a high level of confidence in the basic plan; however, we have run into a few, uhh, *challenges*... and it's the latter that we have to discuss and come to some quick decisions about –"

"I'm not following you," countered the President. "About *what?*"

"As General Anderson's aware," continued the director, "Under the auspices of Operation One-Two Punch, the Agency undertook to centralize the human-assets to be weaponized for use against the alien, in an unacknowledged high-security holding area, which happens to be located underground on the island of Amchitka, in the Aleutians –"

"Am... *huh?*" asked the *nouveau*-President. "Where's that?"

"Alaska, sir," explained the director. "Just south of the mainland, facing the Bering Sea and the North Pacific. The island is basically deserted, which of course makes it a good place in which to locate a 'no-eyes' facility of this nature... may I go on?"

"Yeah... sure," muttered the U.S. leader.

"Right," said the CIA director. "So... the Agency undertook to locate not only the members of the former Billings party, who of course were prime candidates for non-voluntary weaponization, in the Amchitka facility, but also – and here, let me again apologize to the General, since it appears that we might have had – ahem – a slight breach of protocol, in this case –"

Anderson glowered and made no attempt to hide doing so.

"But we – the Company, that is – we also transported the former Mars mission astronauts, that is, Jacobson, Tanaka, White and Boyd – to the same location. All appeared to be going according to plan, and we were very near to being able to engineer a cascading stress-event against the alien, when – as far as we can tell – something went, uhh, *wrong.*"

"What do you *mean*, 'went wrong'?" shot back the replacement President. "I mean... we're talking about four astronauts and a bunch of stupid nobody civilians, here – *please* don't tell me that you guys at CIA can't handle –"

The General bent over and whispered something at length in the new President's ear, and, after hearing this, utter bewilderment appeared on his face.

"You've *got* to be kidding!" breathed the U.S. leader. "Was my predecessor told of this?"

Anderson smugly nodded.

"I... see," stammered the *nouveau*-President.

He turned to address the view-screen. "Continue."

"Before I do... do you have any new information that might be pertinent to the situation, sir?" inquired the CIA director.

"Maybe," guardedly answered the President, to Anderson's obvious displeasure. "Just tell me what you know, for now."

"Very well," offered the director. "The bottom line here, sir, is... we have reason to believe that the situation at Amchitka, has been degenerating into a large-scale riot. We're getting reports of confrontations, some of them involving gunfire. There have been significant casualties among local protective-staff, all over the facility, and it appears that we may have lost contact with the lower-levels of this underground building. Furthermore –"

"You know," interrupted the replacement President, "If I weren't a nice guy, I'd say that you people in the Agency have been doing a pretty piss-poor job of running a jail – I mean, isn't that what we've got a CIA *for*, in the first place... like, 'throw 'em in the hole and throw away the key', kind of thing? And why don't you just send in some of those, uhh, 'wet-ops' guys – you know what I mean – and restore discipline in the good old-fashioned way?"

"I appreciate your frustration, sir," smoothly answered the director, as if reading from a script, "But the facility was lightly-patrolled, on the reasonable assumption that its detainees would already be in an – uhh – weakened condition, and that they'd have nowhere to run, if they were to temporarily escape. While we *are* in the process of air-lifting some of the Agency's best people to the area – also a larger number of guards from GrayWar Corporation – frankly, Mr. President, given the size of the Amchitka facility and how it's constructed, it could be up to a week before we could be sure of clearing it all out – *if* we don't run into organized resistance. Unfortunately... that doesn't seem to be a safe assumption, given the reports that have been coming in, recently. Now, if we had suitable support from the *military*..."

"What do you mean? What kind of support?" inquired the U.S. leader.

"Two options," requested the CIA director. "One – our preferred course of action – would be for us to receive a substantial ground-forces reinforcement... say, a battalion of airborne or special-ops troops – and have them rapidly deployed to the surface of the Amchitka facility, to accompany our own people as firepower backup, as we go underground and liquidate the leadership of the disturbance. At the same time, we'd of course also be seeking out and re-capturing the aforementioned Billings- and Jacobson-group human-assets, for immediate re-weaponization, in case the alien makes another appearance."

"And the second?" nonchalantly asked the *nouveau*-President.

"Well, sir," elaborated the director, in a colorless monotone, "It's reasonable to believe that if we could simultaneously terminate *all* of those within the facility – and here, I'm referring specifically to the Jacobson and Billings parties, who we have to assume are hiding somewhere within the complex – then we might still have a fighting chance of dropping this 'Karéin' creature, once and for all. I've asked the General for his go-ahead to deploy the necessary military assets to ensure the success of this option; but so far, he has chosen to defer a decision to yourself. Hence, why we're on the call, today."

"Okay," grunted the American leader, leaning back in his flex-chair.

"So," he remarked, "If I'm reading the spook-jargon correctly... what you're asking is, 'can we drop a nuke on the place, and be rid of Billings, Jacobson and, hopefully, that pesky fucking alien-bitch, all in one nice big 'bang'... right?"

"The Agency always uses internal declarative language to describe operational matters," answered the CIA director. "But, to put it bluntly, sir... I'd say you're, uhh, 'bang-on'."

Recognizing the unintended pun, he let the briefest of smiles appear on his otherwise expressionless face.

"Might be worth a try," suggested the replacement President, with a non-committal shrug. "Harry... what do you think?"

"Mr. President," Anderson forced out, trying to remain polite, "I think you have to appreciate that whatever our stance regarding the alien's civilian-friends, we have a team of three of the most brave and," – he spoke more slowly, choosing his words carefully – "*unique*, Air Force professionals, located down in the bowels of that facility."

His voice rising, the General now warned, "So, let me be equally blunt here, sir : while all our boys in the Air Force know that the loss of their lives in the pursuit of the mission, is a fact of doing business in our line of work, I *cannot* –

and *will not* – endorse the casual slaughter of Commander Jacobson, Major Boyd or Major White, if there's the *slightest* chance that we can achieve our goals, without needlessly jeopardizing their lives. Should you decide otherwise, Mr. President sir, my resignation will be on your desk, within the hour; and I'd be very surprised, if it's not followed in quick order by similar actions, on the part of the Defense Secretary, as well as most of the other Joint Chiefs of Staff. That's how *I* feel about it... *sir!*"

"I... *see*," parried the *nouveau*-President. "But what if it's our only chance to shoot down the little bitch, once and for all? Would *that* make a difference?"

"I have no doubt, sir," retorted Anderson, "That if Jacobson, Boyd and White honestly believed that the only way in which to ensure the safety of the United States, was to lay down their own lives in her defense, then they'd be more than willing to do it. But that's a far cry from blowing them all to Kingdom Come, on the basis of a poorly-tested theory that – so far – has produced only inconclusive results. I don't think that we've had our best shot at the alien with the rest of our arsenal, anyway. We just need a flat-out battle, on *our* terms."

"I hate to be argumentative, General Anderson," interjected the CIA director,"But wasn't that what you were saying, before the alien destroyed two – or was it three – squadrons of our most advanced fighter-planes, in the skies over the Midwest? Conventional attacks don't *work* against this being – the sooner we all come to terms with that... the better-off we'll be."

"I'd remind you," shot back Anderson, his voice quivering with indignation, "That when 'Operation One-Two Punch' was first proposed, the assumption was always that it would only be the *Billings* party that would be used to, uhh, 'stress' the alien – then, the Air Force finds out that the Agency has kidnapped the Mars team off to the Amchitka facility, for the same purpose. So now, my men are mixed in with all the other detainees somewhere underground in this building, and if we decide to, uhh, 'sanitize' the facility, we have no choice but to target them, along with everyone else there. Mighty *convenient* – wouldn't you say?"

"Mr. President, I don't think this line of conversation is going to get us anywhere," deflected the director.

"Okay, okay, General – point taken," commented the replacement President, motioning for calm. "But can you at least answer me this : *if* – and I'm not saying we will – but *if*, we had to use the, uhh, 'nuclear-option' against this place... do we even have it available? And... could we get a few companies, platoons, brigades, whatever, of boots on the ground, up there on this island? If so, how long would it take?"

"To answer both those questions in sequence," replied Anderson, "Yes, we now *do* have a deliverable nuclear weapon – one only, until at least a week from now – pre-deployed in the Pacific Northwest area; it's a medium kiloton-range warhead, on an air-launched cruise-missile that would have to be fired from a bomber. As for the possibility of reinforcing the Agency's ground-forces, on that front I'll have to defer to General Blanshard, but from what I last heard from him – don't forget, he has his hands tied with the preparations for the assault to re-take the Greater Los Angeles area – I'd be surprised if he can scrape up as much as a complete battalion on short notice. Amchitka is quite far-off the beaten track – so if we want rapid deployment, we're looking at airlift-assets... I'm not sure if what we have now, would be adequate."

"Please see what we can do to get some boots on the ground, up there," requested the acting U.S. leader. "And start preparing for the – uhh – 'other', option, as well... just as a contingency-plan, you understand."

Anderson nodded.

Then, the replacement President directed, "General, let me be plain, here – I appreciate your loyalty to your men... but as C-In-C, I have to consider what's best for the country, however unpleasant the consequences of doing that, might be. Right now, I don't *intend* to drop the bomb – but I won't rule out doing so. Now, if you can't live with all that... well, maybe you *should* be preparing your resignation-papers. Nothing *personal*... but I've got a *country* to run, here!"

Again, Anderson stopped talking for a few seconds.

Then he offered, "Very well – I'll follow my orders, Mr. President; and, I suppose that I'll just have to hope that worst doesn't come to worst, in this situation. May I at least request that – when and if the Jacobson team is located – they be returned to the *exclusive* administrative control, of the Air Force?"

"Oh... *certainly*," agreed the *nouveau*-President.

"Sir, I don't think that's an advisable –" protested the CIA director.

"Don't get your shirt in a knot, down there," said the U.S. leader. "We'll get this all sorted out... once we know what the hell is actually going *on*, in this jail you guys are running up in Alaska. We may just go back to the original plan, or we may try something else. We'll see."

"But, *Mr. President* –" pressed the director.

"That's an *order*, from your Commander-In-Chief!" insisted the replacement President.

He motioned to Anderson, who cut the connection, mutely pondering his options.

"General," said the U.S. leader, "You know... I'm starting to like this job, a little more, each day."

The Corner Of Your Eye

After White and Tanaka had spent five minutes or so re-cementing the door, Jacobson motioned for all of them to sit down at the long meeting-table.

"What 'bout *him*?" asked Melissa, pointing at the crippled biker, who had been propped up against a wall.

The man's face was colorless, his eyes had a glassy sheen and he was breathing fitfully.

"Just leave him," directed Tanaka. "He *got* what he deserved. Or less."

"He gonna *die?*" pressed the teenager.

"Probably. I don't know," evaded the woman, as she took a seat.

"Well then we *cain't* leave him," argued Melissa. "Right, Momma?"

Claremont shrugged, indifferently.

"Look, honey," offered Billings, from the opposite side of the table, "There's nothing more that we can do for him – that's just how things *are*, down here. Bugger mouthed off to 'Captain Rhinoceros' over there, and ended up without a leg to stand on... which is likely as good as 'dead', after we leave. If it's any consolation – it's probably a much more pleasant way to die, than everybody else in this rat-hole has been given."

As the teenager fell stonily silent, Jacobson tried to change the subject.

"Bob... how's Elissha doing now?" he inquired.

"Got her spread out between these two seats next to me, with the blankets we found in that storage-closet behind the video-screen," explained the salesman. "Looks a bit better than she did a half-hour ago – skin isn't as clammy as it was, either, but I'm still worried... either she's the drowsiest kid I've ever met, or there's *definitely* something wrong with her. Especially with all the excitement that's been going on... it's not natural for a kid to be *this* quiet."

"Yeah," affirmed Tanaka, with the same concern in her voice. "I'd normally suspect internal-injuries, but when I checked her out before Bob put her on the chairs, there wasn't any evidence of that... and it doesn't look like a pathogen, either... I don't *think*. I suppose it's pointless to mention that she needs medical-attention... right?"

"It is," unhelpfully responded Jacobson. "We'll just have to keep her as comfortable as we can and hope for the best. In the meantime, I wanted to bring some new information to your attention – things that Brent and Devon have pieced together from the documentation that was left lying around, when whoever was in here originally, left."

He shot a glance to White.

"You got that working yet?" he asked.

"Few seconds more, Cap'n," parried the African-American ex-astronaut. "No manual, of course – but it's not that different from what we had up on the *Infinity*, God rest her tin heart."

"Jacobson," inquired Billings, "Exactly what you want us to see?"

"Well," answered the former Mars mission commander, "Brent and I had a quick look at the paperwork – it's disjointed, parts are missing from the binders – but there's some fairly interesting stuff. First of all, there's a table that looks a lot like a prisoner-manifest... it goes on for 20 pages or more, 50 rows per, so assuming it's complete and up to date, that gives us a total of about a thousand detainees, down here –"

"Let me see that," demanded the salesman.

Jacobson slid a three-ring binder across the table, and immediately Billings buried his head in the thing.

"Good thing that I don't need those glasses, since Sari..." he muttered, his eyes scanning rapidly up and down each page.

"Go ahead... keep talking," he requested.

"Right," continued Jacobson. "Secondly – as you'll see from some of the charts and tables just after the manifest – there's a breakdown of 'who's who' in the prisoner-population – about 30 per cent under the 'gangsters and common criminals' category, 30 per cent 'domestic subversives', as our friends in the CIA are describing them, roughly 25 per cent 'foreign detainees', 10 per cent 'other' and 5 per cent 'special' –"

"I suppose we count in the last five," commented Tanaka. "Bully for *us!*"

Claremont let out a weary sigh.

"Y'all can lay your head on mah shoulder, Momma," offered Melissa.

It was a gesture that was immediately accepted.

"Ready any time... I think," interrupted White.

Jacobson was about to assent, but Billings spoke up.

"Well, there I am... and look, they even gave me my own ID number : 'W15M6D'," he ruefully spelled out. "Strange, though... found Whitney, Melissa, Curtis, codes for them, too... but not Tommy. And none of *your* names are in the register, Commander. Don't know what that means."

"We – ahh – didn't quite check in at the registration-desk, in the manner that they had anticipated," explained the Mars mission commander. "They probably didn't have time to properly enter us in their database. More's the pity."

"Y'all can say *that* again, Cap'n," grunted White. "But you think they took him somewhere else? Karéin's son by choice, I mean."

"No," spoke Tanaka, with a far-away look in her eyes. "He's *here*."

"Yeah," confirmed Billings. "He *is*."

"How y'all know that, Mista Billins?" queried Melissa.

"I guess I just *do*, honey," replied the salesman, to a knowing-nod from Tanaka. "I spent some tough times with him... tried to help..."

"*Bob*," compassionately mentioned Tanaka.

"It's okay, Professor," quietly answered the salesman.

"There's something else – something even *more* interesting," elaborated Jacobson. "Again, it's incomplete, but in *this* one," – he pointed to a larger, differently-colored binder – "There's a more detailed schematic of the layout of this place, compared to what we've so far had access to, on the key-cards. And wait 'till you *see* what's on it."

He stood up, leaned over the table and opened the binder, spreading a double-legal-size floor-map in front of seven intensely-interested pairs of eyes.

"Hey – that's not paper... is it?" observed Billings.

"Nope – some kind of polymer... plastic, basically," said the former Mars mission commander. "Here, we have what I believe to be the level we're on – not much really new, except there's a short-cut to the next set of stairs, which is sort of useful."

"So what's the big deal?" demanded the salesman.

"Yo – you got *another* page under that one, Cap'n," noted White.

A smile showed on Jacobson's face.

"Yep," he confirmed. "Now, as you'll see," he added, folding the top page and revealing the one below it, "This is the level below us – the lowest one, if the map isn't missing any pages. Have a look."

They all crowded around.

"Well... that's 'bout as useful as tits on a bull," muttered White. "Half the damn thing's *blank* – oh, wait a minute, yeah, figures... y'all see that little 'REDACTED'-stamp, right in the middle of the part they cut out?"

"At least we can see the other half," commented Boyd. "Interesting – layout's much different from the levels that we've so far been through... look at all those wide open-areas... should be easier to check out a few big ones, rather than all the little rooms we've run into on the upper-levels."

"True... but there's something *else*," teased Jacobson. "Do you see it?"

"Uhh... nope, Cap'n Jacobson," said Melissa. "There just a bunch of doors 'n rooms 'n such."

"Do you *see* it?" he repeated, with a strange, electric tone of voice.

"What y'all mean?" asked the confused teenager.

A delighted, serene smile came to Tanaka's face.

"Oh, *Sam*..." she started. "Yes – I *do*... *now* I understand!"

Boyd spoke up.

"Holy snappin' arseholes, Batman – I see it too, Professor," he exclaimed. "That thin set of parallel-lines and other symbols – leading off the periphery of the map-area, to the north-west – in the 'more-purple-than-purple' –"

Tanaka arose and stood close by the teenager – one arm around the girl's shoulder, the other on her arm – which the woman took hold of, and pointed at an apparently-blank part of the map.

"Melissa, daughter of the new people," cooed the Professor, with an eerie ocular-glow and soft, ethereal music playing somewhere. "Look out the corner of your eye, dear... like you're straining to see something, and it's almost pitch-dark, and you don't think you can possibly make anything out... but keep trying."

"But Miz Cherie," protested the teenager, "Ah don' see –"

With staring eyes, Melissa fell silent, as Tanaka's beaming face turned to look on the teenager.

The girl rubbed her eyelids, then again opened them.

"Wha' *that!*" she gasped. "Ah ain't never... Momma – y'all *seein'* it? Like them posters Curtis had on he wall, wid that color like it glow when y'all turn th' lights off... but they still *on*..."

An equally-amazed Claremont nodded.

"Start lookin' for what's 'more purple than a grape', sister," quipped White, with a cheery grin.

"*Um'b'as'ài*", added Boyd.

"Oomba-*wha*'?" asked the teenager.

"That's the name for it," explained the ex-astronaut. "In the language of the Storied Watcher, who you knew as 'Sari'. And guess what, Melissa?"

"No... what?" she replied.

"Remember how the Professor said that you were going to evolve your own powers – just like the rest of us?" prompted Boyd.

"Uh-huh," warily answered the teenager.

"It's *happening*, Melissa," he said.

An Update For Sebastian

"Any idea what we should *do* with her?" asked a worried Abruzzio, as she regarded the twitching, fidgeting figure of the sleeping Storied Watcher.

Groggy-eyed, the others who she had forced awake from badly-needed cat-naps, tried to focus on the scene.

A soft, unhappy whimper came from the alien-girl's direction. It was accompanied by waves of psychic-disquiet, which somehow reverberated unpleasantly in the minds of those who had the temerity to venture so close.

They thought they heard something like *call – oh call!* but it might have been their imagination, for the words could not have been in English.

"Dunno," replied Ramirez. "It's a totally-weird feeling, Sylvia – you on the bad end of it, too? It's like the closer that I get to her, the more tense I become... I guess it's a good thing that I can't get *too* near, on account of the fire coming out of that armor she's got draped all over her..."

"Yeah, Hector, I sure *can* feel it – like having to sit through a long meeting with someone you can't stand, but ten times worse... Wolf, can you offer any guidance, here?" asked the female scientist. "You and Misha have had more experience with her."

"Got me *there*, pardner," parried the bounty-hunter, as he scratched the top of his skull and ran his hand over the back of his head. "I *did* see her sleep, but she was always more, uhh, *relaxed*... if you know what I mean. Can't imagine what's eatin' her like that... hey, Russkie, you got any idea? You've known her longer than me."

"I *have* seen her agitated – that much is true," observed Misha, "Although not like *this*... she was awake, very angry... if I am interpreting her emotions properly – and there is a very good chance that I am not – I would say that she is having a bad dream; and as the Storied Watcher apparently does not sleep very frequently, this must be a very unpleasant experience for her."

"Well what do you think we should *do*?" pressed Abruzzio, bending over the somnolent creature's reclining body as close as she dared, before the heat coming from *Vîrya Ahn'jë* made doing so unbearable.

"Who says we got to do *anythin'*?" countered Wolf. "Just leave her be... she'll be okay."

"I don't think you understand what I *mean*," cautioned the scientist. "You've seen the amount of power that's contained in that shapely little figure down there – no, I take that back, all of us have probably only seen a *fraction* of the power contained within her – and if she should lash out, in her sleep –"

"Whoa... yeah," agreed Ramirez. "Like, sleepwalkin', you mean, Sylvia? 'Cept, in *this* case... it'd be 'sleep-*flying*' – at a few thousand kilometers per hour..."

Another pained whimper came from Karéin-Mayréij, along with the clearly-audible words, "*no danger... can hear you... from dream-world...*"

"Heh," grunted the bounty-hunter, with a broad grin, "*Told* you! Little Miss Atom-Cracker's been listenin' in, all the while. But for the record... I kind of don't blame you all for bein' a bit concerned – I seen more than a couple sad stories where somebody thought it was a bright idea to sleep with a gun by the side of the bed, or even in their hand. Well – you *know* what happens next, when they have a real *bad* dream... right?"

"I would have expected her to be aware of us, given the comprehensiveness of all her other defenses," commented Misha. "Karéin – can you hear me?"

The sad vibrations and fidgeting continued, but there was no answer.

"There's the difference between hearin', and payin' attention, pardner," sarcastically remarked the bounty-hunter.

"Well, I still don't think that –" started Abruzzio; but she was cut off by a yelp, coming from the direction of the bedroom.

"Hey, *hey*, there – take it *easy!*" exclaimed Kaysten's panicked voice.

There were confused, crashing-sounds, as if things were being tossed about.

"Mr. *Kaysten!*" called Chu, as – gun at the ready – she strode across the main room in front of the picture-window, heading for the sleeping-quarters.

In the same instant in which the heads of the four ex-humans arrayed around the Storied Watcher turned to regard the commotion, the alien-girl had awoken, and was standing straight up behind them, with her complete arms-and-armor set arrayed in ready-to-don fashion.

"Sebastiàn wakes – as do I," she quickly remarked. "Minn-ee, *wait –*"

Now Chu was standing in the doorway between, the main area and the bedroom.

"Let *go* of him!" she commanded with steely determination, addressing someone that the others could not easily see. "*Now!*"

"*¿Quien es usted, mujer?*" they heard coming from the sleeping-area.

The Storied Watcher disappeared.

No more than two seconds later, she appeared, as if out of thin air, dressed only in skimpy, scale-mail-bra-and-panties, right next to where the *Mara* gangster had put Kaysten in a head-lock, near the small window in the bedroom.

"*Sebastiàn,*" she called, in a calm and friendly voice, "*Soy su amiga... y esta gente es también sus amigos. Le rescatamos. ¡Lance por favor a Jerry!*"

Though Kaysten was in fear for his life – and despite not having been, well, "intimate", with a woman for years – his mind still raced in unrequited directions, with his first glance at Karéin-Mayréij.

God... above all else, don't let me die with a hard-on like this, his frustrated mind called out.

Can't help it – with her so damn close – and irony of ironies, I don't even –

The alien-girl winked insouciantly at the helpless Chief of Staff.

"*¿De dónde usted vino, señorita?*" demanded the startled and confused gangster. "*¿Y còmo sabe usted mi nombre?*"

"*La respuesta a esas preguntas es complicada. También... muchas de esta gente no entienden español. ¿Usted habla inglés?*" she recounted. "*Yo sé muchas diversas idiomas incluyendo español... pero esta otra gente aquí sabe solamente inglés.*"

"*Sì ,*" he answered.

"Do you *mind*?" peevishly requested Kaysten, his voice barely audible through the choke-hold that the *Mara* had put on him.

Sebastiàn warily looked back and forth; then, after a few seconds, his grip relented, and the Chief of Staff dashed around the bed to get out of his tormentor's vicinity.

"Who the fuck *are* you people?" accosted the gangster.

The Storied Watcher, struggling inwardly to restrain her aura of attractiveness, caused a pillow-case to remove and wrap itself around her figure; then, she patted the surface of the bed next to her, inviting the man to sit down.

Slowly, he complied.

"Three guesses 'bout what *he's* thinkin'," grunted Boatman to Hendricks, from their outside vantage-point.

"Can hardly keep it in my pants from back here," muttered the duly-impressed third agent.

"Sebastiàn," she inquired, "What is the last thing that you remember happening to yourself?"

The *Mara* pondered for a second or two, then replied, "I guess I was hit – shot, I mean, *señorita*... shot up *bad*... figured my time was up..."

His voice tailed off.

"It *was*," remarked Chu, who had lowered, but not holstered, her service weapon. "She *saved* you – saved your life, that is."

"More than that," commented Misha, who was also just outside the doorway.

"Listen – you all slingin'... cop-pieces, but so what – this, all of downtown L.A., I mean – this is *Mara* turf," bluffed Sebastiàn. "I don' have to tell you *nothin', hombre. Mis compadres* will be here to fish me out, sooner or later."

"Hate to break it to you this way," joked Wolf, who was tall enough to be able to see easily over Chu's head, "But what you just got yourself into... well, that's something a few *planets* too far for them *muchachos* of yours to deal with."

"*Ustedes* talkin' *la mierda*," challenged the gangster. "I seen that Uptown stuff they dressed in, pieces they carryin', before – them's *Federales, mi hijo*. This is some kind of set-up... entrapment, you know? Well – I ain't fallin' for it! What you gonna *do*... put me in a 'copter and fly me out of here? Ain't no jails workin' anywhere within twenty miles, 'round here."

"See that lip-smackin' little toss-up next to you?" taunted Wolf. "She don't need no 'copter, no airplane – or no pair of lil' feathered wings, neither, if she wants to fly you somewhere. *Trust* me on this one, pardner."

Sebastiàn looked thoroughly confused, now.

Chu could not resist an urge to laugh.

"Listen, Sebastiàn – that's your name, right?" she spoke, "Far be it for me to agree with the big guy behind me – he's 'Wolf', by the way... but, while I *am* Minnie Chu of the FBI – and here are Agents Otis Boatman and Will Hendricks, also of the Bureau, just behind me – we're on a mission that's far, *far* more important than what happens to a single gang-banger who's on the run from a bunch of other gang-bangers. Do you know who it *is*, that's sitting next to you?"

"Yeah, you all noticed anythin'... *different*, 'bout her there, by any chance?" added Boatman.

The Storied Watcher smiled demurely, batting her eyes.

"*Señorita* sure *is*, uhh... *chiquita*, if you know what I mean," he answered. "I don' follow you, Mister FBI-Man."

Though he could hardly see through the jumble of bodies crammed in at the doorway, Misha called to the gangster.

"She is Karéin-Mayréij, the Storied Watcher, the Destroying Angel who saved us from the 'Lucifer' comet, my friend," advised the Russian. "You sit beside the most powerful being who has ever walked the face of this *planet!*"

The *Mara* pointed a contemptuous finger at the young-looking woman.

"*Her*?" he incredulously stated. "Now I *know* you shittin' me, *hombre*. Can I have any of the *yayo* you been snortin'?"

Karéin-Mayréij closed her eyes for a second, then slowly opened them, bathing the gangster's gasping face in an ethereal, blue-green glow.

Sebastiàn jumped back toward the bed's back-rest, by at least a foot.

"*¡Que sea una demonia!*" he stammered, fumbling for his gun and finding only an empty holster. "You keep the *fuck* away from me!"

"Aww, now, Sebastiàn... I am not *so* bad... *am* I?" she coquettishly replied.

Her regal, divine aura washed over all who were present; by now, it was old hat to the rest of the slowly-transforming ex-humans, but the gangster was frightened half out of his wits. He compressed himself against the bed-stand, inching to the right as if preparing to run; but he could not possibly have gotten past the crowd that was jammed into the bedroom doorway.

Chu advanced into the room and sat on the right side of the bed, across from the Storied Watcher, in front of the *Mara*.

"Let's use a little common sense here," suggested the Asian-American FBI-agent. "Before you try running off, what does it hurt just to listen to what she's got to say? And, anyway – we're *not* giving you back your gun, so what do you think your chances would be, out there, completely unarmed? When Karéin found you, Sebastiàn, you were basically already dead; the rest of us aren't precisely sure how she *did* it, but she brought you back – though she still hasn't properly explained why. The least you can do is be a little *grateful*."

The gangster didn't reply, but the tension in his shoulders lessened slightly.

Now the Storied Watcher put her legs underneath her trunk, yoga-stance-style, and levitated herself to a position hovering about an inch over the surface of the bed, right next to Chu.

His eyes bulged in disbelief.

"You – you see *that*?" he gasped, toward the FBI team-leader.

"Yeah... so what?" answered Chu.

"Well she's right *next* to you, *Federale*," he protested. "An' she's... *floatin'!*"

"Does not everyone?" quipped Karéin-Mayréij, wryly arching an eyebrow.

He fell silent for a second or two, evidently considering his options.

I can take any of these putos – 'cept maybe that big hombre with the tattoos and the long hair... he looks like a freelancer, silently considered the *Mara*.

But too many of 'em – without mi arma – and then, there's... her...

"I am not your enemy, Sebastiàn," counseled Karéin-Mayréij.

Now her tone changed, becoming more serious, more dignified.

"I come not to harm and rule... but rather to help and serve," she continued. "If you will accept my love, I will redeem you from the cruel past from which you flee, as surely as you run from the men with the guns, far below us. I will extinguish your guilt... if you will but let me."

She extended her hand.

"What if I don' *want* to be 'redeemed', *chica*?" he half-sneered.

"That's easy," offered Boatman. "Then you gonna *die*."

"You fuckin *touch* me – I'll slit your throat, *puto!*" he growled.

"No, *no*, Otis isn't threatening you – none of us are!" hastily interjected Chu. "What he means is, you've been contaminated – more specifically, you're *radioactive*. Left untreated, it will kill you... maybe quickly, maybe it will take longer as you die of cancer in a year or two."

"*Nasty* way to go, man," echoed Hendricks, from one side of the doorway. "You'd be better off suckin' on a .45. Be less of a mess that way."

"You *lie!*" he retorted. "I feel *fine!*"

But in fact... his legs already felt unnaturally weak.

Wolf called out to the alien-girl.

"*Told* you it was a waste of time bringin' him in here, Karéin," he complained. "You know what 'bad to the bone' means?"

"*No-one* is beyond redemption, if he or she but resolves to re-trace steps wrongly taken," she patiently observed. "Evil is a *choice*... not a heritage."

"Besides," argued the gangster, "If I got such a bad glow in the dark on me, then how come *ustedes* ain't scared of havin' some of it comin' your way, *Federale*? 'Splain me *that!*"

"Because it – apparently – makes us stronger," countered Chu. "According to our friend here," – she pointed at the insouciantly-smiling Storied Watcher – "We're not *human*, any more... by virtue of hanging around *her*."

"And you know what the *real* fun-thing is?" added Boatman.

"No... why don' you tell me?" shot back the *Mara*.

"*You* ain't, either," said the big black man.

"Ain't... *what*?" asked the gangster.

"*Human*," answered Chu.

"You talkin' *shit* again, *Federale!*" protested Sebastiàn. "I got one head, two legs, two arms, just like you – least you got 'em now, 'long as you don' stand in my way, when I decide to fuck off out of here. You understand what I'm sayin'?"

The FBI team-leader rolled her eyes and addressed the Storied Watcher.

"Another time that I hate to agree with Wolf," she said, "But I don't know what you *see* in this guy – look, Karéin... both the bounty-hunter and I, my fellow-agents, too, we've had a lot of experience with gang-bangers like this – they're hardened criminals from early childhood... most of them have a murder or two under their belts by the time they're fifteen. Doesn't matter *what* they say – you can't turn your back on one of them for a *second!* I'd like the opportunity to interrogate him for a while, then let him go back to wherever he came from. He's not worth your time... you've got more important things to deal with."

"You are wrong, Minn-ee," answered Karéin-Mayréij, with a far-off glow in her eyes and the dim sound of subconscious, graceful music. "I was *guided* to find Sebastiàn, rescue him... *redeem* him. He also is important, in his own right. I will *not* give him up – not, at least, until he has had the same chance as Jerr-ee."

"Gee... *thanks*," called Kaysten's irritated voice, from outside the bedroom.

Now the Storied Watcher turned to directly address the gangster.

"Sebastiàn," she stated, "I know that this is all, ahh, 'coming at you rather fast', but such have been the realities of life for many of us, lately; and there is little that we can do, except try to accept and adapt, as best we can. Considering your background – the unforgiving life of a bandit-warrior who dare not show weakness, at any time – I do not blame you for not immediately trusting Minn-ee Choo and her eff-bee-ai friends. Indeed... she, they and I, also – neither are we in a relationship of complete trust, regarding each other."

Perhaps the *Mara*'s tension eased a little more, since they saw him recline against the bedroom wall, hands folded behind his back.

"What you mean, *chica demonica*?" he guardedly inquired.

"Easy," replied Karéin-Mayréij. "Would it help to know that not a fortnight ago, I set about to *warring* against them – not to mention the 'President' and entire government, of this 'United States' empire, in which you live? And that I warned them, their 'Director'-lord and the President himself, that – should they not resolve a grievance done against me and others who I love, and promptly – I will destroy this entire *country*?"

"*You*?" he half-sneered, though less forcefully than before. "Okay... you got weird eyes and some kinda magic-trick 'bout floatin' in mid-air. So *what*."

"Uh-oh," muttered Boatman. "Listen, *hombre*... y'all better take her a bit more seriously, if you know what's good for you. She ain't shittin' you 'bout all that. You seen what's been goin' down lately – Rushmore, D.C. – all that stuff?"

"I kinda been on the road, last little while," replied the gangster. "Only had them *mariachi*-stations on the radio."

"The Storied Watcher there in front of you," calmly recounted Chu, "First destroyed the entire Rushmore National Monument – that is, she shattered most of the side of a whole *mountain* – then, she removed the top of the Washington Monument – something that weighs thousands of *tons* – and dropped it into the South Lawn of the White House."

"She could kill all of us with a blink of that pretty little eye," noted Wolf.

"Actually... it would not take an entire eye-blink," unhelpfully corrected the alien-girl. "A half-second is quite a long time, as reckoned in the heat of battle."

"*Sì... por supuesto*," sarcastically commented the gangster.

"Misha," inquired the Storied Watcher... you have Sebastiàn's gun... right?"

"Yes," confirmed the Russian.

"Shoot me with it," she ordered. "Aim for the head."

"Karéin..." he complained, "I know what you are trying to demonstrate – but *please*, do not make me do this... what if something goes *wrong*?"

"It will *not*," she firmly replied, her eyes focused not on Misha but on the gangster. "There is much more chance of me being hurt by choking on a poorly-chewed piece of food."

Now Abruzzio – formerly silent – spoke up.

"Karéin, *listen* to him, please," she pleaded. "We shouldn't risk –"

"I love you, Sylvia," interrupted the alien-girl, "But please... just watch."

"You want *me* to do it, pardner?" offered Wolf, in Misha's direction. "I got faith... or somethin'."

"No," refused the Russian, as he pushed through the crowd and stood with a clear line-of-fire. "Bu – for the record – Karéin... even if the risk is as low as you claim, this is both unnecessary and imprudent."

"Misha, I love you, but – oh, for the sake of the *Gods!*" grumbled Karéin-Mayréij, "I have spent the last few-score days evading the most lethal attacks – rocket-arrows, death-light-beams, and so on – that the 'President' of this kingdom, could muster... and now I cannot convince anyone to fire a single pistol-bullet, against me. Would you like me to trigger the gun remotely, so that nothing weighs upon your conscience?"

"Three," counted the Russian. "But what if it ricochets?"

"Thank you," said the Storied Watcher. "And worry not... I will catch it."

"Two," he continued.

"Watch," directed the alien-girl, to the gangster. "And all of you – note that I carry not my war-children on my frame."

"Your... *what*?" asked Sebastiàn.

"One," warned the Russian.

Wincing, he pulled the trigger.

There was a sharp 'crack'-sound, followed, – microsecond later – by a painfully-intense wave of heat.

The Storied Watcher's right arm flicked at supersonic-speed from her side.

She held out her hand in front of the *Mara*. It contained a small, heavily-deformed, pitted bullet-slug.

"*Souvenir*, Sebastiàn?" she coyly proposed.

"What the *fuck*..." he incredulously observed. "An' no – you keep it."

"*Your* own gun, *muchacho*," interjected Wolf. "Ain't no fake bullshit about what you just seen. This here's the *real deal, mi amigo!* You're in the *big* leagues now... but for the life of me, I can't figure out how you got here."

"The same could probably be said of both you and I, Madame Chu and her agents as well," reminded Misha, as he holstered the gangster's gun. "Though probably not our two scientist-friends."

"Okay – I *get* it... *ésta es la magia auténtica*," grudgingly admitted the *Mara*, still shaken by what he had just seen. "Ain't *nadie* – nobody *normal* – who can do *that*, an' you don' have enough clothes on to be hidin' no shit on you, anywhere... but what you want from *me, señorita magia*? I'm just a lieutenant, if you understand what I'm sayin'. An' anyway... all *mis compañeros*, they's back in Texas, not here... I barely got connections in this town. I can't get you no *armas*, no synth – not even a lot of *yayo*... you know?"

"How about you start by telling us how you ended up with that nice lil' ol' glow on you?" suggested Boatman.

"Don' have to tell you *nada, Federale!*" shot back Sebastiàn. "I only work with *her*."

He pointed at the Storied Watcher.

"We're all working together," contradicted Chu.

"*Really*, Minn-ee?" counter-contradicted the alien-girl.

"Well... I *thought* –" argued the FBI team-leader.

"We *might* be," commented Karéin-Mayréij, "If your government finds and returns my family, unharmed. If *not*..."

Wolf called out to the *Mara*.

"See?" he joked. "'One big happy family' here, pardner. But – correct me if I'm wrong, here, Karéin – me 'n the Russkie, we're still in tight with you... right?"

"Uhh... what?" stammered a confused Storied Watcher. "*Misha* has been 'in tight' with me – but Wolf, you and I, we have not yet had a private moment to... oh, *wait* a minute..."

Sheepishly she looked at a bevy of vicariously-embarrassed smirks; and if a half-goddess could blush, there was more than the usual acid blood in her cheeks.

Eventually she grumbled, "Another one of your accursed Eng-lish slang words.... correct? I *thought* that you meant – but of course we are friends until the end of days, if you will have me... oh – *forget* it."

She sat and stewed, trying to clear the color from her face.

"Now there's *one* thing that she can't outwit everybody else about," cackled Hendricks. "Fuckin' *ay!*. Oops."

Abruzzio rolled her eyes.

"Your personal life isn't, uhh, the concern here, Karéin," stated Chu, to a grateful look from the Storied Watcher. "So let me fill you in on what the true situation is, Sebastiàn."

"Yeah... why don' you," agreed the gangster, his tone heavy with suspicion.

"Well," explained the FBI team-leader, "Our alien-goddess-friend over there, befriended a number of humans, after she, uhh, fell to Earth, following the 'Lucifer' comet-incident – surely you must know about *that*, right – but they seem to have been kidnapped by some other government agency. According to Karéin, these unfortunate people – who she considers to be her 'family' – are being held in an unknown location, where they're being brutally-abused, as we speak, for reasons that are currently a complete mystery to FBI –"

"Oh... *sure*," sneered the *Mara*. "*Usted no sabe nada*, 'bout all that... do you, *chica?* Well – you show up in *mi barrio*... we don' know what we do to the *Federales*, neither," he spat.

Trying to maintain her composure, Chu continued, "My team was authorized by Bureau to help her locate this 'family'... although since she 'airlifted' us all to downtown Los Angeles, our effectiveness in that department has been zero. By the way... neither the President nor the rest of the government know that we're here, with Karéin. That's lucky for us, because – for reasons that we don't understand – every time that the military has been able to get a fix on her, they've fired off just about everything in their *arsenal* against her, and... well... *she*'s still here, but a lot of soldiers and airmen aren't –"

"I did not kill *anyone*, Minn-ee... I do not *believe*," interrupted the alien-girl. "Except for one spy-warrior down in Tucson – aand *his* intent, was my own death. It was terrible... but my hands are stained only with justly-spilled blood."

"You've sure *threatened* to," argued Boatman. "Kill lots of people, that is."

"The future is different from the past," replied the Storied Watcher. "It can be better, or worse. I hope the former... but I am ready for the latter."

"Do you want to take over the briefing?" demanded an irritated Chu.

"No... you go ahead," demurred Karéin-Mayréij. "Sebastiàn seems to be listening; and that is, ahh, 'the main thing'."

"Go on," requested the *Mara*, of the FBI team-leader.

"Right," said Chu. "As to the others in the audience here, Ms. Sylvia Abruzzio and Mr. Hector Ramirez – don't know if you can see them back there – but they're space-scientists from NASA, who developed a rapport with the Storied Watcher, when she was on the return-leg of the *Eagle* and *Infinity* mission to Mars... that's where the whole thing, uhh, started, when our alien-friend was first brought back to life –"

"I was *always* alive, Minn-ee," noted Karéin-Mayréij. "Sam and Cherie – may the Gods protect them wherever they are – simply awakened me."

"I stand corrected," Chu went on. "You've already sort of met Wolf and the Russian – oh, and by the way, Misha's an ex-SVR agent, he's kind of 'persona non grata' to both the American and Russian governments – so the only one who I haven't introduced, is Jerry Kaysten. He's the White House Chief of Staff – that is, the most senior private advisor to the President –"

"*Wait* a minute!" interrupted the gangster. "If he's some fuckin' big *tamale* like *that*... then what's he doin' here in the middle of *Mara*-turf, in L.A.? Ain't too much the Man can do to back him up down here... *verdad*?"

"No *shit*," called out Kaysten, from behind the crowd. "Why don't you ask that cute little Martian-lady who's floating over the bed, to explain *that* one."

As Sebastiàn's gaze met that of the Storied Watcher, she calmly explained, "You see... I paid a, ahh, 'courtesy-call' to the White House, vainly hoping to find the President and teach him a hard lesson. Instead, he had left an impostor in his place – who, out of mercy, I refrained from reducing to ashes; however, in exploring this fine white palace, I happened across Jerr-ee, and – let us say – when I gave him my most special kiss, he swooned. Not wanting to just leave him there with the gun-bullets a-flying... I *had* to take him with me. We are still, as you humans would put it, 'getting to know each other'... right, Jerr-ee?"

"Oh yeah... *sure* we are," complained Kaysten. "Like nitro and glycerin, the Hatfields and the McCoys –"

A second later, they heard a yelp, then a frustrated groan.

"Not *you*... again!" he protested. "Look – I didn't mean *anything* by it, really! I *like* your mother, honestly I do... but she's a hard woman – I mean, hard *alien* – to please... you know?"

A confused *Mara* asked, "I thought you say... this is all of you? Who he *talkin'* to?"

"Her shield," answered Chu, matter-of-factually.

"Her... *what*?" he asked.

"My war-daughter – *Vîrya I'ëà'b'* – whose form is of an arm-buckler," explained the Storied Watcher. "She – along with all my other war-children – adorns my frame, when I outfit for battle. If you will lay down your mistrust and hostility, Sebastiàn – or just withhold it – you will meet them, when you venture outside this room. I am different from anyone who you have ever *met*, man; and I offer wisdom and counsel – yet, far more important – I offer enlightenment and a second-chance... if only you will follow me. What *say* you?"

"Offer of a *lifetime*, pardner," cajoled Wolf.

"No," softly contradicted Abruzzio, from behind. "Of *ten thousand* lifetimes."

"*Carajo*..." muttered Sebastiàn, under his breath, utterly at odds.

They waited.

"Well... a 'lifetime' ain't too long, in *mi barrio*," offered the *Mara*. "An' I go out there on the streets without my piece, *mi vida será mucho más corta, sin una duda... ¿entiende?*"

"*Lo entiendo*," answered the Storied Watcher. "*Sìgame, mi hijo querido.*"

"No promises... right?" he demanded.

"More than one has already been made – by me to you – in love and good faith," noted the alien-girl. "It shall be up to *you* to decide, if you will be noble, and return the blessing."

He nodded affirmatively.

"Didn't quite catch your name there, *chica*," inquired Sebastiàn. "There was a lot goin' on, lot to take in... still is."

"I am Karéin-Mayréij," she stated. "Though these friends of mine seem to use just the first half of my name, out of familiarity. Oh... and my title is, 'The Storied Watcher'. You may refer to me by either one."

"The 'Storied', *what*?" he replied. "*¿Que quiere decir este?*"

"Mortals tell stories about me," offered the young-looking woman.

"Yeah?" he snorted.

"Yeah – like, 'savin' the whole damn *planet* from a comet," interjected the big, African-American FBI-agent. "You all think *that's* worth a story or two?"

"*Her*?" asked the gangster. "*¡Que va!* A comet's pretty big... *verdad*?"

"That was the *other* 'me' – the *other* 'Karéin-Mayréij'," the alien-girl tried to explain. "The other 'me' is an immortal demi-goddess, with the wisdom of thousands of human-like lifetimes... much of that greater part of me bled away when I threw my ultimate attack against the 'Lucifer' comet – and it was not just *that*, but also my nobility, my god-knowledge, my moral and ethical superiority – all these sustained *terrible* damage... I was afflicted, made unclean, *polluted* in ways that you cannot understand... But I am coming back – I feel myself becoming mighty again, greater, every day... my visage will shine with the light of Heaven..."

Uncomfortable looks appeared on the faces of the ex-humans, as each dreaded to say what he or she was thinking.

Finally, Abruzzio – having been barely able to squeeze into the room past the crowd at the door – was able to protest, "Karéin, do you have any idea how *intimidating* it is, for us to hear you saying things like that? If I wasn't a scientist I'd be very insulted hearing this kind of commentary."

"Yeah, I do, Sylvia – this is what dear Bob Billings said to me, on one of our last nights together," quietly answered the Storied Watcher. "I know *exactly* what you are thinking... and not by reading your minds. You are in the presence of a much more powerful being who can disintegrate you with but a *thought* – one who, right now, you cannot effectively oppose – let alone, defeat. I do not blame you for being afraid of me."

"How would *you* know how we feel?" complained Chu. "We're just 'insects'... remember?"

"Because, I am *also* one of you – mostly, a human woman, who is almost as much afraid of the greater 'me', as you are... who above all else wants you to love me – while the god-like 'me' wants to lead you to the path where you can become more like me, share my nobility... and both of me are talking to you right now," remarked Karéin-Mayréij. "I breathe the same air that you do, I eat nice food and revel in the taste of it, I do my toilet, I take pleasure by the touch of sex... and, lately, I seem to have been re-discovering the repose of sleep... just like you do. Except that... I do *not*. I can live forever – alone if necessary – without *any* of these things. Except that I so much do *not* want to be alone... I want to be with you, all of you, for ever and ever."

"You all followin' that?" quipped Wolf. "Better hope she ain't got no skill-testin' quiz set-up for later."

There was a distant look on Misha's face.

"You know," he reflectively commented, "It may just be wishful-thinking... but I believe that I *am* following... some of it. *Amazing...*"

The alien-girl smiled warmly at the Russian.

"May your eyes be opened," she quietly inveighed.

"*Dios mio*," muttered the gangster.

He stared in half-shock at Karéin-Mayréij for a second or two, then mumbled, "You... uhh... you mind if I sit down?"

"Please," she requested, pleasantly, motioning to a spot near the head-board, where her telekinetic-force cleared away the bed-covers and pillows.

Chu – for her part – sat down, with the chair-back to her chest.

"Karéin," she requested, "Mind if I ask him a few questions?"

"Of course not... but I will not force him to answer," replied the alien-girl.

"Oh... no problem," said the FBI team-leader. "Confessions under duress went out about a century ago."

"*Suure*," interrupted the bounty-hunter. "Tell us another one, just like the other one, lady. If *that's* true – then how come I keep meetin' guys that got taken in by the Man, and come back missin' eyes, fingernails and half their dicks?"

Abruzzio winced.

Chu looked up at Wolf, with possibly-feigned offense.

"I meant within the *Bureau*," she parried. "About the other agencies of the Government... I can't vouch for them."

"*I* can, Madam!" commented Misha, his voice cold and unsympathetic. "At SVR, we have a mandatory training course for field-agents, on 'how to lie when being tortured by the American CIA'. The longer that one lasts, the higher one's grades. I made it to fifty-three seconds – which was a record, at the time."

"The official response from the Government," offered the voice of Kaysten, who was peering over Abruzzio's head, from outside, "Is that reports of tactics like these are all propaganda... lies, put out by America's enemies –"

He abruptly stopped talking, frozen in place by a look of sheer hatred, in the eyes of the Storied Watcher.

The air became suddenly molasses-thick with psychic-tension.

"*Shut the fuck up*, Jerr-ee!" she cursed. "Does your lovely government torture people? As the heavens attest my words – it *does!* I have *personally* felt the agony of it – many times – as your President's cruel dungeon-masters have afflicted poor Bob, Whitney, Curtis, Melissa and – worst of all – Tommy. Though this would again make me scream in pain... I can pull these hateful memories from the deep recesses of my mind, wherein I have learned to exile them upon first sharp stab, then to share them with you. What do you say, Jerr-ee? Ready for the, ahh, 'experience of a lifetime'?"

"Karéin –" admonished Chu, before the abashed Chief of Staff could stammer out an apology, "Vaporize me or not – you *know* that I have to try to stop you from doing that – I *have* to protect him! So do Otis and Will. Please, I'm asking you not to –"

"You need not endanger yourself out of loyalty to duty," countered Karéin-Mayréij. "I would only do this if Jerr-ee is brave enough to endure a few seconds, of what his empire inflicts on the helpless for minutes, hours, *days*, *weeks*, *months*... is he even the *least* bit curious about how his, ahh, pay-stipend, is being generated? Well? What will it *be*, Jerr-ee?"

"I... uhh... I get the point," retreated an ashen-faced Kaysten. "And... no... no, thank you. I'm a *civilian*, after all. Probably couldn't even get past basic training, you know."

"Come here, Jerr-ee," ordered the alien-girl.

As reluctantly as anyone could, he slowly shuffled through the worried throng, to stand in front of her.

This time – if it was any consolation – her attractiveness was manageable.

"*Listen*," she compassionately counseled, "I want you to know... I do not regard you as a coward, for having refused my request – it is an experience that I do not want anyone to *ever* have to undergo."

Uncharacteristically, her chin was quivering, as a tear appeared in one eye.

"Please excuse me, when I lash out, thus," she whimpered. "I do not mean anything by it... but I cannot *bear* that they are doing this – maybe as we speak – to my friends, my family... my *son*... I am the 'mighty hunter', the 'unavoidable-tracker'... yet I have *failed* them, all of them... what is to *become* of them... how can they ever forgive *me*..."

With the hovering-skill faltering, the Storied Watcher dropped on to the surface of the bed. She lowered her head between her knees and began to issue soft, sobbing noises.

It was like each atom in the air was crying along with her.

"I guess that's the 'human' part of her talking," whispered Ramirez.

Most of the others were completely at a loss, but Misha rushed over to comfort the alien-girl.

"It is alright, Karéin," he consoled, embracing her by the shoulders and cradling her body next to his own. "You are doing all that you can. You say that your actions are 'guided' – and for my part, looking back on it, I do not know exactly what drove me to attend that 'seminar' at the Tucson hotel; it was risky, with a low chance of success... yet I just could not stay away. If there is provenance at work here, I have faith that all will be as it is meant to be, in the end. An 'angel' should have that faith, as well... should she not?"

"May the Holy Light bless you, my love," came her grateful voice.

"Can I... uhh... go?" requested the Chief of Staff.

"No... please *stay*," she replied, lifting up red-lined eyelids.

She held out her hand.

Kaysten found a place to sit near the foot of the bed, and he took grasp.

The Storied Watcher laid a kiss on the top of his hand, an – although it was obviously meant only in a platonic manner – again, he had to concentrate like the Dickens to avoid an embarrassing physical-reaction.

"So... where were we?" he started.

"I was going to ask our friend Sebastiàn some questions, before we got, uhh, side-tracked," mentioned Chu. "May I?"

"Yeah... go ahead," assented Karéin-Mayréij, still being held in the arms of the Russian, with a wave of her hand. "And pay no more attention to the pitiful excuse-for-a-goddess who sits whimpering next to you."

"Can we say, 'mood-swings'?" whispered Hendricks to Boatman.

The black agent nodded, and – though the level of the comment was so low that not even the others next to the two FBI-agents could possibly have heard it – the alien-girl let out a soft, rueful chuckle.

Greetings From *Mailànkh*

Tanaka hugged the teenager, whose demeanor – matched in like-step by that of her mother – demonstrated both excitement and fear.

"Listen, team," Jacobson went on, "There's something almost as important – maybe more – revealed in the lines on this map. As we've all just had vividly demonstrated, this part of the schematic is only visible in ultra-violet – even the little bit of it that's being emitted by the fluorescents that are overhead in this room is enough for *us*... but it'd be completely invisible to a normal human, *except* if illuminated by a powerful source of UV, like a black-light or something. Which implies that it was *intentionally* made to be a secret, 'hidden in plain-view', as it were... something meant to be hidden even from the staff who'd be looking at this map, all the time. And if I were to hazard a guess, I'd say that –"

"*Damn you, Jacobson!*" gasped an instantly-overjoyed Billings. "You beautiful, smart space-jockey – you just earned your pay for the next thousand years! A secret tunnel – a way *out*... right?"

"Thanks for the compliment, Bob," answered the former Mars mission commander, "Although I'd remind you... 'a thousand times zero, is still nothing'."

"I'm sure hopin' y'all right, Bob," remarked White, his eyes trying to squint out every last detail. "But maybe we shouldn't get our hopes up too much – what if we're just interpretin' it wrong, Captain? I mean – there's no writin' on it, no key-codes, no *nothin'*..."

"But why would they deliberately hide a service-conduit from the people who are running this accursed jail, anyway?" asked Tanaka.

"Whatever the case – and I guess we'll find out, one way or another – I'll remove the map from the binder, then," said the Mars mission commander. "We'll undoubtedly need it for reference."

"Listen, Jacobson," asked the salesman, "You mind if I keep the manifest, as we travel?"

"No... go ahead," said Jacobson. "But what for?"

"A souvenir, I guess," offered Billings. "Or toilet-paper... if we get desperate."

Melissa guffawed, to the consternation of her mother. She looked at the four Mars astronauts, pointed at the salesman and observed,

"Bob – ah don' care what they says 'bout all this 'Sari' stuff makin' us into super-heroes 'n such... but y'all the same ol' Bob that y'all *always* been."

Billings grinned, appreciatively, as he reached over the table and removed a number of pages from the first binder.

"Glad you're so sure of that," he mentioned. "Only thing that *I'm* certain about, these days, is that I'm going to get you, your mother, your brother, and Tommy – *especially* him – out of this rat-hole. No idea *how*... but I'm gonna."

"Y'all know, Bob," opined White, "If I didn't know y'all better, I'd even say y'all got *faith* 'bout this thing."

"Death and taxes – I got faith about *those*," muttered the salesman. "More about the latter."

"Devon," interrupted Jacobson, "You got the AV-stuff working?"

"Think so," replied the black ex-astronaut. "Want me to try it?"

"Sure – go ahead," said the Mars mission commander. "There don't seem to be any removable-media around here – other than the printed materials, of course – but maybe it has a content-menu or something. Anything more that we can learn about this place might be helpful... although we can't waste too much time watching movies."

"Yeah," ruefully agreed White. "Places to go, people to see... and kill 'em, don't y'all know."

He studied the remote control device for another few seconds and announced, "Here goes."

He pushed a button.

Nothing happened.

Then he tried another... no luck.

Finally – on the third try – an interference-pattern showed up on the video-screen, followed by a blue background.

White fumbled about, but couldn't get anything else to appear on the screen.

"No labels on the damn buttons," he complained. "Kinda shootin' in the dark, here, Cap'n."

"Well I don't blame it for being that way... anybody down here's *bound* to have the blues," commented Billings.

"You have a talent for understatement there, Bob," wryly mentioned Tanaka. "But I'm having an *amazing* experience just looking at it – so keep it powered up, if you don't mind, Devon."

"What you mean, Professor?" asked the African-American ex-astronaut.

"It's kind of hard to put into words," explained the woman, "But it's like I can... oh God, how would I describe it... it's like I can see... no, *not* see, not that, but *like* that... I can *feel* the signals going back and forth on the screen, the pulses, their rhythm, their beat... I have to concentrate to turn it off, or it'll hypnotize me... *crazy* stuff..."

Tanaka bowed slightly down and began to rub her forehead.

"Didn't Karéin say something about, 'I can ride the trail of electro-pulses, from ISS2 to the *Infinity*, and back', and so on?" reminisced Jacobson.

"Definitely," affirmed White. "If y'all remember, it was quite a trick, considerin' the low power of the signal, against all the background-noise out there... never *could* figure out how she did it."

"You might also be interested to know that she kept telling me – when we were back in Tucson, that is – that she could, uhh, 'smell' things like radio-signals and so on," remarked Billings. "Spooks from the government – I'd assume the same ones that shanghai'ed all of us down here – they dropped a bunch of bugs on my house, and Sari claimed that she had shut 'em all down, simply by, uhh, 'broadcasting' on the same frequency; but she also said that there was a limit to it... there were only so many that she could jam at one time. I only half-believed it... suppose I should have paid a little more attention..."

"There have been a lot of 'could have beens, should have beens' lately," reminded Boyd. "Like... for *my* part, 'why did I believe so much as a *word* that the President said, when we landed back on Earth'. If I had just –"

His voice was cut off in mid-sentence, by the utterly-unexpected image of what must have been some kind of military control-center, complete with camouflage-bedecked men sitting at various computer-consoles, appearing suddenly to fill the monitor, while a red light began to issue from a small, fish-eye-like glass-thing just above the top of the screen.

A stern, no-nonsense face, that of a robust, crew-cut twenty-something soldier, stared into the screen.

They saw him turn and shout over his shoulder, "Legion Commander – come *quickly* – we've got the link back!"

In no more than two or three seconds, an older – but still tough-looking – face crowded on to one side of the screen.

This man remarked, "Well, thank God for small blessings... we thought we'd lost contact with you guys in the lower-levels, once and for all, and –"

A perplexed, then suspicious, look appeared on the older soldier's face.

"Who *are* you?" he demanded. "Identify yourselves!"

What y'all want me to say? came White's fast-thinking broadcast, into the minds of all in the deep-below room.

Want me just to turn it off?

No, silently responded Jacobson.

I'll talk to him.

"Hello," greeted the former Mars mission commander, toward the video-screen. "I presume that we have a two-way conversation going, here?"

"Identify yourselves!" barked the top-side gendarme-commander.

"Oh... *certainly*," replied the ex-astronaut, with an insincere half-smile. "My name is Sam Jacobson, formerly of the U.S. Air Force. Who would I have the, uhh... *pleasure*, of addressing, today?"

"I don't have to tell you that," countered the other man, "But I'll choose to do so, anyway. My name is Captain Nicholas Cowin, in charge of security for the R.B. Cheney Special Agency Interrogation Facility. I *demand* to know the reason why you're on this channel – as well as what happened to the Facility-staff who I had expected to be on-line, as of when we re-established the communications-link. You had better have a damn *good* reason for being in a prohibited area... especially under the current circumstances."

"GrayWar," whispered White to Boyd.

The other ex-astronaut nodded.

Jacobson shook his head, suppressing an urge to laugh.

"Do I... do we... have a good reason, for being down here?" he muttered. "I *honestly* don't know what to say to that, 'Captain'... but let me ask *you* a question – do you have any *idea* about what's going on, here?"

"You're in no position to ask *anything!*" gruffly retorted the soldier. "Identify yourselves *immediately* – starting with the Jap-woman to your side."

"He's *so* much 'asking for it', Sam," complained Tanaka.

"You want us to 'identify' ourselves?" sarcastically commented Jacobson. "Oh... by all means. If you can see everyone around the table here, then let me introduce Majors Brent Boyd and Devon White... also Professor Cherie Tanaka – she's uhh, the 'Jap', although she's of course native-born American, not that it'd make much of a difference... after all, this is a truly, uhh, 'international' facility... isn't it? We also have Mr. Bob Billings, salesman from Tucson, Arizona, and Melissa and Whitney Claremont, who are friends of Bob's –"

"You wanted to know what happened to the buggers who were supposed to be in this nice little board-room, before we got here?" interjected Billings, toward the screen and camera. "Well... let's just say that the inmates are running the asylum, these days, and some of us are crazier than others... funny thing – being tortured for weeks on end *does* that to you! I'll bet your little white-frocked 'doctors' lasted about five seconds, when the rest of the prisoners – err – *victims*, showed up here. Too bad; I'd really have enjoyed seeing it. Maybe you captured the video? Send me a copy, some time, if you don't mind – I'm sure it's even better watching, the second, third, fiftieth times around... you know?"

White half-suppressed a guffaw.

"Got another seat in your the-ater room, Bob?" he whispered, with a grin.

They saw the top-side gendarme whisper something to an associate, who ran rapidly off the camera's field-of-vision.

"Now, what we all have in common, down here, 'Captain'," continued Jacobson's barely-suppressed-fury voice, "Is that we all seem to have been kidnapped by the government – certainly including the CIA, and who knows how many other agencies – and have been forcibly and illegally taken to this damnable prison... where several of us have been subjected to the most cruel and inhuman abuse *imaginable,* for reasons that we now know about – but that I'm going to leave to your imagination."

After taking a second to cough, the Mars mission commander warned, "But here's the kicker : *we're* on the loose now, *we* know where we're going and what we intend to do when we get there... and if I were *you,* I'd be looking for the next flight out of town... off this island, I mean. You *don't* want to be around, when we come looking for whomever is behind this disgraceful situation. Oh – and make sure to mention it to your superiors, whoever they are – tell the Air Force, too, because in sending my team and I down here, the brass have committed the great *grandfather* of all fuck-ups. Compared to what we're going to do to them when we get out, they'll think that Custer had it *easy.* You got *that,* 'Captain'?"

For a second, the other man hesitated, but then, he returned to script.

"You're escaped prisoners, then?" he challenged. "Because if so, you should be aware that a *very* large contingent of Legion-soldiers, backed up by other, highly-skilled riot-control professionals – who I choose not to identify – are currently on their way to the lower-levels of this facility, to restore order. You're instructed to lay down any weapons in your possession, remove all belts and shoelaces and proceed to the nearest elevator... sit down with your hands over your heads, while awaiting the arrival of our guards."

"Maybe we *should,*" taunted White, *sotto voce,* to Boyd. "Run up our body-count by a few, don't y'all know."

Boyd returned a grin, while the gendarme went on, "If you're foolish enough to ignore this order, the Legion and facility staff are authorized to use deadly force against you, without any further warning. I need your answer within thirty seconds – or I'll cut the connection and assume that you've refused and have understood the likely consequences. Starting now."

Jacobson chuckled, with a savage-looking smile on his face.

"That's more or less what I *expected* to hear from you little amateur soldier-boys," he shot back. "And all I can say is... *you're* warning *us* about 'likely consequences'? Well – get ready for the '*un*likely consequences', coming soon to a bunch of in-over-their heads mercs, near *you.* You got *no* idea!"

Boyd stood up.

"I have this uncontrollable urge to give them a 'shiner', Commander," he spat, with almost-invisible streams of smoke coming from clenched fists. "Please let me, uhh, *enlighten* them!"

Jacobson put up a cautionary finger.

"No... use your gun... you've got a few rounds left, don't you?" requested the big man.

"More than a few... lots, in fact," replied the scowling ex-astronaut.

He quickly un-slung his auto-rifle, pointing it directly at the reverse-direction video camera above the video-screen.

"Greetings from *Mailànkh*, fucker!" cursed Boyd, as he pulled the trigger.

That Nasty Little Glow

"So... Sebastiàn," inquired the FBI team-leader, "Can you please tell me, where you would have been, that could account for you having been, uhh, contaminated?"

"Why should I tell you *anythin'*?" he curtly answered.

"Like I said a while ago – I can't *make* you say anything," replied Chu. "But it's in our mutual interest to be as honest as possible with each other. What're you *afraid* of? Neither I nor Agents Boatman or Hendricks are in a position to arrest you – we're also 'on the run' from the government... *most* of it, at least. If it means anything... we won't use what you say against you in court."

"Hey... you done read him his rights, Minnie?" joked Boatman.

"What *you* say, *chica*?" the gangster asked of the Storied Watcher.

"Truth given freely, is ever better than lies extracted by hurt," she quietly remarked. "*Why* must each generation of mortals re-learn the lesson?"

"I think that means a 'yes', pardner," commented Wolf.

"¡*Carajo!*" muttered the *Mara*. "Well... I 'spose you right about one thing – ain't *nadie* comin' to spell you down here L.A.-way, so... okay... here's what it is. See... I never even wanted to end up in this fuckin' *puto* town, anyway – *mi barrio* is back in Texas... south Houston, specifically... I'm the shot-caller back in my hood... anyway, *el jéfé* – he get some kind of special fuckin' shipment, captured goods after a deal out in the eastern-counties went down wrong – we lost six or seven *compañeros* in that one, by the way – should never have even tried it with out-of-staters who we don' know – an' just after that, *el jéfé*, he make some kind of other deal to get this box off *sus manos*, so I'm the 'lucky one' who gets to haul it cross-country to L.A. –"

"Whoa," interrupted Boatman, whose knowing gaze was quickly exchanged with those of Hendricks and their mutual boss.

"Wait a *minute, hombre*," directed the big black agent. "You all said, it was a 'box'? What you mean?"

"Jus' what I *say*, Mister FBI-Man," retorted Sebastiàn. "It was just a big fuckin' box... that's all. Fit in the back of my van... but *no mucho* room to spare afterward, you know?"

"Let's not jump to conclusions, here," advised Chu.

She bent forward to query the gangster.

"Sebastiàn," she demanded, "What, *exactly*, was inside this box? Drugs, weapons, money, subversive literature – Muslim-books, for example – or pirated movies or computer-programs... stuff like that?"

"Got no *idea* what was in it, *mujer*," he countered. "It was sealed tight, 'cept for a couple of little holes in one side, but too dark to look inside an' see anythin'. An' anyway, 'drugs', 'cash'... that kind of shit? No *way*, man! *El jéfé* not gonna send a lieutenant like me *that* far, dodgin' the Man for the whole trip – we had to detour all over the place, to beat the roadblocks – even for top-of-the-line synth or guns... we got plenty of both back in the *barrio*, home-town-wise. Like, maybe it was heavy-duty shit – you know, rocket-launchers, machine-guns, *esa clase de materia*? Always a premium for those – can't just buy 'em where we come from... you gotta go to the Uptown gun shops... *sabe usted*?"

"Listen, Sebastiàn," pressed Chu, with deadly seriousness, "Think very, *very*, hard – all our lives may depend on what you know. Where did you deliver this, uhh, 'box'? Who's got it now? Do you know what its intended use was?"

"*No mujer*," argued the *Mara*. "*El jéfé* jus' tell us to drop it off with one of his *amigos* in Chino, but we never made it that far... see, before we make it into L.A., *strange* shit was happenin' in the back of the van – *muchachos* was raggin' 'bout gettin' sick or somethin' – so we was fixin' to pull over for the night, but we hit a roadblock, popped the tires, we goin' nowhere... then a bunch of fuckin' Aryan skinheads show up, well you can guess what happens next – I barely got away *con mi vida*... 'far as I know the rest of *mis compañeros* went down right there, like a gangster should, with they boots on, you know?"

"But you didn't... die... there... right?" challenged Boatman.

"After it go hot for *unos minutos*, I was outnumbered *veinte al uno*, *mi amigo*," explained Sebastiàn, "So I get the fuck out of there... don' know the turf, hide here an' there, lookin' for brother *Maras* – mind you they can be almost as bad as the other 'bangers if they don' know you – but all I run into is them nig... uhh, *lo siento*, Mister FBI-man, I mean... them Bloods an' Crips an 18th-Streeters. Thought I found some of *mis hijos* in one place, but turned out they was them fuckin' *Zetas*, had to run for my life for over a mile before I shake 'em off. An' finally, I end up here. Things is *loco* out there, *hombre*... they shootin' at *anybody* they don' know to see – one of 'em got me, I guess, but I got him first, *por supesto*."

"Anything else?" asked Chu.

"That's about it," he answered. "*Never* should have taken this fuckin' trip," he added. "Didn' want to, in the first place. But where I come from, you *don'* say 'no' to *el jéfé*... if you don' wanna be eatin' your balls for breakfast the next day."

"Minnie," warned Boatman, trying to contain his mixture of excitement and fear, "I think he ain't kiddin' about it bein' 'heavy-duty' stuff."

"Yeah – and if you're right, it's here in L.A. with us, man," added the third agent, with a good imitation of Kaysten's former ashen complexion suddenly showing. "Hello, Kingdom Come. Anybody bring a Bible?"

"Karéin," stammered Abruzzio, "Have you been following this? You have to get us all out of here, *immediately*. If it goes *off* –"

"I will protect," promised the alien-girl. "But to what peril do you refer?"

"I think you just failed *your* quiz, Miss Mars Goddess," interjected the bounty-hunter. "Remember them Paki-bombs they said got jacked awhile ago, when the whole thing went south, over there? They already set one of 'em off, somewhere... nasty damn scenes on the TV, *that's* for sure. If them camel-fuckers managed to smuggle one of 'em past the border, we're shit out of luck... especially if it's anywhere near here."

"Oh... yeah," she replied. "The atom-smashing ones. Right."

"Well?" nervously demanded Kaysten.

"Well... *what*, Jerr-ee?" retorted Karéin-Mayréij.

"Are you going to just *sit* there?" complained the Chief of Staff.

"What do you want me to *do?*" she deflected.

"What if it's in the basement *below* us, or something?" he implored.

"It is not," she reassured. "I do not smell anything... *dangerous*, in this vicinity. At least... nothing like *that*. The only shine-glow around here, is on Sebastiàn."

"What if it's, uhh, just past where you can detect it?" suggested Ramirez.

"Then it is probably far enough away, so that my 'bubble' can protect all of us," claimed the alien-girl.

Uncharacteristically, the *Mara* now spoke up.

"*Oyeme, chica*... you ever *seen* them things go off?" he stated. "I see one on TV, once. Pretty fuckin' big bang, you know... you stop a bullet – *bueno*, I can just see some kinda *loco* magic stuff doin' *that* – but, ain't no *way* you livin' through a bomb. *Carajo*... an' I was right next to it... assumin', of course, that these FBI-guys ain't just makin' the whole thing up."

"Their mind-emanations do not speak of deception," noted the Storied Watcher, majesty rising in her voice with each syllable. "And as to the whole atom-thing... in my desperation to find the power to deal with the comet, several times did I fly through the void, recklessly close to your star, the better to take in its infernal energy, welcome it into my breast; a 'Sun' such as this is like *millions* of your atom-smashing bombs, all going off at once, all the time. It hurt *terribly* – my whole body was on fire, I glowed like a short-lived spark in the night – but behold how I survived *that*..."

"My *God*," gasped Abruzzio. "So *that* was what you were doing, when we thought you had disappeared? After you left Jacobson's ship, that is."

Karéin-Mayréij nodded, with a far-off look, as a shudder of some sort, accompanied by the music of ethereal power, reverberated through the building.

"The other 'me' hopes that some day, Sylvia," she half-sang, "You will come to understand a small portion of what I had to do, in those fateful times, when – unlike so many years ago – at long last, the noble and mighty Storied Watcher, did not flinch from the challenge that the Immortal Light laid before her... death was at every turn... but she was at peace, after all..."

Her voice trailed off.

"The 'noble and mighty'," Ramirez quietly stated. "*Seguro... es lo verdad.*"

"I'd go for that," echoed Abruzzio.

For a few seconds, everyone was silent.

Then, Wolf questioned, with an arched eyebrow, "So you'd be right at ease, havin' somebody set one of 'em off, right underneath your feet?

"Uhh... no," admitted Karéin-Mayréij. "I am a *powerful* Destroying Angel..., not a stupid one. I did not live for eons, by taking reckless chances. And I am now but a sad remnant of my former self, dear friend. Far more powerful than any of you here on Earth, but far less than she who saved your planet. Until... she comes back to me..."

"Amazing, and – understood," acknowledged Misha. "But at what distance *can* you detect the presence of nuclear radiation, Karéin? If we knew that, we might be better able to evaluate the risk."

"That is... *complicated*," she explained. "It depends on where I am – the range is a lot more, if I am flying through the air – and also on how much of the particle-leaky-stuff is there – how concentrated it is... if it is hidden inside a special container designed to conceal the energy-waves, then I may not be able to detect it at all, I suppose. But I might *infer* its presence, by other trail-signs."

"Then, when do we leave?" pestered Kaysten. "You just admitted that the damn thing could be on the next *street-corner*, and you wouldn't have any idea that it's there... right?"

"I did not say anything of the *sort*, Jerr-ee," countered the Storied Watcher. "Oh-kay, you want the truth? I have not yet had any practice in sniffing out this manner of weapon – I have been *avoiding* having atom-smashing bombs dropped on my head; why, then, would I intentionally go *looking* for such a thing? All that I honestly *can* say is... the smell of the glow-particles is still pretty strong, on Sebastiàn's body; so I would have to assume that this 'bomb' you speak of, must not be very well-wrapped-up, for its essence to have so contaminated him. If it were anywhere near *here*, I would know of it."

"Well – I'm not willing to risk *my* life on that kind of guesswork," argued the Chief of Staff. "I'm not hanging around here for so much as five more minutes!"

"Door's that way, pardner," shrugged Wolf. "I'm bettin' you get a block and a half before one of them gangsters out there gets him a nice new blond-haired main-boy. I hear they *like* 'em thin 'n tall."

"Come *on!*" half-begged Kaysten, toward Karéin-Mayréij. "You *know* that our lives are in your hands. I'm asking you, as humbly as I can –"

"Karéin," interrupted Chu, "I know that the Director – and I – had an arrangement with you... but this information, if correct, has completely changed our situation, and you have to *understand* –"

"How has it changed 'our situation', Minnie?" retorted the alien-girl. "Bob, Whitney, Curtis, Melissa and Tommy are still somewhere out there, in a private hell of your President's making, your government is still hunting me and seeking to kill me, I still have, ahh, a 'score to settle', and this problem with the, uhh, 'Moo-slim bombs', was going on before I even awoke on *Mailànkh*... from my point-of-view, very little has changed. I have no interest in whatever squabbles that your President has with these kingdoms. What would you have me *do*?"

"My primary duty now, has to be to protect the Chief of Staff – and the only practical way to do that is to get him out of the Greater Los Angeles area, before whoever has that bomb, decides to set it off," declared the FBI team-leader. "Perhaps just as important, I have to warn the Director of the weapon's likely presence here, so that the Government can take appropriate measures to either recover it or neutralize it."

"Yeah... and what's *that* mean, lady?" grunted the bounty-hunter. "Like, you phone home and tell 'em, then, one minute later, the Air Force flattens everything for ten blocks of where you *think* it is? Better hope them skinhead fuckers haven't figured out how to rig a dead-man's fuse."

Chu was about to reply, but the Storied Watcher beat her to it.

"Wolf... if you do not mind my asking?" inquired Karéin-Mayréij, "What is a 'dead-man fuse'? There are none upon this world who know how to animate the dead, make them walk as zombies –"

"Somethin' that the Muslims cooked up a ways back, 'far as I know," explained the bounty-hunter. "It's basically a trigger... disarmed, 'long as you're squeezin' it in your hand – but the minute you get shot, well, that kind of relaxes your muscles, you know – and when you let go... 'boom'!"

"It is a standard terrorist-tool, used especially in hostage-situations," added Misha. "The Muslim Salvation League is known to devise very sophisticated versions of this trigger; some, for example, will detonate if they no longer detect a pulse or a heart-beat, upon the human who is rigged with the bomb."

Now, the Storied Watcher's eyes had again taken on the far-away stare.

"Do any of you know," she requested, "Between the time when one of these triggers is activated, and when the explosives detonate... how long is that?"

"Usually, no more than a quarter-second," stated the Russian. "Depending on the equipment that is being used for the firing-mechanism."

"I... *see*," she enigmatically remarked.

"*Look*, Karéin," demanded Chu, "I'm not going to get into a bitch-session with you, over who's done the worse slights to who, between you and the President, I mean – there's no *time*. If you're not willing to airlift the Chief of Staff and my team out of here, then the *least* you can do, is permit me to call the Director – I still have my mobile-communicator, remember – and request that the Government send a helicopter, or something, to take Jerry to safety."

"*Now* you're talking!" interjected an elated Kaysten.

"Yeah... that is, if she's *willin'* to let any of us go," mentioned Boatman. "Don't suppose I should really be sayin' this – but as long as Mr. Kaysten there's around here, maybe the Air Force won't be takin' no pot-shots at her."

"I give you my word of honor," offered the FBI team-leader, "That we won't go with the Chief of Staff, when he's transported out of L.A.. my team and I will all come back here and rejoin your group, if that's what you want."

"We *will*?" peevishly spoke Hendricks. "Do I get a vote?"

"FBI ain't a democracy," philosophically noted Boatman.

"How many seats *are* there, on that helicopter?" quipped Ramirez.

"I do *not* take hostages," curtly commented the alien-girl. "And I can defend myself quite adequately, without risking Jerr-ee's life, in any event. Oh, and by the way, I neither indiscriminately slaughter helpless peasants – nor do I torture captive children. Unlike some leaders familiar to you."

"*Well*, then?" pressed the Chu.

"Now, *you* look!" argued Karéin-Mayréij. "If you, uhh, 'tel-ee-phone' back to your Director from this city – then surely he, and probably the rest of your government, Air-Warrior Force included – will reason that I am, also, located here; else-wise, how would you have moved so quickly from the big canyon, to this city? What is, therefore, to stop your President from dropping one of these atom-smashing bombs on Los Angeles, hoping to, uhh, 'take out' both myself and this 'Moo-slim' weapon whose presence you suspect, all at once?"

"But I'll ask him –" protested the FBI team-leader, until she was cut off by the alien-girl's upraised index-finger.

"And *then*," continued the Storied Watcher, "When the outcry comes, he can blame the whole thing on the latter being the source of the explosion, as was done after the battle at the Tucson hotel – the only difference would be one of magnitude... and I have already seen that your government cares scarcely how many it kills, when trying to strike me down. I came to Los Angeles precisely *because* it seemed like the last place where I could be hunted – now, you propose for me to stand up like a target-bird let loose from a wicker-basket! Does it sound like a wise thing to do, Minn-ee-Choo?"

"Hey... I *like* it!" cracked the third agent. "It rhymes."

The alien-girl sent him a malicious smile.

"*Usted sabe*, Missus FBI-Lady," commented the gangster, "If *chica* here really all they *say* she is... you bitchin' the wrong person. Bad idea to dis' somebody who out-gun you."

"Thanks for the friendly advice," amicably countered Boatman. "I'll look y'all up, if I want some more trainin' on 'relationships'."

"I take it that's a 'no', then?" shot back a peeved Chu, at the alien-girl.

The Asian-American agent stood up, glowering.

"*Fine*, then!" she exclaimed. "Will, Otis, get your things together... we'll escort Mr. Kaysten to a suitable distance away from here – as far from the Chino area as possible, opposite direction, I mean – and then we'll just have to hope that we get a signal."

"Uhh... just the *three* of us, Minnie?" inquired the black agent, with a worried expression. "We might have to walk for a few miles, you know."

"Four, if you count the Chief of Staff," answered the FBI team-leader.

"Gee... *thanks*," muttered Kaysten. "Do I get a gun?"

"Ms. Chu," advised Misha, "I understand your frustration, but this is *highly* inadvisable. We are much safer in a group, with her protection –"

The FBI team-leader stormed out of the bedroom and began to collect some of the items that had been strewn hither and yon, in more convivial times.

The rest of the bedroom-crowd followed closely behind, though Sebastiàn stopped dead in his tracks when he saw the smoldering forms of *Vîrya Ahn'jë* and her war-siblings, in the middle of the room.

"I've had *enough* of her 'protection', Misha!" savagely called Chu. "It'll get us all *killed*... probably sooner rather than later. You know, Karéin – for a 'goddess', you're a pretty damn self-indulgent one, what with the possible incineration of an entire *city* full of innocent people, at stake. Jerry – you ready to go, yet? Get your shoes on."

Now, the Storied Watcher had also come to her feet; and, slowly, she walked over to confront the FBI team-leader, standing in front of the Asian-American woman in the large, open, central-area.

"Well... what are you going to *do?*" challenged Chu. "Wave that magic sword at me – chop my head off – or something? Go *ahead*, then – show all of them how 'noble' and 'godly' you are, Karéin!"

"Minnie – don't *push* her, for God's sake –" cautioned Boatman.

But unexpectedly, the alien-girl got down on one knee, submissively looking up at her accuser.

"Minn-ee... you are a woman of iron-strong principle; you remind me greatly of another – whose own words of reproach, uttered at no slight personal risk – also set back my pride," softly recounted Karéin-Mayréij. "You cannot know... it is *so* hard, balancing my own safety, against what I should do... what I *must-do*... forgive me, I beg! I meant no offense."

Nonplussed, the lead FBI-agent replied, "If that's how a, uhh, 'goddess' apologizes... then, 'apology accepted', Karéin. Get up... will you? You're making me *uncomfortable!*"

The Storied Watcher rose to her feet, with restored dignity and majesty issuing from every pore.

Though unnerved, Chu added, "But it's *not* going to change my position – I *have* to warn the Director. I hope you understand."

"I do... but the risk is to *me* – and I have a question," responded the alien-girl. "I assume that your tel-ee-phone signals would work, from far up, on high?"

"Uh-oh," joked Wolf. "I *know* where this is headin'."

"*Sure* they would – less interference," confirmed the FBI team-leader. "Provided that they're within range of a cell-tower, which can be several kilometers under ideal conditions, or, with a line-of-sight to a satellite... but there aren't a lot of the latter working, these days. What are you getting at?"

"Well... to meet you 'half-way' in this dilemma, I reckon that you need to call your 'Director', the better to find out what to do with this supposed Moo-slim bomb... Jerr-ee as well," remarked Karéin-Mayréij, with a mischievous gleam in her eye. "While for my part, I do not want my location to be too easily traced, back to this domicile, nor to any fixed spot on the surface of your planet, where homing-weapons could conveniently be aimed. So... I was thinking..."

"Oh, no – now, *wait* a minute, Karéin!" protested Chu. "You're not suggesting – *are* you?"

"We can – ahh – 'take off', from the top of this building, and travel far enough away so that we cannot be easily found," continued the Storied Watcher, with a wry smile. "You will have to let me smell the signal that your little box sends out, so that I can open enough of my 'bubble', and let the electro-pulses go where they may; should your Air Force still contrive to target a missile or two on us, by tracking this same signature, from – say – two leagues above this city... those, I will easily be able to evade by closing my bubble and doing a few quick maneuvers. What say you, Minn-ee Choo?"

"Hey... there you go again," cracked Hendricks. "Otis – did you bring that harmonica? You could make a *song* out of this."

Boatman wearily shook his head.

"Just the two of us?" asked Chu, with considerable trepidation.

The Storied Watcher cast her gaze at Kaysten.

"You are not afraid of heights... are you, Jerr-ee?" she teased.

"Oh no – no *way!*" he stammered. "That last trip was bad *enough*... and we at least had something underneath our feet."

"It is not *so* bad," commented Misha. "I actually became quite used to flying with her... although I would advise you to, ahh, stay away from those two daggers, if you can."

A weird, annoying sound issued from the pile of armor and weapons that the Storied Watcher had left in the room.

"Shh!" cautioned the alien-girl. "*Væran Ss'éth'ch'* and his war-brother both heard that. You will hurt their feelings."

"Sorry to upset 'em," offered Wolf, "But what the Russkie means is, "Get too close to either of them, and you got your choice of bein' freeze-dried or microwaved, while you fly coach."

"I usually do not stray far from my war-children," explained Karéin-Mayréij, "But here, we are only going a short distance upward... to make it easier, I will leave you all in the safekeeping of *Vîrya I'ëä'b'* and her siblings. That way, you will not have to endure any, uhh, 'discomfort' – though in the long-run, it were better that you would learn to tolerate the heat, cold and energy-glow, which are the essence of my children."

"How does one 'become used to' being right next to something that looks like it just came out of an oven?" demanded Ramirez, pointing at *Vîrya Ahn'jë*.

"Easy," parried the Storied Watcher. "The answer is... 'slowly'."

"Don't wear a suit that you can't afford to lose, pardner," grunted Wolf, ruefully reflecting upon the many burn-marks on his prized denims.

"Karéin," asked Chu, uncertainly, "What happens if the Director says to pull the Chief of Staff, and or my team as well, right away?"

"Then," calmly answered the Storied Watcher, "I will honor his request, and safely deposit all of you, or some of you, – including Jerr-ee, if so demanded – at a safe distance. Then... I return to... *war*."

"I, uhh... *see*," grimly acknowledged the FBI team-leader.

"Well," she added, "I guess we had better get going. Are Otis and Will supposed to come with us? Up to the roof, I mean."

"If they so desire," confirmed Karéin-Mayréij. "Jerr-ee can come too."

Her gaze fell upon the armor-pile.

"I *know*, dear Little Tornado-Diamond-Curtain," she spoke out loud, in a gentle, motherly voice, apparently to no-one. "But the measure of love is sometimes, to be ready to let go... if that is what must be."

The buckler slowly floated to a spot near the burning armor and slid underneath it, making a pitiful, whimpering sound all the while.

Kaysten looked genuinely upset, though he tried hard not to show it.

"Coming?" Chu called out to Boatman, Hendricks and the Chief of Staff.

The three men shuffled forward, casting awkward glances over their shoulders at the gangster, the bounty-hunter, the Russian and the two scientists.

"Oh – I forgot," said the FBI team-leader, as they neared the door to the outside hallway. "Anything that I should bring?"

"That depends," replied the alien-girl.

"On what?" asked Chu.

"If I must out-fly the missiles of your President," counseled Karéin-Mayréij, "The force-stresses so imposed, could seriously injure, perhaps kill, a normal human... not you, Minn-ee Choo. None the less, the experience might be, ahh, *unpleasant*... so, I would ask that you bring a wash-towel."

"A 'towel'?" queried the woman. "What *for*? I'm not understanding you."

"And... that you face outward from myself, if you please," requested the Storied Watcher.

With A Voice That Big, It Can Only Be...

After gathering up everything of use that could conveniently be carried, they had broken camp from the 'boardroom', Billings alternating with Claremont and Melissa in carrying the drowsy little girl.

To the great relief of all, the child had woken up once or twice to ask for water and candy; the first request was fulfilled out of the salesman's purloined-along-the-way water-bottle, but the second could only be half dealt-with, by the provision of a few soda-crackers.

None of them had had a lot to eat, and – though the Storied Watcher's strange energy kept them going, the lack of simple comforts like food, drink and, above all, a chance to *unwind* – was starting to wear on the group.

After going through and ice-cementing the first door on the left – nondescript as every other, and one that would certainly have been missed, were it not for the new-found map in Jacobson's possession – they now stood in the half-light, in front of another portal, this with a small, square window in its middle at about eye-height.

"Same idea as before?" suggested White. "'Cept I sure don't want to get another whiff of that damn gas they had back on the other stairs."

"Gas?" nervously whimpered the teenager.

"Yeah," explained Billings. "*Nasty* stuff, too – Professor was saying that if we hadn't got our butts out of it, we might not be here talking to you, right now."

"More than a few seconds of exposure to it might very well have killed a normal person," added Tanaka. "Not you, Melissa, neither your mother... you're anything *but* 'an ordinary human'... but we don't want to push our luck, and we're not sure about little Elissha there – so if you smell something 'funny', warn us immediately and move away from it, as quickly as you can... you understand?"

A grim-faced Claremont and her daughter, both nodded vigorously.

"We've run into traps on a number of these stairwells," commented Jacobson. "Mostly guns, on swiveling-turrets mounted on the walls, and they seem to target you automatically. Occasionally we've received verbal warnings from the owners of this jail... sometimes we haven't, so don't assume you'll have a lot of time to decide what to do, once the bullets start flying. If you see a bright light shining right at you – Cherie, can you protect Whitney and Melissa?"

"Definitely," confirmed Tanaka. "Ladies – remember that thing that you saw encase us, back in the room where we first encountered you?"

"Yeah – thang that look like a big soap-bubble?" asked the teenager.

Claremont gestured affirmatively.

"It's actually a force-field," explained the professor. "I've discovered that it will stop pistol- and rifle-bullets – though I don't know how well it would do against anything with more, uhh, firepower... hopefully we won't have to find out. So if we're attacked, crouch down as close as you can to me, and you should be fine. I'll shout the word, 'Shield', just before, or when, I power it up... okay?"

Melissa nodded.

"You mean that thang come from *y'all*, Miz Cherie?" she exclaimed. "How y'all *doin'* it, anyways? An' why don' y'all just keep it up, all th' time... we be safer that way, wouldn' we?"

"Yep – it's powered right from yours truly," answered Tanaka with a proud half-smile. "And the truth *is*, honey, I don't really *know* how I 'do it'... I only know that I *can* 'do it', also that lightening-bolt that you saw me fire, back in the room. And as for why I don't have my 'Shield' going continuously – well, when your own abilities mature, you'll start to understand why... it takes a lot of concentration to keep it going – not to mention, it's, uhh, *draining*... kind of like the feeling you get after spending two hours writing an exam, you know?"

"Uh-huhh," bluffed the teenager.

"One other thing," noted the former Science Officer. "I'll call out 'Sword', before I use my attack – that's a warning for anyone in front of me, to get out of the way. Same goes for Major Boyd – he'll call out either 'Midnight' or 'Shine', and Devon's trigger word is 'Sno-Kone'. You got that?"

"Ah gets it, bein' as Major White makin' it like Christmas," replied Melissa, with a wry smile. "But what Cap'n Sam 'n Bob be usin'? For *they* super-hero words, ah means."

"Oh, no – you're not going to get me to say *that* word again," countered Billings, with a friendly wave of his finger. "Been there, done that! Want me to disappear for good? Well then... get me *out* of here."

"I don't talk – I just express myself, uhh, *kinetically*," added Jacobson. "Listen, enough with the briefing – Brent, do you want to recce this one out?"

"No, but that's what I get for being able to cover my tracks... so here I go," muttered the ex-astronaut.

With gun at the ready, he motioned for the rest of them to back off from the portal-area, a request that was quickly honored; then, Boyd used his boot to pry open the door by a crack.

"Mars eyes don't see anything," he whispered, as he pushed the door wide open. "Okay, I'm proceeding in – what the – *shit!*"

Boyd started frantically waving his arms, as if doing a clumsy impression of flying like a bird.

A half-second later, he did a pratfall back into the tenebrous corridor.

"*Brent!*" exclaimed Tanaka, as she rushed up to be beside him. "You hurt? What happened?"

"What, 'happened', Professor?" he retorted, with a frustrated tone. "Can't tell you *that*... but I *can* tell you what *didn't* – namely, a staircase."

"Huh?" asked White, who had come up from behind.

"Just what I *said*," explained the ex-astronaut, after slowly coming to his feet. "I stepped out into thin air, only barely caught my balance – damn stairs aren't there at all, and it's got to be a hundred feet down to what looks like a floor. I *think*. It might just be a deeper hole... hard to tell."

Boyd winced.

"Landed right on my gun, got me in the small of my back," he complained. "Don't take my word for it... see for yourself."

Tanaka opened the door by about a half-meter of clearance, stuck her head through the gap, scanned for a few seconds, then retreated into the corridor.

"Brent's right," confirmed the crestfallen woman. "It's a *long* way down there – much further than our last little 'leap of faith' – and although I think I see some kind of entrance right at the bottom, opposite side from us here, at least it's definitely a solid surface... you guys all know how much I was straining just to land us in one piece, in getting to *this* level. Now, we have two more bodies to add to the load... I don't know. There's an excellent chance that if we try the same thing, I might not be able to hold us to a safe descent-speed."

"Let me see," demanded White.

He took his own look through the opened side of the door, then himself returned to the corridor.

"Too far down there for me to do the 'icin'-on-the-cake' type thing," he grumbled. "Can't focus on where I want it to appear. I *could* make some from up here, but I don't see how that helps... other end of it would just be stickin' out into thin air. 'Fraid that snow 'n ice don't make much of a trampoline, neither."

"Hold on," interrupted Jacobson. "Everybody be quiet, for a second."

They were.

"You hear *that*?" he requested.

"Yeah – shouting – long way away – no, something else –" remarked Billings. "Damn – sounds *familiar*... not possible, can hardly *hear* it –"

Claremont's eyes started staring in alarm, or joy, or... something.

"What *is* it, Momma?" asked Melissa.

A second later, the teenager's face also wore an astonished look.

"Y'all *sure*, Momma?" she pressed.

"*Whoa*," interjected White. "Shootin – real far – yo, check *that* out –"

"What *is* it?" asked a perplexed Boyd. "Like it's a mile away... but also sounds damn loud... like a jet plane, or waves crashing on a beach."

Suddenly, a low shudder reverberated through the building. As much as any of them could tell, it came from the direction of the doorway, far below.

Claremont strode forward and pulled on Jacobson's sleeve, her bulging eyes pleading for attention, while her tongueless mouth made futile, croaking-noises.

"Whitney," gently counseled the big man, "Look at me and think on what you want to say – what you want to communicate to us. We'll all understand."

Instantly, came the reply.

Mah son! she sent, her mind radiating the primal fear of a terrified mother.

He in danger, *he cryin' for me –*

Ah gots *to go to him – help me –* help *me, Lord... help me!*

"Curtis?" exclaimed Billings. "You mean *Curtis*? *He's* down there?"

A heartsick Claremont nodded rapidly.

"Jacobson – we've got to *do* something!" demanded the salesman. "If that's really *him*, he's an eight-year-old boy against a bunch of armed GrayWar assholes. Somebody's *got* to go help him!"

"I *get* it," stammered the former Mars mission commander. "We need to think *fast*, here – okay, look, Cherie – how many can you carry with you, and be sure of a safe landing?"

"None," she unhelpfully replied. "That's one *H* of a long way down. But I'm willing to try with two, say, Brent and Devon –"

The sound from below, re-occurred; and now, it was loud enough so that even human ears could have heard it.

This fact was evidenced by the little girl awakening and whimpering, "Uncle Bob, what's *that*?"

"*Nothing*, sweetie," he consoled. "Nothing at all."

"Negative," countered Jacobson. "That would leave nobody except myself to cover our rear-flank, up here. Bob, give me the girl – why don't *you* do it –"

Billings – never one for heights – was about to argue; but he was beaten to the punch by Claremont.

She rushed to Tanaka, the mother's eyes telling what she wanted to do.

"Whitney," compassionately cautioned the professor, "You're unarmed, and we're about to jump down by more than thirty-five meters, right into a fire-fight. We don't even know if we're going to land without broken bones – nor do we know if you can withstand the amount of energy that I might be giving off, in doing all that. Are you *sure*?"

Frantically, the black woman nodded.

"Momma say, 'he mah only son'," pleaded Melissa.

"I'm hearin' gunshots gettin' closer," warned White.

Firm determination on her face, Tanaka called to Claremont.

"Put your arm around my shoulder, brave woman," breathed the ex-Science Officer. "And don't fear the power that you will see... that you'll *feel*. *Welcome* it, drink it in, Whitney; make it *part* of you."

The professor's eyes started to glow, as Claremont and Boyd arranged themselves on either side of her.

Ooo – ai-ooo – ooo-ai...

Flashes of energy started to light up Tanaka's body. A sweating, grimacing Claremont groaned, as the charges shot into her.

"Whitney?" asked the professor.

The black woman, her eyes closed, gave a 'thumbs-up' gesture.

A palpable roar – the after-effects of which shook the entire area – echoed up through the atmosphere, from down below.

"Ride the *Fire!*" cried Tanaka, as she led the three out into the darkness.

A second or two after the scientist and her two compatriots had gone forth, Jacobson, Melissa, White and Billings – the latter with Elissha, who was now semi-awake, cautiously edged forward.

Billings stood slightly behind, while the teenager and the two men got down on hands and knees to survey the situation.

"Where – oh, wait, *there* they are – *shit!*" inveighed a worried White. "Y'all see *that* – rough landin'. But at least they're movin'."

Professor? he sent.

Y'all okay?

There was no reply, other than mental-static.

To the immeasurable relief of the throng in the top-portal, as her music subsided, Tanaka was seen to stand up and call out, as loudly as she dared, "Devon – was that *you*? I heard a faint thought..."

"I tried that 'radio-your-mind' thing," he shouted back. "Guess I was out of range. Y'all okay?"

"Just bruises, I bet," the professor called back. "Whitney looks fine, too."

Gunfire sounded from close on the other side of the bottom-portal.

The black woman rushed for the door, but was quickly caught and restrained by Boyd.

"I understand how you feel, Whitney," he related, looking her straight in the eye, "But it isn't going to do Curtis – or anyone – any good for us to get ourselves killed by rushing into an ambush."

Claremont tried – helplessly – to say something.

"Okay," interjected Tanaka.

She turned to Boyd.

"Ready?" she asked.

"As I'll ever be," he replied. "But *listen*, Professor – if Whitney's kid really *is* down here, just like we discussed about our entire party, further back – we have to be careful about him being caught in a crossfire. I don't know how much control you have over that 'Sword' thing – but I got almost none over my own attack... I kind of raise my hands, close my eyes and hope for the best. In otherwords, it's anything *but* a 'precision-weapon'... and even if I just stick to my gun... well, you get the idea."

"Yeah," agreed Tanaka. "I've found that it's easier to aim my attack if I point at something – the 'fickle finger of fate', as it were – but even *then*, I wouldn't stand too close to the intended target, if I were you, because –"

Her voice was overwhelmed by a strange roar, something like a lion on rock-concert amplifiers, issuing from behind the door.

This one was so loud as to rattle the floor-tiles.

There were gun-shots, right afterward, and they sounded close.

With desperate eyes, Claremont struggled against Tanaka, pulling her sleeve in the direction of the portal.

The Eurasian woman nodded and began to stride toward the door, with a combat-ready Boyd on her flank.

They had advanced by no more than two or three steps, when the same brutally-loud noise assaulted their ears; except, somehow, they could tell that they were hearing only the half-part of it.

"J.H.C.!" exclaimed Boyd. "What the hell's *that?* Sounds like somebody just set off a bomb on the other side of that door – should be blown to bits – I know it's locked, but –"

Ah goin' down fightin'! came a wholly new mental-signature.

Jus' like ah promise y'all, bro' –

Son! cried Claremont's mind.

Momma! came a child's frantic reply.

There was a muffled banging-noise, as if someone were pounding fists against the opposite side of the door.

Another roar, this one – if such a thing was possible – even more deafening than before, left the ear-drums of the three ringing with pain.

There were sounds of things falling and crashing, far ahead of them.

A half-second later, there was the much less potent but more ominous noise of bullets impacting against the far side of the portal.

With a heartbreaking look of frustration and fear on her face, Claremont stood crying, her arms extended into fists at her sides.

Little brother, hold on – we're coming! broadcasted Tanaka, to whoever was on the other side of the door.

"Brent," directed the scientist, with a flick of her finger.

Boyd, his visage as grimly-determined as that of the professor, took a place right next to hers.

Now, Claremont saw that the familiar glow from Tanaka's eyes, as well as her body-lightening, had – albeit less brilliantly – appeared also in the man.

Odd, she sent to Boyd and the black woman.

Door's a third of a meter off the floor... but no matter, easy to step up to...

"Pull," commanded Tanaka; and a *tsunami* of *Amaiish* converted into telekinesis, tore a reinforced-steel door from its hinges, sending it flying inward, almost to impact with the feet of the more-than-humans.

A ragged-dressed, tear-streaked, wounded and bloodied – but still defiant – African-American schoolboy, turned to look in shock and amazement at his rescuers.

"*Momma!*" he wailed, ducking two or three incoming rifle-rounds while sprinting into the sobbing Claremont's outstretched arms.

"Protect them, Cherie!" ordered Boyd. "And shut your eyes!"

Smoke was pouring from his tiger-strike-pose hands.

Hey, Brent – I like the electric-guitar, sent a smiling, buttoned-up Tanaka.

But too fast a beat for me to dance to...

As an elfin-thin, soap-bubble *thing* descended over two half-crouching adult women and a black kid with a mother's hand over his squirming face, Boyd – his eyelids closed to a sliver, his body illuminated ominously from within – stepped forward to face down into the corridor.

"*Shine!*" he snarled.

Minnie's Secret

The Storied Watcher had shattered both the door and the lock securing access to the building-top, with but a malevolent glance. Leading the way, she, Chu and the three men clambered out on to the tar-and-sand finish of the roof.

"'Cept for them few gunshots way off... I don't remember L.A. ever bein' so quiet," observed Boatman, staring out over the edge of the building into the distance beyond. "Looks can be deceivin', I 'spose. Probably quiet 'cause all the gangstas had to go home to reload."

He looked up to the skies.

"Be dawn, soon," he added. "Guess I could have used a bit more sleep – but it's nice to catch a bit of that there ocean-breeze, before it gets hot in the daytime, again."

"I know what you mean, Otis," agreed the alien-girl, in a friendly way. "Even in the din of war, a time may come when it is wise to be still and dream of peace... be that but for a cherished second."

"You know, Karéin," offered Chu, "I hope you don't take this the wrong way, but sometimes hearing you speak is like listening to poetry – even though you're threatening to do things we think are disastrously wrong. It's hard for us to rationalize these both coming from the same being."

"Difficult for me, too, Minn-ee," reflectively noted the Storied Watcher. "Does the goddess, Karéin-Mayréij, hold the Destroying Angel, Karéin-Mayréij in check, lest she debase herself to atrocity... or is it the other way around? All of me, can but speculate. When I counsel myself, I mostly do not know which 'me' speaks at that moment."

"Well, we can hardly check you into the nut-house, for being schizoid," commented Kaysten.

"Actually I like 'nuts' – they are crunchy, nutritious, and... *oh*," she replied. "I, uhh, 'get it', I believe. But what is 'mad' to one, may just be devious method, to another... right?"

"I'll take your word for that," he wisely evaded.

"And another thing... are you *sure* that you don't want to, ahh, 'gain a higher perspective on the city' with Minn-ee and I, Jerry?" teased Karéin-Mayréij.

"You'd need *two* barf-bags, at least," he argued.

"Umm-humm," she murmured, rolling an eye and arching an eyebrow. "Any of the rest of you, then?"

"Would y'all believe, I didn't remember to bring a parachute?" smartly answered Boatman. "Don't fly without one... usually."

"Listen... I *would*," demurred the third agent, "But, it's, like... uhh... it's a bit too... uhh... *stimulating*, being that close to you... you know?"

Her smile beamed at him, through the eighth-light of the approaching dawn.

"The heat of man for woman – or desire of man for man or woman for woman – is nothing to be embarrassed about, Will Hen-dricks," replied the bemused alien-girl. "Ahh... if we only had the time and occasion to become more, ahh, 'familiar' – surely, *that* would be a joy to the both of us... do you not think?"

"Yeah," he muttered, "But FBI's got *regulations*, you know..."

"Only if they catch you," quipped Boatman. "You could say 'I didn't want to blow my cover', or some-such thing."

"Can we ditch the trash-talk, and get *on* with this, please?" requested an irritated Chu.

In between eye-blinks, the Storied Watcher appeared right at the FBI team-leader's side.

The alien-girl draped an arm over the team-leader's own and then quickly planted a kiss on her cheek, whispering in an ear, "I think that *you* are pretty cute, too, Minn-ee. In a long lifetime, one learns many ways of pleasure."

"*Karéin-Mayréij!*" retorted a shocked Chu, like a mother remonstrating a wayward child.

With an insouciant look, the alien-girl replied, "Ready to be *alone* with me for a while, Minn-ee Choo? Oh, but know *this* – one can never tell when may come a new experience, which will change one's entire, ahh, 'perspective'..."

Sweat breaking on her brow, a blushing Chu tried to avoid looking at the Storied Watcher.

"I... I have my communicator ready," she stammered.

"Hey – any chance I can take back the thing about flying off with you?" cracked Hendricks. "*This*, I gotta see."

"That's *enough*, Will!" snapped the FBI team-leader.

Boatman motioned "cool it" to the third agent.

"Oh, *relax*, Minn-ee," reassured Karéin-Mayréij. "My intentions to you are, as dear Bob used to say, 'nothing but honorable'. Now mind you, if I had decided to kiss you on the *lips* – well, another saying I recall... 'with each setting of the Two Suns, is another chance for two to bed'. Sorry – it sounds much more, ahh, *arousing*, in my native *Makailkh*. Perhaps when this is all over, I can teach you a few words? Ready for 'lift-off', Minn-ee?"

"This was anything *but* funny," shot back Chu. "Why do you insult people like this? You're displaying *very* bad manners here, Karéin!"

The Storied Watcher stared silently and forcefully at the alarmed and wary human women, to whom she was closely joined.

None of your feelings are hidden to me, Minn-ee – none *of them,* she gently sent to the FBI team-leader.

You should not be ashamed of who you are... or of who you desire, when the moment so moves you.

Your human life is too short to be ruined by guilt.

There was a pause, then the message was followed by, *I am ready, whenever you are.*

"I'm ready to execute our plan to inform the Director," spoke Chu, staring ahead and avoiding everyone's stare.

"Oh-kay," announced the alien-girl, with a saturnine smile.

The Storied Watcher's song – perhaps slightly fainter than its habitual norm – began to echo from roof-mounted (but inoperative) air-conditioning units, as well as the sides of nearby buildings and microwave-towers, while the humans saw bursts of *Amaiish*-power envelop most of her body.

"Ohhhh," moaned the FBI team-leader, upon contact with the energy-charges; and neither Boatman nor Hendricks nor Kaysten could really tell whether the sound was evocative of ecstasy or agony.

Like a Roman candle at a State Fair, Karéin-Mayréij and her reluctant passenger streaked skyward. In no more than two or three seconds, they had disappeared even to the slightly-enhanced vision of the three more-than-men waiting below.

"Stop – that's high enough," demanded a worried Chu. "I can *feel* the air becoming thin – okay now, but I don't want to pass out halfway through our conversation."

The alien-girl, her body still faintly glowing within the elfin-thin force field that encased the two, gradually halted their ascent.

"*Impressive*, Minn-ee," she offered, with a pleasant smile.

"'Impressive'... how?" inquired the FBI team-leader.

"I deliberately did not make my bubble proof against the issue of atmosphere... and from what I recall reading," explained the Storied Watcher, "Were you not to have my gift, already would you have swooned. Ahh... but maybe *had* you so done... things would have been... *easier*."

"You mean it would have been easier for you to sexually assault me, if I was unconscious, Karéin?" defiantly countered Chu.

"*Such* over-statement," lightly answered Karéin-Mayréij, with a casual head-shake. "It is not 'assault', if it is something *welcome*... right, Minn-ee?"

"*Look* – you – I've had *enough* of –" protested Chu.

"Minn-ee... *Minn-ee*," patiently counseled the Storied Watcher, "You forget who you now address! I am not some dinner-party acquaintance who you can – ahh – 'bullshit', with an off-putting remark. I *know* your dispositions and desires; you wear them – as do all of your former species – like a big bright prize-ribbon, clear as day to these eyes."

A frustrated and cornered Chu tried to look away, while the alien-girl continued, "For example – consider our friend Jerr-ee, who waits patiently far below. Have you noticed how he – oh, what is the Eng-lish word – 'hangs around' strong and tall Wolf, all the time? Like you, he hides this aspect of his personality, or at least he *believes* that he does – but I could tell within three seconds, of him being in the presence of my disciple, Mister Half-*Makailkh* bount-ee-hunter. It was funny, actually – when first she became aware, *Vîrya I'ëà'b'* asked Jerr-ee why he did not just go up to Wolf and request that they, uhh, 'walk to the room with the bed, together'. I had to give my war-daughter specific instructions not to speak of this to Sylvia and Hector – lest the, ahh, 'companionship' of our group be unnecessarily upset... after all, we have enough distractions to deal with as it is... right?"

"No... *no*..." whimpered the ex-woman.

"Minn-ee," softly advised the alien, "When human beings pretend that they can choose to ignore the feelings and desires with which the Gods blessed them, much time – and many pleasures – are thus wasted... but you are no longer of that race... and you will live far longer. The sooner that you accept who you are – and who you would love and share a warm touch with – the happier will be your time, on this plane of existence."

Her face was uncomfortably close to Chu's own.

Her sweet breath fell upon the other's nostrils.

"With but a kiss," cooed the Storied Watcher, "I can unlock all that."

"Karéin," pleaded the FBI team-leader, with a tear of desperation in her eye, "You've got to *understand* – even if I was to accept that everything you're saying was true... okay – damn it – it *is* true – are you happy now, you prying, smug, shit-disturbing alien-goddess – things aren't that *simple*, and they haven't been in this country for twenty or more years! They've passed *laws*, thrown people in jail, for just 'admitting who they are' – and that applies both to Jerry and me."

"So?" mischievously countered Karéin-Mayréij.

"Look – we've got *careers*, a *lifetime* of work and accomplishment to lose... and I've got a boyfriend in New York, if you're interested. We're *engaged*, for God's sake – wedding's set for next year in Hawaii. You want me to throw all of *that* to the wind, just for a roll in the hay with a female – at least that's what you look like, and God help me, what you *smell* like – from another *species*? Can't you see it from my perspective, Karéin? Or from Jerry's? Just once? *Please!*"

The alien-girl's countenance somehow changed from lust to that of sympathy, or, maybe, pity.

Fire appeared on her mouth for a second, followed by faint, quickly-dispersing wisps of steam or smoke.

"I have a boyfriend too, Minn-ee," she quietly remarked. "A man who I love and desire very dearly. And look at the, ahh, 'bright side' – at least, *you* would be fucking someone with one head, two arms, two legs as well as only one set of gender-organs. Much different has been *my* lot, throughout the ages."

Her hands extended much too fast for the nonplussed Chu to react, cupping the captive woman's ears and drawing her face inexorably forward.

With no warning, the Storied Watcher passionately kissed the team-leader, then withdrew from her lips.

"Please... *please!*" helplessly whimpered a sweating, panting Minnie Chu.

For a few interminable seconds, her mind and body raced with prohibited, suppressed urges; but, mercifully, she then restored a semblance of rationality.

"They... they said that once you kiss someone... there was no turning back..." gasped the un-made more-than-human woman.

"There *is* none... unless I clean the water from my mouth, beforehand," explained the Storied Watcher. "Minn-ee... I will not force myself upon you – nor will I do so by guile. You must make the decision to lie with me by yourself; and mark this, neither should it – nor *will* it – mean that you cannot give yourself to he who will call himself so lucky, as to be your husband. One kind of love does not negate the other – indeed, the opposite is the case – each magnifies and perfects the other. Why you are ready to, uhh, 'do it'... so will be I."

"Damn you, Karéin!" answered the woman, crying. "I love you... I *love* you! All of them down there do, too... but with *me*, it's different in that special way... and you bloody well read me like a dirty book from the first time we met, back there in the Canyon – must make you feel pretty *superior*, having that kind of advantage over a mere mortal like me... right?"

"No," gently argued Karéin-Mayréij. "But hearing it brings pleasure to my ears. I love *you*, too, Minn-ee, as woman to woman; just as I love dear Cherie Tanaka, likewise as I love Bob, woman to man... and even if our desire for each other never be consummated, neither shall that ever diminish the joy that we both feel. Love is not just physical – it is metaphysical and spiritual as well. You will live long enough to fully understand this... and I would help you so to do."

Chu stared longingly in the alien's eyes, but eventually she was able to force out, "Great, now I've said *that*, too... nothing left to admit or to humiliate myself with. I *never* should have agreed to go on a, uhh, trip, with you."

The Storied Watcher beamed at the other, with a look and aura that combined lust, sisterhood and friendship.

"I will tell no-one unless you authorize it, Minn-ee," she reassured. "Now... how would Bob say it... I know... 'you got a phone call to do'?"

"Yeah," replied Chu.

"But it's, uhh, strictly *business*... you know?" she added with a rueful, half-girlish giggle, which the alien-girl happily echoed.

The FBI team-leader entered a few codes on the keypad of her communicator. Her eyes followed the device's screen-messages.

"No response," she complained. "I think this 'bubble'-thing of yours is blocking it, Karéin. Can't you drop it just for the length of the conversation?"

"There is a risk if I do that," countered the Storied Watcher. "The sky-warriors of your empire are ever-vigilant."

She touched the communicator and stated, "I think that I know what its electro-cant is... try it now."

The team-leader complied, but the same error messages re-appeared.

"No good," she muttered. "Look... back at headquarters in the training-sessions, they said something about these things being 'frequency-agile' or whatever... I'm not an expert in communications-security, but as I recall, it's some system by which it jumps from one wavelength to another every few seconds – if *that's* what it's doing, it might be quite difficult for you to selectively allow or block. If we don't want this whole little trip to be a complete waste of time, I don't think you have much of a choice, other than to –"

"Even if we never talk to your 'boss', Minn-ee," answered Karéin-Mayréij, "From *my* perspective, this was anything but 'wasted time'... do you not think?"

"No, I... I guess not," admitted Chu. "But can't we try at least once with the – uhh – 'bubble', down?"

The Storied Watcher sighed and rolled her eyes.

"As you wish," she unenthusiastically agreed. "But I give you fair warning – this must, then, be a short conversation. Hold your little box tightly; for should I sense the approach of war-missiles, expect a quick end to your 'chat', followed by some *very* abrupt maneuvers. Oh, good... I see that you *did* bring your towel."

Overcome with nervous exhaustion, Chu erupted in gales of laughter.

"God, Karéin," she chuckled, "Did I say that I like your sense of humor?"

"Then," answered the alien-girl, not missing a beat, "There *is* something that you *do* like about me... right, Minn-ee?"

Still involuntarily laughing, Chu again tried the code.

This time, there was a soft chiming sound, followed by the words "AGENCY SECURED CIPHER 2033".

"Bingo!" she announced, holding the communicator up to her ear. "This is the Director's personal line, but it may take some time before he... *hello?*"

"At least he does not make you wait long minutes before he will speak," peevishly observed Karéin-Mayréij. "Unlike your President, while I was on a large air-ship, which I could, at any moment, have reduced to fragments."

"Sir... *sir?*" asked the FBI team-leader. "Yes, it's me – Minnie Chu," she spoke. "What? Well... let's just say that I'm in an, uhh, *elevated* position – I'm with Karéin, there are only two of us here... may I put you on speaker?"

There was a slight pause, then she said, "Okay... go ahead."

Ochoa's voice, faint but still clear, sounded over the remote link.

"This is the Director," he said. "I presume that I'm now addressing the Storied Watcher – that is, the alien – as well as Agent Minnie Chu?"

"Correct," confirmed Karéin-Mayréij. "But this call is not about me – Minn-ee has something very important that she needs to explain."

"Go ahead, Agent Chu," he directed.

"Sir," quickly recounted the FBI team-leader, "We have intelligence on the likely presence of a loose nuke, somewhere in the Greater Los Angeles area. I say again – *a nuclear weapon, in Los Angeles*. We don't know precisely *where* it is... but our confidence is high that it *is* here, somewhere. I recommend immediate recovery-action, including evacuation of the surrounding area, when the location is determined."

"My... *God!*" gasped Ochoa. "Are you *sure*? Wait a minute – I'm not following you, here... how do you know this?"

"I smelled the energy-particle-shine on the body of a – uhh, 'gangsta' – who has come into my group of friends and followers," interjected the Storied Watcher. "This man said that he had traveled across-country – from the 'Texas' principality, that is – to deliver this atom-smashing device, which looks like a big, iron-bound box, to his – uhh – 'homies' here in Los Angeles. There was no scent of a lie when he stated this... so I *believe* the story to be true, and so does Minn-ee."

There was a long pause, then Ochoa replied, "Okay... I understand. Listen, need it be said, this is going to change a *lot* of things... Minnie – what is your current status? That is, your team, the Chief of Staff, and the others."

"Alive and doing – ahem – very well," coughed Chu, trying to avoid the wry smile of the Storied Watcher. "They're all with us –"

"Where are you now?" he interrupted.

"Am I allowed to tell him that?" she requested of the alien-girl.

"If you do, I will have to move us again," sniffed Karéin-Mayréij.

"*Fine*," grumbled Chu. "Sir, we're in downtown Los Angeles... I don't think it would be prudent to say more than that."

"For Christ's *sake!*" cursed the Director, "That whole area is being run by the *gangs!* What on Earth are you doing down there?"

"It seemed to me, sir," diffidently offered the Storied Watcher, "That the spies and assassins of your empire, would have more of a challenge, in trying to ply their trade against me, in this place. In other words... it is *safer*, here."

"'*Safer*'..." muttered a frustrated Ochoa. "*Look*, Madam, this just isn't going to *do* – you need to get everyone, preferably including yourself – out of there as soon as possible! I would have asked this even without the information that Agent Chu has just revealed... but with the possibility of a nuclear explosion happening at any time... you've *got* to be reasonable, here!"

"I do not 'got' to be, or do, *anything*, sir," retorted Karéin-Mayréij. "Or had you forgotten that if you keep not your part of our bargain and lead me to dear Bob Billings and my second family, you will face devastation far in excess of what a single 'bomb' can do. If it is of any interest... I believe that I can protect my entire group from one of these atom-splitting blasts, save it be directly below us, and my arts are sufficient to detect its approach to anywhere that close. However, if Minn-ee –"

"No time to argue this," brusquely interrupted Ochoa, "Agent Chu... you said that you don't know exactly where this thing is – but can't you give us at least some clue where to start looking? Did this 'gangsta' say what direction he took, in approaching the L.A. metropolitan-area?"

"We *did* ask him... but apparently he was lost, when his van was ambushed by a bunch of white supremacists," explained the FBI team-leader. "This guy – Sebastiàn is his name, by the way – didn't know much more than that. But, sir, knowing the disposition of the Aryan Nations and so on, it would seem logical that they'd try to deploy the device against a minority-dominated area, so I'd guess that it wouldn't be in Bel Air or Simi Valley... it could be on the move to somewhere like East L.A., or Compton, or the South Side, or –"

"*Wait* a minute," requested the Storied Watcher, her demeanor suddenly reflective and far-away. "What did you say there, Minn-ee?"

"Well, just that the white-supremacist gangs would probably pick an African-American or Latino area, in which to set off the device," repeated Chu.

"Agent Chu, we can discuss this stuff later," demanded Ochoa. "We need to work out a plan –"

"Hold your tongue, Mister Director, sir!" shot back Karéin-Mayréij. "What were the names of those places, Minn-ee?"

"I'll tell you – then we *have* to get back to the Director," replied the FBI team-leader. "I said, 'East L.A., or South Side, or Compton' –"

"Oh ye *Gods*... would *that* be... where one would find Compton Primary School Twenty-Three?" pressed the alien-girl, her eyes staring intently at Chu.

"I'd *assume* so, Karéin," answered the other woman. "Why?"

There was a look of thunderstruck worry on the face of the alien-girl.

"I must *save* them!" she pledged, with her music now sounding.

"Who?" asked a perplexed Chu.

"The little ones. The *children*, I mean," stated Karéin-Mayréij.

"*Which* children?" pressed the FBI team-leader.

"Those who go to Compton Primary School Number 23," forcefully re-stated the alien-girl, with fear and apprehension all over her countenance. "Serena and Jamal and... Latisha. *Especially*, Latisha. Minn-ee – if that bomb is anywhere *near* them –"

"Those names sound familiar, somehow," noted the voice of the FBI Director. "But how would *you* know anyone in Los Angeles, Ms. Mayréij? I don't believe you've ever been there, except for in the last day or so... right?"

"You do not *understand!*" answered the Storied Watcher. "When I was with Devon White – when I was weak and afraid, when I was unwilling to accept my quest... these little ones, they sang to me, made me *strong* – I owe them the ransom of my life and so do you... so do all those who inhabit this world. Minn-ee – we must *go!*"

Her music began to echo through the clouds.

"Waiit... *now* I get it," remarked Ochoa. "That was one of the few episodes on board the spaceship, that we were able to independently collaborate with Earth-based-recordings. Well, Karéin... it would seem that we now have a certain commonality of interest – we should co-ordinate plans –"

"I can tell you what *my* plan is," interjected Karéin-Mayréij. "I will find Jamal, Devon's son, Serena and Latisha, plus all the others who were there, plus their teacher, gather them together and safe them away."

"But the best way to do that," argued Ochoa, "Would be to help us find the bomb, lead us to it so we can –"

"Yeah... how would Bob have said, 'so you may then turn right around and try to drop it on *me*'," she contemptuously shot back. "Try again, Mister Director sir... this time, with a little *creativity*, the better with which to fool a being a thousand generations your senior."

They heard a frustrated sigh at the other end of the line.

"Look, Ms. Mayréij – we'll obviously have to agree to disagree on this issue, although I should tell you that we will have no choice but to launch a recovery mission of our own against the device, with or without your assistance or participation. However, there's something else – namely, it's my understanding that you still have the Chief of Staff, Mr. Gerald Kaysten – in your custody... is that right?"

"I would not say, 'custody'," she replied, "But he is *indeed* here with me, along with a number of other people, my beloved friend Minn-ee included."

Chu cringed, hoping that the video-part of the communications-link was being jammed.

"*Really,*" professionally offered Ochoa. "Well, in view of this new factor – the bomb, I mean – I have to ask you to return the Chief of Staff to us, as soon as we get off this conversation... we cannot risk his continued exposure to this threat. I'm open to suggestions as to how we could best arrange his hand-over –"

"You are in no position to make such a demand, sir," officiously countered the alien-girl, "But... I might be talked into a compromise."

"Huh?" blurted Chu.

"What do you want us to do?" asked Ochoa. "*Anything*, within reason, would certainly be considered."

"Simple," requested Karéin-Mayréij, "You show me where Bob, Tommy and the others are being held."

"We're *trying*," argued the FBI director. "You *know* that."

"I know *nothing*, sir," she replied. "I am no further ahead, than I was during our last conversation... and time is fleeting past –"

"There's new information," hastily added Ochoa. "We've done a careful correlation-trace on the events at the Billings residence and workplace, down in Tucson, had to pull some strings with the military and Secret Service... we now have a high level of confidence that another branch of government intelligence almost certainly *was* involved –"

"Which one, sir?" inquired the team-leader.

"Until we're absolutely sure, I'd prefer not to speculate," he evaded. "All I'll say is... if we're right, we may be facing an almost *unprecedented* situation, where a government department has – for reasons we can't yet guess – openly defied the President's most specific orders, regarding the al – I mean, Ms. Mayréij. This is an *extremely* sensitive situation, and we have to watch our step to avoid it blowing up into a complete disaster –"

"Interesting... very so," observed the Storied Watcher. "And I will await any more information with which you can provide me. And do not think that I do not appreciate what your eff-bee-ai spies are doing on my behalf; at least the three with whom I have come into acquaintance, seem to have some honor and integrity."

"Gee... thanks for the ringing endorsement, Karéin," muttered Chu.

"And as to your request, the fulfillment of which would perhaps convince me to save dear Jerr-ee – *assuming*, of course, that he freely decides to leave – the trouble of walking his way out of this place..." continued the alien-girl.

"Just tell me what you *want*, for Pete's sake!" demanded a frustrated Ochoa.

"Naught... save that dear Minn-ee should ask me *nicely* so to do," serenely replied Karéin-Mayréij, to a frustrated, upset look on Chu's part.

"I think there's something going on there that I'm not fully understanding," remarked the FBI director, "But in the interests of moving forward... Minnie, I assume that you'll issue the request in whatever way that she wants to hear it?"

The Storied Watcher winked at the blushing FBI team-leader.

"Oh... of *course*, sir," sighed Chu.

"Well, it appears that we have managed to agree on one thing," offered a satisfied Ochoa. "Now, regarding the weapon itself, I'd propose that –"

"*Silence!*" exclaimed Karéin-Mayréij, her countenance instantly marked with alarm. "We are under *attack* – Minn-ee, turn it off, *right now!*"

"But –" protested the ex-woman.

In the next split-second, the Storied Watcher's telekinesis rudely yanked the communicator from the FBI team-leader's hand, causing it to go dark immediately, and the near-human woman gasped upon full contact with her mentor's maddening, exhilarating power.

Bolts of lightening-like energy enveloped them both.

Restrain not your breath... neither try to take air into your lungs, silently commanded the alien-girl, as the two of them rocketed skyward.

Drink your lungs of the Fire – she will give you life... my... love.

But with a face cruelly-deformed by a hundred or more G-forces of positive acceleration, a panicked Chu could manage no more than a desperate croak.

She felt the blood draining from her head and received shrieks of pain from every bone and nerve-ending, elsewhere in her body.

Perhaps two full seconds later – already high enough to see the curvature of the wonderful blue-green planet called Earth – came another bone-crunching turn, performed impossibly abruptly at almost a right-angle.

As near as the FBI team-leader could tell from the disappearance of the coastline far below, they were now streaking to the west, out over the Pacific.

Her lungs begged for air, but there was no pain. *Something* – an indescribable *whatever* – was keeping her alive, and all too conscious of the peril of her situation.

Even without my war-children – behold how I throw off their rocket-war-arrows, Minn-ee, came a strangely calming, warming thought; all the better, considering the thin film of frost that was forming on Chu's skin.

Oops, sheepishly added the mind of Karéin-Mayréij.

I forgot that you are, ahh, 'less used to' the cold of the near-void.

I shall make the bubble proof to the outside...

"Karéin," attempted the team-leader; but, in the rarefied air of this altitude, almost nothing audible issued from her lips.

If you think it while you try to say it – I will understand, sent the alien-girl.

"*Where are we going*?" demanded the beleaguered more-than-human, aware that the sounds weren't coming out.

"*Uh-ohh... slow down – for God's sake, open a hole in this thing –*"

With no additional warning, nausea did its worst and Chu's last meal came shooting out of her nose and mouth. But the ever-vigilant alien-girl had already caused the towel to block this bile-soaked issue, and in the next instant the entire mess burst into flames.

A second later, it was somehow frozen solid and was then ejected out the rear of the bubble into a hypersonic slipstream.

Tears congealed in the cold, marking the team-leader's miserable face.

Close your eyes... and ponder a thought that you now chew on a spicy red-pepper, sent Karéin-Mayréij, *And the unpleasant taste will be burned from your mouth, dear Minn-ee.*

Then bury your head next to mine own... hold me tight.

We will circle back and descend.

Utterly at a loss, Chu complied, and – to her amazement – the nauseating taste of stomach-acid was replaced in her mouth with something like the remnants of a joint "smoked, not inhaled".

The crushing-forces returned, still brutal – but not equal to – their former fury.

I hate you... I love you! thought the ex-woman.

Wake me when we get there.

Bob's Leap Of Faith

"Damn... maybe I had better close 'em all the way, next time," ruefully muttered Boyd, as he blinked repeatedly and tried to massage the dazzle out of his half-blinded eyes.

"You okay?" asked Tanaka, with her bubble abating.

"Yeah... fine... just *fine*," replied the ex-astronaut. "Anyway, I'm not hearing any more gunshots – are you?"

"Nope," she confirmed. "But you know *them* – they have a habit of coming back. I'll keep it brief, until we figure out how to get the others down here."

She looked down at the mother-and-child scene unfolding next to her, and counseled, "Whitney – I know you can't introduce me properly, so... Curtis, my name is Cherie Tanaka – and this guy here, 'Mister Flash-Bulb-Hands', I mean – he's Brent Boyd. Along with some more of our team, who are up there in that opening, way up in the wall – including Bob Billings and your sister Melissa, by the way – we're all friends of Karéin-Mayréij – the Storied Watcher – who you knew of as, 'Sari'. Commander Sam Jacobson, Major Boyd, Major Devon White, Sergei Chkalov and I, we brought Karéin back with us in our spaceship... and if we *hadn't* – well... there wouldn't *be* much of an 'Earth' left, by now. You keepin' up with me there?"

The little boy looked up with wide eyes and silently nodded.

A second later, he piped up.

"Y'all mean y'all one of them *astronauts*? That went all th' way to *Mars*?" he gasped.

"You *bet!*" smiled the professor. "And it was *us*, who first met 'Sari'. We've all come a very long way, I guess."

"*Wow...*" he offered, with obvious delight.

Now Tanaka got down on one knee, with a more serious look on her face.

"And Curtis – here's *another* thing that your Mother and Melissa already know," she quietly and forcefully commented. "Dear son... like the rest of us, you've been greatly blessed, by the wise and mighty Storied Watcher. Just a little while ago, I explained to Melissa that she will inherit some of Karéin's powers, as has already happened with us – as no doubt you saw when Brent unleashed his attack against whomever was chasing you. Okay, so far?"

In a small voice he replied, "That *great*, Miz Cherie... but we gots to go help mah bro'."

"Who do you mean?" she asked, with utmost interest.

"Tommy," replied Curtis. "He close to where ah was... ah tries to spring him – like Miz Sari did for us back at the jail up north – but ah couldn't... *couldn't!* Had to run, *had* to – they was shootin' at me..."

He hung his head.

"Son," spoke Boyd, also down on one knee, "We'll get your friend out – I *swear* it! Or die trying."

Again, the boy nodded in silence.

Boyd arose and quickly walked over to a spot diagonally underneath and in front of the portal.

"Hey!" he shouted. "We've got Curtis – had a bad scare but I think he's physically okay. There's important news – kid knows where Tommy is... which is further in on this level. We need to get you guys down here, ASAP."

"Acknowledged," called back Jacobson. "I've been surveying the surroundings – no traps that I see, fortunately; but I had expected a drawbridge or something like that... you see anything like a set of controls down there?"

Boyd looked back and forth.

"Negative," he answered. "Don't see anything on the walls except those grates – probably for air-vents, right up at the top of the chamber. I'd agree, it's weird – no way to get down here from where you are... maybe they expected everyone to take the elevator?"

"If Tommy's down there," demanded Billings, "We better get on our way to him... *now*. Not a *moment* to lose!"

"Great idea, Bob! And how do you propose to get down there?" mordantly asked the former Mars mission commander.

"Well... don't ask *me*," retorted the salesman. "I never pretended to be the brains of this operation."

"Wait a minute... *I* got it!" he added. "Let's get the Professor to fly up here and bring us down, one by one."

He turned to face into the chamber and put a hand to one side of his mouth.

"Hey!" shouted Billings. "Tanaka! Any chance you could zip up here and give me a ride down there?"

The professor turned to Boyd, with an annoyed look.

"Easy for *him* to say... *he's* not the one burning out all of his synapses with over-use of *Amaiish*," she complained.

"'Am-eye-ist'?" inquired the boy. "Wha *that*?"

"The great power of the Storied Watcher – which grows now in *you* as well, Curtis," she noted, with a perfunctory sidelong glance.

"*Wicked!*" gloated the child, with a big grin, which was almost matched by a smile by his mother.

"Curtis!" called Melissa from above.

"Yo!" he replied, waving back.

"I got a better idea, Bob," shouted Tanaka.

"Yeah?" he answered.

"*Jump!*" she demanded.

"Sure, okay... *what*?" retorted the nonplussed salesman. "You out of your *mind*? It's a hundred feet or more!"

"So what's your *problem*?" she called back.

"*Gravity*," he sarcastically commented.

"*Look*, Bob," argued Tanaka, as she walked forward to take station alongside Boyd, "My mind's reaching out, right now – I'm very close to you, I can almost grasp you, even from here... if you jump out and start to fall, I'm *sure* that I can lock on and lead you down to a nice, low-velocity landing. If I propel myself up there, I first have to expend enough energy to lift me, then reverse-levitate the weight of both of us back down. Since it would be that much more difficult if we did more than one person at a time – Elissha maybe excepted – I'd then have to repeat that process at least four times."

"So?" he challenged.

"The point is," continued the professor, "I think I have enough – uhh, 'reserve-power' – to float the four of you up there, down here... but if we do it *your* way, I might falter on one of the later trips. You understand?"

"I understand all too well," he complained. "In particular... I understand what happens if you miss. Easier for *you* to miss *me*, than for me to miss the floor."

"Come on... *try* it, Bob!" she shouted. "Besides, don't you remember how you just about drained my *Amaiish*, the last time that we were at close quarters?"

"Uh-uhh," countered Billings, with a negative head-shake. "Anybody got a parachute?"

"We're wasting *time*, here!" peevishly remarked Tanaka. "Anybody else want to try?"

"Steppin' out into thin air ain't the *stupidest* thing I done lately," muttered White. "But it probably comes damn *close*. Okay, Professor, I'm game... what y'all want me to do?"

"Stand as close to the precipice as you can, Devon," counseled Tanaka, "And give me a three-count – then take a little hop off. Wouldn't hurt to see if you can use some of your own telekinesis to augment my own... you might not even need my help."

"Yeah, well... it's kinda like when you learn to throw a hand-grenade," he grunted. "Y'all want to leave the teachin' of how to do it the first time, to *professionals*, if y'understand what I'm sayin'. Ready?"

"Yep," confirmed Tanaka.

"You're *nuts*, you know," mentioned Billings, to the black ex-astronaut.

"Listen, Bob," countered White, "I was nuts to go on that-there Mars trip... I was nuts to go along with openin' that tomb she was takin' a nap in... I was nuts to... well... y'all get the idea. If I listed 'em all, we'd be here all day – whatever day it *is*, that is. Professor?"

"Yeah?" she called, as the energy-pulses began to flash within her body.

"Three!" he began.

"Jacobson – you gonna let him *do* this?" pressed the salesman.

The Mars mission commander shrugged. "I can't *tell* him to do anything... or *not* to do anything," he evaded. "I can only, 'suggest'."

"Two!" called White.

"Didn't you say not to 'volunteer' for anything?" desperately spoke Billings.

"Only thing *I'm* 'volunteerin'' for, Bob," quipped the black ex-astronaut, "Is gettin' my ass out of this place... and doin' the jump gets me one big step further, in that direction."

Billings was about to plead some more; but White then counted, "One," and did a good impression of a bunny-hop, off the ledge.

The salesman tried to avert his eyes, but couldn't.

At first, it appeared like his worst fears had come true, because he heard a panicked, *"Whoa-oa!"*; but in the next second – to the amazement of everyone except perhaps Tanaka – White's trajectory stabilized; upright and apparently in good balance, he proceeded to a point that was perhaps ten feet over the floor.

Then he said, "Yo, Professor! Stop, if y'all don't mind!"

"Look, Devon – this is taking a *lot* of concentration... not to mention *Amaiish,*" she protested. "Why can't you let me just put you down?"

"Let go, gradually," he requested.

"You're still ten feet in the air, for God's sake!" exclaimed the woman. "*Plenty* of distance in which to break bones and rupture organs."

"Y'all want to argue and blow a fuse, or let go?" he shot back.

"It's *your* neck," she cautioned. "Stupid idea, but... letting go... *now!*" she warned.

For the briefest of seconds, another worried look appeared on White's face, but then, he slowly and deliberately floated down over the remaining distance.

"Y'all want a bird to learn anything," he remarked, with his trademark grin, "You got to *make* it flap them wings."

"*Impressive,*" allowed Tanaka. "But how were you so sure about it?"

"Believe it or not, Professor," offered White, "Last time y'all took the dive – off that walkway, that is – yours truly was takin' notes, y'all know?"

"Should've guessed," answered the woman, with a wry smile.

She turned her attention to the upper ledge.

"One down... three and a half to go," she shouted. "Who's next? Bob?"

He sent a pained look to Jacobson.

"*Fine,* Bob," shrugged the former Mars mission commander.

"Here – give me Elissha," he requested. "Less for you to worry about, when your turn comes up."

"You're bigger than me," argued the salesman. "I'll keep her, if you don't mind. Spread the weight around... you know?"

"Anything you *say*, Bob," muttered an unimpressed Jacobson.

He got up to the ledge.

"Ready, Cherie?" he shouted.

"As ever," she replied.

"Three – two – one!" Jacobson quickly called out.

He jumped.

The Mars mission commander's drop went smoothly, except for a strained look on Tanaka's face, just before he reached the chamber-floor.

"Is there a *problem*, Cherie?" he nonchalantly remarked, upon touchdown.

"You've been putting on weight?" she sighed, wiping her forehead.

"Not from what we've had served to us down here," he evaded, with an insincere half-smile. "And certainly not for lack of exercise... must've been all the junk-food at that Air Force place we were stuck in... right – *that's* it. Yeah."

Tanaka rolled her eyes and shook her head.

"Okay," she called out to the ledge. "Hopefully neither of you have been neglecting your push-ups... next, please."

Billings looked at Melissa, trying to think of some excuse, but eventually he said, "Can't be last one behind the young lady, I suppose... can I? No, I guess I can't, damn it... listen, Professor, mind if I close my eyes? Since we don't seem to have any blindfolds up here, 'condemned man' kind of thing –"

"Oh... quit with the bellyaching, Bob," complained Tanaka. "Just jump and be done with it, *will* you?"

"Fine, *fine* –" he peevishly replied.

"Mista Bob," interrupted Melissa, "Why don' y'all let *me* take 'Lissha? Y'all be weighin' less, then... you know?"

"You *sure*, Melissa?" asked the salesman. "What if she starts acting up?"

"Are we going for a *ride*, Uncle Bob?" piped up the little girl.

"Yeah... listen, honey, Uncle Bob has an idea – would you mind, uhh, 'going for a ride', with Melissa, here?"

A brief frown appeared on Elissha's face. "Why not with you, Uncle Bob?" she whined.

"Uncle Bob's a bit... uhh... I mean – he's quite a *load*, for Miss Cherie to hold up, all by himself," Billings tried to explain. "It'll be a more fun ride, if you go with Miss Melissa. Don't worry, sweetheart... she'll take good care of you."

I hope, he thought.

As in, "ten seconds longer to live"...

"Okay," allowed the child. "Miss Melissa is nice. But *she* needs a bath, too."

The teenager held out her arms, and with obvious reluctance, Billings passed Elissha to her.

"Hey – ah likes *y'all*, too," said Melissa to the little girl, with a friendly smile. "An' ah gonna take a shower for an hour long, or mo', when ah gets out of here."

Now the salesman – his eyes seemingly closed, but in fact very slightly open – inched up to the edge of the upper-portal.

"Want me to count it out?" he called, his heart racing.

"Just *jump*," shouted Tanaka. "I know exactly how to do it."

"Send greetings to next of kin," muttered Billings.

He jumped.

Whoa, flyin' down fast – Professor, any time now – he thought, panic rising.

"What the – *shit!*" yelled Tanaka. "*Can't lock on!*"

Billings started tumbling end over end, his life flashing in front of his eyes.

White charged up to Tanaka and grabbed her arm.

"*Now!*" he demanded.

Two minds took firm hold of the salesman and guided him to a safe – if unceremonious – pratfall on the chamber-floor.

Hyperventilating with terror, Billings looked up at Tanaka with near-hate.

"*Convinced*, now, Professor?" he spat. "That it was a *bad* idea, I mean."

"Look, Bob... I'm sorry, *so* sorry!" she stuttered. "You've got to *understand* – I had no trouble at all with Devon or Sam – well, okay, Sam *was* a bit more than I had bargained with, but it was completely different with you... the first time that I tried to use telekinesis on you, it was like... like... like trying to 'tickle' a fish in a stream – I couldn't get a *grip*. As you approached, it got easier... finally I locked on, and not a second too soon – you were getting close to maximum-velocity –"

"*I'll* say, 'not a second too soon' – that was a nice 'end-of-life' show I got on the way down," the salesman retorted, staggering to his feet. "I give you fair warning... I'm *never* trying that, again. Did I mention that I'm afraid of heights?"

"*Chill*, Bob," intervened White. "She ain't shittin' y'all – it was damn weird, like, when I started pushin', I was gettin' drained... don't know if I could fix y'all up with as much as an ice-cube, right now. Professor, how *you* doin'?"

"Weakened, greatly," she uneasily admitted. "It's *got* to be that accursed *Amaiish*-resistance of his... but I think –"

Claremont grabbed Tanaka's sleeve and began to silently say some words.

"What *is* it, Whitney?" she queried.

A second later, all of them looked up at the ceiling.

There was a red light recessed into the wall, near its top... and it was flashing, on and off.

"Momma! Miz Cherie!" shouted Melissa. "Y'all see *that*?"

"Sure *do*," exclaimed Jacobson. "A light – might be a warning – *uh-oh...*"

A trickle of water began to issue from one of the grates at the top of the wall, just below the light.

"We've *got* to get out of here!" suggested an alarmed Boyd. "And we've *got* to re-seal the door. If this damn place is a *reservoir* –"

A shocked look appeared on every face.

"But they's lots of po-lice wid they guns, back through that-there door!" warned Curtis. "An' they ain't 'fraid of shootin' em!"

"Don't worry," reassured a crouching White, "Y'all and your homies, we'll take care of 'em. But my bro' Major Boyd, he's right – we need to go, sooner rather than later. Professor – y'all better tell Melissa to jump."

Fear was all over Tanaka's visage.

"I... don't think I... *can*," she half-whimpered.

"*What?*" nervously exclaimed a nonplussed Jacobson.

"To paraphrase Devon, I'm feeling very weak, *Fire*-wise... I can *try*, but I feel like lifting a basketball would be a lot, right now. You remember the scene back in the *Infinity*, when Karéin bade me lift that cup of coffee?"

A thin film of water was advancing across the floor, toward them.

Jacobson strode forward, bent over and wet a few fingers, then returned them to his lips.

"Interesting... I *thought* I smelled it out right," he observed. "Sea-salt. So unless they've got a desalinization-plant going here, I'd say this whole set-up is more of a trap, than a reservoir of potable water."

"No *shit*," ruefully agreed White.

"Should have airlifted the two of them and left me up there," muttered Billings. "At least then the crash-landing would have got the last of us down."

"We all heard 'bout hindsight," answered White. "Listen... I can try to help, Professor, but y'all know I'm not doin' too well, either... maybe *both* of us would be enough?"

Claremont's worried stare, clearly stated her opinion.

"Melissa's carrying the kid," noted Boyd. "If you *can't* hold her up –"

Two or three of them moved back, to avoid wet feet.

"Well... what's our alternate plan?" argued Jacobson. "This damn thing's going to *flood*, any minute!I'm not too good with telekinesis, but if Brent and I join up with the two of you – he pulled off a *door*, after all –"

"That was mostly the Professor, to tell you the truth," stated Boyd. "But I'll certainly try."

"*Look!*" warned Melissa, as she pointed to the wall-top-grill.

Water started pouring out of the thing.

"Let's *do* it!" ordered Jacobson. "Hands together, Mars-folk."

"The rest of you get as near to the doorway as you safely can," directed Tanaka, as she, Jacobson, White and Boyd stood together.

The water enveloped their feet, up to the heel.

"Melissa – on the count of three... okay?" shouted Jacobson, barely over the torrential sounds coming from the wall.

"Here we go, baby-chil'," cooed the teenager. "Want to close yo' eyes?"

"Nope," demurred Elissha, with naïve confidence.

The water was gushing down the wall, now.

"No count – just *jump!*" demanded Tanaka.

"Here ah goes," called Melissa.

She took a short-run and hurtled off the ledge, rather further than any of the others had so far done.

A second later, the teenager and her young passenger began to fall, almost in the same manner as had Billings.

"Where *is* she – you're getting in my way!" cried Tanaka.

"You're too weak, Professor, *back off!*" yelled Boyd, as Melissa and Elissha rocketed downward, to the horror of the onlookers below.

"Oh my *God!*" shrieked Tanaka.

Then, a split-second later, her voice stopped.

"You holding her?" loudly inquired Jacobson.

"Not me, Captain," mentioned White. "Yo – check *that* out!"

Delighted squeals issued from the little girl, as Melissa and the child rapidly reversed direction, soaring upward, then cruising effortlessly back and forth.

Just like me in the Infinity, *the first time*, thought Tanaka.

But that, *was in zero-G. And she's carrying extra weight!*

Right at the water-vent, Elissha extended a hand and wet it, splashing two or three times.

"It's just like that big waterfall," she chattered. "Come on... let's go somewhere else, Miss Melissa."

The water in the chamber had now soaked boots and shoes.

Melissa looked downward.

"Oh... sorry," she sheepishly shouted. "Guess we gots t' come down... right?"

Claremont, her eyes beaming with pride and amazement, nodded.

The teenager flew a graceful corkscrew-pattern downward, eventually stopping at a hover about a foot above the rapidly-advancing water-surface.

With moist eyes, Tanaka gushed, "Oh *Melissa*, dear child... that's something that even *I* can't do! I *told* you that it would come... didn't I?"

With a smile that could have done battle with White's own, Melissa acknowledged the compliment.

"And not a *moment* too soon," observed Jacobson.

"How you learn to do that?" asked a plainly-jealous Billings.

The teenager pondered for a second or two, then offered, "Dunno, really, Mista Bob... ah just *had* to – so ah did. It like divin', when y'all jump off a board an' go swimmin', ah guess. 'Cept in the air, 'stead of the water."

With the little girl still draped over her shoulder, Melissa flew down to hug her brother.

"Ah never forgot 'bout y'all, an' neither did Momma," she softly advised Curtis. "We pray an' pray, ev'ry night!"

An ashamed boy wiped a tear.

"*Riight,*" muttered the salesman. "Well, speaking of water... hey, that's a *joke*... you know?" he nervously added, looking at the shin-deep liquid that was perilously close to the level of the doorway.

"You *got* it," echoed Jacobson. "Let's get out of here... as much as a *minute* or two more, and we might flood the corridor, too. Brent – can you do a check? Any hostiles in sight?"

Boyd sloshed his way over to the portal.

"Negative," he replied. "But there's a *lot* of damage about thirty to fifty meters ahead – they might be hiding *anywhere*. Devon – you got enough ice to seal the door, if I manage to lift it into place, behind us?"

"Prolly not," advised White. "Considerin' the amount of pressure that's gonna be on the other side, when this-here chamber fills up, hundreds of tons of water in there. I might be able to freeze it enough to hold it for awhile... *maybe*."

"Everybody out!" ordered Jacobson.

As they all headed for the corridor, he asked, "Cherie – how about you?"

"It's coming back to me... but slowly," explained the woman, as she emptied out her shoes. "I might have enough *Amaiish* to weld the hinges into place, but not the whole door – that is, if you want me to be able to stop so much as a *spitball,* when the going gets rough, later on."

"*I* could try – at the risk of blinding all of you," remarked Boyd. "But I got next to no aim – I might put a hole in it, or – even worse – blast out half the door-jam. Then it would be, 'bring your bathing-suit' time, I'm afraid."

By now the last of them had clambered out of the chamber.

Thin rivulets of water were starting to advance across the doorway.

Boyd stood just behind the entrance.

He concentrated, sweat beading on his brow, as the force of his mind lifted a heavy, metal-and-something door from beneath several feet of water, guiding it into place with a full-throated "*thunk*".

"There's a chance that it'll stand up, or block the water, all by itself... as long as nothing shakes it loose," he stated, still with his back turned to the corridor. "Not a chance we should *take*, though – Professor, Devon, over to you... I'll keep it upright as long as I can."

"Listen, kid," started an apologetic, pensive Billings, as he took hold of the boy's shoulders. "I just wanted to *say*... I'm sorry for all the things that I –"

"Y'all don' gots to 'splain *nothin'*, Mista Billins'," interrupted Curtis. "Ah *heared* y'all bein' strong for us – in mah haid, that is... 'an Tommy do, too – y'all keep us goin', when we's thinkin' we's *daid* –"

"Curtis," called Tanaka. "Come here – there's something I want you to see."

"Let's go," said a slumping, mentally exhausted, but grateful, Billings, to the boy. "Rain-check on the sniveling-stuff."

Curtis smiled. "Y'all got it, Mista Billins'," he agreed, dashing over to the side of the door, where the professor had parked herself.

Abruptly, he stopped in wary astonishment, upon seeing the faint but very evident glow in Tanaka's eyes.

"Take my hand, son," she requested.

"Momma?" he asked, turning his head to address Claremont.

The African-American nodded her permission.

"Y'all look like – ah means, y'all *feel* – jus' like Miz Sari," offered Curtis.

"I was the first person that the Storied Watcher – your friend and mine – entrusted with her power, Curtis," explained Tanaka. "The eyes are just one sign of it. Do *you* want to be mighty and strong? Then hold on, and feel it flowing into you... *through* you. Ready?"

The boy, at last aware that this was no practical joke, hesitated.

"It's okay, bro'," encouraged Melissa. "Miz Cherie – she *wicked* powerful, but she nice... an' she one of *us*. Hadn' been for her an' Cap'n Sam 'n all of 'em, Bob too, Momma 'n me, we still be back there with them... *bad* folk."

Uneasily, the boy extended a hand, and he flinched as he felt Tanaka's energized touch.

"This," she said, "Is... the *Fire.*"

The professor pointed a finger from her other hand at the door's top-most hinge, and an incandescent bolt of energy struck the mechanism, melting much of it upon contact.

"*Whoa!*" breathed Curtis. "That... that... it like when y'all touch one of them live-wires... but it don' hurt... it feels *nice*. Y'all do it again? *Please!*"

Tanaka, her eyes still shining eerily, smiled at the boy.

"Of *course*," she agreed.

Another shot fused the second hinge. It was followed, with Curtis still tightly gripping on, by a third bolt of *Amaiish;* then a final one, which melted the lock and door-handle.

"Hey, you didn't say..." officiously complained Billings.

Tanaka, the glow subsiding, looked up at him.

Wearily, she replied, "Bob... I'm so damn tired, it feels more like a 'toothpick' than a 'sword', when I fire it."

"I suppose that *I* gotta take credit – or the blame – for a lot of that," he admitted. "Sorry."

The woman shrugged and stated, "My fault – not yours – for forgetting your other little... *peculiarity*."

She turned to Curtis.

"Show's over – at least for my part, I'm afraid," she announced. "Devon... over to you."

White now advanced.

He advised, "Y'all might want to back off a bit. My little trick is a lot less, uhh, 'precise' than the Professor's, don't you know."

They retreated from the portal-area, just before White gave the familiar 'Sno-Kone' invocation. But to his obvious disappointment, while the door *was*, indeed, frozen solid – and while a thin patina of ice *did* form over most of its surface and edges – the results were a pale imitation of what the ex-astronaut had been able to manage in earlier trials.

"*Told* y'all," muttered a long-faced White. "If anybody finds us a six-pack down here, I can still serve y'all up a cold-one... not much more than that."

He yawned.

"Professor," inquired the ex-astronaut, "Y'all figured on how long it's gonna take before we get back to, uhh, 'a full tank of gas'?"

Tanaka gave an open-palms gesture.

"Your guess is as good as mine, Devon," she commented. "I think I'm regenerating faster than I otherwise would – what with all of our brothers and sisters around here – maybe their *Amaiish* is rubbing off on me, like human body-warmth helps everyone, in a confined space in the winter-time. Don't call *me*, I'll call *you*... you know?"

"Yeah... 'zactly," agreed White.

A second later, his face clouded over.

"What *is* it?" asked Jacobson.

"Just remembered," said the black ex-astronaut. "We didn't seal that other door, up top... *did* we?"

The Mars mission commander shrugged.

"True – but it's not *our* problem, now... is it?" offered Jacobson.

"Yeah," confirmed Boyd. "Not only *that*... but if it starts flooding up there, those GrayWar-pricks will need some scuba-gear to keep following us – at least if they want to take our exact route... right?"

"There had better be more than one way to get down here," observed Tanaka, "In case we were wrong about those markings on the map."

"Yeah," echoed White. "'Specially if that door don't hold long."

"Point taken, Devon," said Jacobson. "Just before we get going, though... Curtis – mind if I ask you a question?"

"Sure, Cap'n Sam... what y'all want t' know?" eagerly replied the boy.

"What *was* that we were hearing, while you were running from those guards?" inquired the big man. "Prior to when the Professor and Brent pulled the door off and rescued you, I mean. It sounded like the roar of an explosion, or... I don't know. Were they firing something bigger than a gun at you?"

Curtis pondered intently for a second or two, then explained, "Ah'm... not sho', 'zactly, sir. Like, first... Tommy 'n me, they put us together, then they come in, grabs both of us, and they was fixin' to take him off by heself... ah figures they was gonna hurt him even badder than they already done, so ah yells '*stop*' at 'em – sorry, Momma, maybe ah be usin' one or two cuss-words there, it goin' down real *fast*, y'all understand – an' somehow, it come out wicked *loud*, like, things was comin' off th' walls, they fallin' over, holdin' they ears, so ah kicks at they legs an' do the jet... keep yellin' at 'em, but they was too *fast*, started shootin' at me before ah could get to Tommy... they drag him off, 'an ah *had* to run, or they would have got me for sure, 'an that's no lie..."

The boy looked miserable.

He hung his head, whimpering, "Ah'm *sorry*, Cap'n Sam – ah *tried* to save mah bro', ah really *did*... guess ah'm just no good..."

Both Claremont and Tanaka hurried to his side.

"Hey... *hey!*" consoled the Eurasian-American woman, as Curtis' mother hugged him close. "You're just about the bravest little boy that I've *ever* seen;

and let me tell you, Curtis... I've seen a *lot* of bravery lately. And you know what? I think you just told us of your own special gift. When you shouted at the guards and the other sonofabitches that they've got down here, you say it knocked them back a step or two?"

"More than *that*, Miz Cherie," elaborated Curtis. "At first, they just was holdin' they ears – guess they don' like the sound of mah voice, or somethin' – but after they chase me down them hallways, back 'n forth, ah kinda put more into it, like when Momma tell me 'y'all gots to sing from the bottom of your lungs, boy' – it even knocked 'em full over, a few went down, bleedin' out they noses 'n ears... but some of 'em had them helmets an' black suits on, and they jus' got back up 'n went back to shootin' at me. So ah jet any way ah could, but then ah ends up with that door behind me, an' ah couldn' get it open. Thank y'all for savin' me, Miz Cherie – ah don' know *how* ah can make it up to y'all. Them guard guys wanted me *daid*, ah figures."

Now, Tanaka also embraced the boy.

"We all depend on each other, dear son," she breathed. "And soon – I'll need your help, in turn."

The professor pointed at Curtis and Melissa and turned to look at Claremont.

"You must be very proud of them," quietly remarked Tanaka.

The black woman nodded, closed her eyes, and forced out a thought.

Y'all sound so much like Sari, Miz Cherie, sent Claremont.

If ah didn' know better... ah'd reckon she right here with us all.

We prayin' to the Lawd that she okay.

Tanaka grasped the woman's hand as Melissa, still carrying the little girl, joined the three.

"Ah was missin' y'all *terrible* bad, bro'," said the teenager.

Claremont, her two children, Elissha and Tanaka shared a private moment, with the latter explaining the details of the group's standard procedures to the other four, *sotto voce*.

"Listen... while they're, uhh, busy," mentioned Jacobson to the rest, "Can you come over here, please?"

Silently, Boyd, White and Billings complied.

Jacobson rolled out the map, with the rest of them onlooking.

"If I'm interpreting this correctly," he stated, "The section marked 'Redacted', over to the left – looks like it's quite far-off in that direction – while our potential escape-route – can't really make it out in this light, mind you – that's way off to the *right*, from the four-way crossroads ahead of us. If I had to bet on it, I'd say that they probably dragged Tommy off to the hidden-area... what do you think?"

"As good a guess as any, Cap'n," confirmed White. "So we're goin' off to, uhh, 'Terra Incognita'?"

"Unless you've got a better idea," offered the former Mars mission commander.

"While I agree with heading as quickly as possible toward the objective, Commander," advised Boyd, "We'd better keep the plan as flexible as possible... we got a few new issues to keep in mind, here. For example, we now have quite a large party – almost so much so as to be unwieldy – and there are four non-combatants tagging along, people who can't really defend themselves –"

"What about the Claremont boy?" queried Jacobson.

"Yeah – I'd hate to hear him from too close up, with that big mouth of his," grunted Billings.

"Kid used the only weapon available to him," commented White. "Can't blame him for *that*."

"Not disputing you there," muttered the salesman. "All I meant was, knowing Curtis as I do, well... it *figures*... about his 'gift', that is."

Boyd allowed himself a chuckle.

"Yeah – remind me to get my fingers in the ears, before he lets fly," said the ex-astronaut, "But the point is... we have to assume that if they're sequestering Tommy, they may already understand how important he is... which, in turn, suggests that they'll counter-attack with everything they've *got*, the minute that they think we're getting close to him."

"Yeah," noted Jacobson. "So we had better be ready and willing to fight our way in... as well as, out."

"Got any *other* cheery news?" mordantly observed Billings.

"Only that we should re-do our marching-order," parried Boyd. "I don't mind going on point, again, for whatever *that's* worth... Professor, how's the 'Shield' thing, coming along?"

"Poorly," she complained. "I can probably protect you against a volley or two... after that, you're on your own, I'm afraid."

"Understood... but last *I* checked, you're still the best force-field we've got," quipped the former Mars mission commander. "So I think you should go immediately behind Brent and Devon – that way, we'll have some firepower up front. I'll cover the rear, and Bob – can you please follow just ahead of me, so you can make us invisible to anyone who attacks from that direction – I'll use my gun, if needs be – everyone else should be in the middle. They know the drill?"

"Sort of," remarked Tanaka. "But Curtis doesn't yet have a 'power-word'. If I were *you*... I'd cover those ears, when you see him taking a deep breath."

"Ha... got you *there*," agreed Jacobson.

"Stations, everyone," he directed.

Finally, The Big Man's On Our Side

"Why did you request this meeting?" asked the *nouveau*-President, from a solitary perspective inside Air Force One's on-board conference-chamber. "I'm quite busy, you know – dealing with the latest currency-crisis... crap like that."

"Are we speaking privately, sir?" reverse-questioned the CIA director. "That is... you're alone?"

"Yes," indicated the former Vice-President.

"This is for your ears only, sir," cautioned the other man. "But I have extremely important new information, which I think will radically change our current situation... not to mention forcing both of us to take some very difficult – but necessary – steps."

"Yeah... like, *what?*" grunted the American leader.

"Less than an hour ago, NSA's domestic communications-intercept people detected a suspicious wireless transmission originating from the Los Angeles area, so they flipped the capture-file to the Agency for cryptanalysis," explained the CIA director. "It proved very difficult to crack – we had to devote almost all our super-mainframes to the task, so at first we thought it might have been from a deep-cover Russian, Chinese or maybe Brazilian agent, *et cetera* – but when we finally managed to decipher it, to our surprise and disappointment, it turned out to be a *FBI* code –"

"So *what?*" sniffed the *nouveau*-President. "So the Bureau's got a few people keeping track of what gangster's sliced the balls of what other gangster, down in L.A.... I'd have *expected* Ochoa to be doing something like that."

"But... *sir,*" protested the CIA director. "First of all, the originating-location of the outbound call was traced to a point over ten thousand feet *above* L.A. –"

"So Ochoa put some of his guys in a helicopter," argued the U.S. leader. "Make senses to *me*... out of pistol-range, I'd assume."

"Maybe you'll understand the gravity of the situation when I tell you that the conversation appears to have been a three-way one... between the FBI Director at the other end – he's back in D.C., incidentally – and a Bureau-agent who we've identified as a 'Minnie Chu'... she's a senior field-officer assigned to the Red Rover project. The other, appears to have been the *alien*, itself."

"Uhh... *what?*" stammered the nonplussed *nouveau*-President. "Come again? Why didn't *Ochoa* tell me about this?"

"We've done voice pattern-matching on this 'Chu' person, on what we know of the alien, as well as with the FBI Director's own voice-print," explained the other man. "They all confirm, 95 to 100 per cent."

"I... *see,*" muttered the American leader.

"Sir," continued the other man, "The implications should be obvious – we have FBI communicating with, and – as I can prove from the content of the conversation – *co-operating* with, the alien; and they're keeping this all hidden not *only* from yourself, Mr. President sir... but they're also doing it behind the backs of everyone else in the Government."

"Who else knows about this?" requested the former Vice-President.

"We passed target co-ordinates to the Air Force – without disclosing the details of the intelligence, of course," noted the CIA director. "They reacted with commendable speed and took their best shot, but from the feed-back that we've seen, they aren't claiming a kill. Furthermore, there's something else of *crucial* importance."

"Well... other than for giving me a reason to have Ochoa hanged for treason," growled the *faux*-President, "What could they have said, that would be so important? Wait, don't tell me – he told that monster where to come find *me?*"

"Luckily, not that we know of – but given this display of disloyalty, sir, I certainly wouldn't want to assume that he *hasn't* done so in some other conversation," smoothly cajoled the chief-spook. "So I'd strongly suggest that after we get finished here, you take appropriate countermeasures – for example by changing to some other command-aircraft. However, most of the discourse appears to be concerned with the fact that FBI Agent Chu claims to have discovered the location of an uncontrolled nuclear device – it's apparently somewhere in the Los Angeles area –"

"*Damn!*" inveighed the American leader. "Did she say which one it is? Paki – or the one that Air Force got jacked out of, near Barksdale?"

"We have no information on that," commented the other man, "But based on what we've heard from the capture-file, I'd guess the former. In any event, sir, I think you and I have some quick decision-making to do, here."

"*I'll* say!" ruefully acknowledged the President. "I'll of course have to hear the entire conversation myself before proceeding further... but was there anything else there that I should know?"

"Yes," answered the CIA director. "Two more things... although the first of them is very puzzling. You remember what happened to the Chief of Staff? Mr. Gerald Kaysten, that is."

"Yeah... poor bugger," confirmed the *nouveau*-President.

"Well – based on what's on the recording – he *may*, in fact, still be alive," remarked the other man. "In the course of the conversation, Ochoa demands that the alien 'return Jerry to the government'... although, 'Karéin-Mayréij' is non-committal on this request. If the discourse wasn't deliberately-staged, we'd have to assume that the alien somehow faked Kaysten's demise, for reasons that again, we don't fully understand."

"I sure wouldn't bet the farm on some spoken promise made by that vicious little harpy," stated the American leader. "Until I see him standing unharmed in front of me, I'm still assuming that he's dead."

"You *do* have a point there, sir," the director agreed. "Also – and this is a real 'break' for us – the creature mentions something about 'rescuing' the children of a school in the black ghetto-parts of Los Angeles, from being harmed by the nearby nuclear device. Since we know where she'll be going – as you'll appreciate – this gives us a possible targeting-window. However, we'll have to move *fast*, if we want to take advantage of the opportunity."

There was a pause at the substitute Air Force One end.

"Sir?" inquired the CIA director.

"Just... *thinking*," replied the ex-Vice-President. "I have my own ideas; but I'd like to know what you'd recommend, first."

"Well, sir," answered the director, speaking slowly and carefully choosing his words, "Based on this evidence, I'd have to conclude that Mr. Ochoa has – for reasons that I can't comprehend – decided to cut some kind of back-room deal with the alien. As I understand the law, as well as Executive Office precedent, deliberate insubordination of *that* type, would be grounds for immediate dismissal – although perhaps Ochoa has somehow fallen under the alien's mental-control... which would make him mentally incompetent to run the Bureau. Sir... in view of all this, I think it would be *highly* inadvisable for you to allow the Bureau to remain under its current leadership. Who *knows* what the alien's planning to do? She – it – may be planning a *coup d'etat,* or some other subversive activity, even as we speak."

"You're damn right," declared the *nouveau*-President. "As a matter of fact – I'd go further than *that*... but before I do, I need to come to terms with you – CIA, that is. You know what I mean?"

"I *believe* so, sir," answered the CIA director, in his poker-faced monotone. "But would you mind elaborating?"

"Look... let's not beat around the bush," spoke the U.S. leader, his voice tough and business-like. "You and I both know the 'ins and outs' of how this country is *really* run, as opposed to the bullshit that we feed the stupid voters – and if you're interested, my predecessor let me know about your *own* little act of 'insubordination', shortly before I stepped in to fill his shoes. The difference between *him*, and *me*, is... what *I'm* all about, is *power* and *income*, not all these candy-assed niceties concerning 'constitutionality' or other legal crap –"

"I can align with that point-of-view," evenly observed the other man. "Please continue."

"Okay," agreed the President. "Now... *my* problem is – and I'll let you know about this regardless of the outcome of this conversation, if I'm going to purge FBI – and I'm not stopping *there*, oh no, no *way*, I'm going to remake this government in the way that it *should* be set-up – that is, a 'benevolent dictatorship', not some fucking touchy-feely 'let's all have a hug' democracy – you and I both know, I'm going to need the Agency, NSA and the military as well, on-side. Unlike my predecessor, I'm not so stupid as to believe that I can piss off you guys and your little poison blow-darts and live to tell the tale – but at the same time, you need *me*, too... right?"

"Oh... of *course*," cooed the CIA director. "And for the record, the Agency would *never* threaten a President... we just had a minor, ahh, 'misunderstanding' with the last resident of the Oval Office. I hope you know that."

"Right – sure – anything you *say*," answered the *faux*-President. "So let's get down to brass-tacks. What I'm proposing is that you – the Agency, that is – and I work together, to clean out the deadwood... get a new team in place, you know? Starting with FBI. If you want, I'll have the Bureau's senior leadership replaced by the Agency-staff of your choosing. We'll be making some changes within the Executive Branch – that's actually already underway, mind you – but I'll ratchet up the pace and get rid of *all* of my predecessor's people, not just some of them, as was previously the plan. And we'll replace some of the senior members of the Armed Forces, whose loyalties might be suspect... issue will be finding members of the brass who *get* it, about how things are going to be done, from here on in –"

"The Agency may be able to give you some modest help there," said the director, only barely able to contain his glee. "We have a number of people inside the highest levels of all four branches of the military. In some cases, rapid promotions would be necessary... but we're just talking about a couple of pay-grades – nothing that would attract undue suspicion."

"Good," grunted the American leader. "Now the *quid pro quo* in all of this is, while I expect to be informed – ahead of time – on what the Agency's up to, unlike my rather naïve predecessor, I'll keep my nose out of *your* business... as long as you keep yours out of *mine*. Have your fun, shoot a few people, 'disappear' as many as you want, pull out their fingernails if that's how you get your jollies... just keep it under the radar-screen – and leave running the rest of the government to *me*."

"That would work for us over at the Agency, sir," deadpanned the director.

"I *bet!*" offered the *nouveau*-President. "See... I've got a lot of friends on Wall Street who want to have fun spending their money... *they're* my constituency, not those fucking Bible-Bangers that Horn and Kaysten have been catering to, all these years. I got snookered into taking on that 'Harold' guy as my 'personal Bible-tutor'... but other than for *him*, there's going to be a clean sweep within the Executive Branch, and I need to know that CIA's going to be on *my* side – not just now, when the heads start to roll, but on, into the future, once we deal with the alien and the fucking Paki-bombs, once and for all. You got that?"

"I think that such an arrangement would be optimal, sir," stated the CIA director. "However, just to prove good faith... would you disclose some information to me?"

"Sure... what do you want to know?" asked the *nouveau*-President.

"About the former Mars astronaut-team," inquired the other man. "Your predecessor was *very* evasive about them. What is their exact status? Why were both he and Anderson so *protective* of these four people?"

"Hah – I'd have thought that you'd have figured it out by yourself, by now," chuckled the replacement President. "Well... let me clue you in. Bottom line is... they're really not, uhh, 'people', any more. Seems that while they were in space with her, or it, the alien taught them how to use some of these super-duper powers that she's been taunting us with. Air Force considered them their 'crown jewels', had big-time plans to make them into 'America's super-hero team' or some-such nonsense – I never believed a *word* of it – so when your Agency kidnapped 'em and sent 'em to that jail up in Alaska, well, Anderson was more pissed than I've *ever* seen him. *Which*, incidentally, is one more reason why I'm going to give the General his retirement-papers – as I believe you noticed in our last three-way, he's still very protective of Jacobson and company... can't have that getting in the way of making tough decisions."

"*Wow*," said the director, in an expressionless parody of an exclamation. "That would explain the many – ahh – *unusual* things, that we've been hearing coming from the Amchitka situation. For the record, sir, I completely concur with your decision, in this regard. However... in view of what has been going on at the northern detention-facility, would I be correct in assuming that you now consider them to be a 'disposable asset', sir?"

"Oh... *definitely*," airily pronounced the *faux*-President. "Too bad, really; but you can't make an omelet without breaking a few eggs... right?"

"I'll violate an Agency-rule, and descend into slang here, sir," commented the director. "I'll say... 'I like your cooking'."

"Thank you," said the U.S. leader, with a mild laugh. "Alright. I suppose we both have a lot on our respective agendas – on the 're-org' side, that is – but in the short-run, we have some co-ordinating to do. First – on the L.A.-situation – did you say that you think you know where the alien's going?"

"That's right," answered the other man. "We *were* considering dropping in a termination-team – the expected location is a school in Compton, by the way – but we're *critically* short of trained 'wet-ops' staff... we have so *many* commitments in this area – everywhere from domestic ghettos to Cuba to the Indian subcontinent, not to mention the ten or so that we're airlifting to Amchitka right now – that we're having to fall back on trainees who barely know how to use a silencer. I'm afraid we can't guarantee you *anything* for the L.A.-situation – and that includes the loose nuclear weapon... given the minority nature of the local population, our remaining agents would, uhh, 'stick out like a sore thumb', down there."

"Don't worry about L.A.," assured the *nouveau*-President. "I'll have Air Force blast everything in the area – I guess that's Anderson's last kick at the can, before I send him packing... if he *gets* the bitch, so much the better; if not, there's my excuse to do a little house-cleaning at the Pentagon. I got to tell you, if it wasn't for Bel Air and Beverly Hills – yeah, some of 'em *are* Democrats, but they still got money, nice houses, good parties, investments, so I suppose they're 'our people' – I wouldn't shed too many tears if the fucking thing went off and did a little quick 'n dirty 'urban renewal' down there. Best-case, Army finds out where it is, shoots it with a tank-cannon, we get a little uranium scattered here and there; worst-case... well... bigger 'omelet', you know?"

"In *my* line of work, sir," diffidently replied the CIA director, "One learns quickly that keeping our loyal, mainstream Americans safe and secure, sometimes – sadly – requires sacrificing a smaller number of our less... *obedient* citizens. I wish it weren't so... but we work with the world the way it *is* – not how we would want it to be."

"Okay," said the U.S. leader.

"One last thing, sir," interjected the other man. "What about Kaysten?"

"What do you *mean*, 'what about Kaysten'?" shot back the *faux*-President.

"It was stated in the custody of the alien... or was traveling with her, or it," explained the CIA director. "If he's really still alive, he *is* – technically – a member of the Executive Branch; he's thus entitled to the full range of government protective-services... though we'd have to assume that he, too, has been brainwashed by this 'Karéin-Mayréij' creature. His presence in the alien's entourage might make targeting her rather difficult... would it not?"

"Why's *that?*" replied the American leader, feigning surprise.

"Ah... I *see*," said the director.

"Just one more egg in the omelet," observed the President, in a straight-forward manner.

"*Pity*," remarked the other man. "With the right... *encouragement*, perhaps he might have given us some insight into the creature's weaknesses. Or he could have been added to the team of 'recruits' for 'Operation One-Two Punch'."

"Well... if you want to pick his brain, you're welcome to parachute a few agents in there," offered the *nouveau*-President. "But considering what I'm going to order Air Force to do, I wouldn't send anybody who you don't mind losing."

"I think the Agency will have to respectfully pass on that opportunity, sir," replied the CIA director.

"I'll speak to you tomorrow," proposed the U.S. leader.

"Very good," answered the other man.

He cut the connection, and was finally able to reveal a broad smile.

Do You Feel A Tingle?

After a few seconds of shuffling about in the near-darkness, the troupe began to advance.

"No doors anywhere on the walls," said Boyd to White, as the two men, guns at the ready, walked cautiously forward, avoiding the many piles of debris that littered the hallway.

"Yeah – and y'all see them tiles and stuff lyin' everywhere about?" replied the black ex-astronaut. "Like somebody took a fist to 'em."

"Kid sure has a way of making his opinions known," acknowledged Boyd.

A half-second later, he had to jump backward by a foot, as a strongly-reinforced-wall, covering the entire corridor in front of them, suddenly dropped from a hidden recess in the ceiling.

"*Damn!*" growled the ex-astronaut, as he regained his balance and tapped his knuckles against the barrier. "Solid steel... or something like that. We must've set off a floor-plate or something – maybe Curtis was too light to have triggered it, when he came this way –"

"Rats in a cage," complained White. "No, second thought – roach-trap, looks more like it, y'all know... 'they check in, they don't' check out...'"

"Yeah... I'm beginning to see why there weren't too many escapees from this level," ruefully allowed Boyd.

A scent of ozone started to taint the stale, bottom-of-dungeon atmosphere.

"Whoa – bad smell," warned Billings. "Gas?"

"*Gas!*" cried a half-panicked Melissa.

"No – not that... at least, not what we ran into before," quickly noted Tanaka. "Smells more like... *wait* a minute... listen, do any of the rest of you have a, uhh, 'tingly', feeling in your toes?"

"Yeah, Miz Cherie – got it all over mah feet, matter of fact," confirmed the teenager. "Feel real strange... but kinda good, you know... what *that*, Momma?"

Melissa hesitated for a second, then added, "Momma say she feelin' th' same thang."

"Me too," commented Billings.

He looked down.

The soles of his shoes, already badly beaten-up from previous travails since he had arrived in the place, were starting to give off wisps of steam and smoke, rather like Boyd's signature power-sign.

"What the *f –*" he cursed. "Professor, I'm feeling *warmth –*"

"Yo – me too," confirmed Melissa.

The little girl woke up and started crying.

"Oww – oww – *owww!*" she wailed.

"My *God*, if I'm *right –*" gasped a horrified Tanaka.

She wrung out some water from a pant-leg.

It fell on the floor, sizzled and evaporated.

"The whole damn floor's *electrified!*" she exclaimed.

Claremont started dancing, but in the next second, Jacobson had scooped up her slender frame, while Melissa invoked her new ability and withdrew her feet from the surface, floating uncertainly, about a meter-and-a-half off the floor.

"Curtis – get yo' butt *up* here!" she demanded. "Ah think ah can hold y'all an' 'Lissha, too!"

The boy complied, and though his sister's flying-height suffered somewhat, Melissa managed to stay aloft.

"We can't *all* levitate off of this!" cautioned Jacobson.

"Whoa, Professor, I think you're right," interjected a worried Boyd. "I'm feeling it too, and it's ramping up quickly – need a plan – *fast –*"

"Damn – but doesn't it feel sort of nice," added Billings. "That is... it *would*, if my shoes weren't about to catch fire!"

Tanaka went to a crouch, periodically moving her feet so that her melting soles wouldn't stick in place. She extended her arms, palms-down, and to the gratified amazement of the others, little charges of lightening began to leap from the floor to the woman's fingers and hands.

Wincing, she managed, "I'm absorbing as much as I can... hurts and soothes, at once... can't hold it forever... *Sam* – that damn wall in front –"

"There's no *way* I can smash my way through that!" protested the former Mars mission commander. "And even if I *could*... the impact would probably dislodge the door behind us – we'd be immersed in water on top of this electric-trap – and we have no idea of who's on the other side –"

Now even White was stepping gingerly from side to side.

"*Shit!*" he howled. "That was nice a second ago – startin' not to feel nice at *all* – Captain – we better take our chances!"

He levitated a bit, but was not able to consistently stay off the floor.

"Brent – take Whitney," ordered Jacobson.

Boyd rapidly complied, and his former commander put his back to the right-hand wall.

"*Shield!*" forced Tanaka, her eyes taking on a glow.

A shimmering wall appeared between Melissa and Curtis, separating the party from the precariously-sealed door and the flooded chamber behind them.

Now, Jacobson closed his eyes, clenched his hands into fists and started to deep-breathe, almost as if he were hyperventilating. His music – thundering, percussive, profound, like African drums combined with elements of the *Ride of the Valkyries* – began to reverberate in the minds of the troupe.

With blue-green flashes running the length of his body, the big man rocketed forward, much faster than any normal person could possibly have done, with no more than five or six feet in which to get to a run. He impacted with the left-hand wall, causing a mighty 'crash', leaving a minuscule hole and large cracks extending radially outward from it.

From his vantage-point on top of his sweating, panting, air-floating sister, Curtis looked backward and quickly called, "Yo! Door's leakin'!"

And so it was. Thin rivulets of water were seeping from five or six points around the recently-re-attached portal's edges. They formed an advancing pool at the door's bottom.

"Cherie – hold it off as much as you can!" demanded Jacobson.

Tanaka's eyes were glowing brightly, but there was a pained look on her perspiring face.

"God – I'm feeling *drunk!*" she groaned, as the charges of electricity shot up from her hands into her arms and body. "Too much of a good thing... Sam I can only keep this up for another *minute*, at most..."

"Understood," he said.

Again, the former Mars mission commander put his back to the opposite wall, and brought his power and music to a crescendo.

The others noticed that his body was encased in a subtle, translucent, azure-and-gold outline.

Like a more-than-human juggernaut, with clenched fists and an eye-shine only slightly dimmer than that of his former science-officer, Jacobson charged right through the left wall, leaving a gaping, jagged-edged hole, along with shattered bits of wood, metal and gyp-rock, starting about a foot off the floor.

With private satisfaction, he noted that he had smashed through at least six inches of better-than-average, well-reinforced, interior wall-structure.

The mission commander, his aura, music and power abating, cast his gaze rapidly to the left and right.

This mercifully-uninhabited place was small – only barely large enough to accommodate the party, had they all been in there with him – and it had shelves filled with various utility-items on the left and due ahead, while on the right there was an evidently inside-locked door.

"It's gonna *go!*" yelled Curtis.

Melissa and Billings looked behind them.

Jets of water were spraying, lawn-sprinkler-like, from the edges of the doorway to the reservoir.

"*Get out of there!*" shouted Jacobson.

As quickly as they could manage, they all dashed through the wall-hole; all, that is, except for Tanaka, who slowly backed out until only her head and midriff were bending forward into the corridor.

Concentrating on keeping her force-field between the cistern-door and the exit-hole, the woman never took her eyes off the door and the advancing water, which sizzled and steamed as it contacted the far edge of the electrified floor.

"We've got no more than twenty to thirty seconds!" she estimated, shaking her head as if trying to wake up from a deep sleep. "I can slow the water when it gets through... but I can't keep it from flooding us. Think *fast*, guys!"

While Jacobson fiddled with the handle to the right-hand door leading to parts unknown, Boyd side-saddled next to Tanaka.

"Devon – get your butt *over* here!" he demanded, an order that White immediately obeyed, appearing on Tanaka's other side.

Boyd turned to the woman.

"Listen," he commanded, "Door's big enough to cover this breach – if our minds can grab it when it pops, we can pull it over the hole – as long as we wait until the water stops surging, pressure should hold it in place."

"Yeah – let's all lock on at the same time," added White. "Flip it over on its side just before it gets here, put the bottom of it flush to the floor, so it can't slip down... ready?"

"Best plan we *got*," agreed Tanaka. "I'll take the middle – Brent, you take left – Devon, you take the right – *uh-oh* – get ready, boys, here we *go* –"

As the weight of the water behind the far door finally overcame the *ersatz* reinforcement-job that had been done only a few minutes before, the more-than-a-woman winced and, trying to channel all of her energy to the mind-grabbing-skill, dropped her force-field.

A Niagara of cold seawater surged into the just-vacated corridor, becoming lethally-electrified, as it hit the nearby floor.

Salt water sloshed up to and over the remnants of the bottom of the wall that Jacobson had smashed through.

Three straining minds locked on to the door and – working mostly but not completely in sync with each other – drew it forward, until it completely covered Jacobson's impromptu exit-way.

"*Keep pulling!*" demanded Tanaka. "We got to keep it tight, until the water calms down!"

"Whoa, Professor... maybe that's a lil' taste of what y'all was doin' out there," exclaimed White. "I'm gettin' some go-juice from all that electricity out there... must be flowin' from the metal on the door. I think I can cement the edges and seal in the hole so it don't leak – okay to try?"

"Sure – but Brent, don't let go, until it's stable!" requested the woman.

"*Sno-Kone!*" pronounced White, as he extended his hands in claw-like fashion.

Instantly, a thick film of ice covered not only the visible part of the door, and a good three to four inches within and over the edges of the hole, but also a centimeter or two of Boyd's cheeks, nose and chin, not to mention Tanaka's hair and forehead.

"Uhh... *oops!*" sheepishly apologized the black ex-astronaut. "Y'all okay?"

The former science-officer, her eyes aglow and rolling simultaneously, turned to stare at White.

A flash of *Amaiish*-powered lightening illuminated the front and top of her head, vaporizing the ice that had encrusted her features.

"Want me to clean Devon's little facial, off *you*, too, Brent?" sarcastically suggested Tanaka.

"No... I *got* it," he replied, with a confident shrug.

Closing his eyes, Boyd used the force of his mind to shatter the ice on his face into a hoarfrost-like cloud, which quickly dispersed.

"Oh, well... that's, uhh, good to see," muttered White. "I ain't got this Mister Freeze thing completely *down* – still gettin' my personal *English* on it, y'all understand?"

Tanaka bent down her head and laughed with nervous exhaustion.

"I think we can let go now, guys," she said.

Plans And Confessions

The alien-girl and her half-willing, part-human passenger had arced out several kilometers over the Pacific, but had then doubled back, streaking invisibly over coastal and downtown Los Angeles.

After taking but a second or two to admire the burgeoning dawn, they set down on the top of the building that served as home-base.

"We are here," stated the Storied Watcher, matter-of-factually. "Are you feeling any better?"

"Don't know... legs are awfully wobbly... oh, okay – yes, in a bizarre way, I feel ridiculously confident... but I shouldn't, especially in view of how our little chat with the Director ended up," muttered Chu, as she bent forward and took several deep breaths. "Karéin... being *this* close to you for so long, and especially while you're doing that damn roller-coaster thing up there at ten thousand feet –"

"Ten to twenty thousand *meters*," corrected the young-looking woman. "I prefer to work further up, and in – how do you say in Eng-lish – the, uhh, 'metric' measuring-talk."

She turned to address no-one in particular.

"You guys can all come out, now," she announced.

Cautiously, the heads of Kaysten, Boatman and Hendricks appeared from various hiding-places.

"Fine... whatever," said the FBI team-leader. "What I *meant* to say is, 'I feel like I've just been body-slammed by a brontosaurus'... every joint and tendon in my body is talking back to me – and what they're saying isn't very nice. Two days on one of those medieval torture-racks would have been easier to shake off... did you really *have* to do all those abrupt maneuvers?"

"It is only because I evaded the homing-arrows by a fast ascent and rapid turns, dear... *friend*," explained Karéin-Mayréij. "Would you have preferred that I try to befuddle their little thinking-brains with the issue of, uhh, ten thousand micro-wave ovens' worth of unseen energies; or, perhaps, to have exploded them each as they approached? I did not have time to request you cover your ears, in the latter-case. And count yourself blessed, Minnie – for your power now grows rapidly, on account of your bravery and resilience. Would it be of interest to know that even *one* of those 'maneuvers', would have instantly crushed the life out of an ordinary human being?"

"*Damn*," interjected Hendricks. "You givin' any more rides?"

"Stick around me," deadpanned the alien-girl, "And I am sure that you will have your turn."

"We saw some flashes, heard some 'booms', even from down here," remarked the big black agent. "What happened?"

"Don't know, Otis," answered Chu, "But we were obviously targeted – and then attacked – by a bunch of missiles, probably fired by the Air Force. Karéin had to zoom away from them, and if you hadn't already guessed, let's just say that when she gets going, she *really* gets going... I can *personally* attest to that."

The FBI team-leader winced.

"Listen, friends," spoke the Storied Watcher, "There will be time for such pleasantries later – but right now, we are wasting valuable time... and we must rapidly away from here. Wolf – can you please hurry back down to the staying-room, collect whatever foodstuffs and other essentials that you can easily carry and guide the rest of your brothers and sisters up here?"

"Thought you hadn't seen me," complained a voice from behind a rooftop air-conditioning unit.

"You are becoming more skilled at self-hiding," she consoled. "I believe that it is a weirding talent, growing in yourself. Later, I will counsel you on encouraging it, as one waters a flower, to see it bloom. Now... please, away with you! I have preparations to do, up here."

"What do I do, if they don't wanna come with me?" he pressed.

"Tell them that I will then have to come down myself – and I will be, uhh, 'pissed'," cheerily replied the alien-girl.

"*That* oughtta do it," he muttered.

"Listen, Wolf," requested Karéin-Mayréij. "I need to ask you a question."

"Yeah... what?" he replied.

"How familiar are you with the neighborhoods of this city?" she inquired.

"Well... I been here a few times," offered the bounty-hunter. "Mostly on out-of-state warrants... but I don't do those that often – hard to get 'em to pay for all the travellin'-expenses, you know?"

"But if I'm understandin' what you mean, Karéin," he added, "I wouldn't say that I'm that good at gettin' around... usually, I'd navigate with one of them satellite-things, the ones that show you exactly where you are on the map. That is, I *would*, if I had my car... which I don't. What's it *to* you, anyway?"

"Curses," she grumbled. "You see... I need to find 'East Compton Primary School Number 23', and though I no doubt could do so of my own device, it would take much valuable time – this is a *very* big city, and there would be many schools to check in this 'Compton' quarter, before I would happen upon the right one. However, I wonder if –"

"Couldn't help overhearin'," interrupted Boatman. "What you say that place was, again?"

"'East Compton Primary School Number 23'," repeated Karéin-Mayréij. "I need to find it – quickly."

"Now what's *this* all about?" questioned Hendricks.

"I will explain later, good friend," parried the Storied Watcher. "But did you say that you knew where this school is, Otis Boat-man? If you could guide me there, I would give you much love and would be *greatly* in your debt."

"Whoa – now *there's* an offer I can't refuse," joked the black FBI-agent. "But I'm 'fraid I can only give you a bit of help here, lady – I *did* do some work in L.A., not too far from Adams and Vermont, matter of fact, when I was goin' through my first field-trainin'... that was a long time ago, mind you, but somehow that school-name sounds familiar, you know? I might still know what it looks like, if I got down on the street-level. Which – needless to say – I'm not too crazy 'bout doin'... without a *real* good reason."

"There sure *is* that good a reason," answered the alien-girl, almost pleadingly. "What would you need, to get us close enough to tell if we are in the right area?"

"A map, I guess," suggested Boatman. "I could take it from there."

"Curses, again," groaned a frustrated Karéin-Mayréij. "Those 'maps' are only available through the com-pu-ter things and sky-satellites, many of which, ahem, seem to have lately fallen from the skies, after being too near a comet –"

"You're only half-right there, Karéin," contradicted Wolf. "I was tellin' you about the maps that are *easy* to use – the automatic ones, that is. They still got 'em in good old-fashioned paper-format... you don't need a computer to use 'em, all you need is a workin' pair of eyes – I'd assume that yours would do just fine. Not completely sure – but when I was rummagin' around the lobby on the main floor, I thought I saw a whole *rack* full of 'em somewhere down there... you want me to take the stairs and have a look-see?"

Her countenance brightened only scarcely less than the unexpected advent of a supernova.

"Praised be the *Gods*," she sighed. "And no... I shall go and check by myself, Wolf – it is not that I doubt your bravery or gun-skills, but I can go there and return much faster, and with zero risk, besides. Do not worry... if it is danger that you seek, I am sure that plenty of it, awaits all of us."

"Not sure if I like the sound of that... even if I *am* hangin' with a radioactive hottie from Mars, all the while," observed the bounty-hunter.

He pointed a finger at her and said, with an arched eyebrow. "But I'd say that you *owe* both Mr. Otis and me one... you know?"

"I owe so many that I have almost given up counting," replied Karéin-Mayréij, with one of her strange, girlish giggles. "And I am skilled at remembering long numbers. I will repay this debt, along with all the others... *someday*. In the meantime, we both need to be on our respective ways. I will meet you back here shortly... oh-kay?"

"Got it," concurred Wolf.

Damn... and I'm negotiatin' with a fuckin' goddess, he reflected, as he turned for the roof-top door.

Wish them teachers who told me I'd never amount to anythin', after I flunked Grade 11, could see me now.

Indeed, came an unrequited, yet affectionate, thought.

Power is not just from a fire-sword or from compulsion : it comes equally from thinking, helping... from simply being a friend.

My love to you, too... big, handsome one.

They saw a brief glimpse of a tall, powerfully-built back, followed by the sound of the roof access-door, closing.

They didn't see the broad grin on the bounty-hunter's face.

"Well... maybe he could use some help," remarked Kaysten. "With convincing the scientists, I mean."

The Chief of Staff followed the bounty-hunter down the stairs, while Chu could not help sneaking a bemused half-smile, with the alien-girl.

"Nice of that guy to sneak up on us," complained Hendricks.

"Yeah, but funny, I *should* have seen him – *should* have heard him – when he came up through that-there door," commented Boatman. "I ain't hardly *never* been jumped or walked into no ambush, 'least if I had any say in the matter. Peculiar... *that's* for sure."

"Wolf was just practicing his abilities," pleasantly stated Karéin-Mayréij. "You would be well-advised to do so, once the same, come to you."

"Huh?" asked the third agent.

"His skills," explained the alien-girl. "Those special powers that the Gods will have granted to you, through myself. And if you are interested – Wolf was not, technically, 'invisible'. If I have correctly identified it, this ability is called *'Amaii-'h'é-Gozà'y'é'* in my language. It is basically a mind-trick; the user of the art is still there, plainly in sight of hostile eyes – for example, a vid-ee-oh camera would show him as it would anyone else – but the mind of an opponent is commanded to simply ignore, what it sees and hears."

"*Wonderful*," complained the big, black agent. "'And here I thought we only had *one* person 'round here, screwin' with our minds.'"

"If I wanted to do *that*, dear friend," advised the Storied Watcher, "You would *really* be, ahh, 'screwed'... *believe* me. But you do have a defense : concentrate on the idea, 'someone is hiding, but I can see him, I can *see* him'. Eventually, he will be revealed to you – though not to an ordinary human, who would have no recourse against strong, tall and manly Wolf."

I am like you, in that preference, Minn-ee, she enigmatically sent to Chu.

See? One way of love does not preclude another.

"Damn," half-gasped Hendricks. "You mean he's becoming like, uhh, Batman... Spider-Man... Wonder Wart-Hog kind of thing?"

"Really *should* be going... but, ahh, 'for the record', I am not familiar with most of those... although back on the space-ship, one of my dear first family – Devon White, I believe – told me about a fictional character named 'Super Man', who he compared to myself," added Karéin-Mayréij. "At the time, I was flattered; for this 'Super Man' was apparently akin to a god... ah, if only that were the case, for she who now addresses you. But you all shall eventually be far more than men and women. As your abilities wax, the truth of this will be as clear as day, to each of you."

"What am *I* gonna to be?" pressed the third agent. "Like, what kind of super-hero?"

"Channelin' sports-games without a TV," joked Boatman. "That's what *I'm* bettin' on."

Hendricks was about to reply, but he was cut off by the alien-girl.

"I must leave, though I will return in a few minutes," she remarked. "We ought not to waste time, since no doubt, your 'President's army will be looking to again drop some bombs on my head."

"Where are you going?" requested Chu.

But the Storied Watcher had already disappeared.

"Minnie," asked the black agent, "In whatever time we got while them all is off lookin' for stuff, can you fill us in on what happened, up there? Especially this wild-goose chase that she's now off on... the one with the school, I mean. What's that all 'bout?"

"Some of it's, uhh, *private*," stated the FBI team-leader, uncomfortably, "But here's the 'Cliffs Notes' version. We went up – *way* up, by the way – and Karéin had to drop this protective 'bubble' of hers, for my communicator to work. We got a link to the Director, and thank God we were at least able to fill him in on the 'loose-nuke' thing... and now, there's yet *another* complication –"

"Whaddya mean?" inquired Hendricks.

"Well," explained Chu, "During the conversation, Karéin claimed to have suddenly remembered some kind of connection she has to the children of the elementary-school in Compton that she referred to, a few minutes ago... apparently, they, uhh, 'sang' to her at the right time, or something – and now she's on the warpath to get them out of L.A. before the bomb goes off."

"Could be good news," commented the third agent. "*If,* that is, it's a reason for her to get our butts out of here, on the same flight."

"Yeah," agreed the team-leader. "The Director and I were negotiating with her on this, trying to convince her to help us locate and defuse the damn thing, but then she had to abruptly cut off the call when we were attacked. She rocketed – and I *do* mean 'rocketed' – both of us into the stratosphere, did some unbelievable maneuvers that should have squashed me like a *bug*... then we both ended back up here. That's about the long and short of it."

"Well, that explains the school... and just what we *need,* young man... more business to keep her 'round here, waitin' for the bomb to blow us all to Kingdom Come," observed the big black man.

He waited for a second and then added, "But was that *really* everythin' that was goin' on, up there?"

"What do you *mean*... 'really'?" retorted the man's superior agent.

"Listen, Minnie," he offered, slowly and gently, "You and me, we known each other for quite some time... and we's friends, not just 'boss 'n hired help', you know? 'Least that's how I see it – and I don't know how to put this, so I'm gonna just come out and *say* it – but... your private-life ain't none of our business, I think Mr. Will 'n I both understand that... but Minnie, we need to know if your, uhh, relationship with Little Miss Martian is anythin' more than *professional.* If you know what I mean."

"Keep your nose out of my fucking *life,* Otis!" growled Chu. "You're right... it *is* none of your business."

"Hey, Minnie – chill *out,*" interjected Hendricks. "The big guy doesn't mean anything by it – and for the record, neither of us gives two shits who you're sleeping with... that's not the point. What we're both concerned about, is whether she's got you under her spell – that's all. Man, I wouldn't blame you if you, uhh, *did* it, up there, between phone calls... I can hardly get *near* her without having Mr. Jimmy standing to attention, you know? What I'm trying to say is, it's not *natural*... *nothing* about her is. Don't blame yourself. *We* don't."

A miserable-looking Chu barely kept control of a quivering chin.

She wiped a tear.

"Thanks, guys," she replied, in a low voice, trying to squelch a blush. "I... I don't know what to *say.* Is it *that* obvious?"

"Funny... that's pretty much what *I* was thinking, last time I got too close to her," mentioned the third agent. "You sure got company, in feeling like a horny 13-year-old... only we're talking about the same person. *Totally* stupid, man."

"Minnie," quietly reassured Boatman, "We ain't gonna tell nobody. Don't *worry*."

"Okay – you want the *truth?*" she forced out, with watering eyes. "Well the truth is, it's *not* her... not *completely*, anyway. I've known about, uhh... God it's hard to say... about liking *girls*, for years – and you've got to *understand*, it's not that I don't like guys... I *do*, I mean, I'm *engaged*, for Pete's sake! But the Bureau finds out even a *whisper* about this – uhh, how are they calling it, again, 'personality defect' – and there goes my lovely old career in one shot, dishonorable discharge and all –"

"Yeah," muttered Hendricks. "Knew two guys who got the ax for *exactly* that, comin' out of field-training. They were damn good, too... fuckin' *idiocy*, if you ask me."

Chu ruefully nodded and continued, "You guys both know how it's been, since three Administrations ago... what with all the religious 'back to moral-basics' crap showing up everywhere. I've been able to keep it under control until now... but with *Karéin*, dammit – she makes *one* pass at me and I just swoon like a teenager. Yes, *part* of it might be that she's next to irresistible to both genders; but if it hadn't been in me from way back before, I would have just given her a slap and told her to keep her hands to herself. But I couldn't... I *couldn't*, and it's not just that alien-BS that she uses all the time. I *wanted* her to. And she would've known it, if she was just a plain old human being."

She paused for a bit, then added, "So that's how it is. I'm sorry... I guess I'm not much of a professional role-model. Even if she was the best-looking guy that I had ever met, I still shouldn't be counting off the seconds until I can... *well*. I'll try to behave myself better. I really *will*."

"Minnie," remarked the black agent, "You're bein' a little *hard* on yourself, don't you think? Shit – she's some kind of crazy punk-ass *goddess*, after all! It's impossible for any of us to tell if these is normal human feelin's, or if it's part of some subtle kinda mind-control thing'... maybe she don't even *know* that she's usin' it, or maybe she can't control it – after all, isn't that how we all got pushed down the path to becomin', uhh... whatever we's becomin'? And from my point-of-view, at least half of any blame to go around – if any's due – should be laid at *her* door, anyway. What with her fightin' a war against the whole U.S. government, you'd think she'd be a little too busy to be chasin' every damn skirt and pair of pants in the neighborhood –"

He stopped talking, as his gaze turned suddenly to the left.

"Now *that's... different*," offered an awed Hendricks, upon seeing the outline of what had once a Greater Los Angeles Transit System Inter-City bus, slowly float over the low wall, at the edges of the rooftop.

I Wanna Be Like That Man

"Not hearing anything outside," half-whispered Tanaka, now taking her ear off the door of this confined, maintenance-tool-crammed room.

"How long's it gonna hold?" requested a worried Billings.

"Your guess is as good as mine," answered Boyd. "I figure, 'at least as long as Devon's little ice-up job keeps it anchored in place'. After *that*... we're hoping that water pressure will do the trick."

"And if it *doesn't*?" pressed the salesman.

"Get out your swimmin'-trunks, Bob," cheerily advised White. "'Course, whether there's anywhere that you can breathe some air from... that'd depend on how big where we's goin' is... hopefully, bigger than that cistern back there."

"*Wonderful*," muttered Billings.

He looked down at his shoes.

"Damn," he added. "Soles are burned right *through* – two or three places."

"Yeah," noted the black ex-astronaut. "Mine, too."

"Same here... and judging from the level of energy that I felt flowing through me, as well as the physical evidence," speculated Tanaka, "I'd bet that at its peak, the voltage in that floor could have killed an *elephant.*"

She looked kindly at Melissa.

"Are you aware, young lady," mentioned the scientist, "That you probably saved Elissha's *life?* By getting off the floor in time, that is."

"Well thank y'all, Miz Cherie... but why y'all say that?" responded the teenager. "Ah means, it didn' hurt th' rest of y'all... leastaways, not *too* much..."

"It appears that we all can, however uncomfortably, handle enough electricity to kill a normal human being," explained Tanaka. "I'm not nearly so sure about the child. Something to keep in mind, for next time. Good work, honey. *Really* good work!"

"Yes Ma'am," acknowledged Melissa, with a proud smile as her mother embraced her.

A second later, the teenager's demeanor became more wary.

"Miz Cherie," she carefully observed, "Momma aksin' me, like... y'all took *all* that-there 'lectricity, into yo' body? But y'all still doin' fine?"

"Yep," answered Tanaka, with a saturnine half-smile that all around her, save the little girl, knew well from previous experience with another.

For a second, the scientist allowed her eyes to glow.

"As a matter of fact... *better* than 'fine'," she confidently purred.

"You glad she's on *our* side, yet?" joked Boyd.

Claremont vigorously nodded in the affirmative.

"Wow," exclaimed Melissa. "Jus' a second – what, Momma?"

She giggled, then related, "Momma say, y'all bein' our walkin' jump-starter, 'case we need one for Bob's car, again."

"What she means, Professor," interjected Billings, "Is that up north, we tracked down my SUV, which I had abandoned before we got dragged into the

Jesus-Jail... battery was dead until Sari started it up – with her bare hands. That was when we started to realize that she was, uhh, just a bit... *different*."

"Y'all *think*?" sarcastically quipped White.

"Folks," observed Jacobson, "What this last near-disaster – back in the corridor, I mean – shows us, is that we're not dealing with, uhh, 'deterrent'-type traps, any more. They're shooting to *kill*... so don't count on second-chances. We're going to have to be *very* careful, from this point on."

"Listen, Commander," proposed Boyd, "In view of that, I have to again *strongly* suggest that we send out an advance-team on recce – I *know* the Professor's feelings about splitting us up... but if we run into yet another of these lethal man-traps with a half-asleep kid –"

"I'm wide awake, now," protested Elissha. "You're a bad man!"

"Oh... he ain't *so* bad," commented Curtis. "He 'n Miz Cherie, they done sprung me from them bad guys wid dey guns."

Boyd, trying to suppress a grin and not doing a very good job of it, took a few steps and motioned for Melissa to give the girl to him.

"Hey, there, princess," he stated, as he reached out toward the pouting child, "Did you know that your Uncle Brent has kids, too?"

"So *what!*" complained Elissha, crossing her arms in typical brat-fashion.

Boyd withdrew his arms. He put his knee up on a box and spoke to the girl.

"Well, the thing is, when you're a daddy like I am... you start to get *worried* about what happens to your kids – and I'm kind of starting to think of you like that... you know?" mentioned the ex-astronaut.

"You didn't *ask* me if you could," argued the child.

"Okay... can I love you like you're *my* little girl?" asked the smiling man.

"Oh, I *guess* that would be alright," she answered.

"*Insufferably* cute," muttered Billings.

"Thanks," acknowledged the ex-astronaut. "Now, Elissha... if *your* daddy asked you not to do something – like, for example, crossing the street without looking both ways... would you obey him... or would you do it anyway?"

"My daddy's *dead*," immediately retorted the girl. "I *saw* them kill him!"

Boyd's smile disappeared and he hung his shaking head.

"Kind of walked into *that* one," he quietly stated.

"Honey," offered Tanaka, "I think what Uncle Brent means is, there might be some really *bad* people out there – like the ones who we rescued you from. He just wants to go out and look around, so he can, uhh, get rid of the bad folks, before they can try to do any more mean things to you. Would that be okay?"

"I *guess* so," allowed Elissha. "As long as he comes back. I *want* him to come back, so that Uncle Brent can see his own kids, again."

"Thanks," weakly answered Boyd. "And... *thanks*, Professor."

"I'm not endorsing the concept of dividing the party, Brent," pointed out Tanaka. "But maybe it *would* be a good idea if some of the, uhh, more physically-fit of us, go on ahead... if only so we don't all get caught in the same trap with nobody on the other side of it –"

"I like the sound of that," spoke Billings. "Especially, the 'fit' part of it. Kind of rules me out... wouldn't you say?"

"Compared to *who*, Bob?" grumbled Jacobson. "Melissa, Whitney, Curtis or Elissha?"

"Okay... *okay*," hastily retreated the salesman. "Can I at least have a gun?"

"He's got a point," agreed Jacobson, to the three members of his former crew. "But – and this is very open to discussion – maybe we should keep the recce-crew just to you two guys? Brent now has at least some ability to cover his tracks, and we may want to keep Cherie as our, uhh, 'ace in the hole'. If you'd like me to go along with you, I'm more than willing to do that... but we should give Bob a gun... maybe that pistol that you scrounged further back up there, Brent? Both of you – Devon and Brent, that is – have a built-in weapon... so does Cherie, and so do I, sort of... Bob's ability is primarily defensive –"

"Y'all forget me, Cap'n Sam?" spoke up Curtis. "Want to hear me shout yo' ears off?"

"No – that's *quite* alright," demurred the Mars mission commander, squatting down to look the boy in the eye. "But *listen*, son... something that we forgot to deal with, back there... all of us have a warning-word that we use, when we're about to activate our own, uhh, little abilities, so that everybody in front can get out of the way... for example, Brent's is 'Shine', Cherie's is 'Sword', while Devon's one is 'Sno-Kone'. Oh, and Bob's is 'Taxi'; when he calls out that, in the next second, you won't see him at all. I'd suggest something like 'Shout' for you – what do you say, Curtis?"

"'Shout', yo – ah goin' for that, fo' sure, Cap'n Sam," replied the boy, with an enthusiastic grin. "Can ah be slingin' a piece, too, so ah bein' a gangsta?"

Claremont lightly cuffed her son, in the back of the head.

"I'm afraid, young man, that were you to meet some of the 'gangstas' that we've so far run into, in this hellish place," warned Jacobson, "You'd quickly find out that they're anything *but* a good role-model – so nix on the gun, for now... I think your mother wants you just to stick to your vocal-chords. But – something that applies to everyone – this isn't a *game* that we're playing, here, Curtis... and if we get caught in a desperate situation, I want you to use *any* weapon at your disposal, to stay alive and help the rest of us. If that means hurting one of the bad-guys, maybe even worse than that – I don't want you to think about doing it, or to hesitate, for so much as a *second*... just *do* it – okay?"

Suddenly without the bravado, a wide-eyed Curtis replied, "Yes, sir. Ah will, ah *promise*. Ah *seen* what they doin' to Tommy, 'an ah owes 'em back for it. Gonna take 'em down *hard*, Cap'n Sam!"

"Glad to hear that," remarked the former Mars mission commander, with a gentle smile. "And, for the rest of you, need it be said... if you hear a small voice calling out 'Shout' – cover your ears, unless you want to hear a really *big* voice."

"He bad 'nough, without this 'alien' thang makin' him worse," observed Melissa. "So mah hands goin' up *real* fast, when ah hears *that* word."

"You ain't just whistlin' Dixie there, kid," muttered Billings.

Claremont rolled her eyes, but there was a proud smile on her face.

"So here's what I'm proposing," continued Jacobson. "Brent and Devon go and recce out as much of this place as they can. Bob gets Brent's sidearm, he and I cover the immediate vicinity of whatever's just past the door, until the recce-team gets back. Cherie stays with the civilians, so that if the plug on the hole behind us – God forbid – starts to loosen, she can warn us and hold it in place, as long as possible. Anybody got a better plan?"

"Don't like this... but I guess I'm outvoted... right?" complained Tanaka.

"Y'all want to come with us, Professor?" challenged White.

"And leave them all back here? No *way!*" countered the woman.

"Good... I *always* feel more secure inside a force-field," joked the salesman. Tanaka shot Billings an exasperated glance.

Boyd removed the shoulder-sling, holster and pistol that he had been carrying since the first battles. He handed these accouterments to Billings.

"Know how to use one of these?" asked the ex-astronaut.

"Yeah," replied the salesman. "Got one at home, as well as a few rifles. Don't count on me to win any awards for target-shooting, though – just a 'recreational' thing for me, you know?"

"High-energy rounds, partial composite-construction for the gun," said Boyd, professionally. "Twelve in the mag, one in the chamber... here are the other three clips I found on the guys who, uhh, 'donated' it, plus... let's see... eight loose rounds. I'd suggest you aim and fire sparingly, because there's no guarantee of ammo-replenishment."

"Depends on how many people we kill and loot, I guess," commented Billings, with a vacant shrug.

Boyd knowingly arched a eyebrow, as he responded with a low "Yeah."

"What *we* 'sposed to do, Cap'n Sam?" requested Melissa.

"I'd suggest that you, Curtis and your mother, look after Elissha and catch up on current events from the Professor... there's a lot that we need to fill you in on," answered Jacobson. "And try to keep the noise down while you're chatting, of course... if we have to call upon you to do something, be ready to do it at a moment's notice. Oh, by the way, sweetheart... how are *you* doing?"

"I'm okay," said the little girl. "But I'm *hungry*, Mister Sam!"

"I *know*, honey," he compassionately stated. "Next time I find something to eat or drink, I'll make sure you're first in line to have a bite or sip."

"Okay," chirped Elissha.

The former Mars mission commander turned to address White and Boyd.

"Listen, guys," he explained, "We don't have a precise way of measuring time down here – no wristwatches, communicators, *et cetera* – but none the less, let's set an expectation about how long you're going to be out... just so we know when to assume that there's been trouble and we've got to come looking for you. Fifteen minutes, maybe?"

"Make it twenty," requested the black ex-astronaut. "Lots of, uhh, 'distractions' down here."

"Works for *me*," confirmed Boyd. "And as far as warning about 'trouble' goes... I noticed that I can only hear the 'speaking-in-my-mind' stuff, precise words, I mean, at fairly close-range, within eyesight or less than that; but the less focused, 'feelings' part of it, works much further out... does that correspond with your own experiences?"

"Yeah... pretty much," concurred White. "'Specially when it's folks fearin' for their lives, don't y'all know."

"Whitney was able to, uhh, 'read' her son from a fair distance – so maybe it has to do with family-relationships," observed Jacobson. "But in any event, if you get into a jam and can't shoot your way out – start broadcasting; at least *that* should give us an idea of what direction to take when we come get you."

"Roger that," said Boyd.

He turned to the black ex-astronaut.

"Ready?" he asked.

"Got clips, gettin' my chillin'-thing back," replied White, his voice strong and purposeful. "Let's go, bro'... got some *business* to do!"

Cautiously – guns at the ready – they opened the door, peered out and exited this confined place.

As they left, a wide-eyed Curtis pointed at where White had been.

"I wanna be like *that* man, Momma," declared the boy.

Magic Bus

Gradually, the Los Angeles Transit System bus came to a stop, landing with a low 'thump', about three meters from the group on the building-top.

"I had to inspect *six* of these things, before I found one whose door and windows were intact," explained a pleasant-sounding alien voice, a split-second before the Storied Watcher appeared to their eyes.

"If I have calculated correctly," she added, "It can accommodate all of you, your brothers and sisters from the room below – grrr, where *is* Wolf, I had expected that he would be back with them, by now – as well as those who we shall shortly rescue. I hope that you like it... I selected one with nicely-padded-seats. Oh, and *here*" – she caused a collection of at least ten carefully-folded, shiny-paper items, to float toward the FBI-agents, Boatman in particular – "Are all the 'maps' that I could find, down in the ho-tel lobby. Can you please review them as soon as possible?"

"Now *there's* what I'd call 'an emergency-detour added to the transit-schedule'," joked Boatman. "Wonder if she's gonna let us off between stops."

"Only if you *behave* yourself," deadpanned Karéin-Mayréij, without missing a beat.

"Doot doo doo, Magic Bus," cracked Hendricks.

"It's just a *bus*," claimed Chu. "Nothing 'magic', about it."

"Just *wait!*" countered the Storied Watcher, with an enigmatic smile.

"Who gets to be the driver?" asked the third agent.

"I think that 'co-pilot' would be a better description," answered the alien-girl. "And – as dear Bob used to say – 'Did I not just hear someone vol-un-teer'."

"Oh no, now *listen* –" stammered Hendricks.

"You may want to become familiar with the little wheel which tells it where to go, while I go down and find what my trusty boun-tee-hunter friend is busying himself with... not to mention the map that Mr. Otis is now reviewing," cheerily stated Karéin-Mayréij. "Here... the door is open."

"Yeah... but how do I steer it? While it's flying, I mean," he inquired.

"I have not yet, ahh, 'worked that out'," she breezily admitted. "If you have any good ideas about adding the necessary controls, tell me when I return – oh, never mind... so *there* you are, Wolf. What, uhh, took you?"

"Don't bitch to *me*," complained the bounty-hunter, as he led Kaysten and a bee-line of alien supporters and hangers-on, out of the stairwell to the rooftop. "Tell your gangsta-friend that when you say 'jump', it's 'how high' –"

He stopped, upon seeing the bus.

"Better than standin' on a rock while you fly cross-country, I guess," Wolf commented, with a shrug. "Where we goin'?"

"Next stop Compton," said Boatman. "Y'all might want to put away your gang-colors, if we land on the wrong side of Whatever Street."

By now, Sebastiàn had clambered out, and he just caught what the black FBI-agent had been saying.

"Whoa, *hombre*," he complained. "You don' want to go down *there!* Nothin' but fuckin' Bloods and Crips an' enough bullets to keep *la guerra* goin' for a fuckin' *century*."

"Have faith in me. And in yourself," patiently counseled Karéin-Mayréij, with a strange glance at the gangster, right in the eyes.

"A *bus*," marveled the Russian. "Karéin, you never cease to... well, I suppose it makes about as much sense as anything else that I have so far dealt with. I can only hope that this one cannot be – uhh, 'pulled over' – by the local authorities, like the last one was."

"Ain't no Highway-Patrol at ten thousand feet," chuckled Boatman. "And besides, didn't work out so bad that we ended up with you and Mister Bounty-Hunter... could have been the same guys as got the rest of her friends, after all."

"I suppose that you are right about that," ruefully confirmed Misha.

"Listen, Karéin," mentioned Abruzzio, "We tried to carry that armor of yours up here... but we couldn't get it to budge, and it was far too hot to carry –"

"I *was* actually able to, uhh, 'chat' with 'Daughter Tornado-Diamond-Curtain', for a while, until the heat from her sister became too intense," interrupted Ramirez. "But she was unable to, uhh, convince her siblings... or that was the impression that I got. It's hard to understand exactly what a being like this, really means to say. The words were first in English... but then it sounded like she was trying to switch to Spanish, maybe for the sake of practice."

"Well... *duh*," joked Hendricks. "I can hardly figure out my laptop computer, either. And *its* commands are all in *American*."

Abruzzio sighed and rolled her eyes.

"Do not worry, Hector," responded the Storied Watcher, with a wry smile. "My war-children heard you perfectly well; and it is their habit to travel while hidden, in any event."

She turned, as if to address the sky, and exclaimed, "*Vîrya Quü'j!* Now bring thee my children, to mine frame!"

In a quarter of an eye-blink, a creature who had been clad just in disheveled suburban rec-room garb, stood awesomely in front of them, with bright-glowing eyes and flaming battle-gear, and even those such as Wolf and the Russian – who had seen most of this before – reflexively stepped back.

Suddenly, *Væran Fàiagàryuu* jumped into her hand, causing no little consternation among the onlookers.

The alien-girl removed her sunglasses, their TV-snow pattern dimly visible in the lenses, and placed them to cross the shaft of the sword at its hand-guard. Then she brought her lips near to these two strange animate-beings, whispered something, and blew a kiss upon them.

The *katana* and its newfound companion streaked upward, rapidly disappearing from sight.

"What was *that* all about?" inquired Abruzzio.

"I bid *Væran Fàiagàryuu* to, ahh, 'interface' with *Vîrya Ahn'jë*, so we may be forewarned of an incipient attack," explained Karéin-Mayréij. "The eyes of my war-daughter will be useful to him... they are better than his own."

"An integrated military communications-network," observed Misha. "*Impressive*... and very necessary."

The Storied Watcher allowed herself a wry half-curtsy.

"Yeah – but why didn't you send the shield?" asked Kaysten. "What with it being able to fly all over Hell's Half-Acre?"

"Because *Vîrya I'ëà'b'* wanted to stay down here with *you*, Jerr-ee," diffidently answered the alien-girl.

"Oh... *right*," he replied.

"Teach you to ask stupid questions, pardner," quipped Wolf.

"So what are you going to *do*, Karéin?" asked Abruzzio. "With the bus."

"*Watch* me, sister Sylvia," replied the Storied Watcher; and as she spoke, they noticed that a thin, translucent energy-membrane had appeared some ten meters above them, over the rooftop and those that it accommodated.

With movements so fast that their eyes could barely follow, and with the feverish assistance of *Vîrya I'ëà'b'*'s cutting-edge, as well as that of *Væran Ksé'l'ch'* and that of his freezing, violet-blue war-brother, the Storied Watcher's burning gaze – and a faint, silver-green glow, that the group had heretofore not seen – transformed the bus, both inside and out. Its already-tinted-windows became darker still, its former stainless-steel outside was smoothed and changed into a dull-drab tint; and even the smallest of holes and protuberances upon the vehicle's exterior, including the windshield-wipers and the rear-view mirror, were either melted down or covered up.

When she was done – a process that took perhaps ten to fifteen minutes – the bus looked like nothing so much as a rotund, battleship-gray torpedo, with barely-distinguishable windows and nary a joint or attachment-point visible to the untrained eye.

"*Whoa!*" exclaimed Ramirez. "Quite a remodeling-job you done there."

"No shit," added Wolf. "I could hire you out for top dollar, moddin' out cars down on the street in Tucson, girl."

The Storied Watcher darted over to the bounty-hunter, and, much to his enjoyment, planted a friendly kiss on his cheek.

"Thanks, dear friend," she said, "I will keep that in mind, if I ever need a – uhh – 'day-job', as my beloved Bob Billings used to say; although – the last time that I tried such – things did not turn out so well. I *do* have a few, uhh, credit-card-debts to pay off."

"If *only* we had beaten those bastards to the house, and the tile-shop," regretfully commented Chu. "How different this all would have been."

"You *tried*, Minn-ee," affectionately replied Karéin-Mayréij. "That means *so* much to me."

Turning to address the rest of them, she explained, "Now to answer the obvious question – namely, 'wherefore these changes'... while I will do my best to protect all of you, and those who we now go to rescue, as well, with my arts, it may come to pass that so doing may be inconvenient, difficult or even impossible. So my war-children, *Vîrya Quü'j* and I have, ahh, 'fixed up' yonder vehicle, to give it a measure of proof against such surveillance and attacks as the American President may direct against it. Furthermore, if we have done our work right, those inside this thing, even ordinary humans, will find refuge – of a sort – against harmful energies and rapid movements, provided of course that they, uhh, 'fasten their seat-belts'. I would advise you not to rely on it too much, since we are as yet not completely familiar with the ways of techno, and we did not have much time to do the necessary preparations. Still... a chariot hastily-built, is better than to war on one's feet, is it not?"

"I'm at a loss for words," stated an amazed, awed Abruzzio. "But... how does it *fly?*"

"Oh – *that* part is easy," answered the alien-girl. "I throw it up in the air, and there it goes. By the way... it is also partly proof against evil magic. I counseled that doing this would not be necessary... but *Vîrya Quü'j*, insisted upon it."

"What do you mean, 'there it goes'?" demanded Kaysten. "Has it got a rocket-engine, or something?"

"Just what I *said*, Jerr-ee," noted Karéin-Mayréij, with a shrug. "It 'goes', until the forces of gravity again cause it to come to ground... unless something else keeps it aloft."

"Huh?" asked the Chief of Staff. "Now I'm *completely* confused!"

"Not much of a change," muttered Hendricks.

"Anybody want to try flappin' their wings?" joked Boatman.

"Hey, Karéin... do I still get to be the driver?" requested the third agent.

"Sure," confirmed the alien-girl. "But I would advise you not to pay too much attention to the little dials and instruments that are arrayed around the uhh, 'driving-seat'. *Vîrya Quü'j* and I do not have a great deal of experience in connecting techno to the *Fire*... except for my war-children, that is."

"Yeah, okay... but does the steering-wheel work?" he inquired.

"I believe so... but only in two dimensions," she responded.

"What if I want to go up or down?" pressed Hendricks.

"You will have to figure *that* out by yourself, I suppose," she shrugged.

"*Riight,*" he said.

"Consider yourself lucky," noted Misha. "I wanted to be a test-pilot back in Russia... but they were only accepting individuals with better-than-average eyesight. Too bad – I believe that I would probably pass those tests, now. If, that is, they were not to *shoot* me, beforehand."

"Life's a bitch, *amigo,*" grunted Wolf.

"So here's where I *think* we need to go," offered Boatman, pointing a big finger at a point in roughly the center of one of the maps, as the Storied Watcher came instantly and uncomfortably close beside him. "Somewhere between Adams and Exposition on the north and south, an' South Western on the west an' South Vermont, on the east. Ain't no way that I can talk you out of it... is there?"

"Otis," she remarked, casting a serious, determined glance, "These are *your* people – *your* children. In a way, you – and everyone on this *planet* – including myself, owe them our lives. We *must* go to them. Do you understand?"

He did a double-take, then commented, "Yeah, well – I *could* argue the point of just savin' one school's worth of kids as opposed to a whole *city* of 'em... one school's better than nothin', I guess. But wouldn't it just be simpler to get that damn bomb out of L.A.? Then these kids you're so keen to save – they'd be fine, along with all the rest of them."

"And what if these, uhh, 'skin-heads' that Sebastiàn speaks of, set the device off, as soon as I draw close to it... thereby killing not only myself, but everyone else in the city?" countered Karéin-Mayréij. "I have many arts that *might* work to neutralize this evil creation... but they might *not,* and furthermore – were I to unleash my greatest powers against the atom-smashing bomb – this would almost certainly slaughter many thousands of mortals, whose only transgression would be that they were in the area, at the time. I will leave *that* kind of wanton blood-letting, to your President and his courtiers, Otis Boat-man."

"Touché," commented Abruzzio.

"Your house is fixin' to burn down, you get your family out of it first, before you go off and join the volunteer fire-department, pardner," added Wolf. "She's just doin' what you'd do or I'd do, if we were her."

"That's another one that I'd argue on another day, Mister Bounty-Hunter," argued Boatman, "Listen, Karéin... you want to keep this map? Don't know how you can, though, with that fire on your gloves..."

"No... it is oh-kay," she demurred. "I have formed a mind-picture of this area – big multi-streets on the north and east, grass marching-field to the south and east, farther still in yonder direction there is the big stadium for chariot-races, gladiator-battles and so on –"

"Wish that were true – be a lot more interesting, for sure – but hate to disappoint you, all they got is ball-games in there, these days," interrupted Hendricks. "No blood and guts... that is, if you don't count 'no-holds-barred mixed martial-arts."

"I shall have to introduce you to my own skills of body-combat, some time," mentioned the alien-girl. "They are very effective, with or without using the weirding-powers to enhance them. But let us away... sand flows through the narrow middle."

Now, Karéin-Mayréij stole around to the right-hand side of the bus and caused its front portal to open, though neither a handle nor, indeed, anything upon the outside of the vehicle, disclosed that an entrance was there.

As the sword fell from far above to return to her hand, and as the strange sunglasses affixed themselves to her head, she commanded,

"'All aboard'... for to rescue the children!"

All The News That Can Fit

There was the familiar combination of electronic-music chimes and the comforting, background 'squeak-squeak-squeak' sound that heralded the opening of the evening news; then, those few in America who payed much attention to current affairs – their ranks, admittedly, temporarily swelled by recent events – settled back into loafer-chairs and living-room sofas, juggling TV-dinners and cans of weak beer, as they went.

"The Disney Evening News, with Martin Krystal reporting," confidently intoned the voice-over, as the 'hat-and-ears' logo, combined with the slogan, "All The News That's Fit To Entertain", scrolled across the screen.

"Good evening, ladies, gentlemen and kids," said the smartly-dressed, rock-jawed and blow-dried, Caucasian anchorman, from the modernistic, glass-and-stainless-steel set. "Our lead story tonight concerns a major announcement from the federal government, about the apprehension of a subversive spy-network of *unprecedented* size and scope. Our man in Washington – Charles D. Taylor – has the details. Charlie?"

The camera switched to a location in front of the White House – its exterior-damage made almost like new, although there was still that awkward big thing in the South Lawn, now dressed up as a 'monument to our boys in Cuba'; but as the on-site reporter spoke, television-screens in America's living-rooms showed scenes of stone-faced, business-suited men and scowling, medal-bedecked military-men being carted off in handcuffs.

"Martin, the White House tonight issued a press-release, which reads in part, 'Over the past 24 hours, the Secret Service, acting in co-operation with certain other federal security-agencies, has executed the final phase of a long-ongoing investigation, entitled 'Operation Cleanse The Fatherland', into subversion of the government, at the highest levels," explained the reporter, he almost a clone of the anchorman.

"The statement goes on to say," continued the reporter, "That while the details remain classified, the Government is cracking down not only against the forces of international Muslim terrorism, but also against the dangerous alien calling itself 'Karéin-Mayréij' – who, it has recently been discovered – has been conspiring with atheists, homosexuals, pacifists, Communists, illegal immigrants and other subversives, to establish itself as the Muslim ruler of America. The White House's Special Religious Counsel, incidentally, issued a separate news-release, praising the government's recent activities as – and here I quote – 'the first of many blows that we must strike against the sinister tentacles of the Anti-Christ, which extend throughout our sinful, wicked, Godless society'. Other government spokesmen were apparently unaware of this comment, although they have not disavowed it."

The reporter went on, "While the White House has not released a full list of those who have just been apprehended, independent sources have confirmed that it includes former FBI director Cesar Ochoa, former Air Force chief Harry Anderson and former Presidential Science Advisor, Fred McPherson, as well as a large number of others from the previous administration. These individuals are all being held in precautionary detention-facilities, pending in-camera trials under the provisions of special emergency national-security legislation, while wide-ranging warrants for the arrest of numerous others are still in the process of being executed."

The television-screens showed scenes of homes being broken into and yet more arrests.

"The White House has refused all requests for further information," concluded the on-site correspondent, "Although it has said that more details may be provided, once the government is sure that all of those under suspicion, have been apprehended. Martin?"

"Well... it certainly seems that something *big* has been going on, today," noted the anchorman, in his friendly, laid-back style. "Back here in Washington, the Democratic caucus issued its own statement, denouncing the activities of the alien, and specifically denying that anyone from the minority-party had anything to do with the spy-ring, saying, 'Americans should take note of the fact that all those who have so far been apprehended, have been *Republicans*, or were appointed by Republican administrations; therefore, who should our citizens conclude, is the greater threat to national-security'."

"The White House also refused to comment on the Democratic statement," continued Krystal, "But the Chairman of the Republican National Committee *did* say, 'That's rich of the lib-rals to talk about patriotism, when they opposed both the liberation of Cuba and our strikes against the Muslim League in Pakistan'. Sources on Capitol Hill, however, predicated that this dispute would remain an 'inside-the-Beltway' issue, since Congress is currently tied up in a filibuster against cuts to subsidies for gasoline, rural-prison-construction and deep-well water drilling."

The anchorman turned to face another camera.

"In other headline news," he said, "Fifty million dollars bail was posted today for the famous teenage starlet Blaine Maine, after her 'wild night' in New York's club-district, in which – according to a federal grand-jury complaint – Ms. Maine directly or indirectly caused the destruction of two limousines, two ambulances, one helicopter, three luxury hotel-suites, one exclusive nightclub, the Downtown Hospital Emergency Handling-Room, as well as injuries – some severe – to at least sixteen citizens of New York State."

With an arched eyebrow, Krystal related, "According to her press-office, quote, 'Blaine Maine denies all responsibility, because – she maintains – the incident was caused by the refusal of the New York Police Department to 'give her space in a time of personal crisis', unquote. Knowledgeable sources indicate that the cause of the altercation may have been the starlet's ongoing frustration at not being able to return to her sprawling 700-room mansion and regular upscale shopping-haunts in Beverly Hills, due to the continuing disturbances and resulting restrictions against travel into the Greater Los Angeles area... although the use of prohibited substances – long rumored to have been a problem for Ms. Maine – may also have played a part."

After drawing a breath, the anchorman added, "The spokesman noted that she is currently 'seeking the help of a personal values-therapist', somewhere on the East Coast, but that she has every intention of showing up for the trial. When asked 'What about the last two similar incidents', the spokesman replied, 'Those were *clearly* different, because Blaine should be pitied, as a homeless-person'."

"And," he concluded, "Disney News Entertainment Corporation *does*, of course, maintain a financial interest in the 'Blaine Maine' movie-franchise, so we're disclosing that here. Turning to sports..."

In an average American living-room, an citizen belched over his beer.

"*Knew* them Commies and eco-freaks was all throughout the government!" he complained. "No *wonder* taxes is so high!"

"It was the *Muslims* that they caught, Kelvin," corrected the *hausfrau*. "Not the Commies. Don't you ever *listen* to what's on the news?"

"*Sure* I do!" he grunted. "When something comes on, that ties it all together. Like the Ben Gleck show, you know... can't *believe* how smart that man is – findin' out about how them Muslims even go to *Christian* churches – just to make real Americans think they's just folks."

He paused, staring vacantly at the screen, which was showing some advertisement about a new drug that 'grows hair, not to mention something else that you've always thought was too short'.

"Get me another *beer*, Mildred!" he demanded.

Unlucky Shot

The area that Boyd and White had entered, after almost closing the door on Billings' nose as he and Jacobson followed, would have been pitch-black to human eyes; and even the three ex-astronauts, as well as the ex-salesman, could only discern the faintest of details in their surroundings.

"Can't see *shit!*" complained White. "No lights. That look like a wall?"

"Might be... too far-away, I think," answered Boyd. "I'm only seeing in *Um'nàhr'é* – and poorly at that. I don't see *anything*... no, *there's* something – but even fainter, in the other directions. Only one way to find out, I guess."

"Yo, must be the same here – damn, looks like dark-red on one of them velvet wall-paintings. Now if I could only *pronounce* it, as well as see it... sort of. Which way y'all want to go?" asked the black astronaut.

Those damn weirdo 'gifts', Sari – no chance without 'em, thought Billings.

I hope you know how grateful we are...

"Unless you've got a better idea... straight forward," suggested Boyd.

"My 'better idea' would've been, 'don't join the Air Force'," muttered White.

As their footsteps slowly receded, Jacobson wished them, "good luck", *sotto voce.*

"Yeah... good luck," quietly added the salesman.

Cursing himself for not having done so earlier, he looked upward.

Shouldn't there be a ceiling, somewhere? pondered Billings.

Onward went White and Boyd, each man using half-steps, while probing with a gun-barrel, hopefully to give some warning of a trap-wire.

"Damn – this place sure is *big*," whispered the black astronaut. "Can't be just a corridor. It's at least as wide as a basketball-court, between where we're at now, and where we started from."

"Yeah," agreed Boyd, also whispering.

Briefly, he looked over his shoulder.

"Devon," he asked, "You see Bob and the Commander?"

"Barely," said the black ex-astronaut. "Few meters further, an' I'll lose 'em."

Captain – can you hear me? sent Boyd.

Nothing but mental-static, came back.

"There's your answer, 'bro," noted White. "Or lack of same. We can keep goin'... but might be easy to get lost in a place this big."

"Well... it's gonna sound pretty stupid if we come back from a recce-mission, they ask us 'what did you find', and we say, 'absolutely nothing'," argued Boyd. "Kind of makes the idea of 'reconnaissance' a moot point."

"Your logic is impeccable, man," grumbled White. "Let's go."

He took three steps forward, and there was a startlingly-loud, rattling, crashing-sound, followed by something that sounded like a gruff, human voice, shouting a challenge.

Both noises echoed through this cavernous place, but then abruptly stopped.

"*Devon!*" incautiously called Boyd.

This exclamation was followed by another, from the direction in which they had just come.

The second sound quickly died down.

"I'm okay," reassured the black ex-astronaut, to the relief of his partner. "Ran into somethin'... *moved* when I hit it, like it had wheels... yeah, here it is..."

"Damn funny... couldn't see at all – now I *sorta* can, but looks different than that 'oomnari' shit everywhere else," continued White. "Y'all seein' this?"

"Yeah – only a bit," confirmed Boyd. "I guess it *would* be shiny, if there were any light."

There were faint clinking-sounds.

"One of them 'medical' instrument trays," said White. "Just what I *wanted* to find, don't you know."

"Well, it *could've* been a trap," said Boyd. "*Whoa...*"

He craned his neck back to cast the sweep of his vision upward.

"Will you look at *that*," he quietly gasped.

"Look at *what?*" asked White.

"If I'm correctly interpreting what I see," explained the ex-astronaut, "This isn't just a basketball-court – more of an auditorium, or, a theater. You see *that*, ten meters up? Looks like a balcony, maybe."

"I don't – oh, *wait* a minute," replied a duly-impressed White. "But it's just an outline, 'far as I can see... y'all *might* be right. I'd agree that there sure ain't no eight-foot ceiling 'round here, though... I can't see any end to it, up there. Bottom line is... we're not gonna know until we can trace out the outsides, with our hands, if necessary. But somethin' don't add *up* here, bro."

"Like what?" inquired the other man.

"If this place is so honkin' big – gotta be half the size of a whole one of them upstairs-levels, if it's an inch – then why ain't we runnin' into any guards or such?" commented the black ex-astronaut. "Seems awful strange that they'd be crawlin' all over the place elsewhere... but not here."

"Watch out what you wish for," stated Boyd. "You might just *get* it..."

His voice trailed off.

"Brent? Y'all *okay?*" queried White, although he could see his partner as well as anyone could see anything, in the near-total darkness.

"I'm... *fine*," mumbled a confused-sounding ex-Mars pilot. "*Thought* I got a mind-message... must've been imagining it."

"You mean, like just before we sprung Bob's two ladies, back there?" asked the black ex-astronaut.

"Gone now... no way to really tell," answered the other man. "I guess we had better get going."

"Yeah... okay," affirmed White.

They both stepped forward, but after perhaps another six or so meters, it was Boyd's turn to intemperately raise his voice.

A small shower of sparks momentarily lit up the place, but neither of the ex-astronauts adjusted their eyesight rapidly enough to take advantage of it – except, perhaps, to notice a very large, metal-bound container, directly in front.

"*Shit!*" Boyd cursed, rapidly withdrawing his foot from something upon which he had stepped.

A small, baleful red light began to silently shine, off in the distance.

"What *happened?*" anxiously said White. "Damn... what's that smell?"

"Electric-shock – and a fucking *powerful* one!" remarked Boyd, as he strained his eyes at the singed tip of his boot. "And ozone, no doubt."

Cautiously, he bent down on one knee.

"Gotta try this, sooner or later," he said, extending a palm as far forward as he dared. "Let's see if the Professor's lessons have sunk in to her first-year class... *owww!*"

A brilliant bolt of electrical-energy surged up from the floor about six inches from the front edge of Boyd's boot, to the tip of his index-finger. He stuck the abused digit in his mouth and tried to suck out the pain emanating from it.

"Yeah... if I'm estimating the voltage right, that's a 'people-killer', for sure," warned the ex-astronaut. "Whatever else you can say for the assholes who run this place... they're nothing, if not *consistent.*"

"Yo, hate to ask y'all," requested White, as he came up to Boyd's left side. "But I almost got a good look 'round here, when y'all lit up your life, there... want *me* to take a turn?"

"Might as well use the flashlights – except they're nowhere as bright as that thing... hah, I guess I could just fire off my own little trick, at risk to anything in its way," countered Boyd. "But I think I sort of got the hang of this... start looking, okay?"

"Eyes, off with the Mars-shit," joked the black ex-astronaut, turning his back on the other man.

Though there was no-one who could appreciate the gesture, Boyd reflexively winced, as his mind made contact with the trap-plate and baited the lethal power within it.

A scent of ozone drifted through the air, as multiple bolts of synthetic lightening jumped up to the astronaut's fingers and palm, providing a faint but effective illuminating glow.

This time, he did not flinch.

"Man, Devon..." slowly commented Boyd, "You *gotta* try this... broke an arm, got morphine... like that, only better... Gatorade on synth and steroids, God I feel... *strong*... gotta control how much you get, hurts if... too... much..."

"Take your word for it, man," answered White. "Y'all seein' our new little campground, like I am?"

Boyd – though struggling through every second of it – managed to look up and scan the surroundings.

And what he saw, both in the faint conventional-light and in the near infra-red, forced an immediate double-take.

When he had earlier spoken, he had been right about one thing : it sure *looked* like an auditorium; or, perhaps, a better simile would have been a huge, indoor sports-stadium.

The two ex-astronauts were about three-quarters of the way toward the center of a large, flat area with a round periphery; above this, starting about eight to ten meters higher, was a glassed-in observation-balcony, extending to overhang perhaps a third of the bottom-floor, that accommodated five or six rows of comfortably-padded-seats.

The bottom-level was haphazardly strewn with the now-unpleasantly-familiar captive-restraining gurneys, wheeled-trays containing torture-implements, upright-standing metal-cages with various types of computer-equipment and flat-screen video-monitors within. There were a couple of soft-drink-and-junk-food dispensing-machines and – last but not least – at least three very large, gold-colored, steel-reinforced, rectangular-boxes, each roughly half the length of a shipping-container, although just as high as the latter; these were arranged in a sort of triangular-pattern at equidistant points on the floor.

Boyd was sweating, now, and his eyes had a glassy, detached stare. The energy was still arcing into his hands, causing fumes to issue from the distal arm-sleeves of his Air Force fatigues.

"Listen, bro – y'all better –" started White; but immediately, his voice was pre-empted by a shout from the left of the two men.

"Under arrest, prisoners – hands *up!*" bellowed a demand, from someone in a hidden position.

The interruption seemed to bring Boyd to his senses, and, slumping to his knees, he cut the connection to the electrical-trap.

The auditorium was again plunged into near pitch-darkness, alleviated only by the completely inadequate red warning-light that had earlier been activated.

My Mars ears is hearin' whisperin', off to our left, noiselessly sent a crouching White to Boyd.

Y'all okay?

"We got *guns!*" yelled the voice. "Count of three – then we start shooting!"

Got so much of that Amaiish-shit in my belly, that I'll puke if I eat another gram of it, ruefully responded the other ex-astronaut.

The left, you say? I was, uhh, too busy to hear it.

You want to rush 'em?

"Three!" shouted the voice.

There's at least one more of these big boxes between here and all that stacked-up stuff near the left wall, mentally answered White.

If we step on another one of these fuckin' traps –

"Two!" warned their hidden opponents.

Gonna try something... play along with me, silently requested the ex-pilot.

He turned his head and shouted back, "Hey, don't fire! We give up! I've dropped my gun!"

And indeed, Boyd had allowed the auto-rifle to fall noisily to the floor.

"Say *what*?" interjected a nonplussed White.

You might want to shut your eyes, real soon, mentally counseled Boyd.

Fuckin' ay! sent a smirking White.

"I'm walking forward – if you've got night-vision or something like that, you should be able to see me clearly," loudly exclaimed the ex-astronaut.

"Yeah – we see you," retorted a voice. "Go forward twenty feet... then stop."

"Twenty and stop... *sure*," parroted Boyd. "But, listen – it's really dark – I can't see you... so I gotta take this *slow*, you understand?"

He lied.

In the darkness, the more-than-human man could easily detect three – maybe four – warm-shapes, peeking out from behind a collection of storage-units, at a distance of about fifty feet. One of these was evidently equipped with some kind of vision-enhancement-gear, judging from the "coolness" of where his or her eyes should have been.

"*Move!*" ordered the voice.

"Okay, okay... I'm coming forward," acknowledged the ex-astronaut.

"Wait!" demanded the self-imagined hidden opponents. "Don't try to bullshit us! There's *two* of you, we can see – tell him to get up, or –"

"Am I allowed to turn around to ask him that?" meekly inquired Boyd.

"Yes," confirmed the voice.

"Can I ask one more question?" continued the ex-astronaut.

"*What?*" growled the irritated voice.

"Do you like the old rock-group, 'Pink Floyd'?" unctuously inquired Boyd, hoping that they couldn't clearly see the smirk on his face, or the wisps of smoke that were starting to seep from the pores on his fists.

His energized ears could just make out confused discourse to the effect of, "Where the fuck's that *music* coming from?"

"You're wasting our *time*, asshole!" warned the voice. "What the hell's *that* got to do with anything?"

"It's just that they had this old song – it's going through my head, and I can't quite remember the name of it," evaded Boyd. "Something about, '... On, You Crazy Diamond', you know?"

Uh-oh, sent White.

Where'd I put that fuckin' white cane?

Love your song, 'bro.

"Stop stalling!" shouted the supposedly-hidden enemy. "This is your only warning-shot!"

There was a gun-flash, and a bullet whizzed over Boyd's head.

"Oh... *wait* a minute," he nonchalantly offered, closing his eyelids and calling upon the power to protect them.

"*Now* I remember. It was..."

"*Shine!*"

In the next fraction-of-a-second – even though his own eyes were tightly-shut – White was still completely bedazzled by the murderously-brilliant discharge that – despite being fired from way to one side of him, and aimed at a yet more distant target – assaulted every optic-nerve in his head.

Shit man, like bein' inside a halogen-bulb... hot as hell – turn it off! silently begged the black ex-astronaut.

Intermixed with screams, there were sounds of shots being fired – to little effect, because none of the bullets came anywhere near White or Boyd.

It was impossible to tell whether the ex-astronaut had fired his alien-power for less than a second, or several times that; but in a trice, the entire area was again plunged into almost-complete darkness.

Boyd's war-song abated, as well.

Moans and curses came from the left, as he picked up the auto-rifle and shouted out, "Propel those guns out in front of you, toward me... or the *next* time, I won't stop until the boxes you're hiding behind, are reduced to cinders and slag... you *got* that?"

"Can't... can't... *see*... where to throw them..." came a whimpering voice.

"Then drop 'em at your feet," loudly ordered Boyd.

"*Brent!*" came a far-off shout from behind them, along the track that they had followed.

White had now more or less shaken the stars and after-flashes from his eyes and had come to his feet.

"Yo, Captain – that *y'all?*" he challenged.

"Yeah," answered Jacobson's familiar voice.

There were rapid footsteps, as the former Mars mission commander came within speaking distance.

"*Finally* I can see you... sort of," he mentioned. "What the H is going *on?* I was looking the other way when you let fly, there – Bob wasn't so lucky... I'm sure he'll be alright, but you'll no doubt hear some choice language when next you see him. I've got my gun –"

"Don't think it's necessary," offered Boyd. "Took some shots from the left, over there; but, well, the enemy appears to have been rendered 'combat-ineffective', as the saying goes."

"You'd better make sure of that," requested the big man. "How many?"

"More than one," remarked the ex-astronaut. "They were armed... but they're – ahem – probably having a hard time aiming, these days."

"We should flush them out," ordered Jacobson. "I'll back you up – oh, *there* you are, Devon... ready?"

"Sure am... but Cap'n, watch where y'all step – there's lots of them damn 'fry-you-in-two-seconds' high-voltage-things, all over the place," warned White. "If y'all walk slow, y'all can kinda feel the tingle in your toes as y'all get near 'em."

"Hmm... like about ten feet to the right and ahead?" pondered Jacobson. "I think I sort of... *feel* some energy from that direction."

"That'd be it," confirmed the black ex-astronaut.

"Lovely brand new way to die, every day down here," ruefully muttered Jacobson. "Okay... let's clean 'em up. Keep those guns at the ready."

Slowly, the three – Boyd in the vanguard, with Jacobson and White behind and to the left and right, respectively – advanced.

After about twenty feet, the leading ex-astronaut warned, *sotto voce*, "Electrical-trap just ahead... turning left 30 degrees."

He turned and shouted, "No funny-business – you *hear* me?"

"Yo Brent... d'y'all notice, *this* one ain't got no big box inside it," commented White, as he and the other two men delicately navigated around the lethally-electrified area.

"Yeah," said Boyd. "Doesn't make a lot of sense... at least I can see the trap-outline, now – in *Um'nàhr'é* – faint, but still visible enough to get around..."

"Wish y'all'd stop usin' that Mars-talk," complained the black ex-astronaut. "I can see it – but I can't *say* it, y'all know?"

"Hey –" started Jacobson. "I see an outline – a human-figure – he's moving, crawling, I think he's trying to get away –"

"*You*, there!" suddenly exclaimed Boyd. "Yeah – *you!* We *see* you! *Freeze!*"

Either the fugitive didn't hear; or, more likely, he ignored the astronaut's warning, because – down on all fours – he headed rapidly for the as-yet-unexplored depths of the room, away from the three more-than-humans.

A second later, there was a bright flash, followed by a shower of sparks, the smell of burnt flesh and a sickening moan, then... nothing.

"Well... I *told* him," muttered Boyd. "Ugh – I can *see* the heat in the body. Just a few feet further – there, I got a lock-on –"

The astronaut's telekinesis pulled the fugitive's body out of contact with the trap, which had just been his nemesis.

The darkness returned.

God help me, that *felt good, too... it's like some of the electricity channeled back to me over the Amaiish*, mentally advised Boyd.

'One man's poison'...

"Yo, *assholes!*" called White. "One of y'all peeps just got his ass fried real good for tryin' to sneak out of here... weren't *our* doin' – but we'll *take* it, y'understand? If y'all knowin' what's best, I'd sit tight... *real* tight."

There was no answer, but neither was there another break-out attempt.

"If it's of any interest, Captain," quietly reflected Boyd, with barely-suspended disbelief, "That charge that killed the poor guy... from the trap, I mean... only a few minutes ago, I was happily, uhh, 'tripping out on it' – like the Professor did back in the corridor that got flooded. It felt sickeningly... *good*. And yet to a normal human being, just one touch and... 'bang, you're dead'. I guess I really *am* turning into something... different... *better*... but I guess I'm having a hard time coming to terms with it."

"Oh – so *that's* the series of flashes that Bob and I saw, from way back where we were," acknowledged the former Mars mission commander. "And as to being self-conscious... well, I know what you mean – busting through a reinforced-wall or two, or getting shot in the leg and being fine an hour later... those kind of *do* things to one's sense of perspective, I suppose. *Terra incognita* for all of us."

"Yeah... no shit," grunted White. "I really got to try Brent's little trick myself, one of these days... 'real soon now'."

"Listen," mentioned Jacobson, "You see any movement, over there?"

He paused for a second, then added, "Quite *amazing*, how my eyes are picking out the details... looks 'warm'..."

"Welcome to *oomna*-whatever," grunted White.

After another fifteen seconds of careful trap-avoidance, the three ex-astronauts had come almost up to the place from where the gun-shots had issued.

This had been a hastily-assembled temporary strong-point – set-up as if its inhabitants had been expecting intruders – and originally, the position had been built out of storage-boxes, equipment-lockers and other semi-movable types of equipment, up to approximately man-height, with room for no more than one person to enter or exit through either end.

"*Shit*," gasped the black ex-astronaut, as his more-than-human eyes beheld the results of Boyd's attack. "Look at them holes all over the wall that they built – *dozens* of 'em, size of a baseball or more, and still damn *hot* – must have been where y'all hit home. Did I mention I don't want to be anywhere in front, when y'all let fly, Brent my man?"

"As a matter of fact... you *did*," answered Boyd, with a satisfied smile. "I wouldn't mind trying to teach you a bit of it – once I figure out how the hell I *do* it in the first place, that is."

"Time for Boy Scout achievement-badges later, guys," counseled Jacobson. "I'm not hearing anything... no, wait... there's still breathing... *You*, behind the boxes! How many of you are there?"

"Th... three," came a weak voice. "Gildencrantz, he... he was the one who made a break for it."

"Sound off. Names!" ordered Jacobson.

"C-Caravano," spoke the first voice.

"Bickler," said a second.

There was nothing from the third opponent.

"You said *three*," retorted the former Mars mission commander. "We're coming around to get you – and be aware, we've got guns and we can see just fine... one false move and we won't *hesitate* to fire... is that clear?"

"Yeah," complied the first voice. "The other guy, he's... he's... Rosenstein."

"Brent, Devon, take the left – I'll go around right," whispered Jacobson.

Cautiously, pushing their new-found visual-abilities as much as possible, the men rounded the damaged, faintly-smoking remains of the strong-point.

Suddenly, White yelled, "*Look out!*"

One of the ghostly figures had raised a small form-factor auto-gun with some kind of attachment underneath it. This assailant began firing wildly in Jacobson's direction; and – although he could not possibly have seen the former Mars mission commander – a lucky shot from something larger than a normal bullet, struck home just above the belt and below the bottom of his flak-jacket, causing a loud, spark-filled explosion that propelled Jacobson backward and to the floor.

Moaning, with hands clasped over the wound, he slumped, then fell.

A half-second later, this act of treachery was repaid in full by a fusillade from both Boyd and White, which splattered Jacobson's assailant all over the nearby landscape.

"*Motherfucker!*" screamed the black ex-astronaut, as he emptied a full auto-rifle clip into the body of the dead opponent; if there hadn't been much of White's victim beforehand, that fact was more than assured, now.

Boyd rushed up to Jacobson, hardly stopping as he sent a vicious side-kick to the head of one of the remaining enemies.

"Commander... *Commander!*" cried the ex-astronaut.

White put the boot to the same man as had Boyd, more to kick the opponent out of the way than out of anger. The black ex-astronaut noticed, however, that there *had* been three enemies behind the barrier : the kicked-man, who was now crumpled up beside a box, the one that had just been shot to death and a third, who lay prone and unconscious, with ugly-looking, hot burns on his face.

"Ohhhh..." groaned Jacobson.

"He's hemorrhaging!" warned an alarmed Boyd. "See the *Um'nàhr'é? Blood!* Get something to cover it!"

He wasn't exaggerating – warm-infra-red-bright rivulets of more-than-human life-essence were pouring out from the afflicted Mars mission commander's abdomen, forming an eerie-looking Day-Glo pattern on the floor.

Moving with panicked speed, White pulled out a bandanna and handed it to his compatriot.

"*Figured* we'd need this sometime – Captain – y'all *hear* me? *Say* somethin', for the love o' God!"

All they could hear from their former commander was pained breathing, but as Boyd pressed the jury-rigged bandage over the gun-wound, with a tone of wonder, he described, "*Shit* – he took a good-sized round there, hole's gotta be twice the size of a silver-dollar –"

White took a quick glance at the dead assailant's gun and spat, "Fuckin' 20-milimeter grenade... should have killed him, *would* have killed me, for sure – fuckin' split a normal man in half –"

"I can *feel* his power on my hands," observed Boyd. "He's fighting to stay alive! Keep *with* it, Commander... I'm here for you... sending you my strength..."

"Listen, bro... I could... try to freeze it up a bit, y'all know..." stammered White, hoping that Boyd could neither see him wiping a tear, nor hear the desperation in his voice.

"Get Tanaka, ASAP!" was all that the other ex-astronaut replied.

"Yeah... for sure!" quietly agreed White. "Be back in five or less!"

As he left, he called to the one remaining enemy.

"Get any closer than you is now," he cursed, "And I'm gonna fuckin' do y'all *hard*, bitch!"

With his alien-powered eyes showing the way, White dashed for the closet-room, praying for the life and soul of his boss and brother.

New-People... Behold Now Your Gifts

"Any of you *see* anything?" half-shouted Abruzzio, over the roar of air rushing by the 'Magic Bus', as it hurtled over Los Angeles.

"Can't see *squat!*" complained Kaysten. "And it's not just because of the tint she put on those windows."

"Get used to it," commented the FBI team-leader, from her seat just behind Hendricks, who was, unconvincingly, pretending to steer the vehicle. "Because the alternatives – if she lets anything leak through that 'bubble' of hers – are either us getting blown out of the sky by a bunch of missiles, or a roller-coaster ride like you've never lived through, before... if you *do* live through it, that is. Funny, though, that I can hear the wind... couldn't, when she took me up there. Maybe she can filter sound-waves, too."

"*Ulp...*" gagged Ramirez, as the bus unexpectedly dropped like a stone.

Good thing she made us do up the seat-belts, thought the Hispanic scientist.

He looked green, only to hear Chu remark, "Ah... this is just the merry-go-round, Mr. Ramirez – just wait until she takes you on the – uhh – 'Tilt-A-Whirl'."

"Sounds like *fun*, there, darlin," offered the bounty-hunter, with a smirk.

"Let's just say that it was a wise move, making me bring that towel," ruefully noted the FBI team-leader.

Down, down, plunged the vehicle – so fast and far that its inhabitants felt sure they must be coming in for a crash-landing.

They braced themselves, a few silently saying a prayer... but then, the bus simply... *stopped*.

There was a barely-perceptible shudder of tires making contact with concrete, followed by a slight 'hiss' of out-rushing, pressurized air.

The front door opened... as if by itself.

"We reside in an off-alley, fair on to the middle between those grand thoroughfares of which you spoke, Otis," informed a sweet-sounding, female voice. "There is some cover with which to secrete our – uhh – bus; especially, it will not look too out-of-place, from above. You may now all disembark."

"*Whoa!*" exclaimed a half-shocked Kaysten, as he stepped out and surveyed a scene of utter urban-disintegration; but the gangster, Wolf and Boatman just shrugged. The rest followed behind, cringing at the heat being given off by the Storied Watcher, who was standing rather too close-by the bus-door for comfort.

"Oh," she sheepishly commented. "Maybe I – uhh – 'stand out', too much?"

She looked down and whispered something obscure. There was a brief flash, after which the alien-girl had returned to her disheveled street-clothes.

Her war-children had vanished – apparently, into nothingness.

"You ever gonna to get those duds pressed?" idly asked Hendricks.

"I will add that one to the list," deadpanned the Storied Watcher. "Perhaps for the next time... I shall sojourn on the surface of warm *Hlà'ter'ah*. 'Pressure' in abundance, one would have in *that* place! "

"Whaa?" inquired the third agent.

"You probably don't want to go there with her," offered Abruzzio.

"Why's *that?*" he followed up.

"Bit on the 'hot'-side, *señor*," offered Ramirez, with a grin.

Hendricks scratched his head, trying to puzzle it out, while the Russian chuckled at the joke.

They were – indeed – in a back-alley, too narrow in which to fully turn around an average-sized car, running behind a stretch of perhaps ten dilapidated, single-story dwellings on each side. The back-road was littered with rotting, stinking, vermin-infested trash – almost knee-high in some places – as well as with the burned-out hulks of various vehicles at regular intervals.

This neighborhood must have traditionally been a down-and-out one, since the homes around here were plain-looking and were in a generally poor state of repair, but there were obvious signs of something more sinister going on; many windows had been either completely smashed-in, or were pock-marked by bullet-holes, and almost every vertical surface in every direction was covered with inscrutable gangland-graffiti. In at least three directions, black, oily-looking trails of smoke wafted skyward.

Intuitively, many of the group – including even Karéin-Mayréij, whose age-wise eyes had seen cityscapes and populations more exotic than humans would ever know – realized that this should be a *busy* place, with citizens heading about on errands and chores and children playing in back-yards. Yet – other than for the familiar crackle of gunfire, some of it sounding uncomfortably close-by, more of it off in the distance – the place was eerily silent, as if most of the people had simply gone elsewhere.

"Y'all got that map?" asked the black FBI-agent.

"Yeah – okay," he agreed, as Hendricks passed it to him and the rest of them all gathered around. "What's that street sign down at the end of the alley?"

"It says, 'W 35th Pl'... whatever *that* means," remarked the alien-girl. "Oh – and the one at the other end, says, 'W 35th St'. They certainly *do* like 'thir-tee-five', here... perhaps it is a lucky number?"

"Only lucky number *I* know of is, 'seven'," stated Abruzzio.

"And there's ten of us," added Wolf. "But don't worry... spend too much time 'round here, and maybe we'll hit seven yet."

"*That's* the spirit," unenthusiastically muttered Kaysten.

"I don' *like* this place," grunted Sebastiàn. "Smell like *Crip*-turf to me."

"How you know that?" asked Ramirez. "As opposed to some other gang?"

"Signs all over the *walls* here, *hombre*," warily replied the gangster.

Boatman cast the *Mara* a knowing glance. Then the black FBI-agent's big finger pointed and traced out an imaginary path.

"Now... if I'm *remembrin'* right," he recounted, "These two streets here, they's bigger ones – and all we should have to do is just walk east, cross, uhh, what's this one – yeah, cross Normandie... and we're there. School's on the other side of the street... see it there?"

"Don' make no *sense*," argued Sebastiàn. "Name's different... even *I* can see that – an' I don' do English too good."

"You don't *say*," unhelpfully commented Kaysten, to a glower on the part of the gangster.

"If I was you, I wouldn't pull his chain, pardner," whispered Wolf to the Chief of Staff, in one ear. "Boys like *that*... they're half-*loco* at the best of times."

Kaysten nodded appreciatively and apprehensively.

"Yeah," elaborated Boatman, "See – I know it by its old name... don't know if you remember, but a few years back, they started, uhh, 'de-emphasizin' the contributions of black-folk throughout history – some kind of damn-fool directive from the Federal government, up there in D.C., or somethin' – so they changed the name just to 'East Compton Primary #23'. Map must be out-of-date... that's my guess. If you all's got a better idea as to where to start searchin', now'd be the time to tell us."

"I can't speak to *that*," evaded the Chief of Staff, "But what's the point of going to the school in the first place? I mean – most of L.A., this area included – is a no-go zone for anybody without a gun and a death-wish... you aren't going to find the kids *there*, anyway... right?"

"That is true, Jerr-ee," replied Karéln-Mayrélj, "But I know not where all of these children live – and perhaps within this school, there may be documents which would lead us in the right direction... from what I saw when I took to researching American-empire society, children must line up each morning and be accounted-for; thus, the teachers would need a, uhh, checking-list for that purpose. Maybe such a list would have names or living-addresses."

With a wry smile, Chu remarked, "Karéin – are you *sure* that I can't interest you in a FBI-career? What you just suggested is pretty much *exactly* what I'd have wanted to do."

The alien-girl returned the pleasant look and, with a wink, answered, "I have had a *long* time in which to learn how to follow a trail, Minn-ee – though that has not helped me very much with kind Bob, and my dear son... *has* it? In any case... I doubt that I would, uhh, work out as an eff-bee-ai agent, since I do not just investigate what I am told to."

"Well... if you ever want to apply, I'll put in a good word," offered Boatman, "*If* I live through this all, that is."

"Thanks," replied the Storied Watcher, with another smile. "Let us go forth – I will lead the way, and do not be surprised if I disappear to your eyes, as I will scout out the path. Those with weapons should guard the others, until all of us can do so without 'fire-arms'; but use these guns, only when necessary – we are on a rescue-mission and the wars that rage down here, are not *our* affair... although – if challenged – it would be shameful not to defend ourselves. Do any of you disagree?"

"What you *mean*... 'do so without fire-arms'?" incredulously demanded Hendricks. "What are we *supposed* to fight with... harsh language, maybe?"

"Wait and *see*," serenely answered Karéin-Mayréij.

Her face bore one of those trademark odd-looks.

"I disagree about coming down here, in the first place," peevishly complained Kaysten. "But I guess I'm out-voted."

"If you so request... I will drop you off at the nearest, uhh, 'bus-stop', as soon as I retrieve the children, Jerr-ee – I *promised* you that... remember?" answered the alien-girl.

"Yeah," he admitted, shuffling his feet, as if wishing to take back something said in haste.

"Same marching-order as before?" asked Chu.

"I guess... 'cept the Russkie and me – at least we're packin' now," spoke Wolf. "Where you want Mister Gangsta to go?"

"I go anywhere I want to," retorted the *Mara*.

"Would you want to go just behind me, Sebastiàn?" requested Karéin-Mayréij. "Ahead of Minn-ee Chu and the others, that is. You are more familiar with this type of place than are they... is this not correct?"

"Sì – I know my way 'round the streets," he proudly answered. "Like – *por ejemplo*, that sign over on the wall – that's Mexican Mafia... but it's faded, *chica* – so they probably ain't been down this way for a while. You got to keep your turf-marks fresh, or they think you not patrollin' no more... *ustedes lo saben*?"

"Yeah... that's what *I* always do," parodied Boatman.

Ignoring the taunt except for a sneer while he talked, the gangster continued, "See... now *this* one, on the back of the garage-door, nice red Blood colors there, but it been over-sprayed by them Crips – an' the paint's pretty bright – not only *that, pero mira còmo* they put them marks underneath... that's special for sayin' they diss they enemies, so we got some disputed-turf here, maybe we right in the middle... ain't nothin' new for the line-of-demarcation to be a street, or an alley like this. Point *is*... you go someplace like *that* – you *don'* expect a lot of questions, before some *puto* open up on you... *comprende*?"

"I'm feeling *very* uncomfortable, Karéin," protested Abruzzio, "And I want you to know that."

"I do not blame you, Sylvia," responded the Storied Watcher, "But the risk is much less than it appears to be... as long as I am near."

"Yeah – but what if you aren't?" asked Ramirez.

"Then you must learn to use your *own* powers, with which to protect yourselves," answered the alien-girl.

"*What*, 'powers'?" pressed Hendricks. "Like... 'the power to kiss your ass goodbye'?"

She walked over to him, took his hand in her own – a gesture that produced the usual, involuntary reaction, though he had sort of learned to suppress its outward-manifestations, by now – and enigmatically offered, "When the situation is dire and the time is near... *that* is when it will happen; and upon that instant, you shall be well-aware. A voice will say, '*this* is what I should do – though I know not how', and you will think, 'this is crazy, I cannot *possibly*' – but you *will*, dear friend... you *will*. And afterwards, you will realize what a great bridge you will have crossed; likewise, how great you will at once have become. Just do not let the pride of it overcome you; for – like with me – mighty power often overwhelms weak ethics. It will happen soon enough... this I *promise*."

"You... don't... *say*," he stammered, and in so doing, the third agent was merely vocalizing thoughts that had overtaken all of the other more-than-humans in this place.

Karéin-Mayréij turned and looked off into space, as if suddenly in a trance.

"Ready to go, everyone?" asked the FBI team-leader.

She looked at the alien-girl, who seemed to still be lost in contemplation.

"Karéin?" uncertainly queried Chu.

"Minn-ee," requested the Storied Watcher, "Would it be oh-kay if Wolf and Misha followed just behind Sebastiàn, but ahead of you and your eff-bee-ai people? And spread out a bit. I need to be able to see each person."

"I *suppose* so – I don't really have any administrative control over them, anyway," replied the FBI team-leader. "But... why, Karéin?"

"Training... and revelation," spoke the alien-girl. "For *you*, too... beloved."

Damn you, Karéin... can't you be the least bit subtle? peevishly thought Chu.

The Storied Watcher paused for a half-second, then added, "It *comes* to me... see how I know the truth, about each single one who now hears my voice. Did you all think that I brought you down here, just for *company*? As we are here in 'Comp-ton', I can save the children by myself. But for *you* – and all your brothers and sisters, their families and their progeny – today shall be the *greatest* of your days, Minn-ee!"

"Uh-oh," warned Ramirez.

"What?" shot back a confused, but alarmed, Chu.

The 'other' addresses you now... mortal, came back the fearsome reply.

Listen well!

Slowly and deliberately, the Storied Watcher moved to stand in full view of the rest of the group.

There was an odd, "off there somewhere" look in her eyes, which had – predictably – started to give off the now-familiar glow.

Her gaze – a visible beam of *something* – washed over them, lingering for a full second on each one.

A breeze came out of nowhere, rustling sun-dried leaves and garbage. Subtle, inspiring Celtic-rock-hymnal-music – accompanied by ethereal violins – began to be heard; and something sounding eerily like a choir, started to play in the background.

It was like in the canyon, as if the second hand on the clock had decided to go forward at a slow walk, instead of the normal rapid pace.

"Listen to my testimony... for enlightenment comes this day – and forever shall it set the path ahead of you," sang Karéin-Mayréij, in the godly voice. "The onset of nobility is *now* to begin. Do any here, *not* pledge to use the Gods' blessings, in the pursuit of wisdom and justice? I will *not* say, 'refraining from all violence'... for though the use of such indeed *will* taint you, there may be no other way, against a greater evil."

Silence – even from the gangster – was what rewarded her ears.

The mind of the Storied Watcher invaded those of all in her presence.

My friends... my disciples.

Never forget these words... and be proud of who you are about to become!

"Many fine things shall you all have in common," stated the Storied Watcher. "Among these are strength and litheness of hand and foot, tolerance for fast-turning that would kill a human outright, and... long life and good health – much better than could do your now-inferior, human-kin."

"Already," she related, "Your eyes can see – your ears can hear – subtle things that are hidden from mortal men and women; and soon, your minds will more clearly hear the voices spoken without words or sounds. But like the mind-speaking, many of the Gods' gifts have no starting-point within your previous experiences – so you shall have to summon and trust the wisdom from down deep inside you, to be guided as to their use. No human can tutor you in how to wield these arts; you must teach each other, with those to whom it comes easily, leading those to whom it does not."

Is this really... happening? thought all of them.

"For example," continued Karéin-Mayréij, "You shall all – in some measure – learn to turn the waves of gravity to your own advantage, thereby to make objects move, as you bid them do; and this *may* – if the Gods so will it –

carry you unto the fair skies above, or even beyond; for your own bodies are feather-light to this weirding-skill, and can thus be propelled hither and yon with minimal effort. When your arts come full-flower and danger beckons, you shall instinctively make a scarcely-visible fortress of ethereal armor to protect yourselves against foemen-arrows, -bullets, bomb-blasts... or just from the force of the wind, as you hurtle through the sky. Initially, she will protect only your own bodies – to perhaps a finger's-distance from your skin – but with practice, you can bid her also to shelter those within an arm's-length; and she may only be robust as clay-brick for some of you – yet steadfast as adamant, for others. So test her not against gun-bullets... save that the need be valid and dire."

Did I just hear what I thought *I heard?* excitedly pondered Abruzzio.

That's how she's able to fly, and how she resists kinetic-impacts at high-speed –

Oh, come on, *Sylvia – you don't seriously* believe –

"Know that a living thing – especially if of sentient-mind – can resist the invisible-push-and-thought-pull forces," tutored the alien-girl, "And it will do so vigorously, if the integrity of its body be threatened, or if it opposes you consciously, instead of passively. Conversely, one who wishes to be so 'grasped', will feel very light to your mind-pull, whatever his or her true weight. But the greater the willpower, concentration, wisdom and intelligence of he, she or it who resists, the greater your challenge shall be – still more, if the object of your attack itself knows the *Fire*."

"The same," she added, "Is true of those arts which dominate the will : an intelligent creature – much more so if its mind be disciplined by suspicion or training – can refuse your command, where one of dull intellect will obey, even, sometimes, unto death. And if a friend – human, or a being akin unto yourselves – is grievously-wounded, you can lend them a portion of your force of life, thereby to postpone their final day of reckoning. Be careful with this – as your own safety can be threatened, if you give too freely."

If ever a teacher had an audience of utterly attentive students... this must have been it.

"Is... anybody... taking... *notes?*" whispered an entranced Abruzzio.

Misha shook his head, never taking his gaze off the alien-girl.

"Foremost among these," explained Karéin-Mayréij, "Is the grace of the *Khùl-Algrenàthi'i*, who is called '*Amaiish*' – the *Fire* – as lesser mortals say her name. Many marvelous things can she do to save and succor; rarely shall you fail you – though, like all such, her gifts are not without limit and may not be able to save you forever. But in general... when there is no air left to breathe; when the demons of hunger and thirst weaken your resolve; when you are wracked by pain; when your body fails; when the bite of a winter-storm or the heat of an oppressive summer-sun afflict you; or, when you are *afraid*... call upon the *Fire*, within."

Nothing – except what the Storied Watcher related – mattered, any more.

"It is said by my ancestors," she counseled, "That if the hour is dire and if you truly *believe*, she *shall* empower you in exact measure to what is needful to win the battle – no less, no more; so one day, you may be as a god, but the next, your guise may be just that of an 'ordinary' hero. And the ears and minds of those around shall hear the unique melody of *your* personal *Fire*... of your *own* greatness; your war-song will oft come of her own – but if you learn to hum her melody, fast will she manifest, and the more potent yet, shall your own arts be. Foremost shall your song fortify those who love truth and justice, secondly to warn the enemy to flee; though sometimes, shall she be evident only to some but not to others... according to forces that not even I, may comprehend."

A shared thought, from they knew not where, simultaneously came to all.

What will my *song sound like?*

"Know," she advised with gravitas, "That the power of *Amaiish* should *never* knowingly be used by one of you against a fellow-brother or sister, for doing this would offend both myself and the Heavens; and, for the most part, it would not work, for you all have a measure of immunity – not complete, but none the less, substantial – from each others' most dangerous skills. And mark you – this is not just an idle precaution against unlikely treachery or unwise testing the-one-against-the other; it has a very practical, day-to-day meaning. As a foot-soldier kneels and heeds the warning of an archer in the second-rank, before a volley is fired... so should each of you do, when the attack of a brother or sister is imminent against an enemy. Stand not your back in front, in such a case, unless you would risk a terrible wound – or worse."

"Learned that the first time I saw her throw them knives," muttered Wolf, to Misha. "The part about 'heads-down'... that is."

The Russian turned his head, sent a confirmatory look to the bounty-hunter, and mutely nodded.

"Now... I turn to the matter of those specific blessings – unique to each one who hears my voice – which shall make you as demi-gods among mortal men and women," pronounced the Storied Watcher, her eyes glowing cerulean, her face shining as gold. "Know that these are supplementary to those gifts which pertain to all of you; thus – for example – an art that turns a foe-arrow back on he who launched it, can be used with or without the aforesaid mind-fortress, that shall eventually come to you all."

Goddamn, Karéin, mused Wolf, *I'm sure glad that fuckin' force-field-thing – if that's what it was – worked for you back in that hotel meetin'-room...*

No wonder you were just pissed – not scared – when they let fly at you...

Wait for your own blessing to be told, my brother, came a thought.

You will know the reason why what you surmise... is the truth.

As the bounty-hunter grinned maliciously, Karéin-Mayréij pointed at the *Mara* gangster with an unusual, two-handed gesture.

"Prince-of-bandits of the proud name 'Sebastiàn'," remarked the alien-girl, "The Ways of Venom shall live within you; an angered bite and finger-claw-scratch, by your will, can afflict even a foe who stands close-by a poor soul suffering your first-strike; yet, shall you *not* be victim of any such, save my own. Speak to the crawling-things of this world – serpents, spiders, insects and the like – whose fang or sting is deadly – and they will counsel you. Ask for their help, and some of them will come to fight, even unto death, by your side – so long as you do not take their sacrifice for granted. If you desire someone, the essence of your mouth shall make them swoon and join joyfully with you, for a time. The same shall come of the scent of your body, should you so will it to issue... though the effect will be less in each case."

At first, it appeared that Sebastiàn thought this to be a joke, but he quickly got the message; a thunderstruck look came over him.

"Concocted substances which stupefy the minds of mere humans – should you willfully partake thereof – shall *not* make you dazed and ill of judgment; rather, shall they make your strength, vitality, quickness and body, the equal of a fell-demon," promised the Storied Watcher. "You shall know danger, or the fear in minds of others, by its aroma; and by the marks on your skin – especially, the blue-and-white-tattoo of your war-clan – these shall empower and tutor you in other ways, if you stop and pay due attention. When hide you wish, only the most expert shall tell you from that which surrounds... though be aware, this is more useful within shadows, and when you save from moving."

"Neither shall you be overcome with pain," she went on, "Nor by all save the most grievous wounds, nor by the energy-particle-glow; and the flow of these little things, be they through the air or from a wire of metal, shall empower – not harm – provided that you learn to drink in small measure, at first. Quick and near-errantless to strike, shall you be; and when you land a blow, the life-blood which flows from an afflicted enemy, shall re-invigorate you in like proportion. Use this dread art sparingly, I beg; as too much of it, can bring evils that I pray that you shall never come to know."

"Even... *con mi arma*... I mean... with a *gun?*" half-whispered the *Mara*.

"Even *that*... eventually," confirmed the alien-girl, "Though at first, only a blade which draws blood, will bring this type of succor. And lastly, Sebastiàn... know that mortals will run in terror or quail in awe, when you would so afflict them; but also, shall they see you as their good-and-true leader, when needs be. Balance these two imperatives – rule with wisdom, show the humans that there is a way other than war, for its own sake – and noble *indeed*, shall you be!"

"¡Santa... Maria!" he gasped.

Now, Karéin-Mayréij pointed at the bounty-hunter.

"Who is called 'Wolf'," she addressed, as his pulse quickened with electric excitement. "Like your namesake – who shall shortly come to your side – your war-cry shall restore strength to fellow-warriors and warn doom, to whomever you oppose. If so you desire, walk in hidden-guise among humans, because their eyes shall not see you – though techno still can. Majesty also shall you have in the eyes of mortals... but not like your brother Sebastiàn can do."

The bounty-hunter crossed his arms and stared intently at his new-found mentor, who offered, "Fear you neither the strike of projectiles nor of gun-bullets or swords; for your mind shall deflect these – and your skin shall be the like of hard steel, against the lesser of them – even if they are not stopped by your latter-showing force-screen. Only your brother from the Empire of Russia can pierce this defense; but if it please the Gods... never shall he tilt against you."

"In the spark of a gun-shot, when you came to mine aid of free will, this next blessing was decided, dear friend," continued the Storied Watcher. "So hear these words : burning-warmth from most things will henceforth not trouble you; and as concerns the Little Spirit of Fire, she is your friend and companion... she shall come to most things – save living-flesh – upon which you lay your gaze and pray for her to manifest herself, though she will come faster if you make the open-palm-sign to the target... and faster still if your hands or fists strike directly upon what shall burn. If you so will, none shall suffer to come within many paces of where you stand, lest they be consumed by the infernal-glow that your mighty arts shall exude; and anything that retreat not, will go to ashes. Yet in time, such a conflagration shall not vex your breathing, seeing, or hearing – nay, even shall your senses, and your vitality, be magnified by it."

"Holy Sweet *Jaysus!*" he breathed, unable to avoid stealing an admiring look at his upturned hands, which felt suddenly, strangely warm.

"If you respect and love the Little Burning One, Wolf," counseled Karéin-Mayréij, "Never shall she harm you, but ever shall she heed you; plead her to make a circle around, and folly it will be for an enemy – or a foe-weapon – to approach too near; and later – as your skills and her own wax – even shall she lift you to the very clouds and beyond. Take the counsel of the war-child of the lesser me, whose name is *Væran Ksé'l'ch'*; for he will teach you the Ways of the Flame – and terrible *indeed*, shall you eventually be."

"Now I *know* why I went to that damn seminar," he boasted. "Best single round I ever fired."

Wolf would have said more; but a regal, warning glance from the Storied Watcher made him stop the smart-Aleck talk – with a knowing-nod to his alien tutor – before it had a chance to get started.

"Now, as concerns Misha, beloved companion of the lesser Karéin-Mayréij," announced the alien-girl, with perhaps a more tender tone than for the previous two, "Already, exploding-blast, fire, cold are not to be feared, lest they be of great potency; and in the latter-case, shall you soon learn to wield the arts of my war-child, *Væran Ss'éth'ch'* – such as the lethal Skin and Touch of Ice, which affect human-flesh, as does a splash of liquid-air –in war."

The Russian concentrated furiously to ensure he remembered every word.

"But also," remarked Karéin-Mayréij, "Are you skilled in the human arts of non-weaponed-combat; and behold how far greater shall this shortly be, for the speed and potency of each blow and maneuver shall be empowered by the *Fire*; none – save me – shall stand against you for so much as a two-second of Earth-time. Yet unequalled shall be your arts in building cunning weapons-of-war, and in quick-learning the use of these, even if made by others. Chains shall not bind you – since your cold-touch in anger, shall shatter them in like measure as against an opposing sword; traps, snares and those who mean evil, will give up their secrets, if you but concentrate upon a latent peril; and were a cricket so large, still could he not leap as high, nor do so, while appearing as but an eye-blink to the untutored."

"Always – save once or twice or when you desire only to wound," she continued, "Shall you strike home with a grievous blow, against the foe's least-guarded spot, when take you aim – even when you must move or fight only by means of what you hear and perceive... not see. Soon, you will find that these other senses are *indeed* the equal of what human eyes can view. Like your brother Wolf – though less than him – your mind shall make arrows, bolts and bullets sent in anger against you, miss their target, even when your mind-bubble is not raised. When your skills go to full-flower, such foe-missiles shall be turned back on the assailant... or, they shall be launched at your will, becoming substantial regardless of supply, simply by the power of the *Fire*. In silence shall you move, when needs be, and waver not when the task is to run many leagues, for this shall be as but a field's-length."

Enigmatically, the Storied Watcher added, "And greater powers *still* – bestowed of purpose that another beloved-one, who now hears these words, should guess – await you, Misha; these shall soon be manifest, by a cruel gaze. Their coming will make awe, in the eyes of ordinary humans."

The Russian bowed solemnly.

"Thank you, Karéin," he quietly answered. "You will not regret this!"

The Storied Watcher nodded. "Not *me* who blesses... but the Gods, favored male lover of the mortal Karéin-Mayréij," she observed.

Then she pointed at the Chief of Staff.

Well... that clears things up, ruefully reflected Chu.

You lucky bugger! jealously mused Wolf.

"Step forward, dear friend, 'Jerr-ee Kay-stenn'," commanded the alien-girl.

Reluctantly, he complied.

"Even Misha shall you out-hurry, both as regards distance and speed of travel; and you shall turn aside modest obstacles and airborne things, all along the way," she explained. "Indeed, when fully-practiced you become, no steed – nor even any wheel-chariot – shall out-pace you; and you shall see and hear with the eyes of a prey-bird and the ears of a night-bat, when at speed. And the purposeful moving of your body, even without – but even more, when amplified by such war-arts as I shall teach you – will eventually make you more deadly than even the most quick-arrow, ever launched into flight. Though you must take caution; for, should you stumble while in full-charge, much damage may come... your mental-fortress-shield-arts will gradually negate the peril – but it is easy to exceed this safeguard, without knowing it. Yet more skills of travel and escape shall be revealed, if tutored you be, by my cherished war-girl-child, *Vîrya I'ëà'b'*."

She paused for a second, then mentioned, "And, Jerr-ee... wise and of good conscience among men shall you latterly become, if you listen to your heart and reflect upon what is right... against, what may appear to be, 'convenient'. Thus, the fine arts of music, poetry and word-crafting will bless you, and your voice shall sing with beauty; it will convince any mortal of any sensible thing, provided you deceive them not too far. Side-wise, your tongue shall have the gift of risibility... thus, when a mirthful tale you tell, if it be affected by the *Fire*, human beings shall be overcome with humor, even – if you wish – to being made helpless, thereby, for a time. I counsel you to take care with this art... since it affects different beings in various ways, and can even cause permanent harm, if you devote your all-power to it. And when a foreigner speaks, still shall you understand, though never were you schooled in that tongue. Thus *shall* it be."

"The 'Killer Joke'... *okayyy*," happily acknowledged Kaysten. "And... thank you *very* much, Karéin! Kind of makes up for the bite... you know?"

"*Figures*," whispered Boatman to a ruefully-smiling Chu.

The alien-girl sent the Chief of Staff a full-fanged smile, which, by this time, and to his inward surprise, did not bother him in the least.

He searched all around, looking for the little shield.

"*You*, too... wherever you are," added Kaysten.

A strange, "above-the-range-of-human-hearing" little giggle, sounded.

"Hector Ramirez, who guided the mighty Storied Watcher through the void, who thankfully survived the deluge of her coming," addressed Karéin-Mayréij, turning her gaze to the Latino scientist. "Know the composition of substances, by the smell thereof, as long as you ponder and commit to memory. Lay hands on most things, and bid the tiny-parts therein to re-arrange, thus becoming something alike, though different; the mundane – such as ice to water – shall come first to you; but later, even the very rocks, stones and air, shall yield to your command. This is a *most* useful art; and in time, I will teach you the higher-skills of its employment, for example in the making of weirding-garments – even body-armoring – that can accommodate and magnify the abilities of your brothers and sisters. Start today, by caressing the clothes that you wear – modest blessings will come... but these are but a fore-taste how you shall later empower vestments, and other things."

The Philosopher's Stone, thought Ramirez.

I'm... it!

There was more.

"En-magicked items shall not waver you," she counseled, "Since your touch, done so upon in anger, shall drive foul magic from most any enchanted thing – save mine own war-children... for they are alive by their own spirits, and can therefore defend. Your will shall cause a large-part of the air- or water-atoms close-by, to come or go, given that some of each be there in the first place, thereby to make the pressing-forces greater or lesser as you wish. Potent gas- or liquid-flows can be so mastered, with care and attention, and things carried by these can be as deadly as a hail of gun-shot, provided that you learn how correctly to wield this art; also, can it carry you high, far and long, with a great wind under your feet. In time, dear Hector, even shall you overcome the twisting-tempest; you shall work your will upon it, and subject to your whim, shall it be. Receive this gift... and be glad."

"*Dios mìo!*" he exclaimed. "This is a *wonderful* thing... a priceless treasure to a scientist like me... it will not be wasted. *Thank* you!"

She smiled warmly at Ramirez, then turned to his distaff companion.

"Mortal-woman called Sylvia Abruzzio... dear friend – who spoke as a sister to me in the short days of the greatest test – with the love of knowing things," stated Karéin-Mayréij, addressing the trembling, Italian-American scientist.

"Your powers of reason and insight have always been foremost," remarked the Storied Watcher, "But behold how they are strengthened and fortified. Especially powerful – as judged against your brothers and sisters – shall be your mind-pushing-skill; as it flowers, even rods of steel and walls of stone, shall yield like wet-clay, under the force of your will. Never shall you fall to the beguilement of the mind; instead, you shall know the way to the solving of problems... be these mundane or vexing. When I must guess correctly or suffer terrible consequences, one-less-than-never do I twice make the same mistake – you have inherited some of this, cherished companion."

"And as you begin to smell what the energies are like," instructed Karéin-Mayréij, "Happily partake of these, learning how to generate and send them back in stronger-form; for then, the little techno-boxes will be at a loss. Be aware that in time, this skill shall wax, and the sending of too much of it – especially as you learn to focus it in a particular place – can be dangerous, even lethal – to living-things... use its highest potency, only when there is no other choice."

I always wondered what radiation really feels *like,* mused Abruzzio.

Now... I guess I'll find out.

"Indeed... you *shall*," agreed the alien-girl, who continued, "So, when afflicted by too much warmth, or cold, or straightened-particle-light, or electro-charge, or particle-glow – but be warned, not a solid war-spear or arrow, for that requires your mundate mind-fortress-shield – think of a rainbow, and it shall come to protect you... even, to reflect such an evil back upon your enemies, all the while replenishing your vitality... in time, you shall make your colored-shield protect your brothers and sisters. If even *Um'nàhr'é* or the like, be not there to guide your eyes, bid your body – or part of it – to light the way... and this shall come to pass."

Migod, thought the scientist.

She wasn't kidding, about the 'you're a demigod, now', stuff...

"Later," elaborated Karéin-Mayréij, "You shall craft ingenious and subtle images, with the light-and-radio-bending-skills, dear Sylvia; for example – as you become more comfortable with the fine-points of this art – illusion-making that can stupefy any human, will be as second-nature. Imagine yourself, as seen in a mirror – and so shall such a deception appear, if you can keep a portion of your mind committed to the replenishment thereof... whole scenes, lifelike yet ephemeral, will form, on your command; and – when your skills come to full-flower – even shall such illusions have sound, and smell... yea – *everything* – save physical-substance."

"I'm not... *worthy* of this, Karéin!" gasped a flustered Abruzzio. "I'm just an ordinary *scientist*... no smarter... middle of the class at CalTech..."

"Yes – you *are*," serenely corrected the Storied Watcher. "More than all the rest of your 'class', put together. The next time when you must solve a hard riddle... this will be clear."

Nonplussed and wide-eyed, Abruzzio fell silent.

Now she turned her attention to the third agent.

"Step forward, who is called 'Will Hen-dricks'," she commanded.

Though tempted to try for a joke, he wisely said nothing.

"My brother," she advised, "Misha shall in most cases be better, as concern the arts of blade-fighting and high-jumping; Wolf shall exceed you in safe-making from projectiles of malice, as will Jerr-ee, in running past all other men... though still, shall you be justly feared by any other mortal who dares contest your abilities, in any of these; but when you come to learn the skills of hand-combat – using naught but your own body as a weapon – swift defeat shall come to all those who stand against you. And in the arts of love, shall you be unsurpassed – as befit the desires of female for male; for, others shall have this blessing, as woman in the eyes of man –"

"Yeahhh!" he enthusiastically interrupted, to the obvious envy of Ramirez, Sebastiàn, the bounty-hunter and the Russian, while the alien-girl indifferently continued, "And accursed magic shall do you no harm... but instead be turned back against your assailant."

The strength... the I-don't-know-what... I feel it surging through me... bad, no... good drugs, man, thought Hendricks.

"Over the coming days and years, dear Will," promised Karéin-Mayréij, "As with your brother Misha, I shall teach you some of mine own Dance of Death to magnify the war-arts, as you are ready to take heed thereof.... and as your days go on, you shall learn the arts of crafting spirit into things that your hands shall touch and love, noble more-than-human man. Now... hear my voice, as I speak of the most valuable blessing which the Gods have bestowed upon you – for, additionally upon such innate-arts, should one of your brothers or sisters do so of free-will – and should you set to the study thereof – you can learn *any* skill of the *Fire*... though within deep limits, compared to those for whom it is natively-come."

Whoa, realized Abruzzio.

The Jack of All Alien-Powers...

As the blanching, delighted third agent tried desperately to avoid falling at the alien-girl's feet and worship, abruptly, she stopped.

"Something *wrong*, Karéin?" asked Chu.

"Perhaps... there is... oh, no, no – do not *go!*" cried the Storied Watcher, as if sleeping through a nightmare.

"You *okay*, honey?" inquired a worried Wolf.

"Yes, cherished more-than-mortal companion," she replied. "It is just that there is someone *else* that Will Hen-dricks can learn these arts from. *So* close... my other mind *almost* contacted his own..."

"Who do you mean?" asked Abruzzio.

"A friend... a dear friend..." she replied, absent-mindedly. "No name..."

Karéin-Mayréij closed her eyes.

Concentrating, she commanded, "Step forward, Otis Boat-man."

Reluctantly, he complied, as she opened her eyelids.

"A tower of strength and fortitude are you, in the moral and the physical, though in both none the less," counseled the Storied Watcher. "No-one shall ever control or cause terror to your mind, nor shall any – not even your brother Jerr-ee, with his guileful-tongue – say a falsehood in your presence... save that you should know of same, and if the taste of blood or other evil be present, you shall be aware. Likewise – a scene displayed for your eyes shall give up its secrets... if you but call upon the inside power."

"Umm-hmm," quietly acknowledged the big black agent.

"No venom – not even that of your brother Sebastiàn – shall afflict you, neither the burning-acids, besides," she elaborated, "But take care of your eyes... for they can withstand but a splash. Like your brothers Wolf and Misha, fire from normal things shall not suffer you – nor shall cold, nor shall the pressing of great weights of liquid-and-gas-substances – and as the months and years go by, even more proof against all perils, physical and mental, shall you be, until – at the zenith of your arts – men shall say that a castle of adamant, lies upon your skin... and *that* shall be additionally, to your own fortress of ethereal mind-shield."

Well, now... won't that be handy? mused Boatman.

'Specially when I can't find a flak-jacket that will fit me...

"And, noble Otis," remarked Karéin-Mayréij, "If down come your boot, with the force of the *Fire*, upon a surface where you stand – even, in time, the very face of this beautiful world – so shall it be rent by a great shock and shaking; thus, fissures can be opened, and tall-standing structures built thereupon, can be made to come crashing down. And a final, sinister art awaits you – the laying of your hands in anger, shall *themselves* cause the dissolving of things according to how steadfast they are; at first as washing-soap melts in small measures... but later, as a sand-castle is washed away by the incoming tide, though as you learn, the process can be reversed, to make things solid again. This can be a terrible skill, dear friend; for if done with full power against a living being... it is *very* lethal. Use it thus not, if there is any other way."

"You can – uhh – be shore of *that*," he offered. "This is gonna take some gettin' used-to, I guess."

"It will be as using your arms, legs, hands and feet," replied the alien-girl, evenly. "For a mortal akin to yourself, the challenge lies in knowing how to judge... when all mortal-beings around – save your new-found brothers and sisters – are far inferior."

"*Riight,*" uneasily answered the big African-American agent.

Silence fell, as each kept the same thought to himself or herself.

What about... her, they wondered.

Finally, the Storied Watcher walked slowly and deliberately, to stand beside the FBI team-leader.

"Yes, Karéin?" spoke Chu, with mock-indifference.

"Are you not *curious,* dear mortal woman-friend?" inquired the 'angel'.

"Oh, no... not in the least," replied Chu. "I mean, I've got a team of – uhh, *super-beings* – to back me up. Who could ask for anything more?"

She lied, of course.

"'*Super*-beings'," offered Karéin-Mayréij, with her godly essence visibly-waxing. "I like the sound of that – though let not the pride of it, go to a conceit. But... would you like to know about the *greatest* of this group, Minn-ee Choo?"

"*Do,* uhh, enlighten me," feigned the more-than-human FBI-agent, unable to fully dampen the anticipation in her voice.

"Well," purred the Storied Watcher, "She has inherited one of her mentor's most valued abilities; that is – to be warned of the advent of danger, before the trap is sprung so it cannot be evaded. Do you know the nerve-wracked feeling of anticipation on the back of your neck, when you walk through a benighted place? Be aware that the next time it come, this is no false-reaction; if life you wish to continue, stop and turn in all directions – for the sensation will be strongest, when facing where peril hides – and sometimes, even its nature and weakness shall come to your mind. This art is not based on the mundane senses, but rather the metaphysical ones – it cannot be evaded or counteracted... at least, never has this occurred, over past years uncounted."

"Wow," commented a duly-impressed Chu.

"To this leader among disciples of she who is called 'Karéin-Mayréij'," continued the alien-girl, "Many other excellent gifts come as well. More than any other of her brothers and sisters, she can resist any attack given force by the *Fire* – though, be advised, not always the physical-manifestation thereof; at least, not in the same degree. As with her sister Sylvia, the force of her mind is very strong – even, eventually, unto soaring through the skies – and she shall smell the signals in the ether, blocking these, when needs be; as with her brother Otis Boat-man, she shall see forthwith the clues that tell of worrisome events in a place; and as with her other brother Misha, but yea – even *more* than he – she shall react and move much faster than any mortal could hope to do... *so* fast, in fact, that for a trice – when matters are urgent – time will seem to slow down, the better to ponder the most auspicious course of action."

"I'm... not... uhh... *ready* for this, Karéin..." pleaded an overwhelmed Chu; but the Storied Watcher ignored this entreaty, and went on, "Her gaze, if taken deep into the eyes of a human, shall beguile these lesser-beings into her command – though she should use this sparingly – since even human minds resent such domination, especially if repeatedly done in a short time. And... there *is*... one *other* thing..."

Wide-eyed, the FBI team-leader managed, "What'd *that* be?"

"Take my hand," requested Karéin-Mayréij. "And let me into your mind. Resist me not... though you can."

"*What*?" asked a worried Chu.

"In this minute, I am not the half-mortal who desires to love and pleasure you, female to female," imperiously answered the alien-girl, to looks of surprise, shock and weary indifference, among the rest of the group. "She is within me – she speaks as well – and will come back shortly. Right now, you address a being akin to a demon or a god, Minn-ee Choo. You had best heed my request."

"Uhh... *fine*, then," sighed the woman, not resisting as the alien-girl draped herself over her shoulder and took hold of the her right hand.

Were it not for another, different, gentle, supportive and affectionate force that bolstered her psyche, Chu would have instantly succumbed to a terrifying flood of incomprehensible, other-dimensional thoughts.

I am here, my love, came the other voice.

Do not be afraid.

I will not let the other 'me', hurt you.

"Stare at that wooden fence yonder – the one with the round symbol with the dot at its mid-point," commanded the Storied Watcher. "Consider nothing else. Focus your entire gaze upon it."

Still feebly trying to defend herself against a cacophony of sanity-destroying thoughts and mind-images, the FBI team-leader tried to comply.

"Now turn your *hate* on that little spot in the middle," demanded Karéin-Mayréij. "Wish it to *die*, to be consumed in fire... and imagine that a cloud of red has come over your eyes – like a pair of colored sun-glasses."

"Oh my *God!*" whispered Abruzzio. "I *know* what this is –"

"Yes," gravely nodded Misha.

"*What?*" protested Chu, both verbally and mentally. "What do you *mean*, 'hate a *spot*'? It's just paint over wood –"

"I will show you – the trigger-thought comes now to your mind, woman!" replied Karéin-Mayréij.

A drug-like rush of confidence fleetingly invaded the team-leader's psyche; but this was instantly followed by an agonized rush of pain.

It felt like a pair of vinegar-soaked, red-tinted contact-lenses, had been dropped right into her eyes.

Chu doubled over – blinking in discomfort – as tears flowed profusely.

She had missed the sudden surge of power, the lightening-like, subtle discharges around her eye-sockets, the orange-red ocular shine, the little bursts of body-energy and the other-worldly, warbling-, chiming-sound, that accompanied this misery. But the *rest* of the group saw an dimly-visible beam of *something*, akin, perhaps, to a faint laser pointer from a college lecture-hall, flash for a split-second, then impact with the fence, a foot or more from its intended target.

It had burned a round, charred hole somewhat larger than a quarter, right through. Small, blackened fragments of wood, which had exploded from the periphery of the hole, fell, hissing and smoking, to the ground.

"Holy *shit!*" exclaimed an over-awed Wolf. "Lady... remind me not to get 'the look' from you!"

An overcome, grimacing Chu let go of the Storied Watcher's grasp, mercifully freeing her mind from alien, unfamiliar things.

Remaining bent-over, she furiously wiped her closed eyelids and tear-streaked cheeks.

"Has... anybody... got a cold... compress..." moaned the more-than-human woman. "What are you... trying to *do*, Karéin... leave me walking around with a white cane? Ohh... my head *hurts*..."

"Minnie," offered Boatman, as he came swiftly her way and held her close within massive arms, "Do you all know what you just *done*, there?"

"No... but by all means *tell* me," she muttered, aching eyelids still tightly closed, palms on thighs, propping up her torso. "Feels like somebody just threw toilet-cleaner into my eyeballs!"

"Well – that ain't much of a surprise... considerin' what must have been goin' *through* 'em," remarked the big black man. "If I remember what I read 'bout them Army laser-beams... it's gotta be a few Watts, or Joules, or... whatever."

"Yeah – more than enough to melt a Standard Issue Human Mark 1 Eyeball into water-slag," added Hendricks. "The bounty-hunter ain't kiddin' there, Minnie – thats sure one *hell* of a dirty look you got going for you! Wood in that fence is nearly an inch thick, I'd bet."

Barely able to look up, Chu squinted through bloodshot eyes in confusion.

"What are you *talking* about?" she asked.

"Welcome to the *Gaze of the Makailkh*, woman!" interjected a satisfied-sounding Storied Watcher. "This most noble and deadly skill is the Glance of Fire... but many others – some of still *greater* potency – shall eventually issue forth... if you are bold and will suffer for the learning of them."

To others as well, she sent to the Russian, whose face suddenly wore a satisfied smile.

"'Suffer', is *right*," ruefully echoed Chu.

She looked up at the alien-girl.

"But... I *will*, Karéin," pledged the FBI team-leader.

Hendricks, Abruzzio and Ramirez had by now joined Boatman in close proximity to their field boss.

"Listen, Ms. Chu, I *know* this may be a bad time, but... what does it *feel* like?" inquired the female scientist. "If you don't mind my asking, that is."

"Like *hell!*" complained the more-than-woman. "Think of a migraine combined with, uhh, a week's worth of trying to read bulletins in four-point type, all at the same time..."

Finally, she was able to straighten up and review the damage to the fence.

Chu stared off reflectively into space, though she still appeared to have a bad case of conjunctivitis.

"If it's of any interest, though," she stated, taking deep breaths all the while, "It's... *thrilling!* I feel... incredibly... *powerful.*"

She did not notice the dim light-flashes that flickered below her blouse, as she said that last word.

"You *think*?" guffawed the bounty-hunter. "For a second or two there I felt like *I* was holdin' a nice hand... but I guess Little Miss Martian dealt you four aces there, pardner... I'm just hopin' she doesn't teach you how to fly, on top of it, or the rest of us are all gonna be 'fifth on race day'... you know?"

I shall not teach her, Wolf... neither you, came the inevitable reply,
For you shall learn for yourselves.

"We'll see about *that*," interjected Kaysten, unsubtly tapping his feet.

"Well that's fine, *señor* – but where you gonna run *to*, 'round here?" challenged the gangster.

Kaysten shrugged and suggested, "Away from the bomb... I *hope.*"

The Storied Watcher's Stentorian, demi-godly voice again sounded.

"Wolf... you speak in the common-tongue, but your words carry truth," observed Karéin-Mayréij. "The Gods – through myself – have blessed every one of you to be as giants among human men and women; and, throughout the ages, there have always been *two* sides to nobility : the power that you already have... and the wisdom to know how to use it. Now I tell you of a third... for in *these* times, it may prove just as important. Can you guess?"

All of them pondered, though the female scientist had an odd, surprised look, as if she had been suddenly-enlightened, in some way.

"I don' know, *chica*... maybe you want us to clean up the streets down here?" postulated Sebastiàn. "That is... if we really *can* do all this *magia* shit that you talkin' about."

"A good idea," replied the alien-girl. "But not so important as the *real* one. And trust me... when you need to use your gift... you *will* know how."

"Can't wait to put *la mordida* on them Crips 'n Bloods," he tried to joke, although a withering look from his mentor, made the gangster abruptly stop.

Sheepishly, he added, "Bueno, *bueno*, I *get* it... you the shot-caller, *chica*. I cut 'em some slack... but not *too* much, *usted lo sabe?*"

Regally, she nodded.

"You know, I liked the 'other' Karéin – the one who I can talk to in 'non-god-mode', I mean – a bit little more," complained Chu. "No offense, of course."

"None taken, Minn-ee Choo," replied the Storied Watcher, amicably though imperiously. "Both of me are speaking right now. What is *your* guess?"

"Maybe... we've been given these powers – oww, my *eyes*, they *still* hurt – so we can be better able to help you rescue the children... or even assist in tracking down the Billings party?" suggested the FBI team-leader.

"Indeed," mentioned the Storied Watcher, "Valid points, all. But not the most *important* one."

"Help you whack the President?" maliciously proposed Wolf.

"I can do *that*, by myself," countered the alien-girl.

"Well... how about *I* do the *Vice*-President, while you're busy with his boss, then?" quipped the bounty-hunter.

Finally, they saw the previously-forbidding being called 'Karéin-Mayréij', actually laugh.

"My brother, maybe that *is* one of your hidden powers – to amuse even the greater 'me'," she commented. "Doing so is *quite* an accomplishment. But none the less, your idea is far from the truth. Do any of the rest of you –"

"Karéin," interrupted Abruzzio, "I think I know... but I'm reluctant to *say* it. Out loud, I mean."

"Why?" asked the Storied Watcher.

"I'm afraid you might be, uhh, *offended*," said the scientist.

"Counsel given of true heart by a friend should never make anger," stated the alien-girl. "Say what you think, Sylvia. It will not 'offend', me."

"Okay," uneasily started Abruzzio. "See... as you were denominating all of these, uhh, alien-powers, that we supposedly now can employ – particularly this 'danger-warning' thing that you bestowed upon Ms. Chu – it occurred to me that they're at least a subset of your own abilities. Now... there are probably a lot of different reasons why you'd want to do that – some of them have already been mentioned, but... you consider yourself the 'guardian' of the Earth... do you not? The most powerful being on the *planet*... that is."

A broad, delighted smile showed on the face of Karéin-Mayréij.

"Indeed I do... indeed I *do*," she softly replied, "And I know what you are next to say."

"Well then I'll just come out and *say* it, then," continued the scientist. "We humans – when I was one of them, I mean – we have a phrase that sums up a dilemma : 'who guards the guardians'. Or in this case, 'the guardian'... singular."

The alien beamed lovingly at the more-than-woman.

"Is it *us*, Karéin-Mayréij? Is that *our* job?" forcefully pressed Abruzzio.

"Yes – mark my words, never to forget – it *is!*" answered the Storied Watcher, as if confessing a secret. "And... behold the first use of your *own* gift, dear friend. The subtle insight of the *Makailkh* comes swiftly to you... ever may it flower, and ever may it help you correct me... when from the path I stray."

"Wait a minute – *wait* a minute – let me get this *straight*, Karéin," protested Ramirez. "You mean you want Sylvia, me, the rest of us, to, uhh... keep *you* in line? You *gotta* be joking!"

"Not just *me*," answered the alien-girl. "My war-children, too."

"Yeah, *you* know – the sword that disintegrates things on touch, the shield that slices through mountains and those two daggers that freeze Lake Superior and melt Pikes Peak," muttered the third agent. "When do we get *started*, man?"

"As soon as possible, Will Hen-dricks," came back the inevitable reply.

The gangster guffawed.

"What are we 'sposed to *do*, if you're off base?" asked the Latino scientist.

"You *tell* me that I am straying," said the alien-girl.

"And what if *that* doesn't work?" he argued.

"Then use your powers to restrain me," she noted, matter-of-factually. "Though I pray that matters shall never come to that."

"The scene in the motel-room, between you and me," knowingly remarked Misha. "It all makes *sense*, now."

"You took a huge chance there, my love," recounted Karéin-Mayréij. "My fury *could* have consumed you – but you stood your ground and tried to reason with me, both there, and at the lake in the canyon; these are moral-actions for which I shall *eternally* be grateful. And still, you cannot hope to overcome me, or constrain me, by yourself, alone... but, in time, with the help of all of your brothers and sisters... perhaps... you *may*."

She knelt before them.

"I will lead you and teach you – with power akin to that of a *god*," promised the Storied Watcher. "But I *will* heed your warnings, and I *will* make amends, when my followers will rebuke me. Only thus, can I escape the long fall to evil."

"What you're saying is undoubtedly wise, Karéin," interjected the FBI team-leader, "But I wasn't aware that I was one of your – err – 'followers'."

The alien-girl arose.

With her godly visage eroding with each second, she said, "Only *you* can decide, Minn-ee. Will you leave me? Will you go *away*?"

It almost sounded like she was pleading; and more than a few of the more-than-humans noticed that her eyes looked unusually moist.

There were a few long, uncomfortable seconds, during which an obviously torn Chu stood and silently pondered.

"No," softly answered the more-than-woman. "I'll go with you, Karéin. I guess I'm... in.... too deep... you know? And besides – there's got to be *someone* to back up Ms. Abruzzio, about keeping you on a tight leash."

She did a double-take, and blanched.

"Uhh... did I really *say* that?" Chu stammered.

The Storied Watcher unsuccessfully tried to hide her joy.

"Not exactly how *I* would have described it," she amicably commented. "But close enough. You are *all* answerable to me... as am I, to all of you."

"Yeah... but who makes the final decision?" queried Kaysten. "I mean, there's *got* to be one person in charge... 'where the buck stops', I mean."

"No – there does *not* have to be," countered the alien-girl. "We will *all* make decisions together. *Except*, of course, for things like 'saving Bob and Tommy'."

"It won't *work!*" argued the Chief of Staff.

"That's just because you are not familiar with anything other than your own Empire's way of leadership... and you are not used to making demands of a demi-goddess," countered Karéin-Mayréij. "You will learn how to do so."

"Haven't you read any of those books about 'managing your manager', dude?" joked Hendricks.

"But I won't make any promises on behalf of my fellow-agents," warned Chu. "It's up to *them* – if they want to stay, that is."

"Oh, come *on*, Minnie!" wearily remarked Boatman. "If we *don't* go the distance with her... just *what* you s'pose the Government's gonna do with us, the second they find out how we's been, uhh, 'changed'? Probably just string us up somewhere and pull the lever, so's they can get back – they *think* – at her. You're right, there – we're in up to our necks by now – joke not intended – and the funny thing is... I *still* can't figure out where we stepped too far over that line."

"That is easy," answered the Storied Watcher. "It started, when first you let me call you 'friend'. You *could* have run... but you did not. From that point, a propitious fate came upon you."

"I'm 'in'," confirmed the third agent. "And no regrets there, lady. Damn – but don't I feel *great!* Or great*er*. Or... *something*, man."

She smiled at him.

"Listen, Karéin," offered Wolf, "There's an old joke that says, 'I'm from the government, and I'm here to help you'. Well I got it beat – 'I'm a space-alien and I'm here to be your friend'. I wouldn't take nothin' back, mind you – not for a minute – but... talk about 'unintended-consequences'... you know?"

"And more of these 'consequences' yet await," she evenly foretold. "But at least now, you are fit to prevail over them."

"Yeah," reflectively observed Chu. "I bet we *are*... aren't we?"

"I feel... *different*," added the bounty-hunter, flexing his more-than-admirable biceps. "*Bitchin'* drugs, girl! Ain't no synth comes *close*."

Karéin-Mayréij nodded, with a proud look, akin to that of a parent attending a graduation-ceremony.

"It is time that we went to save the children," she advised.

Chu looked behind her shoulder, at the crowd.

"Form up... super-agents!" commanded the FBI team-leader.

Toughest Gang In East L.A.

Some garbage – in fact, a *lot* of it – had been piled up next to, and over, the 'Magic Bus', so that it was hardly recognizable as a vehicle at all. Then, the group – led by the mufti-clad, "little-girl-lost"-looking Storied Watcher, herself followed by Wolf, Misha and Chu – had proceeded down the alleyway, until they were at the junction of a large, multiple-lane street.

In more auspicious times, it would probably have been as much as taking one's life in one's hands, to try crossing anywhere other than at a stop-light. But on *this* day, the only traffic was in the form of omni-present rats, pigeons and the occasional feral dog. A few ravens, or blackbirds, or whatever, picked away at unknown dead things.

Directly across the street, was what might – at one time – have been a school; except every square inch of it was covered in indecipherable gang-graffiti, and all of its windows had either been smashed or shot out. The place was of decent size – two stories, with an semi-detached gymnasium – but was deserted.

Karéin-Mayréij stood just ahead of the rest of them.

Slowly she looked up and down, right and left.

"Minn-ee," she announced, "Portentous things await. And... do you detect them? The hidden-ones, I mean."

Chu, her eyes marked with the same, seemingly-vacant stare, advanced to stand next to her mentor.

"I don't *see* them," she slowly spoke. "But I *know* they're there... I *feel* them, I can, uhh, *smell* their minds... but not what they're thinking. Behind the third car, the upside-down-one missing the front wheels... two of them. Three behind the low wall made up of concrete blocks. Four in that five-and-dime store just to the left of the driveway up to the school... five in various places. Boy... is this ever *strange*."

A saturnine smile came to the other's face.

"Stand ready," she ordered, taking a step out into the street.

"Shouldn't we, uhh, *suit* up, Karéin?" asked the FBI team-leader.

"Behold how *Vìrya Quü'j* adorns my breast," answered the alien-girl. "My war-children see through her eyes... if dispute we must with those who inhabit this place, right now I would prefer not to show my full glory... the better to deceive both your President's spy-planes and simple brigands. And I have another reason besides – namely, the exercise of your new arts."

She looked to her left.

"*Wolf*," calmly designated the Storied Watcher.

The bounty-hunter winked back her; then he simply... *disappeared,* from the sight of all around.

A few notes of a new war-song, sounded dimly, in the ether.

"*Misha*," she commanded.

With a second melody briefly adding its chords to the first, the Russian initially hesitated, casting his gaze from one dilapidated low-rise residence to the other.

Then, bracing himself, he took a short-run.

To the amazement of all save the Storied Watcher, he bounded all the way up to the roof of a nearby house on the right, crouching behind an inoperative air-conditioning unit.

The leap must have been over a distance of twenty meters if it had been an inch, and – though undoubtedly it was still within his possession – Misha did not seem to have his gun drawn.

"Otis... Will... we may be looking at *trouble*, here," warned Chu, over her shoulder. "Protect the rest of them – and be ready to take cover."

"Copy that," confirmed the big black man.

Gravely, Hendricks nodded.

The ex-*Mara* gangster had taken cover behind an overflowing garbage-bin.

"I'm holdin' *aces*," he complained, *sotto voce*. "*Necessito mi arma!*"

"No... you are not," contradicted Karéin-Mayréij. "*Y ha llegado el momento para que usted pueda utilizar sus habilidades, Sebastiàn.*"

"First test," she confided to the FBI team-leader, "I will safe you from any undue risk, regardless, but if urgency comes upon us... blink your eyes, and the second-hands will tick slowly as moves a snail... but only for a short time, so use the brief moments well. I will protect – but you and your brothers must strike."

"Umm-hmm," answered Chu, never taking her eyes off the scene in front of and all around, while she discreetly felt for the holster of her sidearm.

"Let us go forward, stopping halfway," requested the alien-girl.

Slowly, she and her more-than-human understudy, stepped into the street.

They had actually only advanced about a third of the distance to the faded center-line, when a thickly inner-city, African-American male accent, shouted.

"Five pimpin' – six limpin'!" it challenged.

Neither female in the vanguard of the rescue party, answered.

"Five poppin' – six droppin'!" shouted the voice, loudly and aggressively.

Finally, Chu felt the need to reply.

"Our – uhh, group, just needs to get across the street – to that school over there," she called back. "*Please* let us pass by, in peace. We don't want a fight!"

"Y'all on *Blood* turf now, Chinese biatch!" warned the gangsta voice. "Two choices : one, y'all 'n that cute lil' ba-donka-donk white ho', comin' over to *our* side, an' we get y'all into a party... or two, y'all stand there – an' we *still* havin' a party. Either way, we havin' some *fun*... y'all understand what ah'm sayin'?"

A different voice yelled out from the side, up the street to the left.

"*Fuck* them lies, Blob!" it shouted. "C's up, B's down – y'all on *Crip* turf, yo! *Includin'* that school. Y'all be retreatin' or we be gettin' to the gate, sooner than later... want to *ride*, bitch?"

"Fuck *y'all*, Crab pussy ho'!" angrily shouted the first voice. "Y'all up 'gainst a *lot* of 311's this way over here!"

"Karéin – it's *crazy* to go on with this!" whispered a worried Chu. "You and I might end up in the middle of a crossfire – and there's *nowhere* to hide, except for this light-pole beside me. Can't we we should move back to the alleyway? I'm hearing concealed foot-steps on both sides of the street."

The Storied Watcher gestured in the negative.

"These ruffians need to *fear* us," she argued, in a steely tone. "We would run into the same, at some point, in any event. It is an ideal chance for you and your brothers and sister to practice the exercise of your new arts. If the hidden brigands move to take a life on our side... then they cannot fairly complain, when their own are forfeit."

"Really?" muttered Chu. "Was *that* your strategy, at the Tucson hotel?"

"Yes," coldly replied Karéin-Mayréij. "How did you *think* that I lasted a thousand-score of your ages, Minn-ee – by not fighting back, when someone means to *kill* me? A *mountain* of unwise dead, can testify to this."

"Yeah... and you're an 'angel'... right?" complained the FBI team-leader.

"Umm-hmm,"confirmed the alien-girl. "And what is more... I am an 'angel', who *loves* you."

A frustrated Chu shook her head and reviewed all the nearby hiding-places.

The Storied Watcher took a half-step forward and, slowly pivoting in place until she had done a full, 360-degree turn, allowed her voice to rise.

"My friend Minn-ee speaks the truth; we mean not to disturb either side in this contest... but we *must* have safe passage to yonder school," she announced. "And we have our own war-geared soldiers, who follow behind. It would be *most* unwise for you to dispute our march... we are not at all as we seem. We have lethal skills and weapons which you cannot *possibly* defeat! Shoot, and in the next several seconds, most of you will be *dead!* This is fair warning – I give the count of five to decide!"

"*Five!*" loudly counted the alien-girl.

"Y'all ain't even *strapped up*', bitch, we can *see* that," growled a voice. "Gonna *teach* y'all 'bout dissin' Triple Zeros... 'cept for bein' nice lil' hoodrat frog dime, y'all be knocked, already."

"We do not *want* to kill or injure any of you – but neither shall we *hesitate* to do so – so stand aside and let us proceed, and maybe we *will* 'party' with you, at a time of *our* choosing. *Four!*" spoke the Storied Watcher, now two or three paces closer to the street-center.

"*Three!*" she counted. "*Please* just let us pass... *save* yourselves! We will then be on our way without the stain of spilled-blood... your 'gangsta-wars' are no business of ours!"

A breeze from somewhere, carrying the Storied Watcher's beautiful – yet foreboding, *ooo-ooo-ooo* melody – rustled the garbage in the street, causing startled birds and dogs to abandon their prizes.

But this time, the song was echoed by three more tunes, each faint though distinct; there was an ominous whispering-, crackling-beat from somewhere on the left, something a bit like the graceful melody of *Eugene Onegin* from the right; and finally, there was the timbre of fast-paced, synthesizer-sounding music, from a few feet behind the alien-girl.

Karéin-Mayréij allowed the glow in her eyes to wax, though this was as yet visible only to the first group of gangsters, in their hiding-places on the far side of the street.

"*Two!*" she warned, and like some fearsome harpy, the Storied Watcher levitated by a few centimeters and raised her arms, causing a wind-storm to envelop herself, while she started to advance with quickening determination toward the eastern side.

Chu stepped slightly back and momentarily closed her eyelids.

I call upon the power! she savagely vowed.

And it *came* – along with a susurrating, exciting, 'everywhere-and-nowhere' back-beat, like the rush of some impossible, consciousness-enhancing drug.

You can do anything, *Minnie Chu!*

They don't stand a chance!

"**Fuck y'all, 'ho!**" screamed a ghetto-voice.

Gun-flashes – apparently all targeted on the Storied Watcher and with the predictable negligible effect – suddenly erupted from multiple places on the far side of the street.

A feral dog yelped in pain, as a stray bullet caught it in the hind-quarters, and at least two birds were in the wrong place at the wrong time, as they tried to fly away.

A half-second later, a second – and then a third – volley of gun-shots, some apparently aimed at the alien-girl, but more sent in the direction of the rival gang, began to issue from hidden assailants on the western-side of the street, mostly from the left but a few from the right and south.

I have to decide! raced Chu's panicked mind.

Amazing... looks like everything's slowed to one frame per second...

God, if one of them hits me *– okay, assholes, one shot for each of you –*

Though she could not see because she was looking forward, the FBI team-leader heard, or felt, two of her own side, appear to the left and right.

No – left and above to the right – what the hell *– ?* she puzzled.

The team-leader crouched, aimed at the first gangster-in-hiding, and fired.

She heard a scream.

From his perch on the roof, Misha's enhanced eyes, ears and other senses, had little difficulty in precisely identifying where the gangsters – both the red-marked Bloods on the far side, and the blue-marked Crips on the side nearest him – were located, although he could not locate those he knew must have been on the other side of the alleyway, to the north and west.

Very well, mused the Russian.

You will have to deal with those yourself, my big, primitive friend.

Listening to the Storied Watcher's countdown, he had tried to concoct an elaborate, 'least distance between target points' plan of attack, but before this could be fully reasoned, the eastern-side gangsters had both literally and figuratively jumped the gun.

Behind the concrete-barriers, the overturned, burned-out car and inside the smashed-in store-front – I see them... or... sense them, he noted.

But if I go for the ones in front, the rest will have an easy shot at me... and they will probably not hesitate to fire right into a crowd of their own kind.

Can I jump as long as the broken-in window?

Very far – five times the distance from the ground, up to here – but partly downward... we shall see – only one way to find out...

Absent-mindedly, Misha fingered the little finift Mary-and-Christ-Child icon-locket attached to his neck-chain, silently cursing the FBI-agents for having confiscated its hidden, written endorsement from the Patriarch of Moscow.

Blessed Virgin Mother... this fool now asks your protection, in a cruel place far from the motherland, he silently prayed.

A half-familiar thought entered his mind, as he moved to the rear edge of the roof, so he could get a running start.

Be of faith, came the message.

And... believe in yourself!

As the grim-faced, utterly-determined Russian strode forward across the slight upward-slope of the rooftop – moving with a speed that shocked even himself – he knew that this was no idle counsel.

He felt powerful, confident... *superior.*

True is my aim! proclaimed his mind, as the sounds in his subconscious brought back memories of a symphony from back home.

As Misha reached the roof-crest, his legs tensed and then released, propelling him in Olympic ski-jump fashion in a slightly-curved trajectory, directly over the heads of Chu, the alien and dozens of gangsters.

Somehow, he avoided tumbling head-over-tail, while so doing.

A lesser-being would have been startled and confused by what happened next; in the midst of the flight, his normal eyesight momentarily failed, leaving him able to navigate with only a strange 'black-light' that softly illuminated the surroundings in a manner akin to the detail of a photo-negative.

However – an uncomfortably-long second later – the ex-SVR agent was again able to see as do human men; but then, upon approximately the same interval, the second-sight re-manifested itself, and the pattern repeated until he was hurling down right in front of the store-window, with his boot in classic drop-kick fashion.

"What the *fuck!*" came to his ears from behind and below, audible despite the relentless, loud 'crack-crack-crack' sound of multiple gunshots.

His first victim's skull was struck with such blood-splattering force that it was obviously crushed, from the first split-second that Misha made contact. Amazed at his energized reflexes – he was moving so fast that the four – no, three, now – thugs in this place, seemed to be working in slow-motion, turning lazily to try to bring their guns to bear.

He rolled and dodged so as not to continue his motion down the building's inner hallway like a complete idiot, then charged at them.

I made almost no noise when my boots hit his head... or when I braced against the far wall, he thought.

Excellent!

Almost involuntarily, the tempered-steel steak-knife that Misha had appropriated from the downtown hotel-suite, came to his hand, and again, the weird 'visible light blinking in-and-out' effect beset his eyes, although by now he was almost becoming used to it.

As if unable to properly track their target, despite his proximity to them, the gangstas were firing wildly in almost every direction.

One thug – a thin-faced guy – was shot dead by a misplaced bullet from a mountain-like, rotund Blood, and Misha feared that just because of the volume of gunfire, he must be struck; but though he was grazed by at least three rounds – one of which opened a superficial bleeding-wound – none hit solidly home.

The gangstas – however – were nowhere *near* so lucky.

Punching with ferocious, bone-snapping force with his left fist – the impact of which on bare skin, the delighted Russian noted, left ugly, frost-covered, blackish-blue welts – as he alternatively slit carotids and jugulars with the knife and delivered vicious knee-cracking kicks with his boots, all three of the remaining thugs lasted only for a few more lightening-like martial-arts attacks.

Despite the man's massive girth, it took only one well-placed heart-stab to kill this largest of his opponents; then – all the while alert against the advent of hostile reinforcements – the ex-SVR agent allowed himself a second or two to survey the results.

Like fighting cripples or children, he half-ashamedly mused.

They move so... slowly!

And... the power within tells that I can still do better, move even faster...

But they would have killed me without hesitation, had they the chance, he reminded himself.

These would not be the first *whom I have sent to the next world, while 'working under orders'.*

He looked down, for a second, still minding all the entrance-ways.

Good – I can recover those two combat-knives – almost bayonet-size – from the bodies, 'hardly-used', as the Americans say... and there is an AK, looks authentic – not a cheap knock-off, with two spare magazines, he noted.

Though that Mexican-American thug, will probably now want my pistol.

Come here, old friends, he sent to the weapons.

By now, he was no longer amazed that the fighting-knives, and the gun, as much moved into his arms, as he moved, to grasp them.

You want *me, my former 'wet operations' associates?* mused the Russian.

"Then... come and *get* me!" he whispered with a thin smile, before taking a last shoulder-glance and heading down the hall, looking for a back entrance.

Though he had heard the first gunshots, the bounty-hunter had to go further to the north and west than at first anticipated – almost half a block, in fact –

before he stumbled upon the main group of blue-kerchiefed inner-city thugs on this side of the street.

Still effectively invisible to his opponents – but not yet ready to trust his life to this supposed weirdo-trick – he cautiously peered around a damaged front door-frame, with his gun at the ready.

Wolf surveyed the situation, while the furious gunfight to the south continued to rage.

"Y'all *smoke* them Blob fuckers!" shouted a gangsta, evidently the leader.

"Homies few doors down," remarked another. "We be backin' 'em up?"

"Yo," commanded the first one.

"Bit of mah blunt to go," argued a big, muscular Crip. "Y'all waitin' up sec or two."

Seven of 'em – an AK – at least one SMG... and the rest all are packin' as well, thought the bounty-hunter.

Can't possibly fire that fast...

Well, Karéin – either you're shittin' me... or you ain't, he resolved.

Might as well find out...

Get that 'back-from-the-dead' stuff powered up...

Immediately – though there were no words – a feeling of confidence and support flooded into his mind.

"Hey, boys!" he exclaimed, causing the entire group of gangstas to immediately turn in the direction of the sound, guns drawn.

Wolf put away his gun and withdrew behind the door – though he did not hide – and, with a momentary thought, disabled the 'you-don't-see me' trick.

What she call you again, was it... 'Little Burning One'? he mused.

Honey... we ain't acquainted, but now's as good a time as ever... either you show up when I tap on your hot little shoulder, or you'll be lightin' a candle at a funeral, I reckon...

But how do I get you to... wait – there's an idea...

Almost before he had finished this soliloquy, the bounty-hunter was confronted by three or four surly, grimacing 'nigga gangstas', each of which had an obviously ready-and-loaded gun aimed squarely at him.

"What the fuck y'all *doin'* here, white-boy?" snarled the biggest of them. "Step out – or we's smoke y'all right there!"

"Guess I got lost," evaded Wolf, with his hands in the air. "*My* bad!"

He stepped through the doorway and on to the sidewalk, noticing that he now had a line-of-sight to another group of perhaps six Crips who were firing at an unseen enemy, from behind obstacles further to the south.

"Y'all slingin'?" demanded another gangsta. "One fuckin' move and y'all goin *down* right there, biatch!"

"Here," indicated the bounty-hunter. "In my belt. Ain't *got* nothin' else."

Roughly, one of the thugs advanced and pulled out his pistol.

"Y'all *pop* that weasel!" commanded the leader, *sotto voce*, to the big, drug-cigar-smoking Crip. "Got no *time* for such thangs!"

The gangster lifted his gun; but Wolf's alien-powered ears had easily heard his putative death-warrant, and – with half-sincere fear – he pleaded, "Hey, *hey* – there, pardner – how 'bout just a last hit from that turbo, before you do me... *please*? Only fair... I'm *beggin'!*"

"Make it a *good* one, bitch!" spat the big gangsta, as he handed the drug-laced cigar to the bounty-hunter. "Ten *seconds*... you fuckin' fugly AB'er."

Them 'Aryan' boys?

Ain't my *posse*, he thought.

I got a much *worse one, pussy!*

Wolf took a deep drag.

"Got one last thing to say," he offered, staring deliberately at the smoke's dull-glowing tip.

"Which would *be*," he drawled, as Wolf's eyes took on a sinister, orange tint, while a feeling of limitless, incomprehensible power surged through his mind and bloodstream, and as an odd, whistling, flute-like melody – mixed with the growl of something akin to an electric-guitar – began to come out of nowhere.

"*Baby – **light my fire!**"*

Instantly, a dancing, shining, sparkling little thread of flame shot out of the cigar, then – much too quickly for human eyes or reflexes to track or react to – it grew into a roaring jet that raced around the bounty-hunter's body, about a half-meter from his skin, enveloping him from head to toe in a mantle of brilliant, yellow-orange-red fire.

Touch mine feel new master, love new, came a mad, child-like, mental voice, speaking not words but instead symbols and pictures.

Together quest we thine world in, me thee and!

To everyone else within ten meters, the heat was blistering – terrifying – *unbearable*; but to Wolf, all that came backward on the inside, was a warm, invigorating feeling, as if he was enjoying the after-effects of fine whiskey.

Play my game, he tried to reply, *And I'll love you forever, darlin' Little Magic Candle... 'long as you tell me what turns you on.*

Give me a space so I can see... okay?

He was about to bend over to pick up his gun, which had been dropped in panic, but somehow, it flew up to his hand of its own accord.

The handle felt hot – almost painful to the touch.

Jaysus! silently reflected Wolf. That's *how hot it is in here.*

How come my duds ain't flamin'?

Desire to them that do thee, master? came the infant voice.

Uhh, no... that's quite alright, honey, he quickly thought back.

Shrieking, agonized gangstas – exposed parts of their bodies already seared – scattered in every direction. One or two were unlucky enough to have the street as the only available escape-route, and they were quickly cut down by enemy gunfire from the other side, but at least five others were more or less able to stay under cover as they retreated south.

Screaming obscenities, they opened up with everything that they had.

Almost every shot taken at the advancing bounty-hunter hit the terrible column of fire surrounding him and was thus vaporized into nothingness; but reflexively, Wolf raised his arms to cover his head, the moment when he saw gun-flashes through the newly-opened gap in the fire-shield.

He felt two or three sharp, bee-sting-like strikes upon his forearms.

"*Fuck!*" he cursed, as something hit the pavement with a tinkling sound.

Then he noticed arm-welts, each in the precise place of impact.

Master angry not me with? apologized a frightened little voice.

Failed thee! Forgive – beg – oh!

The bounty-hunter stared down in disbelief.

Two pistol-slugs lay at his feet; and again, he felt an irrational surge of confidence, of raw, inchoate power.

Peace, darlin', he mused.

We're good, and I'll never *blame you, not for nothin', no-how.*

Now show me your stuff...

Burn, baby... burn!

The one who, less than a full month before, had been little more than an obscure, semi-pro bail-enforcer, no longer doubted.

With his eyes now glowing a sinister, bright red-orange, Wolf opened his arms as if ready to embrace a friend; but nothing amicable was in *his* advance. He walked slowly and deliberately – with a wicked, cruel sneer – his psycho-music playing stirring, but frightening, symphonic fear within the minds of all about.

He looked like a *devil*.

Fire burst out everywhere in a straight line with his outstretched palms, as the terrified gangsters, only a few having the guts to stop and get off a shot or two, raced away to the south.

You know this *one?* he snickered, to his unseen, spiritual companion.

I'll bet you do, *but just in case... here, I'll sing it to you in my head, darlin'.*

I'm on the High-way To Hell... High-way To Hell, mused Wolf, stepping forward, while the conflagration raged all about.

Hey Momma! Look at... me!

I'm on my way to the... Promised Land!

Minnie Chu – caught in the open except for the street-light pole and its completely inadequate cover – silently cursed against the imperious alien who had so unnecessarily risked her life.

But – while the Storied Watcher just floated about a foot over the pavement, effortlessly deflecting a hail of bullets – the FBI team-leader alternated between desperately dodging incoming-rounds, and methodically returning fire against several other, hidden assailants.

With weirdly-enhanced reflexes and uncanny precision – hearing screams, obscenities and moans – Chu aimed and pulled the trigger; and, one-by-one, the red-side gangstas took pistol-rounds that shredded hands and arms... or, for the less fortunate, which impacted lethally, with faces and heads.

Okay... I did take precision target-shooting back at the Academy, she ruefully self-acknowledged.

But I never *could zero in like* this... *like I can't miss!*

Although a mighty commotion was going on somewhere inside the storefront, there appeared to be a momentary lull in the gunfire directed at the two in mid-street.

The team-leader was about to say something; but then she heard a shrieking curse, from behind and to her left.

"Fuckin' Fed-Ral bitch!" screamed a well-hidden Crip.

Almost simultaneously, he fired a shot so close that she could feel its hot, malicious air-trail. The round almost grazed her thigh, leaving a tear in the lower-parts of her jacket.

A shower of gunfire erupted from this direction; it seemed a miracle that the Chu was not struck multiple times.

Shit! One inch *closer – caught me with my back turned!* she panicked.

Can I get around fast enough – God, no, I can't, he's going to fire again –

Can't protect my body – my head –

In the next split-second, something *hot* and tremendously energetic – like a lightening-bolt impacting a burning smokestack – sizzled past her and overhead. It must have been aimed at the source of the nearly-deadly gunshot, and as Chu wheeled, she saw where the Storied Watcher had unleashed her fury.

Maybe – at one time – it *had* been a multi-bay garbage-bin, or something like that; but now, there was only a black-streaked smear within a rut on the pavement, behind a jagged set of charred, red-glowing metal-fragments.

Chu blanched at the realization of how much power must have been directed at the vastly-overmatched gangster who had met his maker, in the last couple of seconds.

"Jesus, Karéin!" gasped the agent. "You *vaporized* that poor guy!"

"He was aiming to *kill* you... and he suffered much less than the five whose lives you have lately ended, Minn-ee," replied the alien-girl. "Just a brief flash – then... the next life. Another who your aim has taken, will probably not live to see the end of this day. There were two more near by the one who I targeted to save you from being shot in the back... but they have retreated southward."

Then she looked in the direction of the just-disintegrated thug, quickly went down on one knee, made some kind of inscrutable air-gesture and threw an instantly-appearing tear in the same direction.

"Absolve me from this evil... and bid all souls who today meet my sword, to the peaceful Planes Beyond," whispered Karéin-Mayréij, although the FBI team-leader could easily hear.

"*Five*?" wailed Chu, as the 'fast-thinking thing' ebbed and tears came to her eyes. "I killed... *five*?"

Grimly, the Storied Watcher nodded in the affirmative.

With suddenly-weak knees, Chu bent over and threw up.

"I've... I've never... *killed* anyone, before, you know!" sobbed the FBI team-leader, turning her face in the vain hope that the alien-girl couldn't see the tears.

"*Damn* you, Karéin – damn you to *hell!*" she cursed. "*Why* did we have to get into this fight, in the first place? *Why* did we have to kill those men? You *knew* they didn't stand a *chance!*"

"Minn-ee... I am *sorry*," quietly offered the Storied Watcher, "I know that the guilt of this, tears at your soul – as it does mine – but it was *necessary*; you *must* learn how to defend yourself, even unto taking human life. If it will make you feel better, I accept the shame of having thus tainted you –"

But before she could finish the sentence, their attention was involuntarily forced to the north-west side of the street, where a fusillade of gunfire – strangely not directed either across at the fleeing Bloods or at the alien-girl's own party – erupted without warning.

Chu – though sick to both her heart and stomach – managed to look up.

A plume of smoke was coming from just north of the source of the gunshots. A second later, the more-than-human woman, as well as the alien one, saw greedy little orange tongues of fire, consuming well-nigh every piece of inflammable material, on or around the far north-west side of the sidewalk.

"Do you *hear*, Minn-ee?" remarked an obviously-impressed Karéin-Mayréij. "The song of the Little Spirit of Fire, who has found her master!"

"Wolf?" asked the FBI team-leader.

The alien-girl nodded, stating, "He uses his new-found arts... he drives his opponents toward us."

"Karéin," pleaded Chu, "They'll be trapped between us and Wolf, in no more than thirty seconds or so, maybe less – what are you going to *do*?"

"They are armed and will try to kill us," explained the Storied Watcher. "What would you *expect* me to do? What will *you* do – fight back... or be slaughtered *by* them?"

"You want me to be your *conscience*?" spat the woman. "Okay, *fine* – show them a little *mercy*, for God's sake!"

"They are only humans... savage and cruel ones, at that," countered Karéin-Mayréij. "You want to be 'merciful', then *you* do it... I will stay here, but if matters get out of hand, you *know* what happened to the last one who might have killed you... right?"

"Yeah... I know," muttered the Asian-American agent. "Just 'humans'... just 'insects'. You need *help*, Karéin."

"I *know* that I do... and I am counting on you and Sylvia to provide it," softly admitted the Storied Watcher. "*Go!*"

Trying to turn on the 'fast-thinking' trick all the way, Chu trotted a diagonal path to the north and west.

Coming as close as she dared to the source of the gunfire, she yelled, "Listen, you stupid fucking gang-bangers, you're *surrounded* – come any further down the sidewalk toward my voice, and you're *dead!*"

My God... I can feel the heat from here, she mused.

What the hell has she turned him into?

"Fuck *y'all*, bitch!" shouted a voice.

The raging conflagration was inching its way south. Entire storefronts were starting to light up, to the accompaniment of a strange, sinister-exciting melody.

"Let me *talk* to you, damn it!" retorted the FBI team-leader. "I'll stand out here in the street – I'm holstering my gun!"

Perhaps twenty feet away, a scowling, African-American head peeked out from behind a derelict truck, while gunfire still crackled just behind.

"What the *fuck* that, bitch?" desperately growled the gangsta, pointing to the fire-storm behind him.

There was an odd half-smile on Chu's face, as she stared directly into the man's eyes.

"I won't hurt you – my name's Minnie... I'm your *friend*," she cooed. "Tell your homies to put down their guns, lay 'em down on the pavement... come out with your hands up. Then, the fire will stop advancing, and I'll tell you all about it. You get your pieces back when we go 'cross the street. You understand me?"

The Crip – his face wearing a vapid, stunned look, stumbled backward.

There was some rapid-fire discourse, and the gunfire stopped.

"*Wolf!*" called Chu. "Hold it right *there!*"

"That *you*, Lady FBI?" responded a voice. "And... why *should* I? This is *fun*, man!"

"Battle's *over!*" she demanded. "It's going to your *head* – or hadn't you noticed?"

After a slight pause, Wolf, his voice reflective despite the roar of the fire all about him, offered, "Yeah... maybe you got a point there, lady. She fuckin' ain't *kiddin'*... this shit's like a drug – once you're on it... ain't *no* goin' back."

"Who y'all fuckin' *talkin'* to, 'ho?" came a voice from under cover. "Nothin' but big fuckin' fire, up there."

Chu heard the Storied Watcher mention to someone, "She is over there... hurry there, if you please."

The bounty-hunter's voice was now directed at the gangstas.

"Listen, peeps," he shouted. "You all want to get barbecued – go right ahead and pick up them guns... I'm tellin' the hot little monkey on my back, to lay it off – for the time bein', that is."

Too quietly for human ears to detect – but easily within Chu's earshot – he whispered, "Okay, darlin'... jump back inside... warm my heart. And... *thanks*."

Wolf's psycho-music slowly abated.

Something mighty strange *going on there*, mused the FBI team-leader.

Uhh... would that be a surprise?

The close-cropped, serious face of the Russian appeared alongside, and to Chu's encouragement, he was toting an automatic-rifle.

"I have dealt with most of those on the far side of the street – those who did not run," explained Misha. "I will cover you – but what is going *on*, to the north of us? It appears that half the *block*, is on fire! Did Karéin unleash her powers against the ruffians up there?"

"No – it's Wolf," commented Chu. "You've got a rifle, now?"

"Ahh... the 'fire' thing," observed the Russian. "I should have *guessed*. As for the gun... its last owner will not need it, any more. Nor will the others who I encountered."

The team-leader grimaced.

"I'm going on to the sidewalk – then I'll advance and take the guns you dropped," called Chu, in the direction of the trapped gangstas. "Don't try running out into the street – do that, and if my own team doesn't shoot you dead, the Bloods up the street on the other side, will pop you for *sure!* Understood?"

There was no answer, though the FBI team-leader's alien-powered ears could hear various curses and obscenities.

"I'll take that as a 'yes'," she shouted. "Here I come!"

Slowly she reversed her track, heading back to the intersection of the alleyway, where she saw the *Mara* crouched behind a garbage-container; though at first, Chu had completely missed him, because Sebastiàn's normally-Mediterranean complexion, had somehow taken on the same tint as the fence to his side – complete with a swath of red, to match one of the gang-slogans sprayed upon the barrier.

Wonder how long it'll take him to change back, she idly wondered.

One way or the other... if Karéin's predictions come true... I wouldn't want to be a gangsta fighting it out with him, for 'who's the worst thug in the 'hood'.

Another glance showed Kaysten, Abruzzio and Ramirez being protected by Hendricks and Boatman, between Sebastiàn and the two FBI-agents.

The third agent began to shout, "Hey, Minnie"; but Chu put a finger to her lips, as she cautiously looked to the north, around a burned-out car.

Five black gangstas, each with blue Crip colors marking various vestments, stood about ten meters away. Three were standing with hands in the air, while one was writhing on the ground in obvious pain. A fifth was staring off vacantly into space, his fore-body propped up against the wall of a storefront, his legs stretched out in front.

Behind them, just in front of a wall of flame, was the bounty-hunter.

"Wolf – you alright?" loudly queried the team-leader.

"Never better, Missus FBI-agent," he called back.

"You should move," she warned. "Fire's creeping down towards you!"

"Oh... don't worry your pretty little head about *that*," he offered, with an oddly-confident tone. "The whole 'fire' business 'n me – we kind of got things figured out, you might say."

"FBI?" angrily interjected one of the less-shaken gangstas, as Chu puzzled at the bounty-hunter's comment. "What the *fuck* y'all doin' down *here*? Ain't none of yo' posse even twenny mile out, an' we almost downtown –"

"Long story," answered the woman. "Kick those guns down to me."

"Fuck *y'all*," cursed the Crip. "We's *daid* widout some heat!"

"Well, boys," mordantly chuckled Wolf, from their other flank, "I thought you had all the heat you needed, for today... but if you want, I can send a little – okay, a *lot* more – your way. Three-count, 'fore things get *warm. One...*"

Chu's mind jumped with alarm upon seeing the evil, orange glow in the bounty-hunter's eyes.

Did I see him licking his lips? she wondered.

"Check *that!*" cried a panicked gangsta.

"Do like th' China biatch say," he ordered, as quietly as he could.

A small arsenal of handguns and automatic-weapons was sent careening southward, down the sidewalk.

"Otis!" called Chu, over her shoulder. "Need you up here."

"Wolf," she pleaded, "That's *enough* – okay? The situation's under control!"

"Anythin' you *say*, my dear," came back the unctuous response.

The bounty-hunter's eyes returned to normal.

In record-time, the big black agent came trotting down the alleyway and up the sidewalk.

"Can you get the guns, please?" requested the FBI team-leader.

"*Whew*," whistled Boatman. "Shore done some *damage* there, Minnie!"

"Yeah, lots of firepower –" she started.

"No, that *fire* up there... behind Mister bounty-hunter," corrected the black agent. "Young Will 'n me – scientists too – saw the smoke. Growin' by the *second*, looks like it's almost out of control... gonna be *problems* if we light up the whole neighborhood. No Fire Department these days, you know?"

Again, Chu shot a glance over her shoulder to the other side, this time directing her comments at the Storied Watcher.

"Karéin," she shouted, "We've got a problem up there, just past Wolf! He's set fire to half the block, and it's *spreading*. Is there anything you can do?"

Karéin-Mayréij half-glided, half-stepped to join Chu and the Russian, while Boatman collected the gangstas' reluctantly-abandoned arsenal.

"The Little Burning One lives in the separate reality of the Immortal Flame," she tried to explain. "Ever would she 'make her current surroundings to be like home' – our friend Wolf, has just not yet learned how to – uhh – 'set limits for her'. Here... I will quench the fire... but first I must check something."

The alien-girl stepped on to the sidewalk, in full view of both the Crips and the bounty-hunter.

"Wolf," she called, "Is your new companion within you now... or does she dart and delight, within the conflagration behind?"

"If I'm gettin' you right, Karéin," he replied, "I got her on a leash – I *think*. And if it's anythin' to you... I think I'm startin' to understand what it's like for you to keep all them 'war-kids' of yours, from chargin' off and remodelin' the local landscape, whenever they have a hissy-fit. She's a neat little thing – but I can see how lettin' her go off half-cocked, would be a *bad* idea."

A gangsta spoke up.

"Wha tha dilly yo?" he complained.

"Will – bring the others up here," commanded Chu.

"If I correctly interpret your cant, let us just say," calmly stated the Storied Watcher, in the direction of the Crip, "That he who stands in your path to the north, has a new companion-spirit – whose flaming kiss, I believe, some have already suffered. Did I not *warn* you stupid brigands, that battle against me and my followers, would be *suicide?* Behold, the *truth* of it... my hands, and those of my beloved friends, are now stained with human-blood. The fault was yours... but the guilt is, equally, mine."

"Sure... and I bet you're *real* sorry, lady," grunted Boatman, with a dismissive shrug.

After bowing in his direction and silently, gravely nodding acknowledgement, Karéin-Mayréij half-rolled her eyes, so they focused on a spot somewhere overhead, held out her palms as if giving a benediction, and commanded, "Væran *Ksé'l'ch'*, drink thee of the blaze which now consumes the buildings – take such inside thyself – then stay by him called 'Wolf', to parley with the spirit within him; *Væran Ss'éth'ch'*, extinguish what remains, that it not again flare to threaten domiciles 'round here... then return to me. *Go!*"

The two little daggers appeared as if from nowhere, tracing an interlaced, cork-screw path right over the heads of the beleaguered Crips.

As the yellow-orange one passed behind Wolf, the fire behind it and to its sides, vanished, and was replaced, a split-second later, by a coat of ice and frost.

In less than three seconds, the fire had been extinguished; the bounty-hunter stood still, as if mesmerized, while *Væran Ksé'l'ch'* hovered in front of him.

The other dagger returned faithfully to the Storied Watcher's grasp, and its aura of killing-cold began to emanate outward from her arm.

"Fuck – *fuck...*" quailed the Crips.

Her eyes glowing malevolently, with charges of *Amaiish*-energy suffusing her trunk, the Storied Watcher took several steps forward.

"After I finish speaking, take your injured fellow-bandits and make away to the north, through the newly-fallen snow," she demanded. "This will cool and succor the fire-wounds suffered in your recent dispute with my follower, 'Wolf of the Burning Forest'. We will take those few of your weapons which will be of any use, and leave the rest for you in yonder wrecked vehicle, for you to regain, when we go on our own way. Tell *all* who you encounter of what happened here – and, hopefully, we will not have to again give proof of our war-skills."

The alien-girl knelt on one knee, momentarily bowing her head.

"You should grieve for your fallen... as do I," she advised, before arising.

"That's *big* of you, Karéin," morosely complained Chu. "While you're at it, would you mind saying a few words for the five poor people who I shot dead?"

"*Whoa!*" exclaimed Hendricks, who by now had arrived with the rest.

"You must learn to do *that*, yourself," replied Karéin-Mayréij. "It *hurts*... does it not?"

She paused for a second, then added, "And so it *should*. The first step to absolution, is to stop and meditate upon it... if only for a moment."

The FBI team-leader awkwardly attempted to emulate her mentor, but only managed to start bawling her eyes out, as she wobbled briefly up and down.

"*Damn* you..." she impotently cursed.

The Russian came over to console Chu.

"You have never killed before... is that right?" he asked.

"No... no... haven't," she confessed, fumbling for a tissue from an inside jacket-pocket.

"Have you ever shot anyone?" pressed Misha.

"Yes – no – not *exactly*," tearfully admitted Chu. "*Aimed* at a few... *might* have hit one, on a field-assignment, six years ago..."

The gangstas started to guffaw.

One of them teased, "Chinese biatch sayin' she done bust a cap – but she prolly just jet every time, yo."

"*Listen!*" growled Boatman. "Angel-lady over there – yeah, she's the one with the *eyes*, don't you know – she told me that I got my *own* lil' magic-trick, like that dude way up yonder, the one who's havin' the deep-chat with the orange dagger. And mine's even worse than *his*. You all don't get the *fuck* out of here, now, and you gonna find out how *I* do it! You understand what I'm *sayin'?*"

The third agent waved his pistol.

"Fuckin' *move!*" he shrieked.

One of the gangstas had enough of a sense of group-solidarity to kick a moaning, badly-burned compatriot, so that the other got up and stumbled away.

The rest followed, cursing and spitting. They ran right past Wolf, who was almost within easy earshot by now; although, they wisely did not confront him.

Hendricks turned his attention to Chu.

"It's cool, Minnie," he consoled. "Don't bum yourself out on doing what you had to. The rest of us are just glad that you came through it in one piece."

"Aye," agreed Karéin-Mayréij.

"You have nothing to apologize *for*, Madam Chu," offered Misha. "These hooligans – both groups of them – would *certainly* have killed you, and us, had they the slightest chance. If it is of any consolation, I have three more dead to my, uhh, 'credit', as of this most recent battle... in the storefront, on the other side of the street."

"And that doesn't *bother* you?" countered Chu, regaining her composure.

"Of *course* it does," he argued. "To take a human life is *always* terrible! But sometimes, this cannot be avoided... except at unacceptably high risk to one's own. Look *around* you, Madam – this is one of the most lawless, violent ghettos anywhere in the world. Pacifism is not a realistic option, down here."

He paused for a second, then added, "Karéin and I have already debated this subject, in another setting... as I believe she will recall."

"Aye," repeated the alien-girl, with a nod.

"It's just that I think – I *wish* – there could have been another way," whimpered Chu. "If we had just avoided the entire situation."

"Let us speak of that sad topic later, I pray," requested the Storied Watcher.

She stopped the eye-glow, closed her eyelids, made some kind of gesture, and both the orange and blue daggers rocketed skywards, vanishing at approximately the same overhead point.

"We should go to the school before the bandits can regroup and again dispute our way," proposed Karéin-Mayréij, "But Minn-ee, Will, Otis... you are all better-versed in the fine points of these 'guns' – apportion them as you will, but leave at least one spare – so my promise to these 'Crips' is ever-truthful."

"Yeah... okay," said Boatman. "Let's see... got one AK, wait – Brazilian copy, but still shoot you dead... MAC-15 as well, spare mags for both the rifle and the SMG... one auto-Glock, plastic body, looks full... other three are cheap snub-noses, not much stoppin'-power, and some of 'em are almost fired-out... I'd say we ditch the revolvers, and keep the rest. Anybody think different?"

"*Dame el nueve!*" demanded the onlooking *Mara*.

The black FBI-agent frowned.

"Karéin?" he checked.

"Yes?" she responded.

"He wants an automatic-weapon... is that okay?" asked Boatman.

"No – it isn't!" interrupted Chu.

"Why is that?" inquired the Storied Watcher. "He is your brother – is he not? And we have several of these weapons to allocate."

"What I mean," complained the FBI team-leader, "Is that he's – no offense – a *gangster*. Who *knows* what he'll do with that kind of firepower? Especially, if he's behind our backs."

"What you worried 'bout, *chica*?" retorted Sebastiàn. "That I gonna go off an' shoot someone? Seems to me, *usted acaba de hacer lo mismo, comprende*?"

Chu sat down on one of the nearby concrete-barriers, hung her head and waved affirmatively in resignation.

Gloating, the *Mara* grabbed the submachine gun and began to carefully check over its every feature.

Boatman accosted the bounty-hunter.

"You want the AK?" he asked.

"'Fraid not," demurred Wolf. "Might even have to drop off the piece I already *got*, in fact."

"Huh?" blurted a confused Ramirez. "When we first landed here, weren't you complaining about not having a gun?"

"Let's just say, pardner," explained the bounty-hunter, with a scarcely-concealed smirk, "That lately... things have been gettin' a mite on the *hot* side, in my neck of the woods – and the *last* thing I need, is to have bullets cookin'-off, at the wrong time. Seems I *can* stop 'em, in fact... but it still hurts plenty."

"You can tell her not to cast her kiss, where you so prohibit," mentioned Karéin-Mayréij. "She will obey; and thereby, that place on your person could indeed be used to carry dry parchment... never would it ignite."

"Who on *Earth* are you *talking* about?" inquired Abruzzio.

"My new little alter-ego, darlin'," remarked the bounty-hunter. "She's a real, uhh, 'hottie'... if you get my meanin'."

"Wolf, in a time of sadness, always do you have good mirth to share," commented the alien-girl, with an appreciative smile. "Keep your gun for the while, but as to the others... Otis?"

"Guess I'll take the AK, if that's alright," spoke up Hendricks. "Upgrade from what I got now, you know?"

Boatman handed the auto-rifle to his fellow-agent, then said, "Minnie, Glock's a bit better that my existin' weapon... so I'm hopin' you don't mind if I switch 'em. That leaves Will's service-gun, and my old pistol. We gonna give 'em to Sylvia, Hector or Jerry? Unless, that is, Little Miss Angel there, thinks *she* needs a piece."

The Storied Watcher sighed and rolled her eyes.

"Does one replace a legendary sword, with a pickle-fork?" she complained, to Wolf's obvious delight.

"I'll take your gun, Otis," requested Chu.

Ruefully, she added, "After what happened a few minutes ago, it probably has more rounds left. Ms. Abruzzio? Mr. Ramirez? Mr. Kaysten? Do any of you know how to fire a gun?"

"You gotta be kidding me," sniffed the Chief of Staff. "I'm a *civilian!*"

Sebastiàn cackled maliciously.

"I will take one," agreed the Mexican-American scientist. "I would not call myself an expert – but years ago in the *barrio,* I learned how to aim and shoot reasonably well. It was sort of a 'survival-skill'... or *would* have been, if I had not been awarded a scholarship."

"Count me *out!*" demanded Abruzzio. "I'll probably hit one of you, the first time I fire."

"That leaves us with one spare," noted the FBI team-leader. "Otis – empty out the bullets and even up the ammo, between the remaining service-guns."

Boatman nodded and set to work.

After only a minute or two, he had all the pistol and rifle-rounds apportioned. Then he threw the surplus firearms into the same burned-out vehicle as had earlier been indicated by the Storied Watcher; after – that is – carefully emptying all the bullets from the revolvers and strewing this ammunition in various, hard-to-find places.

"The bandits appear all to have fled," advised Karéin-Mayréij, "But let us make way to the school, ere they return with reinforcements."

"Well... based on what I seen goin' down out there," offered the black agent, "I'd say they could bring on an Army-battalion or two, and the outcome would be more or less the same... right?"

"Would our opponents lose? Yes," answered the Storied Watcher, as she led them out into the street. "Would many *more* of them die? Yes – and I would avoid that; because though blood be shed, better the less of it, than the more. And you are not quite correct, Otis Boat-man; from what I know, the army that answers to your 'President' can call upon *very* potent weapons, which the rest of you are not yet ready to safely defeat. Another reason, in other words, for us to find the information about where the children live, find the little-ones themselves, and then – may you pardon the slang – 'get the hell out of here, before the Army Boys come a-callin'. Did I do that right? Bob told me something similar, one time."

"A few more months down here, Karéin, and you'll pretty much fit right in," muttered Abruzzio.

"Except for the *teeth*, man," joked the third agent, as he strode alongside on the right-flank, his eyes still searching the surroundings for signs of straggling Bloods or Crips. "You gotta *do* something about them... you know?"

She flashed him a brief, malicious, fang-bedecked smile, then retorted, "You assume that I *want* to – uhh – 'fit in', Sylvia... the more time that I spend in this 'America' kingdom... the less is my motivation to stay."

Cautiously, the Storied Watcher stole behind an obstruction on the eastern-side of the street, momentarily vanished, then reappeared.

"There are more guns here," she grimly observed, "But I think that you might be better off avoiding them, none the less. Particularly *you*, Minn-ee. I think that some of those who lie here, were –"

"You don't have to *say* it, Karéin," interrupted a still visibly-upset Chu. "And yes... I'll go the other way, by that big pile of trash... I don't remember anyone having been firing from there... so, please God, there can't be anybody, uhh... lying around."

The alien-girl mutely nodded and stood in place as most of the rest of the group followed the team-leader's route, though Kaysten made the mistake of going with Boatman, Wolf and the *Mara* as they walked past the Storied Watcher.

Upon seeing the carnage that Chu's almost-inerrant target-shooting had inflicted, the Chief of Staff dashed to one side and emulated Chu's actions of a few minutes prior.

"Oh *God!*" he gasped, trying to wipe his mouth on a sort-of-clean piece of nearby newspaper. "I *knew* this stuff was, uhh, *ugly*... but... was that just a pistol-bullet, that did *that*?"

Gravely, the Storied Watcher again confirmed with a nod.

"You see, Jerr-ee," she quietly stated, "That it takes not take one of *my* ilk, to quickly snuff out human life. I take some solace from the fact that most of my victims' suffering is over with, before they have time to fear, or scream... *most* of them, that is."

"We don't have lightening-bolts to disintegrate people with," grunted the big, African-American agent. "We gotta do it the 'old-fashioned way'."

"*Wait* a while, Otis," counseled the alien-girl. "Maybe something just as terrible – or worse – will shortly come to you."

"Can't *wait*," he unenthusiastically answered.

"What the *matter*, *muchacho*?" sneered the Latino gangster. "You ain't never seen no *cuerpo muerto*? Come on down where I live, *seguro*... you get enough to last you a lifetime."

"*Sure*," bluffed Kaysten. "*Lots* of 'em. On TV."

As the *Mara* held his fist to his mouth to avoid a probably impolitic guffaw, the bounty-hunter spoke up.

"Well – nothin' quite beats bein' there in person... *does* it?" he commented. "At least *these* boys ain't been lyin' there too long... come back in a few days, if you want a *real* treat."

The Chief of Staff sarcastically replied, "Thanks for the tip," as Wolf and Sebastiàn shared a rare, half-in-contempt wink and grin.

"Trouble him not, nor Minn-ee," ordered the Storied Watcher. "I bring death in ways that you cannot comprehend, and I have done so over ages untold; but *always* – and ever – does it grieve me. Kill if you must – but do not shame yourselves, by believing the demise of any thinking being, to be a trivial thing."

"Yeah, okay – I *get* it," muttered the bounty-hunter. "I was just tryin' to say that –" he was about to argue; but, in the next second, to the shock and dismay of all around, the alien-girl's eyes rolled; she let out a sickening, agonized moan, and then crumpled to the ground, as if suffering a crippling body-blow.

"*Karéin!*" shouted Misha in alarm.

Trying to help, he rushed toward the convulsing, apparently helpless Karéin-Mayréij, as did several of the others in the near vicinity; but this effort was frustrated by the appearance of the alien's accoutrement of arms and armor, which quickly covered her frame as had been the case earlier, in the hotel-room.

But they could still see her sweating, pain-lined face, which was a portrait of despair. The alien's fanged teeth were locked in a ghoulish-looking grimace, and tears poured from her intermittently-flickering eyes, while she tried – mostly unsuccessfully – to force out a pleading word or two.

"Wha' the fuck's goin' *on* with *chica*?" demanded a perplexed Sebastiàn. "Look like she took a round in the gut!"

"Might be they got to another one of her *amigos*," explained Wolf. "Maybe even *smoked* one of 'em... judgin' by how she's doin' there."

He crouched down, as close as he dared to get to the war-children.

"Karéin," he whispered, as compassionately as he could, "We *know* what yer dealin' with – hurts just to *look* at you. There anythin' we can do?"

But the alien-girl just continued shuddering and gasping in pain.

"We've *got* to try to help her!" exclaimed a worried Abruzzio. "This looks really *serious!*"

"What would you suggest, Sylvia?" argued Ramirez. "We know very little about her physiology... remember? Even if we *could* get close to her, we might just make things worse."

The Storied Watcher rolled over on her side and began to cough up blood-tainted saliva, which sizzled and hissed as it contacted the pavement.

"*Wow,*" offered Boatman. "No point on tryin' a bandage, even if she had a wound... just melt, the next second. Not the easiest patient... *that's* for sure."

Chu, trying all the while to avoid showing undue emotion, stared in alarm.

"Well – *you're* the scientist, Ms. Abruzzio," she demanded, "*Surely* you can think of something? Are we just going to stand around and let her *suffer?*"

"What you *want* her to do, Minnie?" interjected Hendricks. "We don't even know what's wrong with her!"

After pondering for a few seconds, Abruzzio again spoke up.

"You're right about *that*," she commented, "But we can find out."

Steeling herself against the infernal heat of *Vîrya Ahn'jë* – as she knew she previously could not have – the scientist knelt and placed both hands on the shield, which had assumed its normal position on top of the armor.

Abruzzio – with closed eyes – repeated her side of the conversation out loud.

"Daughter Tornado-Diamond-Curtain – it's Auntie Sylvia," she mumbled, as if in a trance. "It's about Mommy... her friends and I – we're concerned – we're *afraid*... I know, I *know*, honey, they're *bad* dumb-ass people who did this to her... oh thank God – *all* of you are? But she's not getting better... yes, of *course* I will... I've never done this, it's scary for me... no, no, I didn't mean – okay... I won't fight... go... ahead..."

Apparently unconscious in the next instant, the scientist slumped forward, her head and hands resting on the shield, the rest of her body perilously close to the flames of *Vîrya Ahn'jë*.

"*Sylvia!*" shouted an alarmed Ramirez, but as he approached, a strange look appeared on his face.

"I think... I think she's trying to help," he mentioned, to the others.

"What do you *mean*... 'help'?" incredulously countered Kaysten. "It looks like your scientist-friend just *passed* out! I'll help you pull her free... as long as Little Miss Buzz-Saw Shield doesn't slice me in half, in so doing."

Several of them expected a reaction from *Vîrya I'ëà'b*'; but there was none.

For a few seconds, there was silence, but then – unexpectedly – they saw Chu removing her jacket and pistol-holster.

"Minnie," uneasily asked Boatman, "What you fixin' to do?"

"Make a fool out of myself – get myself killed – turned into a zombie, or... maybe, help someone who I really *care* for," replied the FBI team-leader.

"Oh, wait a *minute* there, girl, you ain't gonna –" protested Boatman.

But he was too late.

Chu had joined Abruzzio, placing her hands on the shield, just next to those of the scientist. A second later, she swooned, idle strands of her hair smoking and melting as they contacted *Vîrya Ahn'jë's* burning scales.

Confused, 'what-to-do-next' glances went from one more-than-human to another.

Eventually, Hendricks, doffing his own jacket and gun to Boatman's obvious dismay, also got down on his knees, taking the one remaining place by the alien's side.

"Three girls and one guy," he cracked, weakly. "Chance of a *lifetime*, man!"

Upon contact with *Vîrya I'ëà'b'*, he – too – fell apparently unconscious, his head forming a trio with those of Chu and Abruzzio, upon the top of the shield.

A sad-faced Misha regarded the scene.

"I am not much given to hope," he pointed out, as he took a sitting-place on nearby piece of concrete-barrier. "But perhaps in this case, I will make an exception."

"So what we do *now?*" asked Kaysten. "There goes half of our firepower, as well as our only half-safe way out of this rat-hole."

"More like ninety-nine per cent, pardner," corrected the bounty-hunter, taking his own place on the sidewalk. "I guess we wait... unless you got somethin' a hell of a lot *better* to do."

They noticed that the *Mara* had been edging further and further away from the still-agonized body of the Storied Watcher and its somnolent hangers-on.

"Yo!" called Boatman. "Where you think you're goin'?"

"What's it to *you*, Mister FBI-Man?" shot back the ex-gangster. "Just checkin' out the *barrio*. Maybe them *putos* back there drop a *primo* or somethin'. Ain't had none in two days, *hombre* – got to keep me fresh... *comprende?*"

"Well... you oughtn't be," argued the big black man. "Just gonna bring on more of them Crips or Bloods – and we're short of Minnie, Will and Little Miss H-Bomb here. We can't *afford* another shoot-out."

"*¿Y que?*" sneered Sebastiàn. "I don' answer to you! If I want to, I can just walk off, set up as *el jéfé*... anywhere I pick, down here. *¿Lo sabe usted?*"

"Yeah," wearily confirmed Wolf, "But you ain't *gonna*."

"*¿Por que piensas este*, Mister bounty-hunter?" replied the *Mara*.

"Same reason *I* ain't," offered the big, long-haired man. "Because this here is the fuckin' best thing that ever *happened* to you, *hombre*... and, more to the point," he said, leaning back with a far-off look, "Because... you *can't*. Because you're *hooked* on her" – he pointed to figure of Karéin-Mayréij, which seemed, mercifully, to have stopped its spasms – "And because, just like the rest of us... you can't *get* enough. *That's* why."

"You don' know that," countered Sebastiàn. "I can leave *any* time. *Quiere verme hacerlo?*"

"Be my guest," answered Wolf, with a half-smile and a hand-wave.

The ex-gangster stood there for a moment or two, then turned and began to slowly walk back in the direction of the hidden bus.

"*Listen* – you all shouldn't have done that," whispered Boatman. "Ain't you never heard, 'better inside the tent, pissin' out, than outside, pissin' in –'"

"*Peace*," smiled the bounty-hunter, with a yawn, as Sebastiàn was almost out of sight. "Everythin's goin' according to plan."

He looked down at the Storied Watcher.

"'Cept... maybe, for *her*," he admitted.

The *Mara* was now totally out of sight.

"One of us needs to go after that guy – talk some sense into him," proposed a worried Boatman. "Hey, Mr. Russian – he don't like me, but maybe he'd let you talk to –"

Boatman noticed that all eyes were trained on the entrance to the alleyway.

"Welcome back," called the bounty-hunter, in the direction of the re-emergent Sebastiàn, as he slowly stepped out of the alley.

There was a strange, yet somehow familiar, look on the *Mara*'s face, as, dragging his feet, he shuffled back to confront the group.

"*Bueno*," he mumbled, with a shrug. "Maybe I hang around... just to keep an eye on *todo el mundo... ustedes saben*? You *muchachos* don' know your way 'round, down here – somebody got to keep your asses clean... *verdad?*"

"Right," lazily offered Wolf.

"An' you know what?" he added.

"What?" replied Sebastiàn.

"You made the right decision there... all by *yourself*, pardner," said the bounty-hunter.

Whitney's Talent

Tanaka – sprinting like a gazelle – had been the first to arrive at the scene, but only because Claremont had ordered her daughter not to fly ahead into unknown territory. Only a few seconds behind the Eurasian-American scientist and Melissa, came the rest of them, with Billings carrying Elissha.

They found a kneeling Brent Boyd, his head slumped, as if in mourning.

He looked up at them; and even in the infra-red, the despair on his face was as plain as day.

"I think... we've... *lost* him," a despairing Boyd quietly remarked. "Last ten seconds, I haven't felt a pulse. Tried CPR... *nothing*."

"*Sam!*" cried Tanaka, as she rushed to the blood-splattered, gun-victim's side and began to smother Jacobson's body with her alien-power.

Her psycho-musical song reverberated to and fro.

"Please, Sam, come *on*, you're okay – *speak* to me, Sam, for the love of God!" she wailed, while holding his shoulders and shooting purplish-yellow-white charges of *Amaiish* into his motionless body.

After three or four seconds, the woman slumped across him, soaking his face and neck with tears, while her shirt was itself stained by the blood welling from his wound.

"I can't... I can't reach his mind," she sobbed. "It's all... *black!*"

The professor howled with a sadness that none had ever seen, as White, his own eyes watering, tried to console her.

"Should have taken that round *myself!*" he spat. "Should have been a half-second faster – should have fuckin' *wasted all* of them, ahead of time!"

The African-American ex-astronaut stood up and faced away.

"Fuck!" he screamed, to the darkness beyond.

"*Nooooo*," whimpered Billings, down on one knee. "Don't *do* this to us, Jacobson you damn decent bastard – you've got places to go – people to rescue, yet. That's an *order*, man!"

The little girl started to cry; but other than for this and for Tanaka's own, grief-stricken sobs, there was silence.

"Somebody *do* something, for Christ's sake!" desperately shouted Billings.

"What do you *want* us to do, Bob?" wearily retorted Boyd. "Mushroom-shot frag-grenade like that would have insta-killed a *normal* man – or you, or me – outright... problably blow either of us, right in half. The big guy lasted a minute or so longer, but... unless you've got an emergency operating-room handy... face it, Bob, if even the *Professor* can't bring him back –"

Somehow – without a sound – Boyd was interrupted by Claremont, who was advancing toward Jacobson's body with a strange, glassy, far-off look.

She tapped Tanaka on the shoulder, bidding the scientist to get up.

"Momma want y'all to stand aside," solemnly announced Melissa. "She gonna say a prayer."

"Is that *all*? Is that all we're going to *do*?" pleaded Billings.

"I... think... maybe y'all better do what she's askin'," suggested White.

"Yeah, okay... fine... *not* fine," muttered the salesman, as he sat down and silently looked away from the terrible scene, so they could not see the wet despair in his eyes.

Now Claremont – with a clearly-visible, silver-white glow in her eyes – knelt beside Jacobson's body. She put her palms together, prayer-style, and, staring off into space, her lips began to noiselessly form words whose meaning none around, could discern.

From everywhere and nowhere, a new song – its ethereal chords somewhere between *Kumbaya* and another, gentle, dignified, but unknown melody – played through the psyches of the dispirited, overwhelmed group.

Claremont – her mute voice still repeating some kind of indecipherable psalm – laid her hands on Jacobson's torso.

Immediately, she winced in apparent pain, with sweat breaking out on her brow and tears tracking across her cheeks.

"*Momma!*" called an alarmed Curtis.

He started towards her, but was quickly restrained by White.

"Son," he quietly explained, "Your Momma's doin' *God's* work, now. If y'all want to help her, best way's to bow your head and ask the Lord to send an angel or two down here... y'all understand?"

"Yes, sir – ah will," answered the little boy, with utmost seriousness.

Several of the rest did the same, but alarm invaded their minds, when they observed and heard what came next – the black woman, her sweat-drenched body wobbling precariously, her breathing pained and short – began to bleed from almost the same area as where Jacobson had been struck.

"Momma givin' up her *life!*" cried Melissa. "Somebody make her *stop*, please! *Please!*"

"Come here, child," demanded White.

The panicked teenager reluctantly complied.

"Melissa," counseled the ex-astronaut, "Whitney's doin' '*zactly* what the Lord wants her to – don't know how, but... I *know* that. Y'all gotta have *faith* that He knows what's best for her... and for us. Come and pray with Curtis 'n me, now."

Crying, Melissa joined hands with her brother and Devon White, the three of them forming a semi-circle, while the ex-astronaut – his head bowed – began to whisper a private invocation.

Tanaka – her eyes closed, her hands tightly clasped – again crouched beside Claremont and Jacobson's body, whispering, "I can't go where you're going, blessed woman – take *my* life, too, Whitney... of my own free will... take *all* of it... *take it...* "

Warm-glowing blood seemed to be issuing from every pore in Claremont's body, soaking both her clothes and Jacobson's body, in a strangely sweet-smelling – yet frightful – weirding-essence.

After two or three more fateful seconds, a loud, agonized groan came from Claremont's otherwise mute throat. Her eyes rolled and – apparently unconscious, or worse – she fell at a right-angle across Jacobson's trunk.

A split-second later, Tanaka fainted, falling sideways and only narrowly avoiding a concussion, thanks to Boyd's quick reflexes.

"Momma – *no!*" shrieked Melissa, dashing over to hold her mother close by.

A weak cough came from the mouth of Sam Jacobson, and he began to breathe, although almost imperceptibly. His wound – while still ugly-warm – looked like it had shrunk by at least a third.

"*Captain!*" joyfully shouted White. He did a double-take as – along with every other member of the party – he crowded around the three motionless bodies, Claremont's piled on top of that of the former Mars mission commander.

"Brent – help me get her off here," he demanded.

Billings handed Elissha to Curtis, and the boy held her in his arms, even though she was not far-off his own size.

The black ex-astronaut was immediately joined by his ex-Air Force compatriot and the salesman.

"Thank you Lord above – she's still got a pulse," breathed White. "Let's get her down here beside him. One – two – *three!*"

The men gently moved Claremont to a prone position between Jacobson and Tanaka.

"Man – even in *Um'nàhr'é*, all three of them are *horribly* pale," offered a mentally-exhausted, but elated, Boyd.

"But... *alive!*" countered Billings.

Not caring that they could hear the passion in his voice, as he took back the little girl, he added, "*Alive.* God *bless* you, Whitney Claremont! The *greatest* power of them all – *that's* what she gave you!"

"No doubt 'bout *that*, Bob my man," confirmed White, as he tried to make the victims as comfortable as possible. "No doubt at *all.*"

He stopped for a second, then mentioned, "But... I'm not sure it was... *her*, that done give it to Whitney. Just a feelin'... y'all know?"

"Yeah, well... I can understand how you might say that," allowed the salesman, with a knowing-nod.

White turned to look at Curtis and Melissa.

"Y'all got a *very* brave Momma," he commented. "She was ready to do it... all the way, give her *life* for the Captain, I mean... y'all *know* that... right?"

"Yes sir – ah does," answered Curtis. "But weren't her time to go up to heaven. That's what ah thinks that th' Lord be sayin', when ah talkin' wid Him, Mista Devon."

"Me too," echoed Melissa. "Ain't the *first* time that Momma risk her life for somebody else. Ah just hope 'n pray that it's the last."

"I wouldn't bet any money that you don't want to *lose*, honey," muttered Billings. "But for the record... can it just be somebody *other* than Whitney, next time? Even, *me.* As long as *she* gets out... along with the two of you, and Tommy... I won't complain."

"Don' talk that way, Mista Bob... we's *all* gettin' out. *Together!*" firmly contradicted the teenager.

The salesman permitted himself a weak chuckle.

"Okay – we'll do it *your* way, then, Melissa," he replied. "*Promise?*"

"*Promise!*" replied the two children, in unison.

"I got heads and feet elevated, via spare clothes," remarked Boyd. "Though it's pretty pathetic treatment, compared to what we've just witnessed. Pulses and breathing all seem to be okay, of course the Commander's is the weakest... but I'm not complaining about that."

"So what we do now?" requested Billings. "Not to run down anybody else's reputation, but... let's *face* it, guys, without the help of two of those three stretched out on the floor – particularly the good Professor – we're sitting-ducks down here, the next time we run into the GrayWar-goons. I'm no medical-expert, but something tells me that it probably isn't a great idea to move them."

"Well then... that makes it easy, Bob," offered the black ex-astronaut.

"What you mean?" inquired the salesman.

"We *wait*," proposed White.

"Just... *wait*?" pressed Billings. "That doesn't sound like much of a *strategy*, if you don't mind my saying so."

"Got a better one, Bob?" said Boyd.

"Yeah," answered the salesman.

"No... what would *that* be?" wearily inquired the black ex-astronaut.

"Deck of cards," explained Billings, with a wicked grin. "Lifted it out of that conference-room, back above. Poker in the dark, anyone?"

White, his mind exhausted from the stress of recent events, laughed altogether too loudly.

"Yo... I'm 'in'!" he said.

So Near... Yet So Far

"I'm glad you finally found that switch on the far wall," remarked Billings. "Even if it *is* still a bit dim down here, with half the lights being out – or on low power – or whatever. Poker's just not the *same* when you gotta look at the cards in that weirdo 'more-than-red' stuff – I can hardly tell a king from a queen!"

"Ain't *my* fault that y'all thought y'all had a royal flush when y'all didn't, Bob my man," crowed White. "Besides... I made me twenty bucks on that hand."

"Only if you live to *collect* on it," grumbled the salesman.

"Always a 'catch' to things," muttered White. "Just somethin' else I can't cash in, when I cash out myself, don't y'all know."

"Good – because I'm 'out'," announced Billings. "*Would*'ve done better if I didn't have to play all that time in the dark. I'm becoming personally acquainted with every deuce and three in the deck... time to try something else, I think."

"Well... we must have been at this for an hour and a half – maybe two – by now," said Boyd. "I need to stretch my legs – think I'll do another check of those doors on the upper-level... see if I can secure 'em better."

He yawned and got up, grabbing his rifle in the process.

The ex-pilot cast a glance over to the pile of storage-boxes that his 'gift' had pock-marked and charred, just before Jacobson's unfortunate ambush.

"No action over there," he observed, looking at the heavily-bound, gagged smock-men, who were tied together, just in front of a crate.

"*Wise* move on their part," he added, menacingly.

"Doubt they's much value in the way of bein' hostages," indifferently offered White. "I'd have wasted 'em and be done with the whole damn thing – 'cept that it should be the *Captain*, who gets the fun of pullin' the trigger."

"Yeah," concurred the other ex-astronaut.

"Any more signs of life from our three hospital-patients, there?" called Billings to Melissa, who had parked herself right next to her mother, Jacobson and Tanaka. "And the little one – what about her?"

"They's breathin' a lot better, Mista Billins," replied the teenager. "But that's 'bout it. Y'all know... Momma always used to tell Curtis 'n me, 'somebody hurt, y'all just let them sleep and let th' Lawd take his time healin' 'em up'... so that's what ah'm doin'. Elissha' sleepin' like a baby, after y'all give her that fruit-bowl from th' machine."

"That's good – because I got quite a headache usin' my tele-stuff to pull the lock off of it," complained White. "And all y'all left me, was that foam-cake thang with the whipped-cream inside... and it was *stale*, too."

"I'd *kill* for a coffee," grumbled Billings. "Why'd the buggers drink all the Hi-Test Cola and leave just fruit-punch, for us? Just another set-up, I bet."

"Speaking of set-ups and plans – Melissa's got as good a one as any currently available to us," ruefully noted Boyd. "Although I got to admit, I'm becoming more nervous about this whole situation, minute by minute... I mean, it's great that we've been able to rest for a bit – get something to eat and drink – bathroom-break, *et cetera*... but tactically, I'm really starting to wonder why we haven't encountered more, uhh, 'resistance', by now."

"No surprise there – 'least from the way we came," commented White, as he also slowly stood up. "I'm pretty sure I froze up everythin' back there well enough to keep the water out, for a while – second time I went back to shore it up, I filled half that damn *room* with the cold-stuff, after all – so they ain't comin' from *that* direction, unless they got scuba-gear... even *then*, they're prolly in for quite a surprise, when they get anywhere near that electro-walkway. As for the other directions, your guess is as good as mine, Brent my man... I'd go recce out past that door leadin' to the corridor, the one with the big iron-wall... but I don't think it's a good idea to run into any more of them GrayWar-pussies, until we get the Professor, the Captain and Whitney back."

"Problem *is*," remarked Billings, "We have no idea *whatsoever* how long that might *be* – another hour, another day, a week... our friendly local Gestapo-ypes are *bound* to come knocking in less time – I'd bet you good money on that. It might be a good idea to do a little looking-around... if only to find this secret back-door that Jacobson's map spoke of."

"Yeah... but it's not a great idea for just one person to go off without any back-up – and if, say, you and I go, that just leaves Devon to cover our whole home-base," argued Boyd. "If, all of a sudden, they show up –"

"That ain't *true*, Major Brent!" interrupted a boyish, over-confident voice. "Mista Devon still got me 'n Melissa to cover our homies. Ah be shoutin' them down *real* good – an' she can drop stuff on they haids."

"Laws *sakes*, Curtis!" groaned the teenager. "Don' y'all 'member what Momma say 'bout such thangs?"

Boyd smiled broadly, a gesture that was mimicked by his fellow-astronaut.

He crouched so as to be more or less able to address the boy, face-to-face.

"Listen, Curtis," counseled the ex-astronaut, "Let me explain something to you – a military-concept, that is. You ever heard of a 'special reserve-force'?"

"Oh... *sure* ah have, Mista Brent," answered the boy.

"So can you tell me what that is?" teased Boyd.

"It's... it's – why don' y'all tell me *yo'* idea of it, so ah can be sure y'all ain't got it wrong?" prevaricated Curtis.

"Oh... *absolutely*," gently replied Boyd, with a grin. "Now the concept is, to have kind of a 'secret-weapon' – something that the enemy doesn't know about, or they think you don't have at your disposal – and you always keep it back at home-base, and you never commit it to normal combat... except when something really *bad* happens, and you've got your back against the wall. It's kind of a really nasty surprise for the enemy – to set them back one when they think that they've 'got you'... you with me so far?"

The boy nodded vigorously.

"Okay," continued the ex-astronaut. "So that's more or less the role that I'd like you and Melissa to play for our group... and your Mom too, when she comes around. Devon, Bob... do you approve of this tactical-arrangement?"

"Was gonna suggest the same thing – but y'all beat me to it," smiled White.

"Good idea," added Billings, trying to sound authentic. "As long as it doesn't involve him doing any tests of his own little – uhh – 'secret-weapon'."

"But, Major Brent," countered Curtis, "What 'zactly we s'posed to *do*, while we's this 'reserve-force' thang? Jus' sit here, waitin' for them bad-guys?"

"No – not at *all*," hastily explained Boyd. "We need you and your sister, on recce. Stay clear of these electro-traps that we've marked with the spare computer-cables and scout out this entire area – look for hidden-entrances or -exits and check out where there might be good firing-positions. As you do your rounds, take note of anything that's changed, from the last time when you did it. When you've done a few passes – say, once every twenty minutes or so – then come back to Major White, Bob and myself, with a plan for how we should defend this place, if and when we're attacked. Just make sure that you don't leave the Captain, the Professor, your mother and Elissha, for too long. Think you can do that?"

"Shore *can!*" eagerly responded the boy, giving a mock-salute.

"Then get *going*, soldier!" commanded the ex-astronaut.

"Yes *sir!*" exclaimed Curtis.

He rapidly walked over to Melissa.

"Come on!" he demanded. "We gots *work* to do!"

"*Mercy*," complained the teenager, rolling her eyes, "Okay, *okay*... ah's comin... but y'all ain't givn' me none of them *orders* – y'all hear? Or when she wake up, ah'm tellin' Momma, an'..."

"Just point them in the right direction," cackled the salesman, as the boy pulled his unenthusiastic-looking sister toward the periphery of the big, wide-open-area.

"Actually... it's not a bad idea for us to do, either," suggested Boyd. "Since the external-recce thing's probably not practical until the others are at least awake – and for the record, I'd prefer to wait until they're combat-ready – we might as well see if we can get any useful information out of the data-systems down here. Like, for example... these three humongous metal-boxes, down with us on the floor – wonder what *they're* all about..."

He stared off into space, with a surprised expression.

"Somethin' eatin' y'all, bro'?" inquired White.

"Oh, it's... uhh... *nothing*," replied Boyd. "Must have been my imagination."

"Imaginary things have had a habit of coming true, since last I hitched up with Sari," countered the salesman. "What were you thinking about, Major?"

"I had a fleeting image of a little boy calling to me... he was shouting, banging his fists on a glass-wall... or something," said the ex-astronaut. "But..."

"But... *what*?" pressed Billings.

"Of course there's no objective way to assess any of this," explained Boyd. "Though I'm trying to compare the characteristics of what I felt there, with the thought-images that the Professor and I saw back in our original Air Force holding-facility... as well as with what I felt upon encountering yourself, Whitney and Melissa – there's something that doesn't match."

"Doesn't... 'match'?" asked the salesman.

"It's like a picture that's partly out-of-focus, when you know that it should be easy to see... some of it looks like it's right in front of you, but the rest of it is crazily far-away... out of perspective. That's the only way how I can describe it," elaborated the ex-astronaut.

"Somethin' tells me, might be *heavy*," offered White, with a serious tone.

He closed his eyes.

"Karéin," he said, looking away, "If y'all listenin', lady – which I realize y'all probably ain't, probably got more important things to do, like maybe savin' some other planet or such – but on the off chance that y'all *are*... well – help us figure all this out..."

His brow furrowed and White twitched involuntarily, as if beset by an unrequited thought of his own.

"*Damn!*" complained the black ex-astronaut. "Felt like I was *gettin'* somethin' there, for a second. Then it cut out. But..."

"I'm repeating myself," mentioned Billings, "But... what?"

White stared at Boyd.

"Y'all thinkin' what I am, bro'?" he plaintively observed.

"*Gotta* be!" confirmed the other ex-astronaut. "Feeling it in my *bones*."

"Holy *crap!*" interjected a thunderstruck Billings. "*Now* I get it! Where the hell *is* he?"

White's gaze caught one of the big, metal-clad boxes. "Pick one, Bob."

The salesman did a double-take, then protested, "Look, guys – I'd *love* to believe this... but come on, how the hell could we have been camping out here, right *next* to him, and not have the slightest idea that –"

"That's the point," noted Boyd. "Why didn't we figure it out before? Because we just *did*, a second ago."

"Why didn't they invent the wheel, before they did, Bob?" added White.

"Wait a minute – *wait* a minute, folks!" argued the salesman. "We're doing this completely on one of these mumbo-jumbo 'visions' that – okay, I'll admit – have mostly been accurate... but, for example, when you 'sensed' the presence of Whitney and Melissa, it was *easy* to see them in there... in the room, I mean. We've been going back and forth between these damn boxes for over an *hour* – maybe two – and there's been nothing of the sort. What makes you think that he's here, as opposed to in some other rat-hole in or out of this prison?"

"Man's got a *point*," allowed White. "We better check out these honkin' big boxes, and sooner rather than later."

"A fine idea," said Billings. "And how'd we do *that*?"

"Ahh – I wish we had the Professor here with us," murmured Boyd. "No doubt she'd have a better plan, but... okay. Here *goes*."

He went up to the box nearest to them and extended a fist, as if to knock on it, but quickly withdrew his hand.

"Bloody thing's charged like a trap – see?" warned Boyd, as he nonchalantly brought his hand close to the container and drew an otherwise-lethal bolt of electricity harmlessly into his body.

"Boyd – you're really going to have to teach me how to *do* that, one of these days," muttered the salesman.

"Even so... I'd prefer not to knock," answered the ex-astronaut. "If there's a human in there, who happens to be in contact with the outside surface..."

"Yeah... I get you," agreed Billings.

He cupped his hands and began to shout.

"Tommy! Tommy! TOMMY!" called the salesman. "*Answer* me, kid!"

There was no reply, except from the voice of Curtis Claremont, who had somehow – probably, courtesy of a free ride from his sister – managed to infiltrate the viewing-balcony.

"Yo, Mista Billins'!" excitedly exclaimed the boy. "Y'all find mah homie? He okay?"

"Don't know," answered Billings. "We think he might be in one of these big boxes, but don't you get anywhere *near* them – they're hotter than a high-tension-tower. We'll let you know if we get a message from him."

"Y'all *sure* ah cain't help, Mista Billins'?" pressed Curtis. "Tommy 'n me, we *tight!*"

"So are we all, son... so are we all," quietly responded the salesman. "Keep doing what Major Boyd asked you to do... I'll keep you up to date."

"Yessir," acknowledged a disappointed Curtis.

The boy vanished behind a row of chairs, discussing something with his sister, in so doing.

"Could be one of these other two," offered White.

He rapidly paced to the second of the boxes.

"Yo, *Tommy!*" he shouted. "Y'all *in* there?"

There was no reply here, either.

"One more to go," noted Boyd, advancing to the third box, while skirting the electrical-traps in its vicinity.

"*Tommy!*" he called. "Tommy George! You have friends outside – we're here to let you out! Answer, please!"

Boyd turned his head and listened intently; but no sound, not so much as a pip's-worth, came to his ears.

"Effin' *great!*" he muttered. "And just by getting *near* it, I can tell that this one's rigged as nastily as the first one... I'd have to assume that the box you checked out, Devon, it's the same way. Any bright ideas, guys?"

"Don't associate me with anything 'bright'... you'll ruin my *reputation*," quipped Billings, trying to lighten the mood. "But... if there really *is* anybody – Tommy or some *other* poor bugger – inside one or more of these boxes... there'd have to be some way for the assholes running this place, to communicate with him... wouldn't there? If only to hear the kid's screams, I mean. I didn't see any doors on any of the boxes – maybe they're hidden or something – but it could be some kind of closed-circuit thing... right?"

"Bingo," confirmed White. "Problem is... there's consoles and terminals all *over* the place – we got no idea which one patches in to what box. And don't forget – we hit the wrong button, we might be givin' them GrayWar-pussies a front-row-seat about what's goin' down... *if*, that is, they ain't lookin' in already."

"What about blowing a hole in one of these boxes?" suggested the salesman. "That scary light-show thing that you fired at the buggers over by the pile of crates – the one that just about blinded me from a hundred feet away – maybe you could zap a hole right through?"

"That's a *great* idea, Bob!" sarcastically commented Boyd. "The operative phrase here is, 'right through'... though my light-weapon would probably just bounce off something that shiny and durable. Can we test the theory by having you stand behind a corner of one of the boxes, and then have me fire at that precise spot? If you end up with a few holes in your head, we'll know that my attack will be effective against the container."

"Uhh... *riight*," sheepishly admitted Billings. "I guess I *could* try my hiding-trick... it might deflect your attack... then again, it might not."

"What's the matter, Bob... y'all afraid of a few lil' ol' scientific-tests?" joked White. "And I *know* what y'all going to say next, but all I can do is ice it up... might give whoever's in there a bit of a chill – but I ain't gonna put so much as a dent in it, with my own little thing. No point tryin'."

"Listen... why don't you two just, uhh, rip the damn things apart, one by one?" demanded the salesman. "I mean – I've *seen* you using those telekin-whatever powers that she bestowed upon you... didn't you rip that door off its hinges – in the cistern – that is, just before we rescued young Mr. Claremont? And maybe doing that wouldn't set off the electro-trap... no physical contact, right?"

"Bob my man... I wish y'all could relate to what I'm about to say," countered White. "It ain't *nearly* so easy as it looks. Can't speak for my bro' here, but I can barely keep my own weight floatin' for a few seconds, before my head starts talkin' back and sayin' things y'all wouldn't want your Momma to hear. No *way* I could rip that amount of metal apart, without pushin' it so far that I'd pass out. Brent – y'all got anythin' to add to that?"

"Well it's true that I *did* pop a few bolts from the hinges of that door down there... so maybe I'm a bit further ahead in that department than Devon is," remarked Boyd, "But the thing with the telekinesis is, it seems to come and go... one minute, I feel like I could toss a battle-tank – the next, I'm straining to lift a coffee-table. Over time, it's becoming more consistent, but I honestly don't know... and the *Professor* did most of the 'heavy-lifting' with the door... which, you will recall, is why we had her catching people as they dove off the ledge –"

"Don't *remind* me of that!" complained Billings.

"Okay... *almost* catching people," corrected the ex-astronaut. "But it's *extremely* unlikely that even Devon and I – working together – could inflict enough damage on any of these containers so as to free whomever's inside. I doubt that we could do it even with both Tanaka and the Captain helping. And it might *still* set off the trap that we know about – not to mention others that we might not yet have discovered. You understand where I'm coming from?"

"Yeah," muttered Billings.

Dejectedly, he pulled up a chair and sat on it, one leg over the other.

"It's just that if your 'vision' was right, it's so effing *unfair* that we're so *close* to the poor kid... and there's nothing we can do to free him – or even communicate with him," argued the frustrated salesman. "I – I've got a few things that I need to *say...*"

The two ex-astronauts did not need any alien-skills to read the sorrow and guilt in Billings' voice.

"Look, bro'," proposed White, in Boyd's direction, "Y'all probably right about the risks, but Bob's got a point, too... there's a pretty big risk that if we fuck around with these console-controls, 'specially without us spendin' some quality-time figurin' out what does what – we'd just set the Man back on our trails. I'd be willin' to try the old 'mind-pull' thing on these boxes, 'long as we have a little side-deal that if anything *strange* starts happenin', we turn it off, ASAP. What y'all say?"

"Yeah," wearily concurred the other man. "We gotta do *something*, I suppose."

Straightening himself and summoning the power within, he strode over to stand beside White.

"Three-count?" asked Boyd.

"Three," confirmed the black ex-astronaut.

"Two," answered his former Mars mission partner.

"One," counted White.

"*Go!*" forcefully called both, together.

Now the *Fire* of two energized, more-than-human minds, latched on to the immense container, sending a trickle of electrified-feedback as White and Boyd tried, as best they could, to pull in different directions.

The box shuddered a bit, but showed not the slightest sign of damage.

The two ex-astronauts continued for another three or four seconds; then, both of them slumped backward with mental exhaustion on their faces.

"*Shit!*" gasped White. "Y'all damn *strong* there, man! For a while I thought y'all 'bout to pull *me* apart – not that honkin' big box."

"Uhh... sorry!" apologized Boyd. "It's kind of like an arm-wrestle, I guess... except that you don't have any idea if you're up against a school-kid, or a gorilla, until you try it... if it's any consolation, Tanaka would have had *me* screaming for mercy, one second after starting. Ready to try the next one?"

"No – but let's do it anyways... get this shit over with," muttered the black ex-astronaut, as he shuffled over to the container at which Boyd had shouted, some time before.

"Three... two... one... *go!*" counted White.

Sweat broke out on more-than-human brows; but again, there was no visible damage.

"Sorta gettin' the hang of it," indicated White. "Trick is to push *off* of y'all, not *against* y'all... if *that* makes any sense."

"There's probably some funky word for how you do that, in *Makailkh,*" commented Boyd, "But it escapes me right now."

"Mak-whaa?" inquired a confused Billings. "By the way... I'd help you guys if I could... I really *would*, you know. Especially how it looks – uhh – *intense* – what you're doing, I mean."

"Thanks for the moral support there, Bob," grunted White.

"*Makailkh*", explained Boyd. "It's the Storied Watcher's native language, or – at least – *one* of her languages. She sort of taught it to me while we were all on the *Eagle*, while we were on the way back from Mars –"

"Wow," interrupted the impressed salesman. "That must be quite some accomplishment, being the first human to learn an alien language... I can hardly speak *American*, after all."

Boyd – his face showing fatigue – propped up his torso with palms on thighs, and chuckled resignedly.

"I wish I could claim to be some kind of linguistic-genius, Bob," he mentioned, "But how I learned it was, well... let's just say that's another story. I don't think that I could *speak* it... but somehow, when she would talk to me in *Makailkh*, I could understand every word – at least, when she wasn't describing concepts that have no equivalent meanings down here on Earth. Something that I fully intend to catch up on, if and when I ever get to see her in person, again."

"Yeah... may we live to see that day," intoned White. "One left, 'bro."

"Let's *do* it!" agreed Boyd, as the two sauntered over to the container near which they had been playing cards.

"I'll do the count," said White.

"Three... two... two and a half... two and a quarter..." he started, before paroxysms of laughter broke out.

"Well... if *y'all* had to do this shit, without no headache pills in sight, *y'all* would be playin' for time too, Bob," said the black ex-astronaut.

"That may be," replied the salesman, "But *I've* been playing for time, ever since those assholes in the black limo shanghai'ed me."

"S'pose y'all got a point there," offered the ex-astronaut. "Okay. Ready, Brent my man?"

Boyd wiped some sweat, nodded and looked up at the looming container.

"Three... two... one... *go!*" exclaimed White.

"Whoa... *whoa!*" immediately called the other man. "You *feel* that, Devon?" he half-shouted.

"*Damn* – yeah!" confirmed the black ex-astronaut. "Can't fuckin' lock *on*, at all! It's just like when I tried to grab Bob – when he took that swan-dive – back there in the cistern. What y'all think's goin' down here, bro'?"

"Don't know," reflectively commented Boyd. "But I've got an idea."

"Yeah, what?" asked White.

"Try icing it up – just a *bit* of it, say, right in the middle of the side wall there," requested the former Mars mission pilot.

"What if it sets off that third-rail-type trap?" argued a worried White.

"I'm betting it won't," answered the other ex-astronaut. "Because I don't think you can even *do* it."

"That sounds like a *dare*, y'all understand," noted White.

"Mind cluing me in on what's going on?" demanded Billings.

"Just a *theory*, Bob," evaded Boyd.

"Go ahead," he directed, pointing at the middle of the thing's flat, rectangular side.

"Okay," uneasily answered White.

With a deep, determined-looking stare and flashes of *Amaiish*-energy racing up and down his trunk, the African-American ex-astronaut held up a claw-mimicking hand and exclaimed, "*Sno-Kone!*"

A blast of brutally-cold air – accompanied by a hail of tiny ice-chips – flew backward at White, its billowing frost-cloud also enveloping the other two men.

But nary an icicle nor a snowball marked the side of the box.

"Now *that's, interestin'*," philosophically observed White. "*Thought* I had a lock on it – like, I *was* able to get my thing goin' – but somethin' slipped, I guess. But I must have gotten a good fix... because my attack still went off. Totally weird... y'all want me to try again?"

Boyd was about to reply, but then he again winced and braced himself.

"Sort of like the problem you had with, uhh, 'locking on' to me?" interrogated Billings. "What's *that* mean?"

"Owww-ohhh...," stuttered Boyd.

"Y'all *okay*, bro'?" exclaimed a worried White, as he rushed over to the other ex-astronaut.

"Clear, *clear,* picture – with some effing *uncomfortable* feelings along with it," explained Boyd, looking up and pointing up at the box. "From in there."

He shook his head and straightened up.

"I'm alright, I think," he added.

"You said you saw a picture," pressed Billings. "Of *what?* Or... *who?*"

"Kid looking at himself in a mirror," described Brent Boyd. "About eight or nine, I think... Hispanic... Jesus, the *wounds*... how can he even *stand up*..."

With no additional warning to anyone, Billings charged at the container, being thrown back on his posterior by a flash and shower of sparks, as – though apparently none the worse for wear for having attempted it – he collided with this bizarre, sinister, high-tech prison-cell.

"*Tommy!*" howled the salesman.

Boob, Tube and Rainbow

A good half-hour had passed, luckily without further gangster-encounters, by the time when, with no warning, Chu, Hendricks and Abruzzio all fell at once in reverse-motion, from their seance-like positions on top of *Vîrya I'ëà'b'*.

The FBI team-leader was only saved from a painful headache – or worse – by Boatman's quick sprint to avoid her head impacting with the pavement, while Ramirez – who had been parked right behind his fellow-scientist – taking observations and notes each ten minutes, broke Abruzzio's backward fall.

Hendricks touched *Vîrya Ahn'jë*, yelped in so doing and was fully awake before any further damage could be done.

Moans and groans came from all three.

"Damn... that was... *intense*..." muttered the third agent.

Chu tried to stand up, wisely gave up when confronted by wobbly-knees, then half-reclined on the pavement, searching for her jacket, which was helpfully supplied by the Russian.

There were tears in the woman's eyes.

"Will... Sylvia... brother and sister," she managed.

"Yeah," answered Hendricks. "Hell of a *perspective*... isn't it?"

"No *words* for it," commented a dazed, awed Abruzzio. "I could... I could *be* you. *Both* of you. As *you*... were *me*. Did you find it as thrilling... as *frightening*... as I did?"

"Fuckin' *ay*," confirmed the third agent. "And listen – I didn't *mean* to, but you know, when I wanted to find out – like, it's kind of one of those things that as a guy, you always wonder about... you know?"

"Don't worry about it, Will," offered Chu, with a weak smile. "So us women have no secrets from you, any more... well, so *what*... seems to me that when we're all in there, things work both ways... right?"

"Minnie..." started Boatman, "What you all *talkin'* 'bout? If you don't mind my askin', that is."

"It's kind of... uhh... *private*, if you know what I mean," evaded the FBI team-leader.

"The *hell* it is!" contradicted Abruzzio. "There were at least *four* people – okay, three ex-people and one alien, in on the whole thing – right, Minnie?"

"You're not counting 'Daughter Burning Mountain', 'Daughter Tornado Diamond-Curtain', 'Brother Ice-Fang' and so on," ruefully noted Chu. "By my count, that makes... six plus three... nine, uhh, 'minds', involved here."

"Ha!" offered Misha. "It seems that Karéin's war-children have received some of the 'education' that she strove to impress upon them. Though there would have been better ways in which to do this."

"And... you forgot... Grandmother Wise One..." half-whispered the still-weak voice of the Storied Watcher, to the joy and relief of everyone around. "Though... none... of it... is... new... to her..."

A malicious smile showed on Wolf's face.

"Now *there's* a threesome!" he joked. "Of course, that's probably not the right word – but I never learned what one you'd use for nine or ten at once."

"There... *is*... a... word," stated the Storied Watcher. "Trust me. But... your... imagination... runs wild, good... friend. Minn-ee, Sylvia and Will... they lent their... power... to help me... gather my... strength..."

The alien-girl tried to raise her head, but gave up on this venture, instead choosing again to recline.

Tears came to her eyes.

"Thank you," she softly spoke. "Thank you all, *so* much! I am... so... in your debt..."

Chu crawled over and addressed Karéin-Mayréij.

"We helped... didn't we?" she asked.

The Storied Watcher, painfully managing a semi-reclining position, answered, "Yes, you did, Minn-ee... you *did*. All of you. Even those who were, uhh, just 'standing around'. I felt your love... your support."

"Karéin," inquired Abruzzio, "I realize that this may not be the right time, but... exactly *how* did we – and your 'war-children' – assist you? I felt your mind, even though fighting off pain, guiding me... and there was another one as well... but it was mostly a jumble of bizarre shapes and ideas. Except for Will, Minnie and, uhh, the 'kids'... I had no idea if I was really helping or not."

"*All* beings have the force of life, Sylvia," explained the alien-girl. "The addition of others' can reinforce and empower one's own. For you and your brothers and sisters, I have unlocked the secret of how to pour the fullness of your life-force into someone else, in times of peril; but in fact, humans have been doing the same thing, indirectly, over many ages. When you 'wait upon' an ill or injured loved-one; when you stay in their presence just to be there... this, all by itself, lends a fraction of your life-force to theirs. Partly, it is why you feel 'drained' – 'exhausted' – upon leaving afterward, though this has never before been measured by humans... yet it has always been there."

The Storied Watcher bent forward and caressed her 'war-children'.

"And I owe all of ye blessed-ones," she quietly congratulated. "*Twice* now have ye saved thy Mother. Never can I repay – I love ye *so!*"

Rescue that would we Mother if would all die, if gladly so thee, came back a chorus of small voices; and this time, a few of these inscrutable words echoed in the minds of Abruzzio, Chu and Hendricks, as well.

Unsteadily at first, Karéin-Mayréij rose to her feet.

Then – taking deep breaths, staring forward with eyes whose glow waxed until they were painful to behold – she began to flex muscles and limbs, almost *Tai-Chi*-style.

The familiar, electricity-like charges of *Amaiish*-energy suffused her body, as the breeze carried her war-song hither and yon.

Ye Gods, thought Abruzzio.

Moments ago, I was touching minds with this being.

Or... with one of, this being.

Both of me, came back the inevitable reply.

I honor you, noble, more-than-mortal friend!

As the alien-girl cast her glance at *Vìrya Ahn'jë*, and in the next second, the war-children shot upward and vanished – although the shield tarried somewhat before she joined her siblings in their invisible hiding-place.

"Listen, Karéin," spoke Kaysten, "Mind if I ask you a question?"

The look of majesty slowly waned from the Storied Watcher's demeanor.

"Umm-hmm?" she replied.

"Not sure exactly how to say this," he continued, "But... well, I'm used to seeing you as a kind of 'unstoppable-force'... you know? So far, you've handled everything that's been thrown at you, with about as much trouble as a pro linebacker at a Pee-Wee game... but whatever happened there – that *really* knocked you for a loop. We were all very worried that you weren't going to come out of it at all. What the hell *happened* to you, anyway?"

"Oh, come *on*, Jerr-ee," she shot back. "As if you do not already know."

"No, I *don't*," he prevaricated.

The Storied Watcher sent a glance to Boatman.

"Otis," she asked, "Use your newly-given arts. Was that an answer in honesty-given?"

"What – you all mean, 'is he lyin' through his teeth'?" chuckled the big black man. "Well, the answer's 'yes', of course... but I didn't have to use no fancy-dancy alien-stuff to be sure of it."

"Skills of Ho-Mo Say-piens – skills of the *Makailkh* – ever the truth is the same," muttered the alien-girl. "But if I *must* spell it out, Jerr-ee Kay-sten of the Empire of United States, what afflicted me a few moments ago was a wound – and a very bad one, at that; though, Gods be praised, I think not a fatal-one – suffered by a person who I dearly love, probably due to torment inflicted by others within your government. Each time, I recover... but I remember the pain. A long account, is being thus built up! And I intend that every last coin of it *will* be paid, by those responsible."

"This is probably poor consolation," offered Misha, "But at least it is proof that those in the 'Billings' party *are* still alive... does it not?"

"I do not know," replied Karéin-Mayréij, with a far-off stare into nowhere. "This one did not feel like Bob... or Tommy... it was... someone *else*. But it *was* still a dear friend... of *that*, I am unfortunately sure."

She turned to address Kaysten, again.

"So, Jerr-ee," requested the Storied Watcher, "Should you exercise the option to go back to, ahh, 'where you belong'...would you tell your President, on my behalf, that his little weapon of punishing me – through the torment of my loved-ones – has worked quite well? It will not prevent him from eventually being reduced to atoms; but it *has* certainly left me gasping and rolling in agony... as a warrior, I must congratulate him on the ingenuity of finding this one weak-spot in my defenses."

The Chief of Staff came up rather too close to the alien-girl for comfort.

Being much taller, he had to bend over to make his point.

"Look, Karéin," he defended, more expressively than normal, "It hasn't been my style to apologize for the behavior of my government, and I'm not going to start now – you talk about going back on *your* principles being 'shameful'; well, if I was going to start bad-mouthing the man to whom I've devoted my entire *career*, that'd be about the same thing... wouldn't it? All the same, I want you to know that none of this was *my* doing – and, had I been asked for my opinion about it – which, believe me, I was *not* – I'd have told them that it was the stupidest idea since invading Pakistan. The *second* time, I mean. These military-guys, and the Agency-spooks – all they understand is brute force... I was always more a 'let's talk it out' kind of guy... you know?"

He hung his head for a second or two, then added,

"I want to be your friend – I really *do!*" he half-pleaded. "And I don't care if my saying that, is just you fucking around with my mind... what they're doing to you and these people that you picked up in Idaho – it *stinks* – it's *wrong!* If I ever *do* get back in front of the President, I intend to say that to his face... *whatever* the consequences. I don't make a lot of promises... but *this* is one that I intend to keep. Whether or not you or Mr. FBI-Swami over there, thinks it's the truth."

She jumped forward and extended him a big hug, causing Kaysten to concentrate only on suppressing one awkward physical-reaction.

"Of *course* I believe you, Jerr-ee," she happily replied. "But I needed to *hear* you say that."

The alien-girl paused for a second, then added, "And I do *not* expect you to repudiate your loyalties... though, I would hope that maybe you can also have such to myself. Learning how to balance these, is one sign of becoming more than who you were, before. And do you know what else?"

"No... what?" he inquired.

"My ears, my mind – they heard your arts, a few seconds ago," she noted, with a satisfied tone. "*Reflect* upon that. You become *powerful*, Jerr-ee!"

"I... *see*," he replied, with a pensive expression.

The Storied Watcher had an even more odd-than normal-look on her face.

"Who calls, across the void?" she spoke, apparently to no-one. "I *will* – take my love – oh, *no*, no, do not *go*..."

"¿*Que*?" asked the *Mara*.

"A plea from afar," explained the alien-girl. "Which I *tried* to answer... but it slipped away. Oh, *curses*! So *pitiful* am I!"

Her fangs showed, as she scowled and spent a tear, in frustration.

Suddenly, Chu spoke up.

"What's *that*?" she exclaimed. "I'm hearing something."

"Me too," echoed Hendricks. "Over there... underneath those big boxes in the alleyway by the side of the dime-store, the ones with the scrap-metal in 'em."

"Indeed," added Karéin-Mayréij. "The sound is... Wolf – go to it."

"*Sure* you're okay?" he answered back.

"I am fine, now," she assured. "Faster than this, have I many times had to recover, from a grievous blow. *Ach*... I am *so* badly out-of-form... yet another after-effect of my long fall, I fear."

The bounty-hunter gave a confused shrug, then – pistol at the ready – he went in a slow trot toward the source of the noise.

After about ten seconds – at a distance of perhaps three or four meters from something in front of him – he stopped, shook his head and called back.

"Dead dog – decent size, too, almost big as a Shepherd... must have taken a round in the hind-quarters during the fire-fight," he remarked. "Trail of blood all the way back, but I can't figure why – oh, *wait* a minute... *there*'s the reason –"

"What you mean?" asked Ramirez.

"Got a den underneath the boxes," said Wolf, as he stashed the gun. "Poor bugger must have been tryin' to make it back. At least a couple of 'em in there, lemme see – **oww!**"

Rapidly, he withdrew his right hand, which had been subjected to a solid nip from half-wild puppy canines.

"Hey – they *like* you!" joked Hendricks. "Just their way of sayin' 'hi', you know?"

"*Perritos* in the *barrio como* your 'junkyard-dogs', *hombre*," offered Sebastiàn. "Full-grown, they take you down in ten seconds, 'cept if you packin'. Even if you got a knife, *hay que tener cuidado*, 'cause they go for the throat."

"Yeah... I know that," ruefully muttered the bounty-hunter. "These ones is a few weeks old, but I guess I forgot how fast them teeth grow along with 'em."

He got up.

"False-alarm, folks," he announced. "I'll catch up to you all on the driveway goin' to the school... I can just cut across the back of the store."

But the Storied Watcher had other plans.

With the half-glow in her eyes, she calmly walked over to the scene with the bounty-hunter and the wild-dog nursery.

"Let us get down on our knees, in front of where these fierce little things make their home," she demanded.

"Huh?" queried Wolf. "What's your *game*, Karéin?"

She pointed at the ground and knelt, facing the den.

The bounty-hunter, fighting both his gonads and resentment at being perfunctorily ordered about by a woman – even *this* one – again shrugged and did the same.

The alien-girl took his hand in hers, causing the expected reaction, which he was able to keep under control only with considerable effort.

"I ain't been with a girl in – well, *you* know, since this whole damn business started to go down," he mentioned, *sotto voce*. "So don't get pissed, if –"

Luckily, he was able to communicate this before the rest of them managed to get close enough to crowd around.

Karéin-Mayréij planted a dry, affectionate kiss on Wolf's cheek and winked at him. Then she lifted the little amulet-and-chain from her neck – in so doing whispering something to it – and draped it over the bounty-hunter's own.

As his mind raced with utterly incomprehensible – yet somehow wise and friendly – thoughts, he heard her intone, "Venerable *Vîrya Quü'j* will guide you in this ancient ritual. But even were she not here, you would know what to say... what to think."

"What... uhh... are we *doin'* here, exactly, darlin'?" he asked.

"Call to your totem, Wolf," softly counseled the young-looking woman, with a song sounding dimly in every syllable. "Ask her to take a place at the side of her master – who will love her as long as she live."

The eyes of the others – especially the two scientists – were focused with laser-like fascination, at the unfolding scene.

"Well, okay, but... how do you know it's a female?" he argued.

"What did Bob say, about such issues?" ruminated the Storied Watcher. "Ah yes... 'fifty-per-cent-chance'... that is what it was."

He shook his head and chuckled.

"Walked right into *that* one... didn't I?" he grunted. "Alright – here goes... hey youuu, little doggie... come ouuut, little doggie..."

The alien-girl sighed, rolled her eyes, sighed and looked skyward.

"Oh, come *on!*" she protested. "Put some *effort* into it, man – you are calling to the spirit of a living, thinking, being, asking her to entrust her *life* to you. Remember my words to yourself, when we were in the ho-tel, in Tucson? Think of how I spoke to your *heart* – how I told you honestly, of the enlightened-path that was then offered. Try it again... and *this* time, sing to the animal who you would call your companion – and ask the spirit newly within you, the Little Voice of Flame... request that she manifest and join in your song; for it will help you to send your trust to this noble animal."

"*Love* to!" argued the bounty-hunter, "But *karaoke*'s about my limit... and anyway, I'm not quite sure how to get her to show up, you know?"

"What – who you talking about?" inquired Kaysten.

"*Shussh!*" remonstrated Karéin-Mayréij.

The Chief of Staff wisely shut up, though Chu motioned to him and began to whisper what she knew both to Kaysten and Ramirez, off to one side.

An astonished visage showed on both.

"In fact... you need only concentrate for a trice, thus requesting that she take something easy to flame – paper, plastic, whatever – that you can touch... and the Little Burning One will come," explained the Storied Watcher. "Here."

A small piece of an oily rag floated over to a spot just ahead of the two kneeling individuals.

"Go ahead," instructed the alien-girl.

Wolf, his eyes flashing momentarily orange-red, stared at the cloth-piece.

"Baby – *light my fire!*" he inveighed.

To the shock of many in the audience, the rag burst into flame. And, while Wolf grinned with pride, his song – distant and low, but crackling, whistling and ominously-exciting – began to issue from everywhere and nowhere.

"Nice to see ya again, darlin'!" mentioned the bounty-hunter, his eyes transfixed on the burning cloth. "How you doin'?"

There were more gasps as the tongue of fire shimmered back and forth, with a weird, below-hearing, chirping-rhythm, as if in mute acknowledgment.

"Shee-*it!*" muttered Boatman.

"Yeah... *never* should have let him near that candle," whispered Hendricks.

"Omigod – I can't *believe* I'm seeing this!" commented an awed Abruzzio. "It's... it's... *sentient!* All the science-books – out the window..."

"Behold how the universe works as it *will*... not as you imagine it," allowed Karéin-Mayréij, never taking her eyes off the matters at hand.

Ramirez silently nodded in acknowledgement.

"Hold open your fist," requested the Storied Watcher, of the bounty-hunter.

He complied; and the flame jumped in its entirety, to a point no more than a millimeter above the inside of Wolf's palm. It flickered – but appeared to be continuing apace – yet with no apparent source of fuel.

"Does it... *hurt*?" inquired a fascinated Abruzzio.

"Feels *fine*... no, second thought, *she* feels great," contradicted the bounty-hunter. "I'd say, 'try her yourself', but –"

"Pray we now," interrupted the Storied Watcher. "You do not have to close your eyes... but ask that your words be guided by the divine powers who you may worship, and by wise *Virya Quü'j;* as well, to be echoed by she who dances now with brilliance, before our eyes. *Sing* to your totem, Wolf! Plead for her loyalty!"

Knowing that the time for jokes was over – with one eye on the flame-spirit and the other on the den – the bounty-hunter reluctantly opened his mouth, acutely aware of his total lack of vocal-finesse. But as he did, the fire-song's volume slowly increased.

"I guess 'How Much Is That Doggie In The Window', is right out?" he muttered.

The annoyed Storied Watcher whispered, "You *think?* Something *serious...* something from *inside* you, Wolf."

"Well... okay," he replied. "Only *other* one I can really think of, right now," he added, as he tried to force out a tune.

"*Me 'n you 'n a dog named Boo, travlin' and a-livin' off the land,*" sang the bounty-hunter, with a Willy Nelson-esque grace and finesse – almost as if someone had turned up a stereo in the background, playing the same song – that took the others aback.

A few noticed that the flame appeared to be matching the beat.

"*Me 'n you 'n a dog named Boo... how I love bein' a, free man,*" he concluded, not realizing how good it had sounded to the crowd.

The big man paused and pondered for a second or two, then again spoke up.

"Hey, you sharp-toothed little gal, in there – I'm 'Wolf' – not exactly my real name... kind of my stage-name, you know?" he spoke. "I'm sorry about your mother – *real* sorry... I can't change *that* – but I *can* give you a new lease on life, somethin' that the best show-dog on this whole damn *planet* can't match... *if* you'll have me. Ain't gonna be easy, travellin' with yours truly, and this hot-stuff you see right here, *she* takes a little gettin' used to, as well, but... I guess I'm still learnin' the whole nine-yards, myself. I'd like to take you along for the ride – and as long as I live, I *swear* that I'll never be nothin' but a good master. That's from the *heart*, babe. What'd you *say?*"

Well done! came a thankful, proud, outside thought.

The Fire *within, was there long before the Little One came to your side and your heart, dear friend!*

The music gradually ebbed to nothingness, and, for a few seconds, there was almost complete silence.

Then, to the delight of all the more-than-humans – not to mention, privately, Karéin-Mayréij – a small, nervously wide-eyed, furry face cautiously poked its coal-black little nose, out of the den.

As – step by wary step – it slowly emerged, they could see the resemblance to its fully-grown, deceased parent : the dog was a mongrel, for sure, but it definitely had the long-legged, pointed-snout blood of German Shepherds and perhaps a stouter breed – possibly something like a Staffordshire Terrier or a Pit-Bull – within its recent ancestry. Its short fur was an odd-looking mottle of black stripes on a chocolate-brown background; and it had intense, almost-yellow eyes.

The feral-puppy cast its gaze at the fire dancing in the bounty-hunter's palm and yelped in alarm, retreating halfway back into the den-entrance.

"Hey, *hey* there, honey," said Wolf. "Nothin' to be scared about – this here's just my hot alter-ego... she ain't gonna hurt you none. That's a *promise*, pardner!"

"The Little Burning One is now a *part* of you, Wolf of the Burning Forest," advised the Storied Watcher. "And as you are proof against her incandescent-touch, so will be your progeny... including such as this, who answer your call as totem and companion in all things."

The bounty-hunter looked at the flame and requested, "Well... would you mind takin' it to one side there, darlin'? Seems that doggie's havin' a bit of a hard time tellin' you apart from a plain old garbage-fire, or whatever."

The fire-spirit leaped to a spot between him and the Storied Watcher, who whispered something incomprehensible. Though considerably diminished, to about the size of a candle-flame – perhaps because it was now above the concrete, and still entirely without fuel to burn – it flickered on.

"C'mon over here, girl," ordered Wolf, to the dog.

Gradually – its eyes darting to and fro at the forest of towering more-than-humans arrayed around the scene – the puppy took step by tentative step, staying well away from the weird fire-thing, until it came within reach of the bounty-hunter's long arms.

He retrieved a small chunk of beef-jerky from a hidden pocket and tore it in half, offering one part to the animal.

"Last piece I got *on* me," he explained, as the puppy downed the jerky in one bite. "You can have the other half, if –"

"What's up?" asked Boatman.

"See for *yourself*," chuckled Wolf. "Got a brother or a sister, in there."

And so it was. Another little face and nose had showed itself, at the entrance to the den.

"Hey, there!" called the bounty-hunter. "Listen, little guy... hadn't counted on this, and I'm not goin' into the whole thing that Angel-Lady had me recite, again, but, I'm makin' you the same offer... get that furry little butt out here, and old Wolf gonna treat you right, come rain or shine, good times or bad. Deal?"

With maybe a bit less trepidation, but with the same wary stare directed both at the onlookers and the bizarre flame-thing, the second puppy – this one, slightly larger, and obviously a male – slowly made its way out of the den.

"Your turn," said the bounty-hunter, as he tossed the one remaining piece of food so that the second puppy had an easy shot at it.

"Look at that tail wag, eh?" happily remarked Wolf, to the rest of the group.

"I'm glad you didn't have to shell out for a purebred," offered the Chief of Staff. "A good one will set you back a *lot* of money."

"Wouldn't *want* one!" replied the bounty-hunter, as, with an odd-looking stare, he silently motioned to both of the puppies, with a 'come-hither' gesture. "Us mutts gotta stick together, I guess."

Amazingly – considering how little time had yet passed – both of the dogs came close to Wolf. They licked his hands affectionately, when he extended the latter to pet them.

"These are *special* animals, Jerr-ee," advised Karéin-Mayréij. "Strong and valiant spirits are they – as *Virya Quü'j* so confirms. You would be lucky to have *one* such companion... Wolf has *two*. It is a great honor!"

"Oh, uhh... *sure*," he agreed, trying to avoid another *faux-pas*.

Kaysten bent down, and attempted to emulate the bounty-hunter's befriending of the wild pups – only to have the smaller one snarl, jump up and miss landing a nasty bite, by no more than an inch.

Immediately, he jumped back in a start, while several of the group did a bad job of suppressing laughs.

"*Hey* there, honey!" counseled Wolf, to the animal, "He ain't so bad, once you get to know him. Kinda like Little Miss Bunsen-Burner over there... 'cept I can't make him come and go, like her."

Wagging its little tail, the doggie came over to the bounty-hunter and let him pick it up and hold it close to him. The male animal quickly joined in, and, for the first time in a long while, all saw Wolf's more gentle-side manifest itself as he became acquainted with his new pets. Seconds later, the amulet-and-chain levitated from his neck and regained its normal place with the Storied Watcher.

"Karéin," inquired Abruzzio, "From what I know of semi-feral animals, it's very unusual for them to develop trust with a human master, *this* quickly... is Wolf using an, uhh, alien-power, here – or is something else at work?"

"A totem-animal is a kindred-spirit to one's own, like how a beloved human mate would be to a man or woman... it is not exactly the same principle – but is none the less, not an inferior relationship," explained the Storied Watcher. "It is *meant* to be joined with its master in life-long loyalty and partnership – and will always do so – if humbly and honestly asked. And in the case of those of you who are blessed with mine own weirding-gifts, such a companion will become compatible with these – for example, these will, over time, stand unharmed in his fire – and may also develop their own arts. Does *that* answer your question?"

"'Totems' – 'fire-spirits' – 'Planes Beyond'!" complained Abruzzio. "I don't *know*... it's just that you're leading us away from science, back into mysticism and superstition... you're overturning *everything* that rational-thinking, logic and the scientific principle have taught us, for hundreds of years. Can't you see how that's a bit – uhh, 'distressing' – for people like Hector and me?"

"Absolutely *not!*" countered the alien-girl, while the bounty-hunter continued to enthusiastically roughhouse with the two puppies.

"What do you *mean?*" pressed the scientist.

"These things are only 'mystic' or 'superstitious', because you are not accustomed to them... because they were heretofore outside your sphere of reference," countered Karéin-Mayréij. "For example, take the Little Burning One, who – in part – energizes and magnifies Wolf's fire-skills, who burns within his heart... and, soon, within the those of his new little companions. She is both very intelligent and very much 'alive'... though not in the way that your human-kin, understand these terms. The same could be said of my war-children. Why is this so hard for you to come to terms with?"

With her still-half-in-disbelief-gaze focused on the little fire-thing flickering unaided beside the bounty-hunter, Abruzzio argued, "Yeah – let's take, uhh, her, as an example, Karéin. An intelligent being, made completely out of elemental *fire?* That's *impossible* – fire isn't a *substance*, it's just the byproduct of rapid oxidation! Saying that you could construct a living creature out of *that*, makes about as much sense as saying that you could make a being out of rust, sunlight or darkness. It simply can't be *done!*"

"Oh yes... it *can* be!" contentiously contradicted the alien-girl.

"Then explain me the processes of physics and chemistry that would enable something like fire to 'live' – that is, bonding into complex, organic-molecules, never mind developing sentient-thought," demanded Abruzzio.

"What if the natural laws of physics and chemistry are not always the same as here, elsewhere in the universe?" elaborated the Storied Watcher. "What if there are places – other Planes, other dimensions, call them what you will – where human flesh, water or these 'organic-molecules', would be instantly destroyed... but other elements of matter or energy, could still be of living spirit? Life is *everywhere*, Sylvia... it can come to almost *anything*, if the will be there and the Gods – or God – so permit."

"You speak in *riddles!*" complained the scientist. "And suppose that what you say is true... how does it exist *here*, under *our* natural laws? On *this* planet, in *this* reality, fire requires fuel – not to mention *oxygen*, for Pete's sake!"

"Maybe she can draw her life-essence from somewhere else... or from the Holy Fire in her master's heart," offered Karéin-Mayréij. "A 'symbiotic' relationship – as is normal for many creatures – both here and on other worlds. Have you considered *that* possibility? And please... do not say, 'it'. You may *offend* her!"

Abruzzio shook her head and muttered something impolitic, though the Storied Watcher thoughtfully did not repeat it.

"Wolf," she requested, "I do not want to unduly interrupt your, ah, 'private-time' with your two new faithful little friends... but may I ask you to bid the Little Burning One to your palm, then to show her close to Sylvia's face, if you please?"

"Sure," he agreed. "Okay, darlin'... I guess we got some more intros to do."

The fire-thing vanished from its previous spot, and in a split-second, it reappeared, its size and glow enhanced, exactly where it had been so ordered.

The two puppies stopped moving and sat on their hind-quarters, their wide little eyes tracking what was going on with close attention.

"Tell her that our scientist-friend here, thinks that your fire-companion, cannot possibly exist," requested the alien-girl.

"You sure she's going to like hearin' that?" he replied.

"She already *has*... have thou not, noble spirit?" spoke the Storied Watcher.

The flame did a strange kind of shimmer, like a candle subjected to a puff of wind.

"Now, Sylvia," explained Karéin-Mayréij, "As a scientist, what you have here, is proof – one would say, pretty *clear* proof – that the Little Burning One, who has come to inhabit and obey Wolf's soul, *is* definitely 'alive' – that she definitely *can* hear statements in Eng-lish – and that she certainly *does* respond to an external stimulus. I fail to see how her presence here could reasonably be considered as 'superstition', which is – if I correctly understand that Eng-lish word – 'belief in something for which there is no plausible evidence'."

She paused for a second, then got up on one knee and bowed in the direction of the flame.

"Please excuse, O Bright-Burning Child," apologized the alien-girl. "I mean not to treat thee as a lab-or-a-tor-ee subject... it is just that these others are ignorant of thy ways. Over time, they will learn... and will thus respect thee also."

Again, the fire-thing wiggled and darted.

"You know, Sylvia," offered Ramirez, "All these things she's been showing us, they sure *do* challenge our current understanding of the world, but... all it goes to prove, is how little we have really known, all along. I mean, if it's *real* – and it's not 'magic', we should be able to test it – oh, sorry there, *her* – under controlled-conditions... just like we'd do with any other unexplained-phenomenon... right, Karéin?"

"For the most part, the answer is 'yes', dear friend," answered the Storied Watcher, in a friendly manner. "I do not do... 'magic'! You must, however, understand that beings such as she who dances in Wolf's warm hand – not to mention mine own war-children – are *alive*. They have feelings, they must be treated with dignity, and if they are not disposed to be subjected to these 'lab-tests' – then those wishes must be respected. Would you allow some other sentient being to come up to *you* one day, and *tell* you – not *ask* you – to 'undress and jump up on this table, for a few months, while we do a few tests'?"

"If it was one of those funky 'war-kids' of yours – like the ones that can freeze-fry you in a half-second, telling me to do it – it'd be 'how high should I jump, sir'," joked the third agent.

"Oh... *good*," deadpanned Karéin-Mayréij. "I shall make sure to pass on that message to *Vîrya Ahn'jë*... her sister and brothers as well. Such 'co-operativeness' may be *useful* at some time in the future."

"Whatever," sheepishly evaded Hendricks.

"*Listen*, everybody,' interjected Chu, "Between the fire-fight and our, uhh, tour-guide's little problem back there – both events which might have attracted the attention of the Government's espionage-systems, with possible consequences that I don't have to spell out – we've wasted quite a bit of time. It's bound to take us a while to find the home-locations of the school-children that Karéin is out to 'rescue', then considerably more to actually track them down – assuming that they're still here, of course. Can we get going? To the school, I mean."

"Yeah... suppose we should," concurred Wolf.

He winked at the fire-thing, which jumped right at his arm and disappeared, in so doing burning a small but clearly-visible hole in one sleeve.

"Remind me to *tell* her somethin' 'bout that," he muttered, bending over and picking up a licking, affectionate puppy in each arm.

The bounty-hunter started to walk away; but with each step, the dogs became more and more restless, yipping and squirming, as if not wanting to leave the area.

"Hey – *hey* – settle down there, boys and girls," remonstrated the big, long-haired man. "What's *eatin'* you guys?"

Both dogs pointed their noses at the den and yelped.

"Ah," remarked the Storied Watcher, with a wan smile. "I think your young friends do protest, that one of their kin remains behind."

"Yeah, maybe so, but... uhh – don't take this the wrong way, but – I already *got* two – good match for the number of arms, you know?" argued Wolf. "I *love* dogs... but it's a bit much to ask me to take a whole *litter* of 'em –"

The alien-girl had by now sat down very close to the den-entrance.

She lowered her fore-body and looked inside.

"Aye... there she is," explained Karéin-Mayréij. "Cowering in yonder far corner."

She turned to address the rest of the more-than-humans.

"A little one – only two-thirds the size of the female that now adorns Wolf's arms," she stated. "What shall we *do*, friends?"

"Don't ask *me*," evaded Kaysten. "Got a cat at home... and *that* was a stretch – it's supposed to be a 'no-pets' apartment, anyway."

"Sebastiàn?" asked the Storied Watcher.

"Runt of the litter?" sneered the *Mara*. "*No mujer!*"

"Minn-ee?" inquired the alien-girl.

"Can't!" parried the FBI team-leader. "Bureau-regulations – no relatives, friends or pets on assignment... unless it's a properly-trained police-dog. That covers Agents Hendricks and Boatman as well, by the way."

"Yeah, but *Minnie*," joked the third agent, "What if your relatives have had police-dog training?"

"Remind me to ask the Director about that, next time I speak to him... before the missiles start flying," deadpanned Chu.

This obtained a giggle on the part of the Storied Watcher.

"Unfortunately... the same rules apply for SVR," observed Misha. "I suppose I *could* be convinced – since I have already given them more than enough broken rules to justify shooting me – but I would suggest that you try the others first. As much as I like dogs... they are rather, uhh, *inconvenient*, for an undercover-agent."

"Very well!" stated Karéin-Mayréij. "It then falls to Hector and Sylvia, to decide what fate will befall this poor, well-nigh helpless, little animal. Whether – in other words – she will be left here, to fend for herself in a cruel world; or if she will come with us. What say you?"

"*Love* to," mentioned Ramirez, "But I'm allergic. When I got married, my wife had to get rid of her cats. Was a big scene! Sorry."

"You are not any more, you know," replied the alien-girl. "Allergic, that is."

"How you know that?" he asked.

"I just... *do*," she said. "Like most all ailments... this, too, shall be banished, by way of the gifts that now empower you. Sylvia?"

"Oh – I *couldn't!*" demurred Abruzzio. "I've got no way of caring for the little guy – or gal – or whatever you call them... I mean, what would we *feed* it?"

"Come here and sit down, Sylvia," ordered Karéin-Mayréij.

"Come *on*, Karéin!" argued the scientist. "I've never *had* a pet – not even as a small girl. Mother said 'they're messy'... and she was the *ultimate* Italian neat-freak. I'm – uhh – *scared* of dogs, to tell you the truth."

There was the same, strange look on the face of the Storied Watcher.

"Close your eyes and *sing* to your Heaven-sent companion, dear friend!" she directed.

Desperately – Abruzzio looked to the others for support – but found nothing other than a malicious pointing-finger on the part of Hendricks and a bemused smile from the Chief of Staff.

"Well – for Pete's sake – what am I *supposed* to sing, Karéin?" complained the scientist. "I don't *know* any dog-songs... other than for the ones that Wolf has already laid claim to."

"Clear your mind – and then hum the first thing that comes into it, when you ask for your song," calmly replied the Storied Watcher. "It need not speak of a 'dog' – all it should do, is come from your heart."

"Fine – just to get this exercise-in-futility over with... here *goes*," unhappily answered the frustrated woman.

She sat down next to the Storied Watcher.

Now, the chords of an old tune began to reverberate, both through the surroundings and through more-than-human minds. It told of 'colors in the air, like a sunset going down, shooting-colors all around'; it told of a rainbow.

"Oh... *yeah*," quietly offered Wolf. "Last-century stuff – but still *got* it. Good choice, lady!"

The two puppies in his arm trained their eyes on the den-entrance.

Haltingly, while the music took on a life of its own, a tiny, furry face appeared. It looked outside, then scurried, squealing, all the way back in.

Karéin-Mayréij stroked the amulet and gently cooed something in the direction of the den.

Again, the runt-of-the-litter poked its raisin-like nose outside. It sniffed a few times, then – with agonizing slowness – took to advancing by a paw's length, then another, then retreating.

"Hi there," softly spoke Abruzzio, and the others noticed that her previous reluctance had vanished, because the scientist's tone was completely different, now. "I'm Sylvia – I've never *had* a puppy-friend before, but... well, something in my soul is telling me, that this is the right time. Can you hear me, little one?"

Unexpectedly, the animal sat down on its hindquarters and began to stare.

Her voice was becoming more melodious and dignified, with each syllable, while her face seemed lit up by some invisible light-source, just below her chin; and her music gained the sweet, sighing sound of other-worldly strings,

375

becoming like an orchestra of electric violins accompanied by a hypnotic back-beat. A few tiny, multi-colored motes of light began to dance around her, like a wind-blown kaleidoscope in motion.

"*Listen* to Sylvia's music!" whispered Chu, to Ramirez. "*Beautiful...* isn't it?"

"I should *do* so well," he replied, *sotto voce*.

Even the *Mara* was impressed.

"So... I bet you heard from that big, tough-looking guy over there – the one with your brother and sister, I mean – about how he's going to be a good master for them?" continued Abruzzio, to the little dog. "If you'll have me... I'd like to be *your* master – and I promise that I'll love and protect you just like I would one of my own kids. I think... I think... you're *my* 'totem'... aren't you... *Rainbow?*"

For the briefest of moments, there was a weird, multi-colored effect in the puppy's eyes. Then it gave a short 'yip'... and cautiously took step by step, until it reached Abruzzio's proximity.

"That's *always* been your name... hasn't it?" half-whispered the scientist, as if she was stating a plainly-evident fact.

"Will you *have* me, dear little Rainbow?" she pleaded.

The pup went right up to her lap, its tail wagging; and as she took it to her breast, there were tears streaming down her cheeks.

"*Thank* you, Karéin!" she breathed.

Abruzzio looked down.

"And thank *you*, little lady!" she added. "I guess this is a kind of life-changing experience for both of us... isn't it?"

The puppy looked up and gave a friendly 'yip', along with a lick to the woman's face, too close for comfort to her lips.

Sputtering, the scientist quipped, "I can see how we're going to take some time getting used to each other."

Karéin-Mayréij crouched beside the scientist and her new friend.

"Sylvia," she remarked, "You *do* know that in time, this fierce little one will inherit your gifts... and yet may she have her own, to magnify and enhance all of these together?"

"So I've been told," allowed Abruzzio, "But since I don't have a *clue* how to turn on these 'gifts', I'd say that it doesn't make much of a difference. Anyway... I'm sure that just having her for company, will be worth the effort... right?"

This was rewarded by another puppy-lick.

"The hour when your arts will be needed – and will thence come to flower – is near," counseled the alien-girl. "Keep careful watch over little 'Rainbow' there – and mark anything she does on your behalf; for she will try to communicate to you, when she need use her own special gifts."

The Storied Watcher looked up at Wolf.

"This is advice for *you*, too," she advised. "For example, when your two start doing tricks with fire – you will know that *their* time has come."

"Oh... I'll be sure to keep an eye open for *that*," confirmed the bounty-hunter, with a wink. "When I tell 'em to go fetch, and they bring me a stick from the middle of the bonfire... *that'd* count too... wouldn't it?"

"Especially if you hear their primitive voices in your head, when they prepare so to do," noted the alien-girl.

"Uhh... just what does a dog's mental voice *sound* like?" inquired Boatman.

"It sounds nothing like that of a human, or of a more-than-human," explained Karéin-Mayréij. "It is akin to a barking-noise – except that you can understand what each sound means... from the perspective of the animal, of course. So – for example – if your companion is confronted by danger, you will perceive a bark infused with alarm; if he or she merely wishes to rejoin you, it will be filled with love and longing. It is not like *any* human language. You will just have to become used to it... there is no other way."

"What about a rabbit?" joked Hendricks. "Lots of words for 'carrot', maybe? Or a gerbil. What's *that* sound like, man?"

"I do not know," parried the Storied Watcher. "I have never tried it... and would not want to, because too great a difference between minds, carries risks – some of you have already experienced this, when touching with the greater 'me'. Mind-talking is confined only to intelligent, or – at least – semi-intelligent, creatures... and, in the latter-case, only those with whom you have a close personal relationship. Such as – for example – with a totem-animal."

"We're wasting *time*, again," warned Chu. "We can deal with these questions later. Can we get going?"

"Well... before we *do*," requested Wolf, "There is one little thing –"

"*¿Que pasa?*" grunted the *Mara*. "They shit in your arms?"

"No – I told 'em to save that for next time when *you* grab 'em, pardner," smoothly riposted the bounty-hunter. "What I *meant* was... seeing as Ms. Scientist has tagged her little friend with 'Rainbow'... I guess mine need names, too. Do I got to clear it with you, Karéin?"

"Not at all – although I would suggest you refrain from having either of them sound like any of us – our names, that is," suggested the alien-girl. "In the heat of combat, one does not call a comrade... only to be answered by a bark."

Wolf chuckled.

"Guess *not*," he noted. "Well now... I think I'd like to name the first one 'Boo', since that was in the song –"

"Can't!" officiously interrupted Kaysten. "*That* music's probably 'protected-property' – you can get life in prison – or worse – for using a copyrighted or patented tune... or even a couple of words from it. Been that way since the Government handed over the whole criminal trial-process concerning 'intellectual-property', to the entertainment-industry, a few years back."

"Oh, come *on*," complained Wolf. "Who's gonna *know*?"

"Hate to *say* it, but he's right," commented Chu. "Until they turned the whole thing over to the recording-industry, the Bureau was spending fifty per cent of its time chasing down home video-pirates – a complete waste of time, terrorists were going free, because we were raiding people's basements six days per week and confiscating home-performances of 'copyrighted' sheet-music. Why don't you just pick another name and be done with it?"

"*Okay*, then!" muttered the bounty-hunter.

He looked down at the female puppy, touching its wet little nose.

"How you *doin'*... Boob?" he maliciously asked.

"That's a *vulgar* word!" protested Chu.

"But it ain't 'copyright' – or *whatever* the hell that is... right?" argued Wolf.

"He's *got* you there, Minnie!" interjected Boatman. "Can't 'copyright' a swear-word... remember the 'Legion of Decency', Supreme Court decision?"

"Why would one's breasts, be 'vulgar'?" inquired the Storied Watcher. "They are a source of nourishment, pleasure... and the pride of being female."

"They just *are* – in our language, at least," offered the FBI team-leader. "I don't make up the rules... I just report them."

"Yeah, I know, Eng-lish – like 'get happy', 'get going' and 'get stupid'," complained the alien-girl. "Well, for the record, Wolf... I think 'Boob' will do just fine! But what will you call the second one – the male dog, that is?"

The bounty-hunter stopped and thought for a second or two, then looked at the other puppy and remarked, "Since you're gonna be right by your sister all the time – and since she's a 'Boob' – then I figure what suits you best, would be 'Tube'... right, pardner?"

The little dog gave an enthusiastic 'yelp'.

"So there you *go!*" stated Wolf, with a grin. "Any of you'se ever got a hankerin' for TV... why, I'll always have my 'Boob Tube' here, 24 hours a day."

Chu groaned – but could not think of anything to say back – while the Storied Watcher giggled appreciatively.

"So can we go, now... *please?*" demanded the FBI team-leader.

The bounty-hunter cast a glance at the animals being cradled in his arms, then he did the same for Abruzzio and her new puppy.

"Get *alonggg*, lil' doggies!" he crooned, turning toward the schoolyard.

Better Talk While You Can

Billings had been throwing anything and everything that wasn't bolted down to the floor, at the looming, metal-bound container, and had only stopped when the two ex-astronauts threatened to physically restrain him.

"Give it a rest, Bob," admonished Boyd. "We're all just as – well, okay, *almost* as – motivated to get him out of there. But chucking things at it, isn't going to accomplish *anything* – except, maybe, set off another defensive-system. We got to think with our *heads* here – not our hearts."

"You don't *understand!*" countered the salesman, his voice still shaking with desperation. "I was tied down right *next* to him, when they did their – uhh –

worst, to both of us. It wouldn't be so bad if I could at least *talk* to the kid... but I can't even do *that!*"

By now, the Claremont boy and his sister, despite orders to the contrary, had returned.

"Ah hears y'all yellin' 'bout Tommy," exclaimed Curtis. "What 'bout him?"

"We're pretty sure he's in there," explained Billings, pointing to the container. "But we can't contact him, and there's no way to get him out – bloody thing's impervious to every attack that we throw against it... including the Mars-weirdo-stuff. On top of *that*, his little iron prison-cell seems to be electrified... so don't touch it, unless you want to get a shock that might kill you."

"Damn!" gasped the boy. "Well, ah *could* shout at it, Mista Billins'... bang it up some, like, before Major Brent an' Miss Cherie done rescue me... ah yellin' mah lungs out at them bad-guys, an' roof-tiles was fallin' all *over* th' place –"

With a half-smile, Boyd bent over to address the Claremont boy.

"Don't blame you for wanting to try, Curtis," he consoled, "But we're worried that anything we direct at the outside of this thing, might also affect Tommy, even though he's inside. Remember – a lot of our, uhh, 'powers', are *very* destructive. Can you *imagine* what might happen if, for example, you were behind a wall, and the people who were trying to get you out, fired a tank-cannon at it? Sure, there'd be a nice big hole in the wall... but there might not be much left of you to take advantage of it, you know?"

The crestfallen boy's eyes looked down at the ground.

"Yeah," he quietly acknowledged. "Ah'd do *anythin'* to git Tommy out... *anythin'!* But ah don' want him to get hurt on 'count of me... no *way*."

"That goes for all of us, son," sympathetically agreed the ex-astronaut.

"Major Brent," asked Melissa, "If'n y'all cain't talk to him or see him... then how y'all knowin' he really *in* there?"

"I had a – uhh – *vision*," answered Boyd. "*Saw* him in there, standing up and looking at himself in a mirror... an ugly sight... the kid's been badly hurt."

"How y'all know it not just a dream, though?" pressed the teenager.

"Because it was pretty much exactly what both I and the Professor had, just before we rescued you and your mother," explained Boyd.

"Oh," quietly answered Melissa.

"Listen, bro'," commented White. "Don't forget that according to Curtis, them GrayWar-pussies dragged Tommy down here, after his little homie-pal sprung free. Which – of course – leads to the question of where the hell did *they* go... along with what the hell were they doin' to him in this damn big box. Leavin' aside Bob's need to catch up on their friendship... It might be a good idea to find out about all that stuff – and the only way we can really do *that*, is figure out how to communicate with him."

A frustrated Boyd ran his hand over the back of his head and neck.

"Jesus H. Christ – I sure wish the Professor and the Captain – or any one of them – were here with some bright ideas!" he complained. "Okay, *look* – first things first. Curtis, Melissa... you see anything *suspicious*, while doing the rounds, up there?"

"No sir," replied the teenager. "They's five doors leadin' off somewhere, up on th' top-level – th' one wid all them chairs, ah means – but we didn' open any of 'em, tried to lock 'em an' put some chairs up 'gainst each one, but ah don' know if we did it right, cain't test it from outside, of course... 'an it seemed like they was locked already, 'near as ah could tell. Didn' hear nothin' comin' from any of 'em, not that we spent a lot of time listenin'. Them chairs is nice an' comfortable, an' they's lots of trash up there – half-full bags of popcorn, candy-bar wrappers 'n such... like they was watchin' movies, or somethin' –"

"Oh, *sure*... like, 'Matinée Night for the Gestapo'," sourly muttered Billings.

"Yeah," agreed Melissa. "But it look like them guys done the jet pretty fast – 'cuz they's lots of garbage-cans up there, but they didn' put any of they trash in 'em... just left it at the seats. Glass between the viewin' level an' here, it pretty thick, inc'dentally. That 'bout it."

"What about those assholes that we've got tied up, over there?" suggested Billings. "*They* might know how to get an intercom going between one of these terminals and the box... or, better still, maybe they can even *open* it."

"Worth a try, for sure," concurred White.

He paced rapidly over to a point within normal human hearing distance and shouted, "Yo, peeps! Yeah... *y'all!*"

A couple of trussed-up heads turned to regard him.

"Now listen up – and listen *good*," demanded the black ex-astronaut. "We know that y'all got one of our folk locked up in that big box back there," – White pointed to the container with his other hand – "And we want to know how to get him out of there. *Talk*, muthafuckers... while y'all still got tongues to do it with!"

A weak voice replied, "We don't know *anything!*"

Angrily, White strode until he was close to the tightly-bound smock-men.

He put the boot to the one nearest by, not paying much attention to whether or not it had been this man who had answered.

He crouched down, until he was almost level with those of the captives.

"Okay," he growled, with mock courtesy. "Now, see, here's the *thing* – y'all's the sumbitches that shot my CO, and just between y'all 'n me, I don't give two shits if y'all live one minute longer – but here's a *promise*... I can make that minute the *longest* one y'all ever *had*, before the lights go out for good. Here... let's try a lil' ol' dry-run, if y'all understand what I'm sayin'!"

He grabbed a foot and called upon the power.

A scream reverberated throughout the area, as the smock-man instantly felt the pain of many days' worth of frostbite, coming in a half-second.

The black ex-astronaut stood up and bellowed furiously, "If y'all don't *know* shit, then I might as well waste y'all right *now* – *got* that? So start *talkin'*, muthafuckers, or I'm gonna tell the kids to turn their heads the other way – ain't gonna be pretty, don't y'all know."

"No – *no!*" wailed several of the captives.

"We'll *talk* – we'll tell you *everything!*" pleaded another.

White leaned back against a blackened, pock-marked storage container.

"Better be *good* – better be some *quality*-info," spat the ex-astronaut, menacingly. "And don't forget... whatever y'all tell me – it's gonna be tested, sooner rather than later. I don't think I got to explain what happens, if I find out y'all been feedin' me any more bullshit. *Talk!*"

"Oh-oh-kay," whimpered a smock-man, his voice trembling. "You... you say that your friend... he's in that box over there? The one that all the others are standing beside?"

"Yeah," affirmed White. "Now tell me how to get him out."

"Can't," answered the captive.

He saw the immediate reaction from the black ex-astronaut and immediately added, "You *got* to *believe* me! Boys and I – we were *late* on all this, we didn't get the code for the lock... *nobody* but the Big Man back at home-base has *that*... and furthermore, it's got some kind of an internal-trap in it –"

"What that *mean?*" immediately demanded White.

"They didn't tell us exactly what it does," explained the smock-man, "But what they *said* was, 'you try to drill into it from outside, and you can kiss the ass of whomever's *inside*, goodbye'. Technology's supposed to be designed for gangsters, terrorists and so on, who the Company leaves out as bait... just makes sure that they don't go away with the goods... you know?"

"Yeah – I know... and *fuck y'all!*" cursed the black ex-astronaut, giving the captive a kick in the shins.

"Assuming I *believe* you – and I *don't*," coldly stated White, "Who the hell's the 'Big Man'?"

He got a perplexed look back from the smock-men.

"Why... the *Director*, of course," one of them said.

"Brent – y'all better come over and hear this," shouted White.

Rapidly, the other former Mars mission crewman approached, followed by Billings, just behind.

"Peeps here sayin' that only the 'Director' – Agency, that is – got the code to spring Tommy out of that damn cell," explained the former Mars mission navigator. "They're prolly full of shit... but y'all see a *pattern* emergin' here, Brent my man?"

Grimly, Boyd nodded.

"Yeah," he acknowledged. "Couple of things : one, high-level endorsement, as well as hands-on control of the whole, pardon the pun, shootin'-match; two, something that can resist our, uhh, 'special' abilities... which would suggest –"

"Oh – *whoa!*" exclaimed Billings. "You mean... a *trap?*"

"*Could* be," offered Boyd. "It would explain a *lot* of things... like – for example – the fact that this place was almost deserted, when we got here... when it should have been *swarming* with guards and torture-goons, and so on. But if it's a trap... I don't think it was meant for *us*."

"Huh?" inquired the salesman.

"Figure it *out*, Bob!" interjected White. "Assholes back at the Agency couldn't have known that *we'd* go on the loose, once they marched Brent, the Captain, the Professor and yours truly down here – we done made *that* little 'deviation from the plan', all up by ourselves. Maybe they meant to sit *your* ass down here in one of these other big boxes, beside Tommy, just because the person they *really* wanted to trap would come lookin' for the both of y'all – we *know* who we're talkin' about, don't we, Bob? She was *your* main girl... y'all understand what I'm sayin'?"

Billings looked bemused as he spoke.

"Well... that might *be*," he mentioned, "But they might as well try to 'trap' a grizzly-bear in a cardboard-box. Just before all the bad-stuff went down in Tucson, she told me that in a few days, she'd be 'carrying ocean-liners around as if they were a spare luggage-trunk'... or something like that. They're effing *crazy* if they think they can corral her like this. I'd like to see them *try!*"

"Oh... I don't *know*, Bob," countered Boyd. "There are all *sorts* of things that a smart – but totally-unscrupulous – opponent like who we're probably up against, might think of to do. For example... they could rig up Tommy's jail just like they have, so anybody showing up trying to free him would have to be *very* careful about doing so... they could rig it so that he gets put in excruciating pain each time the structure's attacked. Maybe Karéin *could* eventually get around something like that – she's damn smart, after all – but while she was busy figuring it out... now *that* would be an excellent opportunity for them to hit her – and anything *around* her – with everything they've *got*... don't you think?"

Billings gulped.

"Yeah... I guess it *would* be... wouldn't it?" he worriedly commented.

"It gets *better*," added the ex-pilot. "The confinement-cell obviously has some way of resisting *Amaiish* – at least at the energy-levels that we're able to put into it. If it can do *that*, it's reasonable to assume that it may also have some kind of an alerting-mechanism that says, basically, 'you detect *this* kind of energy anywhere around here, it's bombs'-away-time'. Remember – when they rigged the thing up, the only person that they *thought* was capable of using *Amaiish* in the first place, was the Storied Watcher herself. So..."

"And we set it off... is *that* what you mean?" nervously asked the salesman.

"Maybe," said White. "*Could* be just speculation... worst-case possibility."

He turned to re-address the smock-men.

"Tell us everything... *everything!*" he barked. "Before I make it 'the day after New Years at the North Pole, after a night out without your hat and coat'."

"Well... well..." stuttered one of the men, "We never... got much of a briefing on it... 'need-to-know' principle, you know?"

The black ex-astronaut kicked this guy, causing Boyd to try to restrain his partner, while Billings faked an indifferent whistle and looked idly by.

"Okay – *okay!*" whined the smock-man. "Here's all they told us – like I said, the whole thing is remotely-managed from H.Q... or, *somewhere* like that. And it *does* have a trap of some kind, or maybe more than one – all they said was, "touch it and you die, take the prisoner out without authorization from all the way to the top, we shoot you,' kind of thing. All *we* were allowed to do was monitor the prisoner from one of the consoles – *that* one over there, it's ten feet to the side of the confinement-box – it's got two-way-communications, if you patch in to the camera –"

"Y'all gonna set that up, five seconds after we say so," ordered White."

"But it requires *authentication!*" protested the smock-man. "Fingerprint or retinal-scan, only. No, sorry – *both* of them. One alone, won't do."

"Makes no difference to *me* if I got to slice off your hand or gouge out your eyeball," shrugged the black ex-astronaut. "So y'all best be fixin' to remember any codes that y'all might have to type in."

The man mutely nodded.

"What else?" demanded Boyd. "What were the plans for the 'prisoner', since that's what you're calling him?"

"Not much more I can tell you," protested the sniveling Agency-staffer. "We were told that gaining information from this particular prisoner was 'a life-or-death, highest-priority matter of America's national-security'... so at first, we gave him almost the full business –"

At this, Billings put the boot in – and hard.

The man squealed.

"I know all *about* the fucking 'business', jackass!" cursed the salesman. "Because I was right next to the poor child who you did all this to, *while* you were doing it... to him and me both. You're damn lucky that I don't recognize you having been there at the time – otherwise you'd already be torn limb-from-limb. And if Major White over here doesn't eventually deal with you... well, there's a whole *jail* full of us who'll sport him the favor!"

"You aren't giving him much of a reason to talk," counseled Boyd, who now crouched down beside the tied-up smock-men.

"Now *listen*," he calmly but angrily inveighed, "The *only* chance that you sons-of-bitches have of getting out of here alive – I won't mislead you, it's a slim-one – is for you to be very, *very* cooperative, and tell us absolutely *every* last detail – no matter how irrelevant that it might seem – about what was going on down here, especially concerning the boy in that big box over there. Apparently, your masters were planning for Bob, Devon and I, to also become your victims... and, so far, we've killed *plenty* of assholes like you, in avoiding that outcome – so two or three more, doesn't mean *shit* to us! With me so far?"

The man vigorously nodded.

"I'm with you... I'm *with* you!" he pleaded. "I wasn't involved in his interrogation... not *directly*, anyway... I was just the, uhh, records-keeper... I was responsible for tracking the, uhh, *assets*... you know?"

"Yeah... we know," grunted White. "Keep *talkin'!*"

"So we had gotten lots of talk out of the – uhh – *prisoner*, while he was undergoing preliminary-interrogation... but it was all low-value, mumbo-jumbo stuff... like 'my new Mom is going to bite you with her poison-teeth' and 'you don't know who you're dealing with'... didn't make any *sense!* H.Q. got some of these rantings and ravings, and to our surprise they were interested in them... so they told us to – uhh – 'turn up the heat', if you know what I mean – listen, don't hit me again, *please,* I'm trying to be *honest* with you – and we had been doing the really *intensive-stuff* for less than a day down here, when all of a sudden we started to get reports of some kind of a riot on the upper-floors. Everything went into lock-down... protocol in a case like that is, we move all the high-priority assets to this level and wait for rescue."

"Well... consider yourself 'rescued'," muttered the salesman.

"We were just getting set-up when another one of the priority-prisoners – another kid, would you believe," continued the smock-man, "Somehow got free and started doing some *weird* shit... I wasn't there, so I don't know what really happened, but there was a fire-fight right on this level... next thing I know, GrayWar drags in the first kid... they call H.Q., the box opens and the asset gets thrown inside, kicking and screaming all the way. Frankly, I'm *amazed* he had any fight left in him... never *had* one who could put up with all *that,* and still –"

"Do you effing *know* who that kid is – or how he was able to survive the torture that you bastards inflicted on him and me?" cursed Billings; and again, he had to be physically-restrained by Boyd.

"No – I don't... I *swear!*" pleaded the smock-man. "You have to *understand,* to us, they're just, uhh, a *product,* something that we're expected to get output from! Just doing our *jobs* –"

"Fucking son of a *bitch!*" screamed Billings, as he evaded the ex-astronaut.

White and Boyd saw a yellow-green flash – sort of like a discharge of off-colored electricity – jump from the salesman's claw-like hands, as he grabbed the prisoner and began punching his victim with the power of a prize-fighter.

"*Bob!*" shouted Boyd, grabbing on and only barely managing, with White's assistance, to pull Billings away.

The overwrought salesman slumped back on a nearby chair, bent forward with his head covered by hands and began to sob.

"Can't *take* this... can't handle it..." he whimpered. "Hate's welling up in me like a fart in the bathtub... can't *help* myself... *should* care what I do to them, 'do unto others'... you know? But I *don't* care... just... *don't...*"

White went over and offered a sympathetic pat on the back.

"Nobody blames y'all, Bob," he consoled. "'Far as I'm concerned, these muthas done lived twice as long as they ought, anyway. But we got to think it through... when it's time to *do* them, I'm gonna leave that to y'all – and I'll fuckin' sell *tickets* to the event... y'all know?"

"Yeah," wearily breathed Billings.

"Come on back when y'all feel up to it," suggested the black ex-astronaut, as he returned to the smock-man, who had by now sort of come to.

"What... *was...* that..." quavered the drooling, semi-convulsing prisoner. "Felt like a Taser on steroids – he *burned* me!"

"Two things, muthafucker," growled White. "One – it's *us* who's askin' the questions. Two – aww, that's just too fuckin' *bad*, peeps! Sorry y'all got a little taste of what y'all been doin' to all your – uhh, 'assets' – for your whole damn career. Don't talk *real* fast, Brent 'n me gonna make what Bob did to y'all feel like a fuckin' walk in the *park!* Got that?"

The frightened man nodded.

"*Then* what happened?" demanded Boyd. "After you imprisoned the boy."

"It gets even *more* strange," replied the man. "Most of the regular bottom-level-staffers see some kind of message on the terminal – me and the boys were over here by the boxes, we were busy doing an asset-count – then, all of a sudden, the regulars march up the stairs, right out the balcony-doors... they were escorted by GrayWar. By the time we realized what was happening, they were almost all out... we charged up behind 'em, but the exits were all locked by the time we got up there. It all happened so *fast* – we used the console to unset the upper access-doors, and we tried to follow where they went... but we ran into barriers, locked-portals... S.O.P. for lock-down, unfortunately. So we tried to call upstairs, but the circuits were down... then we camped out here, figuring that we'd just have to wait before they came back looking for us."

Boyd turned his back to the prisoner, motioned to White, took several steps back and addressed the other man.

"I don't like the *sound* of that," he whispered. "It's consistent with an evacuation – prior to an all-out-attack."

"Yeah," concurred the black ex-astronaut, *sotto voce*. "But we got no damn idea if we got a minute, an hour or a *day*, before it's goin' down... and anyway, we're pretty much stuck here, 'long as the kid's still in the box and the Professor, Whitney and the Captain's all recoverin'. Leastaways... I figure there ain't no H-bomb under Tommy's cell – because if there *was*... we'd all be atoms floatin' around in the stratosphere by now."

Boyd nodded.

"Somehow," he remarked, "I think that I'd have, uhh – *felt* – the presence of that much Oralloy or HEU under our feet... you know?"

While Billings looked confused at the comment, Boyd and White re-traced the path to the prisoners.

"Lucky it's *us* who 'found' you," grunted the black ex-astronaut. "Look at the bright side – y'all might get out of this alive... just, 'might'. Could've been them gang-bangers we ran into, 'few levels up... I think you'd make a damn good main-boy for some of them, but they might be a bit *big* – might *hurt* when they do it... if y'all understand what I'm sayin'."

The smock-man stared with wide, alarmed eyes.

Eventually, he managed, "Well, we thought that you might be, uhh... them... like, gangsters. Which is why we, uhh, *engaged* you, when you showed up."

"Yeah... *sure*," muttered Boyd. "Anything you *say*. But now it's *my* turn to explain some things. Put your listening-cap on there, asshole. First... the boy who you tortured and then locked into that cell is named 'Tommy George'. He's the adopted son of the alien-being named 'Karéin-Mayréij' – the one who Captain Jacobson's exploration team, including myself, Major White and Professor Tanaka, took back with us from the planet Mars. Maybe you remember her – she saved this whole sorry *planet* from the comet –"

"That... the 'alien'-stuff... just a PR-story, 'keep everyone's hopes up' kinda-thing," stuttered the man. "The *Air Force* blew it up... *everybody* knows that!"

"I am – correction, I *was* – Air Force myself... and I can assure you that it's a pack of lies; but you believe what you want to believe," countered Boyd. "Here's something that you *should* believe, though – we think the reason why you had Tommy in the first place, was to lure Karéin down here, presumably to trap or kill her. There's just one little problem – she has the powers of a *goddess*... she'll probably vaporize everything within twenty miles – maybe the entire United States as well – the minute she finds out what you've been doing to her child. So if you don't want your whole *country* wrecked, you'd better help us get Tommy out and fix him up as best we can, before she makes her appearance."

"What if I don't?" the man asked.

"Oh... then we kill you," indifferently remarked White. "Your bum-buddies, too. But it ain't the *worst* thing that might happen to y'all."

"What could be worse than being *killed*? quavered the man.

"Bein' killed by the Storied Watcher – that's another name for Karéin-Mayréij, by the way – herself," coolly explained White. "She got about a *million* lifetimes of experience on how to make it last a long, *long* time. Bullet in the head be a *lot* easier."

"What... exactly... do you want me to *do*?" asked the sweating man.

"You know how to work that terminal?" demanded Boyd. "The one that supposedly can communicate with the prisoner inside the box?"

"Y-yes," confirmed the smock-man. "I... think. I wasn't on the, uhh, 'interview-team'... but I watched them fire it up lots of times... my credentials should work on it."

"Well... that's *good*," offered the ex-astronaut. "That buys you another hour on this good Earth, or until Karéin shows up – whichever comes first."

"On your feet!" he ordered.

"I'm tied-up!" the man protested. "The other two guys are out – they're weighing me down. I can't get up. At least – untie my legs!"

"I have a *better* idea," retorted Boyd.

With a grim, determined look on his face, he called upon the power.

The astonished smock-man stared at the ex-Mars pilot's dimly-glowing eyes and energy-infused body; no less amazing, was the subtle-but-powerful music that began to play, as the ex-astronaut's telekinetic-powers lifted the pack of captives to an upright-position.

"Who – who the hell – *are* you?" gasped the prisoner.

"Oh, you'll have to guess at *that*, but... funny you should mention Hades," calmly replied Boyd.

"Why?" said the smock-man.

"Because... though I'm down here in that place with you," stated the ex-astronaut, "I'm waiting for an... *angel*."

At The School

If an alien demi-goddess could mope, that was the emotion evident on the face of the Storied Watcher over the second half-hour, while the group was inside the graffiti-and-trash-covered remnants of the school.

News had evidently traveled fast, because the few gangsters that she and her followers had detected on the way in, had quickly decamped for safer places.

"Even Daughter-Burning-Mountain cannot get these accursed things to function," complained Karéin-Mayréij out loud, to no-one in particular, in what was once the main school office. "I understand this not – why would they smash these com-pu-ters – save the few that were hidden away – into little pieces... rather than making some use of them, or at least selling them? It makes no *sense!*"

"Maybe same reason that you all's takin' so much care not to get on that-there cell-phone," philosophically offered Boatman, while his big fingers tried to brush layers of dust off a stack of printed paperwork. "*Everything's* on them networks, these days... don't hardly work at all, if you can't connect. But if you *do,* well – that means that friendly ol' Uncle Sam can look right back at you, through the same connection. Gang-bangers probably figured that it wasn't worth the risk... so they took a baseball-bat to 'em. Happens all the *time*."

"Or maybe they was just pissed because they couldn't turn 'em on in the first place and get at all that nice hot Neo porno," added the bounty-hunter, as he opened a filing cabinet. "No juice in the power-plugs."

He bent down and gave a pat on the head to the two puppies that had taken to following his every move.

"You find anything down there, Boob?" he asked the first one. "How 'bout you, Tube?"

One dog rolled on to its back and got a belly-rub as a reward, while the other gave a little 'yip' and contented itself with chewing on a chair-leg.

With carefully suppressed pride and satisfaction, Wolf noted that where the second dog had done its teething, there were the expected fang-marks; but each of these was subtly blackened, with almost imperceptible wisps of steam or smoke issuing for a second after the puppy had released its grasp.

Wolf winked at his prized pets.

"It hasn't been a *total* loss," mentioned Hendricks. "Like... I don't know *how* the gang-bangers missed all those cans of baked-beans and soup down in the cafeteria – but I'm glad they did. That's one H of a handy trick you've got going there, Mister bounty-hunter – don't even need a portable-stove to heat something up for cooking it."

"Glad to oblige, pardner," acknowledged Wolf, "But it's really *her* – Little Miss Bunsen Burner – that you should be thankin'. Anyway, I can't really claim to be that much of a good guy... puppies needed feedin', you know?"

"Quite amazing, *that* I have to admit," remarked Chu. "I *needed* something to eat, after all we've been through, lately. I only wish they hadn't wrecked the washrooms... ye *Gods*, what a *mess!* I won't go into what I had to do, to get by."

""Get by'?" inquired the alien-girl. "What stood in your way?"

"It means, 'improvise one's way through a challenge', *et cetera*," explained the FBI team-leader.

"Well, I had *Vìrya Ahn'jë* send the proper electro-waves into two or three of these 'smart-paper' things," grumbled Karéin-Mayréij. "With the direction going back and forth every split-second – it was very tiring for her, but she persisted... to no avail. Their fake-techno-brains are all dead; none of my war-children could make contact. Minn-ee – is there anywhere else that the location of these children might be determined? A Temple of Knowledge – a – uhh – 'library', I mean. Or perhaps a place where all citizens of a city are registered?"

"Could we piece it together?" replied Chu, as she studiously examined the contents of an old-fashioned file folder. "*Sure*... if you give my team and I, a couple of weeks of doing research... on second thought – a couple of *months* – if all the computers around here are 'down'... which they obviously are. Sorry, Karéin, but I'm afraid in the present circumstances –"

The voice of Abruzzio sounded, from down the hall.

"Think I've *got* something!" she shouted. "Come see!"

Rapidly, everyone headed out of the office, with Kaysten in particular moving quickly, though he careened clumsily from one wall to another, altogether overshooting the entrance to where the scientist had been working.

They found Abruzzio behind an old-fashioned hardwood desk, her hands supporting her upper-body, while she carefully reviewed an unfolded, glossy-paper book of some kind.

"You get the addresses, so we can get the H out of here?" hopefully inquired Hendricks.

"Not... *exactly*," answered the scientist. "But *this* might be a start."

"What you mean?" asked Kaysten, who had finally managed to make it through the door.

"See for yourselves," offered Abruzzio, taking the book by its cover and flipping it so that the onlookers could review its contents.

They beheld something that looked quite like a school yearbook, except that it seemed to be devoted entirely to children's sports.

"Take a look at this page," she requested. "Specifically, the one entitled, 'Class 4a Inclusive Intramural Softball-Team'. See anything *interesting* here?"

They peered forward.

After a second or two, a deflated Kaysten said, "It's just a bunch of kids... yeah, there's some names and phone-numbers – but all these pictures, like, the one on the other page – they've all got the same thing. So *what*?"

"You should have been watching your tee-vee screen, when last I spoke to these dear little ones... and their wise teacher," reprimanded Karéin-Mayréij. "See you not her name?"

"Yeah... 'Jones, Atasha'," replied the Chief of Staff. "Well... what would you *expect*, down here, anyway? Oh, *sorry* – no offense meant, you know..."

"Sure, *Señor Gran Tamale*, gov'ment-man," muttered the *Mara*. "*Nosotros* just folks... *verdad*?"

"Little Serena... Jamal... beloved Latisha, whose words braved me to duty... Martin, dear Devon's own *son*..." recounted the Storied Watcher, with excitement building in her voice with each word. "You have tel-ee-phone-numbers for all of them, right here – correct? We cannot use the phones – the related infrastructure is likely not working – but could the numbers not be compared with some other source of information, to find out where they live?"

"Sure... if you got a phone-book handy," commented Boatman.

"I am certain that I saw one back in the headmaster's office," added the Russian. "While working, ahh, undercover, it is worthwhile to take note of such things... the more information that one can get without consulting the computer-networks, the better. Do you want me to find it for you, Karéin?"

"Thank you – but *Vîrya I'ëà'b'* will retrieve it," she answered, looking up briefly and whispering something in her melodious, whistling language, followed by words like "foh-hoh-nee boo-ook".

The shield blinked into view for a half-second, then shot off in the direction of the main office, making several of the onlookers reflexively duck as it passed treacherously-close over their heads.

"Not sure how up-to-date it might be, though," cautioned the black FBI-agent. "They stopped printin' them altogether in some of the suburbs a while ago, put everything on the computers –"

There was the sound of something falling – or being dropped – from quite far down the hall.

Two or three people started heading to investigate, but the alien-girl called them back, saying, "Do not worry about it... nothing is amiss."

"Like I was sayin'," continued Boatman, "They put it all on the network, so they could de-list your business immediately if you didn't pay your phone-bill. But in an, uhh, *urban* community like this, it might even be this year's version. Got nothin' to lose by tryin', I s'pose."

As soon as he had finished, the buckler retraced its previous course, flying a bit higher this time. It stopped and hovered in front of the Storied Watcher, its concave inner-surface carrying a newish-looking copy of the White-Pages, with the outside cover half ripped-off.

"*Vîrya I'ëà'b'* became a little, ahh, 'excited', and she flew too fast," explained Karéin-Mayréij. "Thus, the book was damaged by the wind."

She turned to lay a kiss upon the shield, as she again spoke in *Makailkh*.

Vîrya I'ëà'b' rocketed toward the ceiling and promptly disappeared.

"It's going to take us a few minutes to match up the phone-numbers to the names," advised Chu. "For example, 'White', 'Jackson', 'Adams'... there are bound to be a lot of these in the book, so maybe we should divide the work –"

"Give it to your sister Sylvia," demanded the alien-girl. "There are how many? Twenty, not counting the teacher? This should take her no more than five to ten minutes, at most."

"Whoa!" protested Abruzzio. "Wait just a *minute*, Karéin... this is *very* picky work – a lot of small type, I mean. We don't want to make any mistakes... I'd like some *help*, if you don't mind."

"You do not *need* any help," patiently noted the Storied Watcher.

"Don't we want somebody to at least check her work?" argued Kaysten.

"Sylvia," directed Karéin-Mayréij, "See how there are so many little numbers and letters, on the page in front of us, here?"

"Yeah... of *course*," answered the scientist.

"Let us find the number for Jamal's family," counseled the alien-girl. "Wash your gaze up and down the page, looking for the word 'Kingsley'; and while you do so, ask your eyes to make the number, which one is it again – ah yes, '122-310-635-0831' – stand out as if the Holy Light were to shine upon it... keep that thought in the back of your mind. The key is not to try too hard – do *not* puzzle or concentrate! Let the *Fire* guide you."

"Fine... just to get this *over* with," muttered the scientist. "Here goes!"

They noticed that the color of her normally brown eyes, had changed measurably, with a subtle, multi-tinted effect infusing them; and as Abruzzio reviewed the database, she absent-mindedly began to hum, evidently not noticing the delicate, uplifting melody that sounded within her voice.

The woman stared at a two-page spread of phone-numbers, identities and addresses, all displayed in minuscule 6-point type. Her eyes traced an up-and-down pattern over the listings on the left-hand leaf of the book, and – in no more than two or three seconds from when she started – her finger quickly pointed to a number in the middle of a column of names.

"There we go," she announced.

Abruzzio looked up at the group.

"This is... uhh... hard to explain," she stated, in a hushed, reflective voice. "I just *looked* at it, and... there it *was*. Like a car with no wheels, or a red banana in a bunch of yellow ones. I couldn't – uhh – *miss* it, if I tried."

"*Jaysus!*" gasped the third agent. "There's gotta be more than a *thousand* addresses on that page! Sure you got the right one?"

"Check it for yourself," answered the scientist.

"I already *did*," commented Ramirez. "That's the correct one, alright. You know, Sylvia... you havin' *that* kind of mind, it's sort of, uhh, *intimidating*."

"I don't *feel* any smarter," evaded the woman. "It's just a *trick*... that's all."

"Oh no – it is not," countered the Storied Watcher. "It is the key to unlock the powers of your mind, those that you never knew that you had... but you always did. How does it *feel*, to have a taste of the insight of the *Makailkh*, Sylvia? Tell them honestly – for much, *much* more of the same, yet awaits!"

Abruzzio paused for a couple of seconds, then, with a far-away look, replied, "You want the truth? Okay, here it is – it feels... *wonderful* – like when you first understand a principle of mathematics... like the pure joy of simply knowing what you didn't know, one minute before. But the person who's most intimidated right now, is 'yours truly'. Even as her head races with excitement."

She sat back in the chair – her stare vacant and contemplative – but in the next second, her reverie was interrupted by the advent of her puppy hopping into its mistress' lap, licking her arms and being generally mischievous.

Abruzzio sat up and petted the dog.

"You also feeling smart today, Rainbow?" she quipped, with a big smile. "Then help Mommy find all these names... okay?"

As she bent over the book, the others noticed that the puppy, its tail wagging enthusiastically, had taken to standing with its hind legs on the woman's lap, while its two front paws held its fore-body half-erect.

The little dog's kaleidoscope eyes stared almost as intently at the phone-book as those of its owner, while Abruzzio began to match the numbers in the sports yearbook with the identities and addresses in the White-Pages.

"Will you look at *that!*" commented Boatman. "If I didn't know better, I'd swear it was readin' along with her."

"It appears that it *is*," even-handedly stated Misha.

"We should let her work," suggested Chu.

She motioned to the Storied Watcher and went out into the hallway.

The alien-girl obliged, and soon Abruzzio and her canine-understudy were left by themselves in the sports-office, busily cross-referencing data and recording the results on a nearby notepad.

"Karéin," requested the FBI team-leader, "Now that we've got this – uhh – 'breakthrough'... we should review our next steps. Specifically, how we go about tracking down and retrieving these children who you're after. There are quite a few questions that we have to come to an agreement about."

"I believe that I know what you are thinking about, Minn-ee," replied the Storied Watcher. "But go ahead."

"Well," started Chu, "First of all, 'are we all going to proceed together in the same group' – if we do, it might be safer... but on the other hand, we'd take a great deal more time chasing everyone down. *Second*, 'what do we do, if one of the children wants to bring his or her family, along for the ride'. Particularly with how things are on the streets, parents are unlikely to release their kids into the custody of a bunch of complete outsiders, like... us. *Third*, 'what do we tell the children and their parents'... I mean, do we knock on the door and say, 'Hi, we represent Karéin-Mayréij, Earth's favorite space-alien, and we've come to take your kids off to her castle in the sky – please have them packed in five minutes and don't forget your toothbrush'?"

"Hey,,, *I'd* go for that," joked the bounty-hunter. "Who gives a shit if it's a bunch of lies... it's *gotta* be better than bein' cooped up in Compton in the middle of a gang-war... right?"

"That is *entirely* the wrong message," wryly countered Karéin-Mayréij. "I only have a 'Magic Bus' - not a 'sky-castle'."

"Come *on*, Karéin!" pressed Chu. "We got to be *serious*, if we want this to work. Oh, and one more thing – what do we tell the parents about how long we're proposing to have their kids with us... and do we tell them the *truth* about what's going on? My vote would be 'no' – if only to avoid total panic."

"I think I'm done," called Abruzzio, from the other room.

"I shall be there in a minute, Sylvia... and thank you, from my heart," replied the alien-girl.

Turning to again address the FBI team-leader, she continued, "To state my own viewpoint, and in order... as to the issue of one party, I believe that your arts are now well enough developed so that you should be safe from the ruffians who inhabit these quarters... but in case you end up, ahh, 'in over your heads' – as Bob used to say – perhaps I should hover over the area in hidden-guise; call my name as you did when first we met, and I will hurry to reinforce you. There are three of you eff-bee-ai agents, and all have a badge of office... correct?"

"Yeah, that's right," confirmed Chu.

"Thus there should be three search-parties, with yourself, Otis and Will in charge of each," proposed Karéin-Mayréij. "Plus a few people to guard the bus, as we retrieve our quarry. You can show your 'badge' to those who we seek, as a credential of authority... do you think that might work to convince them?"

"*Federales* ain't too popular *en este barrio*," remarked the gangster. "Might make 'em shoot at you, rather than do what you say."

"Well that might be true – but I 'spect it's still better than you showin' up with them *Mara*-colors at a Crip-house," Boatman pointed out.

Abruzzio now walked up to the group engaged in the discussion.

"I matched every one of them, and I marked the locations," she proudly announced, holding the map up for inspection. "That's the *good* news. The *bad* news is... as you can see, five of the kids seem to live quite far from here – at least a good half-hour's walk for the nearest of them – and the teacher's house is even further. Which means – inevitably – *more* delays, unless somebody's can drive us there... and even *then*, it might be quite risky to go through the 'wrong' neighborhood... you know?"

"I have a *bus*," noted the Storied Watcher. "It should be no trouble to move it back and forth, both to position you to each correct location, in turn, and then to bring you and those who you rescue, back... and we will be going *over* these areas – not through them. You can signal to me by throwing a stone high into the sky, as high as you can manage; my war-children and I should see it on the first try... but if I do not come immediately, just keep doing it and I will arrive."

"How about a nice, hot flare?" suggested Wolf, with a wicked smile.

"Ha!" she replied, acknowledging his pride. "But *that*, might attract somewhat too much attention, dear friend."

"*Thought* you'd say so," he chuckled.

"Now... as to the other issues," continued the alien-girl, "I believe that the truth would be the best approach – as long as we are not too generous in providing it. We can simply say that 'the Storied Watcher wants to meet with the children who helped in the deepest hour, to give them their love' – and this is of course true, in part. If a family refuses, admonish that they are denying their child 'the opportunity of a lifetime'... and if they *still* will not relent, then – *only* then – may you offer one parent, the chance to accompany their young-one, on our, uhh, 'Magic-Bus-Ride'. Does this sound reasonable?"

"Sure," interjected Hendricks, "But you *know* that a few of 'em – maybe more – probably won't listen to *anything* we say. If *that* happens, you want us to pull out our pieces and *make* 'em come along with us?"

"No," demurred Karéin-Mayréij. "Instead – take one parent aside and quietly tell her or him the *real* truth, explaining that it is better that a few should survive, against the chance of all perishing. Give them a minute or two to say a farewell – and if tears come, add your own; for the Gods look with pity on such, and may – in the end – grant a favor. Then – when you have he or she for whom you have come – tell the other parent to take the rest of the family out of this city, as quickly as possible, braving all perils so to do. I would suggest going westward to the sea... then north or south. Does anyone object?"

"Whole thing's a *huge* waste of time," complained Kaysten. "Yes, *yes* – I *know* I'm talking out of turn, Karéin, and I'll do my best to help you – but I wanted to state that, for the record."

"When you see the little-ones who you have saved, Jerr-ee," she answered, "Your conscience will speak to you... as it did to me, while I was in the cold void of space. I would suggest that in that moment... you should listen."

"Yeah... I suppose," he muttered.

"It's gonna be a *challenge*, you know," remarked Wolf. "Wouldn't be surprised if half or more of 'em aren't even *there*... what with all the shit goin' down outside their front-doors... anybody with a brain and a hundred bucks, probably already bailed on this town. But we'll *try*, Karéin... least we can do for you, after what you've done for us. That goes for all *four* of us – right, kids?"

The two puppies 'yipped' enthusiastically, provoking a laugh from everyone around – even the *Mara*.

"Listen, Karéin," asked Ramirez, "Can we tell the people about these – uhh – 'special'-abilities, that you've given us? What I mean is... if they're not convinced that we're really there to represent yourself... maybe a small demonstration might help prove it."

"I would prefer that you do so only if *absolutely* necessary," replied the Storied Watcher, "But if it would be the difference between rescuing one more child or not, then you may certainly proceed. Just do not burn down any houses, or show off your war-skills, if you please."

Smiling, the Mexican-American scientist joked, "Maybe I'll just transmute some nickels into gold... *that'd* get their attention, wouldn't it?"

"I would suggest that you start by practicing how to change ice into snow, or the other way around, Hector," answered Karéin-Mayréij, with an arched eyebrow. "With no experience in this art, you are more likely to turn these coins into sand-stone, mud or mica... on a, ahh, '*good* day'."

There was another polite laugh, then Chu again spoke up.

"Since we've got one agent in charge of each team, we should decide 'who's going with who'," she stated. "Also... if we're to have people guarding the bus, while you're hovering overhead and not moving it, whoever's doing that should have combat-training. Can I make some suggestions?"

"Sure," said the Storied Watcher. "What do you propose?"

"Misha and Sebastiàn should be the bus-guards – no offense, gentlemen, but both of you – for different reasons – might not be very easy for us to pass off as being, uhh, 'from the Government'... you know?" explained the FBI team-leader. "Now as for the others... the Bureau typically uses two-person teams for normal field-operations – *this* one was, ahem, a little different, obviously – so I'd suggest that Team One – which will cover north to south-east – should be myself and Sylvia; Team Two – for south-east to south-west – should be Otis and Hector, while the third group – for south-west to north – should be Will and Jerry. Wolf can either stay at home-base, or go with any of the field teams, as he so desires. That's how *I'd* do it."

"I have no objections," agreed the alien-girl. "Does anyone not like this arrangement?"

"*¡Bueno!*" chimed the *Mara*. "Less I see of them Bloods, Crips an' 18th-Streeters... *lo mejor*. You don' mind if I ask if they got anythin' to smoke, when they get to the *autobuse*, do you? *Everybody* down this way, got some."

"You may want to work with Hector," advised Karéin-Mayréij, not missing a beat. "After a few tries, he should be able to transmute lawn-grass to the, uhh, 'good-grass'; and even *better*, if he makes a mistake and crafts a poison, the worst it will do is give you a nose-ache."

"No pain – no gain, pardner," quipped the bounty-hunter.

The two little dogs looked up appreciatively and wagged their tails, as if acknowledging the jest.

"I'm just curious," inquired Kaysten, "But is there any reason why each person is paired with each other one?"

A bemused Abruzzio answered the question before Chu could speak.

"Think of your 'gift', Mr. Chief of Staff," she instructed. "You're supposed to have a silver-tongue... right? And both Ms. Chu and Mr. Boatman here, are also apparently blessed with special-abilities to beguile people... or at least find out when they're not telling the truth. But I'd like to suggest a change – I think that Wolf and I should stay back at the bus. That would free Misha to join you."

"Why?" asked Hendricks.

"Didn't Minnie say that the Bureau doesn't allow pets on field-operations?" replied the scientist. "It's going to look a little, uhh, *strange,* for me to claim to be FBI with Rainbow here tagging along... not to mention Wolf, with those two miniature hell-hounds of at his feet. Right?"

"Smart *lady!*" congratulated Boatman.

Abruzzio smiled.

"The *Makailkh* rarely forget a fact," commented Karéin-Mayréij.

"Unless, that is... they happen to fall hard from the sky," she ruefully added.

"Okay, *fine* – I'm not really dressed for the occasion, anyway – and neither are Boob and Tube," conceded the bounty-hunter. "But what you gonna do about that accent of his?"

"Sounds Israeli to me," offered Abruzzio. "They're on *our* side... I *believe.*"

"Ha!" replied Misha. "Many of those currently in *Mossad* or *Shin Bet*, are of Russian-ancestry, in any event. But would you not say this is something of a role-reversal, Ms. Chu? I mean... not a fortnight ago, I was your prisoner, as well as being a captured foreign-agent – and we all know how *that* usually ends... do we not? How *quickly*, fortunes may change!"

"You *still* don't get a badge," deadpanned the team-leader. "'Agent', Grishin."

"But I *insist* on keeping my AK," he pleasantly demanded.

Chu shrugged and half-rolled her eyes.

The Storied Watcher stepped back, stood up straight, looked upwards, and in half a human eye-blink, she was bedecked in war-garb, with a powerful song echoing from everywhere at once; her infernal heat caused all around, especially the dogs, to cringe, though none were really harmed by the display.

"I will bring the bus," she promised, one second before she disappeared.

Tommy, Can You...

White – his gun still obviously at the ready – sauntered back to the encampment.

"Just checked it out," he announced. "No leaks – but I iced it up a bit more, none the less. Did the same for that door leadin' to the store-room... might buy us a minute or two extra, if the main-one goes."

"That's nice to know," grunted the salesman. "No life-jackets anywhere?"

"'Fraid not," offered the black ex-astronaut, with a slight smile. "Which is too bad, if the Professor ever takes y'all up on that suggestion of airliftin' us up over the Pacific.'

"Still no sign of life from any of them?" asked Boyd, casting a perfunctory glance over his right shoulder.

"Not that I can see," answered White.

He called to the teenager.

"Melissa... they doin' any better?" he inquired.

"Think so, Major White," she stated. "Breathin' even better now... an' they feelin' warmer to the touch. But they's still out cold."

"*Wonderful*," grumbled Billings.

"Yeah, well – it *could* be worse," countered Boyd. "As you know. Okay. Drag him up here... will you?"

"My pleasure," agreed White.

He turned his gaze to the smock-man, who had been tightly tied to a chair equipped with rolling-casters for wheels, fixed a deliberate stare on the seat, and used his mind to pull it forward.

When the man and the chair had almost collided with the computer-console off to one side of the huge, iron-bound cell, the black ex-astronaut bade it stop.

There was a slight commotion from the direction of the three wounded party-members, and for a second or two, the hopes of their three adult comrades surged; but all that had in fact occurred, was that Elissha had awoken. She began to act up, but evidently Melissa was able to calm her, and the two began playing some kind of "pat-a-cake" game.

"Now... y'all know the drill," forcefully mentioned White, to the captive, as he maneuvered the chair into position and untied the man's arms and hands, though not his waist or legs. "Fire it up – get us talkin' to him, and no damn tricks – you try one, lose a finger, two and that's two more gone... y'all understand what I'm sayin'?"

"Yes," nervously replied the smock-man. "But you'll have to turn it on, first... use the un-marked black switch, underneath the keyboard-assembly."

Boyd reached under the desk-like structure and felt for a toggle.

A second later, a number of dials, blinking status-lights and other electronic paraphernalia appeared to power up.

"So far, so good," he neutrally commented. "Now it's *your* turn."

The captive nodded and extended a finger to a touch-pad on the console, just to the left of the keyboard.

"Listen," he babbled, "Something I forgot to mention... I'm ninety-nine per cent sure that this is going to work, but... each session's limited to no more than fifteen minutes of continuous communication into the cube – then, it automatically cuts out. You can re-authenticate and start up another session... but only after a delay of thirty seconds from when the last one ended. If you try to re-initiate before the delay-period is over with, then it disables your ID for twenty-four hours. *And* you go on report for 'failing to follow Agency protocols'."

"*Really*," indifferently stated Boyd.

"'Failing to follow protocols'," muttered Billings. "Is *that* what they say when you pull out people's fingernails in the wrong order?"

"Yo, good one, Bob," remarked White, with a cynical smile.

"It's the *truth*," answered the man. "Considering the, uhh, *circumstances*... I just don't want you guys to run into any, uhh, *surprises*... you know?"

"Yeah, well, peeps, this whole thing, since we got off from Mars – that's been one big, bad surprise after 'nother," riposted the black ex-astronaut. "Get on with it."

Again, the smock-man nodded.

He typed something at the keyboard, ran his finger over the biometric touch-pad and bent forward so his face was in clear view of the small camera-lens at the top of the cardboard-thin computer-monitor.

Gradually, a picture began to form out of the previously-black pixels of the screen. It revealed something that very much resembled the barren, Spartan confinement-cell in which Billings had been stuck, when first he had been seconded to this accursed place. There was a wash-basin, a toilet and a bed without anything upon it that could have been folded or twisted into a noose. On the far wall, there was a polished and highly reflective piece of stainless-steel, which extended from the floor to roughly man-height.

In the middle of the antiseptically-cold, white-tiled floor, was a skeletally-thin, dark-haired boy of about eight years of age, dressed only in filthy underwear, lying motionless in a fetal-position. Though the exact extent of his injuries were difficult to discern, it was clear that he had suffered numerous wounds, including some that were nowhere near healed.

"Vital signs display shows low to nominal – although with *this* one, I remember that we had a lot of *strange* readings," explained the captive, pointing to a series of fluctuating, multi-colored bar-graph symbols on one side of the computer-image.

"Testing, testing, one, two, thr –" he started, only to be roughly shoved out of the way, in mid-sentence.

"*Tommy!*" cried the salesman. "Can you *hear* me!"

The boy remained motionless.

"*Tommy!*" shouted Billings, even louder, now. "It's Uncle *Bob!!!*"

Still, there was no reaction.

The two ex-astronauts were both staring intently at the screen.

"Poor kid must be in shock," observed Boyd. "Can't blame him, really."

"You don't know the *half* of it, Major," retorted the salesman. "I only *barely* kept my sanity... what little is left of it, that is. I can't *imagine* what it must have been like to be subjected to that... as a *kid*."

Propping his upper-body with extended arms, Billings hung his head and tried with all his might to avoid wiping a tear.

"Hey, Bob," consoled White, "'Least we know he's okay... sort of."

The black ex-astronaut turned to address the smock-man.

"Y'all sure he can see us... *hear* us?" asked White.

"Visual-display at his end's disabled by default – requires higher-level authority to turn it on... that's what Headquarters told us," answered the smock-man. "But he *should* be able to hear what we're saying – unless we squelch the audio-feed. Frankly, this kind of thing is 'par for the course' in kids... they tend to withdraw into their shell... you know?"

"I guess you have a *lot* of experience in dealing with children... right?" spat Boyd, with hate in his eyes.

"No, no – not a *lot*," evaded the man. "They're actually pretty rare down here. Usually don't have any useful information on 'em... and like I told you, I don't *do* any of the rough-stuff – I'm just the records-guy."

Somehow, Elissha had managed to wander over to join the four men – a fact that thoroughly alarmed Billings, Boyd and White – when each of them realized that she might easily have stepped on one of the trapped-areas.

"Hi, Uncle Bob," she said, in her sweetly innocent, childish voice. "Who's the little boy on the tee-vee? Can he come out to play with Curtis and me?"

Billings quickly reached down, scooped her up and took her off to one side.

"That boy is Tommy George, Elissha darling," explained the salesman, as he involuntarily planted a kiss on the child's cheek. "He's Curtis' best friend – and he's also the Angel Lady's son. Not to mention, being someone who Uncle Bob thinks of as *his* own son, as well. The problem is, we can't figure out how to open the door, so he can come out and join us – but the moment we do, we'll make sure to introduce him to you... okay?"

"Okay... I'd like that!" chirped the little girl, giving Billings a very well-appreciated hug.

"Now, listen," instructed the salesman, "Uncle Bob's going to take you over to where Melissa should be – and he wants you to *stay* there until she gets back, and I don't want you to go wandering off by yourself... you understand? There are some dangerous places around here – and if you walk on to the wrong one, you could get a really *bad* 'owwie'. Promise me you'll be a good girl?"

"*Promise!*" pledged the child.

Taking a sad last glance at the boy in the box, Billings slowly walked toward the resting-place of his three injured comrades.

"Y'all don't get a lot of kids down here – that right?" sneered White.

"Yeah... that's right," the man answered, trying to maintain a poker-face.

"Well, that's damn funny... because we already run into *three*, now – countin' the one y'all just met, as well as Tommy, that is... and countin' Elissha's poor brother, that you muthas *tortured* to death, 'couple of levels up from here," added White. "And if we hadn't showed up, y'all would probably have done *her*, too. Fuckin' *coincidence*... wouldn't y'all say?"

Wisely, the smock-man looked down and did not reply.

"Alright!" barked Boyd, as he manually and roughly wheeled the smock-man, still affixed in his chair, out of easy hearing-range.

He returned to the area of the console and monitor and addressed White.

"We only got a few more minutes until the damn thing cuts the signal – and we can't be one hundred per cent sure that Mister Amateur Gestapo-Asshole back there will be in a mood to get us hooked up again," noted the ex-astronaut. "Furthermore, Bob's too *close* to all this to be completely-objective... not that I blame him for that. You got any ideas?"

"Yeah, bro' – I sure *do*," ruefully grunted White. "My main idea, is 'why the *fuck* can't we get the Professor to wake up'."

"You and me *both*," agreed Boyd. "But in the meantime... I don't like the idea of us just *sitting* here, waiting for things to happen. We need to wring every technical detail that Mister Jackass over there, knows about this place... manuals, communication-channels, defensive-systems... the *works*. Let's do his bum-buddies as well – that is, if they're in any shape to survive the treatment. At least we know that the kid is physically okay – we got to take our wins where we can get 'em."

White nodded, adding, "'Long as y'all keep in mind... every second word, bound to be a lie."

A second later, the screen flickered and apparently went dead.

"Okay – maybe *one* thing that bitch said, might have been true," allowed the black ex-astronaut.

"Time to find out what *other* little secrets he knows," proposed Boyd, as he motioned to Billings and walked toward the chair-bound smock-man.

"Top Dog here," spoke the calm monotone of the CIA director, into the high-confidentiality mobile-communicator. "My ID-value is Anthill 456, Geranium 89, Torus 3A. Confirm-code, please."

"Little Birdie at this end," came back the reply. "ID-value is Ice-Cube 809, Sycamore 2137, Diamond 0F. Sir, I have some *very* high-priority information. From the special-site."

"Go ahead," stated the director.

"Are you capable of receiving a video-transmission?" asked the remote voice. "I see that max security is enabled."

"I am," confirmed the director. "Initiate at your discretion."

"Sending now," replied the other operative.

There was a delay of a second or two, then the director again spoke up, saying, "Transmission stored at this end. I am reviewing."

Uncharacteristically, he let out a soft whistle.

"Well... *well*," he gently chuckled. "Now this *is* an interesting development, indeed! Do we have IDs on these captive-assets?"

"High-confidence positives on all of them," answered the remote voice. "The first male to appear – albeit briefly – is one 'Ira Bickler' – he's an Agency Class 7 Special-Methods Interrogator assigned to the R.B. Cheney facility... although why it was *him* who initiated the link is problematic... I mean, there should be higher-ranking staff with higher priority. The other three are, in order : Robert K. Billings Jr. of Tucson, Arizona; Major Brent Boyd, of the U.S. Air Force Mars expeditionary team, and Major Devon White, same affiliation... we can't account for them being all the way down there, since they were last checked at ingress – and even with the maximum program, that's a twelve-day cycle, after all. Oh, and sir... there's also apparently a female child of approximately five to seven years of age, but we have so far not been able to get a name for her... we're still running the records."

"Okay," impassively offered the director. "Well... the girl was probably a bonus from a parental-rendition, anyway – lower-priority, look her up by all means – but don't waste too much time on it. We've got bigger fish to fry, here!"

"Acknowledged, sir... but we need a MOP, from this point on," requested the remote voice. "Frankly... we're concerned about a breach of protocol."

"We've already anticipated this kind of development," explained the CIA director. "We'll need a precise fix on the location, of course; but for the time being, only deviation from normal process should be to pipe any new data, directly to my personal mobile. Under *no* circumstances are you to initiate – or reply to – communications associated with this endpoint. This order will maintain until I countermand it – is that *understood?*"

"Understood and accepted, sir," answered the other man.

"Very well," said the director. "I'll be going now... I need to do a few calls."

"Yes, sir," stated the remote voice.

"Top Dog out," concluded the Agency's head honcho; and his face showed just the slightest hint of a smile.

Mrs. White... Here's Your Travel-Ticket

Each of them somehow knew that by now, they *should* be exhausted, both mentally and physically; but they persevered, with their psyches, bodies and spirits constantly reinforced by the self-styled 'blessing' that had been laid upon them.

None the less, the frustration of having to cajole and plead with the fearful and suspicious residents of Compton, California, over and over – in support of a Quixotic quest that none of them really fathomed – was beginning to wear down the patience of even the most Stoic of the troupe.

"I don't think we been goin' about this, in at *all* the right way," offered Boatman, wiping the sweat from his brow with a now thoroughly-filthy handkerchief. "If she'd just show up each time we knock on a door, I'd bet you that we wouldn't have *any* convincin' to do. But *this* way – we been damn lucky not to have been shot at."

"Can't argue with *that*," replied the Mexican-American scientist, stopping to take a breather, with one foot on the first step leading up to the suburban house – with boarded-up windows and a bit of graffiti defacing its walls, but still notably bigger and in better shape than any of the surrounding buildings – that was in front of them. "I'm amazed that we got every one – except for that place that was abandoned – to come along with us. We're quite a team, I'd say."

"Welcome to the Bureau," ruefully agreed Boatman.

"What *I* can't understand is, why she's still stayin' invisible, once she drops off the bus where we gotta load 'em up," complained Ramirez. "It's makin' us look bad – 'specially when we got to tell 'em that 'you get to see the alien when you come with us'. You *saw* their faces when that *estupido* gangster greeted everybody... I'm surprised that none of them turned tail and ran right there. I guess just the fact that the bus showed up out of nowhere, was weird enough to let 'em know that this wasn't any trick. Hasn't been *easy*... that's for sure!"

"You know, Mr. Agent," continued Ramirez, "Since this whole thing started going down, it's sure been interestin'... but I got no *idea* what she means by all this stuff about 'Hector, you can transmute elements, and you can manipulate air-pressure'... like, it's pretty clear that *some* of 'em – for example the bounty-hunter, maybe Sylvia and the Russian, too, *they've* figured it out – but as for me, I think she forgot to tell me where the 'on' switch is, you know?"

"Heh – know what you mean," agreed Boatman. "'Disintegrate shit by just touchin' it'... as *if!* Been on some *strange* assignments – but *this* one, pretty much takes the cake."

Wearily, he added, "But there's *one* good thing – if I'm countin' right, and the other teams are holdin' up their ends of the whole operation – this should be the last one... right?"

"You forgot the teacher," corrected Ramirez. "Gotta do *her,* last... remember?"

"Yeah," confirmed the big, black FBI-agent. "Well... I 'spose we better get it over with. I'll do the knockin', this time."

"Go for it," directed the scientist.

Boatman slowly ascended the stairs, checking carefully for signs of danger.

Finding none, he stood on the landing in front of the main entrance to the house and tried to ring the doorbell.

There was no sound.

"Power's off," he muttered. "Remind me to remind myself of that."

His huge fist rapped on the door.

"This is the FBI!" he called, in a loud – but non-confrontational – tone. "We'd like to speak to Martin White... or any of his parents."

For a few seconds, there was no reply.

Then, a woman's apprehensive, defensive voice replied, "What y'all want? My son ain't done *nothin*" – and y'all ought to *know* that there ain't no point in comin' after him, or us, for skippin' school... ain't been no classes since the comet stuff went down. Leave us *alone!*"

"Is that Mrs. White?" asked the black agent. "To answer your question... no, Ma'am – we're not here for anything like *that.* My partner and I, we're from the Federal Bureau of Investigation, on a special field assignment. We need to talk to you about somethin' very important. This is *serious*, Ma'am, and we don't have a lot of time."

They heard the sounds of multiple locks and catches being disengaged; then, the door slowly opened, revealing the fear-twisted face of an otherwise very attractive, early-thirties African-American woman.

There was a handsome, tall boy of about nine years, hiding behind her skirt.

With a trembling voice, she softly pleaded, "No... please, *no* – not Devon, please God, *no*..."

"She means Major White," immediately interrupted Ramirez. "The *astronaut*, that is."

"Oh – *terrible* sorry to give you that impression," hastily answered Boatman. "This isn't about your husband, Mrs. White; as far as I know, he's – uhh – fine. We're here to ask you if –"

"Where *is* he?" demanded the woman. "My husband was 'sposed to be back home *weeks* ago – he's a *space-hero*, and he's disappeared off the face of the Lord's green earth – Air Force hasn't told us but *shit*, right from the start. Y'all government-folk got some kind of *nerve* comin' here and askin' *us* for things, when I can't even get straight answers 'bout Devon!"

"Ma'am – may we come in?" requested Boatman. "I'll do my best to tell you what I know about that, but it's not safe for us to be standin' right out here... as I'm sure you're aware."

Suspiciously, she grumbled, "Oh yeah... we're sure up to date on all *that* – ain't seen no police 'round here for four months. They done ransacked the upper-levels here couple of times, and if it hadn't been for that reinforced 'safe-room' that my husband set us up with before he left for that space-trip, we wouldn't have nothin' left to eat at *all*. We're about to run out any day, if you're interested to know."

She motioned for them to enter, quickly closing and locking the door after Boatman and Ramirez did so.

A second or two later, a girl of perhaps five or six years of age – dressed in a rather unkempt yellow dress and sporting pig-tails – skipped into the living-room.

"Who's these folk, Momma?" inquired the child.

"Just some men from the Government, Francelle honey," explained the woman. "Y'all and your brother go and play downstairs."

"Aww... but Momma – we already done all them board-games, ten or twenty times," whined the girl. "Ain't *nothin'* to do down there, 'long as y'all don't let us run the computer off the battery."

"Now I don't want no back-talk –" started the woman; but Boatman stepped in to the conversation.

"Don't blame you for wantin' them out of your hair," he sympathetically offered. "But, actually... this is kind of *about* them... about your *son*, anyway. I think he should hear what I have to say... if that's okay by you."

"I got no idea what's goin' *on*, here," she replied with a worried stare, "And it might have been a mistake to even let y'all in here – but just to get this all over with... Martin, Francelle, y'all sit down – and mind your manners... hear?"

The two children rapidly complied.

"Speakin' of manners, Ma'am," started the FBI-agent, "I'm sort of forgettin' my own. Name's Otis Boatman – I'm with Special Project Red Rover, reportin' to Field team-leader Minnie Chu... who I'm hopin' – if all goes well – you'll be meetin' with quite soon. This here's Hector Ramirez, who's – ahem – one of the special scientist liaison-people for our mission."

He flashed a badge at the woman, which she briefly examined.

Ramirez extended a hand.

"Hector Ramirez... Houston Space-Center," he stated. "I was assigned to the *Infinity-Eagle* Mars exploration mission... maybe you saw it on television?"

"We were tuned in to it twenty-four hours a day – until the power went out, that is," commented the woman, as she accepted the handshake. "I'm Saquina White. Now... what's this all about?"

"Well, briefly, Mrs. White," explained Boatman, "And I know this is going to be – uhh – kind of hard to believe, but... do you remember, just prior to the 'comet'-thing goin' down, a situation where your son participated in a video-conference with the alien-lady callin' herself 'Karéin-Mayréij'... otherwise known as the 'Storied Watcher'? From the school he used to attend, that is."

"Of *course* I do!" forcefully confirmed the housewife. "Martin couldn't hardly talk 'bout nothin' *else*, all the while. Now – mind y'all – there was also a lot of rumors that the whole thing was staged – faked, like – 'just to keep everybody's spirits up', kind of thing... but I never believed that, because Devon told me *specifically* that it was true, afterwards. He used to go on and *on* 'bout this 'Storied Watcher' person, how wicked *amazin'* she was, and such... these days, I honestly don't know *what* to believe, though. All I want is my husband back and be done with it. Get back to something like us bein' a *normal* family, with no more of this crazy Air Force stuff... y'understand?"

She noticed that a broad grin had broken out on Ramirez' face.

"What *you* so happy 'bout?" she complained.

"Oh... sorry... I didn't mean to upset you, Mrs. White," he quickly apologized. "It's just the way in which you said that, I guess."

"Huh?" asked Saquina White.

"What he *means*, Ma'am," continued Boatman, "Is... this stuff about the alien – it's no lie, and it's no joke; 'matter of fact, it's about as far from that as you could possibly imagine. I'll get right to the point – we were sent to this here house specifically by Karéin-Mayréij *herself*, to see if your son wants to come along with her – and us – on a little bus-ride that she's arrangin' for all the children in Mrs. Jones' school class. She's waitin' out there right now... but we don't have a lot of time before she's got to be goin' on her way... so we pretty much need to know now if Martin's comin' along. If you please."

Unable to comprehend what had just been said, White's wife stood in place with a 'deer-in-headlights' look on her face.

Eventually, the flustered woman managed, "Y'all *got* to be kiddin'... now tell me what's *really* goin' on – expectin' me to give up my *child* to two men who show up totally un-announced on my doorstep, with some kind of crazy-ass story about an *alien* hangin' in my 'hood, and she's drivin' a *bus*? If she's from outer-space, then why ain't she here in a flyin'-saucer? Sorry, boys – but in *this* house, we don't smoke nothin' – and whatever *y'all* been doin', it ain't helpin' your heads none. I'll ask you to make your way out, if y'all don't mind."

"Mrs. White," interjected Ramirez, "I realize how improbable that this story must seem – and please *believe* me, if you only *knew* what has happened with Otis and myself, since the comet-incident – what I'm tryin' to say here is, it's been one crazy thing after another, for all of us. But what he's saying is one hundred per cent true... and it's *critical* that Martin should come with us!"

"Why would it be 'critical' for *him*... but not the rest of us?" demanded the woman, with a jaundiced eye.

"Well," stammered the scientist, "It's just that... you see... your son was in the school-meeting, and... oh, *you* tell them, Agent Boatman. I'm no good at this kind of thing."

"I'd prefer to go into that just between you and us, Mrs. White," proposed Boatman. "In private."

"Is it about Devon?" her panicked voice replied. "Y'all tell me right *now!*"

"No – like I said, as far as I know – as far as *we* know – he's okay, but we have no idea of where he is now... that's just one more part of a very complicated story," evaded the FBI-agent.

"Y'all tell me all of what y'all know, right *here!*" pressed Saquina White. "And I don't care if my kids hear it. *They* got a right to know the truth, too."

"Okay," wearily conceded Boatman. "You want the *truth*, Mrs. White? I'll tell you, provided that it goes no further than this room – and that applies to the young'uns, as well. So here it is... we ain't just here to get Martin... although that *is* the main objective. See... it has come to the attention of both the Bureau and the Storied Watcher, that there may be one of those 'loose nukes' – a terrorist H-bomb, that is – located somewhere within the Greater Los Angeles area. For all we know, the damn thing could be over on the next block –"

Upon hearing this, the housewife mumbled, "Oh my *Lord...*"

"Now... I don't know if your husband mentioned any of this while you was talkin' with him while he was in outer-space," elaborated the big FBI-agent, "But 'Karéin' is extremely, uhh, 'protective' of those who she considers to be her friends – and that *definitely* includes young Martin here... I'm *certain* that she'd also extend the invitation to yourself and your daughter, if you'll accept it. She wants to get all of you out of here, before the bomb has a chance to go off. By the way – as to the bus, let's just say that she's kind of fixed it up a bunch – it sure ain't anythin' that you'd recognize from the L.A. transit-system... you'll understand what I mean, once you see it. Any questions?"

"Sweet Baby *Jaysus!*" she gasped, her face blanching. "Now *listen*, Mister FBI-Agent. In *this* house, we take the Bible *very* seriously. Are y'all willin' to swear on the Holy Book that everythin' y'all said, is God's own truth?"

Boatman held up his hand.

"I was in the choir at the North St. Louis Baptist for twenty years, Ma'am," he attested, "And I got no problem about doin' that. Now we had better be goin', and *soon*. Every extra minute, may be one that we can't afford to waste."

White's wife turned to the children.

"I want the two of y'all to go get one change of clothes and your toothbrushes, right now, and be back in thirty seconds," she demanded.

"But Momma, can't I take –" pleaded the girl.

"*Get!*" exclaimed the mother. "*Now!*"

Both of the children knew that tone... and that it meant *business*.

Rapidly, they disappeared around a corner.

Her hands trembling, Saquina White fumbled absent-mindedly through a haphazardly-strewn collection of mementos, distributed over a mantel-piece.

"Found it," she stammered. "Family Bible. All the dates goin' back to my husband's great-granddaddy."

Boatman stepped forward and examined the book.

"Don't blame you, Ma'am," he wistfully mentioned. "My Momma's got one like that, back home. Said I'd get it, when she passed on – 92 years old, but she's still goin' strong."

"*There* it is!" remarked the housewife as she grabbed a small, glass-encased portrait of Air Force Major Devon White, smartly dressed in a formal Air Force uniform.

At this, the two children returned, each one carrying a crumpled mass of school-clothes, although the girl had also brought a stuffed toy-tiger.

"Honey, y'all can't –" admonished the woman.

"It's okay," reassured Boatman. "We got a few more who brought some stuff. And 'far as I know, the cargo-hold in the bus is still workin'."

"I'm not so sure of that," advised Ramirez. "Remember how she sealed all its exterior-cracks and -bumps? She said something about 'the little energy-particles go off in all directions'... I think it was the 'stealth' treatment, that is."

"Let's should find out about *that,* when we get on board, if you don't mind," countered the black FBI-agent. "Well, now that we're all ready to go..."

With tears in her eyes, White's wife looked back into the house, as she walked through the door.

"He done bought this place for me on our weddin'-day," she quietly observed. "Said it proved that goin' into the Air Force was the right thing to do... made him proud he could finally support us."

"You may yet come back here," noted Boatman. "None of this is a done-deal – but we got to do the right thing and get you out of harm's way, until we're sure it's safe."

"Mister," inquired the boy, as the five descended the steps and headed down the front walkway toward the street. "Are we gonna meet the alien? The space lady, I mean."

The big FBI-agent grinned.

"Yeah – you shore will," he promised. "No more than ten to fifteen minutes from now... that'd be *my* guess."

"What's she *like*?" Martin excitedly pressed. "Dad said that she was *wicked* neat. He said she was an *angel!*"

"Your Daddy wasn't exaggeratin'," agreed Boatman, with a far-off look in his eyes. "She's like nothin' you've ever *met* – although she's not so hard to get used to, once you're over the initial – uhh – shock. Only thing is – if she wants to *bite* you... well, in *that* case, personally... I'd ask for a second opinion."

"Say *whaaat?*" retorted a perplexed Saquina White.

"It's a – uhh – long story, Mrs. White," commented Ramirez. "But don't be worried... she only bites people who she really *likes.*"

"You're *silly*, Mister," chirped the girl.

The black agent ceased walking and held up his hand, bidding them to stop.

"Okay," he stated. "We're here, I reckon."

"Now, what nonsense is *this*?" demanded White's wife, the suspicious tone again rising in her voice. "I don't see no bus, no alien, no... *nothin'!*"

"Hold on," he advised. "Hector... you want to do the honors?"

"My *pleasure*," answered the scientist.

He looked down at his feet, searched around and found a small rock, about half the size of a golf-ball.

Imitating a World Series-pitch, Ramirez tossed the stone skyward.

"Ready for the ride of a *lifetime?*" advised Boatman, with a knowing smile.

It's Party-Time

A soft moan – too low to have been heard by ordinary human ears, but very audible to the two ex-astronauts and the ex-salesman – was all it took to send Boyd, White and Billings scurrying over to where the Claremont girl stood vigil.

"Momma?" excitedly called Melissa. "*Momm*a – y'all comin' 'round?"

The African-American woman coughed, rolled on to her side and let out another, slightly stronger sound.

"Give her a few minutes," advised White, squatting beside Claremont and her daughter. "Bet your Momma's been up to them Pearly Gates, but ol' Saint Pete told her she got more work down here on Earth... so she's back with us."

The woman weakly nodded, to the delight of all around.

"Momma – oh – *Momma!*" cried the teenager, draping herself over Claremont's frame and drenching her with tears.

A second later, they were joined by the boy, who hugged his sister and held his mother's hand.

"She say, 'peace... child'," whimpered Melissa.

"Well... that's one out of three," offered a pleased Boyd. "And obviously I'm glad for it – but given what we saw Whitney go through, when she saved the Captain, I'd have expected either him or the Professor, to come to, first."

"How are the other two doing?" asked Billings. "By the way... 'welcome back', Whitney! It's sure good to see you... and that's *another* thing that you wouldn't have had to endure, if you hadn't met Sari and me. I'm doing a lot of apologizing these days, I guess."

"To answer your question... they're still out," noted Boyd.

"I can *see* that!" complained the salesman. "What I meant is – I don't know my arse from my elbow in terms of first-aid... do they *look* any better?"

"Think so, Mista Billins'," confirmed Melissa, slowly getting up from her comforting position. "Might just be mah 'magination... but thought ah hear somethin' from Miz Cherie, 'bout a hour 'go... then she jus' go back to sleep –"

Abruptly, she stopped talking, then re-started.

"What that, Momma?" asked the teenager.

Slowly, Claremont managed to raise her upper-body, supporting her weight with her arms straight and behind.

Though still dazed, her face wore a concerned look.

She cast glances at the still somnolent figures of Tanaka and Jacobson.

"Ah'm not gettin' y'all, Momma," protested Melissa. "Ah don' see *nobody*."

"Huh?" interjected Billings.

"Not sure what she tryin' to say," explained the teenager. "Somethin' 'bout 'men is comin' –"

"Uh-oh," said the worried salesman. "Listen, Whitney, just *think* it – say it in your head, over and over again... we'll hear you."

Now a thought appeared in the minds of all those in the immediate vicinity. *Soldiers is comin' – and they fixin' to do us bad!* sent Claremont.

"*Shit!*" cursed White. "That's just about *all* we need – and with two of our people down for the count!"

He got down on a knee and looked Claremont straight-on.

"Whitney," he spoke, his voice serious, "Thanks for the fair warnin', there. Y'all know where they're comin' from?"

The woman pointed upward.

"Must be the top-levels," suggested Boyd, thinking as fast as he could.

"Well... didn't Mister Gestapo-Jerk over there, say that all the doors up there were locked?" Billings pointed out. "That's *some* protection, at least – maybe we could reinforce them, like pile stuff up behind 'em..."

"They get *that* far – we're fucked, anyway," countered the black ex-astronaut. "We're gonna have to meet 'em as far-away as possible... give 'em a bloody nose and hope for the best, afterwards."

"What do you *mean*... 'hope for the best'?" complained the salesman. "They probably got a small *army* up there, looking for us!"

"Probably," agreed Boyd, "But we still got our secret way out... right?"

"Not without Tommy," persisted Billings. "I'll go down shooting, right beside this box, rather than leave him here!"

"Me too, Mista Billins'", loudly chimed in Curtis; and for this, the salesman took the boy by his side and gave him an appreciative, fatherly hug.

"Let's hope we don't have to quote you on *that* one, Bob," muttered Boyd. "Even if we drag Tommy, the Professor and the Captain all that way... we don't have a *clue* about what we're going to do when we get topside. In the meantime, grab your gun and come with us – we've got to recce out those upper-doors and whatever's behind them. Problem is... there's five of 'em and only three of us – better than 50-50... but not odds *I* like."

"Unless they got teams coming through *each* door," unhelpfully commented Billings.

"Listen, Curtis," said Boyd, squatting to address the boy, "You remember that 'reserve-force'-thing?"

"Yes sir – ah does," answered Curtis, with wide eyes.

"You'd *better!*" warned the ex-astronaut. "Because this is serious business – we may need your help – at full power – any *minute* now."

"Ah'm *ready*, sir," dutifully confirmed the boy.

"Okay," acknowledged the ex-astronaut.

He looked up at the other men.

"Ready?" asked Boyd.

"Just a sec," interjected White. "Gonna drag 'asshole' over here so he can enter the unlockin' codes, when we want to go through. Bob, y'all cover him and make sure he does what he's told, then get your ass up to the top-level with Brent 'n me as fast as y'all can... got that?"

"Yeah," grimly confirmed the salesman. "Backs-to-the-wall time, I guess."

Boyd had a steely look on his face, as he straightened up and slung his rifle.

For a few seconds – as he clenched his fists – the ex-astronaut's determined-looking eyes glowed, a martial-melody sounded, and his body showed the now-familiar charges of the *Fire*.

The display brought immediate hope and confidence to the onlookers.

"Well... that's *one* way of looking at it, Bob," he stated, his voice tough and purposeful. "But I prefer to think of it in another way, entirely."

The salesman sent him a silent, interrogatory stare.

"For *me*," vowed Boyd, "It's... *'party-time'!*"

Welcome To The Magic... And The Bus

Though none of those on the bus – save for the troupe of more-than-human acolytes – had yet seen Karéin-Mayréij, few of these recently-embarked Compton-residents doubted that something *far* out of the ordinary, was underway.

The fact that they had sat down, strapped on seat-belts, and then had felt the vehicle soar rapidly upward, had – at least – convinced them of *that*.

Now, they had come to another full stop, and a few of them – despite the general excitement – had become restless.

"Where *is* we?" asked a mother.

"Can't tell," responded the Hispanic aunt of one of these prized children. "Still pretty dark out there from these tinted-windows, but it ain't as bad as a few minutes ago... couldn't see *nothin'*. Whew! Few things fallin' 'round the *autobuse*... and a lot of dust."

"We're in some kind of building," called Hendricks, towards the back of the bus. "Four-car garage or a car-wash, maybe... she took the front door clean-off, just before we came in for our last landing. I can sort of see out the front."

Privately, he whispered to Chu, "Minnie... you *see* that? Movement off in the distance... but too far to make it out. Not sure what's going on."

The first woman called forward.

"Hey – Mister FBI!" she shouted. "How many more of these damn stops we gonna have? I done counted *twenny*... and it's gettin' stuffy in here, since we landed and they turned off the conditionin' –"

"Actually, this is number twelve," corrected Boatman. "On account of a couple of families not bein' where they's supposed to be... and because of two or more kids in this famous little class comin' from the same family. Anyway, you all will be seein' her real soon now – I'd just ask you to be patient –"

"Well, that'd be easier if you'd tell us where we's goin', after she shows her face," grumbled an elderly African-American man, in the back.

"Yeah... where *is* we goin', anyway?" demanded the aunt.

"Listen, everybody," counseled Kaysten, motioning for calm, "I'd like to mention that I had a lot of the same worries, when first I met Karéin; but when she explained exactly what was going on – the 'wherefores and whys' of it all, I mean – the first thing that I said to myself was, 'Holy *Crow*, Jerry, you mean you were almost ready to walk away from *this* kind of opportunity?' I *know* it's frustrating just sitting there and waiting – but *believe* me, folks, you won't regret it! Karéin-Mayréij will fill you all in on the details, as soon as she gets here."

Whispering, he added to Boatman, Hendricks and Chu, "I... *hope*."

Amazingly, this seemed to quiet the complaints... at least temporarily.

The bemused third agent surveyed the audience, which had turned to discussing the situation, one person to another.

"You know, Minnie," he muttered, "Bullshit baffles brains – but *alien*-BS baffles 'em better than a million channels of Pay-TV. Maybe between the laser-eyeballs and the silver-tongue, Mister Politician here, came out ahead of you."

Chu tried hard to avoid laughing – and was about to lose the struggle – when the front entrance door unexpectedly opened.

Unsteadily, a middle-aged African-American woman in a conservative dress and hairdo, with a figure that had – at one time, been on the overly-plump-side, but which had now been significantly eroded – stepped up the stairs, until she was plainly visible to the throng further back in the bus.

Immediately, five or six youthful voices joined a chorus, shouting out, "'Mornin', Mrs. Jones!"

"Hello... children..." mumbled the teacher, with an odd, glassy stare.

"Oh, *wow*," observed Chu. "I *know* what she did to that poor woman!"

"Huh? What you *sayin'*?" asked Boatman.

"What did she *do*?" inquired Kaysten. "And how would *you* know?"

"Because... *I* can do it, too," quietly remarked the FBI team-leader.

"Atasha – I release my grasp... and I pray that you can forgive me!" called a light, melodious and familiar voice, from the threshold between the bus-door and the outside. "There was no more time in which to argue."

As if stunned, the teacher just stood in place for a second or two.

Then she blinked her eyes, shook her head and looked down into the stairwell.

"*You*... " she started. "How'd y'all convince me to just drop everythin' and head off here to the garage at Kleen-Yore-Truck? Not five minutes before, I told y'all I didn't want to go."

"I dominated your *mind*," answered the unseen voice, in straight-forward fashion. "In other words, a 'mind-f...', uhh, *that* was what my dear lover Bob called it... but as there are so many children here, maybe I should refrain from using that word. I am very sorry that I did this, Mrs. Jones; and after you have heard what I now will say... you will be free to go. I will also do labor for you, in penance. Oh-kay?"

"Yo! Ah knows who *that* is!" shouted an excited child.

Moving effortlessly without apparent effort, the Storied Watcher, clad only in her civilian-clothing, floated up to the main floor of the bus.

With a godly, ethereal glow surrounding her and the same in her eyes, she faced the rear-half of the vehicle, smiled and said, "Hello, dear little ones – your kin and beloved, as well. I am joyed and honored, that you have come to be with me!"

More than a few had to be physically-restrained by parents, relatives or guardians, and two of the children almost made it over the seat-tops, before they were caught.

"Jaysus, Mary and Joseph... it's really *her!*" gasped one of the parents.

"*Told* you it'd be worth the wait!" smugly commented Kaysten, with a pointed finger and raised eyebrow.

"She seems so *short*," whispered one of the adults, to another.

"I am Karéin-Mayréij – the Storied Watcher – with whom you last spoke while I was with my first family, on Sam Jacobson's space-ship," she explained. "I am *eternally* in your debt for singing to me... and preparing me for what I had to do. Know *this* : what you did may have been critical to the saving of your entire *planet*. All people of this place called 'Earth', should bring you grateful homage! I will now do the same."

She got down on a knee, bowed her head and quietly intoned, "I love *all* of you, like you were my own family; and I always *will*... dear, cherished friends."

"Y'all *awesome!*" exclaimed a boy.

With a huge smile, the alien-girl came to her feet and beamed at the child.

Turning to Chu, she asked, "Minn-ee – how much have you told them?"

"Various things," answered the FBI team-leader, right in front of the throng. "Some of them know more or less the whole story... some just came without needing to know a lot of details. They need to hear the *truth*, Karéin."

"The... *truth*?" asked a thin, greasy-looking Hispanic man, involuntarily holding his little daughter close as he spoke. "What's goin' *on*, here?"

"Y'all ain't gonna *eat* us or somethin', is y'all?" demanded one of the African-American parents.

"I am a 'vegetablian'," replied Karéin-Mayréij, with a well-rehearsed shrug.

Laughter rang out.

But in the next second, her countenance darkened, as she stole past the FBI-agents and others in the front of the bus, stopping midway within the vehicle to address the group of newcomers.

"Now *listen*, you all – and listen well!" implored the alien-girl. "We will have much time later, to become acquainted... and I am as excited about doing that as you are – but right now, I must bring you tidings of grave peril. I will speak plainly – your *lives* are in danger... and I mean to keep you safe."

"Sweet Baby *Jaysus!*" swore the teacher. "What y'all *mean?*"

"Some of this will be explained to you by my friends – whose names are Minn-ee, Otis, Will, Sylvia, Hector, Jerr-ee, Wolf, Misha and Sebastiàn – as we travel," replied the Storied Watcher, "But briefly : somewhere within this city, lies hidden one of the 'atom-smashing bombs'; and it may detonate at any time. Now that you are all in one close space, I could perhaps protect you from this... but I certainly could *not* have done so, were you in your own houses. I will take you sufficiently far-away from this 'bomb' so that it will no longer be a threat. However, there is another, even *more* serious danger... one that will not be nearly so easy to deal with."

"What could be worse than one of them bombs?" nervously asked the aunt.

"Your entire *government*... *that* is what," ruefully admitted Karéin-Mayréij. "Since I fell to this planet, your President – for reasons that I do not comprehend – maybe fear of a powerful rival, maybe just stupidity – has been trying to *kill* me! Ordinarily, that would not be a concern, since I can quite easily evade any of your President's weapons; however, lately, he has taken up the idea of trying to hurt me, by abusing – even killing – those who he knows I love and cherish. Sometimes, when one of my beloved kin are so anguished, *I* feel the pain, as well. And since all of *you* who now hear my words, could be counted as my friends – well, I hope that you understand what might happen, when your President's assassins discover this fact... as well as your own whereabouts."

There was an aghast silence.

Finally, one of the adults spoke up.

"Y'all knows, down in mah basement, we had a batt'ry-powered radio... tried to keep up with what was goin' down, after everythin' went to them gangstas, in our 'hood," this woman recounted, obviously choosing her words carefully. "There was this story 'bout y'all doin' some kind of shit at the White House – they said y'all a 'menace to the world', or somethin' like that... guess what ah'm aksin' y'all is... y'all really *doin'* all that?"

"Well ah never hear nothin' like that... an' ah had one of them digital-TV-things that ran off th' generator... somebody said them Muslims did it," countered another parent. "Or was that what went down at that there ho-tel?"

"Did I, uhh, do a little, 'remodeling' of the White House?" answered the Storied Watcher, with a sheepish grin on her face. "Yes, I *did* – although no-one was really hurt, there. But that was *after* your President had declared war against me, and had already tried to kill *me* – several times – starting at the hotel in Tucson. It is a long story, Mrs. Vickers... and once you hear the real truth, I hope that you will appreciate how... *restrained* that I have been, in dealing with this sad and pointless conflict."

"How y'all –" started the second parent, but her voice was cut off.

Suddenly, there was a forceful shudder that reverberated through what was left of the garage, bringing pieces of its interior falling randomly here and there, including upon the roof of the bus.

A second or two later, a sound like a low 'thump', caused another near-avalanche of dust and debris.

"*Whoa!*" exclaimed a worried Kaysten. "What was *that*?"

"The *bomb?*" shouted the Hispanic woman, causing a thrill of panic to start infecting the group. "We gonna *die!*"

Shaking her head, he Storied Watcher held up her hand for quiet. "No – not that," she counseled. "For if it were, we would now either be dead – or would be hurtling away from the blast, like a fire-stone thrown from a volcano. This is something *else* – I must away to determine it, though I will return forthwith."

"Yall *leavin'* us?" cried one of the frightened parents.

"Only for a few minutes," answered Karéin-Mayréij. "And in that time, you must ask yourselves : do you feel safer *with* me... or *without* me? For I will not force anyone who does not want to come along, to do so. Instead, I will bless you and pray that you will never be harmed. Consider it well, dear friends!"

She re-traced her steps until she was near the exit-stairs, then turned her Sirius-bright stare at the fearful, confused throng at the back of the bus.

For the first time, they heard her haunting, sweetly-powerful song of war, its Celtic-electric-violin-rock chords sending excitement racing down their spines like an impossibly potent adrenaline-rush.

With bolts of *Amaiish*-energy all over her body, the Storied Watcher called the words that had become familiar to her more experienced fellow-travelers :

"*Ahn'jë! Fàiagàryuu! Ksé'l'ch'! Ss'éth'ch'! I'ëà'b'!*"

Instantly, she stood before them in war-garb – save for the shield, which for some reason was not in its normal place – with the burning essence of *Vîrya Ahn'jë* causing the startled human passengers to flinch involuntarily backward; despite this, Chu and the others, especially Misha, seemed now to be almost accustomed to the armor's hellish aura.

The more-than-humans did a double-take, as the alien-girl, her voice unusually impatient, called out, "*Vîrya I'ëà'b'!*"

Now the buckler appeared, scooting from a previously-invisible spot somewhere near Kaysten, and affixing itself to the arm of the Storied Watcher, who muttered something in her inscrutable tongue, tapped the shield with a smoking, chainmail-clad finger, and then shot an embarrassed look at the crowd, before donning her interference-pattern goggles and rocketing from the bus.

"Oh... that was just because she *likes* me," announced the Chief of Staff, with a smirk. "The *shield*, that is."

"What on Earth y'all *talkin'* 'bout, Mister FBI?" asked the older, African-American man. "What *was* that thang? Flew so fast ah hardly could see it!"

"She's not an 'it'... she's a 'she'," explained Kaysten. "Her name is 'veer-ya ee-ab', or something like that... and she's kind of got the 'hots' for me, would be the best way to put it, I guess."

He paused for a second, then added, "But the whole thing's *strictly* platonic. I'm just... *humoring* her. Make sure not to tell *her* that, though! She can be a little, uhh, *moody*."

Several of the children giggled profusely, upon hearing this.

After the mirth had quieted down, Chu spoke.

"Just to clear something up," mentioned the FBI team-leader, "Mr. Kaysten isn't technically with the Bureau – he's actually the President's Chief of Staff."

"Well if that true – then what he doin' down here, wid Angel Lady, if she goin' off on some big war against the guv'ment?" asked one of the African-American women.

"That's a little, *uhh*, complicated," evaded Kaysten. "Let's just say that I'm kind of – uhh – 'undercover'."

Abruzzio winced.

"I don't know how long Karéin will be away," continued Chu, "So I'll keep this brief... but I'll try to explain what's been going on. She *believes* that her friends – specifically a bunch of people who she met when she, uhh, 'fell to Earth' – are being cruelly abused by some other government agency. My team and I were ordered to contact her, using Mr. Ramirez and Ms. Abruzzio, the bounty-hunter named 'Wolf' and the other individual named 'Misha', as our, uhh, scientific consultants. We met Karéin some distance from here and ended up in Los Angeles, where we ran across Sebastiàn – who some of you met outside the bus – and it was him, who warned us about the presence of the bomb. Since then, we've been trying to convince the Storied Watcher to call a truce and sit down for negotiations... but, unfortunately, she's still very suspicious of the President's motives –"

"All true, Madam Chu," interrupted the Russian, "But you omitted the repeated attempts against her life, by your government's intelligence-agencies and military. I *personally* witnessed one of these and – like Wolf – I was almost killed myself, in the resulting cross-fire. So all who now hear this, should understand that Karéin's defensiveness is very well-founded."

Addressing the audience, Chu replied, "Yes – I *do* have to admit that, Misha... and it's something that our friends on this bus need to know, right from the start. I'll be honest with you, folks; there's a *lot* about this story that my team and I *don't* know. We're going on instinct, here... and you may have to, as well."

"The point is – as I believe Karéin has already explained," spoke up Abruzzio, "The *minute* the Government figures it out – that she cares about you – there's a real possibility that they'll come looking for *you*, as well. If that were to happen without Karéin being nearby, the outcome would be *much* worse than if she were there to protect you. It's bad news... but it's the truth."

"Y'all talkin' like our lives just been turned upside down," complained one of the African-American women.

"They *have*," quietly confirmed the scientist. "I'm very sorry about that. If it's any consolation... the same thing has happened to Minnie, Misha, myself and all of us. We may *never* be able to go home again."

"Ah refuse to believe that," retorted the parent.

"Come on, Charity!" she ordered, to the little girl beside her, pulling the child to her feet.

"But Momma!" protested the girl. "She say –"

"Bunch of nonsense!" firmly replied the woman. "This all some kind of weirdo-shit that we got *no* business, bein' in!"

With the child in tow and the rest of the passengers looking silently on, the parent strode down the corridor.

Reluctantly, Chu and her compatriots stood aside to let her pass.

The two had only barely stepped outside the bus, when the others inside began to hear the '*thump-thump-thump*' of turbine-powered helicopter-blades.

They heard the woman's voice shout, "Come *on*, child – hurry *up!*"

There were more percussive sounds, but these were different – faster, sharper – compared to the ones that had just been heard.

Screams and the noise of gunfire, began to come from every direction.

"Minnie – sounds like *trouble* out there," barked a worried Boatman. "Big-caliber impacts. We better go after 'em!"

"No – you stay in here with the folks," ordered the FBI team-leader. "*I'll* go. Will – be ready to take the wheel."

"You *got* it!" briskly answered Hendricks.

"Now if I just knew how the damn thing *works*," he added, below his breath, as he jumped into the driver's seat.

With her gun at the ready, Chu dashed down the aisle and out of the bus.

"*My God!*" they heard her shout. "*Stay down!*"

A child's wail screamed from outside.

A few of the more perceptive ones heard, "Can't move – we's *trapped!*"

Something went 'whoosh', apparently directly over the garage; and – a second later – the rear-end of the bus rang like a bell, against the impact of a vicious shock-wave.

Whatever had just went off must not have been aimed directly at either the garage or what was in it; although part of the roof collapsed, there was no immediate fire- or blast-damage.

Wolf's voice sounded.

"Can't light her up – we'll burn down what's left of this place – come *on*, get your ass out from under the bus –"

"*Minnie!*" bellowed Boatman, now terribly afraid for his senior agent.

All those in the back of the bus crouched down, covering heads with hands. Many of the young ones began to cry.

"Stay *in* there!" they heard. "I'm *going* for them!"

Misha was heading for the bus-door, as the hauntingly-pretty song of the Storied Watcher began to echo throughout the air.

"Don't go out, Miss FBI – y'all can't do *nothin'* to that thing –" shrieked the parent's voice, from outside.

Now, there was the hint of *differently*-thrilling music – sort of like a famous guitar-riff from the mid-point of *All Along The Watch-Tower* – along with an odd, warbling-sound, akin to that of a ray-gun from an old science-fiction-show.

A half-second later, these were followed by the noises of metal-parts coming violently-undone, and rotor-blades beating more and more quickly.

"*Run!*" yelled Chu's voice. "*Get back here!*"

The terrified Compton-woman – carrying her child – clambered furiously over piles of broken timber and gyp-rock, back into what was left of the garage.

There was a deafening, crashing noise, accompanied by a wave of heat.

Again, what was left of the garage, swayed and buckled precariously.

"Take my hand!" demanded Chu.

The team-leader was wincing, with tears pouring from her eyes; but there was a regal, proud, powerful air, about her.

"Back in the bus! You *too*, Wolf!" she shouted.

"Yeah, but –" he grunted, then clambered aboard, with Misha in tow.

The Russian was just outside the bus.

"Over *here!*" he exclaimed, waving at Chu and the mother-and-child.

Hendricks was about to close the door, but at the last moment, his boss – her red-ringed eyes closed to a mere squint – demanded, "Where's Sebastiàn?"

"I ain't *comin'!*" called the voice of the *Mara*. "*¡Que se vayan!*"

"Don't be a *jackass!*" cursed the bounty-hunter. "There's Air Force all *over* the place, out there! You'll get shot to *pieces!*"

As if to emphasize the point, a rocket – or a missile, or something akin to those – struck a target not far from the remains of the garage.

"*¡Usted no comprende, cholo!*" shouted Sebastiàn. "I got some *business* with them 'Aryan' pussies. Ask *chica* – *she* knows!"

"He speaks the *truth*, Wolf," came the disembodied voice of Karéin-Mayréij. "He embarks now on his death-quest; we dare not stand in his way – but instead, we should bless and pour out our power over him – and wish him, 'Heaven-speed'. Make proof the door and bid everyone to secure their seat!"

The bounty-hunter tarried for a second or two, looking outward.

With hast – but sincere – empathy, he called to the gangster.

"Well then... *buena suerte* – wish we had more time – let's do a *cerveza* when when this is all over with. *Hasta mañana*, pardner!" offered the big man.

Quietly and reflectively, Wolf added, "And... *vaya con Dìos, hombre.*"

A second later, his blazing alter-ego, chimed in.

Fire of Kiss thee warrior lay I on, came a thought even more alien than those of the Storied Watcher.

"*¡Igualmente a usted, mi amigo!*" came back the voice of the *Mara*, as he began to dash for the opposite end of the garage.

The bounty-hunter – carrying one puppy under each arm – retreated back into the bus and gave a hand-signal to Hendricks (who fancied himself the driver, while hoping none of the others realized he had no idea how to steer the vehicle).

As the third agent closed the door to the outside, Wolf offered, "What I was *gonna* say was, 'well now, we're in here... but they can just as easily aim for –"

Abruptly, he stopped talking, as – waving his arms like a madman – the bounty-hunter tried to maintain his balance; for the bus was now rising at a very rapid pace, with its nose, despite Hendricks' best efforts, pointed at almost an upward 45-degree angle.

Ooo-ooo-ooo, came the thrilling, exciting, inspiring music, combined with alien-power; it blanketed the more-than-humans, and perhaps others as well.

Wolf's gesture proved futile, since he fell backward into the throng in the front aisle, causing a chain-reaction as the two fire-puppies careened into Chu, who – still barely able to see – collided with Misha and then Ramirez.

Chaos broke out as the bus rocketed skyward, with brutal acceleration – almost at the limits of average human-tolerance – crushing passengers into seat-backs, while Chu and her troupe held on for dear life.

Suddenly, the third agent's mind was invaded by an unmistakable order.

Hold it steady, Will Hendricks – let the path not change!

Now the bounty-hunter's name was called.

Wolf – bid your Little Spirit to propel, from below!

Immediately – with orange-glowing eyes that caused yet more fear in those humans who beheld, – he complied.

Okay, darlin' – get yourself down there and make like a blowtorch...

But just make sure to fire down and away from us... you got that?

Master beloved obey I! replied a strange, private thought.

A bright-glowing spark – or something like it – jumped from Wolf's body, plunging through the floor-boards, without making any apparent mark.

Another entreaty – this one, directed to Ramirez – came from the mind of Karéin-Mayréij.

Hector – imagine blowing into a big bal-loon, underneath the bus.

Keep thinking on it, I beg of you!

Don't know what I'm doin', mused the scientist.

But... here goes!

Ramirez crossed himself and looked intensely forward, and – for the first time – there was a back-light visible in his stare.

Frantically, Hendricks manipulated the steering wheel, and – to his amazement – he found that the vehicle was somehow responding to his entreaties... though its trajectory continued to zoom upward.

One last command was sent – this time to Abruzzio.

Sylvia – make a shroud around this ark, implored the alien-girl.

Bid it mix and deflect helpless, every light-beam that should try to intrude!

Extending a hand to Ramirez – which was immediately accepted – she adopted much the same pose as him, while cradling the puppy in her lap.

Guide me, Rainbow! she prayed, with her eyes closed.

Let's make this thing shimmer... like a far-off mirage in the summer heat!

"What *the* –" exclaimed the third agent.

He was used to not seeing very much through the bus's darkly-tinted-windows; but now, it looked as if he was in a circus fun-house, with indistinct, ever-changing reflections of sky and clouds coming from every direction.

"Can't even see where 'up' is!" complained Hendricks. "All I can do to keep her level, is trust my gut!"

With a hand still tightly-locked to that of her fellow-scientist – and the *Fire* flickering under her shirt – Abruzzio slowly opened multi-colored eyes.

Her face – though deep in serious contemplation – wore a saturnine smile, as the scientist's melody – delicate yet with grandeur in its chords – was perceived.

Neither the third agent nor any of the others – save Wolf who had a dim idea of it – could see the amazing scene that was unfolding directly underneath : a jet of fire, its thrust supplementing an invisible pocket of high-pressure air, issued – as if from nowhere – just aft of the rear wheels.

Songs of power – from several of the group – echoed through the bus.

"*Damn,*" shouted Boatman as he struggled to stay semi-upright, while the bus continued to ascend. "Is that *frost* I'm seein' on the windows?"

High over the Santa Monica Mountains, those assigned to the 3-D situation-displays on the airborne command-post, worked their various dials and controls at a rapid pace.

"Neighborhood-Watch – report," commanded a tactical controller.

"High Five, this is Neighborhood-Watch Three," responded a voice, overlaid with the *thump-thump-thump* background sound of helicopter-blades. "Had an anomaly just off the school back there a few seconds ago – building collapsed with a lot of dust for no reason, then one of the guys from the other wing went down – not sure what hit him, saw some kind of a flash... maybe a MP-SAM? Don't think the poor bugger punched out... but no sign of the main objective... havin' a *party* doing the mop-up, though, *lots* of targets of opportunity, down here –"

There was a short pause, then the voice became louder.

"Gunner – 30 degrees right, ground-fire!" it shouted, to the staccato-sounds of a heavy automatic-weapon opening up.

"*Engage!* Oh, *yeaaah!* Good hit... good hit! Busted his black *ass!*"

"Rodge, Neighborhood-Watch – monitor and call in as necessary," mentioned the controller.

He hit a different virtual-button on his touch-screen.

"Rover Splash Golf, over," he commanded. "Top-cover status... report."

"Splash Golf here," responded a ghostly voice, with the radar-returns of the fighter-plane involved, instantly superimposed over the display's holographic-image. "Had a trace – 44.1 positive delta at 252 kph – directly over target-area, but lost track about three seconds later. Lots of odd returns... looks like side-lobe reflections... wait – IR-sig, I think... *shit*, dropped off the HUD... what the *hell*? Hold on... another blip... enhancing to narrow-angle – yeah *baby* – there it *is!* Faint, but I got a clean track now –"

The controller temporarily disabled his throat-mike and turned to the smartly-dressed, crew-cut young Air Force crewman alongside, not paying much attention to how this man reflexively fingered a small crucifix on a chain.

"Where's the *nuke?*" demanded the first controller. "We got a *shot* now!"

"Coming," replied the other. "Need a few minutes to get in range, though. And don't forget it's a slow missile... we got to get the bitch right on *top* of it –"

"Well then – the fly-boys gotta do their stuff," retorted the first controller.

He re-enabled the microphone.

"Rover Splash Golf... clear to engage," he declared.

"Rodge that," answered the voice. "Wingman, follow me – intercept-path, vector south-west, 19 degrees, angels 27. Fox 6 – then Fox 7 at lock. Acknowledge!"

"Rover Splash Hotel, SW 19, 27 thousand, Fox 6 active at launch-point, Fox 7 on lock – acknowledged," came the voice of another fighter-pilot.

"Bank now," ordered the first pilot.

Two more of America's deadliest interceptors, each loaded with lethal guided-missiles, lit their 'burners and roared toward a distant point in the sky.

Angry with this latest attempt on her life – not to mention on those of countless innocent bystanders – the nearly-invisible Storied Watcher, fell down through the atmosphere like an avenging harpy.

The scene below was a Pandemonium of out-of-control fires, with heavily-armed helicopter-gunships shooting auto-cannons at civilians and the occasional lightly-armed gangster, through the ghetto-streets.

A wave of fury washed over her psyche.

They slaughter these poor people just for sport... but I cannot tarry and save all, she sent to her war-children, with disgust.

Ai! Another *one whose blood stains the pavement, right in front!*

What if she be kin of Atasha Jones or the children in her class?

But I can *make some of their assailants, pay,* mused Karéin-Mayréij, *In the short interval, before the ark-on-high, would fall again to Earth.*

Me let Mother strike, pleaded *Vîrya I'ëà'b'.*

The burning gauntlet adorning the arm and hand of the scowling, fang-toothed alien-girl, took grasp of the buckler, tensing and holding the latter close to her breast.

Then go, *Daughter Tornado-Diamond Curtain!* cried the Storied Watcher, as she propelled *Vîrya I'ëà'b'* edge-on at the closest gunship, like a large, other-worldly *shuriken.*

Appearing as if from nowhere, the shield screamed through the air, striking the outer extremities of the helicopter's whirling rotors at an oblique-angle, severing the majority of these instantly. It then continued through the unfortunate craft's main gearbox and turbines, sending the gunship to smash into the ground a couple of seconds later.

Flying a parabolic-course, *Vîrya I'ëà'b'* brought down two other war-birds in more or less the same manner, before she returned to her mother and creator.

Some scores of meters to one side, the alien-girl noticed another military helicopter firing at the stragglers of a crowd, who had temporarily taken desperate refuge in an already-burning building.

Suddenly, it fired two anti-tank missiles at the doomed throng:

With the fast-thinking skill instantly activated, she dropped part of her protective-bubble and sent a mental code to *Vîrya Ahn'jë*'s pseudo-glass eyes.

Then she fired.

A few nanoseconds later, both missiles exploded thunderously – but prematurely – as they were struck by a scintillating, white-and-gold beam of potent energy; and in the next trice, the same fate befell the gunship, as it was struck side-on by the Storied Watcher's lethal gaze.

It crashed straight down in a cacophony of smashed Plexiglas and wrecked component-parts; but somehow, the gunner within – bearing a side-arm – managed to crawl out and stagger to his feet.

Stunned at their delivery from apparently certain death – but still livid with rage at what was being done to them – several of those in the building ran toward the Army-soldier.

"We gonna kick yo' fuckin' *ass*, white-boy!" shouted a ragged-dressed, bloodied African-American. "Y'all smoked *seven* of us! Ain't 'nuff left of 'em to even put in a *coffin!*"

"You fuckin' porch-monkeys *get back!*" the half-dazed – but professionally-aggressive – gunner barked. "Make one move and I'll *kill* you... *nigger!*"

He waved his gun, firing a warning-shot into the air, though it could hardly be heard over the mayhem of the battle taking place all around.

An invisible, hostile voice sounded behind him.

"Behold – how I do the 'kicking', *for* them!" she cursed, her boot coming much too fast for him to react.

The Army-gunner didn't see this fearsome being – whose flaming boot and mind-forces propelled him by the seat of smoke-trailing pants, right over the heads of his erstwhile victims – into the top floors of a nearby, burning building.

Screams sounded briefly, as Karéin-Mayréij popped into view, her burning aura and presence taking aback those who she had just rescued.

"Holy *shit!*" gasped one of the ghetto-dwellers. "Y'all done kicked he *ass* into next *week!*"

With a savage, sharp-toothed half-smile, the alien-girl looked up, at where the man had likely breathed his last.

She called a final insult.

"Then... 'welcome to next week... and the next *life*', 'brave American soldier'!" spat the Storied Watcher.

"Who the hell *is* y'all, lady?" inquired another. "Homies sure could *use* somebody like y'all to help us, down here – they *butcherin'* us! We ain't done *nothin'*... an' we dyin' in th' streets!"

Above Mother ones danger to! warned the internal voice of Vìrya Ahn'jë.

"I tarry not, here," demurred Karéin-Mayréij, her godly demeanor waxing with each word. "Though, I am an ally, who shamefully stains her hands with human-blood – because she cannot... *refrain*. If you would resist this cruel 'President' and his lackeys... then seek you my disciple of new-found nobility, whose name is 'Sebastiàn' – obey his counsel, and he will give you hope and victory. Now stand back... lest you be *consumed!*"

With her cape billowing and her war-song roaring a melody of power and defiance, the Destroying Angel turned away from the crowd and began to run; but after a few steps, charges of lightening issued from her boots, and it appeared as if she was racing up an imaginary set of stairs, with sparks blasting upon each step.

After another second, she was gone, rocketing invisibly into the sky.

"We goin' *down*... ain't we?" shouted a terrified passenger.

"Hate to say it... but... 'yes'," called Hendricks, over his shoulder. "I think it's gonna be alright, though – we're just kind of gliding. Not *dropping*, you know? And at least it's not so cold outside... did you notice?"

Except we're 'gliding' kind of fast, he said to himself.

"We's all scared, back here!" exclaimed a child. "What's gonna *happen*?"

"*Nothing*, honey," evaded Chu, with a forced smile. "We're just coming in for a landing... that's all. Can you please keep your seat-belts fastened? I'll come back to explain what's going on, in a minute or so – but right now, I have to discuss some things with the – uhh – crew."

"Okay," came back a reluctant voice.

The FBI team-leader hauled herself forward.

"Will – how you holding up? Need me to take over?" she asked, holding tightly to everything and anything within reach, to compensate for the very un-airliner-like ride.

"I'm *fine*," he replied, trying to keep his voice down. "But I was being a bit on the 'optimistic'-side, a second ago. We're losing altitude – and we're going a bit faster every *minute*. It's a cinch to steer right and left, not up and down... well, there doesn't seem to be an 'up' stick... you know?"

"Dammit, where's *Karéin!*" complained Chu, over the shoulder of the third agent. "It's a *miracle* that we're still up here and we're still upright – I was expecting this thing to fly like a lead balloon, when the push she gave, ran out –"

"You can thank *me* for that... I *think*," offered the stressed voice of Ramirez, from several rows behind. "At least... partially. What a *strange* sensation – I'm pushing the air together, under the bus, providing lift, stability... I cannot see it, but I *know* that I'm doing it, I can *feel* it happening... but it is *very* exhausting – don't know how long I can keep it up..."

"Same here," added the bounty-hunter. "My little burnin' kid's gettin' tired, and it's blowin' back right into *my* head... she's the one that's lit a Roman Candle under us, keep us movin' forward. I wouldn't mind puttin' down somewhere, so we can take a bit of a breather."

"That's not a bad idea," commented Boatman. "But just where *is* we, anyway? Don't want to land in the ocean, you know."

"Your guess is as good as mine, man," replied Hendricks. "Ms. Scientist's crazy-house thing is making it impossible to see where we're going – and this is a *bus*, not a plane... no compass, no artificial horizon, no... *nothing*."

"Well, if we land in the water, that's probably better than crashing into L.A.," interjected Kaysten, from the last row of the forward-section accommodating his more-than-human friends. "Given what's going on down there, I mean."

"You are assuming that this vehicle is water-tight and that it is buoyant enough to stay afloat," countered Misha. "And even at that, it would probably not be a good idea to land in a current that goes out to sea... like in the direction of somewhere like Antarctica."

"What's the matter... don't you like fresh polar-bear?" joked Wolf. "They tell me it's a bit on the oily-side – but hell, the skin makes a pretty good rug."

"There are no bears in the Antarctic," wearily corrected the Russian. "Only penguins and seals."

"I flunked geography, or animal husbandry, or *whatever*... but no sweat there, pardner," deadpanned the bounty-hunter. "My hot little kid can still roast one or two of 'em up, and you can have a few feathers for your hat, if you –"

"Would you two *please* –" started Chu; but abruptly, she ceased talking, and began instead to stare out one of the windows, though Abruzzio's kaleidoscope-effect made doing so apparently of little practical use.

"What *is* it, Minnie?" demanded Boatman, easily reading her worry.

"*Danger,*" she said, as if in a trance. "Coming at us *fast* – from the right!"

"How you know?" replied the black agent.

"I can... *smell* it," she answered.

"What *kind* of danger?" demanded Abruzzio. "Can you be more specific?"

"This might not make any sense," stated the team-leader, "But it's like a vision – I keep seeing arrows flying right at me... at *us*. Will, we've got to put down, right *now!*"

"Shouldn't be a problem," muttered the third agent, "Considering that's what we're doing, anyway. Listen, Minnie – like I said, I got almost no control in the vertical, but maybe if you tell Hector to ease up –"

"Mr. Ramirez – Hector – can you do that?" rapidly repeated Chu. "We *have* to descend, as quickly as possible!"

"I'll slowly release my grasp," promised the Mexican-American scientist, "Beginning *now* –"

But instead of a slightly faster descent, the front of the bus immediately plunged into a steep dive, like a cannon-ball at the end of its trajectory.

Screams of panic – accompanied by last-minute prayers – issued from the passengers at the rear, while Hendricks frantically – albeit ineffectively – worked the bus controls, desperately trying to regain a modicum of stability.

"I'm *losin'* her!" he shouted, over the roar of rushing air outside. "She's spinnin' like an airplane in a stall!"

"Sylvia – drop that thing you're doing, outside!" commanded Chu. "He can't fix it if he can't see the horizon!"

Abruzzio's eyes flashed momentarily and returned to their normal tint.

Now – to no-one's surprise, but to the alarm of all – they saw that they were in a slow spiral down over the Pacific Ocean, far below, but approaching with uncomfortable speed.

A second later, the scientist exclaimed, "Minnie... did you say, 'arrows'?"

"Yeah," yelled Chu, casting a fearful glance at Hendricks as he struggled with the controls. "No time to think about it, now – we're going to *crash* if we don't figure out –"

"Don't you *feel* it?" shouted Abruzzio. "Radio-energy, on the outside of the bus – from high above and towards the land, I felt it hitting my rainbow –"

"So *what?*" the FBI team-leader called back, as the bus continued its frightening descent.

"'Arrows' and radio-waves, Minnie – what's *that* mean! Use your *brain*, woman!" retorted the scientist.

Misha – moving with supernatural-agility considering the unpredictable tossing and turning of the vehicle – had overheard, and he came close to both Abruzzio and Chu.

"Missiles, Madam Chu – *missiles!*" he warned. "She means that we are being 'painted' by airborne guidance-radars! If we cannot throw them off, distract them, they will follow us all the way down –"

"*Shit!*" cursed Chu. "How are we going to do *that!*"

There was another brief, multi-colored flash in Abruzzio's eyes, then she addressed Hendricks.

"Will," she requested, "We're low enough to open the front door, without de-pressurizing the bus – can you steady our descent so we aren't spinning?"

"Not without any lift!" he shouted back.

"*Hector!*" demanded Abruzzio. "Turn it on again!"

"I'm already *tryin!*" protested the frustrated Latino scientist. "But we're movin' all *over* the place – minute I start the pressure, it's no longer under us."

"Well – *keep* trying!" shouted the woman.

Taking long strides toward the front of the bus and almost losing her footing twice, Abruzzio stopped halfway and looked back.

"No, no, Rainbow, honey," she admonished, in the direction of the puppy, which was trying to follow her. "Stay with Auntie Minnie... you hear?"

"'Auntie'?" quipped Boatman, with a gallows-smile.

"*Whatever,*" sighed Chu, as she took hold of the little dog.

Immediately, the FBI team-leader's face wore a surprised look.

"My *goodness*, puppy," she commented, "*Now* I can feel much more of it... is that *you*?"

The doggie wagged its tail and licked Chu's throat, while the bus continued to hurtle down, its corkscrew-motion abating, but not completely stopping.

"Open the door, Will!" commanded Abruzzio.

"You *crazy*?" he argued. "One bump and you'll go flying without a parachute!"

"I'm not *gonna* fall!" retorted the scientist. "I'm just trying to avoid us getting shot down! Open the bloody *door!*"

"Fine!" he complained, unlocking and pulling a lever.

The front entrance to the bus swung open, causing even more heaving and bucking, as the door interrupted the flow of air over the vehicle's exterior.

Holding on to an arm-rail for dear life, Abruzzio stuck her head outside, closed her eyes and tried to zero in on the source of the impulses.

Make a rainbow as far out as I can, she resolved.

Far away as possible... free of the confusing signals shooting back and forth, inside... no, that's too far... try a little closer... there we go...

God, with this thing careening back and forth, it's like trying to see something that a lighthouse illuminates, a half-second out of a two-second cycle, thought Abruzzio, as she opened her eyes.

Wait... that's it... huh?

Can't see them with my eyes, but can sense them with my mind, two big ones, high and far-away, four really little ones, much closer, all coming fast at me, from over the shore...

Should be much easier to lock on to, but they keep jumping back and forth like a star in an unsteadily-held pair of binoculars, fading in and out... what could that mean? I'm no military-buff, but...

Doesn't matter, she realized.

Whatever *they are, I only have* one *way of trying to befuddle them – here goes – all the colors, visible or not, all the energies, everything – store it up, get ready to release –*

Again, Abruzzio closed her eyes and concentrated.

The little radio-signatures were growing easier and easier to detect with each passing second, like fireflies approaching, on a summer night.

Ready to turn on the flashlight... three... two... one... she counted, *waiting for the rotation of the bus to give her a good line-of-sight.*

Here's a rainbow – coming straight at you!

The airborne command-post-controller touched a point on the 3-D display and spoke into his throat-mike.

"Splash Golf, this is High Five," he solicited. "Need tactical-status – you had permission to fire, you should have engaged by now. What's going *on?*"

"Fox 6 already away," replied the ghostly voice of the lead fighter-pilot. "Weird maneuvers from target – had an intermittent-track blinking in and out, computer was able to predict its flight-path, we kept a good vector... but it cruised at altitude for a few seconds and then went into a steep dive... strange shape on the SAR, it's a large, oblong thing... you *sure* this is the alien?"

"Confidence is high," confirmed the controller. "Alien is known to deploy deceptive ECM. This is probably such a tactic. ETA to impact please."

"Tracking clean, ETA twelve seconds... eleven... ten... nine... eight," smoothly counted the fighter-pilot.

Suddenly, his tone changed to one of befuddled alarm.

"What the *fuck –*" he cursed. "High Five – you get that?"

"Negative," answered the controller. "Still have you, Hotel and the target on the display... returns are clear as day."

"Burst of very powerful multi-band ECM from the target," remarked the pilot. "Must have been highly-directional... my systems shut down completely for a second. And TVM-telemetry from missiles has *failed!* I say again, no response from missile – *shit,* damn things are going *ballistic!* Wingman – you still have track?"

"Splash Hotel here, checking..." sounded another voice. "Mine too, Captain – same thing must have fried their fuckin' *brains!* Sir, this makes no *sense –* been *years* since we ran into that kind of crude jamming, even the *Brazilians* gave up on it two decades ago – need new orders now."

"Continue to target and engage with all available weapons," ordered the controller. "Good shootin', guys – at least we *know* it's the alien, now – couldn't *possibly* be anything else! Patch tactical-display in to me here – we'll calculate optimum firing-position."

"Rodge that," acknowledged the lead fighter-pilot. "Wingman – Fox 7 and gun... are you armed and ready?"

"Armed and ready," echoed the second fighter-jockey. "Let's *get* it, Captain!"

Again, they lit their afterburners.

I left this for too long, self-remonstrated the Storied Watcher, as she flew invisibly upward.

Vîrya Quü'j, she sent to the locket, *on the next time when I dither, shock my mind – I cannot afford more mistakes... be they large or small.*

So much for the famed inerrant judgment of the Makailkh... *it fades from one as polluted as I...*

Friend – old – thee --never –afflict, came the response.

I – but – remind – do – will.

Intermittently dropping the energy-trapping properties of her bubble to permit a good look at what was going on above her, the alien-girl immediately did a horrified double-take.

The bus was falling rapidly – with no more than a half-minute before impact with the surface of the Pacific – while four of the American Air Force's death-arrows were hurtling toward the vehicle. Far off to the east, high and over southern California, were two of the same kind of fighter-planes that she had recently vanquished elsewhere.

Not a moment to spare, she realized, invoking the quick-thinking skill.

But I am leagues away – I cannot focus my gaze on the missiles and be sure to strike the first time, so small are they... and if I miss, I lose surprise...

Speed – I need speed!

Now, Karéin-Mayréij pushed her flying-powers to near their limit, accelerating faster than a just-launched ABM, trying desperately to close the distance between herself and her precious bus-full of friends.

Not caring to mask the incandescent, friction-caused plasma that enveloped her bubble, she streaked upward like a reverse-meteor, only to be distracted a split-second later, as her mind perceived a kaleidoscopic burst of energy, issuing – but *how*? – outward from the bus, in the direction of the missiles.

Scarcely another second later, she observed the latter starting to tumble helplessly, end over end, far from their otherwise-helpless target.

Flying so fast that she could barely maneuver to see the bus, as she rocketed past, the alien-girl could still see someone standing in an open front portal.

Sylvia! called the excited, relieved mind of Karéin-Mayréij.

But the encounter was over in an instant, as even the Storied Watcher's age-old, expert gravity-bending skills could not compensate for the forces of a tight turn, at *these* speeds.

Cannot use the mind-force to carry them with me – the stress would tear that bus apart, she considered.

Upward soared the alien-girl, making a wide arc in the stratosphere, reversing course as rapidly as she dared.

Far below her, two F-32E stealth-fighters closed in for an easy kill.

"*Sylvia!*" shouted Chu. "You *see* anything?"

"What, Karéin?" replied the scientist.

"Huh?" responded a confused Chu, barely audible over the rushing wind of the vehicle's continued descent.

"I saw her... *heard* her," offered Abruzzio.

"Was that the streak we saw fly by? I thought it was another missile," replied the FBI team-leader.

"Leveling out," announced Hendricks. "Thank God... still descending, but I think I got her under control."

Sighs of relief issued from the back of the bus, as it slowly stopped rotating, coming to an uneven, nose-high, but relatively stable, downward glide.

"Uh-oh," warned Abruzzio. "I thought I *got* them... but the two big ones are back – and they're coming in *fast!*"

"What are you talking about?" demanded Kaysten.

"Will," ordered a fearful Chu, "Get us *down* – fast as you can – water-landing or no!"

"Target range fourteen kilometers," broadcasted the lead fighter-pilot. "Good track... damn, that thing's *huge*! What the hell *is* it?"

"Yeah," confirmed the wingman. "If I didn't know it's *her*, I'd say it's a weather-balloon – it's sure big enough on the display."

"High Five, we need TACEVAL on that thing that just shot by our radar-target, a few seconds ago," requested the leader. "IR-sig was off the charts... someone on the ground fire a SAM?"

"Negative, Splash Golf," came the voice of the air combat controller. "Not sure *what* it was. We're deploying assets to investigate, but it went off our screens, too. Continue to engage objective."

"Roger that... Fox 7 on my mark," agreed the fighter-leader. "Two birds each run, second pass if – just a second – some kind of interference on the audio, sounds like rock-music – what the *fuck* – trying to squelch –"

"Mayday! *Mayday!*" interrupted the panicked voice of the wingman. "I'm hit – I'm *hit!*"

"*What –*" yelled the lead pilot, as his rear-view display showed a fireball, from which a seat containing a pressure-suited human-figure, was flying rapidly upward and away.

"Splash Golf – Splash Golf – *report!* Hotel just dropped off the *radar!*" exclaimed the tactical announcer's panicked voice.

A split-second later, the fighter-leader watched in shocked dismay, as the right wing of his own aircraft was neatly bisected, by a red-and-green-glowing *something* that looked like a weird parody of a shark-fin, effortlessly swimming underneath, right through a composite-and-titanium sea.

Its fly-by-wire brain no longer able to compensate, the F-32E spun out of control. Luckily, the pilot's ejection-seat lasted long enough to get him out, just before a similar explosion disintegrated his own war-bird.

As he tried to remain conscious against the g-forces of the rocket-seat, a strange thought invaded his mind.

I spare your life, it told, *to honor Sam, Brent and Devon, who once flew into battle in service of the same "Air Force"... and because it is shameful to slaughter the helpless-without-guilt.*

Do not count on being so lucky next time, American air-warrior – and pass my warning to your fellow-soldiers!

He popped his chute.

"I guess we had better close the door... this thing might not be water-tight, but we leave it open when we hit the Pacific, we're gonna need our swimmin'-trunks that much sooner," advised Boatman.

Though they were descending at a controlled-pace, the surface of the ocean was now looming below.

"But then I can't see those planes, and I can't try to –" started Abruzzio.

Suddenly, there was a thunderous explosion from above, followed quickly by another.

"I see two parachutes," announced the female scientist.

"*Pity,*" growled Misha.

"Well... that's about what I'd *expect* you to say," gruffly retorted Kaysten. "Those guys were just trying to do their *jobs,* you know – they got *families...*"

"If I had let members of your government 'do their jobs', Mr. Chief of Staff," countered the Russian, "I would be dead, many times over, by now."

"Will, time to close the door," requested Chu.

"I can't!" he argued. "It's *stuck,* or something... and... what the H – we've stopped going down."

A relieved smile showed on Abruzzio's face, as she looked outward and beheld the just-arrived Storied Watcher.

"Karéin – where the *hell* have you *been?*" demanded the exasperated scientist. "We could easily have been *killed* while we were up there!"

The abashed alien-girl motioned with a flame-bedecked gauntlet and Abruzzio stepped back. Behind, came the Storied Watcher, her infernal aura causing the upholstery in the vehicle to smoke and sizzle, until she bade *Vîrya Ahn'jë* to restrain herself.

Now, it was impossible to see anything out of the windows, as a black shroud enveloped the bus.

"*There* she is!" shouted an excited child, from the back.

"Hi, everyone!" acknowledged Karéin-Mayréij. "Hector, Wolf – you may refrain from the efforts that you have lately performed, so admirably. I am holding us aloft."

Moving the strange sunglasses-cum-visor to her forehead, the alien-girl knelt and tried to apologize.

"I am *sorry*," she plainly stated. "I thought that those preparations that were made to this vehicle by my war-children and I, would have been sufficient to hide it, and yourselves, from the President's air warriors – evidently I was wrong. This 'America' empire has some *very* sophisticated techno, the likes of which I have never before encountered. I keep underestimating it, but consider the alternative – if I feared it as much as perhaps would be prudent, I might just as well hide myself on some rock in the heavens, and abandon all of you to the tender mercies of your President. Ye *Stars*, my wisdom fails... I honestly know not what to do."

"Well – first of all – you might get our asses *out* of here," suggested Boatman. "There's *bound* to be more of them fighter-planes and missiles comin' on their way, any minute now."

"We are safe for at least a few minutes, from anything short of a near-miss by an atom-smashing-bomb," remarked the Storied Watcher. "I have made my bubble to shut out or deflect every kind of light- or energy-pulse. And – if necessary – I can probably evade all the President's tracking-systems, simply by plunging us deep under yonder ocean... this 'radar'-thing that the fighter-planes possess, cannot see through water... is that not right?"

"No – *not* correct," mentioned Misha. "There are some kinds of airborne- and satellite-radars which *can* do that – not very far under the surface, mind you – although given the situation after the comet, it is likely that many of these would not now be operational. But you would then be subject to attack by submarines, or, possibly, surface-ships that could track you by sonar – that is, echo-location from sound-impulses. Karéin – how fast can you travel, under water?"

"Right now, not very – that element is extremely dense... it requires *tremendous* effort to go at any appreciable speed," explained Karéin-Mayréij. "I can use certain element-changing tricks – such as the ones available to Hector – to make the task easier; but these cannot completely offset the fact that flying through a liquid is far more challenging, than flying through a gas. And do not forget – when one travels with the slightest velocity, great turbulence builds around my bubble. No doubt, this would be easily-detectable by something that hunts by listening for sound. Maneuvering is also much more difficult... I cannot turn or feint nearly as quickly as I can, within the atmosphere."

"After being subjected to your idea of a 'fast-turn', Karéin," muttered Chu, "I'm not sure whether that would be a handicap... or a blessing."

"I'm not sure how confident I should feel, upon hearing all of that," commented Abruzzio. "Considering the recent track-record. But anyway, there's a larger issue that we have to resolve, before we do anything else – namely, 'where on Earth are we *going*'?"

"Oh – that's *easy*," interjected the bounty-hunter, as he petted one of his dogs. "I think the answer's, 'not back there', you know?"

"Well... *duh*," sarcastically echoed Hendricks. "You *think*?"

With a slight smile, Wolf nonchalantly shrugged.

"We need to get *serious* here," persisted Abruzzio, looking down the aisle and speaking loudly enough to be heard right at the back of the bus. "Not to give Mister Walking Gas-Barbecue back here too much credit, but he *does* have a very valid point – given our association with *you*, Karéin, *none* of us can think of ourselves as safe, anywhere within the United States; not, at least, until this dispute between yourself and the Government is finally settled. By definition, therefore, we have to go somewhere else."

"Yes... I agree with you," admitted the Storied Watcher.

"Well then – where did you have in mind?" pressed the scientist. "I mean, *surely* you must have considered this possibility, prior to now... right?"

"*Sort* of," evaded the latter-day 'angel'.

"What do you *mean*... 'sort of'?" exclaimed an exasperated Chu. "What kind of answer is *that*, from an alien 'goddess'?"

"A kind of – uhh – 'incomplete' one?" Karéin-Mayréij tried to joke, with a sheepish grimace and an embarrassed shoulder-cringe.

"For God's *sake*, Karéin!" protested Kaysten, "Please don't tell me that we're all dressed up, with nowhere to go. Since you shanghai'ed me from the White House, I thought this was all part of some big, ingenious plan that you've been cooking up."

"It *is*..." she repeated. "But even the best-crafted strategies can be thrown from their intended courses, by unanticipated-events. Such as – for example – the appearance of an atom-smashing bomb, right in the midst of where reside all the beloved friends, who I have gathered into this vehicle. I will be honest with you – I have had to improvise, to deal with *that* peril. And as I believe that I said before – I am reluctant to travel outside the 'America' empire... lest I inadvertently spread the conflict to yet *more* innocent bystanders."

"I kind of think we're past *that* point," observed Ramirez. "That is... if you seriously want any of us to *live*, past the first hour when you next fly off somewhere away from us."

Half-hanging her head, the Storied Watcher meekly replied, "Oh-kay, then – where would you suggest? You know this planet much better than do I."

"How about, like, Australia?" proposed Hendricks. "They got good beaches there. Not to mention good beer."

"That island-continent is very far-away," countered the alien-girl. "And apart from the fact that you would not enjoy a long flight in these confined-ircumstances – do not forget, I can only transport this vehicle at speeds that our human passengers can tolerate, not as fast as I would normally travel – I do not want to stray too far from where Bob, Tommy, Whitney and her children were abducted. Common sense says that there is a good chance that they are being held captive somewhere right inside this empire... when I find out where, I want to be close enough to quickly effect their rescue."

"Fine, then," offered Chu. "How about South America? *That's* not too far."

"I did some research on your com-pu-ter network about that continent," stated Karéin-Mayréij. "Many of the kingdoms there, are already at odds with your 'America'. My presence there – if detected and attacked by your President – might easily provoke a larger war. I would prefer somewhere else."

"What's *left?*" wearily asked Boatman. "Russia? Europe? India?"

"Too far," interjected Misha. "And – judging from the events in the hotel – I would say that my own country would probably not be much more welcoming, than this one. Particularly, if I were to accompany you."

"As you always *will*, dear friend!" kindly remarked the alien-girl.

"Mexico?" suggested Abruzzio.

"Not unless you want a *whole* country run by the *narco-trafficantes* – as opposed to just a *city*," snorted Wolf.

"Well... how about Canada?" inquired the third agent. "Right next door, and not so cold anymore, after all that 'climate'-stuff started happenin', I mean – and *they* got good beer, too."

"Young man's got a point," noted Boatman. "You can even find rivers that still have fish in 'em, unlike practically everywhere in this country... 'cept the Rockies. Went fishin' up there several times – even caught me two or three that I could *eat*."

"Yeah – but don't doubt for a minute that our government wouldn't hesitate to attack you up there, if they tracked you down," warned Kaysten. "We think of that place as less of a real country, than kind of the 'fifty-second state'... you know? Still – I'd have to say – if you want to hang around the neighborhood, it wouldn't be the *worst* place to go... the Agency, Secret Service, and so on, don't tend to pay it a lot of attention, simply because the Canadians mostly spend their time playing hockey and worrying about how to deal with that Frenchie-state that they've got north of New England. Might buy you some *time*, anyway."

"And we wouldn't be too far from our homes," mentioned Abruzzio. "That'd be a 'plus', as well."

"Hmm... alright," agreed the Storied Watcher. "But as I understand it, this 'Canada' is quite a big kingdom – it has many different areas. Some are wide and flat, like where I met Bob and the others – I would prefer more rugged-terrain, for there would be more places in which to hide."

"And because of the hills and valleys, the airborne-radars of the United States government would face a challenging task in tracing you up there, provided you went relatively far from the border," added Misha. "Do not take that as counsel to let down your guard, however."

"You can be *sure* of that!" ruefully confirmed Karéin-Mayréij. "Those mountains where first I fell... they extend to the north – do they not?"

"They certainly do," explained the Italian-American scientist. "Almost all the way to the northern ocean, in fact. If you're looking for mountains, I'd suggest somewhere outside of one of the resort-communities in the Canadian Rockies... very scenic, definitely out of the way, and we could make town-trips for supplies –"

"Anybody bring any cash?" interrupted Wolf. "Can't use our credit-cards up there... might as well paint a big bulls-eye on our backs, if we did."

"Yeah – I have several hundred, so do Otis and Will... standard Bureau-procedure, so we can – uhh – pay off informants, if necessary," mentioned the FBI team-leader. "Actually, what's funny about it is, I have to account for every last *cent*, when I fill out my post-incident report. I wonder if our accounting-system has a category for, 'sight-seeing trips to Canada with an alien princess'."

"Back in the Executive Branch, we can expense everything from Belgian absinthe chocolates to toilet-paper made out of gold-leaf," smirked Kaysten. "I'm sure Ochoa can figure out some way to fit it in. Oh... and by the way... I only have a bit of cash... I just use it for tips."

"*Here's* a tip, pardner," grunted the bounty-hunter. "'Don't go to Tucson'."

"I'll second *that* opinion," muttered Boatman.

"I have about a hundred and fifty on me," remarked Ramirez. "I was going to buy my mother a present..."

"That should keep us going for a while," said Abruzzio.

"Listen, Karéin," she continued, "There are a number of fairly big resort-towns in the Canadian Rockies, although many of them are far enough south so that they might not be appropriate for us... but there's one further-up, just to the east of the Alberta-British Columbia border, as I recall – and it's several hundred miles above the dividing-line between Canada and the United States. What was its name again – help me out, here, Rainbow – oh, wait, I remember – it's called 'Jasper', I think."

"It's got bars – licensed restaurants... right?" inquired Hendricks. "After what's been going down lately, I sure could *use* a drink."

"You and me *both*, pardner," agreed Wolf. "I'll buy... if they take I.O.U.'s."

"I hate to – ahh – 'burst your bubble', friends," observed the Storied Watcher. "But soon, alcohol will have little effect – your bodies will neutralize it, as a poison. And in any event... I think it not a good idea to frequent such places, until matters have settled down."

The bounty-hunter and the FBI-agent both wore a look of no small consternation, upon hearing this.

The alien-girl paused for a second or two, then stated, "Very well, then... unless anyone objects, we go to this northern kingdom – praying all the while, that we not bring any of its peasants to the wrath of the American President."

Chu stood, went down the aisle and faced the throng of passengers, most of whom had only barely regained their composure.

"Well, folks, that seems to be the plan – anyone object to us all heading off to Canada?" she solicited.

"What happen if we say, 'Ah don' want to go?" asked one of the parents.

"I'd assume that Karéin would drop you off, somewhere... right?" replied the FBI team-leader, with an interrogatory glance over her shoulder.

"Only with the *greatest* reluctance," commented the alien-girl. "I so much want you all to *live!*"

"'Long as you put it *that* way... guess ah gots no objection," said the ghetto-woman, with a rueful chuckle that was echoed by a number of her peers. "'Sides, ah ain't never had enough money to go anywhere 'cept 'Cisco... an' that weren't on *half* as good a bus as this one."

"Not only *that*, dear friend," remarked the Storied Watcher, with a sidelong look at Chu, "But *this* – ahh – 'vacation-trip', shall yet change your life, in ways that you cannot now imagine. I hope you will be deserving of what is to come... for it has already begun."

"*Whoa!*" exclaimed a nonplussed Boatman.

Scanning the visages of his two fellow-agents, he saw that the reaction of Chu and Hendricks – not to mention of several others in her entourage – was the same.

"Karéin," whispered Abruzzio, into the alien-girl's ear. "You can't be *serious* – they're just *children*, for God's sake –"

"So are Curtis, Melissa and Tommy," answered Karéin-Mayréij, *sotto voce*. "My blessing falls upon all who will listen, follow and renounce evil; doing so is yet easier, for those of tender years."

"What y'all *talkin'* 'bout, Angel-Lady?" inquired a young, African-American boy.

With a far-off, saturnine smile, she replied,

"A blessing comes your way, dear Jermaine; and soon now... you will see."

Then her heat waxed and she flew out of the bus, moving in front of the vehicle as Hendricks shut the door.

"Seat-belts, folks," ordered Chu, just before they felt a mighty pull.

Necessity's A Mother

Having been directed thence by Melissa, all three men had been racing up a central wrought-iron staircase to the upper-level; and although Billings didn't handle this challenge as well as Boyd or White, he noted with some pride that he wasn't winded, either.

"Damn!" he exclaimed, as he gawked in both directions. "This place is *huge*... the kid was right about the five doors – but she didn't tell us about how bloody far apart each one is, from the others. What you want to do?"

"What y'all *mean*... 'what y'all want to do', Bob?" grunted White, as he reflexively checked his gun and supply of ammunition. "Gotta meet 'em head-on – *that's* what!"

"No... what I *mean* is," continued the salesman, "Which doors are we going for? Do we all make our own choices?"

"Good point," offered Boyd. "Why don't you take the middle-one, while Devon and I do the doors on the far left and right, respectively. Which – of course – leaves the intermediate doors on both sides untended... but maybe we can hear what's going on in 'em, through the walls. Plain fact is... we don't have enough people; we'll have to take some chances."

"As good a plan as any," reluctantly concurred Billings, "Given that running away isn't an option. If you hear a voice coming from a direction where you can't see anything, hold your fire... okay?"

"Y'all *got* it!" confirmed the black ex-astronaut. "But Bob, don't forget – see any of the bad-guys... y'all *smoke* 'em – understood?"

"Especially if you use your – uhh – 'skill', to get the drop on them, as you should," added Boyd. "We don't want *any* of them reporting back on what they encountered – or even *worse*, about how to counter or defeat it. They aren't giving us any second-chances."

"Yeah... 'smoke 'em', or something," muttered the salesman. "Well... at least I get to take a few of 'em *with* me, I guess."

"Wrong attitude, my man!" cautioned White. "Who was that general who said, 'the objective of war is to make the *other* poor bastard die for his country'... or some-such thing. That's what *I* intend to do. Can't let the idea that y'all might lose, even *enter* your mind – got to tell yourself, 'it's *them* that should be afraid – it's *them* that's gonna go down hard'. And know *what*, Bob?"

"What?" vacantly said Billings.

"Y'all prollly be *right*," cheerily offered White. "They ain't *never* fought anybody like us. Let's make it a real fuckin' *nasty* surprise, my man!"

Grimly, the salesman nodded, as did Boyd.

"Let's go!" commanded the former Mars mission pilot.

He sprinted to the right, while his Mars mission navigator hurried in the opposite direction.

For a second, Billings just stood in front of the central access-door; then, fatalistically, he gingerly extended a hand to the handle upon it, secretly hoping that the smock-man had made a mistake in entering the access-codes.

Alas... it was not to be.

The door was unlocked; so, after cautiously peering inside and seeing nothing but a dimly-lit hallway – extending as far as he could see – he went in.

Nervously, the salesman tip-toed his way down the corridor, which was rather more narrow than those he had been used to navigating. However – as in some of the passage-ways that he had already traversed – most of the overhead-lights in this place were out and others were flashing intermittently, leading to an odd, strobe-like effect.

Might be a good thing, thought Billings.

That much harder for the bastards to get a bead on me.

Sure hope that the key-word works if I just think it... talking out loud around here, now there's the mother all bad ideas...

From far ahead, his newly-sensitive ears picked up the faint sounds of marching boots – *lots* of them – and for a second, he stood, utterly paralyzed.

This is fucking crazy! he said to himself, a cold sweat on his forehead.

I'm no soldier – I'm just a goddamn salesman from Tucson, in way over his head, in more than one meaning of the word.

I'm probably outnumbered ten to one – and there are a hell of a lot more of them lined up around the corner, in case I get lucky and pick off one or two before they plug my ass.

But I can't just turn tail... can I? he despaired.

That's going to look just effing beautiful – 'Bob the coward, who buggered off before a shot was fired'.

And those two fly-boys are right... sooner or later, you'd have to make your last stand beside Tommy, anyway.

Might as well bite the bullet, and... whoa, Bob old boy – now there's a joke, eh?

Keep that in your pocket, while you're lined up outside those pearly-gates...

The sounds were getting closer still – almost to the point where normal human ears could have perceived them.

Okay, he mused.

Cloaked or not, you hang around in front of the bastards – they'll just spray every square inch with machine-guns and show up with the bucket and water-hose, five minutes later.

Gotta out-think 'em, Bob... but there's nowhere to hide, for God's sake!

This thing's so narrow – and despite the starvation-diet there's still a bit too much around the old waist – so there's no way that you could expect them just to walk by without brushing up.

Hold on, came a thought.

What if I was flat out, on the ceiling? Unless they play basketball, there's got to be a foot or so of clearance.

Didn't bring my suction-cups – but this tele-whatever thing that Tanaka and her cohorts are so gung-ho about... yeah, that's got to be it.

Let's give her a try...

Billings closed his eyes and mentally whispered, "*Levitate.*"

Nothing happened.

He tried again... this time with more passion.

He stayed very obviously under the control of Earth's gravity.

The foot-steps sounded like they should appear within eyesight, in no more than a few seconds.

Worse still, there were sounds of gunfire to the left, then to the right.

Fuck this! he said under his breath.

Wrong time to be fiddling around with this kind of thing.

"Taxi," self-whispered the salesman, and instantly, a shroud of Stygian darkness descended all about. But *this* time, he noticed that, in fact, not *all* light was being blocked, by the strange alien-ability; instead, there was an odd, soft, deeper-than-purple glow issuing from various points on the ceiling.

Must be the overhead-light-bulbs, those few that are still lit up, he thought.

Didn't Tanaka, or somebody, say something about that 'ultra' stuff?

All of a sudden, an even more dull, barely-distinguishable figure – then another, plus more in ranks behind – appeared at the limit of his eyesight. All of these were bathed in the same super-violet color that must have been leaking through the dark-bubble.

Just before party-time, mused Billings.

Since I got absolutely no other plan... let's try this again.

How did it feel when they just about dropped me, back in the cistern?

Maybe that'd do it!

He closed his eyes and tried to imagine the sensation.

A moment later – to his astonishment – the salesman felt himself floating gently upward, much too slowly for combat-maneuvers; but he *was* levitating, no doubt about that.

After a few long seconds – all the while listening to the far-off gun-shots and silently praying that his fellow-adventurers were still alive and kicking – he came into contact with the ceiling.

Billings tried to force the effect to push against the lower half of his body – a gambit that required several more seconds of effort, but one which was successful, after a fashion – with only shoelaces not being fully-pressed against the corridor's upper surfaces.

Now all I gotta do is keep it up, he thought.

Quite a strain... but I'll put up with it...

Don't sneeze, Bob...

With a mixture of terror and amazement, the salesman remained affixed to the ceiling and watched first two – then two more – combat-geared gendarmes pass directly underneath him.

As near as he could tell in this strange 'black-light' environment, their gear looked different – more complete, perhaps – than what had been seen on the GrayWar-types, and unlike the latter, these men communicated only by hand-signals or by some other meanhas; because they said not an audible word.

When they were eight to ten feet behind him, Billings slowly released his new-found alien-power, floating gradually down to land almost noiselessly on the hallway-floor.

After a quick glance in the other direction, he readied his pistol. To his alarm, he noticed that one of the soldiers in the front-row had made a pointing-gesture toward the door to the inner-sanctum; and a second or so later, one of the others retrieved a small object about the size of a baseball, from a backpack.

With his left side anchored against the wall, Billings went into the sniper's-crouch that he had learned from the two ex-astronauts and aimed carefully, his enhanced senses making his quarry stand out as plainly as in a video-game on the 'low'-difficulty-setting.

This is for Tommy! he considered, as he pulled the trigger.

Busier than she was used to being, Melissa had been alternating between explaining about Tommy's predicament to her mother, monitoring the status of Jacobson and Tanaka and fetching her brother, when curiosity overcame Curtis and he strayed too far from their impromptu base-camp.

Now, she heard the ominous sounds of gunfire, far-off and above.

Invoking her special-ability, the teenager flew until she was right beside the high-impact glass-barrier between the overhead balcony-level and the main area.

But she saw nothing – other than for three open doorways.

Disappointed, Melissa returned to the encampment, only to see Jacobson's powerfully-built, big-boned upper-body, sitting upright.

"Cap'n *Sam!*" happily exclaimed the girl. "Y'all feelin' better, now?"

His breathing still laborious, he replied, "'Better', yes... 'good' – I'd have to say 'no', to that. Honestly... I thought I was a 'goner' there, that guy caught me completely flat-footed... I won't make *that* mistake again, let me assure you!"

The former Mars mission commander looked around. "What's wrong with the Professor?" he asked. "And where are Brent, Devon and Bob?"

"Miz Cherie helped Momma, when she brought y'all back from goin' to heav'n," stated the teenager. "Momma almost *die* doin' that – she was out for a *long* time, as well... ah 'spose it was hard on both of 'em. An' them three men went upstairs, to where they's all them seats n' such... 'cause we had a warnin' that the bad-guys wid dey guns comin' to get all of us, 'cludin' Tommy."

"*Tommy?*" replied an amazed Jacobson, doing a double-take. "Where *is* he? Can I speak with him?"

"Mah homie in that big box over there," explained Curtis. "It sealed tight, y'all gots to use one of them computer-thangs to talk wid him – 'an last time Major Devon an' Major Brent an' Mista Bob done tried, Tommy didn' want to hear them, ah guess. An' y'all cain't bust him out, neither... they tried, but that box *wicked* strong – they real 'fraid of hurtin' Tommy if they hit it too hard."

"Bugger," muttered Jacobson, wincing as he tried to flex his waist. "To have come *so* far, and... well, anyway."

He turned to Claremont and offered her his hand.

"Whitney..." he gratefully offered, the look on his face already speaking volumes. "I don't know how I can *thank* you... I owe you my *life*. When we get out of here – anything you want, I *swear* –"

Grasping the big man's hand, the African-American woman briefly closed her eyes to concentrate on a thought, which was related by her daughter.

"Momma say that th' only person y'all owe anythin' to, is the Lawd Heself," said Melissa. "An' 'sides... y'all an' yo' homies already saved our lives... so we kind of even, y'all know?"

A puzzled expression came to the teenager's visage, then she added, "But Momma want y'all not to get shot no more – y'*understand*? She say one time was more than 'nuff for her."

Jacobson coughed out a laugh, upon hearing this.

"More than enough for *me*, as well," he ruefully commented.

With pained, wheezing, eye-watering effort, he slowly stood up.

"Where's my gun?" he asked. "I've got to help Devon, Brent and Bob."

"Y'all *shore*, Cap'n Sam?" asked Melissa. "Ah knows y'all maybe feelin' a bit better now, but that was one *ugly* hurt... like they cut a big hole right in yo' belly. And it's just me, Momma an' Curtis here, guardin' Tommy and Miz Cherie. If them bad-guys show up from some other direction –"

There were the sounds of rapid-fire shooting, from the upper-level.

"If they *do*... Curtis, you know what to do – don't you?" sternly advised the former Mars commander, addressing the boy.

"Yes sir... ah does," he replied, smartly. "Major Brent done tell me."

"Well then – f that was good enough for *him*... it's good enough for *me*," agreed Jacobson.

He took two or three steps toward the staircase, then doubled up in pain, though he remained on his feet.

"Hey –" started a concerned Melissa, but the man waved her off.

"I'll be alright," he forced, with a smile that came out looking more like a grimace. "And if it's of any interest – and it sure *is* to me – it's like I know that I shouldn't be able to stand up, shouldn't be able to breathe... shouldn't be able to do *anything*... but somehow... I am. I can *feel* my body stitching itself up."

Jacobson pulled on his clothing so it opened up to reveal where the wound had been. It was closed now – though there was still an ugly scar – but it was dimly-glowing, with energy-charges jumping to and fro, all over.

"*Bless you*, Karéin," he mumbled. "We ended up the creek... but at least you supplied us with a few good paddles."

Then he readied his gun and headed for the stairs.

Feeling both proud at having successfully ambushed the four enemy soldiers and disgusted at having had to kill them, Billings did one last shoulder-check down the corridor, and cautiously stepped back toward the door, checking constantly for the slightest signs of life or movement.

But his aim had been precise, and though his magazine was almost empty – these guys had flak-jackets, but unfortunately for them, most of their protection was to the front – his opponents were quite dead.

Those astronauts will be glad to get this *stuff*, mused the salesman.

Damn lucky I got the drop on the buggers – because if those machine-guns that they were toting had been able to open up on me...

Well... let's just say, my pistol would have been as much use as a point-ed stick...

After a kick to the ribs of each victim just to be one hundred per cent sure, Billings approached the door.

He was about to push it wide open, but at that moment, the sounds of a savage fire-fight began to echo from the balcony-room, ahead and to the right.

Shit! thought the salesman.

That's where White went... isn't it?

He whispered his "Taxi" command to drop the shroud so he could see the goings-on, and put his eye up to the narrow gap between the door and the jam.

The bleeding, stumbling figure of the black ex-astronaut briefly dashed across Billings' view-port.

Despite being seriously-wounded – it was impossible to tell exactly where White had been hit, but he sure didn't look too good – the man was obviously still able to fight, because he quickly took refuge behind a row of chairs, reloaded his gun and let fly at unknown assailants who must have been out of the salesman's field-of-view, to the far right.

A fusillade from the right shredded the row of protective-chairs, and White only just managed to duck in time.

Moving back and forth to shift his perspective, Billings noted with alarm that the ex-astronaut was trying desperately to retrieve something from a pocket.

He must be out of ammo – or almost out, realized the salesman.

White dropped his auto-rifle and raised his hand.

A sensation of chill beset the salesman's face and he knew what was coming, so he reflexively withdrew back from the door-jam.

No more than a half-second later, a blast of brutal Antarctic-style air shot through the crack, and the door itself became painfully-cold to the touch.

There were screams and moans to the right, accompanied with the sounds of retreating boots; but then, there were more gun-shots.

Creeping closer to the frost-encrusted door after another shoulder-check, Billings felt the air-displacement made by bullets whizzing right in front of his nose, only slightly inside the balcony-room. But when he again cast his gaze on White's last position, the black ex-astronaut had disappeared.

A combat-garbed, rifle-armed figure dashed past his hiding-place – then another... then a third.

Now that's *great*, said the salesman, under his breath.

The fly-boys must be outnumbered, or out-gunned, or both...

I got only a few shots left, with a bunch of the bad-guys between White, Boyd and myself.

Still – if it worked once, maybe it'll work twice... right?

Not enjoying such a grim task – but thinking in life-or-death terms – Billings grabbed an auto-rifle – plus two spare clips for it – from the fingers and fatigues of one of his recent victims.

"*Taxi*," he whispered.

Again, his eyes now saw only a scene illuminated in a faint, more-than-purple-glow. He invoked his new trick, this time floating up to the ceiling with little difficulty.

Carefully, Billings extended a hand to the top of the door and gradually pulled it open.

Suddenly – his mind reverberated with panic – as he saw rifle-flashes that must, he decided, be pointed right at him.

That's it, Bob old boy... how'd the prayer go? thought the panicking salesman.

But he was in fact totally unhurt : although there *were* three or four hostile soldiers with a clear line-of-sight – and although they *did* indeed fire, in the same second in which he opened the door – they had – sensibly enough, from their point-of-view – fired only at man-height and below.

The rifle-rounds streaked by, below Billings' hidden, top-hugging figure.

One of the extra-purple-gendarmes – gun obviously at the ready – stepped forward and looked through the door, right underneath his erstwhile target.

"Four down just inside the doorway," he barked to the soldiers in the balcony-room. "Looks like small-arms fire... not exotics. No signs of the enemy – must have gone back down this hallway. Should I pursue, sir?"

"Negative," ordered another one of the shadowy figures. "We must be nearing the main objective... consolidate and advance!"

"Yes, *sir!*" answered the first gendarme.

He wheeled and went back.

Exhaling involuntarily, Billings again tried to slowly open the door.

This time, there was no obvious opposition, and the crossways-gunfire had receded; so, still enshrouded, he floated down and cautiously stepped forward.

Looking in all directions, he saw at least three more fallen figures – none of them, mercifully, resembling either of his comrades – to the right, within a part of the balcony-room that was covered in the remnants of White's boreal attack.

To the left, the enemy soldiers had pressed on. Most of them were past the staircase that Boyd, White and the salesman had ascended to get into the balcony, and they were firing at couple of hidden targets near the far end of this room, but there was one gendarme stationed near the stairs.

Without warning, he began to fire downward.

Bullets flew up from below.

Couldn't be Curtis or Whitney... Melissa, maybe?

Anyway, can't expect any of them to hold off a professional killer for more than a few seconds...

Hang on – I'm coming!

Dashing forward – but still trying to keep cover even though he was deep inside his hiding-bubble – the salesman maneuvered to get behind the soldier at the stair-top.

He pulled the trigger. Nothing happened.

Trying to avoid cursing out loud, Billings tried a second, then a third time.

Safety might be off, he realized, *But can't see worth* shit *in here... the purple-stuff isn't giving me enough detail to figure out which switch to move.*

Fine, then – we'll do this the old-fashioned way!

Dropping the auto-rifle on a nearby padded-seat to avoid making noise, Billings – his mind summoning the hate from weeks'-worth of torment – charged at the gendarme, catching the unfortunate man in the small of the back with complete surprise.

Charges of greenish-yellow, lightening-like energy raged out of the salesman's tiger-strike hands, causing sparks and smoke at the point of contact. The unfortunate man's nervous-system went into agonized, and – likely – fatal convulsions, before he went right through the opening, to the lower-level.

The enemy soldier went careening downward, but the fall was the least of his worries : a hail of bullets from Billings' unseen-ally quickly struck home, reducing the gendarme to a bloody mess.

Damn lucky I didn't lose my balance and go down there with him, mused the salesman, as he got up to a low crouch.

A bullet whizzed by his head, and Billings ducked reflexively.

A second later, it felt like his eyes were being burned out of their sockets, as an impossibly potent burst of extra-violet light – along with some kind of infernal radiation that he could scarcely comprehend – somehow invaded the bubble.

Diving for cover, he fell flat, nestling his face inside the crook of an elbow.

Hope you got *'em, Boyd,* said the salesman, to himself.

If It Moves... It Dies

"Didn't we *tell* you that something like this was going to happen?" complained the uniformed-man with the 'GrayWar Legion' insignia on his shoulder-straps. "You don't have a *clue* about what's been going on down there!"

"*Shut up!*" snarled the other, a tall, muscular man clad in dark-green camouflaged battle-gear, with blue eyes and a large knife-scar. "I'm *busy!*"

He turned to a portable computer-terminal.

"Charlie Leader – Charlie Leader – did not hear your last transmission," he calmly repeated. "Report now!"

A static-distorted voice exclaimed, "That *you*, Commander?"

"MacGammon here," confirmed the scar-faced man. "What's going *on*, soldier? You're *late* with your report!"

"Ran into *heavy* opposition down here, sir," stammered the remote voice. "Gotta be fifty or more of them, judging from how we've been repeatedly-ambushed, and they're using those energy-weapons we were briefed on – we got multiple casualties... request *immediate* reinforcements, plus medevac for eleven grunts, at the very least. We can't go *any* further, without –"

"You *will* execute your orders!" gruffly interrupted the soldier. "We're sending reinforcements now, and we've knocked down one of the laser-projectors – when we get it down there, re-assembly will take a few minutes. In the meantime – fire at will, and use the gas if you need to. Is that *understood?*"

"Copy, sir," answered the static-voice. "Squads are re-grouping right now – we'll do another push in a couple of hours... ran into quite a few other, non-priority escapees down some of the surrounding corridors – liquidated 'em of course – but we gotta make sure the approaches are secure. We're doing a head-count, ammo re-divide. I'll report as soon as we're ready to go."

"Well, get your *asses* in gear," countered the scar-faced-man. "Intel says we got 'em cornered... no way out. Press on the *minute* that you're ready."

"*Hope* so," replied the voice. "But, *sir*... what about the rules of engagement... you know – the astronauts, and so on?"

"*What* rules, soldier?" retorted the man at the console. "My understanding of the situation is, 'it moves... it *dies*'. Simple enough for you?"

"Copy that," agreed the squad-leader.

The Woods Of British Columbia – And What They Portend

The trip to the supposed refuge of Jasper, Alberta – or, more precisely, to the far edge of an isolated camp-site by Moose Lake, just off the Trans-Canada Highway, about a half-hour's drive from the resort-community, on the B.C. side of the inter-provincial border – had taken more time than any of them had anticipated; this was not just because of the Storied Watcher's insistence on making numerous feints and detours, but also because at least twice, she sank the bus deep into the ocean... only to come to the surface several-score kilometers from the point of entry.

Mercifully, she had only advised her passengers of the latter tactic as of their second rest-stop, which happened to be on the side of a mountain glacier in the British Columbia Bendor Mountain Range. Some – notably Chu and Abruzzio – had suspected something like this had been going on, despite the care that Karéin-Mayréij had taken not to enter the water with too big a 'splash'. But most of them – exhausted both mentally and physically – had slept through much of the trip and hadn't noticed anything at all.

Finally, they had arrived – apparently safe and free from the lethal attentions of the U.S. Air Force – and were once again able to breathe fresh air; though, this stuff was unfamiliarly-clean. Mighty, snow-capped mountain peaks, covered to a dizzying height by a dense, tall forest, loomed in every direction.

Mercifully, there didn't seem to be too many mosquitoes.

"So what we do now?" asked Boatman of the alien-girl, who, having wandered off to a large rock on a tree-lined lake-shore, had ordered her war-children to their invisible hiding-place.

She began to methodically and salaciously disrobe.

The black FBI-agent had stumbled upon her accidentally; or, at least, that was what he *wanted* to believe.

"Uhh... listen..." he stammered, "You all want me to turn away, there?"

"Oh... do not worry," insouciantly replied the Storied Watcher. "Since I would not want to scandalize your moral values – I will remove my underclothes, only when I immerse myself."

"Why the hell you want to go *swimmin'* anyway, Karéin?" he asked, secretly regretting that he had apparently spoiled what might have been his only chance to see a naked alien-goddess. "Water in that lake's *freezin'!*"

"To me, it is not," she cheerily answered, as – clad only in a skimpy bra and panties, which soon were removed underwater – she plunged in. "I can make it any temperature that I desire – for more of a challenge, you should try swimming through the molten-rock of a volcano. It *does* take a little, ahh, 'getting used to', I *must* admit. But I am really not aiming for personal recreation, in any event – all that I am trying to do, is to clean out my peasant-clothing... I can compress and heat it afterward, thus removing all the unpleasant stains and smells which have accumulated, over the last few days. Would you care to *join* me, Otis Boat-man?"

"Ha!" he ruefully demurred. "Love to take you all up on the offer – but I got a feelin' that the Director might want my badge, for doin' somethin' like that."

A wistful look appeared on the face of Karéin-Mayréij, which was well-nigh all of her that was above the surface of the water.

"So sad," she sighed. "To me, being close – *really* close, I mean – to one's war-comrades, can only bring more trust and friendship... not less."

"Listen, Karéin," requested the big black man, as he took his own place on a nearby boulder, "There's somethin' that I've been meanin' to ask you... but the bus just wasn't the right place... you know?"

"Umm-hmm?" replied the alien-girl.

"Now, I hope you won't be offended by anythin' that I'm gonna say here... but I wanted to express the opinion – which, by the way, I have no doubt is shared by my two team-members and probably them pointy-headed scientists, I'm not so sure about all the rest of 'em – that you all is doin' with those folk who we picked up back in L.A.... well, it's just downright *wrong!*" stated Boatman.

"How is that?" she disingenuously countered.

"Come *on*, lady – let's not be bullshittin' each other about all this," he protested. "You're affectin' *them*... same way as in which you affected *us*."

"Yep," airily acknowledged the Storied Watcher. "That... I *am*."

"Point is, Karéin," he continued, "You don't have their permission – hell, they don't even *know* what's goin' *on*! Now... I don't know how they do it on Mars – or whatever you call that place – but down here on God's Green Earth, we have this funny old custom of askin' people's *consent*, before you go turnin' every second cell of their bodies into... I don't *know* what. And before you go any further... you *owe* it to them, to tell them what's happenin' – before it's too late."

"Is that *right?*" she replied, with the slightest hint of annoyance in her voice.

"Yeah – that's *quite* right," he argued. "Let me tell you somethin'... when you did all this 'alien'-stuff to myself, Minnie, Will and all the rest of them, it wasn't fair *then*, either; but for most of us, we all *knew* that we was gonna be takin' some chances, by fixin' to meet up with you – in *my* line of work, that goes with the business. But these people is *different*, Karéin – and you've got to *respect* that difference! They's mostly *children* – who can't make an informed decision for themselves – plus a lot of parents and caregivers who got stampeded onto that bus just because of the bomb-stuff –"

"Now wait just a *minute!*" she defiantly shot back, after ducking under for a second and re-surfacing. "It may be true that they ended up under our custody, because of the 'moo-slim' bomb – which, for all that you or I know, might already have exploded, down there in the southern-city – but nothing that we did in *that* venture, was in the *slightest* respect, unfair or dishonorable. Would you have preferred to have them all *incinerated*, by such an evil weapon?"

"You're evadin' the issue," he persisted. "Even if I accept that everythin' that you had us do down there was both the right thing, and that it was done in the right *way* – somethin' that by the way I *don't* accept – it *still* wouldn't make it acceptable to be monkeyin' around with their minds and bodies... maybe their very *souls*. 'Specially if you ain't even *asked* them if they want all these 'blessin's' that you keep talkin' about. Point is – you're an awfully *smart* little goddess... you could have cooked up some way of rescuin' those people, without recruiting them into your special little 'family', at the same time. That not right?"

"Maybe... I do not know," answered the alien-girl, in a small voice.

"*Thought* so," he observed.

"Alright – you want the truth, Otis Boat-man?" explained Karéin-Mayréij. "Here is what I believe... not, what I *know*. First... from what I have observed since I woke up on *Mailànkh*, it *does* appear that just being around me – if you are someone who I love and call a friend – that, causes my power to rest upon you. The more, ahh, 'intimate' my relationship with a human, the quicker and more powerfully, will this blessing come to manifest itself."

"The deepest recesses of my memory," she went on, "Can recall only one place – and it was many eons ago and very far-away – in which anything like this started to occur... at least, without my being able to control it. Originally, on Sam Jacobson's space-ship, my concern was just to impart knowledge of the *Fire* to humans; do not forget that given my quest against the comet, I fully expected not to be alive to pass it on to anyone else... so, because I was – and *am* – only too well aware of how *Amaiish* can work both good and evil, I made dear Sam, Devon, Brent, Sergei and Cherie, to swear an ancient oath, binding them to only honorable uses of this gift. But the possibility of my *Fire* spreading, uhh, *spontaneously*... *that*, I honestly did not anticipate."

"Well... I suppose a lot of us, didn't 'anticipate' a *lot* of things," grunted Boatman.

"Now consider my situation, when I first began to suspect that this was happening," she argued, "I had the following options : one, I could have stolen away from all those who I cared for, quite possibly to end up as a laboratory-experiment staged by one of your 'President's' lovely secret-police forces – a course of action that might have ended up with the *Fire* being given to precisely the *wrong* people – possibly inadvertently, more likely by compulsion. The other – which is what I instead chose – was to acknowledge that the spread of *Amaiish* might well be inevitable... and that I should accept this and first introduce the power to those few who I knew personally, who I loved and respected."

"I feel flattered, you know," he commented. "If you all's includin' me in that second category."

"Of *course* I am!" answered the alien-girl, with genuine affection in her voice. "But in all honesty, I did not *plan* it that way... I *felt* it happening, and Otis, you *must* understand that sometimes – when something is bound to happen anyway, and that 'something' may be other than what one would have chosen – one just has to, uhh, 'get out in front of it'... and try to influence matters as best one can. That is sort of where I am at, today. To prevent the dissemination of my power to humans, I would have to completely isolate myself from your species... or, at least, from those humans who I have come to love. Can you not *see* why I would be reluctant to do that?"

"Neither I nor any of the others can make you do *anythin'*," he carefully parried, "But isn't it possible that you may have to do just *that*? If only to avoid making a bad situation worse, I mean."

"I absolutely *will not* do any such thing – unless and until the present issue between myself and your 'government' is finally and completely dealt with," she shot back. "Neither Bob, nor Whitney, nor Curtis, nor Melissa, nor especially Tommy – not to mention a host of others, ranging from Bob's 'boss' at the floor-tile store to people who I have befriended along my way – *none* of them have deserved the despicable treatment that they have encountered, on account of me. There is a huge debt of justice to be paid here, Otis Boat-man, and I mean to make it right... even if that requires taking this entire 'America' country apart!"

"Now and here I was hopin' that we were gettin' *over* that," he complained.

"Do you think that one defeats Demon-Princes, master-warlocks, ogre-kings and armies of the evil, walking-dead, by giving up *easily?*" regally parried the Storied Watcher, trying to conceal contempt. "If you only *knew* some of the impossible-seeming tasks that I have completed, simply by persevering, my friend. In this case, all that I am trying to do is free one 'sales-man', a woman and three children. Should I just throw up my hands and have a nice time on a 'nood-beach' somewhere, instead of pressing my case? A fine 'goddess' that *I* would be... would you not say?"

"You *got* me there, I guess," muttered the big agent. "But if you're ever headin' down to one of them beaches, don't forget to invite me," he tried to joke.

"I will make a note of that," she answered, with a genuine smile. "As it is now – given my utter lack of effectiveness in this quest – I feel guilt gnawing at my soul with each passing minute; but if search I must-do for ten, twenty, a hundred years... then that is what I *will* do."

Karéin-Mayréij paused for a few seconds, then asked, "Otis... you know how much I value the straight-forward counsel of one who I respect and love – even when his words might not be what I want to hear. So tell me what your heart says is true – what, exactly, would you have me *do* with the newcomers who we have brought with us, to this place?"

"Simple," he replied. "Tell 'em *honestly* what's gonna happen if they keep hangin' out with you – and before you do that, think up a *reasonable* alternative, if they decide to bail on the whole project. Like, 'okay, I'll drop you off on the top of some mountain', ain't gonna *cut* it, Karéin... you got to look at the situation from *their* perspective – that is, a bunch of poor, scared, black-folk from L.A. who never had much of anythin', and who've just had their lives turned upside down, stuck way up here in the land of them guys with the red suits and Smokey-the-Bear hats. It'd be – pardon the joke, *inhuman* – to simply cut 'em loose and have 'em fend for themselves. They're *your* responsibility now... and that's been the case since you trotted 'em all on to that-there 'Magic Bus'. Have some *mercy* on them, lady! They didn't deserve all this, any more than you did – and they're *dependin'* on you, to get 'em out of it."

"I have not even a little silver-dollar of money to spend," protested the Storied Watcher. "Else I would gladly give it to these people, so that they could, uhh, 'move on', if they wanted to refuse my gift. How shall I both protect them – but let them reject me so completely?"

"I don't know, Karéin... I don't *know*," grumbled Boatman. "Funny thing is, here you is with all these amazin' powers – smashin' comets and such, I mean – but there's still things that you *can't* do. Which, I'd imagine, I'd find mighty frustratin'... if I was you."

"A comet is merely big... and its acts are defined by the immutable laws of physics," ruefully commented Karéin-Mayréij. "Unlike Presidents, American peasants and spies of various types and descriptions... it does not have a resentful mind that will try to thwart me, at every turn."

"Yeah," he agreed.

Pausing for a second, he added, "So... you gonna tell 'em?"

"I suppose that I will have to – unless some very nice friend would volunteer so to do, in my place," she answered, batting her eyes with a coquettish smile.

The big black agent threw up his arms.

"Oh, no – you ain't droppin' *that* one on me – Minnie and Will neither!" he protested. "You got yourself *into* this thing; and if you can't – or won't – get yourself out of it... then it's up to *you* to explain why."

"Thanks for all the *help*, Mister Boat-man," she complained. "When I revealed my – uhh – gift to you and your eff-bee-ai friends, as well as Wolf, Misha, Sylvia, Hector and Jerry – also Sebastiàn – by then, I had some personal familiarity with every one of you. But *these* people... I hardly *know* them, though I am trying very hard to love them. I am worried that they will neither love me, nor accept this blessing... especially if its advent comes as a great surprise."

"Hey, look... that don't mean that I won't be there to give you all a little back-up," retreated the FBI-agent. "If they ask me, I'll tell them the truth, which is – as far as I know – 'all this alien-stuff ain't made me grow any little green antennas, yet'... and it'll be up to them to decide if they believe me. Sound fair to you?"

"Almost *nothing* that has happened to me, since I fell down to this little blue-and-green planet, has been 'fair'... so I suppose that your offer looks good by comparison," ruefully admitted the Storied Watcher.

"Listen... I'd better get back to them folks back at the bus," Boatman responded. "Before instincts get the best of me... you know?"

"Life is long – and there are many places in which one can – oh, how did Bob put it – ah yes, 'take a dip'... right?" she teased.

"Yep... I guess," he sighed, turning and testing his ability to resist her.

When he looked back, there was only a ripple in the water, and a pile of clothes piled tantalizingly upon a rock.

"So where'd she go off to, *now?*" demanded an irritated Chu.

"*That* way, according to your FBI-friend," answered the bounty-hunter, pointing toward the lake-edge. "Walk far enough and I'm sure you'll find her... or – more likely – *she'll* find *you*."

"I'll go ahead of you," proposed the third agent, in typical smart-Aleck style. "Didn't Otis say she was skinny-dipping?"

"Fine... if you *must*,' answered the team-leader.

But she had taken only three or four steps in that direction, before the Storied Watcher – her body, garb and demeanor clean and refreshed – immediately came into view.

"Karéin," complained Chu, "Where've you *been*? Otis got back here ten minutes ago – he said you and he had been doing some talking, which is fine... but we've got some *decisions* to make! The passengers from L.A. are getting restless – they want to know what the plans are, from here on in."

"Indeed," confirmed the alien-girl. "Gather the people all around, for I have something to tell; and, something to... *confess*."

Chu stared at the Storied Watcher for a second or two, then said, knowingly, "I... *see*. Well – I guess I had better *do* that."

Karéin-Mayréij merely nodded.

After the Asian-American FBI-agent had hurried to the bus, the alien-girl looked behind, toward the lake.

"I will need something to stand upon, when talking to them," she remarked.

In the next second, a huge boulder – which must have weighed a ton if it weighed an ounce – was lifted from the lakeside by the invisible grasp of her telekinesis, coming to rest right behind.

A throng of tired-looking, downtown African-American and Latino-folk approached, and, without flexing a muscle, Karéin-Mayréij jumped – or was otherwise propelled – upward and backward, to the top of the boulder.

They made a semi-circle and one of them called out, "So... y'all gonna tell us what happenin' next? Mah kids is gettin' *hungry* – and there ain't hardly *nothin'* left on the bus, 'cept for a bunch of frozen burgers 'an hot-dogs that one of the other folk brought along. But we ain't got no way to cook 'em."

"We will deal with that, Mrs. Washington," politely answered the alien-girl. "But I have summoned all of you here for a far more important reason."

"Such as?" asked the Latino father.

"Enriqué, mark this well; I speak tidings of power and majesty, for you and all your kin," she proclaimed, with an elfin glow starting to come from her eyes, as well outlining her body.

"Here's our old *amiga*... the 'other' Karéin," muttered Ramirez, while Abruzzio, Chu and Misha, nodded in agreement.

"What you *talkin'* about?" peevishly retorted the man.

"*I* know, Daddy!" chirped his daughter, staring forward with wide eyes.

But Enriqué rapidly hid behind someone else, at the withering, imperious glance that came back in his direction.

"You think that your lives have been changed merely by meeting me; but this is but the most tiny *fraction* of what yet awaits," explained the Storied Watcher, with an eerie, yet lovely, adrenalin-pumping song, seeming to come from the very rocks and stones. "For just being in my presence, will eventually make you far superior to those among whose ranks you were born. I am the Destroying Angel who brings the *Fire* of Heaven, whose name is 'Amaiish' to man and woman of Earth; and I say to you now – as you stand before me as dear brothers and sisters – that my power has *already* begun to rest within you... if you will but accept it and forswear the use of it for evil or self-enrichment."

"You mean, like... magic?" one of them inquired.

"No, not that... for all that I am – all that I do, and what powers I have – these are of the sensible world, and I obey the laws of nature," she replied. "But if you stay with me – learn from me and help me – you will be *greatly* blessed. Long life and good health shall you always have; but far more shall be your gifts, though different specific powers shall come to each of you, in turn. Some of these shall be like the abilities that you have already seen me exercise; others will similar to those that all your friends and family will have, while a very few – even *I* do not know how, or why – will be unique to one or two of you."

"Well, that's nice," said one of the African-American women, "But y'all still ain't told us 'zactly what y'all *mean*. What *is* all this talk 'bout 'powers', 'n such?"

"I do not expect you to understand all of this at first," stated Karéin-Mayréij. "Though you can come to know some of it, by inquiring of your brothers and sisters, who helped me gather you from the city to the south. And perhaps, by seeing what you will become, your eyes will be opened. Minn-ee... would you care to give our new friends a demonstration?"

"What do you – uhh – *mean*, Karéin?" evaded Chu, as if she didn't know.

"See that tree-stump over yonder?" indicated the alien-girl.

"Umm-hmm," warily confirmed the FBI team-leader.

"Blast it to *pieces*," ordered the Storied Watcher.

"Oh, come *on!*" protested Chu. "You *know* it hurts my eyes like hell, to do that. Besides... you'll *frighten* them!"

"Wrong!" contradicted Karéin-Mayréij. "First... it will be *you* who 'frightens' them – not *me*. Second... it is *indeed* wise to fear someone whose powers could kill with so much as a whim – *unless* one knows that shortly, one's own greatness will wax to compensate. Third... it did not hurt so much, last time... did it? Even though you destroyed an entire hell-ee-kopter war-bird... correct? You are *mighty*, woman! *Embrace* it and be *proud* of yourself! And show your brothers and sisters what they can be – if they will just take my gift, freely offered in hope and love."

Chu stood and pondered for a short while, then addressed the crowd.

"Listen, ladies and gentlemen... and kids," she unsteadily commented, "I have to admit... there's a lot of truth in what she's saying. The being who you see up on the rock – she's unlike *anyone* whose feet have ever stood on this *planet*... I can't pretend that I understand her, or what she's done to me and my fellow-agents, not to mention the others who you met down in L.A. –"

"What y'all *mean*... what she's done?" suspiciously demanded a parent.

"What she's talking about, to put it into plain language," elaborated the team-leader, "Is... if you stay with her, over time, you'll cease to be normal human beings; you'll start becoming something in between *Homo Sapiens*, and – well – whatever species that the Storied Watcher herself, happens to be."

Chu paused for another second or two. Her arms hung at her sides, with her hands flexing repeatedly open and shut into fists, as if preparing for a fight.

Then – with dim flashes of the *Fire* visible under her blouse, a yellowish-white glow coming to her eyes, a waxing grandeur echoing through her voice, and her war-song – an eerie, humming, surreally-hypnotic electro-rock-alike-thing, subtly different from and softer than that of her mentor – resounding in the minds of the throng, Chu proclaimed, "You'll become someone... like..."

"*Me!*"

With no more warning and a warbling sci-fi sound, the more-than-a-woman unleashed her lethal, now yellow-and-crimson gaze against the tree-stump, small, burning pieces of which went flying in every direction, to the shock and astonishment of the awed crowd.

"Oh mah *Gawd!*" breathed one of the parents.

"It's no trick – and no joke," advised the bounty-hunter, as – with a sinister-looking orange-red back-light in his eyes and his own, ominous-yet-entrancing war-song issuing from everywhere – he stepped away from the crowd.

"And," he added, "She ain't the *only* one who's learned a thing or two from Little Ms. Nuclear Angel, up there!"

He whispered something, and instantly, a sweet-singing jet of flame – its brutal heat instantly obvious to the as-of-yet-humans – began to race around him, like some kind of incandescent tornado.

Wolf stared at the charcoal remnants of a nearby, long-abandoned campfire, with his arms and palms arrayed, as if to embrace a friend. Several of the throng exclaimed in surprise and apprehension, jumping involuntarily backwards, as the cold, apparently-depleted shards, instantly burst into a roaring bonfire.

"Even works for *dogs*, too!" he mentioned.

The bounty-hunter nodded at the puppies, and – to the astonishment even of his more-than-human friends – they began to leap up and down, back and forth through the Little Burning One's inferno, without the slightest apparent damage.

After allowing the conflagration to go on for another few seconds, Wolf issued a mental command and all was as it had been before, with neither him nor his dogs being the worse for wear... despite having been inside a mobile furnace.

He used a "come on" head-gesture, and the campfire flamed-out.

Wincing, Chu rubbed her watering eyes and interjected, "Of course... you don't get something for nothing. Getting used to having laser-beam eyeballs has – ahem – been a bit of a *challenge*... I can attest to *that*, for sure."

A delighted child shouted, "Y'all mean *we's* gonna be able to do *that*?"

"Perhaps, Juanita darling... perhaps not," answered Karéin-Mayréij, with a godly – but friendly – smile. "Each of you shall – in turn – be given various powers and abilities, the nature of which only the Gods Themselves will know in advance; all of these are marvelous in their own way. But you must *first* agree to receive my blessing – and here, I must make a heart-felt apology, to you all."

She got down on one knee and bowed her head.

"At first," she quietly confessed, "I could not *conceive* of how a mortal could refuse this blessing; and therefore I had intended to give it to all of you, without first saying the truth, as I now do. But dear Otis Boat-man prevailed upon me that this would be a conceit, that it would be unethical – even, immoral. I am sorry... and I resolve not to do again, if I have any choice in the matter. I am *far* above you – I have the power of the very *Gods* within my body and soul – but I am *not* perfect... nor infallible. When I stumble, I beg you should first correct me... then forgive me, as much as you can."

The Storied Watcher arose, her demeanor still as majestic as ever.

The background psycho-music was almost *irresistible*.

A hush fell over the crowd.

"So today, I stand before you as a teacher and prophetess – but also as a sister and friend – to ask you to follow me, and drink of my power... of my *life!* I beg you to welcome my *Fire* – and welcome she who brings her to you, asking nothing in return – except for your love and gratitude. Almost-gods among women and men, shall you be; but always in *service* to humans – never in rulership – for it shall be your quest to enlighten your brothers and sisters not to fear *Amaiish*, as you go before them in the knowledge of her."

They stood silent, utterly at a loss for what to do or say.

The alien-girl closed her eyes, folded her hands in front, half-bowed her head, and issued the plea that all knew had to be coming.

"*Will* you, therefore, walk with me? Will you *answer* this call? This do I humbly pray," she implored, allowing her music to subside.

Finally, after an eternal few seconds, the voice of the Latino man sounded.

"Yes," he spoke, with equal gravity, and a far-off look. "As for me and my family... we will travel with you, Storied Watcher."

He turned to the little girl, scooping her up and holding her close to him.

"Right, Juanita?" he asked.

"*Right!*" answered the beaming child, with a thumbs-up gesture.

Several others murmured approval, as well.

"I think we have a consensus," remarked Abruzzio, "But we should be sure. Is there anyone who does *not* want to join us... yes – I'll say it out loud – as *disciples*, of the 'Destroying Angel'?"

One of the African-American women put up her hand.

"You're Mrs. Washington... correct?" asked the scientist.

"Yeah... that's right," replied the parent. "Ah gots a question."

"Go ahead," said the alien-girl and Abruzzio, simultaneously.

"Ah actually gots two," corrected Washington. "First... y'all ain't settin' yo'self up as some kind of 'new religion' kind of thang... is you? 'Cuz we's all Baptists in mah fam'ly – and we *ain't* gonna change... not for all the tea in China."

Karéin-Mayréij laughed out loud – perhaps revealing a bit too much of her fanged bite in so doing – although no-one remarked upon it.

"I want you to follow me... to learn from me and take my blessing," she answered. "I desire no worship – and if ever I fall into the trap of demanding the latter, I expect you to remonstrate me, forthwith. And I would be *honored* if you would in turn teach me about this 'Baptist'-faith. I have learned some already from dear Whitney Claremont – may the Gods protect her until I can do so myself. I profess no particular Temple; but instead, I respect, honor and glorify *all* the Gods, never to favor one over another. Neither will I encourage or prohibit you from your own religion... save that doing so be unduly-disruptive of our other activities. Just do not be surprised if – as your own power waxes – your perspective on these things may, ahh *change* somewhat... oh-kay?"

"Alright... ah '*spose*," warily confirmed the woman. "Th' other thang is... if we decide not to want all this 'Am-way' stuff that y'all fixin' to drop all over us – how *that* work?"

"There appears to be only one way to stop you from receiving my gift," replied the alien-girl. "And that is for you to go far-away from me. If you stay in my presence, the *Fire* of the *Makailkh* will come to you... desired or not. The decision ever is your own, and I will not force it – except to ask, 'will you come with me, Bessie Washington?'"

Chu was watching carefully.

She tapped Boatman on the shoulder.

"*Good*," she whispered. "She isn't trying to hypnotize the poor woman. I think our divine little *sensei* is learning that there *are* limits."

At a loss, the African-American mother said, "*Mak* – what? And how y'all knowin' mah name, anyways?"

"'*Makailkh*' is both the name of my species – my kin – and the name of my language," explained Karéin-Mayréij. "I know *many* things... such as the names and motives of those who cannot guard their thoughts from my mind. If you – or others here – wish to go, my friends will pool their mon-ee and divide it so as to give as much as they can spare, so that you can provide for yourself while you find your way back home... if 'home' still exists, of course. And I will transport you to any place, within a reasonable distance."

"Well... nice of you to promise her all *my* travellin'-cash," complained Hendricks. "Don't I get to put a few bucks away so I can buy myself a beer or a hamburger?"

"As you can see," wryly observed the Storied Watcher, her grandeur now diminished almost to its ordinary-level, "Powerful as I may be – I am by now quite used to being, ahh, 'talked back to'. And as for the money, Will – it is up to you, and your brothers and sisters. I have almost none of my own... since the last place in which I had a 'job', came to a rather – ahh – abrupt, end."

"Will you come with me, Bessie?" she repeated.

Even more torn, the African-American woman hesitated for a few seconds, then turned to her son.

"What y'all think, Jermaine?" she requested, *sotto voce*. "This *way* off what we all been doin', all our lives! Y'all see them *teeth*? What if she some kind of *devil* or such?"

"Momma... ah'm not 'scared of her," answered the boy. "An' y'all always done tell me that if we firm in what we believe, then it don' matter if somethin' come 'long, that might be diff'rent. Ah say, 'go for it'."

"Alright," muttered Washington. "Ah honestly don' know what we's gettin' into – but ah 'spose it better than tryin' to hitch-hike back 'cross th' border, with ten dollar left in mah pocket. We's 'in'... ah guess."

A tear came to the eye of Karéin-Mayréij.

"You sound *so* much like dear Whitney!" she softly observed. "Maybe you will help lead me to her – or to my lost son – or just to... 'redemption'."

"How ah gonna do all *that*?" demanded the perplexed black woman.

"You do not yet know – nor do I," noted the alien-girl, "But perhaps in time... we both will."

"Well... I think that's, that," cheerily exclaimed Chu.

"Gotta *hand* it to you, lady," grunted Boatman. "You got 'em all to come along for the ride, just by *askin'* 'em to. Not somethin' *I* could do."

"I had – I *have* – *faith*, dear friend," she serenely replied. "Many times has it kept me from despair, in days much darker than these."

"*That's* a 'plus'," quipped Kaysten. "So what we do now?"

"Before we go any further," suggested the Storied Watcher, "We should all sit down together; for I have much to explain to these folk, both about what has gone on before now, and about what may yet come to pass. You can help explain some of it yourself, Jerr-ee... may I ask you to do that, on my behalf?"

Relishing the opportunity and not caring about the obvious appeal to his vanity, the Chief of Staff replied, "I'd be happy to do that, of course. After all... did you know that I ran the White House Department of Public-Relations, before I got promoted?"

"Really?" she demurely deadpanned. "I would – ahh – *never* have guessed."

"Get them wienies and burgers," proposed Wolf. "I'll make a fire."

Phony-War – And The Real One

"*Taxi*," invoked Billings, in as small a voice as possible.

Cautiously, he peered left and right for the sights and sounds of hostile boot-steps; but seeing and hearing none, he slowly arose to look above the level of the rows of theater-seats.

Which was not difficult – because the backs of the majority of the chairs in his vicinity, had been shredded or charred to half or less of their former sizes, by auto-rifle fire, or by an ex-astronaut's "flashlight-from-Hell" attack.

"Hey!" called the salesman. "Billings here. White, Boyd – you over there?"

"Yeah," came Boyd's voice. "We drove 'em off – I'm pretty sure of that. But Devon's hurt!"

"I'm *coming!*" answered Billings.

As he got to his feet, he looked around and did a double-take, aghast at what the limitations of his 'black-light' vision mode had shielded him from.

There were at least seven dead gendarmes lying in various grotesque positions, and three of them bore the grisly mark of Boyd's attack, with multiple, black-ringed wounds burned right through them.

One dead soldier literally had a 'hole in his head' – and not a *small* one, at that.

Reflexively, the salesman turned away.

A voice came from down below, through the entrance to the staircase.

"Bob? That *you* I hear?" exclaimed a voice very much like Jacobson's.

"Yeah... am I hearing the Commander?" shouted Billings.

"One and the same!" answered the big man. "I'm coming up... is the coast clear?"

"Far as I know," stated the salesman. "Jesus – is it good to hear from you again, Jacobson," he added, as a familiar, stubble-bearded face appeared in the stairwell. "That was one *hell* of a nasty-shot you took there... for a while we thought we'd *lost* you."

Now the former Mars mission commander had made his entrance. He pointed to where he had been shot and winced.

"Let's just say that the feelings remain," he remarked. "I'm still not one hundred per cent... but I'm getting there."

"*Captain!*" called a relieved Brent Boyd. "Thank *God!* Listen – can you get over here and drag Bob along with you? Devon took a round in the arm... and I think he also got hit by splinters in the leg."

Both Billings and Jacobson double-timed their pace over to a row of badly-damaged seats, where the two ex-astronauts had been hiding and firing.

White was propped up against a seat-back. His left arm wore a jury-rigged bandage which was saturated with blood, and there was a smaller red stain on his right leg; but, still in familiar form, he waved with his good hand.

"Yo, Captain!" wheezed the pale-looking, sweating African-American. "One up, one down... I think we gotta... *time* this a bit better, y'all know?"

"Try not to talk," advised Jacobson, as he got down on one knee and examined the wound.

"*Damn...* the one in the arm looks like one of those new metal-composite mushroom-rounds," he noted. "Probably a decent amount of tissue-damage, but look at the *bright* side of it – if Whitney could heal *me* from the brink of death, maybe this'll be a piece of *cake,* for her."

"Let's hope," offered Billings. "Listen, Boyd – as the Commander's still kind of on the mend, I'll help move him back below... get the right arm, okay?"

"Yeah," agreed the ex-astronaut, as the two of them maneuvered White up and under.

Awkwardly, they stumbled forward toward the stairs.

"I was wondering," commented the salesman, "If it's such a good idea, leaving this area undefended... I mean, what if they come *back?*"

"Chance we'll have to take, for a few minutes," replied Boyd. "But Captain – are you well enough to get the bodies discreetly out of the way, and to salvage whatever weapons and ammo we can get off of them?"

"Definitely," confirmed Jacobson. "Ugh – that's one *ugly* job you did on some of these poor bastards, Brent, but I suppose their bodies are the best thing we got, to jam the doors closed –"

"There's more of 'em, just inside the middle door," interrupted Billings, as the big man started to go off in the other direction. "I greased 'em courtesy of a new trick; specifically, I figured out how to, uhh, 'see' – *sort* of – through that dark-field that I do. Everything looked like the 'more than purple' black-light thing... not very much to go on compared to real daylight – but more than enough to aim a gun with, you know?"

"Fuckin' *ay!*" managed an obviously-impressed White. "I guess that means I can hide in there with y'all, and do the same thing... *assumin'*, of course, that I don't buy th' farm in the next half-hour."

As Jacobson went to do his grisly business and as they took a few initial steps down the stairway, Boyd added, "That may *be*... but remind me not to do the same, and then fire my own little trick. Even if that cloak of yours can be jiggered so that it just lets *Um'b'as'ài* in and out, it might *still* stop or reflect everything else back... which might be really *bad* for anyone inside."

"Yuck," muttered Billings. "How about you just don't crawl in there with me, if you don't mind?"

"Not *welcome?* Why Bob... here I thought you *liked* me!" quipped the ex-astronaut.

Down they clambered, looking with apprehension at the bullet-riddled body of the soldier who had been shot by Jacobson.

"Well, there's another rifle and bunch of clips for us – but as you can see, that armor isn't going to stop everything," dispassionately commented Boyd.

Immediately, they were met by Melissa and Whitney Claremont.

"Major *Devon!*" gasped the worried teenager, "What *happen* to y'all?"

"What's it *look* like?" grumbled White. "Guess I kinda zigged when I shoulda zagged..."

"Whitney – can you help him?" requested Billings.

Claremont stared forward for a second or two, then Melissa again spoke up.

"Momma say 'yes'... but she been usin' a lot of her – uhh – prayers, just gettin' y'all an' Miz Cherie well again," explained the teenager. "She might not be too much use for a while, if'n other folk be gettin' shot 'n such."

"That fits nicely in with *my* plans," offered the salesman. "The part about 'not getting shot', that is."

"Okay – let's get him down by Curtis and the others," ordered Boyd.

Quickly, they moved White over to where lay the somnolent Tanaka.

Claremont sat down cross-legged and made a 'come-hither' gesture.

"Momma say, 'put he haid in her lap'," said Melissa.

"He's got a *bad* owwie," added Elissha.

"Are you going to kiss it better?" she asked of Claremont, who extended a hand to the girl.

"Okay," stated Elissha, to an inaudible request. She sat down.

"Major Devon... y'all gonna be *alright?*" interjected a worried Curtis.

Again, they saw Claremont's hand-signal, this time directed at the boy, as White's head was moved into the desired place.

"Yes, Momma – ah shorely *will*," quietly mentioned the boy.

He took a place beside the woman on the side opposite from the girl, held her hand and closed his eyes, as did White.

A gentle, inspiring song drifted through the minds of all about, as a faint blue glow enveloped Claremont, her son and the ex-astronaut. The woman's eyes wore a far-off stare.

"Nothing more that you or I can do here," said Boyd. "Melissa, how are the captives? Any trouble from them?"

"No sir," replied the teenager. "But one of 'em, he smell *awful* bad. He say 'let me out 'cause ah gots to go to the bathroom'... an' ah say, 'well where *that*', an' he say, 'just 'round the corner' – so ah say he gots to wait until y'all be returnin'... maybe y'all come back a bit on th' late-side."

"That's the *least* that the bugger deserves," scowled Billings. "Let him sit in his own shit for a while – see how *he* likes it."

"*Shh!*" cautioned Melissa. "Y'all sayin' cuss-words, might interrupt Momma."

The salesman rolled his eyes, but backed up a bit and addressed Boyd.

"Want me to stay down here?" he inquired.

"Not unless you want to cover that one other entrance down on this level – you know, the one that we reinforced with all the boxes and other junk," indicated the ex-astronaut. "It's pretty clear that they aren't going to come by way of the reservoir – and maybe there's some other reason, a blocked-corridor, for example – why they haven't gone for the main-floor portal... whereas, they very well *might* again try forcing the passageways leading to the balcony-level... if only to recover the bodies."

Billings stopped and considered these facts for a few seconds, then said, "Okay... you got a point. But why don't I just hang out just below the top of the stairs? I'd have a clear line-of-sight to that bottom-entrance – ignoring, for the moment that it's barely visible, in this light – and I'd be just around the corner, if you and Jacobson need me, up top. Deal?"

"Deal!" concurred Boyd. "Let's get going."

To their surprise and relief, at least another hour and a half – perhaps two, or more – had passed, with Billings, annoyed at losing another opportunity to communicate with the boy in the box, fretting in his perch at the top of the stairs.

Relieved at the lull in the action, he had almost dozed off when shouts of excitement began to issue, from the group's temporary encampment below.

Reflexively, the salesman reached for the 'reclaimed' auto-rifle that he had been assigned, as the result of one of Jacobson's scrounging expeditions. He checked its complicated locking-mechanism, trying to ensure that *this* time, the damn thing would actually *fire*, when called upon to do so.

"Mista Billins'! Mista *Billins'!*" called Melissa's excited voice.

"What *is* it?" shouted the salesman. "We got bad-guys? Where are they?"

"No sir," answered the teenager. "Miz Cherie's wakin'! Ya'll tell Captain Sam 'n he two homies up there, if y'all don' mind!"

"You *bet!*" Billings rapidly acknowledged.

He poked his head up into the balcony area and exclaimed, as loudly as he dared, "Boyd! Jacobson! I think we got *Tanaka* back!"

"You mind taking over, here?" requested the former Mars mission commander, coming toward the stairs in a rapid trot, with Boyd just behind. "It's been quiet for a while... we'll only be a few minutes."

"*Go* for it," allowed the salesman. "What with how you got those doors blocked... I think we'll be okay. Just remember that if any of the *heavy-stuff* breaks out, I might not be visible when I open up... you know?"

"Glad you're on *our* side," said Boyd, over his shoulder, as he rushed down the stairs.

"Tell her it's about *time* she got out of her little beauty-sleep," amicably joked Billings, toward the backs of the two ex-astronauts.

Despite Jacobson's promise, his *rendez-vous* with the former Mars mission science-officer dragged on and on, until the salesman felt obligated to temporarily abandon his post, retreating to the top of the stairs and shouting, "Hey you guys, what's going *on*, down there... you playing a few quick chess-games or something?"

"As a matter of fact, Bob," came back a gratifyingly-familiar female voice, "That might be a good idea – *if* we had pieces and a board. Although a few of us found out that playing *that* game against the Storied Watcher was kind of a futile-pursuit."

"Good to hear from you again, Professor," stated Billings. "And – for the record – that was a damn brave thing that you did, helping Whitney bring back Jacobson, that is. How you *feeling*?"

"Like – pardon the expression – 'death warmed over'," grumbled Tanaka, her attractive Eurasian face now appearing at the bottom of the stairs. "I feel 99 and 44/100 per cent, drained. You aren't *kidding* about what a close thing that was, with Sam, I mean... I'm in *awe* of that woman – I wish I had the depth of faith that I felt within her... it's pretty much the only thing that brought all us back."

"Wouldn't be surprised," allowed Billings. "And it might be the only thing that gets our arses *out* of here. Listen – did they tell you about Tommy?"

"Yeah," she confirmed. "It's almost as frustrating for me, as it must be for you, Whitney and the others. To have come *this* close... well, we still may be able to figure something out – but I'm worried about how much time in which we'll have to do it. I heard that you helped Brent and Devon hold the line up there, while Sam and I were out... all I can say is, 'thanks *so* much'! You might have saved our *lives*, Bob."

"My dear, we've all saved each others' lives so many times, I've lost count by now," he gracefully parried. "And for the record, Tanaka... I ain't no war-hero. Seeing those Army Gestapo-guys after I... uhh... *did* them – even the *thought* of it makes me sick to my stomach, to tell you the truth. I'm sure they would have whacked *me*, had they the chance... but all the same, I'm kinda hoping that Whitney can figure out something for me to say, when finally I get called to account for myself, 'upstairs'... you know?"

As quietly as she could, and still be heard, the scientist replied, "We've *all* done some pretty terrible things down here, Bob, and there may be more to come... so maybe I'd better have a talk with Mrs. Claremont, as well..."

"Can't hurt," evenly agreed Billings. "And I'd also suggest that –"

But his voice was cut off by the sound of a thunderous explosion, coming from what had been, a half-second before, the door and passageway that White had defended, before he and Boyd were driven back into the upper area.

Shattered pieces of the door and the frame for it, along with grisly chunks of dead human flesh, were sent flying in every direction, with the bulk of them impacting on the inside of the balcony-glass.

The salesman's first instinct was to yell a warning to those down from and behind him; but lately – for some unknown reason – his mind had been working rather quickly, when pressed by scenes of desperation.

So instead, all that came out of his mouth was that same magic phrase :
"Taxi!"

With This Name... There Is Hope

All of them – save Melissa and Whitney – who had been assigned to watch over the little girl and the boy in the box, had been called into action.

White's sojourn with Claremont had been abruptly cut short, but his brief time with her had still helped substantially; his wounds – while still painfully-present – had already healed enough to make him mobile and alert.

The fire-fight had been raging back and forth for an eternity; which, so far, had taken a little less than an hour.

The rag-tag group of ex-astronauts and ordinary civilians had the advantages of a prepared defensive-position, a well-thought-out battle-plan and their individual alien-powers; they had adapted their tactics to make the best use possible of the latter, for example by using their telekinetic-abilities to send successive volleys of hand-grenades back upon their opponents.

Despite this, as the battle wore on, the weirding-powers helped less and less; each person – save perhaps for Billings – began to run low on the *Fire*.

Their war-songs were ebbing, along with their *sang-froid*.

What's your *score?* absentmindedly sent Boyd, while he and White crouched behind a wrecked chair-row, the ex-astronauts about three meters apart from each other.

Seventeen... I think, came back the psychic message.

Not countin' the ones I greased last time.

But I got nothin' left, bro'... couldn't even chill y'all a beer, right now.

Got you beat, grimly riposted the former Mars mission pilot.

If I'm counting right... I'm up to at least twenty-two.

A second later, White's almost-despairing mind added,

A cold beer on the back deck with my wife and kids...

What I wouldn't give for that, *now...*

Just once more. Wouldn't care what happens after that.

Steady! admonished Boyd.

We ain't done – not by a long-shot. I still got lots of clips – how about you?

Same here... that's the good *news*, mentally replied the black ex-astronaut.

Bad news is, they hit us with another one of them rockets – and without the Professor's shield at full Wattage –

Well – at least she can still deal with the gas, offered Boyd, as he took a few pot-shots at a shadowy figure who was sneaking out of the shattered doorway.

There was a shout from the bottom-level.

"We gots *trouble* down here!" cried Melissa. "Door on th' side!"

"*Shit!*" exclaimed White, out loud. "Where's *Bob?*"

He was rewarded for this indiscretion with a hail of fortunately off-target gunfire, due to the remnants of Boyd's ebon-cloud, which had been deposited over the smashed, burn-scarred, ice-encrusted portal.

"Taxi – on my way!" advised the salesman, as he suddenly appeared just ahead of, and to one side of, the two ex-astronauts.

Yeah... but that leaves only the Captain in charge of the other four doors, silently sent White.

"Tanaka told me she's *completely* out of juice," whispered Billings, as he passed by. "That leaves only *Curtis* to cover our rear-flank!"

"*Go!*" demanded Boyd.

Moving as quickly as he could ever remember himself doing, the salesman dashed down the staircase, pausing for a split-second to focus on what was unfolding below.

On the far right – at the edge of shadows – was a pile of smoking wreckage that had previously been a pile of artfully-arranged storage-boxes; the door that these were reinforcing had evidently been quite a strong one, because although it had been hit from behind by some kind of explosive charge, the blast hadn't been powerful enough to open a clear path into the wide parts of the arena.

Well – despite the shocks – Mister North Pole's re-freeze-job, and that door – are still holding, reflected Billings.

At least we don't have to go swimming in electrified ice-water.

Two cheers for small blessings... right?

Curtis was rushing toward the scene of this latest breach, with Tanaka – her arms unsteadily holding a pistol – advancing behind the boy and calling something at him. Claremont and the little girl were cowering behind an overturned instrument-tray next to Tommy's metallic-prison, while Melissa had gone upward, disappearing in the darkness near the top of the bottom-level.

Just effing great! mused the salesman, as his feet danced down the stairs.

We're defending against a small army of lethally-armed professional soldiers, with a half-goddess whose battery is drained, a flying teenager, an ex-salesman and an eight year-old, loud-mouthed kid.

What else *is new, Bob ol' boy?*

A canister of some kind flew through the hole that had been blasted in the bottom-level door, causing Billings to reflexively cringe; but in the next second, his ears were ringing, after Curtis' *Amaiish*-powered shout – or, perhaps, the dregs of Tanaka's telekinetic-powers – caught the thing in mid-air, throwing it backward, until it hit the inside part of the doorway and rattled to the floor, just below the blast-hole.

There was a dull flash.

"*Curtis!*" yelled Tanaka. "*Stop! Gas!*"

The boy stepped backward and tried to hide behind a computer-console.

Rapidly, the scientist dashed forward. She seemed to be staring at the canister, which self-levitated and then was propelled through the door-hole, toward whoever had first fired it.

There were sounds of mayhem in the corridor behind the almost-breached entranceway.

By now, the salesman had reached the boy and the woman. Looking up, he noticed that more mayhem had broken out inside the balcony level.

They've got their *hands full too*, he realized.

"I smelled it," explained Tanaka. "No, wrong words... *not* smelled... more like... *sensed. Nasty* stuff – worse than what we ran into, back there. I'm pretty sure I pushed all of it back at them... but the doorway's probably contaminated."

"*Damn!*" cursed Billings. "Wasn't that our only way out?"

"Yeah," sighed Tanaka. "But I'm also sensing a *lot* of bad-guys out there – we'd have to *shoot* our way through them... and I'm all thumbs with a gun. Bob – is there anything you can *do?*"

A fusillade flew through the hole in the door, impacting and ricocheting with a faint 'pinging'-sound, off the opposite wall.

"I can disappear and still shoot," he volunteered. "But we'd have to let the buggers get through, first, and if there are too many of 'em –"

"*Ah* get 'em!" exclaimed Curtis, with boyhood bravado. "Ah'm feelin' stronger every *minute*, Mista Billins'!"

Billings crouched down; which – as it happened – was a good idea, for another few rifle-rounds had come flying through the breach.

Immediately, the others followed suit.

"Curtis," he gravely counseled, "This isn't a *game* – one false move, and we could all end up *dead!* Keep your head down and only fire your – uhh – primal scream, when you can take 'em down in one shot. Don't hold back – pour everything you've got into it, if and when you have to do it. You *understand?*"

"Yes, sir," replied the boy, seriously. "And ah *knows* it ain't a game – ah knowed that, since they took Tommy 'n me. Ah ain't *stupid*, Mista Billins'... just real scared."

"That goes for *all* of us, son," sympathetically observed the salesman.

There was an explosion on the balcony-level.

The glass-windows rattled furiously.

"I'm still sensing Sam, Devon and Brent, thank God," breathed Tanaka. "But we're *surrounded*, dammit! Think, Cherie, *think* – there *has* to be a *way!*"

"Devon's ice-up job on the door can't hold up forever under *that* kind of pounding," commented a worried Billings.

"Christ... if Sari were only here," he idly complained. "She'd wipe the *floor* with those bastards! Sari, where *are* you, girl! We *need* you!"

"It ain't gonna do no good," dejectedly commented Curtis. "Tommy 'n me, we callin' for her over and over... she gots to be too far-away to hear, ah guess."

While more bullets – some of them, ominously, making a more potent sound – flew through the door-hole or impacted against the other side of the portal, Tanaka's face had suddenly taken on an inscrutable, far-off look.

There seemed to be a temporary lull in the fighting above.

"Bob," she inquired, "Did you say, you had called to the Storied Watcher?"

"Yes – of *course* I did," retorted Billings, as he double-checked the safety on his automatic-rifle. "More times than I can *remember*... I mean, when they first stuck me in that cell, I had nothing else to *do* except sleep and sit on the john. But Curtis is right... guess she's just off on another planet, or something."

"Bob Billings of Tucson, Arizona," pressed Tanaka, slowly and deliberately, "*Who*, did you call for?"

"I just *told* you!" he complained. "I said, 'Sari, where *are* you' –"

"Is *that* the name you used?" demanded the former Mars mission science-officer. "'*Sari*'?"

"That''s right," confirmed the salesman. "It's what we knew her by – the name she used herself when we all were together... so *what?*"

"And it was the *only* name that you called, man?" she cried, passion reverberating through her voice, tears in her dull-glowing eyes. "Tell me *now* – tell me for *true*, Bob Billings!"

"What's there to tell?" shrugged Billings. "We couldn't have used anything else, except for the weirdo-language-one she had up in space – and I could never pronounce *that* damn thing, anyway. Professor... you *okay?*"

"*Now* – there is *hope!*" she gasped.

A hint of the old light flashed in Tanaka, as she hurried backward, stood up, apparently out of the line-of-fire, and looked upward, with her hands outstretched as if giving a benediction.

"Karéin-Mayréij... Karéin-*Mayréij*... **Karéin-Mayréij!**" she wailed, at the top of her lungs.

Do You Hear What I Hear?

The mufti-clad alien-girl had grumbled about 'having to dirty my mouth with the flesh of animals'; but – none the less – she had still partaken of half of one frankfurter.

The other half had been discreetly fed to Abruzzio's pet, while only a few were in the right place to notice this subterfuge.

"You know," mentioned Kaysten, reclining and licking his lips, "They say that seeing how they make sausages is like seeing what goes on in politics."

"How's *that?*" inquired the bounty-hunter, throwing the last bit of a hamburger, carefully divided in two smaller morsels, to his own two dogs.

"They're both best done in private," explained the Chief of Staff. "I can personally attest to the fact that whoever said that, sure knew how things work in D.C... anybody remember to bring serviettes?"

"That's what your sleeves are for, pardner," remarked Wolf.

"Easy for *you* to say," countered Abruzzio. "Greasy-fingerprints shouldn't be too much of a problem when you can put a blowtorch to them, and not even crease your shirt."

"Learned a *long* time ago, to go with the hand I'm dealt, darlin'," replied the bounty-hunter, with a shrug and a smile. "Grandma on my dad's-side used to say, 'it'll all even out in the end... so it don't matter *squat* what you do, one way or t'other'. But after the past few days, I'm not sure if I still *believe* that, mind you."

"You *can* make a difference," counseled Karéin-Mayréij. "And so you must! Like a herding-dog who guides the flock to safety... you all now have a sacred duty to bring the *Fire* to the people of Earth – spreading its sparks – while not allowing your lesser brothers and sisters to be consumed by it."

"Well, I suppose bein' just a hound-dog – that ain't the *worst* thing that could happen... right, kids?" joked Wolf, addressing the two puppies at his feet.

Both of the little dogs yipped enthusiastically.

"Did everyone have enough to eat?" asked the Storied Watcher.

Most of those arrayed around the campfire, whether sitting on re-arranged rocks or on park benches, nodded or murmured agreement.

"For the time-bein'," observed Saquina White. "But y'all *sure* that water y'all brought, is really safe? I mean – can't drink hardly *nothin'* that's in a river, back home... they're all filled with bacteria 'n chemicals 'n such, these days."

"I burned each bucket of it with the particle-shine, before I set it before you," explained the alien-girl. "Any small, sick-making things within, should thus have been eliminated. And besides... your bodies grow stronger, with each passing minute; soon, the illnesses of humans shall hardly trouble you."

"Guess we'll have to believe y'all on that, Missy," grunted one of the parents. "Because if y'all wrong... well, I don' see no outhouse 'round here."

By now, most of the Compton-refugees had clustered around, eager as they were to observe and interact with their strange new friend and mentor.

"At least we *do* have some picnic-tables," noted Chu. "We got everything out of the bus... right?"

"Yeppers," answered Hendricks. "Such as it *is*... but only three of 'em were bright enough to pack some tenting-gear – so it's going to be a bit – ahem – 'cozy', unless we want to sleep on-board. Which might not be a bad idea... I hear that the bugs can be nasty around here, after dark. But there are a few coolers and probably enough pots 'n pans, as long as they're happy with doing a lot of dish-washing after each meal."

"Bug-spray?" asked Abruzzio.

"Got it," confirmed the third agent. "Three cans, in fact. The latest 'they-die-before-they-land', stuff."

"Marshmallows?" requested Kaysten.

"One bag," informed Hendricks.

"Oh – *good!*" happily commented Karéin-Mayréij.

"Beer?" inquired Wolf.

"Don't I *wish!*" shrugged Hendricks.

"There goes the party," muttered the bounty-hunter.

"I believe that I told you about *Spetsnaz* training... did I not?" mentioned Misha. "Compared to a trip through the *taiga* with nothing but a knife – why, this is a 'luxury-vacation'."

"'Luxury' – like 'poverty' – is mostly a state of mind," philosophically observed the alien-girl. "As long as one has one's weirding-powers, that is."

"How do you mean?" asked Ramirez.

"It is *one* thing," stated the Storied Watcher, "To be trapped in an ice-bound cave with a cruel blizzard raging outside – but still to be able to make the very *rocks* to burn, thence to warm one's feet... quite *another*, when one must resort to rubbing sticks together... and so forth."

"Ah... so *that's* how you 'cope'," teased a smiling Abruzzio. "Not much of a *challenge*, when you have access to all these fantastic alien-powers... *is* it?"

"That depends on the circumstances," argued Karéin-Mayréij. "Find yourself in a place like the surface of the second planet which orbits yonder star," – she pointed up to the Sun – "And without my arts, you will not have much time in which to 'cope', in any event."

"Got you *there*, Sylvia," chuckled the Mexican-American scientist.

"*Sic* 'em, Rainbow," ordered Abruzzio; but the little dog just sat, looked up at its master and wagged its tail.

"*Smart* doggie!" quipped Wolf.

Chu looked up.

"If I'm correctly judging the position of the sun... we're well past noon by now," she observed. "So we really should decide what we're doing, long-term."

"Umm-hmm?" pleasantly murmured the Storied Watcher.

"The point *is*, Karéin," commented the FBI team-leader, "'More-than-human' or not – we've got a couple dozen people out here in the near-wilderness, and we've just used up the bulk of our food. We *could* sleep in the bus, although doing so would be uncomfortable; but the larger issue is, we've got to think out how long we plan to stay here... and – at a minimum – how we're going to obtain enough food, to camp out for that amount of time."

"Might be a good idea to send one or two people into the town – what's its name again, oh yeah, 'Jasper', right – to buy some provisions," suggested

Boatman. "But I don't think they should be any of *us*, Minnie... we might be a bit too easy to recognize, you know?"

"To say nothing of our friendly little alien-goddess there," added Hendricks. "Although I guess she *could* air-lift a couple of these folk from Compton and drop 'em around the corner from the local supermarket. They take American bills up here, don't they?"

"Monn-ee, *again*," sighed Karéin-Mayréij, rolling her eyes.

"Yes, they do," confirmed the Russian. "But only at a steep discount, especially since the closing of the border with the United States; if I remember my last SVR-briefing, the ratio was four and a half American dollars to one Canadian dollar –"

"Hate to break it to ya – but there goes your trip to the bar, pardner," ruefully mentioned Wolf. "Looks like we'll be doin' good to buy us a loaf of bread, or a couple bags of potato-chips. Anybody bring a fishin'-pole?"

"Hey, Karéin," interrupted Ramirez, "Want to give me some lessons on how to transmute these rocks, into gold, or something? If it comes down to either learning or eating, you'll find me to be a – uhh – *motivated* student."

"Hah!" replied the alien-girl, with a wry smile. "If we are trying not to draw attention to ourselves... do you not think that walking in to a merchant-shop and dropping a huge gold nougat on his counter, would be too, ahh, conspicuous?"

"It's 'nugget' – not 'nougat'," corrected Abruzzio. "'Nougat' is a kind of *candy*."

"Well, then – so much the better," smartly replied the Storied Watcher. "I *like* candy; and if I had any money of my own, I would –"

All of a sudden, a thunderstruck look appeared on her face, and – in a half-second – she had jumped to her feet, standing in front of the group like an icon, with bright-glowing eyes and energy-charges beginning to pulse within her body.

A breeze rustled the trees, as a war-song began to play.

"*Karéin!*" exclaimed Chu, immediately standing herself. "What's *wrong?*"

Tears of joy watered the glowing eyes of Karéin-Mayréij.

"Listen, Minn-ee... *listen!*" she gasped, with amazed excitement. "Do you *hear* it!"

"Ah don' –" started one of the parents, but she was quickly silenced by a warning-gesture on Abruzzio's part.

"But I *do*," breathed an astonished FBI team-leader. "Far, far-away... like singing from over the ocean..."

"*I* hear it too!" echoed the now-upright Abruzzio. "From *that* way..."

The scientist pointed to the western mountains.

"Yes... yes!" exclaimed the Storied Watcher. "Gods be *praised*, it is them – at long last – it is *them!*"

"They *call* for you, Karéin-Mayréij," offered the Russian, with stars of his own in his eyes. "You must *go* to them!"

"I *will*," she promised, with hot tears staining her cheeks. "I *will!*"

Now, the Storied Watcher called the names of her war-children, one by one. *"Ahn'jë! Fàiagàryuu! I'ëà'b'! Ksé'l'ch'! Ss'éth'ch'!"* she sang.

In the blink of an eye, she was combat-geared, and – for the first time – the frightened refugees from Compton saw the mighty Storied Watcher in the fullness of her infernal, deadly glory, as pine-needles and other forest-floor debris began to ignite under her boots.

All save Misha, Wolf, Chu and Abruzzio dashed to put space between themselves and the shining, burning alien-girl.

"Listen, Karéin," called Hendricks, while shielding his eyes with his hand. "Just wanted to say... 'good luck'."

"Sì," added Ramirez. *"Vaya con Dìos!"*

Standing impossibly close, the team-leader asked, "Where will you go?"

"To the west," replied Karéin-Mayréij, her greatness waxing with every syllable. "To the rescue of my beloved, whose cries will guide me as surely as the North Star."

"Take us along," pleaded Chu. "This is *our* quest, too!"

"Even *you* would be crushed, dear friend," argued the Storied Watcher. "I will fly with my most-speed!"

A look of despair appeared momentarily on several faces, until Abruzzio interjected, "Then give us a *boost*, Karéin – lift and pull us in the bus, as high and fast as we can tolerate, until you must let go. *We'll* do the rest."

"We'll do *what*?" demanded a nonplussed Boatman.

"We *will* do it," quietly vowed Ramirez. "I *know* that we will."

"Take my hand – all of you!" commanded the alien-girl.

Crowding around, they laid their own upon the smoking, gauntlet of *Vìrya Ahn'jë*, apparently unconcerned at her flaming-touch.

With eyes closed and the little amulet in her other hand, Karéin-Mayréij said an ancient oath in her own language, then continued in English.

"The Destroying Angel now lays the deepest wisdom of the *Khùl-Algrenàthi'i*, upon you," she chanted, while the chords of her war-song echoed through the tops of the trees, like an other-worldly, melodic zephyr. "My war-children and I will call, as the bell-tower counts each score of minutes; and by fixing on this... so shall you be guided, to where I have gone. Do you all comprehend this?"

In unison, they replied, "Yes, we do!"

"Then it is *done!*" exclaimed the Storied Watcher. *"Prepare* yourselves!"

They were standing in the beginnings of a fire; but Wolf looked down at the little tongues of flame spreading over the forest-floor, and – somehow – these disappeared into his boots, causing him to flinch, momentarily.

The Russian nodded at the bounty-hunter with silent respect.

"Team! To the bus!" ordered Chu.

"*Wait* a minute," protested Boatman, as he pointed to the Compton-refugees. "Who the hell's gonna look after *these* folk?"

Kaysten stepped forward, with a look of dignity that none had yet seen.

"You're going off to a *fight*... aren't you?" he asked, of the Storied Watcher.

"Aye!" she confirmed, not caring to hide her savage fangs. "And when I find those who beset dear Tommy and my newfound kinfolk, before you – and all here – I *swear*... I will smite them, even unto the very *dust*."

"Then I'll stay behind... keep the civilians out of trouble," proposed the Chief of Staff. "Unless you have any objections."

"Of *course* I do not, Jerr-ee!" she replied, her voice kind and appreciative. "Hold them safe until I return – which I will *surely* do. Your courage is of a different kind... but brave you *are*, none the less. *Thank* you, dear friend!"

"Otis, Will – give him what cash you've got on-hand," requested Chu.

"Aww, but –" started Hendricks.

A second later, seeing their faces, he sighed, wisely shut up and pulled out his wallet, as did Boatman.

The more-than-humans began to head to the bus, but as they were about to board, a voice called out.

"Hey, y'all!" shouted Saquina White, while Kaysten started to herd the rest of the Compton-refugees off to a safe distance. "Where y'all *goin'*?"

"With *her*," stated the FBI team-leader. "This is a *dangerous* mission – even more-so, than what we've all just been through. It's no place for amateurs!"

"Not without *us*, y'all ain't!" insisted the wife. "Goin', I mean."

Chu re-traced her steps and approached White.

"I understand how you feel," she said, "But you *can't* go with us – you have no *idea* of what it's like flying with Karéin-Mayréij, when she goes at full speed. Saquina – you'll be *killed* if you go on that bus!"

"Y'all don't *understand*," argued the woman. "We *gots* to go!"

"We don't have time to argue," rejected Chu, turning her back.

"Vex her *not*, Minn-ee!" interjected the Storied Watcher, who temporarily restrained her burning aura, so as to safely approach the two women.

She gazed long at Saquina White.

"Yes – you *do* have to come with us... do you not?" reflectively commented the alien-girl.

"*Now* it makes sense," said Abruzzio. "*He's* with them... isn't he?"

Devon White's wife nodded.

"I don' know how... but I *know*. He *needs* me – and I *got* to go to him."

"It is a quest of many perils, Saquina," advised Karéin-Mayréij. "Much may beset you and the little-ones – there is scant time in which to prepare."

"I'm *ready*," defiantly answered White.

"So is we!" chimed her two children.

The Storied Watcher turned her attention to the boy.

"You look and sound *so* much like your father – who gave me hope in my hour of trial," offered the alien-girl. "Consider that as a *great* honor, Martin."

"I *know*," affirmed White's son.

"I love my Daddy very much," added the daughter.

"So do *I*, Francelle," echoed Karéin-Mayréij.

The alien-girl moved her arm and put a palm upward, as if she were checking for rain; but a second later, a previously-unused half-hot-dog-bun was telekinetically retrieved from a nearby food-cooler box.

She divided it into four morsels – each slightly larger than a crouton – and, one by one, touched these to her fangs.

The more perceptive of those standing close by, could tell that a stain had appeared within the pieces of bread.

"The moment when you fasten your seating-belts on board yonder vehicle," directed the Storied Watcher, "Swallow these – one per person – and thereby be opened to my life and power. A deep sleep will come; but when you awake, much greater than before, shall you be. Fail to do this, and Minn-ee's warnings *will* – indeed – come true. Do you understand?"

"Yes," nodded White's wife, as she accepted the venom-infused bread. "But why are there four of 'em? Only three of us, after all."

"What if you lose one?" insouciantly remarked the alien-girl. "Scarcely would I desire to see one of you painfully-die, due to a dropped bread-crumb."

"Welcome to the alien-side, Saquina," quipped Chu, with a wry smile. "She kind of thinks of *everything*... doesn't she?"

"Ah – if such only were *true*," sighed Karéin-Mayréij. "But there is *no* mortal life like the one on which you embark, dear friends. Now... go, and make yourselves well-ready – for in *my* world, there are no 'second-chances'!"

Rapidly, all of them – Chu, Boatman, Hendricks, Ramirez, Misha, Wolf with his two dogs and Abruzzio with her one, along with Saquina White and her son and daughter – headed for the bus, closing its door immediately.

"*Karéin!*" shouted Kaysten, as he saw and felt her power starting to surge, far beyond human comprehension.

Her war-song howled across the sky, its inspiring, exciting tune telling of battles yet to come.

She turned her regal gaze upon him, saying nothing.

"*Mercy for them!*" he pleaded.

The Storied Watcher – her eyes glowing – nodded, in an inscrutable manner that might have indicated agreement, or – perhaps – mere acknowledgement.

Then her fire became overwhelming, and the Chief of Staff was momentarily afraid that the trees would be next to ignite.

But instead, the Destroying Angel rocketed up and away at a steep angle, with the bus being jerked abruptly into the air, following behind like a ribbon trailing an arrow-head.

As his godly former abductor-cum-friend suddenly vanished, relative quiet returned to the forest-scene, and – for a moment – Kaysten began to ask himself if it had all been real.

Then he looked at the burgeoning flames in the spot from which she had taken flight.

"We'd better get some water from the lake," he said, to the others.

Sebastiàn – El Nuevo Diablo

He had been stealing across the garbage-, gang- and vermin-infested streets of urban Los Angeles, trying to retrace his footsteps back to where he and the other *Maras* had been ambushed by the White-Power thugs.

Fuckin incredible *that none of them Crips, Bloods or El-Rukns put the tag on me,* he mused.

Even in broad daylight! Gave 'em the finger... posses walked right by...

Still not tired at all – despite having gone for hours – Sebastiàn paused for a few seconds, his back against the cheap stucco-siding of a lower-class house.

Idly, he regarded at the exposed flesh on his gun-hand, the color and texture of which had – somehow – begun to resemble the plaster on the house-side.

His face wore a satisfied, even smile.

¿Porque? he asked himself.

Chica set me up with everything I need to go somewhere – Sudamerica, por ejemplo – and take over, be top dog, live like el rey.

Totally estupido *to go up against all them fuckin' 'Aryan' putos, mi-mismo...*

No hombre... it ain't, he said under his breath, as he stared out over the low-rise houses and strip-mall buildings, their roofs giving off a steady shimmer that made the bottom of the ghetto L.A.-sky look like a modern-day mirage.

They smoked mis compadres : Reason Numero Uno.

Reason Numero Dos : *I feel like takin' them down... hard!*

Today... if not sooner.

Got nothing to do with what chica *ask me... whole thing started way before I run into her, anyway.*

She couldn't *have known* – verdad?

And Reason Numero Très : *You ain't up against Sebastiàn,* el Mara, *no more, putos.*

You up against Sebastiàn, el... Diablo!

He ran his finger across his teeth, forcing his mind to repeat the last thought, and he put the saliva-covered digit up to his nose.

Though he'd have missed it at first, his spit smelled, well... *strange.*

The same, thin, grimly-determined smile re-appeared, and again, he trotted forth, moving inexorably out of Compton, toward the east.

Song Of The Destroying Angel

Somehow – and none of them knew precisely how – they had appeared to have beaten back the latest attack; but – though none of the more-than-humans trapped in the bottom-level of this abyss wanted to say it out loud – all of them knew that they were being steadily worn-down.

Some of Tanaka's telekinesis had come back to her, and she had used it to advantage, pushing and piling up enough debris in front of the bottom-level entrance to build a good-sized barrier in front of it. White – in one of his few respites from alternatively standing-guard and fighting gun-battles on the upper-level – had covered the pile of *bric-a-brac* with as much ice as his own, almost-exhausted powers could muster, while saving a shot or two for the reinforcement of the breach leading to the flooded passageway.

Now – while the African-American ex-astronaut had gone back to join Boyd in defending the balcony – Billings, Jacobson and Tanaka stood together, some distance from the three children plus the forlorn one in his metal-bound prison, and tried to reason out their options.

The soft, rhythmic chant of the name of the Storied Watcher, being maintained all the while by the two Claremont children, plus the little girl, *did* bring some comfort; though all but the two adult women suspected that this, too, would turn out to be another forlorn hope.

"There's only one thing to do, you know," offered Tanaka.

"No!" answered the salesman. "No *way!*"

"Bob, think with your *brains*... not your heart!" pleaded the woman. "I don't want to leave him down here any more than you do – but it makes no sense *whatsoever*, to get us all killed while trying to protect him. We've *got* to at least clear the way out, while we still *can*."

"Which is just a nice sugar-coated way of saying, 'and when we find that old staircase to the topside, then we've got a good reason to *take* it, and a lousy reason *not* to'," retorted Billings. "Sorry, Professor – I ain't falling for it!"

"*Look*, Bob," argued Jacobson, "I understand how you feel, but from a tactical point-of-view... we have a reasonably-defensible position here; but even with what we've been able to salvage, we're running out of ammunition – after the last fire-fight, Brent warned me that he was down to five clips... and Devon's even worse-off. We've got our side-arms, of course – but it's *crazy* to believe that could defeat whole squads of fully-armed soldiers, with a bunch of pistols. Even if we *were* to try and force that doorway over there, there's an excellent chance that we wouldn't have enough firepower to deal with whoever's hiding behind it. Not without our other – uhh, 'specialties' – being at full-strength, that is... and speaking just for myself, I feel anything *but* like that."

"*Really?*" parried the salesman. "I feel *fine!*"

A frustrated Mars mission commander sarcastically retorted, "Well... having half my gut shot out, kind of *drains* me... Cherie? How are you doing?"

"*Terribly*," complained the woman. "I could barely move all that stuff in front of the door. I can probably keep the shield up temporarily – maybe stop a bullet or two – nothing more substantial – but the minute I have to take a shot at anything with the zap-gun... well, ever heard of 'having shot one's bolt'?"

"Yeah... and that's pretty much what I've been hearing from both Devon and Brent," concurred Jacobson. "We've got to face *facts*, here; we've been doing *amazingly* well, considering everything that's been thrown at us, so far... but whoever's issuing the orders on the other side, knows he can just keep wearing us down, until we don't have anything left to give. It's a classic siege-situation, basically. Bob, we've *got* to get out of here!"

"I *told* you," Billings acerbically countered, "The answer is, 'no'! If *you* guys want to take off, you're welcome to do so... although – for the record – you don't have a *clue* about what you're going to do, when and if you get above ground – remember? As for *me*... I'm staying! I'll hide in the shadows and kill them all with my bare hands, if I have to!"

There was an angry, defiant look on his face.

"*Look*, Bob – maybe they won't do anything more to Tommy," suggested Tanaka, almost at her wits'-end. "By now, they *must* know what an important – uhh – 'asset', he is. They'd be *insane* to kill him, given what he represents to the Storied Watcher! He's their biggest bargaining-chip... he's worth far more to him alive, than, dead."

"*Really*, Professor?" shot back the salesman. "I'm sure that's what somebody said about Elissha's brother... right?"

Tanaka hung her head and sighed, "*Right.*"

She threw her hands up and addressed her former commander.

"I don't know what to *say*, Sam!" she dejectedly protested. "It's *suicide* to stay here, but Bob's right – it'd be *reprehensible* to leave Tommy behind, to the tender mercies of the bastards who run this effing place –"

Just then, two simultaneous explosions thundered : one was somewhere on the upper-level, while the other blew their laboriously-constructed doorway strong-point, into pieces that rocketed in all directions.

Several of these would, for sure, have struck the three adventurers, had it not been for Tanaka's instantly-raised force-field.

A barrage of automatic-gunfire sprayed through the bottom-opening – frightening, to be sure, though nothing new – but to their amazement and dismay, a scintillating beam of light – akin to but much different from Boyd's – came from a point that must have been near to one of the five upper-doorways.

It struck a glassed-in observation pane and reflected from it at an oblique-angle, after leaving an ugly, blackened scar on the window's surface.

A second later, Boyd's almost-panicked mind called out, *Devon, they're using gas, too – whole nine-yards!*

Make for the stairs!

Instinctively, Tanaka fired her *Amaiish*-powered lightening-bolt at the source of the machine-gun fire, causing screams and curses from behind where the doorway had been blown open.

To the relief of the two nearby more-than-men, her shield flickered but – at least for the moment – remained operational; however, to their dismay, a second or two later, more bullets began to issue through the gap.

"Melissa – *hit the lights!*" shouted Billings.

"But Mista Billins', Momma 'n them is wide *open* –" warned the teenager.

"*Do it!*" he shrieked, as he dashed over to protect Claremont, her son and Elissha, invoking his own special-ability.

"*Taxi!*" spoke the salesman.

He disappeared, along with the two kids.

"No, I ain't *stoppin'!*" they heard the boy arguing, as Billings shepherded his three friends out of the line-of-fire, toward the far end of the lower-level.

Karéin-Mayréij... Karéin-Mayréij... Karéin-Mayréij... came the faint call of the little girl, into the minds of the desperate, besieged troupe.

Jacobson crouched and began to return fire, although he knew that he must be heavily-out-gunned.

The figures of the two ex-astronauts appeared at the top of the stairs, each man alternatively sticking an auto-rifle above the opening from the staircase to the balcony, while rifle-rounds impacted all around them.

"Captain – we can't *hold* 'em!" yelled Boyd. "Must be *dozens* – and they've got some kind of energy-weapon!"

As if to reinforce the point, another shot of this infernal whatever-it-was, hit a row of chairs just in front of the entranceway to the lower-level. The seats, or what little was left of them, were melted and charred, with some of the carpeting and other nearby materials being set on fire.

Then there was another explosion, this time directed at the upper-level observation-windows themselves. An entire, more-than-man-size pane shattered, its shards being ejected to litter the bottom-floor.

"*Shit!*" cursed White. "Got a whiff of that gas – *nasty*, man – if it starts driftin' down, now that the seal's gone –"

He caught a brief glimpse of Melissa, who had, despite a hail of bullets fired alarmingly-close to her, flown over to the far wall.

The teenager flipped a switch, and the entire area – except for the balcony, in which a few, dim floor-lights remained operational – was again plunged into near-total darkness.

Good work! sent Jacobson.

We got a chance, team! Tell your eyes to see the hot-stuff!

Tensely, they all waited for the other shoe to drop, more than a few of those in this ill-fated expedition suspecting that they might be living out their last few minutes.

But, for a few agonizingly long seconds, all fell quiet.

Then they heard a gruff voice – undoubtedly amplified by a bullhorn or something similar – make a demand. The sound seemed to be coming from the balcony, or somewhere behind it.

"*Attention, escapees!*" it bellowed. "You are *surrounded*, with no possible avenue of escape. You have the following options : one, lay down your weapons, drop immediately to your knees with hands on your heads and submit to the lawful authority of the Government of the United States, including summary trials which will be held forthwith; or two, continue to resist – and be quickly annihilated. I warn you – we have *overwhelming* firepower, including but not limited to, automatic, high-velocity guns, grenades, rockets, gas, flamethrowers and certain even more powerful weapons, at our immediate disposal. We will not *hesitate* to use these, should you elect to take the second option! You have thirty seconds in which to decide, starting... *now!*"

Though hidden in a way that could probably have defeated almost any means of detection, Claremont seized the hands of both the little girl and her son. The woman began to quietly pray, her entreaties to her God intermixing with Elissha's incessant chanting of an alien-name.

"*Sam...*" whispered a crestfallen Tanaka, crouching beside Jacobson.

"I'm... *so* sorry, it's come to *this*," she managed. "I *thought* – I *believed...*"

"Down but not out," growled the former Mars mission commander. "Don't forget that we can see *them*, and they can't –"

There was a 'popping'-sound; then their infra-sight saw five or six canisters of some type being fired into their last stand, both below and above.

A second later, all – save Billings, who was using the more-than-purple sight, not the warm-sight – had to wince, as bright-burning flares illuminated the area, not as well as had the remaining conventional-lights, but more than sufficiently to allow a human soldier to identify and target an opponent.

"*Shit!*" muttered Jacobson. "Gotta *hand* it to them – they aren't taking any chances, *are* they? Better tactics than I'd have expected from GrayWar."

Captain, came White's mental call, *What's our next move?*

"Twenty seconds!" yelled the voice on the loudspeaker.

Don't think for a minute *that surrendering is going to save our lives,* cautioned Boyd's response.

If for no reason other than the number of them that we've already killed, the same thing will happen to us, anyway... only, more slowly.

I'm for fightin', added White.

They'll take my gun out of my cold, dead, hands.

'Scuse me – out of their, *cold dead, hands.*

Jacobson chuckled, then sent a message of his own.

Devon – I think what I'll miss the most, is hearing those stupid jokes.

Sorry, all you best-of-friends... I really thought *that –*

"Ten seconds!" bellowed the voice. "Company, prepare to fire!"

Y'all don't have to say *it, Commander,* came back White's mordant, but serenely-fatalistic answer.

"*After the Mars-thing... what* more *could possibly go wrong?*"

Teach you 'bout ass-you-me'in things, I guess.

At first, they did not understand the hymn-like thought that came from Claremont's mind.

From the hate of the wicked, thou at long last deliver me, O blessed Lord!

Surely now shall I never doubt thee!

"Momma – ah *hears* it!" incautiously cried an excited Melissa. "Thank y'all, *Jaysus!*"

"I got something to *tell* you little jerk-off, wannabe soldier-boys," taunted a defiant-to-the-last Jacobson, to no-one in particular.

"And *that* is –"

But never would they know, what he had intended to say.

Because...

As eerie, as a mournful wolf-howl, on a deep winter's-night;

As foreboding, as the first winds of a tempest, making landfall;

As clear, as the call of the *Shofar*, on the first day of the seventh month;

Came the stirring, electric-thrilling, impossibly-beautiful melody, for which the beleaguered little group had *so* long waited.

Jacobson, Tanaka, Boyd and White recognized every last note; but somehow, so did the others.

***Ooo-ooo-ooo-ooo*, it sang, while the walls began to shake.**

– *End of The Angel Brings Fire* –

...and be sure to read the exciting sequel to
The Angel Brings Fire...

The Future Burns Bright

www.ingramcontent.com/pod-product-compliance
Lightning Source LLC
Chambersburg PA
CBHW030926020726
47498CB00001B/127